DESCENDANTS OF THE FALL

The Complete Series

AARON HODGES

Edited by Genevieve Lerner
Proofread by Sara Houston
Illustration by James Churchill
Map by Michael Hodges

ABOUT THE AUTHOR

 Aaron Hodges was born in 1989 in the small town of Whakatane, New Zealand. He studied for five years at the University of Auckland, completing a Bachelors of Science in Biology and Geography, and a Masters of Environmental Engineering. After working as an environmental consultant for two years, he grew tired of office work and decided to quit his job in 2014 and see the world. One year later, he published his first novel - Stormwielder.

FOLLOW AARON HODGES...
And receive TWO FREE novels and a short story!
https://aaronhodgesauthor.com/newsletter

ALSO BY AARON HODGES

The Sword of Light

Book 1: Stormwielder

Book 2: Firestorm

Book 3: Soul Blade

The Legend of the Gods

Book 1: Oathbreaker

Book 2: Shield of Winter

Book 3: Dawn of War

The Knights of Alana

Book 1: Daughter of Fate

Book 2: Queen of Vengeance

Book 3: Crown of Chaos

The Evolution Gene

Book 1: Reborn

Book 2: Havoc

Book 3: Carnage

Descendants of the Fall

Book 1: Warbringer

Book 2: Wrath of the Forgotten

Book 3: Age of Gods

Book 4: Dreams of Fury

The Alfurian Chronicles

Book 1: Defiant

Book 2: Guardian

Book 3: Conquest

The Swords of Heaven and Hell

Book 1: <u>Darkstrider</u>

The Four Circles

Book 1: Help! My Wizard Mentor Had A Heart Attack And Now I'm Being
Chased By A Horde Of Giant Spiders!

The Untamed Isles

The Path Awakens

THE KINGDOMS OF HUMANITY

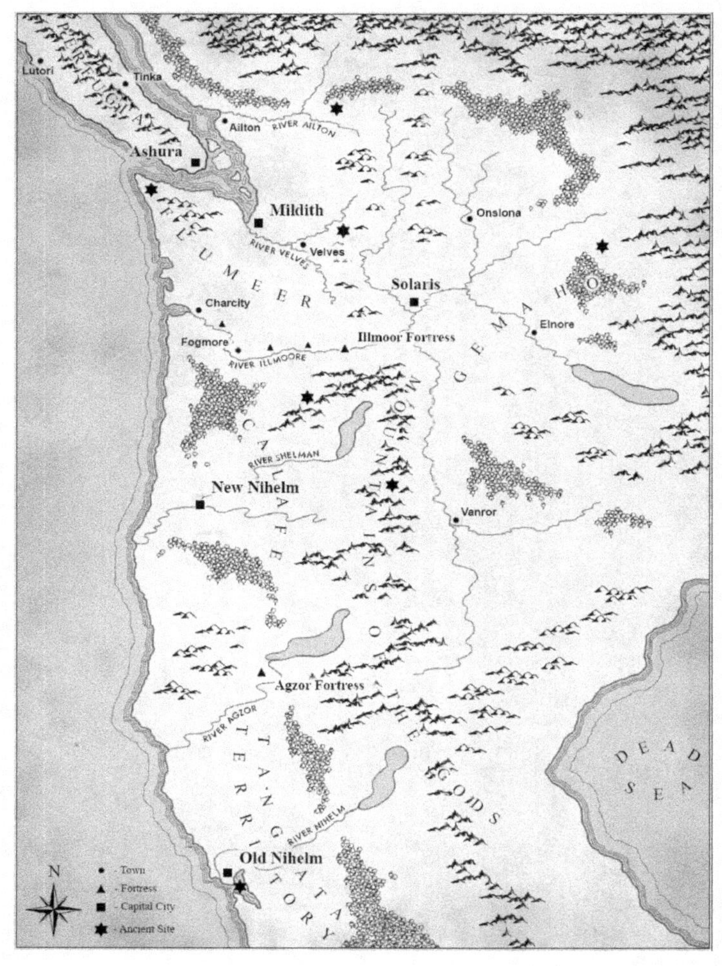

NEW YORK TIMES BESTSELLING AUTHOR
AARON HODGES

WAR BRINGER
DESCENDANTS OF THE FALL

PROLOGUE
THE WARRIOR

Romaine shivered as a breeze shook the treetops and somehow found its way through a gap in his clothing. He pulled the cloak tighter around his shoulders, eager to keep the winter cold at bay. The soft *thump* of falling snow came from nearby and he chuckled as two of his companions flinched. Settling himself more comfortably in the saddle, he flicked the lieutenant a glance.

"Want me to check it out?" Romaine asked, voice serious but the hint of a smile betraying his mirth.

The lieutenant scowled, though Romaine noticed the man loosened his sword in its scabbard before urging his mount onwards. Shaking his head, he let the lieutenant take the lead. The four other scouts fell in behind Romaine, nervous eyes on the dense forest to either side of the deer trail.

They were right to be nervous. Ten miles south of the Illmoor River, they were deep in no man's land, far from the paved roads and walled cities of the northern nations. This was Calafe, a land of seemingly endless forest and great plateaus of tussock, of rugged hills and racing streams, with only the occasional settlement to prove the existence of humanity. This was *his* country, *his* home.

Or at least, it had been, until the Tangata.

Another tremor slid down his spine, though this time it had nothing to do with the cold. For ten years he'd fought to halt the Tangatan advance, ten long, brutal years of war. He'd been a simple woodsman once, but everything had changed with the destruction of their southern fortress, the Castle of Agzor. For a century it had barred the Tangata from the kingdoms of man, but with its battlements broken, its citadel cast down...nothing could halt the enemy advance.

And so those ten years of battle had proven futile. Just a few short months past, the last of Calafe's territory had been lost. The allied armies had fought for every patch of earth, but in the end it had not been enough. The tide of the Tangata could not be stopped.

It had pained Romaine to leave behind his nation. Most of the Calafe army had already fallen by then, and yet more of his fellows had chosen to remain with the rearguard. They had been overwhelmed before the ships could return for them. Injured aboard one of the vessels, Romaine had been forced to watch as his comrades perished.

Thankfully, the enemy had not yet sought to strike across the Illmoor river. Some said they would remain in the south, but Romaine knew it was only a matter of time before they came. After all, people had once said the same of the Agzor Fortress, that it would stand forever against the beasts.

Romaine's horse was struggling now, the snowdrifts growing deeper as they tracked their way eastward into the foothills of the Mountains of the Gods. Ahead, the lieutenant started to curse. Grimacing, Romaine edged his gelding alongside his superior.

"We'd best turn back," he grunted. He didn't bother with any honorifics—he rode with the Flumeerens, but he was not one of them. "If we press hard through the afternoon, we might make the crossing before nightfall."

The lieutenant flicked Romaine an irritated glance. He was a young man, still in his mid-twenties, the son of some minor noble. Romaine could almost see the gears turning behind his eyes. Reaching the river before dark meant shelter over their heads and a hot meal for the night. But if they abandoned their path and missed some enemy movement...

"A little further," the lieutenant replied finally. "We'll turn around if the way becomes impassable."

Romaine responded with a grunt. Pressing his horse forward, he continued along the trail, eyes on the way ahead. The storm had come upon them unexpectedly in the night, howling through the fir trees like a beast unleashed and burying the world in white.

They should have turned back then, but the lieutenant was new, still earning his stripes. Their orders had been to spend three days scouting for signs of the enemy. This being only their second, Romaine should have guessed the lieutenant would be hesitant to return. No doubt he feared the failure would be a black mark against his name.

It was an infuriating thought—evidence that the Flumeeren did not truly understand what came for them. They and the dregs of Perfugia might have fought alongside Calafe this last decade, but it had never been their land at risk, never their families, their very way of life.

That was about to change.

For if they could not stop the enemy at the Illmoor, Flumeer would be the next to fall.

Returning his thoughts to the present, Romaine scanned the path ahead. The snow had thinned again and the horses were making better progress. At least the fresh snow made Romaine's task easier; not even the Tangata could move in these conditions without leaving tracks—

Romaine pulled sharply on his reins, bringing his horse to a stop. Beside him, the lieutenant cursed, but Romaine didn't spare the man a glance. His eyes were on the trees, scanning the upper branches, the shadows beneath the broad trunks, seeking sign, however small, of an ambush. The wind had fallen off now, and he saw no movement. He let out a sigh as the others began to murmur. Breath fogged before his face as he returned his gaze to the trail.

Two sets of bootprints led away from them in the snow.

"What is it?" the lieutenant asked sharply as he got his horse under control. He had not noticed the tracks.

"Tangata," Romaine replied.

The word cut through the whispers like a knife. Silence fell like a blanket over the six riders. The men looked to Romaine, faces as white as the snow all around them. Romaine might have laughed, if not for the racing of his own heart. Unlike the others though, it was not from fear.

This land had been abandoned months ago. There was no one left, not of his people, at least. It meant the general's fears were true. The Tangata were moving north.

Kicking his horse forward, he followed the prints for several yards. In places the strides were separated by as much as six feet—no doubt now, their owners were Tangata.

"We should bring word to the general," the lieutenant's voice carried from back down the trail. He and the other scouts had not followed Romaine.

A smile touched the Calafe warrior's cheeks. "Word of what? A single scouting pair?"

"Our orders were to return if we found sign of the enemy."

"Sign of an enemy *army*," Romaine corrected. "Do you really want to be known as the lieutenant who turned tail and ran at the first sight of the enemy?"

"There are *two* of them," the lieutenant hissed. He edged his horse forward, hands fiddling nervously with his reins. "What do you propose we do?"

Romaine stifled a sigh. The man was right to be afraid—if they'd been on foot, two Tangata would be more than their match. But mounted and with the element of surprise, there was a better than even chance of victory.

"We're downwind of them," Romaine replied finally. "If there's only two, they're no threat to the frontier. But if they're part of a larger force…General Curtis needs to know."

The lieutenant stared at Romaine for a long moment, the muscles of his jaw stretched taut as he contemplated the suggestion. Like before, Romaine could see he was weighing his options. But Romaine's last words about the general were too tempting to resist. The officer who brought such vital information would not soon be forgotten.

"Very well," the lieutenant said, nodding quickly. "Take the lead, Calafe."

Romaine grimaced at the man's cowardice, but held his tongue. He had what he wanted—a chance to follow the creatures, maybe even catch them. The thought of them loose in his land filled him with fury. No, unlike the greenhorns riding behind him, Romaine did not fear the Tangata.

He *loathed* them.

"You should ready your lances," Romaine said, and gave a grim smile when the lieutenant's eyes widened. "Just in case."

It was almost too much for the man. His Adam's apple bobbed up and down as he swallowed, but to reverse his command now would be a show of cowardice.

"Cadet Flagers, ready the lances."

At the rear of the party, the Perfugian recruit dismounted clumsily and started unclipping the long package strapped to the packhorse. Safe on their island nation, the Sovereigns of Perfugia wasted little energy worrying over the Tangata. Unlike the treacherous King of Gemaho, they still honoured the ancient pact each kingdom had signed when the Tangata first appeared. Each month they sent their obligated hundred recruits to fight on the frontlines. Unfortunately, those they sent were generally…useless.

A sharp *clack* sounded as the skins holding the lances together suddenly came undone, sending the weapons tumbling to the ground. Muttered curses followed as Flagers dropped to his knees and tried to pick them back up.

"*Godsdamnit,*" the lieutenant swore as he swung from his saddle and strode to where the recruit crouched. "You trying to get us all killed, Flagers?"

"Sorry, sorry!" Arms clutched around the lances, Flagers stared up at the lieutenant with terror in his eyes.

He was barely a boy, really, untrained and unprepared for the horrors that waited out here. Pity touched Romaine, but he quickly pushed it aside. Against the Tangata, there was no room for weakness, no space for compassion. He'd learned that ten years ago, when the truce had first been broken. He would not repeat the same mistake now.

Instead, he watched in silence as the lieutenant snatched the steel-tipped lances from the Perfugian's hands and handed them out amongst the scouts. Romaine only reached over his shoulder, lifting the giant twin-bladed axe from its sheath and settling it on the pommel of his saddle. Calafe warriors did not learn the lance.

As the men settled their weapons, Romaine cast a practiced glance over his companions. Despite their inexperience, they were well trained other than the Perfugian. They would not back down from a fight if it came to it. Turning to the lieutenant, he offered a nod, before starting off once more.

The bootprints had emerged from the surrounding trees, but even the Tangata apparently preferred a trail over the untamed forest in these parts, for they kept to the animal track for the next few miles. The sun grew higher as their party crossed frozen streams and occasional open meadows, all the while watching for the slightest hint of the enemy. Despite Romaine's earlier reservations, the snow cleared and they made good progress. With the trail beginning to loop northward, they might still make the Illmoor that night.

If they did not encounter the Tangata first.

Romaine kept his eyes on the trees as he rode. Despite what he'd said to the others, he wasn't altogether sure the Tangata did not know they were in the forest. They were inhuman creatures, capable of terrible violence. With so little known about them, it paid to be cautious whenever they were close. He glanced back at the bootprints, noticing how they'd grown close together. It suggested the creatures were travelling slowly…

…the prints changed again.

A curse slipped from Romaine's lips as he pulled his horse to a stop. Ahead, a third set of prints joined the trail. Blood pounded in Romaine's ears as he tightened his fist around the hilt of his axe. Three Tangata was too many, even on horseback. Just one of the demonic creatures was a match for three men.

They had just become outnumbered.

Murmurs came from the men as Romaine edged his horse forward, examining the fresh bootprints. Then a frown touched his face. There was something unusual about the new set of tracks. He dismounted and knelt for a closer look. They had emerged from the forest to the east, the same as the others, but their owner was smaller by several boot sizes. And now that he was close…Romaine realised that the Tangata tracks overlaid the third pair.

The Tangata had not met with this new individual; they had come later.

His eyes travelled ahead and he saw the stride of the Tangata grow longer. They had started running, in pursuit. Could the third set of tracks belong to a Calafe, one of his own? It didn't seem possible that anyone could have survived out here, alone for months with naught but the Tangata. And yet…

Romaine stood suddenly and raced back to his horse. The lieutenant opened his mouth to ask a question, but Romaine was already swinging himself into the saddle. The tracks were recent, their edges still hard instead of crumbling. If they were quick, they might just reach them in time.

"Romaine…" the lieutenant began, but Romaine silenced the man with a glare.

"Whoever left the third pair of bootprints, they're no friend of the Tangata," he hissed.

Then Romaine kicked his horse into a gallop, leaving the lieutenant and his scouts with no choice but to follow.

THE WARRIOR

Romaine ducked as a snow-covered branch flashed for his face. A second later a muffled curse told him another of the scouts had not been so lucky. Without slowing, he glanced back and was reassured that five riders still followed.

Facing the trail once more, he studied the bootprints as they sped past. The snow was thinning now, the trail sloping back down towards the lowlands. Trees flickered past either side of him, but the forest was changing, the dense mountain firs giving way to cedar and maple. The trail split and re-joined around clumps of brush.

Romaine urged his gelding on, coaxing another ounce of speed from the beast. Without the prints to follow, they would struggle to track their quarry. He had to catch them before the last of the snow vanished. Behind, the cries of his comrades chased after him as they tried to keep pace, but this was not their land, not their fellow citizen standing alone against the Tangata, and they were losing ground.

Images flashed through Romaine's mind, of a woman lying silent in the snow, of a boy's pale face, of lifeless eyes in the daylight. Blood pounded in his temples and his vision blurred, blinding him to the forest, the trail, until all that was left to him were the bootprints he followed.

A scream cut the air. At first, he barely registered the noise over the pounding of hooves. But it came again—a cry of terror, of a woman alone, unmistakably human.

"Romaine!" His companion's voices called him back.

He slowed his horse, but only for a moment, to readjust his grip on the axe. Sunlight rippled across the twin blades, then he was surging forward once more, the gelding responding to his urging with a cry of its own. They were still downwind of the Tangata and the horses could smell them now, the unnatural scent of humanity mixed with something *else*, the madness of the enemy.

Suddenly the trees were falling away and Romaine found himself rushing across an open meadow. The pounding of hooves from behind told him his comrades still followed. For a second he was touched with guilt, that he had led them here so recklessly, but there was no time for second thoughts now. Ahead, two figures swung to face the newcomers. At first glance, they could have been mistaken as humans. Neither were larger than the average man— were smaller even than Romaine, in fact. Their clothes were of rough-spun cotton, faded and torn, but not far removed from that worn by a farmer or a woodsman—in summer. In this frozen forest, a human would have perished from exposure long ago.

But the Tangata did not feel the cold.

Each wore its hair in long, unkept braids—one jet-black, the other straw blond—and the finer features of one revealed it was female. Their scouts often hunted in pairs. While little was known of their hierarchy, they were assumed to be mating couples.

Beyond the two, a woman in heavy winter furs staggered backwards, auburn hair flashing in the sunlight. Relief swept through Romaine—they were not too late.

His attention snapped back to the Tangata as growls came from across the clearing. He shivered as two pairs of slate-grey eyes fixed on him. More than anything, this feature marked the beasts as inhuman. Completely grey, the eyes of the Tangata held no empathy, no compassion, no emotion other than rage—and hatred. They were the eyes of the lost, their humanity washed away by the magic they had stolen from the long-departed Gods.

Watching the creatures now, Romaine's jaw clenched with a hatred of his own. These creatures had taken everything from him, consumed a decade of his life, stolen his nation. And still they came, still they sought more. The greed that had first driven them to betray the Divine lived still within them; they would not stop until the world was theirs.

Rage swept through Romaine like a wave, banishing fear and thought. Though the Flumeeren scouts had spread out behind him, in that moment there was only Romaine and the Tangata.

With a roar, he charged. Shouts came from behind Romaine as the gelding leapt forward. He trusted his comrades would follow. Howls met his battlecry as the Tangata sprang towards him, crossing half the clearing in a single bound.

Their speed was terrifying to behold, even on the snow-kissed ground. The creatures carried no weapons, but they hardly needed them. Ice slid down Romaine's spine as the male drew ahead and the slate-grey eyes locked with his. Immediately the beast diverted its path, heading straight for the charging axeman.

A wicked grin split Romaine's face and he rose in the saddle, bellowing a challenge. Let it think him easy prey; this was not Romaine's first encounter with the beasts. He raised his axe as the distance closed, waiting for the moment…

Suddenly the Tangata was airborne, a bound of its powerful legs sending it soaring into the air—straight at Romaine. Beneath him, the gelding screamed and then it was rearing up, hooves lashing the air.

Only that saved Romaine. Instead of him, the full strength of the Tangata struck the horse. A sickening crunch followed as the two came together, iron-shod hooves striking flesh. Yet it was not the Tangata that fell. With almost a sigh, Romaine's mount toppled backwards, body limp.

Cursing, Romaine kicked free of his stirrups and fell sideways, narrowly avoiding being crushed. In one fluid movement, he rolled to his feet, boots crunching on the icy ground, axe still in hand. He had a second to glimpse the now lifeless corpse of the gelding, its head snapped where the creature's blow had struck—then the male was upon him.

It came as little more than a blur, teeth bared, arms raised to tear him apart. In a second it dissolved the space between them, and again it leapt, a scream shaking the snow from the branches of nearby trees.

This time, though, Romaine was ready. He swept his axe up, the twin points of its butterfly blades rising to meet his assailant. Mid-air, the creature could not adjust its attack, and with a soft *crunch*, its weight slammed down into the axe, driving the points deep into the creature's chest.

Triumph swept through Romaine—but a wild fist struck his shoulder. The axe was torn from his grasp as the blow sent him tumbling across the snowy earth. Stars flashed across his vision and he struggled to reclaim his senses, to regain his feet. Desperately he fumbled for the dagger on his belt; the beast could be on him any second. Finally he found the hilt and tore it loose. Swinging around, he gasped for breath, seeking his foe.

But the Tangata had not moved. Romaine's axe remained embedded in its flesh. Blood seeped from the wound, staining its tunic red. Slowly its head turned, and the grey eyes focused on Romaine. Fury flicked on the beast's face and it tried to take a step. The effort was too much, even for this creature. Its legs gave way and it tumbled forward.

Romaine flinched as the impact drove his axe deeper into the creature's chest. It moved no more.

He stood staring at his foe for a moment, but the satisfaction of its defeat was short lived. One more of the creatures was dead, but the death would not fill the emptiness…

A scream came from across the meadow, drawing Romaine's attention back to reality. His heart palpated as he recalled the second Tangata, then fell into the pit of his stomach as he saw the battle being fought across the clearing.

One of the scouts was already dead, eyes staring lifelessly up at the sky, while the Perfugian recruit, Flagers, lay nearby, hands clasping desperately at the silver cords spilling from his stomach. A moan came from his throat as the intestines slipped through his fingers, and his head swung around, eyes fixing on Romaine. He tried to cry out, but his words emerged as little more than a whisper.

Steeling his heart, Romaine forced his attention back to the battle. He had seen such wounds before—Flagers was already dead. But the lieutenant and the two remaining scouts could still survive. They had managed to keep their horses, though only the lieutenant still held his lance. Another lance lay broken on the ground nearby, while the last had been driven through the thigh of the female Tangata.

Though terribly injured, the beast had managed to snap the lance in half. Its tip still jabbed through her thigh, dripping scarlet blood in the snow, but the other half she now flourished like a club, preventing the three horsemen from getting close enough to finish her.

Romaine staggered to his fallen foe and kicked the Tangata onto its back, then retrieved his axe. Silently, he started towards the female, eager to put an end to the creature before it harmed anyone else.

Before he could reach her, though, the female finally noticed its mate's death. A terrible scream echoed around the clearing as it spun towards Romaine, and he saw again the madness in its eyes, the desire to rend and tear and kill.

But for once the lieutenant acted without thinking. The only one left with a weapon, he urged his horse forward while the Tangata was distracted and drove the steel-tipped lance through the creature's back.

The awful howl was instantly cut short, and a *thud* followed as the beast crumpled to the snow. Silence returned to the clearing... only to be punctuated by the soft cries of Flagers.

For an instant, Romaine kept his eyes fixed on the Tangata. Blood pounded in his ears and he still felt the need for battle within him, that terrible rage demanding he charge forward, axe raised, battlecry on his lips.

But the fight was over, their enemies dead, and slowly the pounding subsided.

Despair rose to take its place, and silently Romaine turned to look again at the boy. Before he realized what he was doing, Romaine staggered forward and dropped to one knee beside the Perfugian. There was nothing he could do for the lad—not even a doctor could have saved him from such a wound.

"Romaine?" Flagers gasped, his voice trembling. "Romaine, it hurts...don't know what happened. I'm...sorry."

"It's okay, lad," Romaine murmured. As he spoke, he reached for the dagger on his belt. "It's going to be okay."

"It hurts, Romai…" The words trailed off as the boy's eyes slid closed. A few moments later, his breathing ceased as well.

Releasing the boy, Romaine sat back. His eyes were drawn to the blood pooling in the snow, still seeping from the wound he'd opened in the recruit's groin. A lump lodged in his throat and he felt the boy's lifeless eyes watching him, accusing. It had been a mercy, and yet…the face of another boy flickered into his mind. He lay not in snow but a bed of roses. Romaine scrunched his eyes closed, trying to banish the image.

"Is he…?"

A voice was calling from behind him. Shaking off his grief, Romaine stood and faced the lieutenant.

"Gone," he said shortly.

The lieutenant swallowed, his eyes drawn to the corpse. He held his sword in hand now, its tip trembling. It was probably the first time he had faced the Tangata in battle.

A flicker from across the clearing. The unfamiliar woman was standing beside the body of the male Tangata, staring at its gruesome remains. Her face was unusually pale for the Calafe and freckles dotted her cheeks, but the heavy fur coat and woollen leggings were familiar.

Romaine watched as she knelt beside the Tangata. She seemed more curious than afraid. The woman couldn't have more than twenty years to her name. What was she doing out here, all alone?

Casting one last glance at the dead boy, Romaine let out a sigh, then started towards the young woman. Her head whipped around at the sound of his footsteps, and amber eyes widened, fixing on the bloody axe he still carried in one hand. Seeing her fear, Romaine paused, then setting the weapon on the ground, he continued with empty hands.

"Easy now," he said.

"You killed him," the young woman murmured, rising to her feet and facing Romaine.

She spoke in a strange, singsong accent unfamiliar to Romaine —though that was not unusual in Calafe. His people were a nomadic sort, and there were many groups who would spend months or even years apart from civilisation. The isolation bred strange tones, though if this woman belonged to such a group, where were the others?

"Ay," Romaine replied to her question. "It's dead. You're safe now, lass."

A tremor shook the woman and she raised a hand, as though to keep him back. Her other hung limp at her side, and Romaine realised she had been injured. Well, she'd gotten lucky if all the Tangata had given her was a broken arm—they were said to do terrible things to those they captured.

"It's okay," Romaine said, trying again to comfort her. He reached out a hand. "We'll take you to safety."

"No!"

The woman's voice echoed from the nearby trees as she leapt away from him. But whether from the cold or some unknown injury, her legs failed to support her weight, and she crumpled into a snow-drift with a muffled cry—quickly silenced.

Romaine was at her side in an instant. Her broken arm lay at an awkward angle in the snow and her eyes were closed—she must have lost consciousness from the pain.

"Is she alright?" the lieutenant asked. He approached with sword still in hand, as though the woman might yet somehow prove to be an enemy.

Romaine placed a finger on the woman's throat. Her pulse was racing and erratic, but strong, and he nodded as the lieutenant drew to a stop alongside him.

"Her arm's broken. Passed out from the pain, or maybe shock. We'd better get her on one of the horses." There would be plenty spare, now.

"Poor lass," the lieutenant said as he looked at the woman. "What was she doing out here?"

"I'd like to know that myself," Romaine replied.

"I'll fetch Flagers's horse," the lieutenant murmured, then hesitated. "Shame, about the lad. I told him to hang back, but…" He shrugged and turned away.

Romaine said nothing. What more was there to say? The boy had never had any business being out here, untrained, unprepared. But then, he'd had little choice in the matter. Unlike the citizens of Flumeer or Calafe, Perfugians did not decide their own fates. That was a matter for their betters, a judgement passed down by their Sovereigns.

Rising, he lifted the woman in his arms and crossed to where one of the surviving scouts had gathered the horses. She was surprisingly heavy in her thick furs—or perhaps it was merely exhaustion finally catching him—but regardless, Romaine was relieved when he settled her in the saddle of Flagers's horse. Taking care with her arm, he bound the woman so she would not fall, and then looked for a mount of his own.

The dead scout's horse had emerged from the battle unscathed, and before long they were on the trail once more, riding north. The battle had cost them precious time and the light faded quickly. The sun plummeted towards the western treeline, setting the horizon alight.

It was still an hour from dark when the howling began in the forest behind them.

❧ 2 ☙

THE ARCHIVIST

Erika paused as she leaned backwards over the void, the darkness beckoning below. Only the corded rope looped around her waist held her in place. A shiver touched her, but now was not the time for second thoughts, and with a last look at her two assistants, she kicked off into the chasm. The rope slid through her fingers as she descended, the pitch-black reaching up to embrace her.

Soon the oil lantern clipped to her backpack became the only source of light, as the opening above shrank to nothing. The air grew colder, damp with the breath of the earth, and she shivered again, her eyes searching the absolute dark below for sign of the bottom. The lantern flickered and the black seemed to press closer, as though trying to repel her, to keep her from the secrets that had lain hidden from human eyes for centuries.

There were those who said these places were haunted, that they were the sacred sites of the Gods, or the birthplace of the Tangata. The details changed from story to story, but all agreed that entrance was forbidden, that to step foot in these hidden places was to call death down upon the human race.

As if that weren't already coming.

Erika ignored such superstitions. The small-minded who believed such fancy had held back humanity for long enough. They could no longer afford such ignorance. Flumeer needed every weapon it could find for the war to come.

Fortunately, the Flumeeren queen had finally come to see her point of view. Now Erika just had to discover something of use in these lost places, something that might change the tide of the war.

So far though, her search had proven fruitless. The other sites had been empty; whatever secrets they'd once contained long lost to the passage of time.

And the queen was not known for her patience. She had taken a gamble, supporting Erika in the face of resistance from nobles who preferred to leave the past buried. What would happen if Erika came back empty-handed a third time?

"This is the place," Erika whispered to herself, breath now fogging in the lanternlight. "This time I will find it."

The magic of the Gods.

Those had been the words that had convinced the queen. Erika had spent most of her life studying their long-lost deities, whose magic had once been shared freely with humanity. What wonders had her ancestors witnessed in those glorious times before The Fall? Before the traitors amongst their ranks had grown jealous of the Gods and stolen the forbidden powers?

Only legends told of that time now. The traitors had sought to use the stolen magics to reshape themselves, seeking to join the Divine. But when the Gods had discovered the violation, their rage had been terrible, and instead the thieves had been cursed to madness. They had become the Tangata.

If only the anger of the Gods could be so easily sated.

All humanity had been equal before their omniscient gaze, and so all humanity had been cast down.

A hundred years of darkness had followed.

Fools!

Just the thought of that ancient betrayal caused Erika to tighten her grip about the rope. The Tangata had ruined everything, sentenced humanity to crawl amidst the dirt like common beasts for their avarice. Even when the light had finally returned, humanity had found the Gods gone, returned to their citadels amidst the clouds.

But the Tangata had remained.

Surely there was a design in that, some divine plan. Erika was convinced it was a test, a trial to see whether humanity could put right the mistakes of their ancestors. The Gods would not have left them alone to face the beasts, not unless there was a reason, a chance for victory.

And so she searched in these ancient places, searching for what had been forgotten by the mind of men, for a power left to them by the Gods to defeat the Tangata.

She had dedicated her entire life to it.

Thunk.

Erika stumbled as her feet struck solid earth. She would have fallen, but instinctively she had stopped letting out rope and now it brought her up short. Getting her feet back under her, she straightened.

Overhead, the entrance was little more than a pinprick now. Unclipping the lantern from her pack, she held it high to make sure she was truly at the bottom. On three sides the shaft was hard rock, but on the fourth a tunnel led into the darkness. She swore at the sight of water dripping from the walls. That was as the other sites had been, their contents rotted away long ago.

Not this time, please, Gods, not this time.

Her lantern illuminated walls of white limestone. Stalactites had begun to form in the ceiling, young yet, while water and the relentless passage of time had carved grooves in the stone beneath her feet. Silver threads criss-crossed the air, reflecting light from her lantern, but she saw no sign of the arachnids that had spun them.

Satisfied she had reached the bottom of the shaft, Erika set the lantern on the ground beside her and unclipped herself from the rope. Three tugs signalled to her assistants it was safe to descend. It would not pay to venture too far into this place alone.

She looked again at the walls. So much had been lost to the passage of time, but Erika knew for herself that some powers had remained from the time of the Gods. Her mother had…become a scavenger, digging in the dirt for scraps of metal that she could sell to the local blacksmith.

Their poverty in her later childhood stung Erika even now, though at least her mother's occupation had given birth to her fascination with the Gods. The woman had collected trinkets found during her digging—pieces of glass and strange, bendable materials that were of no worth to the local tradesmen. Most had been inert, remnants of a time long lost.

But one had been different.

Erika had found it amongst her mother's collection—a smooth, round piece of glass. It had seemed no different from the others, but for an impurity at its centre. Some mistake in its crafting, her younger self had thought.

Until she'd squeezed it between her fingers, and a brilliant light had burst forth.

She'd dropped it, so great had been her shock. The artefact had struck a rock and cracked in half, its light dying with a final flash. Half-blinded, Erika had scrambled to put it back together, before she'd smelt the burning.

Only as her vision cleared did she see the tiny drop of moisture that had been expelled from the glass. Solid stone had dissolved at its touch, leaving a smoking hole in the rock. Frozen in terror at what she might have unleashed, her younger self had sat frozen as the house filled with a terrible, molten stench. The stone had burnt for an hour before whatever magic had been hidden within the glass finally consumed itself. It had left a hole almost the size of Erika's fist in the unadorned floor.

Erika had not soon forgotten the beating she'd received for the incident, though today it was the loss of the object she regretted. Who knew what power it might have possessed? She'd found other objects over the years, but none had retained their magic.

The scuffing of boots on stone announced the arrival of her first assistant. A plump Flumeeren man by the name of Ibran, he had been one of the first to record the known locations of these sites. He'd been reluctant to join the expedition, concerned as he was by the wrath of the Gods, but his academic's mind had finally proven stronger than his superstition. Unclipping himself from the rope, Ibran took up another lantern and stepped aside for her second assistant to make his descent.

Sythe was Ibran's opposite in every way, more fighter than academic. The queen had offered his services to ensure their safety on the journey. So far, they had not had to test his skills as a warrior, though his strength had been a welcome addition. He came into view now, descending rapidly, a massive pack looped over his shoulders. A pickaxe was clipped to the side and within were their supplies—rope and food for several days, water, even a blasting cap, in case they had to break through a collapse in the cave network.

She might have travelled with a larger party, but Erika was not the only one interested in the world before The Fall. She'd heard whispers of Archivists in Gemaho who sought the same secrets as herself. With the fall of Calafe, the world was growing desperate for an answer to the Tangata.

When Sythe had landed and unclipped, Erika nodded for him to take the lead. "Slowly," she murmured, "if anything remains, I don't want to disturb it."

"Yes, Archivist," Sythe said with a nod. He was not a man of many words.

Ibran took up position behind Erika as they started off into the caves. He too carried a pack, though like hers, it only held his food and water for the day, along with a few scrolls to help with translating the language of the Gods. Though breathing in the moisture-laden air, Erika felt they might be getting ahead of themselves.

The ancient sites seemed to follow a similar pattern to one another, though the rock that surrounded them was smooth, unbroken by a single joint. Had the Gods carved them from the bedrock itself? The thought of such power sent a shudder down Erika's spine. Surely even a fraction would be enough to destroy the Tangata.

Using sketches of the last site they'd visited as a map, the three wound their way deeper into the darkness. The tunnel branched at regular intervals, creating a maze far beneath the surface. Smaller openings appeared in the walls, revealing all manner of chambers.

The moisture seemed to lessen as they pressed on, though as the hours stretched out, they still saw no sign of relics. Doubt touched Erika. What had she been thinking, pinning her future on a wild goose chase? She should have known nothing would remain of the time before The Fall, not even in these secret places. If only they had been sealed away, protected from the elements. Instead they had remained opened to the world, their contents rotted away, or perhaps even stolen by early explorers.

Steeling herself, Erika forced her chin higher. They had barely started. It would take days to explore the entire network. Plenty of time yet for a discovery.

There would be a chamber somewhere here, something that had been protected, that still held its secrets. She continued on, counting steps, checking each chamber she came too, then continuing. Always they were spaced the same number of steps apart---

Erika frowned, pausing midstride. There should have been another opening ahead, but instead she found only smooth, untouched stone. Still in the lead, Sythe continued on, unaware of the break in pattern, but she stopped.

"Something wrong, Archivist?" Ibran asked.

Shaking her head, Erika did not reply. Had she lost track of her footsteps? No, she had long grown used to keeping the count while other thoughts occupied her mind. Following the pattern of the other sites, there should be a chamber here.

But there was nothing but solid stone.

Erika's heart hammered in her chest as she held the lantern closer to the limestone wall. Not a single crack showed in the silvery stone, nothing to indicate a cave-in had closed off the chamber. Had the Gods changed their pattern in this place? But no, the rest of the site had been a mirror image of the others.

"An irregularity," she murmured, more to herself than her companions.

It didn't make sense. Why change the pattern here? She leaned in closer, inspecting the pale rock. Light from her lantern shimmered as it caught in the thin trails of water trickling down the wall. She frowned as an idea came to her. Wasn't it odd, that these places had been carved from the bedrock—then left unadorned? With the power at their fingertips, why would the Gods choose to leave their sacred places so…plain?

Unless the limestone was not, in fact, the original stone.

"The pickaxe," she said, turning to Sythe.

Sythe raised an eyebrow, but he was a former soldier and accustomed to obeying orders without question. Shrugging the pack from his back, he unclipped the pickaxe and handed it over.

Carefully she stepped up to the wall. The white stone seemed to glow in the lantern light, as though the rock had somehow absorbed the great magics that had once been worked here. Erika cared little for its beauty—only for what might lie beneath. Using the razor-sharp point of the pickaxe, she scraped at the rock, gently at first, then with greater pressure as the limestone crumbled.

She kept at her task until, with a sharp grating noise, the pick struck something unyielding beneath the white rock. The breath caught in her throat and she withdrew the pick, revealing darkness beneath. For a moment, Erika thought it was stone—then Ibran moved his lantern, and light reflected from the black.

"Metal," she whispered.

"Truly?" Ibran leaned in closer, trying to get a better look. "That's...impossible. It would have corroded, rusted away long ago."

"And yet it remains," Erika murmured. That was a question for another day, though. Turning to Sythe, she handed the pickaxe back to him. "Let's see how far it extends."

The warrior nodded. He worked with more care than Erika would have expected from one untrained in the Archivists arts. The queen had apparently chosen her people well. Chunks of stone fell away and slowly a great panel of reflective metal was revealed. Dust covered its surface, but it remained unmarked by the pickaxe. Whatever the Gods had used in its creation, it was apparently harder than steel.

Blood pounded in Erika's ears as Sythe finally stepped back, revealing the full extent of his work. He had removed the limestone a foot to either side of the panel, though here his administrations had only revealed another type of rock. It confirmed Erika's suspicions. The limestone had not been there during the time of the Gods—it had formed later, deposited as a thin layer by the calcite laden waters.

She turned her attention back to the metal sheet. Its surface was unadorned, giving no indication of its purpose. But Erika knew, had guessed it the second she'd uncovered the reflective surface. This panel was the reason for the missing chamber.

"It's a door," she murmured.

"But how to open it?" Ibran replied.

He had a point. There was no handle that might have released the door from its frame. In fact, the steel joined so tightly with the rock on either side that it formed a perfect seal. Erika's hands began to shake. If this door had kept out the moisture, its contents might have been protected from the relentless passage of time.

This was what she'd been searching for!

"Can you knock it down?" she asked, excitement washing away her usual caution.

Sythe flicked her a glance, then stepping back from the door, he lurched forward and slammed a boot into the metal. The panel did not so much as budge. He tried again, and a final time, but it was clear the metal would take more than human strength to move.

Erika swallowed. Dare she risk the explosive charges? They could bring the roof down on them, or destroy whatever lay on the other side. But what other choice did she have? The pickaxe had not even dented the strange metal.

"Sythe," she murmured. "The blasting cap."

"What?" Ibran hissed. "Archivist, you cannot be serious. The risk—"

"The risk is acceptable," Erika spoke over him. There was more than just her reputation at stake—the queen did not take kindly to failure. Especially if she learned they'd been so close and turned back. "Sythe, I trust you can open this door without bringing the ceiling down on top of us."

Sythe was already rummaging in his pack, but he paused long enough to nod. Ibran stuttered something incomprehensible and then started off back down the corridor. Ignoring him, Erika watched as Sythe set the charges. She had little experience with such things, and had to trust the man knew what he was doing. If they ended up destroying what lay within…

No, she could not doubt herself, not now. She needed to know what lay behind this door. Her fate, the fate of Flumeer, and perhaps even humanity itself, depended on it.

Finally, Sythe stepped back from the door. He had set two charges, one high, the other low, both on the left-hand side of the door. Taking the fuse from his pack, he attached it to the charges and then glanced at her.

"Ready."

Nodding, Erika led the way back down the tunnel. If the explosion did cause a cave-in, she didn't want to be anywhere near it. Sythe trailed the fuse out behind them as they went, until they reached the last chamber they'd passed. There they found a sulking Ibran. Erika joined him in the chamber's questionable shelter and then looked to Sythe.

He lit the fuse.

Erika held her breath as sparks leapt from the wire and vanished back into the main tunnel. Suddenly doubtful, she shared a glance with Ibran, but it was too late to change her mind now. Closing her eyes, she held her hands over her ears and waited.

Boom.

3

THE ARCHIVIST

Light seared through Erika's eyelids as the explosion shook the chamber. A shockwave followed and something struck her, driving her to the ground. Breath hissed between her teeth as she dragged in a breath. Dust burned in her nostrils and when she opened her eyes, Erika found herself in absolute darkness.

For a second, she thought the worst had happened and they'd all been buried. But then the weight shifted above her and she heard a grunt as someone picked himself up. The flare of a match illuminated Sythe's face, then the broken lantern and the grumbling Ibran where he had fallen on the other side of the cave. Sythe retrieved their spare lantern from his backpack, though even with it lit, it was near impossible to see with the dust and smoke still obscuring the air.

Erika coughed as she dragged herself to her feet. "Did it work?"

Without a word, Sythe moved to the doorway. The light of his lantern drew them after him. Excitement pulsed in Erika's veins as she stepped back into the tunnel. An uncharacteristic grin split Sythe's face as he glanced back.

"Looks like it worked, Archivist."

She was at his side in an instant, her discomfort forgotten. Dust still danced in the lanternlight, but a gap in the steel panel was now evident. Beyond, darkness beckoned. Hardly able to contain her excitement, Erika staggered forward. The door had twisted in its frame, the blast blowing the bottom half of it inwards several inches, while the rest remained stubbornly fixed in place. Thankfully, the gap was large enough for even Ibran to fit.

She stepped towards it before a sense of self-preservation gave her pause. If this space had remained untouched since The Fall, the magic of the Gods might still prevail—along with any traps they might have set for intruders. She considered sending Sythe first… but no, if the unknown truly awaited, she wanted—needed—to be first.

Gathering herself, she ducked beneath the broken sheet of metal. Darkness swallowed her up as she left behind the lantern and set one foot, then another, on the unseen floor. Holding her breath, she straightened.

Clang.

A scream built in Erika's throat as something clicked overhead and she tried to throw herself back. But in the darkness, she misjudged the height of the hole in the door. Her shoulder collided with the heavy metal and threw her back, leaving her at the mercy of whatever trap she had triggered…

Light flooded the chamber.

Erika's scream turned to a gasp as she found herself face-to-face with the brilliance of the Gods. A magical glow now lit the chamber, stemming from great globes of glass fixed high on the walls—like giant versions of the artefact she had once held as a child. Mouth wide, she turned in a circle, eyes burning from the sudden brightness after the dark, but unable to turn away.

"Archivist?" Ibran's voice came from beyond the door. He sounded nervous. "Is…everything okay?

"See for yourself," she said, too engrossed with the magic to offer any explanation.

Scuffling came from beyond the door as her assistants followed, first Ibran, then Sythe bringing up the rear. Their eyes widened as they saw the source of the light. Erika shared their astonishment. What magic did the Gods possess, that their talismans retained power, even centuries after being abandoned?

"What sorcery is this?" Ibran murmured.

A grin came unbidden to Erika's face. "What we've been searching for."

"Perhaps the doubters were right," he croaked. She looked at him in surprise and saw his jowls quiver as he swallowed. "This… just being in this place, it feels like sacrilege."

The smile slipped from Erika's face. "Nonsense," she snapped, before returning her attention to the chamber.

There was no sign of water damage here—indeed, even after the explosion, there was barely any dust on this side of the door. Instead of limestone, the walls and floor were made of polished grey stone, their surfaces untouched by weakness or imperfections. Her breath caught as she saw a massive pane of black glass fixed to one wall. It would have been worth a fortune back in Mildeth—only the richest of nobles could afford windows of glass.

A table made from a similar metal to the door sat pressed against the opposite wall. Blood pounded in Erika's ears as she stepped towards it. The metal surface was empty. Despite the magic lights, the shining glass and sealed door, there was…nothing.

No!

Erika darted forward as the light glinted from an object she'd almost missed—a glove, lying alone on the table. The way it reflected in the strange lights had camouflaged it. As she picked it up, she realised why. It had been woven from metal rather than wool. A gauntlet? What would the Gods have needed with such an object?

Instinctively, she lifted the gauntlet and slipped it onto her hand. Behind her, Ibran gasped, no doubt disturbed by her supposed sacrilege, but she ignored him. She had come to learn, to gain understanding of the Gods—not surrender to superstition. The time had come to throw caution to the winds.

The cold steel sent a shiver down her spine. She was surprised how well it fit—she had always imagined the Gods as giants. Though she supposed that was foolish, given how small these hidden tunnels were.

Holding the gauntlet up to the light, Erika wondered at how the steel fibres had been woven together. They rippled in the magical glow, seeming almost alive. What was the function of such an object? Her heart throbbed as an idea came to her. Could this be what she'd been looking for, some connection to the Gods and their magic?

"Erika…"

It was Ibran, but she was past listening to his cautions now. Standing there, illuminated by the magic of the Gods, surrounded by their riches, Erika *knew* what she had to do. Forgotten were the warnings, the legends of the Tangata and The Fall. She now held the magic that could destroy them in the palm of her hand, if only she had the strength to command it.

She closed her fist, reaching out with her mind for those ancient powers, seeking to wake them, to bring them forth for the first time in centuries. This was her purpose, the reason she had been drawn to these ancient places, to a lifetime dedicated to the study of the Gods…

Nothing happened.

Her heartbeat slowed and finally she opened her eyes, an exhaled breath whistling between her teeth. She turned her hand over, examining the gauntlet, but nothing had changed. Her elation subsided, the thrill of just moments before fading away. It was no more than an ordinary glove. Perhaps this had been the height of fashion for those who had lived alongside the Gods. A revelation of great interest to scholars like Ibran, no doubt, but for her…

Erika's face warmed as she felt the eyes of her assistants upon her. Clenching her fists at her sides, she continued her inspection of the chamber, though she still sensed their mirth. She forced her mind back to that of a scholar. Magic or no, this was still a great discovery. Those crystals…how long would their light remain? Perhaps they could remove them from the walls, to show the queen that her expedition had not been entirely in vain.

Then her eyes alighted on a picture that had been plastered to the wall. She hadn't noticed it at first, so engrossed had she been in the crystal lights and the gauntlet. Something about the decoration caught her eye now. She took a step closer, frowning. It looked so familiar…

A gasp slipped from her throat as she realised what it was.

"It's a map," she murmured.

The map was so detailed and colourful, she hadn't recognised it at first. Now its true nature practically leapt at her. There was the northern archipelago of Perfugia, and there the Mountains of the Gods, the southern coasts of Calafe. And so much more.

Reverently, Erika stretched out a hand and touched the map. She was surprised to find it was paper—how had such a delicate thing survived all this time? The steel door had truly sealed off this chamber from the world, from time itself, it seemed.

Her eyes continued to roam the lands depicted by the map, making connections. Dots labelled in the language of the ancients must have indicated cities. Erika was not surprised to see many corresponded with modern-day towns and cities—no doubt the benefits of their locations had not changed through the centuries. Several, though, were wastelands today, others the sites of mining extractions.

Footsteps sounded as her assistants approached, but Erika did not take her eyes from the precious paper. There was something else here, something important. Several locations had been marked with stars rather than dots and had not been labelled. They didn't seem to correspond with any modern cities, nor any significant feature that might have proven an advantage for a settlement...

The breath caught in her throat as the pattern clicked into place. Surely it couldn't be so simple? Quickly she tracked the distances, trying to judge the scale, to be sure. Yes, there was the site on the peninsula west of Mildeth. And there was the one in the foothills of the mountains...

"It shows the ancient sites," she whispered. "The hidden places of the Gods."

"Truly?" Ibran gasped, stepping up beside her. "That—"

Erika was barely listening to him, so engrossed was she in the map. It didn't only show those sites they'd visited in Flumeer—it revealed *all* of them! They dotted the landscape, many matching sites already known to the Archivists, others that had yet been identified. Her heart throbbed, sending blood rushing to her temples.

If those sites had remained undiscovered all this time, if they were sealed as this chamber had been...who knew what treasures they might have preserved?

Then a frown touched her lips as she noticed an absence. Of the dozen or so stars on the map, only three were located in Flumeer. The three they had already visited...

Thump.

Erika jumped as something heavy struck the ground. She swung on Ibran, ready to reprimand him for his carelessness, but the words died on her lips. Her assistant lay facedown on the floor, blood oozing from an awful wound in his neck. A scream built in her throat, her sluggish mind trying to put the pieces together, to understand how he had come to be there...

...her eyes fell on the bloody dagger clutched in Sythe's hand.

"What did you do?" she hissed.

"Step 'way from the map," the man said calmly.

Ice spread through Erika's veins. His voice had changed, losing the western tang of the Flumeeren people. He sounded almost...

"I said, *step away*," Sythe repeated, voice deepening to a growl. He took a step towards her, dagger poised to strike.

Instinctively, Erika tried to back away, but the table brought her up short. It took a moment for his words to register. They sent a shudder down her spine. Step away from the most important finding of her career, a map to all the secret places of the Gods? Even if there were no other sites in Flumeer, the discovery was a priceless treasure.

Scanning her surroundings, Erika searched for a way to fight back. The chamber was only ten by ten feet and Sythe was a big man, easily twice her size, and the knife in his hand was almost two foot long. Any plan that resulted in physical conflict would not go her way. But that didn't mean she would surrender her prize without resistance.

"Stay back!" she hissed.

Her eyes flickered to the ruined door, but even if she could grab the map and make it past Sythe, she would never make it through the gap before he caught her.

A smile touched Sythe's face, as though he could read her thoughts. "Hey," he murmured, lowering the point of his knife half an inch. "No need for ya to join 'im, ay?" He gestured to Ibran. A pool of blood was already beginning to form beneath the man.

Erika shook her head, adopting the manner of a terrified youth. It didn't take much to be convincing—the blood dripping from Sythe's knife was enough to drive her to the edge of panic. *This couldn't be happening.*

"Why are you doing this?" she whispered.

Sythe's lips drew back, revealing yellowed teeth. "The King pays well for secrets."

"The king?" Erika said, momentarily confused, before the man's accent clicked into place. "Gemaho!" she gasped.

She hadn't heard the accent often as a child, when visitors had dined with her father. But that had been before the war, before she'd fled with her mother; she hadn't heard the accent in years now. Gemaho had broken the war pact when the allied expedition south of the Agzor Fortress had failed. Afterwards, they had retreated within their borders and barred entrance to all foreigners. Sythe—if that was even his true name—only laughed in confirmation of her suspicions.

"What interest does the King of the West have in my work?" she asked, trying to regain the initiative. Maybe if she could negotiate…

Sythe laughed. "New age is approaching, Archivist," he rasped, accents mixing. "Kingdoms are doomed, without'a new weapon. Or an old one. Whichever kingdom uncovers the magic of the Gods, will rule the world."

"That's insanity!" Erika gasped. "The kingdoms stand united—"

"Ha!" Sythe interrupted. "'ought you were smart. Wars comin', one the king ain't intending to lose."

"But—"

"Enough," Sythe barked. He swung the dagger in a lazy arc.

"*No!*" Erika screamed, flinching against the table and thrusting out her gauntleted hand to fend off the blow.

The attack had only been a warning, but now Sythe's face darkened and he raised the blade high. Erika was sure she had only seconds left. Frustration burned in her soul. So much time, an entire life, wasted on the study of the Gods, and for what? To have someone else snatch away the prize at her moment of victory?

But as the blow swept towards her, Sythe stumbled, and the swing of his dagger fell short. A frown appeared on the assassin's unshaven cheeks and he shook his head, as though to dislodge something in his ears. It seemed to work, and he straightened—but only for a moment.

A scream tore from his throat as he staggered back, the dagger slipping from limp fingers. Hand still outstretched, Erika watched as the blade clattered harmlessly to the stone floor. Another cry came from Sythe as he crashed into the table, upending it on the floor. His screams turned to an awful gurgling as he slumped to his knees. Wild eyes, red with blood, swivelled in his skull, finding Erika standing frozen in place. He stretched out a hand, lips moving, trying to make sounds.

"Pleas—" he managed, as though the word had to be clawed from his throat.

Erika gaped as his face began to change. Blood seeped from his eyes and ears, leaving trails of red down his cheeks and neck. Another groan hissed from the man's throat as gore burst from his lips, splattering the stones between him and where Ibran lay dead.

Slowly Erika's horror turned to fascination. Her eyes moved from the Gemahan assassin to the gauntlet. This had to be its doing. Indeed, while unwatched, it had changed. Goosebumps tingled across her hand and she realised with a touch of fear that the fine wires had somehow become entwined with her flesh. Warmth spread through her hand and up her arm as a glow began in the unknown metal, like that of the crystals in the walls, but darker, more threatening.

Deadly.

Curious, Erika closed her fist. Immediately the light died. A sharp inhale from where Sythe had collapsed to the floor confirmed the traitor still lived, though he made no move to recover his dagger or feet. Soft sobs tore from the man's throat, and Erika wondered what style of agony could inspire such relief at its departure.

Heart pounding in her ears, Erika looked again at the gauntlet. She swallowed. *God magic.* She had hoped for this, prayed for it night and day since childhood. Now, though…she found herself wondering. What cost might this magic extract?

"Archivist?"

The faintest of whispers came from the assassin. He had not moved from where he lay, but now she saw his eyes moving, the bloody irises moving back and forth. Horror touched her and she forced herself to look away. She couldn't dwell on what her newfound power had done. There would be time for that later. For now, she needed to escape, in case others were working with the Gemahan.

The map!

It still hung from the wall, untouched in the conflict. Carefully she leaned across the table to recover it.

"Archivist," the call came again, though each word seemed to cause the man great pain. "Archivist…please…are you there?"

Icy cold slid down Erika's spine, but she ignored it. As she looked down at the map, she caught sight of another star. It lay beyond the borders of Flumeer, but not far, perhaps only two days ride south of the Illmoor. A secret site that no one had ever set eyes upon, that had never been opened. The treasures it might hold… surely they would make even the gauntlet look ordinary.

She rolled up the map and slid it into her satchel, then forced herself to look on Sythe. His eyes still flickered back and forth, but she saw now what the gauntlet had done. Its magic had shredded his corneas. He would never see again.

He tried to kill me!

Shaking off her pity, Erika slid along the table to the wall, avoiding where the assassin was still struggling to stand. Even blind, he might still prove a threat. Only when she reached the broken door did she pause to glance back. Sythe cried out again, crouched now beside Ibran.

"Archivist, *pleaaase!*"

Another cry drew her gaze back to Sythe. He crouched on the floor, pitiful in his desperation, raw terror twisting his face.

Erika turned away. She would feel no compassion for the man. This was only justice. He had tried to kill her—worse, he had tried to steal her victory.

Let him rot down here in the darkness.

4

THE RECRUIT

Lukys's legs burned as he made his slow way up the slope. The weight of his pack and chainmail vest dragged him back but he kept on, teeth clenched, eyes fixed on the ground two yards ahead of his feet. Grunts came from the other Perfugian recruits walking around him, though little was said. After a week of hard marching, few could spare the breath for idle words.

On more than a few occasions, Lukys had wondered whether he could keep on. The way had been a brutal series of mountains, valleys and river crossings, with each night spent camped in the open, with only the canvas tents they carried on their backs for shelter. Exhaustion weighed on his shoulders; he had not enjoyed a good night's sleep since the voyage from Ashura. If only the ship had carried them further south, the march to the frontier could have been completed in a day.

Instead it had deposited them on the docks of Mildeth, the Flumeeren capital, leaving them to walk most of the way. Apparently, the galley was needed for more important tasks, such as ferrying the famous Flumeeren spices back to Ashura.

Many of the recruits felt affronted at the idea, but Lukys's childhood had been filled with hardships far worse than a cross-country march. His parents had been nobodies. That wasn't meant to matter in Perfugia. Children were taken from their families at eight and enrolled at the national academy, so that none would be privileged above others.

But even at the academy, the division had been clear. His dormitory had been old and crowded; the newest facilities given to the noble born. And so had passed his twelve years of study. He was glad to be rid of the place.

Now, at last, he would have a chance to prove himself.

It had come as a surprise when they'd named him. The Perfugian army was renown throughout the four kingdoms; it was a rare honour to serve in its ranks. Lukys's hopes had been for a position as a scribe or doctor, though he'd struggled with both in his final examinations.

But a soldier? He hadn't dared dream of such an assignment.

Noticing the slope lessening beneath his boots, Lukys finally glanced up. A sigh escaped him as he saw the top of the hill was close. Several recruits and the officers on their horses were already waiting there. His fellows were taking the opportunity to sit and rest their legs, while the officers talked softly amongst themselves.

Coming to a stop alongside the others, Lukys leaned against his spear with a groan, then drew out his waterskin and took a swig. The path up the hill had been dry and it felt good to wash the dust from his mouth. Laughter came from the nearby recruits as they looked in his direction.

"Finally made it, peasant?"

A scowl twisted Lukys's lips but he kept his mouth shut. The group were made up of some of the higher born from the academy, men and women who at various points over the last ten years had made his life difficult. He was used to their taunts, though he'd hoped they might have ceased now that they'd all been named professional soldiers.

"I hope we get to march into Calafe," one of them, Dale, was saying to the others. "Let's see how tough the Tangata are when they come up against Perfugian steel!"

The others cheered and clapped his back. The officers on their horses ignored the noise, though the recruits had been instructed to keep quiet as they neared the frontier. If the maps were to be believed, they were close now…

Putting away his waterskin, Lukys moved past the officers. The remaining recruits were still filing up the hillside. Several of the stragglers were at least ten minutes behind; he had time to look around.

The terrain ahead was greener than what they'd just climbed. Trees spotted the rolling hills, though they could not compare to the untouched forests of northern Perfugia. Then Lukys frowned as he noticed a blackened strip of land. Further down the hill, the forest had been burnt, leaving bare earth stretching all the way to the broad waters of a river.

A river…

The Illmoor!

His heart quickened as he scanned the banks of the famous river, searching, seeking, *there!*

Nestled in a bend of the Illmoor was a town—Fogmore. A grin stretched his cheeks as he looked upon the end of their long journey. It faded, however, as his eyes lingered on the town. The stockade walls were tiny, and many of the buildings he could see looked to be made of wood. In Perfugia, even the poorest of villages were constructed of stone, built to last, to endure the wild storms that often bashed the island kingdom's coast. Wood was only ever used as decoration.

He supposed it was all a farming nation like Flumeer could afford on such a distant frontier. Even so, his stomach twisted at the thought of sleeping in such a matchbox—what would they do if a fire swept through the sprawling buildings?

And why had they burnt the forest?

Shouts came from behind, then the officers were trotting past. They didn't spare him a glance as they started down the winding path to the plains below. Lukys let out a sigh as he settled his pack more comfortably on his shoulders. Then he waited for Dale and his friends to go first—no doubt they would react unpleasantly to a mere peasant overtaking them.

The scraggly trees swallowed them up, sealing off the town from view for the time being. The weather had improved over the last day, but now Lukys noticed clumps of snow beneath the trees once more. The dry air of the valley they'd just traversed was replaced with a damp, cloying humidity, and by the time they reached the burnt section of land, clouds had gathered in the sky.

As they continued towards the distant town, Lukys looked on the ruined earth with sadness. Blackened tree stumps stood here and there, but the fire must have burnt hot—there was little remaining of the forest that covered the hillside further up. With the trees lost, the land already showed signs of erosion: deep rivulets carving through the ashy soil, exposed roots dotting the land, even a crumbling cliff that had collapsed across a section of the road.

Lukys couldn't begin to understand the destruction. While they lived in cities of stone, every Perfugian regarded their forestland as sacred.

The aching had begun again in his legs and back, but the knowledge that every step brought him closer to a bed—however flammable its enclosure might be—gave Lukys strength. His eyes sought a fresh glimpse of the fortified town, but it hid behind the rolling hills now between the recruits and the river.

Only as the sun dipped towards the horizon did the land flatten out, bringing the town back into view. Less than a mile off now, Lukys glimpsed the flicker of movement as armoured soldiers shifted atop the palisade. They wore chainmail like himself and their half-helms matched the one hanging from Lukys's pack.

Pale faces turned to watch at the approaching column, though no trumpets sounded to announce their arrival. They had probably been spotted when they'd lingered on the mountaintop. No doubt word of the reinforcements had carried ahead, and Lukys straightened his shoulders in anticipation of their reception. They were not fully-fledged soldiers yet, just at the beginning of their training, but he wanted to at least look the part.

But there were no cheers to greet them, no welcoming applause. The gates facing the road north stood open and a small gathering of onlookers in plain clothing had gathered atop the stockade walls, but an unnatural silence hung over them, more like mourners at a funeral than a welcome party. Lukys let out a sigh: he shouldn't have expected any better from a city at war.

As the column approached the gates, the officers brought their horses to a stop and turned to face the recruits.

"Column, halt!"

A ripple went through the Perfugian ranks as fifty men and women came to a staggering stop. Lukys and the others glanced at one another, wondering why they'd stopped. They were just a few yards from the town now, surely whatever it was could wait…

"Column, form lines!"

Again the recruits looked at one another, but another shout from the officers had them scrambling. Chaos ensued as they bumped into one another, trying to arrange themselves into some semblance of order. Lukys's cheeks grew red as snickering carried down from overhead. The civilians were laughing at them!

He gripped his spear tight and focused on finding his place in line. Let them laugh; what did they know? They might be inexperienced, but they were Perfugian soldiers and they had won their right to be here! The citizens of Fogmore would be reminded of that soon enough, when the Tangata came.

Long minutes later the fifty recruits had organised themselves into rows of five wide, ten deep. Lukys stood with his spear held vertically at his side, eyes fixed straight ahead as he'd once seen the royal guards do when in the presence of the Sovereigns. To his embarrassment, he was one of the few to adopt an official pose—the others lounged in various states of boredom, apparently impatient to finally reach their destination and discard their packs.

"Column, advance!"

At the command, the recruits started forward. Their lines immediately disintegrated as those behind moved faster than the recruits in front, but the officers apparently no longer cared. Turning their horses, they started into the town without glancing back.

And so the Perfugian column entered Fogmore, somewhere between organised soldiers and disorganised mob. Lukys closed his ears to the howls coming from the ramparts—though as they entered, he realised the onlookers stood not so much on ramparts as an earthen mound built up against the wooden walls.

What is this place?

In Perfugia, towns and cities were guarded by great walls of granite and gneiss, topped by crenulations and watch towers. It was why in all their long history of war, no kingdom had ever managed to gain a foothold on the island nation.

Yet Fogmore, command centre for the war efforts against the Tangata, looked to be little more sophisticated than the hilltribes that had once occupied Perfugia's mountain forests. The buildings were indeed made of wood—and looked little better than temporary shacks propped up by nails. Fresh snow was just beginning to fall and Lukys couldn't imagine the shabby walls doing anything to keep in the warmth—or keep out the snow, for that matter.

Lukys exhaled hard, his anger turning to disdain. These people dared to mock them, when not a building in this town could compare to even his parents' modest cottage? The streets weren't even paved—and the passage of men and women had long since made them slick with mud. Back home, not even the most insignificant of towns would have suffered such an indignity. The entire place had a temporary feel to it, as though the Flumeerens had thrown it up overnight.

The column made its slow way through the town, struggling on through the thick mud. The fresh snow only made matters worse, and those at the rear began to lag, though their grumbles did not reach the officers on their tall horses.

It was a relief when the buildings finally gave way to a broad central plaza—though it hardly deserved such a title. The churned earth continued without so much as a street sign, except where several boulders the size of small wagons dotted the ground. For a moment, Lukys thought they might have been placed as ornaments and was impressed. Then he noticed that the rocks were smooth, untouched by so much as a chisel, and realised they probably predated the town. Too large to be moved without great expense, Fogmore had simply been built around the boulders.

No, the square was little more than a muddy paddock. Snow had been piled up in the corners beneath the eaves of the surrounding buildings, but that was the only sign of order present.

Doubt touched Lukys as the column came to a halt, and he found himself looking at the officers. What were they doing in a place like this? Surely they weren't expected to live—and fight— alongside such savages?

"Column, form lines!"

The command came again. This time the chaos was worse, as the recruits became entangled in the thick mud. Several ended up face-first in the muck. Lukys couldn't imagine how anyone could live in these conditions. Did the Flumeerens hold themselves in such low regard?

"Enough!"

The word cracked like a whip over the head of the recruits. Lukys flinched at the unfamiliar voice, freezing in place. Movement flickered in the corner of his eye, and he watched as a man in plain clothing stalked to the front of the assembly. A frown wrinkled Lukys's face at the sight of a civilian giving orders to soldiers. Who did this man think he was?

The thump of boots striking earth followed as the Perfugian officers dismounted. Lukys expected them to reprimand the newcomer for interrupting, but instead the three snapped to attention, backs straight, eyes fixed ahead as the civilian approached. Shocked, Lukys turned his eyes back to the newcomer.

The man stood some five feet and nine inches, little taller than Lukys, though his frame carried far more muscle. Greying hair had been cropped short in the style of the military, but his barber had apparently ignored the strands sprouting from his ears. He wore long silver furs across his shoulders and a heavy cape draped down his back, while beneath he sported a tunic of rough spun wool. Fresh stubble shaded his jaw and frown lines streaked his face, suggesting a man who rarely smiled. Despite his obviously advancing years, his eyes were sharp as they swept the square, inspecting the recent arrivals.

It was clear from his scowl that he was not impressed.

"General Curtis, sir!" one of the Perfugian officers announced. "Your fresh batch of recruits, as scheduled."

Lukys's jaw almost struck the ground. Surely this couldn't be *the* General Curtis. The man was a legend, his career stretching back decades. He had been one of the few who'd warned against a resurgence of Tangata, before their surprise incursion into Calafe ten years prior.

Those had been innocent times, when the kingdoms had thought the beasts contained south of the Agzor Fortress. The attack had proven them all wrong, and hundreds had died before the creatures were hunted down. All because men like General Curtis had been ignored.

At least the general had commanded the allied retaliation. Disastrous as it had ended, the outcome might have been worse yet without his presence. An army of ten thousand had marched south of the Agzor Fortress, intent on crushing the Tangata once and for all. That had been the last time soldiers from all four kingdoms fought together, a noble sight for any who watched them depart, no doubt.

Two months later, General Curtis and the warrior queen of Flumeer had led the routed forces back through the gates of the Agzor Fortress. The enemy had taken them by surprise, surrounding and almost destroying them before the Flumeeren forces had broken free. The Calafe King had fallen in the battle, and barely two thousand soldiers had escaped, but at least some had survived.

Unfortunately, the Tangata had soon followed. The unbreakable Agzor Fortress had fallen in days, and the war for Calafe had begun.

Ten years and thousands of lives later, Calafe was lost, and still the Tangata came.

Lukys shivered, looking at the man with fresh eyes. If ever a soldier had earned the right to repudiate his uniform, it was this one. Where would the four kingdoms have been without his brilliance?

It did not bear considering.

"So these are the best the Perfugian Sovereigns have to offer," the general muttered.

He almost seemed to be speaking to himself, but Lukys drew himself up at the man's words, chest swelling, spear clutched tightly at his side.

"A more wretched bunch I've not seen since your last batch." Shaking his head, the general turned back to the officers. "I suppose you've filled their heads with the usual nonsense of glory and Perfugian superiority?" He snorted. "You're short fifty men."

The officers shared a glance while Lukys and the other recruits stood gaping. What had the general said?

Clearing his throat, the head officer of their column stepped forward. "There were not sufficient candidates of quality this year—"

"Ha!" the general laughed. "You mean these fools were the only ones to fail your preposterous examinations."

Fail... Lukys opened his mouth and closed it. He had failed? Murmurs came from around him as his comrades glanced at one another, but Lukys couldn't tear his eyes off their superiors. *I failed?*

The officers shifted nervously on their feet, but they did not refute the general's claims. What was going on? There was anger in the general's eyes as he looked at the Perfugian officers, but finally he gave them a dismissing nod and turned back to the recruits.

"My name is General Curtis," he barked. "Though while you live, you will address me as 'sir.' I do not expect that to be long."

The whispers started again at his words.

"*Silence!*"

The shout rang from the walls, so loud that Lukys actually leapt backwards. The movement sent him crashing into the recruit behind him. The mud slipped beneath their boots and before either could recover, they both went tumbling to the ground. Shocked, the other recruits stepped back as though they were contagious.

Grunting, Lukys pushed himself to his knees. The mud clung to his clothes and he raised his hands. "Sorry!"

The recruit he'd knocked down looked as surprised as Lukys, but at the apology he only nodded and flashed a grin. "No worries."

Lukys let out a breath as the recruit offered him a hand, but before he could take it, a shadow fell across the two of them.

"What is your name, recruit?"

Crouched in the dirt, Lukys found himself staring into the ferocious eyes of the general. His heart dropped into his stomach and he would have thrown himself backwards again, had terror not frozen him in place. His mouth opened and closed, but the words took several tries to come out.

"Lu…Lukys…sir!"

"Do you make a habit of sitting in the presence of your commanders, recruit?"

"N…no, no sir!"

"*Then get on your Godsdamn feet!*"

Lukys practically flew off the ground as the scream rattled in his ears. Somehow the recruit he'd knocked down was already up, back straight, eyes fixed straight ahead as though he'd never fallen. Only the streak of mud on his trousers betrayed him. Lukys thought he might have been another of the noble born, but did not know his name.

The general flashed Lukys one last look of contempt, then spun on his heel and marched back to the centre of the square. His voice rang from the walls of the nearby buildings as he addressed the column.

"Welcome to the frontier, ladies and gentlemen," he shouted, "though I daresay such titles are above you." Clenching his hands behind his back, he turned to face them once more. "I would say we are pleased for the reinforcements, but it's been a long time since the soldiers of Perfugia were worth more than tits on a bull. I daresay you lot will fare no better."

Lukys's insides twisted. Surely it couldn't be true. The Perfugian military were renown amongst the kingdoms…he had been chosen, honoured…

…yet wasn't this the man who had saved the civilised world? Who was Lukys to question him, to doubt the cruel words he spoke? His eyes fell to the ground and his shoulders slumped, the spear hanging loose in his grip. Could it be true?

"I have no interest in dealing with the discards of your privileged kingdom. We have no resources to waste training failures, so you will be assigned to hard labour. Your beloved Sovereigns saw no more use for you than death, but perhaps you might yet make this dump a little more bearable. At least until the Tangata come." His eyes shone as he appraised them.

"Make no mistake though," he continued, "when the beasts *do* come, it is the duty of every soul in this city to take up arms against them. You *will* fight with us on the frontline."

The man's words turned Lukys's innards to ice. Not even Dale's boastfulness could ignore the fact they were woefully unprepared to face the frightful creatures. They would be slaughtered!

"Perhaps you'll be lucky, and the Tangata will be long in their arrival." He grinned. "I wouldn't suggest holding out hope though."

"We don't even know how to use a spear!" another recruit called out. "How can we fight without training?"

The general did not denounce the interruption, but a cold smile appeared on his lips. He seemed to take a grim amusement from their predicament—but what had they ever done to deserve such cruelty?

"Perhaps you'll get lucky, and distract the beasts long enough for the real soldiers to do their job," he replied. "Regardless, try not to die too quickly. I shudder to think what your beloved Sovereigns would send to replace *you*."

With that, he turned and marched from the square. The Perfugian recruits stared after him, shocked to silence by his words. A pall of terror had fallen over the square, and Lukys found himself shaking his head. Surely this couldn't be real, must be some cruel joke played on new arrivals. The general would return in a moment and reveal the truth, surely…

Whoorl.

The song of a horn cut through the silence.

5

THE WARRIOR

Romaine stood at the stern of the ship, watching as the shores of Calafe retreated into the mist. It had been close for a time, racing through the fading light, seeking the ever-elusive waters of the Illmoor as the howls of the Tangata grew closer. Just their luck that more of the creatures had been in the area.

In the end, the river had come upon them suddenly, the twisted trees giving way to an open field that stretched along the riverbanks. Even then, it had been a nervous wait once they'd signalled the other side, listening to the Tangata coming ever closer.

Now as the mist rose around the ship, Romaine listened with satisfaction as the howls of the hunt fell silent. The creatures had reached the shore and discovered their quarry escaped. Turning from the bow, he shared a nod with the lieutenant. The last hours had rattled the man, but there was open relief on his face now.

The other scouts sat in silence around the galley, eyes distant, as though reliving some waking nightmare. They did not seem to notice the sailors moving about them. Romaine knew that look well, had seen it on the faces of half-a-hundred soldiers over the past decade. It was the look of the guilty, of a man who knew he had survived while others had fallen. But these men were strong; they would rise above their despair, and be better for it. More prepared to face the Tangata when next they came.

Long oars propelled the galley through the rushing waters,

towards the unseen shores of Flumeer. The Illmoor stretched almost a mile wide in these parts. They'd emerged from the forest close to their rendezvous point, but even then, they'd been lucky the ship captain kept his crew alert. The torch the scouts lit for signalling was bright, but in the heavy mist it could have easily been missed by a less attentive captain.

Ignoring the crew, Romaine wandered towards the bow where the horses had been stowed in makeshift stalls. He had sequestered the woman in a nook behind, where the captain stored extra sailcloth and rope. There she was safely out from under the feet of the sailors as they went about their work. Boards creaked beneath his boots as he approached, and Romaine glimpsed movement in the shadows.

Moonlight caught on the amber eyes as she appeared from the darkness, almost feral with fear. Romaine raised his hands to show he was unarmed—he'd left his axe with the horses. He took another step closer and his shadow shifted, allowing a nearby torch to illuminate the woman's face. This time she did not flinch away, though she cradled her injured arm to her chest. Romaine had placed it in a makeshift splint while they waited for the galley, but it would need the attention of a doctor when they reached safety.

"Who are you?" she whispered in that singsong voice of hers.

"Romaine," he replied. "Of Calafe."

Pursing her lips, the woman nodded. She lowered herself down onto one of the benches running along the side of the ship, but otherwise she did not respond.

Romaine raised an eyebrow. "It's customary to offer a name in return."

The woman stared at him for a long moment, and it seemed to Romaine she was weighing him up. Again, he wondered where she had come from, what she had been through to find herself alone in Tangata territory.

"Cara," she said at last.

Romaine offered his best smile, though on his bearded face and in the flickering light, it might have been mistaken for a sneer. When Cara said nothing, he gestured to the bench attached to the other side of the ship.

"May I?"

Again the long stare, but finally she nodded, and Romaine sat with a groan. "Long ride," he explained, then nodded to her splint. "How's the arm? I'm sorry about before, about startling you."

As though his words had reminded her of the injury, Cara cradled the arm to her chest once more. "I fell…" she said, and for a moment her eyes took on a haunted look. "I've never fallen before." Then she shook her head, her expression turning blank as she looked at him. "Where are we?"

"Crossing the Illmoor River, into Flumeer."

"Flumeer!"

Instantly, the woman was on her feet, head whipping around, eyes wide with fright. But in her haste, the injured arm slammed against the side of the galley and whatever she might have said next turned into a moan. Romaine rose quickly as she staggered, ready to catch her if she lost consciousness again. The colour had drained from her face and she swayed on her feet, but eventually she slumped back to the bench.

"I can't go to Flumeer," she whispered, rocking on her haunches. "There's…people there."

"We must," Romaine said softly. "It's not safe where we found you, not anymore. Did your…people not receive the news? New Nihelm has fallen. Calafe belongs to the Tangata now."

"*New* Nihelm?" Cara's eyes were wide. She turned to face the mist. "Gone?"

"I'm sorry." He paused, watching as the wind tugged her hair. He shivered, but in her bulky furs, Cara did not seem to notice the chill. "Your people…" He trailed off, then added, "You were alone when we found you."

Cara nodded, facing him again. "I was lost…"

"Then your family, they're still in the forest, still alive?"

Cara shook her head, and Romaine's stomach twisted as his own grief called out its sympathy. He reached out a hand to pat her shoulder, but at the last moment she glimpsed the movement.

"*Don't touch me!*"

Screaming, she flinched away, coming to her feet again in a rush. This time she tripped over a loose coil of rope and instead of fleeing, she went crashing to the ground. Another cry tore from her throat as she fell and she tried to roll away. Rope and cloth went with her and in a panic she thrashed, tangling them around her.

Romaine had come to his feet, but he dared not try to help her, lest he spur another outburst. Finally her terror seemed to subside. She slumped against the deck, gasping as though she had just climbed a mountain. A tremor followed, seeming to sweep her from head to toe, until her entire body was shaking.

"Are you…I'm sorry, are you okay?" he whispered, hardly daring to make a move towards her.

Cara's eyes slid closed and she drew in a great breath. The tremors slowed, then ceased. Exhaling, she pushed herself up with her good hand. She gulped in another breath, as though fighting against some terrible pain, and slowly unravelled the rope and sail that had wrapped around her. Finally she managed to stand and sink back to her bench. There she pulled her knees up to her chest and closed her eyes, a single tear streaking her cheek.

"I…I don't like to be touched," she croaked when she finally looked at him again.

Romaine nodded, though silently he wondered again what horrors the woman had endured alone in the wilds of Calafe.

"You killed them." A frown crossed the woman's brow as she looked at him. "The Tangata. How?"

"How?" he repeated, then shrugged, recalling the battle, the pounding in his ears, the rush of adrenaline. "It was not the first time."

"You were so fast," Cara murmured. "Almost as quick as them."

"Not quite," Romaine replied. He rubbed his chest where the male had struck him and winced. "But I knew what it was going to do."

She nodded, as though what he'd said made perfect sense to her. Silence fell between them, and Romaine sat back, listening to the soft moaning of the ship, the lapping of water against the hull, the cursing of sailors at the oars. He tried to imagine himself back in the silent winter forests of his homeland, but instead he saw Flagers, lying dead in the blood-red snow.

His eyes snapped open and he rose. To his surprise, the mist had lifted and now the waters around the ship were clear. Ahead, burning torches lit the night and he sighed. That would be Fogmore, where he and the other scouts were barracked. It had been a sleepy town on the banks of the Illmoor once—until the war had come. Now it hosted the command post for the Flumeeren army.

They were closer than he'd thought, and inwardly Romaine suppressed a sigh. Seeing the stockade city only served to remind Romaine of his own loss. With Calafe fallen, he was now a man without a kingdom, forced to rely on the generosity of others for a place to stand, to sleep.

"Where are the trees?"

Romaine glanced sideways as Cara joined him on her feet. Her eyes were on the distant lights and it took him a moment to realise what she was talking about. In the darkness, it was difficult to see the barren hills around the city.

"Some were cut down to form the palisade, others for the new buildings needed to host the army. The rest..." He trailed off, thinking of the infernos that had lit the shores of the Illmoor from ocean to mountains. "They were burnt."

"Why?"

"To keep the Tangata from slipping past our scouts," Romaine replied.

"That's horrible," Cara murmured.

"Can you walk?"

She nodded, and turning, Romaine led her past the horse stalls. As they reached the main deck, the ship shuddered and the sound of wood crunching against gravel carried to their ears. He didn't need to look over the side to know they'd reached the shore, though he noticed the wide-eyed look on Cara's face as she spun around. Unbidden, a smile touched his lips.

"We've arrived," he grunted.

The announcement finally seemed to shake his comrades from their stupor, and rising, they moved to free the horses from their stalls. Romaine made no move to help—the busy work would be good for them. He turned as footsteps announced the lieutenant's approach, and he offered the man a nod, but his attention was focused on Romaine's new ward.

"Awake at last, I see!" the lieutenant said in what he must have thought was a friendly tone. He offered a friendly bow. "Lieutenant Marco, at your service."

Cara only stared at the man, lips clenched tight. The lieutenant turned to Romaine with a frown.

"Does she speak?" he asked.

Chuckling, Romaine clapped the man on the shoulder. "Not to you, apparently," he said with a grin. Nearby, the sailors were raising the gangplank from where it had been sequestered beside the railing. The current had turned the ship side-on to the riverbank, and with a groan of steel hinges, the plank slammed down into muddy shore. "Come," Romaine added. "We'd best get out of the way of these men. No doubt they'd like to return to the safety of the river before the night grows too old."

Ignoring the lieutenant, he led Cara down the gangplank to the shore, then raised an eyebrow at the woman. The faintest hint of a smile touched her lips, but it faded as she looked ahead. Romaine could hardly blame her. Fogmore was anything but welcoming. The wooden palisade waited some two hundred yards from the river, though the ground sloped upwards from where they stood, so that the city seemed to loom above them.

Torches had been lit at regular intervals along the palisade, and the flickers of shadows revealed the guards on watch. Nothing could be seen of the city beyond, though the gates were already swinging open in preparation to admit the new arrivals. Once a gravel path had wound its way up the slope to the gates, but the constant passage of marching boots had turned it to a muddy, rutted mess.

"Welcome to..." Romaine sighed. "To my new home."

Wrinkling her nose, Cara flashed him a glance. "You sure you wouldn't rather the Tangata?"

Romaine blinked, then let out a snort. "They might yet convince me."

Movement came from the gangplank as the lieutenant started down. Gesturing to the path, Romaine started off before the man could reach them. The thump of boots on wood picked up pace as the lieutenant sped up, and Romaine let out a sigh. The man caught them before they'd gone ten yards, puffing softly. It was difficult to move quickly on the muddy path. To Romaine's relief, the lieutenant said nothing and they plodded on.

The other scouts overtook them when they were halfway. They waved from the backs of their horses and continued ahead, broad grins on their faces. Now that they had reached the safety of home, the guilt and fear had receded, replaced by joy at their own survival. Romaine clenched his jaw as he felt himself longing for the men's innocence, for their hope and optimism. His had died long ago.

"Are you okay, lass?" the lieutenant asked as the last of the horses overtook them. "Sure you wouldn't like a ride?"

Cara was managing better than either of them in the mud, though she must have been in pain from her arm. Romaine cursed inwardly that he had not made the offer sooner, but Cara only raised her eyebrows. The lieutenant shared a glance with Romaine, but he only shrugged. Shaking his head, the man returned his attention to the path.

Despite his sorrow at leaving his homeland once again, Romaine still felt a touch of relief at the sight of the city. Packed and chaotic as it was, he would at least be extended a hot meal and a bed. These days, he didn't want for much more than that.

When they were still some fifty yards from the gates, Cara suddenly slowed. Romaine pulled alongside her as she glanced back, the fine features of her face twisting in a frown. For a moment, he thought she was having second thoughts about entering the city. Then her entire body went taut, and she opened her mouth to cry out.

Whooorl.

Romaine's heart lurched as horns sounded from atop the palisade walls, drowning out Cara's scream. Atop the walls, soldiers pointed down at them. No, past them—down at the distant river. Romaine followed their gestures, gaze travelling back to where their galley had landed.

The ship should have been pushing back from the shore by now, but it remained where they'd left it, sailors racing back and forth across the deck...

...No, not sailors.

Another howl sounded in the night, but this time it was not the Flumeeren trumpets.

Tangata!

Dozens of the creatures were swarming over the ship. Their clothes were soaked from the river waters and Romaine could hardly believe what he was seeing.

They had swum!

The sailors didn't even have a chance to scream before the Tangata overtook them. In a matter of moments, their bodies lay scattered across the decks. A *whoosh* carried up the slope as a lantern was smashed against a railing, scattering flames across the wooden boards.

"*Run!*" Romaine bellowed.

Cold grey eyes turned after them as Romaine spun. Forgetting Cara's affliction, he grabbed her by the shoulder and dragged her up the path. A cry came from the woman and she tore herself loose, but whatever panic she felt, she channelled into movement. The lieutenant had already seen the danger and had taken off without a second thought for those behind.

Whooorl.

The horns sounded again, followed by the soft creak of hinges. Romaine's eyes snapped to the gates, just thirty yards away now. Slowly, they began to swing closed.

Fear touched Romaine and he bellowed for them to wait. If the guards heard, they took no notice. The other scouts had already reached the safety of the town. Only the three of them remained outside.

Light burst from atop the palisade walls as bales of straw were set aflame and pushed over the side. Their glow swept down the slope, illuminating the way ahead. And what came behind.

Glancing over his shoulder, Romaine glimpsed shadows streaking up the hill towards them. Moving with incredible speed, the Tangata had already covered half the distance to the town. Another minute and they would be upon them. He set his eyes on the closing gates and pounded on.

A bowstring twanged overhead. Angry shouts followed—a superior reprimanding the archer for releasing his arrow early. The Tangata were still too far away. Even in his desperate state, Romaine appreciated the officer's discipline in the face of the attack.

A dozen Tangata…where had they come from? Why now?

Moments later, a chorus of *twangs* lifted from the ramparts, and fifty arrows flashed past overhead. Romaine didn't need to look back now to know how close the beasts were. Convention dictated a crossbow volley be fired at sixty yards. Ahead, the gates continued to close, the squeal of their hinges sounding their doom.

"Wait!" There was open terror in the lieutenant's voice, but he should have saved the effort.

At least a dozen Tangata came behind them. If even one were to enter the city, the havoc it would wreak amongst the civilians would be terrible. The officer in charge of the watch could not take the risk—not solely for the lives of two men and an unknown woman.

Romaine cursed. He didn't even have his axe. They were just ten yards away now, so close. But they weren't going to make it.

Suddenly the gates stopped moving. A figure appeared in the gap—Romaine recognised one of their fellow scouts, waving frantically for them to hurry.

Then they were through, the gates slamming closed behind them. A *thud* followed just as the locking bar dropped into place, shaking the wooden boards. Howls chased after them, then the twang of arrows came from overhead as the archers fired again.

All sound from outside ceased.

Then the screaming began.

Panting, Romaine straightened to take stock of the situation. His fear deepened as he witnessed the chaos that had taken hold of the city. Men and women raced in all directions, some towards the ramparts, others in seemingly mindless circles.

Terror was spreading.

And the Tangata were at the walls.

"Someone get me my axe," Romaine growled.

❧ 6 ❧

THE RECRUIT

Lukys stood frozen as the trumpets sounded again. Not even the officers moved from where they stood, but all turned their faces to look southward. Darkness had fallen almost unnoticed; the torches lit around the square casting their orange light across the snow. A third call sounded from the direction of the river.

"To arms!"

Lukys never saw who gave the call, but with those two words, the peace was broken. Chaos descended on the square as others picked up the cry. The general's words were proven true as men and women went racing from the nearby buildings, some dressed in chainmail and carrying swords or spears, others in the plain clothes of civilians. Many of these carried hatchets or long knives, a few had construction hammers, one a pitchfork.

Standing in the centre of the square, armed with their spears and protected by heavy chainmail, not one of the Perfugian recruits moved. It was as though a spell had been cast over them. All Lukys could hear in his mind were the general's words.

Death, death, death.

It was like a prophecy, a chant rattling around his skull, demanding deliverance.

The Perfugian officers swung into their saddles, but they said nothing to their charges. Instead, they put heels to flesh and galloped from the square—heading north, not south. Lukys watched them go, mouth wide, his last trickle of hope fading to nothing. Their commanders had fled, had left them here to die.

Death, death, death.

Lukys's heart pounded in his chest as he looked at the spear in his hands. He had carried it all this way, had worn the chainmail, but he had never *used* them. He stared at the spear now, willing himself to lift it, to shout a war cry and race to aid his fellows.

He couldn't.

A moan came from his throat as he looked around, seeking help from someone, anyone. Dale stood nearby, but his face was pale, forehead beaded in sweat. His eyes were fixed to the ground and as Lukys watched, a shudder went through the man, as though he were on the verge of tears. Gone was the bravado of just a few hours earlier.

The Tangata had come, and they didn't care whether your blood was noble or poor. They would kill you all the same.

Death, death, death.

A tremor shook Lukys as the first scream sounded over the blowing of horns. His eyes fixed in the direction of the river. The palisade was hidden by the nearby rooftops, yet it couldn't be far, not if they could hear sounds of battle, of the dying…

Lukys's gaze caught movement in the windows of the nearby houses. Faces peered out at them, an older woman with two young children, their eyes wide with terror. He swallowed, seeing others now, the old and young, the injured and the infirm. They stayed in their homes, unable to fight, only to wait and see who would prevail.

Lukys's stomach twisted in a knot as he looked from them to the Perfugian recruits.

Cowards.

How could he and his comrades stand here, frozen in terror, while others bled for their freedom? What did it matter whether they were failures or heroes, when there were those here who fought with pitchforks? At least they had spears, at least they had *armour*.

A soft *thud* whispered across the square as Lukys dropped his pack. Almost unconsciously, he reached down and tore the half-helm from its strap and placed it on his head. Then he was stepping forward, mud splashing beneath his boots. The spear came up, its tip dropping in what Lukys approximated to be the correct position.

Hairs rose on the back of his neck as he sensed the eyes of the other recruits on him, but Lukys ignored them.

Eyes fixed straight ahead, he walked through the ranks of his fellow Perfugians, towards the distant screams of battle.

Thud, thud, thud.

Lukys glanced around as the sound of objects striking earth came from behind him. Other recruits were moving forward now, spears held at the ready, determined. He glimpsed the man he'd knocked down earlier amongst them, and offered a nod. A woman stepped up alongside Lukys and they shared a glance. He saw a steely resolve in the hazel depths of her eyes, a determination to do her kingdom proud—whatever the bastard general might have said of them.

Movement came from all around now as the spell shattered. Like a wave breaking against the shore, the fifty recruits surged forward with a cry, racing to reinforce their fellows in the battle for humanity's freedom.

Running down the muddy streets, Lukys's heart soared. There was no time to think about what was to come, about strategy or logistics, only to charge, spear raised towards the enemy. The palisade came into view, the sloped earth leading up to makeshift ramparts packed with soldiers.

Lukys's fear came rushing back.

The Tangata did not appear to be attacking this section of wall, but somehow that only made the fear worse. His guts turned to liquid as he listened to the sharp *twang* of bowstrings. Somewhere, men and women were screaming, but ahead a strange peace hung over the soldiers, the calm before the storm.

Lukys's stride faltered and he slowed his pace, allowing several recruits to overtake him. But he didn't allow himself to stop. If he stopped, he'd never be able to start moving again.

Soon the ground was rising beneath his feet. Lukys clenched his teeth and clutched his spear tighter as they approached the waiting soldiers. Unbidden, the recruits spread out along the wall, seeking areas where there was space for them to stand. Screams came from away to their right and Lukys craned his head. Even in his terror, he longed for a glimpse of the villainous Tangata.

Then he was standing atop the fortifications, the spiked palisade stretching up to his waist, a twenty-foot drop beyond. A barrel was burning nearby, casting light out across the ramparts, while below great bales of hay turned the river flats to red.

Ghosts moved amongst the flames.

Death, death, death.

The hairs on Lukys's neck stood on end as he tried to track the creatures below. They were effervescent in the darkness: a flash of their eyes catching the light here, a flicker of shadows there, always moving. Bowstrings twanged along the wall, but Lukys sensed few would find their mark—not in this darkness, not with these creatures.

Taking a two-handed grip of his spear, he looked left and right. Soldiers wearing the red embroidered uniforms of Flumeer made up the bulk of the front ranks—few of the blue-clad Perfugians had been so bold as to step right to the edge.

Thwack.

Lukys gaped as just a few feet from where he stood, a man crumpled to the ground, head caved in from some unseen projectile. The helmet had done nothing to protect him. Other defenders cried out as the *crack* of rocks striking wood came from the palisade—then they were throwing themselves down. Lukys mimicked their actions, though his eyes were still fixed on the dead man. A rock the size of a fist lay on the ground beside him.

What The Fall am I doing here?

Standing amongst the soldiers of Flumeer, Lukys realised in that moment he had no business being on that wall, in that city, on the frontline. He had no idea what he was doing, no clue about how to fight, what to do when the Tangata came.

The pounding of rocks ceased as quickly as it had begun. Maybe the Tangata had run out of projectiles—or perhaps they were only waiting for fresh targets to present themselves. The Flumeerens must have thought the same, for they were slow to regain their feet.

Eventually, some of the bolder archers began to fire into the darkness again. Still crouched, spear clutched at his side, Lukys watched a woman draw back a bowstring, eyes fixed on some point down below…

Lukys blinked. The woman had vanished…no, not vanished—

her body lay a yard from where she'd stood, neck snapped in two, eyes still staring at some distant point.

Something else took her place.

Lukys didn't move, didn't dare even breathe as finally he laid eyes upon the monster that haunted the dreams of every Perfugian child. It could have been human; indeed, there was no outward difference in its appearance. There was no disfiguration, no sharpened teeth or talons, as some of the legends claimed. Nothing other than eyes as grey as stones.

Those eyes swept the ranks of defenders surrounding it, and as one they drew back. The Tangata smiled.

Death, death, death.

The chant had become a cacophony in Lukys's mind now, booming along to the racing of his heart. Fear lodged in his throat, suffocating him, robbing him of strength. The tip of his spear shook; he almost dropped it.

A howl shook the night.

And the soldiers of Flumeer charged.

Sword raised, a man leapt at the beast, steel point aimed for its throat. The Tangata wore no armour, carried no weapon that Lukys could see, but it moved far faster than its foe. It spun, and the soldier's sword found only empty air. A hand flashed out and caught the soldier by the throat. Though he wore an iron bevor, the steel offered little protection against the strength of the Tangata. The creature wrenched its wrist, and then the man was dead.

Lukys's stomach churned as blood sprayed across the mud, but the loss did not slow the man's comrades. Screaming their rage, they struck at the creature, though it was already moving, evading their attempts to trap it, to drive their blades home. Lukys watched on from his knees, unable to find the courage to stand.

He had never understood until now. Sure, he had heard the tales, knew the stories, the legends of these creatures who had dared defy the Gods.

But no one in Perfugia truly understood.

He knew that now. If they did, all the might of their island nation would already be here, battling on to hold the line, to push back against the inhuman hordes.

The Tangata were no ordinary enemy, no human kingdom you

could surrender to. The creature before him was mad, possessed by the magic its ancestors had stolen, utterly corrupted.

If the Tangata could not be stopped…

They were all going to die.

Lukys climbed to his feet, spear held out before him. A second Flumeeren soldier had already fallen. The creature swept up the man's sword before others could converge on it, and a third man fell, head separated from his shoulders in a single swing. Growling, it continued forward.

Screams rent the air as Lukys watched the creature come, unable to move, to run, to do anything but wait for death to find him. It stalked across the rampart, dealing death with each step, and Lukys raised his spear, preparing for a final stand. But the soldiers of Flumeer were not finished yet.

A woman stepped between Lukys and the creature, bow in hand with arrow nocked. Before the creature could spot the danger, she loosed. A howl sounded in the night as her red-plumed arrow sprouted from the Tangata's chest. It stumbled back, grey eyes showing a moment's surprise. But the wound was not mortal, and with a roar, the beast drew back an arm and hurled the stolen sword.

There was a sickening *thwack* as the blade slammed into the woman's chest. Thought fled Lukys's mind as he dropped his spear and stepped forward to catch her. She sagged into his arms, the strength gone from her legs. The chainmail vest she wore had done nothing to save her, and staggering, Lukys lowered her carefully to the earthen ramparts.

Blood bubbled from her lips as she struggled to breathe. Desperately, Lukys tried to recall the teachings of the master doctor. But the sword embedded in the woman's ribs was beyond anything he'd learnt in the academy. With a last sigh, her eyes slid closed and the harsh rattling of her breath faded to nothing.

Lukys sat back on his haunches. Around him, the world was on fire. Winds blew from across the river, catching in the hay below the walls and sending flaming strands swirling through the air. Acrid smoke stung his nostrils as he inhaled, and his throat burned. Terror robbed him of strength.

He drew on what final dredges of courage remained to him.

Clasping at his fallen spear, he forced himself up—and found himself staring into the stony eyes of the beast.

It stood just a yard away, close enough that it could have reached out and snapped his neck at any moment. It didn't. Wrinkles creased its forehead as it watched him. The spear shook in Lukys's hand as he realised this was his chance.

But even as he tightened his grip on the weapon, the Tangata tensed, its features closing over. A smile twisted its lips, revealing yellowed teeth.

Death, death, death.

Laughter sounded in Lukys's ears and the beast raised a hand, gesturing him forward.

Screaming, Lukys leapt, spear held at the ready. He knew he could not win, that this was the end, but in that moment he didn't care. All that mattered was the spear in his hands and the beast.

The tip of his spear flashed out, aimed clumsily for the creature's stomach. The Tangata was quicker, its hand swiping down, catching his weapon by the haft and snapping it in two with a quick wrench. Lukys staggered back, half of his now useless weapon still clutched to his chest. The tip of Lukys's spear clasped in one hand, the Tangata advanced.

A cry escaped Lukys as his boots failed to find purchase in the mud. He crashed to the ground, broken spear tumbling from his fingers. Mouth wide in terror, he looked up, expecting to see death descending upon him.

A warrior stood between Lukys and the Tangata, twin-bladed axe extended towards the beast. The weapon rippled in the firelight as it swept out. The Tangata leapt away, twisting from the path of the blade, but even with its superhuman speed, it could not avoid the blow completely.

A shriek rent the air as the axe sliced the creature's thigh. Blood pulsed from the wound as it staggered. Lukys was surprised to see it bled red. Despite their distinctly human appearance, surely the monsters could not be the same within?

Pain contorted the Tangata's face as it faced the axeman. Then a change seemed to come over the creature, a wave of pure rage sweeping away its agony. Its eyes flashed and it rushed forward—now in total silence.

The axeman did not retreat from its fury. He charged with a shout, words lost in the chaos, massive shoulders sending the axe flashing for the Tangata. Somehow, the creature seemed sluggish by comparison. Perhaps the wound had slowed it. Regardless, it realised its mistake too late, and with a sickening *thud*, the axe slammed into its shoulder, slicing through bone and sinew to bury itself in the beast's chest.

An awful gurgling came from the Tangata as it struggled to step forward, to reach the enemy that had slain it. But not even these creatures could survive such a blow, and with a sharp whistle of departing air, it slumped to its knees and fell alongside Lukys.

The warrior towered over the beast. His shoulders heaved as blue eyes scanned the ramparts, seeking out signs of fresh danger. Another Tangata lay nearby, its body peppered with arrows and impaled by several spears. In the distance, the sounds of battle were fading, an eerie stillness coming over the night.

The battle was won.

Looking up at the massive axeman, Lukys could hardly believe he was alive. If not for the ferocious warrior, he wouldn't be. Only now did he notice the man did not wear the familiar red of Flumeer, nor the blue of Perfugia. Instead, his chainmail had been woven through with the deepest green, remnant of the forest.

Calafe.

He hadn't realised there were any Calafe warriors left. They had passed the refugee camps outside Mildeth, but it was said that the last of their soldiers had refused to leave their land, and had died on the shores of the Illmoor. What did this man fight for now, with his kingdom overcome?

"Need some help?"

Lukys started as the man spoke, dragging him from his thoughts. Seeing the hand the warrior was extending, he took it. His slender fingers were ingulfed by the warrior's giant mitts and he was yanked to his feet. Lukys stumbled before righting himself, his gaze catching on the body of the Tangata once more. The blood had stopped flowing from the awful wound the man's axe had left.

It almost killed me.

Before he could stop himself, Lukys was bent in two and retching in the mud.

Gentle laughter came from beside him. "First battle?"

Gasping, Lukys managed a nod.

"You'll get used to it," the warrior grunted.

With that, he took a hold of his axe. Placing a boot on the Tangata's chest, he yanked the weapon free with a sickening *squelch*, then turned and walked away along the ramparts.

Lukys watched him go, a reply on his lips, though he couldn't bring himself to say it. The warrior was wrong. He would never get used to this. He would never get the chance.

He'd be dead long before then.

7

THE ARCHIVIST

Erika was sagging in the saddle by the time the walls of Mildeth finally came into view. The short winter days had made the journey hard, forcing her to wake in the darkness and ride until long after the sun had shrunk beneath the horizon. Blessedly, it was still high now; her five day journey would be at an end by nightfall.

Now her excitement began to rise as she contemplated what awaited her in Mildeth. They had all been expecting her to fail, every noble in the blasted court. Only the queen had shown faith, and even she had warned Erika that there would be no more expeditions should she return empty handed.

But this time, Erika had succeeded.

This time there would be no reprisals.

This time she would offer Queen Amina the true magic of the Gods.

She had spent the long journey intermittently dreaming of what might lie hidden in northern Calafe, and practicing with the power she now literally held in the palm of her hand. Not long after leaving the caverns, she had discovered the metal fibres had indeed fused to her flesh. It should have frightened her, but instead she found herself relieved the magic could not be taken away.

Each night she had practiced with it, trying to discover its secrets. She had experimented first with its ability to summon light. In her rush to escape the caverns, Erika hadn't realised she'd forgotten the lantern until halfway to the exit. It was only then she'd noticed the magical glow that had followed her, seeping from her hand. Now she could summon not only light, but warmth at will by clenching her fist, though she found if she practiced too long, she grew fatigued.

She'd had less success replicating its more deadly nature. The magic seemed to have no impact on inanimate objects; the trees she'd practiced on hadn't so much as shaken before her power. Erika hadn't dared test it on anything living yet: she would have to trust it would work when needed.

The rolling hills fell behind Erika and the last of the snow with them, while the walls of Mildeth grew larger. Built of red sandstone, they rose from the land like a bloody scar, standing defiant against the wild green of the surrounding farmland. Joining the Queen's Highway, Erika began to overtake wagons. Many were loaded with food goods, broad beans and cabbage and onions, late crops, the last to be harvested before the snows had started. Others were escorted by armed men, their contents hidden by heavy tarps. These would be from the mines, filled with gold or silver or other precious metals. Maybe even marble, cut from high in the mountains and conveyed to distant Mildeth to grow the ever-expanding citadel in the city's centre.

Erika's heart raced at the thought that one of those new apartments might soon be hers. Finally she would be granted the position in court she deserved. But her excitement was short-lived, as ascending the final hill before the city, she looked down at the plains surrounding Mildeth.

A mass of humanity crowded the earth beneath the walls. Here was the fate of the failed, all that remained of the ruin that was Calafe. Flumeeren guards stood at the gates, inspecting each wagon and barring entrance to those who lacked the proper papers. There were simply too many for the city to hold; already Mildeth was bursting at the seams.

And so they gathered without, women and children, the old and crippled and infirm, all waiting upon the queen's mercy. Some had raised worn canvas tents, while others had gathered enough garbage and detritus to create lean-tos or makeshift buildings—though that was perhaps too strong a word for the pitiful structures they had erected.

The Calafe had never been builders. Though many spoke of the beauty of New Nihelm and Fort Agzor before they had fallen, most of its people were said to be nomads, surviving upon the fruits of the forests.

Only there were few forests in Flumeer. Those had given way long ago to farmland, a necessity to feed not only the growing population, but the ever-expanding army.

Raising her hood, Erika drew the cloak tighter around herself and rode on. After the assassination attempt in the caverns, she was wary of being recognised. Though she would be forced to show her papers to the guards, there was no need to shout her arrival to every watcher in the city.

She kept her gaze fixed straight ahead as she entered the crowds, eager to avoid contact. A long line of wagons clogged the road ahead, waiting to be processed and checked, but alone on her horse, Erika was able to press forward unopposed. Even so, she felt the refugees pressing in, their desperate eyes upon her back. Clenching her fist, she summoned warmth to her gauntlet, drawing strength from the magic's presence.

However, it could not keep the stench from her nostrils. Closer to the city, the refugees grew denser, bunching up against the walls in their desperation for shelter. Erika wrinkled her nose as she caught a whiff of another unpleasant smell. She didn't need to ask what happened to their waste in such tight conditions.

Approaching the gates, she could no longer avoid setting eyes upon her poverty-stricken neighbours. They were everywhere, crowding onto the Queen's Highway, pressing at the guards, the wagons. Images flashed before Erika's eyes, of a pale-skinned, dark-haired woman wearing a thread-worn dress. Even the memory made her cheeks grow warm. Her past was like an anchor, ever seeking to drag her back to the poverty she and her mother had experienced when they'd first arrived in Flumeer...

The last wagon in line was being searched as Erika rode past. She didn't spare the contents a glance. Ahead, the gates were open, though a company of soldiers stood at the ready should any of the human debris camped outside attempt to gain passage. They closed ranks at her approach and Erika pulled her horse to a stop before them.

She dismounted as one of the soldiers wearing the badge of a lieutenant pinned to his chest stepped towards her. "Papers, ma'am?"

"Erika, the Queen's Archivist" she replied, reaching into her coat for the documents. As she did, her hand brushed the ancient map and a thrill of excitement touched her. Shaking it off, she offered her papers to the man. "I trust everything is in order," she added, adopting an elevated tone.

The lieutenant cast a cursory glance over the papers, then back at her. He raised an eyebrow. "Long journey, ma'am?"

Erika's cheeks warmed as she saw the judgement in his eyes. She'd hardly had time to find food on the long journey south, let alone bathe or purchase new clothes appropriate for her rank. In truth, she looked little better than the Calafe refugees. But the news she brought could not wait.

"We are at war, Lieutenant," she answered curtly, anger washing away her embarrassment. "I come with urgent news for the queen."

"Yes, I'm sure ancient history is *littered* with urgent news," the man replied drolly. Erika balled her gauntleted hand into a fist, but after a moment he handed back the papers and stepped aside. "Go, though I suggest you bathe before entering the presence of Her Esteemed Majesty."

Snatching back her papers, Erika flashed him a scowl, but the lieutenant was already returning to his men. Stepping back into the saddle, she directed her mare into the gate tunnel. Snickers came from the guards as they watched her go but she ignored them. Their insolence would not be forgotten. Soon she would be one of the elites, a noble of Flumeer. Then the lieutenant and his men would learn the error of their ways.

The shadows of the walls enclosed her as she entered the tunnel. She shivered in the sudden darkness, feeling the weight of stone looming overhead. The passage narrowed as she edged her horse around a corner designed to slow intruders, and in the black she felt herself losing control. Suddenly, she was back in the tunnels beneath the earth, in the realm of the Gods, and Sythe was creeping towards her, knife extended...

She exhaled hard, fighting for control. Ahead, the tunnel twisted again, a shimmer of light promising an exit. She pressed her heels to the mare and with a snort it broke into a trot.

A moment later she returned to the light. The nightmare banished, Erika pulled her mount to a stop and dragged in great lungfuls of air. Lifting her hand, she clenched and unclenched her gauntleted fist. Light danced upon the metal, though in full daylight it was difficult to pick the source. She knew, though…

Nightmares banished, Erika lowered her hand and continued her journey. There were still several more hours of daylight remaining, but the city was large and she intended to call upon the queen before the court retired for the day.

Beyond the gate tunnel, she found herself in a broad plaza with a dozen roads leading off from it. The buildings here were of the same red sandstone as the outer fortifications. They were squat and ugly things, reflecting the average Flumeeren's mind for practicality over beauty.

Erika directed her horse down the central avenue, settling her hood back in place. The walls protected the streets of Mildeth from the worst of winter's winds, but she was still wary of being recognised. Sythe might have died with her secrets, but returning without her assistants would be suspicious. And who knew where else the Gemahan king might have watchers?

Stones clicked beneath steel hooves as she made her way through the city. The streets were peaceful compared to the chaos beyond the city gates, the pavements clear of waste and detritus. Guards stood watch at intersections and citizens made their way through the grid-like streets with smiles on their faces. The occasional wagon rumbled by on the way to and from the docks.

The order restored calm to Erika's soul, banishing the stress of the past week. This was where she belonged, standing shoulder to shoulder amidst the elite of society. Memories of her past were naught but a passing shadow on a sunny day.

It took her an hour to reach the citadel. She made only one stop on the way, a brief detour through a perfumery in which she was able to clean her face and augment the scent of a week spent on the road. This time she would approach the guards with more confidence, to avoid any further delays by men inflated by their own sense of power.

Yet when she turned the final corner to the citadel, she couldn't help a fluttering in her stomach. The sight that greeted her would have intimidated anyone. Soldiers in gold-embossed breastplates and full-faced helms lined the street. Each was armed with shield and spear, with swords strapped to their waists for good measure. To the ignorant, they might have appeared as statues, decorations to bid guests welcome to the towering citadel beyond.

But Erika was anything but ignorant. Behind each of those impenetrable helmets was a veteran of a dozen battles. Soldiers did not earn a place amongst the warrior queen's guard without proving their worth.

Wind whistled between the rooftops as Erika made her way between the silent men. Goosebumps lifted on her neck as she sensed the unseen eyes watching her, but not one of them moved. Silence hung over the street like a blanket, heavy, suffocating, until she wanted nothing more than to scream. She continued, her horse plodding slowly towards the palace gates.

Only there did movement finally come. As she stopped to dismount, she saw suddenly that soldiers had moved behind her, barring the path back down the street. For men in full-plate armour, they moved quickly, and with frightening silence.

"Archivist."

One foot still in the stirrups, Erika spun towards the citadel, and almost ended up face-first in the dust. Thankfully she managed to get a hand on her saddle to steady herself before disaster struck, but too late to entirely save her dignity. Agitated, she finished dismounting and looked to the speaker.

"Your return was not expected for another week," the man continued before Erika could get a word in. Wearing a silken doublet of Flumeeren scarlet, he stood with arms clasped behind his back and a look of carefully crafted indifference on his face. "The queen trusts you have not returned empty-handed…again."

Erika's mouth opened and then closed, her veins turning cold. His words cast her back to that last failure, when she had stood before the queen and her court and begged for one final chance. Most had called for her dismissal—or worse. The queen had been moved by her words, but she had implied another failure would require recourse.

I did not fail!

Clenching her gauntleted fist, Erika straightened and looked the queen's emissary in the eye.

"Take me to Her Majesty, steward," she commanded. "I bring news that will change the future of the war."

8

THE WARRIOR

Romaine sat in silence as the sun clawed its way over the eastern mountains, casting back the dark. Exhaustion hung across his shoulders like a cloak, but he had not slept. Through the long night he had waited, axe in hand, to see whether the Tangata would return. Now as he watched the light reclaim the world, he felt the weight of disappointment on his soul.

It wasn't that he wished to die. Only that…he was so tired of the pain. Every morning when he woke, there was a short moment when he did not remember, the briefest of seconds when his heart was free.

Then the memories would return, and with them the agony of loss.

Exhaling, Romaine looked across the earthen rampart to where Lieutenant Marco lay in the mud. Romaine hadn't seen the man's death, though it must have happened in the first hour of the attack. One of the beasts had torn out his throat. At least it had been quick.

The irony of the man's death was not missed on Romaine. Marco had survived the Tangata in the forest and the crossing, made it all the way back to Fogmore—only for death to find him on the town walls.

Below, the mudflats were silent, the enemy long dead. He should have slept, should have retired to his bed after the long journey. But he could never sleep after a battle. And so he had sat here in the darkness, waiting, remembering.

The light around the mountains grew brighter as the sun reached for open skies, and soon movement began below. Soldiers emerged from the river gates and walked amongst the dead, claiming armour and weapons to be inherited by a new generation of recruits. Slowly the dead were gathered into piles, one for the human fallen, another for the Tangata. The bodies cloaked in red and blue must have outnumbered the beasts five to one.

Romaine was still sitting atop the ramparts when the first of the pyres was lit. By then a soft snow was falling. The ice flakes glistened in the dawn light as they drifted down, settling on the barren earth. Come noon the combination of ice and marching boots would churn the ground to mud. Fogmore truly was a Godsforsaken place.

Only when Romaine's breath began to fog on the frozen air did he finally lift his axe and rise to turn away…

…only to find a pair of amber eyes watching him.

He had forgotten the strange Calafe woman, and the sight of her sitting on a nearby barrel gave him pause. He'd assumed someone had seen her to safety, but in the chaos, he supposed no one had thought to take responsibility for her safety. It was a miracle she had survived.

"What are you doing here, lass?"

Cara shrugged, her eyes lingering on the lieutenant's body. Though she had not known the man, Romaine glimpsed sadness in those amber depths. He remembered having such compassion once. He had lost it long ago, somewhere between the endless battles and death. There had been no choice—caring, loving, it offered nothing but pain in this war. Against the Tangata, death was inevitable. It was just a matter of when.

"I wanted to see," Cara replied, her gaze turning to the burning pyres, and the blackened ruins of the ship that had carried them clear of her homeland.

Romaine frowned. "I would have thought you saw enough last night."

A shudder shook the woman. "So much evil." Her eyes did not leave the flickering fire. "So much death."

"They kill everything that crosses their path," Romaine murmured, pain wrapping its thorny tendrils around his heart.

Finally Cara broke off her watch over the fires. "You have suffered from them?"

Romaine couldn't help but shiver as their eyes met. There was something about the woman's gaze, some ageless quality, as though she had seen far more than her youthful appearance implied. What had happened to her out there in those woods? How long had she wandered, without her family?

After a moment, he realised he hadn't answered her question. He shook his head and forced a grim smile. There was no point reliving that pain; it was enough that he still lived, and that his axe had sent another of the beasts into the abyss.

"We should do something about your arm," he said instead, nodding to his makeshift cast. "You might have other injuries too. The camp doctor should really check you over…"

"*No!*" Cara hissed, taking a step back from him, eyes wide with fright.

Romaine raised his hands, his heart inexplicably racing. "Okay, okay," he murmured, "but we still need to do something about that arm. I'm no doctor, and that splint I made is already half falling off. You don't want the bone to mend crooked."

Lips pursed, Cara looked from Romaine to her injured arm. As if to test his words, she stretched out her hand, and flinched. Pain tightened her face and she sank back to her barrel—though to her credit, she did not cry out.

"I…I might be able to help."

Quick as a viper, Cara was back on her feet, arms raised as she swung on the newcomer. Beyond her, a young man in Perfugian colours yelped and leapt backwards. His feet slipped in the mud before he could flee and sent him crashing to the ground. Landing face-first in the mud atop the ramparts, he thrashed, and would have probably gone tumbling down the slope back to the city had Romaine not strode across and plucked him from the muck.

"Hey…what…get off!" the man cried.

Chuckling, Romaine set the man carefully on his feet. Behind him, Cara mirrored his mirth, her laughter peeling from the ramparts. The man's blue uniform, along with his face, was now stained top to bottom with mud. Pink tinged his pale cheeks as he stood there, head bowed, brown eyes locked to the ground as though it had been cast by some great artist.

"So, what were you saying, lad?" Romaine asked when the laughter finally died away.

The man's eyes flashed as he glanced at Cara, but she only responded with an innocent smile. Whatever the Perfugian had been expecting, it had not been that. Shaking his head, he looked back at Romaine.

"You saved my life," he said softly.

Romaine raised his eyebrows. It was a moment before his memories clicked into place and he recognised where he'd seen the young man before. This was the recruit who had crouched at the feet of the Tangata Romaine had killed earlier.

"It was nothing, lad," he grunted. "I've made a habit of gutting the bastards." A grin split his bearded cheeks. "Though you might want to consider keeping on your feet next time." He glanced at the Perfugian's mud-stained clothing. "Falling over is not a habit I would recommend around these parts."

The pink in the Perfugian's cheeks darkened to red but Romaine only clapped him on the shoulder. From the crispness of the man's uniform, he guessed this was one of the fresh recruits from Perfugia. Word amongst the Flumeeren soldiers was that the column had arrived just before the battle, and had actually participated. It was more than could be said for most of the recruits out of Perfugia, though from the number of blue uniforms amidst the pyres, it seemed their bravery had come at a hefty cost.

"So what's the name, lad?" he asked when the recruit did not respond to his goad.

The recruit started, his head jerking up, as though surprised to be asked the question. "Lu…Lukys," he stammered.

"Romaine." He held out a hand, and after a moment Lukys took it in his. "Now," Romaine continued, "what were you saying about helping young Cara here?"

Lukys blinked, looking at the still smiling woman, then back to Romaine. "What…oh, yes right, her arm."

"Her arm," Romaine agreed.

"It's broken?"

The axe man sighed, already regretting entertaining the young man. "Well, we'd need a doctor to say for sure…"

"Yes," Cara interrupted. She stepped up beside them, arm cradled to her chest. "I fell, out there," she said, indicating the land beyond the river. "I'm sorry for laughing," she added. "I am not used to…people."

Silence answered her words. Romaine glanced at Lukys and saw the youth's mouth had fallen open. His eyes were on the river, and he realised the recruit probably knew nothing about Calafe and his people.

"You…were…you came…from Calafe?" the young man finally managed to stammer.

Laughter danced in Cara's eyes as she shared a glance with Romaine, but this time she was wise enough not to voice it. Instead she nodded to her forearm. "Do you think you can help?"

Lukys glanced from the river to Cara. "I…" He swallowed, then drew in a great breath. It must have helped him gather his wits, for when he spoke next, his tone was almost calm. "I…yes, I think so. They taught us all sorts of things at the academy, to prepare us, you see, may I?"

It took a moment for Romaine to pick the meaning from the man's jumbled words. It took Cara longer still, but after a pause she finally offered her arm. She stood with her back arched, jaw clenched as Lukys gently took her arm in his hands.

"You're a medic?" Romaine asked, attempting to distract the woman from her phobia.

"What?" Lukys murmured, then shook his head. "No, I wanted to be, but I…failed, apparently," he answered before Romaine could repeat the question. He didn't seem to notice the tension in his patient as he carefully removed the makeshift splint Romaine had made. "We…all did, I suppose, all of us here." His eyes flickered and Romaine glimpsed the shame that hid there. "But then, you already knew that."

"We're all failures at something, lad."

Lukys snorted, but this time he did not reply. The last bandage came loose, revealing the purple bruises that marked Cara's pale skin. They spread almost the length of her forearm. It must have been quite the fall, to leave such a bad break.

"Fortunately, I do remember how to treat a fracture," Lukys added finally. He shot Cara a smile, as though to reassure her.

Cara did not reply. All colour had drained from her face and she looked like she might explode from her coat of heavy furs at any moment. The recruit's eyebrows lifted in surprise and he glanced at Romaine in question.

"Will you heal her with your hands, lad?" Romaine asked in response.

"I…" He trailed off, looking around, as though checking for listeners. "I have some supplies in my pack. I left it in the plaza, but I can get them." Carefully he lowered Cara's arm to her side and released her, then turned and hurried down the slope into the town.

In his absence, Romaine turned back to Cara. "You okay, lass?"

Cara nodded, though she had grown pale enough to be mistaken for a ghost. "Are…all the people of Perfugia so strange?" she asked.

Romaine grinned and took a seat on another of the water barrels that stood nearby. "Hard to say," he replied. "We only get the misfits down here. Lad's heart seems in the right place. You sure you don't want a real doctor though? They've got stuff that'll help with the pain."

Cara's face darkened. "No," she said shortly.

After that, they waited in silence for the young man to return. He appeared a few minutes later, large pack strapped to his back. A spear hung from one side, a helmet the other. With a sleeping roll atop, he looked more tortoise than man as he rattled his way up the slope. Romaine watched his approach with amusement, too fatigued to go down and help.

"You carried all that from Perfugia?" he asked when the young man finally reached them.

Lukys was puffing so hard he only managed a nod by way of answer. Uncaring for the mud, he threw the pack down near Cara and started rummaging around inside. When he rose again, he held several rods of copper and a handful of dried herbs. He handed them to Romaine before pulling out a pack of bandages.

Cara flinched as he turned towards her, and he paused, glancing uncertainly at Romaine.

"Only the arm," Cara whispered, drawing the recruit's attention back to her. She lifted the offending limb, as though it were an offering for some sacrifice.

Lukys still hesitated, his eyes on Romaine. The axeman shrugged. "She doesn't like to be touched."

Understanding blossomed in the recruit's eyes. "I'll try to be careful," he murmured.

He gestured for Cara to seat herself on the barrel, then waited until she was comfortable before moving alongside her. Taking the dried herbs from Romaine, he plucked a flower from the tip of one and offered it to Cara.

"For the pain," he explained. "Chew, but don't swallow, or you won't be able to taste food for a week."

"No," the young woman replied, shaking her head.

Lukys raised an eyebrow. "This…is going to hurt. I need to check whether the bone is set right."

"Thank you," Cara said shortly, "but I can handle the pain."

The lad hesitated a moment longer than was wise, but when Cara still made no move to accept his offering, he finally relinquished. Romaine sat back on his barrel as Lukys took Cara's arm in his hands once more.

Her face immediately lost the last of its colour, though this time Romaine wasn't sure whether it was from pain or fear.

With meticulous care, Lukys peeled back the sleeves of her coat once more. "Is this okay?" he asked, placing a finger on the injury.

Cara flinched, and her lips drew back in a snarl. Romaine expected the young Perfugian to retreat in fear, but curiously he stood his ground, brown eyes fixed on his patient. Cara's breath came in short gasps and Romaine feared she was working herself into a panic, but finally she gave a short nod.

Permission granted, Lukys moved his hands softly over the purpled flesh, fingers prodding gently at the bone beneath. Pain flickered on the young woman's face and her jaw remained clenched, though she did not let out even a squeak to show her pain.

"Okay, it's only broken in one place," Lukys said finally, straightening to look her in the eye. "You were lucky."

Cara's face was still pale, but she offered a fleeting smile. "I'll remind you of that next time you break something."

"That's fair," Lukys chuckled.

With his hands at work, he seemed more relaxed than earlier. Taking the copper rods from Romaine, he lined them up with her arm.

"Could you hold these here for me?" he asked, flashing his patient a smile.

The grimace had returned to Cara's face with his touch, but she did as he bid. Lukys placed his fingers back on her arm, and then hesitated.

"Are you sure you wouldn't like the—"

"Just do it," Cara practically snarled.

"Ahh, okay," Lukys said, and pressed his fingers to her wrist.

A shrill keen sounded from the back of Cara's throat as she arched atop the barrel. For a second, Romaine thought she would strike the young man. Veins bulging on her forehead, she clung to the copper rod.

Then it must have been done, for Lukys was removing his hands. Cara let out a short exhalation as the tension fled her body. Her shoulders rose and fell in rapid succession beneath the heavy cloak, her breathing short. Gently, Lukys took the rod from her hands and moved it back into alignment with her newly set arm. Taking up the bandages, he wrapped several layers around the rod before adding a second rod, then finally a third, until Cara's arm seemed twice the size as normal.

"There!" he exclaimed finally. "Done!"

Cara sat back with a sigh, though her face still showed her tension. "Thank you," she murmured. She sounded faint, and worried the woman might collapse, Romaine stepped closer. She waved him back, curious eyes turning on Lukys. "How did you learn to do something like that?"

Lukys only shrugged. "Like I said, the academy."

"An academy." She said the word as though tasting it.

"We all go," Lukys murmured, becoming self-conscious again now that the job was done. He lowered his eyes. "But like I said, I failed."

"Oh…" Cara deflated. She clutched her arm to her chest for a moment, before her head came up again. "But you seem so good at this!"

Lukys scratched a spot of dried mud from his tunic, looking

away. "I…well…" His cheeks grew red, standing in stark contrast to her paleness. "I throw up when I see vomit." The words came from his mouth in a rush.

Laughter burst from Romaine's lips before he could keep himself silent. The recruit's head snapped around, anger touching his brow. Rising from his barrel, Romaine clapped him on the shoulder.

"All got our weaknesses, lad."

"Some of us have a few more than others," Lukys replied, his eyes drifting out across the mudflats.

Pity welled in Romaine's stomach and he saw again the eyes of another young man, staring up at him from the snow, terror in their murky depths. Romaine quickly shoved the memory away. He couldn't afford such sentiment out here, not with the Tangata gathering. He wouldn't survive losing anybody else.

"Romaine." The young man's voice was taut as he spoke, his eyes still fixed in the distance.

Following his gaze, Romaine saw that the pyres had almost burned out, though there were still shapes amidst the embers…

"I don't want to die here."

That makes one of us.

Romaine said nothing. Faces flashed before his eyes, of those he'd lost, of those he hadn't been able to save, all the way back to that night ten years before…

"The general won't train us. He says we're not worth the time. I…I won't last another battle against those things, not without help."

No, no, no!

"Please, I saw you fight. You're a warrior, a great one. Please, Romaine, will you train me?"

No.

It was a fool's request. Even had Romaine been inclined, General Curtis was right. He usually was. It took months to turn an untrained recruit into a soldier—and based on the night's assault, they might not even have a week before the true Tangatan army reached the frontier.

He let out a long sigh, readying himself to spurn the man's

request, to crush this last hope before it could catch light. He faced the young recruit.

"Meet me here tomorrow, at first light." The words leapt unbidden from his mouth. "And we'll see whether there's hope for you yet."

❦ 9 ❦

THE RECRUIT

Darkness.

A full moon over silent peaks. Rock and snow and cold.

Light flashing, a shadow in the night, the hiss of an inhaled breath.

Pounding, the racing of a fleeing heart, the panting of pursuers.

Cold, *rushing water, fire and flames, shouts in the night.*

Loss, failure, death!

Lukys gasped as he snapped awake, sitting bolt upright in his cot—

Crack.

Cursing, he crumpled back into the tangle of blankets, head ringing from the blow he'd struck against the bunk above. Somewhere in the dark, the other recruits grumbled and muttered dire warnings against disturbing their slumber. Outside, a rooster crowed.

Holding a hand to his chest, Lukys tried to slow his racing heart. Already the dream was fading. The rooster crowed again. Beyond the heavy shutters, night still clung to the city. He needed to rise, to stumble out into the cold and meet with the bearded warrior of Calafe.

The thought did not fill him with excitement. By the faint glimmer of a shuttered lamp he could see his breath misting on the air above him. It would be worse outside the dormitory. Surely he could lie here a little longer.

But no, Romaine had said the hour before dawn.

Stifling another moan, he pushed himself up more carefully and swung out the bed. It was a drop of two feet to the ground. The bunks were three-tiered, and being one of the last to the barracks, he'd been left with one of the middle beds.

Unable to light a lamp, he fumbled in the dark for his clothes and quickly dressed himself in every layer he could find. The muttering began again but Lukys ignored it. There was little he could do about the noise. He continued collecting his gear and was just pulling on his chainmail vest when a rough hand grasped him by the shoulder and spun him around.

"What the Fall do you think you're doing, *peasant?*" Dale spat.

Eyes wide, Lukys found himself staring up at the larger man. Dale's lips were drawn back into a snarl and he looked ready to throw Lukys through the window. He quickly tore himself loose and raised his hands in a gesture of peace. Voices rose at the commotion and movement came from nearby beds as the other recruits woke.

"Sorry!" Lukys whispered, trying to get away from Dale.

Across the room, someone unshuttered the lantern, allowing a flicker of light to illuminate the scene. Dale's eyes narrowed at the sight of Lukys fully dressed, though he hadn't quite managed to get the chainmail into place.

"Where do you think you're going?" he snarled. He gestured around the room, though most of the recruits looked like they'd rather be asleep. "Look, brothers, sisters, the peasant shows his true colours! The coward seeks to flee!"

Anger touched Lukys at the recruit's words, washing away his fatigue. He stepped up to confront the man, though Dale was several inches taller.

"Strange," Lukys said, keeping his voice soft. "I did not see you atop the wall, Dale. Where were you, when the Tangata came?"

A flicker passed across Dale's face and for a moment he did not seem able to reply. Lukys spoke into the silence:

"I'm no coward," he said softly, addressing the others in the room now. Thirty-seven of their number had survived the battle. "The rest of you can accept your fate, but not me. I won't let them throw away my life like yesterday's garbage."

"So you are a deserter," Dale snarled.

"No." Lukys flicked his eyes back to the recruit. "I'm going to train."

Dale sneered. "Who would train a runt like you?"

"A Calafe warrior," Lukys snapped.

With that he spun and strode to the door. A cold breeze swirled into the room as he yanked it open. He snatched a spear from the weapons closet beside the entrance, then stepped out into the darkness and slammed the door behind him.

There he paused, half thinking Dale would follow to continue the fight. But no one appeared, and after only a moment's stillness he found his teeth beginning to chatter. A faint glow lit the sky pink and he saw now that fresh snow had fallen during the night. It crunched beneath his boots as he started down the alleyway, making for the section of wall he had first met Cara and Romaine.

Romaine had said to meet there, and judging by the light in the sky, he was already late. He picked up the pace, but the cold had frozen the earth solid, making it precarious to go faster than a walk. Even then, he had added more than a few bruises to his already aching body by the time he found himself standing in the shadow of the palisade.

There was no one there.

Cursing, Lukys hugged his chest and shifted his weight from foot to foot. Where was the axeman? The dawn was still and the cold wind cut like knives through even his heavy coat. Had this all been some prank, some act at Lukys's expense?

His legs were just beginning to go numb when the crunch of footsteps came from overhead. The Calafe warrior appeared, jogging along the tops of the ramparts. He wore his full chainmail armour and the giant butterfly axe hung from a sheath on his back. The man lifted a hand in greeting.

"You're late, recruit," the axeman called down.

Lukys's face grew warm but when he opened his mouth to offer an excuse, Romaine only laughed.

"Relax, lad. Why don't you get on up here? View's better from the top."

Nodding, Lukys started up, but soon found the task more diffi-cult than it appeared. With the earth frozen, the mound was now slick beneath his feet and he had to dig the toes of his boots into the earth with each step. Fortunately, he was able to use the butt of his spear for balance. He was puffing hard by the time he reached the top, but couldn't help but grin when he looked around at the Calafe warrior.

Romaine laughed, gesturing away to the side. "When it's frozen, we generally use the stairs."

Following the man's indication, Lukys groaned when he saw the makeshift steps that had been cut into the earthen rampart a few yards away. He looked into the distance and saw they repeated at regular intervals. How had he missed them earlier?

"Come," Romaine said, turning towards the wooden spikes that topped the wall, pointing towards the river.

Beyond, the sky had turned from pink to scarlet, the rising sun setting the distant mountains aflame. Looking upon those towering peaks, Lukys could almost imagine that time all those centuries ago, when the Gods had rained their fury down upon humanity. The conflagration had destroyed humanity's ancestors, reducing them to little more than animals, scavenging in the remnants of their former greatness. Only pockets of civilisation had survived—places such as the noble city of Ashura, guarded by the open seas.

Lukys glanced at Romaine, but the Calafe's eyes were not on the mountains. The warrior looked out across the river, and though a light mist clung to the waters, obscuring their view, Lukys sensed the man's mind was on the distant lands to the south.

"Do you miss it?" Lukys asked softly. "Your home, I mean?"

A rumble that might have been laughter came from the warrior. "I miss many things, lad," he said, then gestured to the river. "But time, like the Illmoor there, flows on whether we like it or not. Can't go back. If you fight the current, you die. So best just go along for the ride."

"Unless you have a ship," Lukys replied.

Romaine shot him a glare and Lukys's cheeks warmed with embarrassment.

"So," the warrior said, shaking his head. "What *did* they teach you in that academy of yours? About war and that spear of yours?"

"Not much," Lukys murmured. "I thought we would be trained when we arrived here, but..." He shrugged, not wanting to linger on the general's words.

"Good," Romaine grunted. Lukys gave him a sharp look and the Calafe grinned. "Means I shouldn't have to beat any bad habits out of you." His eyes flickered to the spear Lukys held awkwardly at his side. "Why don't you have a go at me with that thing?"

"*What?*" Lukys gasped, eyes widening. He glanced at the spear, its razor-sharp point shining in the sunlight, then back to Romaine. "I could *hurt* you."

Romaine chuckled. "I doubt that very much."

"You don't even have a weapon!"

A smile crossed the Calafe's face, and calmly he lifted the massive axe from his shoulders. Ice spread through Lukys's veins as the warrior shifted into a fighting stance. He clutched the spear in front of him, thinking of that axe flying at his face. The point of his spear began to shake.

Laughter boomed across the wall, and then Romaine was driving the head of his axe into the frozen earth.

"By the Gods, lad, you look like you might die of fright." He shook his head. "Was a joke. Come, most of the Tangata don't have weapons either. Let's see if you can hit me with that thing."

"I…"

Lukys stared at the man. Romaine's hands were empty now. Steel chainmail protected his chest and caked leather gauntlets his arms, but Lukys still couldn't help but fear he might harm the warrior. But he'd been given an order, and gripping the spear in two hands, he thrust out half-heartedly at the axeman.

Romaine moved calmly to the side and batted out with one arm, sending the spear careening into the earth. The shock of the weapon striking ground was almost enough to jar it from Lukys's hands. He opened his mouth to protest, but yelped instead as Romaine leapt and struck at him with an open palm.

Even through his chainmail and heavy furs, the blow to his chest sent Lukys staggering back. The breath hissed between his teeth and he doubled up around the spear. For once he managed to keep his footing, but as Lukys straightened he saw Romaine coming again, face dark, unreadable.

In terror, Lukys thrust out with his spear. A cry left his lips as he realised what he'd done, but it was too late. Romaine moved faster than thought, his arm flashing down to deflect the attack, and he narrowly avoided being skewered by the spearhead. Lukys flinched as the warrior straightened, but Romaine only chuckled and stepped away.

"Well, you're quick, I'll grant you that lad," he said, "but you're also right. You don't know much about spear work."

Lukys lowered his eyes and clutched the offending weapon to his chest. Despair touched him as he saw himself on the ground once more, the Tangata standing over him, that awful chant ringing in his mind.

Death, death, death.

He began to shake. That image had haunted him through the night. It was only a matter of time before the creatures returned. How could he ever hope to face such monsters?

"It's useless," he whispered, voice bitter. "It's too late. That general is right. I'll never learn. May as well just go back to my bed. Least it's *warm* there."

"Maybe you're right," Romaine rumbled. "Might be I'm wasting my time. After all, you're only a *Perfugian*."

Lukys's head snapped up, but the angry words died on his tongue as he saw the humour in Romaine's eyes. Grinning, the warrior crossed to one of the water barrels and sat, gesturing for Lukys to join him.

"You can quit if you like, lad," he said as Lukys lowered himself down. "The Gods know, you've drawn the short stick in this bloody frontier." He paused, steel-blue eyes flickering. "But don't quit because of what some old bugger told you. Even if that bugger *is* a legend. This is war, not bloody architecture. Anyone can learn to hold a spear, if he's determined, if he puts his heart into it."

"You don't really believe that," Lukys muttered.

"Oh?" Romaine rumbled. "You think I'm doing this out of the goodness of my heart then?"

Lukys hesitated. Why *was* Romaine doing this? He glanced at the grizzled warrior but found himself unable to ask the question. A sigh slipped from his lips and his gaze flickered in the direction of the hills. Two of the recruits had disappeared during the battle, but their bodies hadn't been found. Lukys was sure they'd taken advantage of the carnage to flee. If so, they wouldn't get far. The world was at war, and deserters were not treated kindly.

That only left one choice: Learn to fight.

"Okay, Romaine," he said, dragging his spirits from the chasm of despair. "I'll do my best."

The warrior grinned. "Don't look so glum, lad. This is going to be fun. Now, why don't you take a lap around the walls while I get a few things ready?"

"You want me to walk around the city?"

"I want you to *run*," Romaine corrected. "First rule of combat—be fitter than the other man."

"But the Tangata aren't…"

Lukys trailed off as he caught Romaine's blue eyes glaring at him. He hesitated, mouth still half-open, until Romaine reached down and plucked his axe from the mud.

Hefting his spear, Lukys ran.

❧ 10 ❧

THE ARCHIVIST

Striding through the scarlet halls of the royal citadel, Erika struggled to keep the apprehension from her face. The queen's steward walked ahead, while two of the royal guards trailed her on either side, as though they feared she would flee. Their presence made her nervous, with their shining swords and impenetrable helms, and it was with an effort of will that she forced herself to concentrate on her surroundings.

Like the rest of the city, the citadel had a certain practicality to its construction. The plain sandstone blocks did little to assuage the eye and the few windows were squat and high in the walls, allowing sunlight to enter while still keeping out the undesirable. Such designs stemmed from earlier ages, when Flumeer had been a collection of warring tribes rather than a united kingdom.

Even the layout of the corridors had been designed with defence in mind, winding inwards and upwards in a spiral pattern. An assailant would have to circumnavigate the building several times to reach the queen's quarters at the centre. In places, windows in the inner loops of the spiral looked down on the outer corridors, allowing defenders to fire down upon their attackers from a sheltered position.

They passed through several gates, each defended by another squadron of the royal guard, before sandstone walls gave way to marble. From there, they moved quickly through a series of courtyards, most empty on this cold winter afternoon, until finally they entered the inner palace.

Erika's heart began to race as she suddenly found herself before the golden doors of the royal court. They stood closed, their precious surface studded with gems and platinum decorations. Of all the passages they had passed, here alone had no thought been given to defence. Grand windows of stained glass turned the light in the corridor to red and green and blue, and not one guard had been left at the entrance to the court.

The queen's steward turned towards her. His face remained carefully schooled, though Erika could read the disdain in his eyes. He thought her a liar, that she had failed once again to claim the powers of the Gods and came now to beg for further clemency. A tingling came from her fingers, as though the gauntlet yearned to be used. She fought the temptation.

"I am ready, steward," she said to his unspoken question.

He spoke no further, only turned and pushed open the golden doors.

The buzz of voices ensued as she followed him into the chamber, though they died away as the queen's steward marched towards the throne. Row upon row of chairs stretched upward in tiers from the chamber floor, packed with the Flumeeren elite. Erika's legs turned to lead as she sensed their eyes upon her, but it was too late to turn back. She heard her name called through the ringing in her ears. Turning, she saw the steward raising his arm.

"…Archivist to the queen, here with urgent news for the war," he finished, meeting her eyes from across the room. Erika could have sworn his neutral expression broke for half a second, revealing a mocking smile.

A hundred voices erupted from all around, echoing from the domed ceiling high above and ringing across the chamber, almost deafening. Erika felt her legs retreat a step and had to force herself to stand still, to endure. Behind her, the guards who had escorted her this far stood at attention beside the doors, barring her escape.

Steeling herself, Erika ignored the councillors and nobles that surrounded her and stepped up beside the steward. Across the floor of the chamber was a small dais. There were none of the decorations and grandeur of the palace here. The queen sat upon a simple wooden chair, legs crossed and fingers steepled, her emerald eyes on the crowd of nobles above.

Stranger, though, than the woman's plain surroundings, was the full suit of armour Queen Amina had donned. Plain steel covered the woman from her boots to her chest. Only the helm was missing, revealing shining auburn hair and a copper circlet upon her brow. The queen was only thirty-five, barely ten years her senior, but she carried herself with a poise Erika could only imagine. She wore a longsword at her side, and the crimson scar on her left cheek proved she knew how to use it. Indeed, she was not hailed as a warrior queen for nothing.

The sight of the queen in steel gave Erika pause. Amina only wore her armour during times of war. Had something changed on the frontier while she'd been away? Erika's heart quickened. If the Tangata had firmed their hold on northern Calafe, her plans to visit the ancient site were already doomed. But it was too late to change tactics now.

"Your Majesty," she said over the cacophony of voices in the chamber. "I bring a message of hope."

"My Archivist," the queen murmured. Eyes as hard as gemstones regarded Erika from across the room. "Pray, tell me you have brought more than just hopeful words."

"Of course!" Erika exclaimed, her voice rising to an undignified tone. She swallowed, regaining control of herself before going on. "I would not have returned so quickly had my quest not found success."

The queen seemed to consider her words. Then her eyes flickered, as though searching for someone else on the chamber floor. Her lips tightened to a frown. "Then where are the good assistants I sent with you?"

Erika hesitated. "I…" She bowed her head. "Alas, the noble Ibran fell," she replied. "And Sythe…was a traitor."

The room erupted at her words, the entire court of two hundred nobles leaping to their feet and shouting their disdain. Erika flinched at the discordance, but did not look away from the queen. The woman had not reacted to the news, though now she slowly came to her feet and raised a hand. Silence fell. Not even the nobles of Flumeer wanted to risk the queen's displeasure.

"A traitor?" she murmured.

"Yes, Your Majesty," Erika replied, bowing her head. "He killed Ibran, and tried to claim the treasure we discovered beneath the earth. For the King of Gemaho."

This time not one of the nobles said a word, though the revelation was even more scandalous than her earlier news. The queen was still on her feet.

"I see," the woman murmured, eyes fixed on Erika. "Yet you escaped?"

Erika swallowed, hearing the accusation in her voice, and drew herself up. "I did," she said. "I was determined to keep our discovery from the hands of the Gemahan."

"And what did you discover down there in the dark, Archivist?"

"A map, Your Majesty!" Erika replied, drawing the scroll from her pocket. The queen's brows lifted into her auburn locks. Swallowing, Erika quickly went on: "It compiles the ancient sites of the Gods, many yet undiscovered, untouched since the time before The Fall. It was discovered in a sealed room. I believe these other sites might be the same. If so, the treasures within, the magics…this is what the King of Gemaho wanted!" She finished in a rush, cheeks warm, heart racing in her excitement.

The queen did not move from where she stood. She regarded Erika in silence, one eyebrow still raised, iron arms folded across her chest.

"A map?" she said at last. Her voice did not share Erika's excitement. She lowered herself down into the wooden chair. "And where are these sites with their precious treasures?"

"Calafe!" Erika gasped. "In the northern region, there is a site just a few days south of the Illmoor. If we move quickly, I could recover its secrets with a single regiment. Just think, Your Majesty, the power that waits, enough to conquer nations, to destroy the Tangata for good!"

"I see," the queen murmured, tapping idly at the wooden arms of her chair. "Was that not what you promised before this latest venture?"

"I…" Erika trailed off, the words lodging in her throat.

"A venture which cost two persons of some prestige," the queen went on, her voice cold enough to send shivers down Erika's spine.

"And now…now you ask for an entire *regiment?* Do you not realise, child, that the Tangata sit on our very *doorstep?*"

Murmurs spread around the hall, though this time the nobles did not seem angry. They could sense the blood in the water, the rage lurking beneath the queen's measured voice. So instead they watched, waiting for the kill.

"The map was not all I found!" Erika shrieked.

Why had she not mentioned the gauntlet first? Because… because it was *hers.* Her secret, her weapon, the only thing that had kept her alive down there in the darkness. She didn't *want* to share this discovery with the queen. Yet neither could she allow the murmuring around the chamber to continue, to allow herself to be condemned.

"Oh?" the queen asked. She made no effort to conceal the scepticism in her voice.

"Does Your Majesty still keep any of the Tangata captive here in the citadel?" Erika asked, struggling to hide the tremor in her voice.

Images flashed through her mind, of bronzed faces behind bars, of awful screams, of eyes dripping with hatred and rage.

"There is one that survives," Queen Amina replied.

"Bring it," Erika ordered, attempting to project confidence, before adding: "Should it please Your Majesty."

The queen regarded her for a long moment. Then the hint of a smile touched the queen's lips and she nodded. The two guards stationed at the doors turned and vanished into the corridor, presumably to retrieve the captive Tangata.

Sweat dripped down Erika's brow as she stood watching those golden doors, feeling the eyes of the entire court upon her. A lump lodged in her throat and she squeezed her fist tight.

What was she doing? Would the gauntlet even work on one of the Tangata? Could she even *make* it work? She still had not practiced with that ability…

Hinges squeaked as the doors swung open again, admitting the guards back onto the chamber floor. But they were no longer alone. A third figure stood between them, arms and legs chained, face streaked with filth, clothes in tatters.

Grey eyes staring.

Erika shivered as she looked into those eyes and saw…nothing.

A frown touched her forehead. When she'd last been in the capital, the queen had paraded the creatures regularly before the court. Then, the rage that lurked within these creatures had been obvious, their hatred a raw, animalistic thing. But with this creature…its eyes showed only emptiness, only defeat.

"Well, Archivist?"

Erika swallowed, glancing back at the queen. Drawing in a lungful of air, she raised her gauntleted fist. "I found this in the ruins of the Gods," she said softly.

"A glove?" the queen murmured archly.

"No," Erika said shortly. She turned her back on the queen and faced the wretched Tangata. "My Queen, let me show you the power of the Gods."

She didn't wait for permission. Stepping up before the beast, she lifted the gauntlet. The Tangata's head bobbed at the movement, its eyes slowly coming into focus, fixing on her. It made no move to attack, though the guards held its chains tight all the same. Erika hesitated, sensing the beast's despair.

Whispers spread around the room as the moment stretched out. Erika could sense her audience's impatience. She had promised them magic; if she failed now…

Erika opened her fist and pointed her palm at the Tangata.

The screams began.

The beast took long minutes to die. By the time it fell silent, not a soul in the throne room moved. A terrible silence hung over the chamber as Erika stood over the Tangata, looking down at its tormented face. Blood stained its cheeks and turned its eyes red. It had died in agony.

It was a monster. It would have killed you if it could have.

Releasing a breath she hadn't realised she'd been holding, she turned to face the queen. Steel rattled as the royal guards moved between them. They were wary of her now, frightened by the power she had revealed, but the queen waved them back. Rising, she stepped from the dais and moved to stand before Erika.

"You have done well, Archivist," the queen said. Then she held out her hand. "Give it to me."

Erika swallowed, but met the woman's eyes. "Alas, My Queen, I cannot. The gauntlet has fused to my flesh. Its power is a part of me now. But…grant me my request, and I will find you more objects of power, perhaps even greater than this one."

The queen stared at her for a long while, but finally she nodded, and a smile touched her lips. "Very well," she murmured. "You have done well, Archivist. You will have your regiment."

Erika's heart was thundering in her ears and she hardly heard the queen's words. She felt suddenly drained, as though she had just sprinted the length of the city. Was that the gauntlet, or simply the rush of the moment? Hardly knowing how to react, she bowed her head in acceptance.

"You will leave with the dawn," the queen continued. With that she turned and returned to the dais. Only when she reached her throne did she hesitate. Slowly, the woman turned to face Erika once more. "And Archivist?"

"Yes, Your Majesty?" Erika asked, her head jerking up.

"This will be your last expedition," the queen said. Her eyes narrowed. "Do not fail me, or one way or another, I will have that magic."

The ice in her words left Erika in no doubt as to how she would claim it.

THE WARRIOR

Romaine's breath puffed in the cold morning air as he jogged along the earthen rampart, chainmail jingling with each tread of his heavy boots. An ache had taken hold in the small of his back, and at times it seemed his knees were one bad day away from giving in. He didn't know exactly what day his age had caught him. It was like an assassin, creeping up slowly, until suddenly it stood before him with knife in hand.

Gritting his teeth, Romaine pressed on. Weakness meant death out here, and he refused to surrender to its call. Finally he found himself back where he had started and drew to a stop, panting softly in the dawn light.

"Why do you run?"

He spun at the voice and cursed. Cara sat on a nearby water barrel, those strange amber eyes watching him through the morning mists. The general had provided her with lodging on Romaine's request. He'd seen enough of his people homeless without adding another to their number. But what was she doing atop the palisade?

"Sorry?" he asked, straightening and forcing his breathing to slow.

A smile touched the woman's lips as she came smoothly to her feet. Her broken arm hung from a sling, but otherwise she seemed fully recovered from the trauma of a few days past. Hugging the heavy furs tight around herself, she wandered over to where he stood.

"The running," she said. "It hurts you."

Romaine stared at the woman for a long moment, then shrugged. "The Tangata do not care about my pain. I cannot afford to be slow. So I run."

Cara nodded as though he had confirmed some secret suspicion of hers. Her eyes flickered out over the rooftops of the city. The streets remained silent, though soon soldiers would rise to begin their days.

The thump of jogging boots approached and Romaine turned to watch Lukys stagger to a stop beside the water barrel. Gasping, he bent in two, and Romaine chuckled. Truthfully, he was impressed the young man had managed to keep pace as long as he had. The overland march from Mildeth had at least put a little muscle on the Perfugian recruit.

"Cara!" Lukys suddenly burst out, finally noticing the woman. He straightened immediately. "What are you doing here?"

"What, afraid of practicing the spear with an audience, lad?"

"An audience…" Lukys murmured, thick eyebrows knitting together in a frown. "Wait, we're going to practice the spear today?"

The day before Romaine had only taken Lukys through exercises to help build his strength and stamina. But such exercises did little to dislodge the despair in Lukys's eyes. He needed something to restore his confidence, or training the man was a lost cause.

Grinning, Romaine nodded to where two practice staves leaned against the stockade crenulations. "The spear is not my weapon of choice, but it's better than most when facing the Tangata."

"It's…awkward," Lukys said, picking up one of the staves and holding it before him. "Like it's too long for my arms."

"You'll be thankful for that reach when next you encounter the Tangata," Romaine replied, claiming the second stave.

He faced Lukys across the earthen rampart and adopted the basic fighting stance for the spear. Meanwhile, Cara sat herself on the water barrel and pulled her knees up to her chest to watch. A brilliant orange light shone from the horizon and the mist was beginning to lift. They were alone atop the wall but for a few guards, and they mostly kept to their own sections. Voices carried up from the streets of Fogmore as the first citizens rose to greet the day. The faint scent of burning wood carried on the air.

"So," Romaine said, "show me your best strike, lad."

Raising his stave, Lukys bit his lip. His eyes looked Romaine up and down and the warrior smiled. The lad was right to be cautious, but hesitation could prove costly against the Tangata. So with a roar, Romaine took the initiative, his practice spear thrusting out for the recruit's chest. Lukys's eyes widened and he stumbled on the slick mud, unable to move fast enough to avoid the blow. A soft *thump* followed as the wooden stave struck him in the chest, followed by a crash as Lukys tumbled to the ground.

"Stop hesitating," Romaine said, setting the butt of his stave to the earth and offering the recruit a hand. "The Tangata won't wait for you to make up your mind."

"Sorry," Lukys muttered, accepting Romaine's assistance.

He gathered his stave with a groan, lifting it slowly, as though in great pain. Romaine sighed and was about to offer a break when Lukys lunged forward with his weapon. Taken off-guard, Romaine struggled to get his own practice spear into position. Wood clacked upon wood, but he failed to completely deflect the strike. The stave connected with his shoulder, forcing a grunt from the axeman.

Stepping back, he brought his weapon around, prepared to fend off another strike from the recruit. But Lukys did not follow up. Instead, he stood staring at his weapon, as though surprised by what he'd done. Romaine grinned.

"Well done, lad," he laughed. "We might just make a soldier of you yet!"

Lukys looked up from the spear. "I…sorry! I thought you would stop it!"

Romaine only shook his head, still grinning, until laughter came from nearby. Glancing around, he saw Cara's eyes dancing with mirth.

"You're getting slow," she said. "I am not sure the running is working."

The grin slipped from Romaine's lips. "Even the greatest of warriors can be taken by surprise," he said, scowling. "Now, are you going to let us practice?"

Cara nodded quickly, moving her finger across her lips in a strange gesture. Shaking his head, Romaine faced Lukys once more.

"That was good," he said again, ignoring the eyes on his back, "but you almost overbalanced on the strike."

"What do you mean?" Lukys asked, running his fingers over the stave.

Romaine gestured him forward. "Try that again, I'll show you."

Lukys nodded—then thrust out with the makeshift spear. This time Romaine was ready for the strike and he twisted easily from the path of the blow. Then he swung out with his spare hand, snatching at the wooden staff and dragging it forward. Lukys cried out. His attack had thrown his centre of balance forward, and now Romaine dragged him beyond the tipping point. He struck the ground with a *thump*.

"*That* is what I meant," Romaine said.

Grumbling, Lukys picked himself up off the ground. Brushing the mud from his clothing, he flashed a glare at Cara, though the woman remained silent this time. She only raised her eyebrows at Lukys. Scowling, he turned back to Romaine.

"What am I doing wrong?" he gasped, his frustration clear.

"Patience, lad," Romaine responded, stepping forward and patting the man's shoulder. "It's only a matter of balance."

"Oh yes, *only*," Lukys replied with a scowl.

Romaine chuckled. "You seem upset."

The recruit shook his head. "If you hadn't noticed, I tend to fall down occasionally."

A snicker of laughter came from behind them and Lukys's cheeks reddened.

"You think balance is a talent you lack?" Romaine asked, pointedly ignoring Cara.

"Isn't it?"

"For some it comes naturally," Romaine admitted. He shifted so he was standing up straight, feet directly beneath him. "But not everyone is so lucky. Here, try to push me over."

Lukys looked him up and down, obviously expecting some trick. Tossing the stave aside, Romaine spread his arms, indicating he was defenceless. Even so, Lukys approached cautiously. Romaine could hardly blame the lad—he had some fifty pounds on the young recruit.

Suddenly Lukys darted forward, palms connecting hard into Romaine's chest. With his legs directly beneath him, Romaine was unable to brace for the blow. He toppled backwards, feet staggering in search of purchase but unable to find it, and went down like a sack of bricks.

Stumbling to a stop, Lukys gaped down at him, open horror on his face. "I'm so sorry," he gasped.

Grunting, Romaine picked himself up off the ground. Sensing the nervousness in the young man, he took a moment to calmly brush the mud from his clothes. Then he darted at Lukys in a sudden rush.

"Argh!" Lukys shrieked, leaping back, arms raised, face going white with terror.

Romaine threw back his head and laughed, bellowing his mirth out across the town. He would never admit it, but he hadn't had this much fun in a long time. Fighting, slaying Tangata, marching through the open wilderness, practicing with the blade, that was one thing. But by the Gods, he'd missed this, the camaraderie of the army. Why had he avoided others for so long...

A pale face, blue eyes, staring up from a bed of white.

The laughter left him. Letting out a sigh, he nodded to Lukys, who still looked like he half-expected Romaine to throttle him.

"Sorry, lad," he said, adopting a serious tone. "A joke. But you see now? Even a big man like me can be knocked down by a smaller foe if he adopts the wrong stance." As he spoke, he moved his legs so that they were shoulder width apart, left foot slightly ahead, right slightly behind. "Now," he murmured, "try again."

Lukys narrowed his eyes. The laughter had angered him, but he was cautious now of a trap. His chest swelled as he drew in a breath, then he leapt. Romaine did nothing to defend himself, but this time as Lukys connected, he was able to brace. With a grunt the recruit stumbled back, eyes widening as he saw Romaine had barely budged.

"Again," Romaine rumbled.

Hesitation showed in the recruit's eyes, but he obeyed, coming at Romaine in a rush. This time the axeman softened his stance, so that when Lukys struck the blow pushed him back. But with his feet correctly aligned, he simply stepped his left foot back, maintaining balance.

Lukys, meanwhile, had thrown too much of himself into the blow. With Romaine's sudden withdrawal, he found himself over-balancing once more. His arms windmilled and he tumbled forward—

Romaine caught him by the shoulder and set him back upright. "Easy now," he said with a smile. "I can only stand to watch you plant your face in the mud so many times in one day."

Shrugging off Romaine's hand, Lukys shook his head. "What am I doing wrong?" he croaked. He quickly lowered his head, though not before Romaine saw the glint of tears in the young man's eyes. Then he swung around, locking sights on Cara. "I'd like to see you do any better!"

Shocked by the outburst, Romaine took a step back. Across the palisade, a stunned look showed on Cara's face, her eyebrows lifting into her fringe of copper hair. Her mouth opened, as though to shout something back, but after a moment she closed it again. She rose from the barrel and stalked off without another word.

"Well that wasn't very gracious of you," Romaine commented.

Lukys sighed. "Sorry," he murmured, eyes to the ground. "I just…I'm no good at this, Romaine!"

"Lad, you gotta walk before you can run," Romaine replied. "Or in this case, you need to know *why* you fall, before you can figure out how to stay standing up."

"And that means?"

Romaine sighed. "I see this is going to be a long lesson." He gestured to the ground. "Look, a warrior's strength, his balance, his mobility, it all comes from his feet." As he spoke, he shifted so that his legs were rigid and directly beneath him. "A man who stands like this balances all his weight on a narrow base. He cannot move quickly, and is easily toppled." He moved his feet to the basic fighting stance. "But stand like this, and suddenly you're able to brace against an attack, or move easily from offence to defence." He leaned forward then backwards in demonstration, always keeping his feet in the same position.

Frown lines creased Lukys's forehead as he watched. When

Romaine finished, he did his best to adopt the same stance. Romaine shifted his feet a little, placing them closer to shoulder width, and then stepped back with a nod.

"This is what we call a forward stance," he said to Lukys's questioning look. "It's how you avoid ending up on your ass in battle."

This time, Lukys didn't seem to notice the gibe. His eyes were on his feet and concentration was etched across his face. Romaine smiled.

"Now, step forward with your right foot. Keep this stance in mind as you move, so when you place your foot down, you remain in the position." Romaine mimicked the instructions as he spoke, his right boot becoming the forward foot. He waited for Lukys to copy and corrected his stance again before continuing. "Now left foot forward."

They continued in that fashion, advancing and retreating across the palisade to the amused glances of the soldiers on watch. But Romaine did not see Cara's face among them, and he made a mental note to remind Lukys to apologise later. No point in letting animosity grow between those forced to live inside the walls of Fogmore.

"Are you sure this isn't another of your jokes?" Lukys asked suddenly after half an hour of marching up and down in forward stance.

Romaine raised an eyebrow. "Let's see, shall we?"

They were back where they'd left the staves. Romaine swept one into his hands and leapt at the recruit. A yelp tore from Lukys and he jumped back as the wooden tip lanced for his face. The makeshift spear missed him by an inch.

Gasping, Lukys lowered his hands. "What The Fall was that?" he shouted at Romaine.

Romaine grinned. "You didn't fall."

"What?"

He gestured with the baton at Lukys's feet. "You kept your feet in the forward stance."

"I…" Lukys trailed off, looking from the stave to his feet. Realisation dawned in his eyes and a grin split his face. "I did!"

"Good work," Romaine said. Then he tossed his stave to Lukys and swept up the second. "Now, guard up!"

Lukys was still staring at the makeshift spear in his hands when Romaine attacked. This time he didn't move with the same speed, his mind obviously tangled between using the spear and moving his feet, and a muffled *thud* followed as Romaine's stave struck the recruit on the shoulder.

A grunt came from Lukys as he stepped back, losing his stance. Romaine advanced, stave flashing out to prod him in the chest. With a cry, Lukys's feet went out from under him, and he slammed into the packed earth.

Romaine towered over the young man.

"What?" he said, a grin on his lips. "You didn't think you'd become a warrior in just one day, did you?"

12

THE ARCHIVIST

Erika's spirits lifted as her horse topped the hill and started down the other side, cutting off her view of Mildeth and its host of refugees. She had spent the night in luxury, bathing in the royal saunas, sleeping in private apartments reserved for the most important of foreign dignitaries. But despite the extravagance and her aspirations to make such an existence her reality, Erika had felt stifled, trapped by the towering walls.

She felt almost excited to be on the road again, setting off towards distant horizons. There was a freedom to this life, especially now that she rode alone. The queen had offered another assistant to help with her work, but after her experience down in the darkness, Erika had declined the offer. There was no telling who she could trust now; better she ride alone and have faith that the magic would defend her.

There was one drawback to this journey—every mile she rode carried her deeper into the frozen south, back towards Calafe and a past she had thought left long behind.

A shiver ran down her spine and Erika forced her mind to her surroundings. The road ran straight from Mildeth along a valley that cut through the rolling hills of lowland Flumeer. The terrain would provide for easy riding the first day, and regular waystations along the Queen's Highway meant she should not need the canvas tent stuffed into her saddlebags.

Which was just as well, for it had always been Sythe who'd set their camp each night.

That would change once she crossed the Illmoor, but then she would have a full regiment of soldiers to perform such menial tasks. The queen had provided her documents to sequester the force from one of the border cities. By Erika's calculations, the journey would require a total of five days in Calafe land—two to reach the site, one to explore the ruins, and another two back. Surely they would encounter no problems with the Tangata in such a short time. Not in the wide, untouched wilderness of Calafe, at least.

In the meantime, riding through the snow-sprinkled farmland of lowland Flumeer was a far sight more pleasant than her prior excursions.

She rode hard through that first day, stopping only occasionally to eat or walk her horse. The road was well-used and well-kept, and she encountered plenty of other travellers along the way. Some were farmers with wagons loaded up with wares, others merchants from further afield, though these were fewer now that Calafe had fallen.

Many more, though, were refugees—not from Calafe now, but people of Flumeer. They were obvious from the carts they brought with them, loaded up not with wares for sale, but ordinary goods— tables and chairs and kitchenware, the items of worth they had been able to carry away with them. These were the wealthy of the south, those with the power and resources to leave behind their former lives and set out in search of safer pastures. They were leaving now, before the Tangata came. Those who were left behind would not be so fortunate.

Erika nodded politely to those travellers who offered greetings, but her mind remained in the darkness beneath the earth. Now her discovery was known, there would be those who sought to take it from her. She imagined in each of the strangers the eyes of a killer, waiting to slay her on behalf of a foreign king. Whenever they came close, she would raise her gauntlet, ready to defend herself if necessary.

Only when the sun dropped towards the distant horizon did she start looking for a place to sleep. The road had begun to wind between the hills now, cutting off sight of the way ahead and behind. She continued on, eyes alert for an inn, but unconcerned by the empty land around her. The queen's steward had assured her that inns were in plentiful supply on these southern passages.

A half hour later the first traces of worry began to form in Erika's mind. There were no travellers on the road now and she realised she hadn't seen even a farmhouse for quite some time. The sun was already disappearing beneath the horizon, its glow fading by the minute. Without its heat, the temperature plummeted. Pulling the coat tighter around herself, she kicked her horse into a canter.

It was almost dark when she found herself beside a stream. Alone on the road, she cursed winter and its short days. It seemed there would be no feathered bed for her tonight. Out of options, she dismounted and led the mare from the road. At least the creek would provide fresh water.

Directing her horse upstream, she walked a hundred yards through a neighbouring field, until the curve of a hill hid her from the road. If she was going to camp alone in the open, she didn't want her presence known to every rogue and bandit in the area.

She found an old willow tree overhanging a section of river-bank, its twisted limbs stretched far out over the river. Tying her horse's reins to one of its branches, she then rummaged round in her saddlebags and pulled out the canvas tent. Above, the sky was clear, the first twinkling of the northern star just beginning to shine. She hoped that meant it wouldn't snow that night.

The tent was so heavy Erika almost dropped it when she finally dragged it from the saddlebags. Cursing, she stumbled away from the horse to an empty patch of grass and tossed it to the ground. Then she stood staring at the bundle, and for the first time, began to regret not bringing at least a porter. She was unaccustomed to the day-to-day tasks of preparing a camp, and while she'd occa-sionally watched Sythe...she hadn't really been paying much attention.

"How hard can it be?" she muttered to herself.

An hour and several ropes jerry-rigged to the willow tree later, she finally admitted to herself that pitching a tent was perhaps slightly more difficult than she'd thought. Nearby, her horse snick-ered and she rolled her eyes. The tent looked like a strong breeze might knock it down, but with only the light of a half-moon for guidance, it was as good as it was going to get. She would have to pray the night remained clear.

Returning to her horse, she struggled to remove its saddle then threw a blanket over its back. By the time she was done her teeth were chattering and her fingers so numb it hurt to move them. Clenching her fist, she sighed as warmth ignited in the gauntlet.

Only then did she recall Sythe had usually lit the fire *before* it grew dark.

Swearing, she fumbled at the saddlebags for tinder and flint. Thankfully there were plenty of fallen branches beneath the willow, and with little rain the last few days, they were mostly dry. She knelt and gathered the twigs into a pile, the tinder at the centre. Then she took up the flint and struck it towards the wood…

…and cursed as she struck her hand instead. The stone tumbled from her fingers as she leapt to her feet, cursing loud enough to wake the ancients. The cold only seemed to make the pain worse, and she balled her uninjured hand into a fist, wishing in that moment for an enemy she could take her anger out upon—

"Looks like you could use a hand."

Erika's heart twisted in her chest as a woman's voice spoke from the darkness. Pain forgotten, she lurched to her feet and swung around, gauntlet raised as she searched for the speaker. But whoever it was, they stood just out of line of sight—which wasn't far, admittedly, with only the half-moon for light.

"Who's there?" she hissed. "Show yourself!"

"Easy, Archivist," came the response. "I mean you no harm."

The breath caught in Erika's throat. Whoever the woman was, she knew who Erika was. That meant…

A soft glow emerged from the gauntlet, not enough to illuminate her foe, but it gave her reassurance.

"I said, *show yourself*," she hissed.

The woman laughed in response. "Of course," she said, "just as soon as you promise I will come to no harm."

Erika swung her arm backward and forward, but if the gauntlet was working, its range must be limited. There was no choice. She lowered her hand—it would still be a simple thing to strike the woman down should she prove dangerous.

"Thank you, Archivist." Shadows shifted in the night as a

woman stepped forward, hands raised. "I left my weapons near the road," she said quietly, "as I said, I mean no harm."

"That has yet to be seen," Erika replied, eyes narrowed.

Swathed in a black cloak and heavy winter clothes, little could be seen of the speaker but her face. Erika lifted her fist higher, and the glow of her gauntlet illuminated wide, circular eyes and a narrow jaw. The woman's lips pursed and Erika didn't miss how her gaze lingered on the magic. She allowed herself a smile.

"Why are you here?" she asked again. "How do you know who I am?"

"All in good time," the stranger said, lowering her hands before nodding to Erika's stack of wood. "I find winter nights to be more comfortable with a fire. May I?"

Erika hesitated, wondering whether this was some elaborate trick to lower her guard. But if so, she could not see how it could be sprung, not with the gauntlet in her control. She gave a curt nod.

Smiling, the stranger crossed to the woodpile and began moving some of the branches around. Then she took up the flint and struck it twice into the kindling. The sparks caught with a tiny *whoosh*. Leaning close, she blew softly into the flames. Within minutes there was a small blaze burning.

The stranger paused, eyes lingering on something off to the side. Despite herself, Erika's cheeks grew warm as she realised the woman was looking at her tent. She raised an eyebrow, amusement showing on her twisted lips.

"Don't think I can help with that one," she chuckled.

"Enough," Erika snapped, using anger to cover her embarrassment. She pointed her gauntlet at the woman. Though her fist remained closed, the death magic dormant, she was pleased to see the self-assured smile leave the stranger's face.

"I asked you some questions," she said dangerously.

"So you did," the stranger said, straightening beside the fire. Erika flinched, but the woman only held her hands out to the flames. "What a creation, fire," she murmured. "Man's earliest, most important tool, the beginnings of all civilisation." She glanced at Erika. "And the end of many too."

Erika swallowed, looking from the woman to the flames,

wondering if she was making a threat. But her visitor made no move towards her, and finally Erika shook her head.

"What nonsense are you spouting?"

"My master believes the secrets of the Gods could be the gateway to a new era," her mysterious visitor replied, "one without poverty or illness." She turned towards Erika, eyes aglow in the light of the fire. "But in the wrong hands…those secrets could destroy us."

"*This* magic deals only in death," Erika snarled. "If your master wants it, tell him to come and face me himself."

The stranger seemed amused at that. "My master is not interested in trinkets," she replied. "Your map, however, is of far greater interest."

Erika's heart beat faster and unconsciously she reached for the scroll in her inner pocket. No copies had been made—the risk was too great, after the attack beneath the earth.

She narrowed her eyes. "You were sent by the King of Gemaho."

"I was."

"He tried to kill me."

"An unfortunate misunderstanding," the stranger replied. "That was never his intention. He values the work of those rare souls who seek the truth. Your knowledge of the Gods and the ancients who once worked alongside them is irreplaceable. Your death would have been a terrible tragedy to his royal personage."

"I'm sure," Erika said shortly.

"Regardless of such miscommunications, I have been sent in peace, to heal the rift this unfortunate…accident, has opened between us."

"And why should I trust anything you say?" Erika hissed.

"Perhaps you should not," the woman said, extending her hands towards the flames. "It is up to us to prove our worth to you. That is why I was sent, to aid you in your journey."

"And rob me of my prize, should I succeed, no doubt."

"No," the stranger said, standing. "My king offers equal partnership."

Erika sneered. "I already have a partnership—with a monarch who has *not* tried to kill me."

"Not yet," her visitor replied softly, "though she came close, did she not?"

"I…" Erika trailed off, recalling that moment in court, the look in the queen's eyes. Doubt touched her, before anger swept it away. "Enough!" she snarled. "The queen is my ally, has granted me supplies and an army to ensure my success. I need no aid from the cowards of Gemaho."

"The world calls us cowards," the woman murmured, looking out into the dark, "but perhaps we are the only ones who have not been fooled." She shook herself, glancing back at Erika. "I will not fault you for your loyalty, Archivist, though it is misplaced."

"The queen has given me power, lifted me up to the highest of honours."

"Honours which can be easily taken away, should you fail." The woman's eyes bored into hers.

"*Enough*," Erika hissed, lifting her gauntlet. "I am tired of your lies. Tell your king to stay away. I want no part of your kingdom of traitors."

"Very well," the woman replied. She bowed her head, as though Erika's words had wounded her. Turning, she made to go, before glancing back. "But know this: our people are never far. Should the time come and you reconsider our offer, remember my words. In our king, you will always have a friend."

Then she was gone, disappearing into the night as though she had never been.

Erika stood standing beside the fire for a long time, staring at the place where the woman had stood. Her words rang in her ears. Now that she was gone, Erika could no longer deny their truth, could no longer hide from the doubt they had inspired. *Had* she given her loyalty to the wrong person?

No.

She could not trust a king whose assassin had tried to kill her just a week before. Shaking herself, she sat and added a log to the fire.

For the rest of the night though, she did not sleep, and when the sun rose it found her already on the road. For every night after that, she was sure to find an inn long before sunset.

13

THE RECRUIT

Light grew on the horizon as Lukys jogged his way around the earthen palisade. His shoulders ached, seeming to jar with each step, though at least he no longer carried the heavy pack. It had snowed again in the night, and while burning barrels atop the ramparts kept the snow from gathering there, the ground remained frozen beneath his boots.

He kept on despite the difficult conditions, eager today to beat the axeman at his own game. Lukys had slept the night in his clothing and risen early, leaving the barracks in silence to avoid further confrontation with Dale. Now he hoped to complete his loop of the city before Romaine arrived.

The run took him past several ranks of soldiers on guard. Each looked up at his approach, but upon seeing the blue colours of Perfugia, they quickly resumed whatever tasks he'd interrupted. The sight took some of the breath from Lukys. He would show them his worth eventually; for now, he could do little but accept their disdain.

Sunlight set the Mountains of the Gods aflame as he turned the final bend and approached his meeting point with Romaine. The Calafe warrior was only now striding up the steps, a bundle of practice spears carried over one shoulder. Lukys picked up his pace so that they both arrived at the same time.

Coming to a stop before the warrior, he sucked in a lungful of air and stood straight, doing his best to pretend the run had not tired him. Below, life began to stir in the town as its citizens stepped into the frosted streets.

"Early today?" Romaine asked, one eyebrow raised.

There was no sign of Cara. Lukys felt a twang in his chest. He shouldn't have driven her away, but there had been something uncomfortable about the way she watched him, and her laughter... her laughter had made him feel a fool.

Which he was.

Shaking his head, Lukys resolved to find her and apologise later. In the meantime, he offered Romaine a salute.

"Bright and early, sir." After his mortification at knocking Romaine to the ground the day before, he had decided to treat the warrior with the respect owed one of his professors back in the academy.

A scowl darkened the warrior's face. "Enough of that," he rumbled, tossing Lukys one of the practice spears. "I'm no blasted Flumeeren officer."

"I..." Lukys stammered, his cheeks going red. So much for showing respect. "Sorry..."

Romaine only grunted and hefted the spear. Before Lukys could ready himself, though, the sound of pounding hooves came from below. He turned back to the town and watched as mounted men in Flumeeren uniforms appeared, riding in the direction of the river. Each was garbed in full plate mail and carried shield and lance, armed for war.

Heart suddenly pounding in his chest, Lukys swung towards the river. The mist had melted away with the morning light and the waters were clear, the mudflats between the city and the banks empty of movement.

"Looks like the general's resuming the morning patrols. It's usually a half-regiment, different men each day. They'll cover twenty miles before returning," the warrior said in answer. "Dangerous after that attack. The creatures could be setting an ambush. But suppose it's necessary, to keep them from gaining a foothold our side of the river. And looks as though he's given them some rein-forcement."

Lukys watched in silence as the wooden gates swung open and the riders spilled out onto the mudflats. There were at least fifty, a full regiment. More than enough to handle any stragglers that might still be in the area, even a Tangata pair, should they risk a crossing. Even so, Lukys did not envy them the task of facing down one of the creatures in the open.

Turning his back on the departing soldiers, Romaine hefted his spear. "Ready?"

"What? I—"

Romaine lunged before Lukys could finish. He leapt back, bringing up his spear in a rough estimate of the low block Romaine had shown him the day before. The wooden poles came together with sharp *clack*.

"Your stance," Romaine growled, continuing the attack.

Blocking again, Lukys forced himself to be mindful of his feet, of moving through the stances Romaine had demonstrated. He was surprised when he stayed upright, though he knew the Calafe warrior was taking things slow. It seemed the drills were working— he had practiced them during his free time after the last lesson, eager to prove to Romaine he was worth the time.

"You're getting better."

Lukys stumbled as Cara's voice came from behind him. He started to turn, only to receive a solid blow to the hip. Air hissed between his teeth as he staggered back, gasping curses.

"…wasn't ready!"

"In battle, a warrior cannot afford to be distracted," Romaine replied, though he wore a grin. Stepping past Lukys, he nodded to Cara. "Welcome back, lass."

Cara snorted as she walked past, amber eyes fixing on Lukys. He swallowed and dropped his gaze. "Sorry, about yesterday," he said quickly.

Sorry, sorry, sorry.

When she did not reply, Lukys lifted his head, expecting to find anger on her face. Instead, she smiled. "That's okay," she said slightly, gesturing with her bandaged arm. "I shouldn't have laughed; I don't know how to use a spear either."

"Really?" Romaine murmured. He seemed surprised. "Your… parents didn't teach you?"

Cara shrugged. "How to defend myself, sure. Just…not with

weapons," she hesitated, looking up at Romaine from beneath her lashes. "Would you teach me as well?"

The question seemed to give Romaine pause. Lukys looked from one to the other, then blurted out the obvious: "But your arm!"

"My arm?" Cara glanced down at the offending limb, as though surprised to find it was still there. "Oh, right, well, I'm ambidextrous!"

"Ambi…what?" Romaine asked.

"It means she's comfortable using either hand," Lukys explained, frowning. It seemed there was more to Cara than met the eye. He looked to the Calafe warrior. "But still…she can't—"

"Why not?" Cara interrupted. "Afraid of getting beat by a girl?"

Lukys's cheeks grew warm, though it wasn't that. Having the guards watch his ineptness was bad enough, he actually *liked* Cara. He didn't want to appear a fool in front of her, at least, any more than he already had. But unable to say as much, he only shook his head.

"No," he muttered, "but your broken bone, it needs rest to heal."

"Not to worry." A smile brightened Cara's face as she lifted the injured arm and waved it. "I had a good medic. Feels fine to me."

A long pause stretched out as Romaine and Lukys watched her, and finally she rolled her eyes. "I only need the one hand to wield a spear," she insisted. "The other is meant to be for a shield anyway."

"Fine," Romaine surrendered finally.

Lukys supressed a groan as the Calafe gestured for Cara to collect the spare stave. Pushing aside the emotion, he tried to focus on the bright side. At least he was no longer alone. And Cara said she hadn't practiced with weapons before. Perhaps she would be just as embarrassed as him—

"Lukys, *high block*," Romaine bellowed suddenly.

Flinching, Lukys tried to bring up his practice spear, but he'd been holding it awkwardly and the wooden stave caught between his legs as he retreated. Before he could stop himself, he was slamming into the ground. A groan slipped from his lips as he looked up from a puddle of mud.

"Did I at least get the stance right?"

Chuckling, Romaine offered his hand and pulled Lukys back to his feet. "As you've already seen," he said, addressing Cara, "Lukys here still has a lot to learn. Why don't you two pair off."

Steeling himself, Lukys glanced at Cara, but for once she kept the smile from her face, though he still imagined he could hear her laughter, whispering in his ears. He shook his head, dismissing his embarrassment. Cara was just as much a beginner as he was…

Lukys narrowed his eyes, watching Cara as she approached. For the first time he noticed how smoothly she moved, her feet shifting naturally through the stances he had so struggled with the day before, body in constant balance. The breath caught in his throat as he saw the smile tugging at her lips.

"Again, Lukys, high block!" Romaine called, but Lukys hesitated.

"Romaine, I—"

The stave in Cara's left hand seemed to come alive, leaping for his face, and with a cry Lukys shoved his own spear upwards, barely deflecting the blow. He staggered back, struggling to recover his stance, but Cara still came on. The stave flicked out again and this time Lukys couldn't get his weapon up in time. A blow struck him in the shoulder, then chest, forcing him backwards.

Witch!

Though the blows stung, somehow Lukys managed to keep his feet. Enraged, he grabbed his stave in both hands and struck back, using the only attack Romaine had taught him. The practice spear thrust out, aimed at Cara's chest. At the last moment she twisted and the point of his stave slipped beneath her arm, missing its mark.

Faster than thought, Cara dropped her own weapon and grasped his. Lukys cried out as the stave was yanked from his grasp. The scream died on his lips as Cara spun his weapon, the tip flashing up…and coming to a stop just inches from his face.

A smile touched Cara's lips as she lowered the stave, and Romaine's laughter rumbled across the rampart. Lukys's cheeks grew warm and he swung away. A hand on his shoulder stopped him.

"Lukys," Cara called him back. "I'm sorry."

Cursing inwardly, Lukys drew in a breath and faced her. She still smiled, but he could see the apology in her eyes. He sighed and smiled despite himself.

"That's okay," he replied.

Stones crunched as Romaine approached. "Every child of Calafe learns to fight at a young age," he explained.

"I…" Cara started, before nodding. "Yeah."

"Though in this case, it seems young Cara wasn't entirely lying," Romaine added. "Those blows wouldn't have been much good with a spear."

Red creeped into Cara's pale cheeks at the warrior's words, and chuckling, Romaine went on. "Shall we see what I can teach the two of you then?"

So they continued for the rest of the morning, running through stances, spear thrusts, and blocks. The broken arm didn't seem to bother Cara much, and she needed no help with her balance, but using the stave like a spear seemed to give her more problems. Lukys, meanwhile, found himself growing increasingly frustrated about the repetition. Still, there was method to Romaine's madness, and as the morning progressed, Lukys found that the moves began to come more easily. Where before he had to think about each step, now the movements became instinctive, natural.

By the time Romaine dismissed them at noon, Lukys had collected a fresh assortment of bruises, but at least he was finally making progress. He wandered through the town, making for the northern gates. The Perfugian regiment had been assigned to the quarry just outside the city, breaking down shale rock into gravels that could be laid on the streets and ramparts of Fogmore to reduce the incessant mud that followed every rain and snowfall. While Lukys had been granted consent to train with Romaine in the mornings, he was meant to join them by noon.

The sound of steel slamming against rock carried down to Lukys and he belatedly picked up his pace, embarrassed that others were working while he was not. Perfugians did not skirt their duties, however much they might loathe their superiors.

As he drew close, Lukys saw the exposed stone was of a deep red. Pickaxes in hand, the other recruits were already working at the rockface. Or at least keeping up the pretence of work. A quick glance at their barrows showed little progress had been made in the hours they'd already been there.

Not that their overseers cared. The general certainly hadn't chosen his best to care for the Perfugian recruits. The three Flumeerens assigned to watch them had set a table in the shadow of the cliff and appeared to be busy playing cards. As Lukys watched, one even took a swig from a silver flask.

At least they didn't seem to notice his late arrival. Taking a pickaxe and barrow from the pile, he moved to join the others.

"Peasant!" Lukys flinched as a shout came from amongst the recruits on the other side of the quarry. He lowered his head and pulled back his axe to swing at the wall, but the voice came again. "Finally decided to join us, have you?"

Stones crunched as someone approached. Lukys's eyes flickered closed and he released the breath he'd been holding. It seemed there would be no avoiding this confrontation.

"Dale," he murmured, turning to face the recruit. "What do you want?"

"Who do you think you are, peasant?" Dale snarled as he came to a stop in front of Lukys. "Sneaking off, avoiding work. Think you're better than the rest of us, do you?"

"I—"

"You're trash, you hear me?" Dale spat, stepping closer and gesturing with his pickaxe. "You're nobody!"

Lukys reeled back, raising his hands in front of him in a gesture of peace, though the pickaxe he held distracted from the gesture. He was surprised at his fellow's reaction. Dale and his friends had been cold, even cruel, before. Now though...the man's face was pure rage. It shone from his eyes, showed in the veins bulging from his forehead, in the clenching of his jaw. Lukys could not understand it.

"You're right!" he said quickly, eyes on the point of Dale's axe. "I *am* nobody. But Romaine is teaching me to fight." Lukys hesitated, thinking fast. "He could teach you as well."

"I already know how to fight, *peasant*," Dale snapped. "Do I need to show you?" He swung his pickaxe in a lazy arc, forcing Lukys to jump backwards out of range.

He stumbled and almost fell. Anger touched him then and he surged back up...

...just as Dale thrust out with the hilt of his pickaxe. The blow caught Lukys square in his midriff and drove the breath from his lungs. He doubled over, gasping. Laughter sounded in his ears.

The sound cut through the pain like a knife, igniting his rage. Finally he managed to suck in a breath and forced himself to straighten. Dale stood across from him, hands raised as though to accept the cheers of his friends. The smug smile on his lips begged Lukys to take a swing.

Standing almost six feet tall, Dale towered over Lukys. He stood with his feet directly beneath him, just as Romaine had the day before. Clenching his fists, Lukys charged.

Dale saw the danger just as Lukys's shoulder struck him in the chest. Despite the size difference, momentum was on Lukys's side and the other man went down like a sack of bricks, the pickaxe flying from his hands. Grinning, Lukys stepped back, satisfied he'd taught the larger man a lesson…

"Bastard!" Roaring, Dale staggered tc his feet, face purpled with rage.

Lukys flinched, fear suddenly touchirg him as his foe swept up the pickaxe and started towards him.

"Enough." A man stepped between them, hands raised to either side, as though to hold them back.

For a moment, Lukys thought the overseers had finally intervened. Then he realised the man wore the same uniform as himself, the royal blue of Perfugia. The newcomer looked from Lukys to Dale, hazel eyes hard. Light brown hair hung down to his shoulders and he was well-built, shorter than Dale, but no less muscular. It was another second before Lukys recognised the man as another of the noble born recruits—the one he'd knocked over that first day in the plaza, in fact.

A growl came from Dale but the sight of the newcomer gave him pause.

"Travis?" he said, a frown creasing his forehead. "The Fall are you doing?" He tried to shove past, but the recruit held him back.

"I said, that's *enough*, Dale," Travis said, calmly pushing the taller man back.

"The bastard struck me!" Dale spluttered, eyes bulging, teeth bared. He tried to push past Travis again but was rebuffed.

"You insulted him, struck him without warning. You expected

the man to roll over?" He waved a hand. "No, never mind. It doesn't matter." Anger shone in his eyes. "Don't you see, Dale? You cling to this belief that we're superior. But look where we are! We all failed, or we wouldn't be in this cursed place." He looked away, seeming to fix on some distant point, beyond the city, beyond the river. "And now that we're here," he continued, his voice suddenly low, "we have greater concerns than your bruised ego."

His words seemed to drain the anger from the other man. For a moment, Dale stood there, hands balled into fists, jaw clenched. Then in a rush he turned away. Lukys let out a breath as he watched the man stalk across the quarry. His heart was pounding in his ears and he was gripping the hilt of his pickaxe so tight his hand had turned white.

Finally he shook himself and turned to his rescuer. The hardness evaporated from Travis's face as their eyes met, replaced by an easy smile. Stepping forward, he offered his hand.

"The name's Travis," he said. "Now, did I hear something about a mighty warrior of Calafe offering to train us?"

14

THE WARRIOR

Romaine let out a sigh as he lowered himself onto a boulder and sat back to watch the recruits at their practice. Two weeks had passed since his return from the south, and somehow he now found himself the unofficial instructor for the Perfugians. He now had almost two dozen men and women under his wing; half of the regiments surviving number.

Watching them struggle through the drills he'd set, Romaine tried to keep his face impassive. It was times like these that he was convinced the Gods still watched over humanity, if only to make mischief for their own amusement. How else could he have ended up here, when all he'd wanted was to be alone?

A sigh slipped from his lips and he closed his eyes for a moment, responsibility weighing heavily on his shoulders. When he opened them again, he found Cara standing nearby, one eyebrow raised. He cursed inwardly to have been caught in a moment of frailty, but gestured to join him on the boulder anyway. Their numbers had forced Romaine to move the training to the central plaza, where his activities would be known to all. He was still waiting for the general to come asking after him.

"You're tired," Cara said. An uncharacteristic frown creased her face.

Romaine grunted by way of answer.

"Do you not sleep?" the young woman pressed, frown lines deepening.

"I sleep," Romaine replied, though perhaps that was an exaggeration.

He had taken to sitting atop the walls most evenings, watching the darkness. Waiting was not amongst his talents. He longed to return south, to fight back against the creatures that had stolen his nation, that had taken everything from him.

But while the general had resumed scouting this side of the Illmoor, there had been no more crossings. Fogmore had not even found a new ship capable of making the journey.

Silence fell between them and Romaine turned his gaze back on the recruits. The *clack-clacking* of practice spears rang across the square, drawing the eyes of bystanders, though none had complained so far about the commotion. He'd separated the recruits into two groups to practice drills with shield and spear. One side would attack, running through a series of predetermined movements, while the other matched with the required blocks.

"They seem…slow," Cara said beside him.

Romaine chuckled. "Shouldn't you be out there practicing with them?"

Cara shrugged. She had continued practicing with Lukys at first, but as more and more recruits came asking for Romaine's help, she'd joined them less and less. At least her arm seemed to be healing well. Lukys still changed the bandages regularly, and the last time the bruising had almost vanished.

Silence fell between them again, and shaking his head, Romaine watched as the recruits ran through another drill. Lukys stood in the middle, wielding his spear against a taller man they called Travis. The exercise started with a high stab for the opponent's throat, followed by a spinning riposte, and finally an attacking thrust from the enemy's shield. The two performed the drill well with only minor faults, but even so, Romaine could see Cara was right.

"It's not enough," he murmured, unable to keep the words to himself. "I can't help them. Against ordinary soldiers, with a few more weeks or months, maybe I could make a decent fighting force out of them. But against the Tangata…"

"They *are* getting better," Cara replied, glancing at him. "More than you realise."

As she spoke, a grunt came from nearby as a recruit crashed to the ground. It was one from the attacking group. The thrust of his opponent's shield had caught him in the chin and knocked him off-balance. Romaine let out a sigh.

"You were saying?"

"Maybe you're right," Cara said after a long pause, "maybe you're wrong." A smile lit her face. "But it makes no difference to them. Somehow, you've given them *hope*. Can't you see it in their faces?"

Romaine looked at the Perfugians again, but as the drill continued, more mistakes bled into their exercises. Frustration began to take hold. He sighed.

"I see only fear." He should not have been confessing such things to the woman, but he was in over his head, needed to speak. "Only desperation." He swallowed. "I've heard them, after these sessions, whispering to the Gods, thanking them for sending me." His eyes stung but he forced the words out. "If I have given them hope, it is only a false one."

"All hope is false in the face of desperation," Cara replied. She glanced at Romaine, looking older than her years. "If theirs is a false hope, surely the same must be said for that of humanity. You said it yourself: the Tangata are too fast, too powerful. What hope can there be for your victory?"

Romaine swallowed, but caught in her amber gaze, found he did not have the words to reply. Cara spoke into the silence:

"Yes, they're afraid," she murmured, "and desperate. They know there'll be no ground given in the war to come. And so they learn."

A shudder ran down Romaine's spine as Cara fell silent. They sat together watching the recruits for a while longer, until the ice finally left his veins.

Before the conversation could resume, the sound of approaching hooves rattled from across the plaza. They looked around as a single rider emerged from the main street leading north. It was a fine winter's day and she wore a velvet bodice and slim-cut pants of Flumeeren red rather than furs. Despite her obviously recent arrival, her clothes were untouched by the dirt of the road.

Electric blue eyes swept the square, dismissing the blue-garbed recruits at a glance before continuing towards Romaine. Settling on his green-hued uniform, she heeled her horse towards him. Romaine let out a sigh—he knew a royal courtier when he saw one.

"A Calafe warrior!" the woman exclaimed as she approached. "I did not think any of your kind were left on the front lines."

"Where else would I be, lass?"

The woman's lips twisted in a frown and she scrunched her nose, but did not answer his question. Instead she looked away, eyes fixed on the distance now.

"Where is your general, soldier?" she asked.

Silence had fallen across the plaza at the woman's appearance. Her clothing was of a far better quality than that of any of the citizens still in Fogmore. The rich had fled long ago, packing up their possessions and heading north to escape the coming war. Even without the expensive clothing, her long golden hair and bronzed skin was something of an anomaly amongst the Flumeeren and Perfugian soldiers. They spoke of southern heritage, an oddity in itself given the woman's apparent standing in the Flumeeren court.

When Romaine's reply was not quick in coming, the woman swung back to face him. "I asked you a question," she said curtly.

"Forgive me, lass," Romaine said, taking a step towards the horse, "but who in The Fall are you?"

The woman's mouth fell open at his words, her face turning pale. Romaine only folded his arms and waited. The woman's arrogance probably matched her importance, but not technically being a Flumeeren citizen, he was willing to risk the reprimand. He certainly didn't have the patience to play her games.

"My name is Erika, Archivist to the crown, sent by Queen Amina herself!" The woman spouted the words as though they meant something to Romaine. "And you will show me some respect, Calafe!"

Romaine stifled a sigh and decided it was best to make the woman someone else's problem as quickly as possible.

"My *deepest* apologies, ma'am," he exclaimed, exaggerating a bow. "I had not heard of your arrival. I am sure General Curtis awaits your company with bated breath."

The woman seemed taken aback by his sudden change in

conduct. Her eyes narrowed but after a moment she gave a short nod.

"Very well," she murmured, lifting her nose in a way that suggested she was above the apologies of a mere soldier. "You are forgiven. Now, the general?"

"Last I heard he was surveying our defences on the banks of the Illmoor," he said, gesturing in the direction of the river gates. "You should find him there."

The woman faltered, the colour draining from her cheeks. Romaine suppressed a grin. What was this woman doing on the frontier? He watched as she lifted her left hand and clenched it into a fist, and for the first time noticed she wore a gauntlet, though the metal links were too fine to offer any protection. Stranger still, her right hand was bare.

"Was there not an attack here, just two weeks past?" she asked. To her credit, there was no hint of fear in her voice. "What is the general doing outside the walls of this...city?" She said the final word like she could not quite believe the description.

"The Tangata are unlikely to attack in broad daylight, ma'am," Romaine said, attempting to mimic the woman's haughty air. "And the general is eager to bolster our defences. But your fears are... understandable. Perhaps you would prefer to wait—"

"No." The woman drew herself up and set her eyes on the distant walls. "You will take me to the general, now, Calafe. I cannot afford any further delays."

"Very well, ma'am," he murmured, then turned to the recruits. They had stopped their practice at the woman's arrival. It was time they resumed their duties at the quarry anyway. "Off with ya!" he bellowed, gesturing towards the mountains. "We're done here for the day."

The recruits moved off without further complaint. Lukys and Travis waved their goodbyes, grins on their faces, and Romaine nodded back. When they were finally gone, Romaine let out a sigh. Best he get this over and done with. Turning to the woman, he extended a hand in the direction of the river gates.

"After you, ma'am."

15

THE ARCHIVIST

Erika dismounted in front of the so-called river gates and cursed as her boot immediately sank to the ankle. The ground before the palisade had been churned to mud by the passage of horses and men—but she still could not understand why these gates were being used at all. The report she'd received in Mildeth spoke of dozens of Tangata attacking in the night. She was no officer, but it seemed beyond foolhardy to risk soldiers beyond the admittedly questionable protection of the palisade.

She glanced at the Calafe warrior that had guided her this far and balled her gauntleted hand into a fist. If this was all some joke…No, the man had been insolent at first, but had been the model of good behaviour since learning of her importance. Though she was tempted to have him fetch the general back...

But no, she would be venturing far beyond the wall before long. Letting out a sigh, she nodded to her guide. At a gesture from the warrior, the guards on the gate leapt to remove the heavy locking bar from its brackets. These wore the red of Flumeer, marking them as true soldiers—unlike the Perfugian rabble she had observed in the plaza. Why their island neighbours bothered to send soldiers at all was beyond her when those were the best they could offer. They might have copied the Gemaho and just sent no one at all.

The gates squealed as they swung open, revealing a plain of churned-up mud leading down to the black waters of the Illmoor. A shiver ran down her spine as her eyes continued on. The day was clear and in the distance she spied a hint of green—the banks of Calafe. Enemy territory.

Home.

She pushed the memory away. Calafe was *not* her home. Mildeth, with its towering walls and spiralling citadel and noble queen, that was home.

Forcing her mind to the present, she walked past the guards and out into the sunlight beyond the palisade. The Calafe warrior fell into step beside her but before they could go far, racing footsteps chased after them. To Erika's surprise, another woman ran from the city to join them.

Erika frowned, her stride faltering. The woman wore green, though it was so dark it could have been black, and like Erika she wore pants rather than a dress. Was this the warrior's daughter? No, their complexions were too different. Though they certainly seemed to know each other.

"What are you doing here, Cara?" the man rumbled.

The woman ignored him, instead offering Erika a broad grin. "Cara," she said. Her accent was soft, unlike the warrior's.

"Erika," she said reluctantly, still studying the woman. One of her arms was in a sling, though even that could be an act.

"Don't mind Romaine, here," Cara said lightly, pointing a thumb at the Calafe warrior. "He's just tired." She swung back to Erika. "So, what brings you here, Archivist?"

The hackles stood up on the back of Erika's neck at the question and she narrowed her eyes. How did this strange woman know who she was? Could this Cara be another of Gemaho's spies? No. She forced the thought from her mind. The woman had probably just overheard, back in the square.

"I'm afraid that's a sensitive matter," she replied coolly, keeping her eyes fixed straight ahead.

The muddy path was treacherous enough as it was without distraction. She glimpsed movement down near the river and was relieved to see the blue cloaks of her fellow countrymen. So the Calafe hadn't been lying, that was something.

Then her eyes alit on something in the river. A vice closed around her heart as she stared at the blackened ruins sitting just above the water level. Even from a distance, she could see it was clearly a ship. A fresh breeze blew across the mudflats, carrying with it the cloying stench of smoke.

"What happened?" Erika croaked, unable to keep the tremor from her voice. There was no sign of another ship; had they truly been so careless as to lose their only vessel for crossing the Illmoor?

"The attack," the Calafe murmured.

"Poor men," Cara added. "They…were kind to me."

"Where…there is another, surely?"

The Calafe shrugged. "Afraid not."

"But I…" Erika trailed off. There was no point spouting secrets to these two. It was the general she needed. She picked up the pace.

As they neared the river, Erica saw that the soldiers were hard at work driving giant wooden spikes into the mud, the sharpened points directed at the water. They had already covered the entire bank and now seemed to be doubling back to add more.

Scanning the ranks of mud-stained men, Erika searched for the general. The men at work did not wear their helmets, though a group standing off to the side looked ready for war. They would be the lookouts. No doubt she would find the general there. Erika started towards them, but a call from the Calafe drew her back.

"Where you are going, lass?" he called, falling back into his informal manner.

"I can find my way from here, Calafe," she called over her shoulder, continuing towards the group of men.

"Glad to hear it," the man's voice chased after her, "since you're heading the wrong way."

Erika came to a stop. "What?" She glared back at him.

The Calafe wore a broad grin as he turned towards the working men. "General Curtis, messenger from the queen for you."

Amidst those working, one straightened with a groan and looked around. Mud covered his face and clothing, though on closer inspection Erika saw this man was older than the others. Grey hair shone through the grime and frown lines marked his forehead. Otherwise, there was nothing to suggest this could be the legendary General Curtis, veteran of a dozen campaigns and hero of Flumeer.

Anger touched Erika as she realised her mistake in trusting this Calafe. A general of such repute would not be here, digging in the dirt. She swung on Romaine and raised her fist, readying herself to release the magic. She would *not* be made a fool of!

"Romaine!" a voice called from the mud. She looked around as the older man strode towards them. "I heard you were busy wasting your time with the Perfugians. What are you doing delivering messenger girls?"

Erika gritted her teeth as a smug smile appeared on the Calafe's face. Exhaling a breath through clenched teeth, she faced the approaching man.

"General Curtis, I presume," she said, drawing herself up. "And I am afraid the Calafe spoke in error. I am Erika, the royal Archivist, not a messenger. The queen sent me on urgent business."

"Did she now?"

The general made a gesture towards the working soldiers. Groans echoed around the work site as the men downed stakes and shovels and wandered towards the lookouts, who were offering waterskins and strips of what looked like beef jerky.

Satisfied his men were cared for, the general returned his attention to Erika. Smiling, he offered his hand.

Erika studied the filthy digits, struggling to keep the reaction from her face, before finally reaching out to accept the gesture—though she only placed her fingertips in his palm. Grime did not bother her, when it served a purpose. But this…any man could be sent to dig in the mud. What was the commander of the entire allied army *doing* here?

"My apologies for the poor welcome," the general went on. "In wartime, there are little resources to spare for luxuries here in Fogmore. My little city must be quite the change from the capital."

"Nonsense, General," Erika replied, forcing a smile to her lips. "I did not get to be the Queen's Archivist without getting my hands dirty."

"I see," the general replied.

His eyes swept her up and down, no doubt taking in her clean clothes and face. She'd been fortunate enough to find an inn with a bathhouse for her last night on the road, though it had taken some convincing to have the innkeeper prepare the waters. Erika had been the woman's only guest in days.

"I must admit though," Erika added. "I did not expect to find the famed General Curtis working in the mud. Surely we are not so short on hands that a common soldier could not be assigned in your place." Despite her best efforts, she could not keep the disdain from her voice.

The general only chuckled. "I am not always so occupied, but at this moment we have little intelligence about the Tangatan invasion plans. There's not much else to do but ready our defences." He paused, but when Erika only raised an eyebrow, his grin spread. "It does me well, to remember my roots as a common soldier, Archivist. And it is good for the men to see their officers are not above a hard day's labour."

"I see," Erika replied, though she did not understand at all.

The queen did not clean her own privy chamber. To do so would be to invite questions of her authority. Had age begun to erode the general's famed military mind?

"In that case," she continued delicately, deciding it was best to leave that line of thought to others, "perhaps my assignment will be of interest to you."

"Oh?" the general asked. "And what task has our illustrious queen assigned to her young Archivist?" As he spoke, he unclipped a waterskin from his belt and upended it over his head. He used his spare hand to wash his face clean.

Erika bristled at his tone, but forced herself to calm. She could not afford to upset this man, not when the success of her mission relied on his benevolence. If he wished to think of her as a youth… she would manage. Perhaps she might even use it to her advantage.

She offered the general an innocent smile. "Through my research, I have found another of the ancient sites," she began delicately. "One I believe has lain undiscovered since The Fall."

"Another of those underground ruins?" the general asked. Wiping the last of the water from his face, he offered the waterskin to the Calafe. The man waved a hand, declining the offer, and the general returned it to his belt. "I thought the queen had abandoned her interest in those dusty old tunnels?"

Erika frowned at his words. "Clearly your knowledge is out of date, General," she replied. "Through my research, the magic of the Gods has been returned to the hands of humanity."

Raising her hand, she clenched her fist, igniting the cold light of her gauntlet. Silence fell over the men at the sight, while nearby the young woman leaned closer, her eyes growing large. The other soldiers were too far off to notice the glow in the bright sunlight. After a moment, Erika lowered her hand and allowed the light to die.

"So you see, General, why my mission is important," Erika murmured. "With magic on our side, the Tangata will be rebuffed, and Flumeer will stand supreme amongst the kingdoms of man." Her heart pounded against her chest as she faced the general, watching for his reaction.

He laughed.

"Archivist," he said after a moment, a grin stretching his cheeks. "The Tangata will not flee from a pretty light show."

"The magic is much more than just *light*—"

"Oh, I know," the general said, waving a hand as though to dismiss her. "A carrier bird arrived from the capital just yesterday speaking of your demonstration."

"Then why…" Erika trailed off.

"I wanted to see it for myself," the general replied, his grin fading. "Now that I have…" He shook his head. "Archivist, all due respect, but this war will not be won by magic. The ancients thought the same, and look what happened to them—all dead or turned to mindless beasts. No, mark my words, those devices are not for human hands. I'll keep my sanity, thank you very much. We'll win this war the old-fashioned way, with sweat and blood and cold, hard steel."

"I…" What was happening? This meeting was not going at all as she had expected. Why had the queen pre-empted her arrival with a letter of her own? Shaking herself, Erika drew her thoughts together and faced the general. "All due respect to you, *sir*," she said coldly. "That is not your decision to make."

She unclipped her satchel and removed the documents the queen had provided her. Silently she handed them to the general.

"Orders for you to provide me with a squadron to venture south of the Illmoor," she said coldly. "Signed by the queen herself."

Beside her, the Calafe warrior started, his face showing surprise. "*You* want to cross the Illmoor," he gasped.

She faced him, her face carefully blank. "Yes, Calafe. And if you are unable to keep that mouth of yours shut while your betters speak, I would suggest you return to your charges."

The man's face went blank at that, though she could see the rage behind his eyes. She let a satisfied smirk touch her lips. She faced the general again. In stark contrast to the Calafe, he had shown no reaction to her announcement. No doubt the queen's letter had forewarned him.

"You are insistent on this path, Archivist?" the general asked calmly.

"With all due respect, *General*, we have tried your way." Erika lifted her chin, confidence growing now. "It failed. Calafe was lost. Yet still you cling to your beliefs that the Tangata can be defeated by the sword alone."

"In the south, it was not *my* armies that were defeated, Archivist," the general replied, his voice like ice now. "The Calafe, for all their repute as warriors, were not soldiers. They fought alone, and died for it. There is a reason it was our armies alone who escaped."

His words took the impetus from Erika's argument. She was surprised the Calafe man did not speak up, though a glance in his direction revealed his jaw was clenched tight.

"Perhaps what you say is true," Erika murmured, adopting a consolatory tone, "but the time for caution is over. All weapons must be explored if we are to save our kingdom from destruction. Surely you understand that."

"Do not lecture me on the ways of war, Archivist," the general snapped. His eyes drifted down the riverbanks, to where the burnt ship still lay. "You know nothing of desperation, of what it is to face the Tangata, man to beast." He sighed and looked back at her, eyes sad. "I had hoped to dissuade you from this path. But I see now that was never a possibility." He handed her back the papers.

"Then you will obey the queen's orders?" Erika insisted.

"The Tangata are already in the forests beyond the Illmoor," the general said after a moment. "Romaine was amongst the scouts who encountered them. How many did you lose again, Calafe?"

"Two," her guide rumbled, before adding: "Not including the ferryman and his crew."

"Nor the soldiers we lost when they gave chase and attacked the city," the general added. "I still wonder at that. Why did they come here, throw away lives on an assault that could never have succeeded...?" He trailed off, then shook himself, facing Erika once more. "Your devotion to the Gods has blinded you to reality, Archivist. You would need an army to reach your sacred site. But I will obey my queen, as in all things."

"I *will* be successful," Erika said in response to his doubt. "We will travel fast, set cold camps, fight if we must. It is you who does not see, General." She lifted her gauntlet, gaze lingering on the shining threads of metal that had somehow fused to her flesh. "*This* is our future, our salvation. What lies in those caverns, I must find it, claim it for our queen."

"I will not risk our nation on a fool's gambit," the general continued as though he had not heard her. "This river is the only thing standing between our people and oblivion." His eyes took on a haunted look, before he shook himself and looked at the Calafe. "Romaine, take the Archivist back to the city and have my clerics find her quarters. And have them send a message to Charcity, we will need one of their ships."

"What about my regiment?" Erika insisted as the general made to turn away.

"You will have your soldiers," the general replied curtly. "Until the morrow, Archivist."

❧ 16 ❧

THE RECRUIT

Lukys's shoulders ached as he finished the last trip back from the quarry, barrel loaded high with gravel. It was a thankless task, mining the rock and towing it back to the city to lay on the streets each day, only to watch it be stomped into the mud the next morning. There were simply too many people, too many soldiers, in Fogmore for the unsealed street to be maintained.

What they needed was brick, like they used in Ashura. But the Flumeerens he'd spoken to had laughed at the idea. Their nation was too preoccupied with war to waste their energies on enhancing the city.

So instead the Perfugian recruits marched into the hills each day and gathered gravel.

This trip, Travis had taken the first shift with the barrow, hauling the load through the foothills until they reached the Queen's Highway. That left Lukys with the longer shift, though the way was easier, with less hills and potholes to navigate. Even so, he was glad when they finally entered the shadow of the palisade.

Several others from Romaine's group walked nearby with barrows of their own, but Dale and the others had reached the city long ago. They did not work quarter as hard as Lukys and the others, only half-filling their barrows to make the way back easier. Dale had not spoken to Lukys again since that first day in the quarry, though Lukys had noticed the man watching him.

In a way, Lukys pitied those others. Most of the noble born had spurred Romaine's training, but without the Calafe warrior, they had no hope. You could see it in the way they walked, in how their shoulders slumped and they lowered their heads as they returned to the city. They believed what the general had told them, that they were worthless, a waste of resources best done away with. Only the threat of being hunted down as mutineers kept them in line.

A sliver of despair touched Lukys's heart and he quickly forced his mind from such gloomy thoughts. He had to concentrate on the good. They were getting better, getting proficient with spear and shield. With time, they would become true soldiers, not the frauds they had arrived as.

The only question was, would it be enough, when the Tangata came?

"Why so gloomy, Lukys?"

Lukys looked up as Travis spoke, but before he could speak another voice piped up from nearby.

"He's always gloomy," Cara said as she joined them. A smile took the sting from her words.

Though she rarely participated in Romaine's training now, she did occasionally follow them up to the mine. With her arm, she didn't help much with the work and she rarely spoke to the other recruits, but he and Travis had developed somewhat of a comradery with her.

"You're not eating the same slop as the rest of us," Lukys grunted.

Cara only grinned, though his words were sadly true. Despite their progress, the officers of Flumeer still refused to take the Perfugians seriously. They were barred from the common soldiers' mess hall, and received only the sparest of meals. If there was even any left—Dale and his cohort showed little restraint when it came to saving food for stragglers.

Even worse than the food though was the thought of returning to their barracks. Left in those unlit rooms, there was nothing to occupy their minds but thoughts of what was to come. Alone in a room of dozens, it was strange how those times had come to haunt him. The faint hope that Romaine had given them was little match for those unoccupied hours from dusk to dawn.

"I wonder what that woman is here for," Travis mused as they dumped their load of gravel in a pile inside the gates, to be spread on the roads come morning.

They looked at Cara—she'd followed Romaine and the newcomer after all—but she only looked away.

"Had to be someone from the queen's court," Lukys said finally. "Not like it matters though, she won't be sticking around once the fighting starts."

"You *are* in a bad mood today," Travis replied with a grin. "You're telling me you don't appreciate the presence of a beautiful woman?"

"Ahem," Cara interrupted, a scowl lining her forehead.

"Ahh…" Travis grew red, words failing him for once in his life. Cara punched him in the arm with her good hand.

Lukys laughed as the man looked in his direction. He raised his hands. "Don't look at me."

"Hey, there's Romaine!" Travis said quickly, pointing ahead and changing the subject. "I'm sure *he* can tell us more about our new guest—hey!" he exclaimed as Cara hit him again.

Flashing him a final glare, Cara strode past him and headed for Romaine. Still grinning, Lukys joined her, a sheepish Travis bringing up the rear. Despite her time in the wilderness, Cara was more capable than anyone of putting the noble born in his place.

Lukys spied Romaine sitting atop the palisade, his gaze focused on the southern horizon. They often saw him there in the evenings. He seemed to be waiting for something, as though he expected the Tangata to appear at any moment. Just the thought sent a shudder down Lukys's spine and he directed a quick prayer at the Gods for a quiet night.

"Romaine!" Cara called. Gravel crunched beneath their boots as they started up the steps. At least on the walls it remained long enough to be useful. "How goes the watch?"

A smile touched the warrior's face as he saw them. Slowly he rose from the water barrel he'd been using as a seat. "I'm not on watch, lass," he murmured. "Just like to watch the sun set…" He trailed off.

Lukys glanced in the direction of the river. The sky was clear but for the clouds that clung endlessly to the Mountains of the

Gods, and the sun was just dipping towards the distant horizon. Today the fiery glow had an orange tinge. Lukys wondered whether that might be some omen, a warning for rain or snow or another fine day. Distantly he remembered a lesson from the academy. Perhaps if he hadn't failed, he might have remembered…

He shook himself, casting off the memories. The waters of the Illmoor remained brown, polluted by its passage through hundreds of miles of Gemahan farmland. He could just glimpse the trees on the distant riverbanks through the fading light.

"And where are you three headed?" Romaine asked, filling the silence.

"Our mess hall," Travis answered with an easy grin. "Thankfully, we've probably already missed the worst of the pig feed. We wanted to ask you about the woman today—" He broke off as Cara delivered a clean elbow to his ribs.

Romaine grunted. "That one's trouble, if ever I saw it."

"Really?" Lukys asked, his curiosity finally piqued.

The warrior waved a hand. "A worry for the morning," he replied. A frown touched his forehead. "Did you say you'd missed dinner?" He shook his head. "Can't have that. Come, you can dine with me in the soldiers' mess hall."

"Erm…" Lukys exchanged a glance with the others. "We're not allowed—"

"Like The Fall," Romaine interrupted. "You're with me. Come."

He started off down the steps back into town, leaving the three with no choice but to follow. They shared a glance before starting after him. Romaine seemed in a strange mood, and Lukys finally joined Travis in wondering why the strange woman had come. It was bound to be something bad. Surely the queen would not have sent her Archivist so close to the frontier unless it was urgent, not with the Tangata on their doorstep.

His spirits lifted though as they entered the city and Romaine started towards the mess hall. He hadn't eaten a decent meal since they'd arrived—there was no telling what the cooks put in the grey slop served to the recruits; it was barely food.

The temperature plummeted as they made their way through the darkening streets, the thought of a hot meal drawing them on. It was a welcome sight when the lights of the mess hall finally came into view. The guards on the door gave Lukys pause, but Romaine only offered them a nod, and they said nothing as the two recruits and Cara followed the Calafe inside.

Warmth washed over Lukys as they entered the mess hall. The sight that greeted him did not disappoint. Large tables filled the main floor, most occupied by off-duty soldiers, while on the far wall a large window opened into the kitchen. Two men stood on duty behind the window, serving the soldiers lining for their food. A second counter seemed to be used to return the dirty plates. On another wall, flames burned in two great hearths, casting back the winter chill.

Removing his coat, Romaine gestured for them to hang theirs on a rack beside the door. Lukys sighed as he removed the heavy fur. Travis did the same but Cara left hers on—she didn't seem to like even a hint of the cold. Together they followed Romaine across to the kitchen window. A massive Flumeeren man wearing a grease-speckled apron greeted the Calafe with a grin. Bulging eyes flickered as Lukys and the others approached, before returning to Romaine.

"Your pups?" he rumbled. Romaine grunted, and the cook burst into laughter. "Look like they could use a decent feed." He gestured for them to approach the window. "Come, what can old Dante get you lot? Got some fresh mutton tonight, still hot. Mash too, and 'cauli and 'coli, if vegetables are your thing. Take a plate, help y'selves."

"Thank you!" Lukys gasped.

Travis nodded his own excitement. Plate in hand, Cara was already a step ahead of them. Grabbing utensils of his own, Lukys speared a chunk of meat from the platter, then took a generous helping of mashed potatoes as well. There was broccoli and cauliflower too. Once he might have avoided vegetables, but after the endless slop, he'd go for anything with a green shade to it.

Afterwards, they took a seat at an unoccupied table and Romaine disappeared again. Still taking in their surroundings, Lukys noticed that one of the boulders that lay in the plaza formed part of the mess hall as well—one of the walls had been shaped around the giant stone, rather than moving it.

Shortly, Romaine reappeared with four large mugs and a carafe of some deep red liquid. Curious, Lukys wafted it under his nose and was surprised when he detected the scent of cloves and cinnamon. He raised an eyebrow at Romaine.

"Mulled wine," he replied, a grin tugging at his lips. "Hardly touched my quota these past few weeks so there's plenty to share."

They passed the carafe around, each filling their mugs to the brim, and then sat back to take it all in. Mulled wine was considered a delicacy in Perfugia, a drink they had only enjoyed on special occasions at the academy. Breathing it in, Lukys savoured the rich aroma.

"You're meant to drink it, you know," Travis said, raising his mug to cheers.

"Right." Lukys's cheeks warmed and he chinked his drink with the others before taking a sip.

It was sweeter than what he'd tried during the winter celebrations in Perfugia. Stronger too, though the spice of the cloves covered much of the taste. There was still some warmth in it, and he welcomed the sensation of heat spreading from his stomach. Eating and sleeping in their frigid quarters, it seemed an age since he'd last been truly warm.

"It's good!" Cara exclaimed. She sat across from Romaine and Lukys, with Travis. She lowered the mug only long enough to make her point before taking another swig.

Romaine chuckled. "Did your parents never let you try a southern vintage?" he asked. "The Gods help 'em, there's a reason they spice the stuff here. Undrinkable without it."

"Better than your cooking, Romaine," a man Lukys did not recognise said as he lowered himself down beside Travis.

"That so…Lorene?" Romaine said. There was an obvious pause, as though he had trouble remembering the name. "Don't recall you volunteering to cook during our last trip south of the Illmoor!"

The man grinned but said nothing, only scooped a lump of mash from his plate and took a bite. Lukys and the others looked from Romaine to the newcomer. The Calafe warrior grunted when he finally noticed their confusion.

"This is Lorene," he said. "Joined me on a few scouting trips down in Calafe."

"One, to be exact," Lorene replied, and for a moment his eyes took on a haunted look. "Barely made it back with our lives, too. Though I suppose we did rescue poor old Cara here," he added, gesturing beside them.

"Will you go south with the others then?" Cara asked suddenly, lifting her head from the mulled wine.

Lukys and the others at the table started at the announcement, while Romaine fixed her with a glare. She frowned when he did not reply, before her eyes widened and she muttered a curse.

"Oh, right, that's meant to be a secret."

Beside Lukys, Romaine groaned and buried his head in his hands.

"What The Fall, Romaine?" Lorene hissed, leaning forward. His voice adopted a slight tremor as he went on: "They're sending us into Calafe again?"

The Calafe shook his head. "No," he whispered. "It's that Archivist woman. She wants to go south, find some sacred site of the Gods."

A gasp slipped from Lukys's lips. "*What?*"

In Perfugia, disturbing any relic related to the Gods was a capital offence, one few dared to challenge. All knew what had become of the last souls who'd dared to meddle with the Gods and their magic. Now that Lukys had seen the Tangata himself, he wanted even less to do with such powers. What was the woman thinking, risking her life to seek out such a cursed place?

"She's quite mad," Romaine replied, not understanding the true source of Lukys's indignation, "but she has somehow convinced the queen to support her. The general is to supply her with a regiment. He's not happy about it. I suspect he will ask for volunteers."

Across the table, Lorene let out a long breath, the relief in his eyes obvious.

"She's not *mad*, Romaine," Cara snapped, leaning across the table to glare at the warrior.

"Anyone who wants to go back there is insane in my book," Lorene said cheerfully, raising his glass in salute. Romaine's words seemed to have reassured him.

"Perhaps there is more to her than meets the eye," Cara said softly, before glancing at Lorene. "Besides, *I* want to go back."

Silence fell over the table as they all turned to stare at her. Lukys opened his mouth and then closed it again, unable to fashion a response. Calafe was Cara's home, and true, he couldn't understand what it must be like to lose that, but…

"Don't be a fool," Romaine growled, coming slowly to his feet.

Fool, fool, fool.

Lukys shook his head as the words rang in his mind.

"I'm serious, Romaine," Cara said, standing as well. "I have to go home."

Home, home, home.

"Home?" Romaine gasped. "Home is gone, girl! They took it. All we have left are our lives. Don't throw yours away because some madwoman thinks it's safe to wander around a forest swarming with Tangata."

"You don't understand," Cara whispered, eyes shining in the light of the hearth. Silence had fallen across the mess hall as the other soldiers turned to watch the commotion. "I can't stay here, I have to go."

Go, go, go.

"Don't understand?" Romaine raged. "I understand better than anyone! I forbid it."

"You forbid it?" the young woman hissed, eyes growing dark.

Her hands balled into fists and for a moment it seemed she stood taller. Romaine said nothing, only stared at her across the table. The moment stretched out, punctuated only by the clattering of plates from the kitchen. Finally, Cara gave a curt nod. Without saying a word, she spun and marched from the hall without looking back.

Romaine watched her go, a haunted look on his face, as though he had just lost something dear to him. Finally he closed his eyes, head bowing.

"Piece of advice, lads," he murmured, "if you want to avoid my mistakes. There's no room in this war to care. About anything. Do yourselves a favour and burn that crap from your hearts now, before it gets you killed."

With that he turned and walked from the mess hall, leaving the two recruits and Lorene sitting looking after him.

17

THE WARRIOR

Drums pounded against Romaine's skull as he staggered from the barracks and into the street. Silently he cursed the fortified Flumeeren wine. He'd bribed the cooks for an entire bottle and taken it up to the walls. If the watch hadn't found him passed out between the water barrels, he might have spent the whole night up there.

Now he'd almost slept past the roll call the general had announced for noon. He hurried through the streets, head still pounding to the distant rhythm. How long had it been since he'd had *real* wine, from the vineyards of Calafe? Years, surely. It was so hard to find nowadays, impossible in this border city. The Flumeeren stuff was little better than moonshine.

A cold breeze blew down the street as he hurried to reach the central plaza. He barely made it a block before his stomach roiled and he was forced to detour into an alleyway to empty its contents into the mud.

After that he felt slightly better, though there was no way he'd be attempting his daily jog around the palisade. It wasn't just his head that ached; he felt it in his shoulders and back, in his very bones. Maybe it wasn't the wine, maybe time was finally catching up with him. Those who had joined the army alongside him in those early days had retired long ago—those who'd survived, at least. But *he* would not surrender to the creeping erosion of time.

Fool.

The streets began to fill as he neared the square and Romaine found himself searching the crowds for the glint of copper hair. His stomach twisted at the memory of his conversation with Cara. Surely she had not been serious about returning to her homeland? With the light of day she would see sense.

No. He had seen the glint in her eyes the night before. She was determined. A tremor ran down his spine at the thought of saying farewell to the strange woman. He cursed beneath his breath. When had he begun to care for her?

Finally he emerged from the buildings into the central plaza. He was one of the last to arrive, and most of the army's regiments were already in place. With them all standing in line, the differences in discipline was on full display today. Some groups such as the royal guard—the division assigned to the general's protection—stood in perfect rows, eyes fixed to the front, weapons shining in the noonday sun.

Others from the civilian units were only marginally better than the Perfugian recruits, with many slouching against their spears and beards nearly as unkept as Romaine's.

Not being an official part of the army, Romaine himself cared little for Flumeeren regulation. He wandered around the borders of the plaza, seeking out the Perfugian blue.

He found the recruits standing close to the centre of the plaza, their ranks broken by a large boulder in their midst. They too had no official officers in the Flumeeren command structure—other than the louts that supervised them at the quarry—and so their thirty-seven remaining members stood in a semi-organised mess. His heart lifted as he spotted Lukys and some of his other trainees attempting to impose some order.

Romaine couldn't reach them without forcing his way through the Flumeeren soldiers and causing a stir, so instead he retreated to the edge of the square and leaned against the wall of a nearby building. His eyes slid closed, and he sighed to escape the day's brightness.

Unfortunately, the peace did not last long.

The blaring of a horn announced the arrival of the general. Romaine forced his eyes open and watched as General Curtis marched through the ranks of the soldiers until he reached a cleared section of ground in the centre of the plaza. Only then did Romaine spot the Archivist waiting there. Arms clasped behind her back and lips pursed, the woman was impatience personified.

So eager to get us all killed.

Romaine shook his head. He wondered what the woman would do if none of the soldiers volunteered to join her quest. Indeed, he couldn't imagine anyone being so mad, not after the attack two weeks before.

No one except Cara.

Gritting his teeth, he forced his mind back to the general as the horn sounded again. Armour rattled as the army snapped to attention. Romaine rolled his shoulders, settling his own chainmail into a more comfortable position, and watched as the general leaned in close to the Archivist. Whispers passed between them before he turned back and surveyed the gathered forces.

"Soldiers of Flumeer!" he called, his voice ringing from the walls of the nearby buildings. "Thank you for joining me this fine day. Important works are underway and I saw it fit to ensure you were informed of what is to come."

He paused, looking out over the army, eyes cool. Despite the hangover, Romaine shivered. He had no great love for the general, but he couldn't help but respect him. The man was a veteran after all, had been a general even before Romaine had first signed up as a soldier. Curtis had been one of the few to warn about the Tangatan threat. Maybe if more had listened, the war would have gone differently. Maybe the south would not have been so unprepared, maybe…

Romaine tore himself free of that train of thought. There was no point regretting what had already passed…

"In the coming weeks, the Tangata will attack," General Curtis continued. "The Illmoor is our last defence. If we lose the battle here, Flumeer *will* fall. You have faced the beasts, you know the truth. No one can stand against them on open ground." He walked down the front ranks of soldiers, meeting the eyes of every man in the square. "We do not yet know where they will strike, so we must defend the entire river, man every fort and city, use every resource at our command to protect these shores."

Romaine frowned at the man's words, and noticed many soldiers doing the same. None of this was new. Every soul in the city knew the importance of the Illmoor.

"Of course, you all know this." The hint of a smile crossed the general's face and he turned towards the Archivist. "I say it not for you, but for the sake of this woman here. Like many in the capital, with its learned academics and bureaucrats, she thinks this war can be won with myths and fairytales."

The Archivist's face darkened at the general's words, but to her credit, she stared him down. Chuckling, General Curtis offered her a nod before facing the army once more.

"Sadly, I have failed to convince her of the reality of this world. She insists on endangering our very existence with her daydreams. She would have us venture beyond the Illmoor in search of ancient magics!"

Murmurs spread around the square at the announcement, shock showing on soldier's faces. The Archivist's mask slipped as she stepped up to meet the general, giving way to rage.

"I come on the *queen's* orders," she hissed, loud enough for the entire plaza to hear. "It is not your position to question her, *General*."

She pointed a gauntleted finger at the man. Recalling the light she'd summoned earlier, Romaine shivered. Somehow, that strange magic disturbed him almost as much as the Tangata themselves. Even so, Romaine was impressed at the woman's defiance. He looked at Curtis to see how the general would react.

"Fairytales, as I said," Curtis continued as though the woman had not spoken. "I will not allow Flumeer to fall for the sake of a woman's fancy."

"I will have my soldiers, General," the Archivist snarled.

"Ay," the general rumbled, "the Perfugians will accompany you south."

For a moment, Romaine didn't think he'd heard the general right. Silence fell across the square at his words, every soldier staring in disbelief. Curtis couldn't be serious. A journey beyond the river would be difficult for the hardest company of soldiers. For untrained recruits, it was suicide!

"The Perfugians…what…you cannot…no!" the Archivist stuttered into the silence, all colour draining from her face.

"Yes," the general replied calmly. "I will not compromise our borders by sacrificing good soldiers to a lost cause. So you will be joined by a lost cause of their own. That is my final decision."

"I will petition the queen!"

"Do what you wish, Archivist." The general's eyes shone. "Though regrettably, our last carrier pigeon departed this morning. If you wish to dispute my interpretation of the queen's commands, you will have to send a runner for a clarification."

"But…that could take weeks!" the Archivist exclaimed. "The Tangata could have occupied the site by then."

"I suggest you be content with what you have been offered then, Archivist," the general replied, a smug smile on his lips.

"Bastard!" the Archivist screamed. She lifted her magic gauntlet as though to strike the general down, then seemed to think better of it.

Romaine stood frozen on the edge of the plaza, staring as the two faced one another down, still reeling. Lukys, Travis and all the others who had turned to him to save them, they would soon be marching to their deaths, doomed to die alone in the frozen forests of his homeland. He had failed them.

A shudder shook him and he cursed himself for a fool. He had learned this lesson, hadn't he? Long ago, again and again. Was he fated to always repeat the same tragedy, always too weak, too slow to save those he cared for?

"Very well, General," the Archivist said finally, the calm mask falling back into place. "Though know this: when I return and win my place at the queen's side, you will know the full weight of my displeasure."

"That is a risk I am willing to take," the general replied, staring her down, "for my kingdom."

"You damn us all with your cowardice," the Archivist spat back, her composure cracking once more. "What lies beyond the Illmoor will change everything."

"Then you had best make yourself ready for the journey," the general replied. "We received word from Charcity this morning. Your ship will arrive in the night. You sail at first light."

The woman matched his glare for a moment longer, then her shoulders slumped and Romaine knew she was defeated.

"Will you at least provide us with scouts?" she murmured. "Someone who knows the land? Calafe was a wilderness even before its fall. I *must* have a guide to show us the way."

"No—"

"I will go, General," Romaine said, striding forward through the ranks of soldiers.

His heart pounded in his chest as he walked past Lukys and the other recruits. Their faces were white with terror, though to their credit they had not tried to argue. Perhaps they were simply too shocked to put up a fight. He caught a glimpse of Lukys's face amongst the others, saw the flash of hope that appeared in his eyes, and quickly looked away.

The Archivist looked surprised as he walked up. She stepped towards him, words of gratitude spilling from her mouth, but Romaine waved her away. He wasn't doing this for her. His eyes caught the general's.

"Are you sure you wish to do this, Romaine?" Curtis murmured, stepping in close. Romaine only nodded, and he sighed. "Very well. I will place you in command of the regiment. I know you have been training them. Perhaps your presence will give them a chance to survive the woman's madness."

"Thank you, sir," Romaine said shortly. He understood the man's reasoning, cold as it was. Maybe under other circumstances he could have agreed with his decision…maybe.

The general nodded, and turning to the rest of the army, he barked the dismissal. Steel rattled as the soldiers filed from the plaza one line after the other. The general watched them for a while, then glanced at the Perfugians. For a second, Romaine thought he glimpsed regret in the general's eye. Had this been a bluff, to force the Archivist to abandon her task? If so, it had failed.

Finally only the Perfugians remained. Glancing one last time at Romaine, the general offered a nod. Then he turned and marched from the square. The Archivist went next.

Then Romaine was alone with the Perfugian recruits. Turning, he found himself looking into the youthful eyes of Lukys.

"I thought you said not to care?" the recruit whispered.

18

THE RECRUIT

"I thought you said not to care?" Lukys croaked as Romaine turned towards him.

Standing in the front ranks of his regiment, Lukys couldn't keep the horror from his face as Romaine met his eyes. His heart was pounding in his chest, his ears still ringing. It couldn't be true, couldn't be happening…

They were doomed.

"Who here is afraid?" Lukys flinched as Romaine looked away from him, speaking instead to the entire regiment.

Standing at the head of the column, the warrior's red-streaked eyes swept the gathered recruits, seeming to take them all in at once. Lukys wondered what game the man was playing. Every single Perfugian, even Dale, was trembling in his boots. Surely he could see that.

No one spoke, and after a moment, Romaine began to pace up and down the line. That continued for a while. Every man and woman in the regiment watched the warrior, until he came to a sudden stop, and looked at them again.

"I'm afraid," he said unexpectedly, voice soft. "Many of you already know me, but for those who don't, I am a warrior of Calafe. Tomorrow we will be marching into my homeland." He paused, lowering his head, though Lukys still saw the sadness in his eyes.

"But it is no longer my home. It has become enemy territory, the home of our nightmares."

He started to pace again, though now his eyes were on them. He spoke as he walked: "As of tomorrow, we will be brothers and sisters in arms. If we are to stand any chance of surviving, we must trust each other. Even with our deepest, darkest fears." He stopped midstride, looking at them in earnest now. "My name is Romaine, and I am afraid of what we will face on the morrow. But that fear will not stop me."

Lukys swallowed as he locked eyes with the warrior. A shudder passed through him and before Lukys knew what he was doing, he stepped forward. "I am afraid."

A snigger came from somewhere behind him, but already another voice was emerging from the ranks of recruits.

"I'm afraid." Lukys smiled as Travis stepped up beside him, head held high as he looked back at their fellow Perfugians. "But I will not run from it."

"I am afraid as well."

Others followed, then all the recruits who had trained under Romaine, and others too, those who had not joined them, but perhaps had wished to, if only they'd found the courage. The laughter that had come from Dale and his friends died away, drowned out by the whispered admissions. Lukys glimpsed anger in his rival's eyes.

"Very good," Romaine spoke again from the front ranks. "Then we will face our fears together." He drew in a breath. "Well, we only have the day. I will not press you—we will need every ounce of strength for what we find in my homeland. But I must know your capabilities."

Whispers went through the recruits as they exchanged glances. Even those who had not joined Lukys knew about the gruelling training regime Romaine had subjected them to.

"Enough!" Romaine's shout rang from the walls of the nearby buildings.

Silence was instant.

"Enough," the warrior repeated, folding his arms across his chest. "We've wasted too much time already. You lot." He indicated the recruits to his left. "Break off, you will be the defenders. And you." He gestured to the right. "The attackers."

Lukys and those who had worked with Romaine leapt to obey, but the rest stood staring at him until he barked, "*Now!*"

Terrified, the recruits stumbled over one other in their haste, and the square rang with the sounds of confusion. It was only when they'd gathered into the two groups that Lukys realised what Romaine was saying. Attackers and defenders? But they didn't have their practice spears. The regiments had come in full parade dress—full chainmail armour and shields and spears. Sharp. Deadly.

Before he could ask what Romaine planned, the warrior issued fresh orders:

"Form up, two ranks deep, shields to the front," he bellowed.

This time the recruits were quicker to obey, though their movements were still clumsy. It was obvious the manoeuvre would have failed in a true battle. Lukys tried to suppress his frustration as the recruits to either side jostled him. He was in the defending group, while Travis had ended up in with the attackers. Both were trying to inject order to the chaos, but it was an exercise in futility.

Finally the two groups stood facing one another, each two lines deep. Romaine strode down the length between them, surveying the Perfugians with a professional eye. Lukys smiled as he saw Dale in the other group. At least he would not have to fight alongside the man.

"Put down your spears," Romaine said softly as he stepped away from the two lines.

The clatter of wooden shafts falling to the dirt followed as the recruits released their weapons. Lukys frowned—they'd only just begun in the last week to practice with shields.

"In this exercise," the warrior continued, "you'll use only your shields. They will be your most important weapon against the Tangata. Stand together, and you can neutralise the enemy's strengths."

A burst of laughter came from the group of attackers. "No wonder your people are dead," Dale snarled, pushing past his fellows to stand at the front of the line. He still held his spear. "Why should we listen to you, Calafe? I heard only the cowards escaped the Tangata with their lives."

To Lukys's surprise, there was no rage in Romaine's eyes as he faced Dale, only pity. "Because I'm your only hope of surviving what is to come," he said coolly.

Dale snorted. "Think I'd rather take my chances with the madwomen, if you think we can defeat the Tangata with a shield."

Romaine stared at the man for a long moment, then turned and walked to where Lukys stood. "Your shield," he ordered.

Lukys handed it over without a word and the Calafe nodded his thanks. Returning to stand before Dale, he nodded at the recruit.

"Go ahead, soldier," the Calafe said quietly. "Take your best shot."

"I…"

Dale's eyes showed reluctance and despite his bravado, he hesitated. Romaine held only a shield, and Dale's weapon was not some blunted practice stave. Then his eyes narrowed and he seemed to make up his mind. With a roar, he let his own shield fall to the ground, then he rushed Romaine, the razor-sharp blade aimed for the warrior's throat.

To Lukys's surprise, Romaine did not attempt to evade the attack. Instead his stance deepened, bracing his body behind the shield. As Dale neared, he surged forward, taking the recruit by surprise. Off-guard, there was no power behind Dale's blow and his spearhead deflected harmlessly from the wooden shield.

Then Romaine drove the steel-capped rim of his shield into Dale's midriff. Breath hissed between the recruit's teeth and the weight behind the blow put him flat on his back. Lukys winced at the muffled *thump* of Dale hitting the ground.

"The time for games is over," Romaine announced, facing the other recruits.

At his feet, Dale was still straining to catch his breath. Sharing a glance with the Calafe warrior, Lukys couldn't help but offer a satisfied grin. It was about time someone taught the man a lesson.

"Lukys, to the front!"

Lukys jumped as Romaine called his name. After a second's hesitation, he hurried forward, and Romaine returned his shield. Then he gestured Travis forward. He took the shield and spear from him, before sending the man back to the watching ranks.

"Your second strongest weapon is each other," he went on. "A shield is not enough against a creature with the strength to tear you limb from limb. Unless we all stand together, we will die alone." He gestured to Lukys and Dale, who had recovered his spear and managed to stand. "If you want to survive, you must fight together."

"What?" Lukys asked, glancing at Dale.

The man looked just as disgusted at the thought of working alongside Lukys. "You can't be serious."

"Deadly," Romaine replied, then stabbed out suddenly with his spear.

Lukys cried out as the point hammered against his shield, leaping back. Instinctively, he tried to parry with a spear he did not hold. A curse slipped from his lips as alone, Dale charged Romaine. The Calafe caught the charge on his shield and turned the blow aside, then kicked out with a heavy boot, tripping the Perfugian recruit and sending him crashing back to the ground.

"I said *together!*" Romaine bellowed as Dale struggled to his feet.

Panting, Lukys shared a glance with his rival. Without speaking, they took a step closer to one another, Dale on the right with spear held in a two-handed grip, Lukys standing so that the shield could cover them both. A grin split Romaine's face as he advanced on them again.

This time when the Calafe attacked, Lukys stood his ground, using the shield to deflect the spear tip away from Dale. Immediately, the other man thrust out with his weapon. The two-handed grip delivered a powerful blow and Romaine was forced to retreat to avoid being caught by the razor tip. Even in full chainmail, these were live weapons and the risk was real.

Lukys and Dale advanced, doing their best to match one another's strides. Romaine laughed and attacked again. This time Lukys thrust out with his shield the way Romaine had done, turning aside the blow and catching Romaine's shield with his own. A cry came from Dale and he leapt forward, driving his spear for a gap that had opened in Romaine's guard. Lukys's heart lurched in his chest as he realised the blow would surely land.

Quick as a cat, Romaine released his shield, causing Lukys to stagger as the pressure went off his own shield. Still moving, Romaine twisted and narrowly avoided being impaled. The spear spun in Romaine's hands, seemingly an extension of the warrior's own arm, and too late Lukys saw that Dale had stepped beyond the protection of his shield. There was a sharp *crack* as Romaine slammed the butt of his weapon into Dale's chest.

Paling, Dale staggered back, exposing Lukys to Romaine's next attack. He opened his mouth to cry out, but instead found himself staring down the shaft of a spear pointed at his face.

"Together, you had me on the defensive," Romaine said calmly as he lowered the spear and giving it back. He offered Dale a hand. To Lukys's surprise, the recruit accepted. "When you separated, you were defeated."

Turning, he faced the rest of the recruits. "Let that be a lesson to all of you. It doesn't matter how skilled any one of you are, nor how strong or fast your opponent. Stand together, and you can defeat anyone."

Perhaps it was only Lukys's imagination, but it seemed that Romaine's words lit a spark in the eyes of his fellow Perfugians. Smiling, he looked at the Calafe warrior. But instead of confidence, Lukys thought he glimpsed despair on the face of the warrior. A second later it was gone, but still it gave Lukys pause. His heart throbbed in his chest as he lowered the shield and stepped towards the warrior.

Romaine turned away. "We're all afraid of something," he said softly to the men and women gathered before him. "I can't promise that all of you will survive what is to come. But if you stand with me, together as one, I promise you will have a chance." He drew in a deep breath. "Now, form up!"

19

THE ARCHIVIST

Erika tapped her foot gently on the muddy street. She stood before the river gate, rage boiling through every part of her, waiting for her "regiment" to arrive. Bad enough that the general had betrayed her, worse that the Perfugians were *late*. Again, she wondered whether she was making the right choice, gambling her entire expedition, her *life*, on thirty-seven untrained soldiers and a warrior of Calafe. Perhaps she should have sent the message to the capital and risked the delay.

No, she couldn't wait. This was her last chance to discover the true magic of the Gods. She could almost *feel* the power throbbing in the palm of her hand as she clenched and unclenched her fist, but the gauntlet was but a taste. True magic awaited her in the south, she was sure of it. If only she could reach the ancient site before the Tangata swept through the land.

A shiver ran down her spine, though she couldn't have said whether it was from nerves or the cold. It was still dark inside the walls of the town and fresh snow had fallen during the night, leaving a thin layer of white on the slate rooftops. Erika wrinkled her nose as she looked down the torch-lined street. One thing was for sure: she wouldn't miss this damned city. Better the wilderness, the open trees and forests…

The rattle of footsteps finally carried to her from around the corner and she released her breath. They should have already been boarding the ship, but of course the Perfugian regiment would be delayed. Doubt assailed her yet again, and she found herself thinking about that third option, about the strange woman who had accosted her in the countryside...

No, they tried to kill you!

A flash of blue appeared at the end of the street as her regiment marched into view. She straightened her shoulders, determined to make the most of what she had. Almost forty heavily armed soldiers. A Calafe warrior who knew the land. A magic gauntlet that could kill a man with a thought.

No, there was no reason to panic. The general might be determined to see her fail, but Erika would not allow his failures to be her own. She would succeed, would return with the power mankind had sought for centuries. Then the general would know her wrath.

Erika shook herself, forcing her thoughts back to the present. This was no time to get ahead of herself. She must focus on the mission at hand. Watching the approaching recruits, she was relieved to see the Calafe at their head. And the Perfugians seemed to be moving in step now, rather than tripping over one another as she'd glimpsed her first day in the city.

Turning to the city guards, she nodded for them to open the gates. They said nothing, and she did not miss the disdain in their eyes. But after a moment they turned and set to removing the locking bar.

There was no sign of the general, though Erika had to admit, she was pleased at his absence. She wasn't certain she could contain her rage if forced to face him again. Though no doubt it was a sign of disrespect to the Perfugians that he had not come.

Taking the reins of her horse, Erika started towards the gates as her regiment drew near.

"Not bringing a weapon, Archivist?"

She looked around as the Calafe drew alongside her. He too led a horse, though they would be the only two mounted on this expedition. Yet another factor that would slow their journey. She caught his gaze on her empty belt strap, and smiled.

"I don't need one," she replied, flashing her gauntlet.

He nodded, though doubt still lurked behind his eyes. The demonstration earlier had not been enough to convince the general of her power; why would it be any different with this man? Regardless, she started towards the gates, then noticed the Calafe had stopped and was looking back into the city.

"Forgotten something, Calafe?" she asked.

"What?" he replied, glancing at her. Then he shook his head. "No, let's get going. The sun will be up soon."

Erika frowned at the man, confused by his reactions. Had she missed a madness in the warrior that might jeopardise her mission? If so, it was too late now—they would not make it far on the other side without a guide. Together they walked through the open gates.

Below, a galley now bobbed against the riverbanks, gangplank already in place to see them aboard. It was larger than the burnt-out husk that lay downriver, and had probably once been used to trade goods up and down the Illmoor. Those days were long gone; now such vessels were used for the defence of the frontier.

Leading her horse down the winding path to the river, Erika noted that the stakes the general had been planting now sprouted in four or five rows along much of the riverbank. The enemy would not be able to charge the palisade so quickly if they came again, though there was still a good eighty yards of open ground left to stake.

Five minutes later, Erika stood at the railings of the galley, watching as the Perfugian recruits made their careful way up the gangplank. She took the chance to examine them more closely, and found herself pleasantly surprised. Each wore full chainmail and carried shield and spear. They looked impressive in their full kit, almost like real soldiers, and she found herself hoping the general's assessment of them might yet be proven wrong.

The ship quickly became crowded as the Perfugians struggled to find space where they would not be in the way of the sailors. They were almost all aboard when shouts carried down from the city walls. Spinning, Erika scanned the currents swirling around them, thinking the guards must be shouting a warning. But the waters were empty, and a second later the pounding of horse hooves carried to her ears.

Looking towards the city, she watched as a rider erupted through the gates. The young woman, Cara, appeared on the back of a black gelding. Riding at full gallop, she directed the horse down the path towards the last of the Perfugians on the banks. Just as she was nearing the shore, more shouts carried down from the fort, then a fresh group of men came running through the gates.

On the shore below, Cara leapt from the horse's back, and taking it by the reins, led it through the last few recruits still on the shore. Only as she started up the gangplank did Erika realise what the woman intended. Suddenly suspicious, she pushed her way through the crowd on the deck, while the last of the Perfugians followed Cara aboard.

"Looks like that's all of us!" Cara was saying as Erika reached her. The young woman wore an easy grin and her injured arm was no longer bandaged. "Think we'd better get on our way?"

"What The Fall are you doing here?" Erika gasped, looking from the woman to the men still racing down the path towards them. Something was very wrong here. Why would this woman want to get *on* a ship heading into enemy territory? Not unless…she was a spy!

She spotted Romaine standing nearby. "Calafe, get your blasted daughter—or whoever she is—off my ship!"

The smile fell from Cara's face at her words. Romaine stepped forward, his lips drawn tight, frown lines marking his forehead. Drawing herself up, Cara swung to face him, her face betraying nothing of her thoughts. A strained silence stretched out between them.

"Didn't know you could ride," Romaine grunted finally. "How's the arm?"

Cara's shoulders sagged, as though in relief, and the hint of a smile returned to her face. "Better," she said with a nod, then: "And I'm a fast learner."

"Good." Romaine nodded. "You can help me scout the way."

"Scout…" Erika pushed forward to stand between them. "What in the Gods is going on here?"

"Archivist," Romaine said, "Cara is not my daughter, but she is of Calafe. We found her on our last scouting trip south of the Illmoor. She was injured in a Tangata attack, so we brought her back, but…she did express to me her wish to return."

"Oh…*what?*" Erika exclaimed, too shocked by this new piece of information to form a response. She managed to shake her head.

"But…even so…we cannot afford…any liabilities on this journey. I cannot have an untrained woman slowing us down."

"She survived for months alone in enemy territory," Romaine replied, speaking slowly. "I think you'll find she's anything but a liability."

Erika glanced from the young woman to the men still racing down the slope. It didn't look as though Cara had asked permission to take her horse. If the soldiers came aboard, there would be yet more delays. Grinding her teeth, she turned on the ship captain.

"Push off, Captain!" she ordered. "Time we got underway."

The man hesitated, his eyes flicking to the approaching soldiers, but a bellow from the Calafe warrior sent him into action.

"Heave hoe!" he bellowed, moving to the tiller at the rear of the ship. "Get that gangplank aboard!"

The half-dozen sailors raced to obey, taking hold of ropes attached to the plank. As it lifted from the mud, the ship immediately began to turn, the currents taking hold. The sailors stowed the plank alongside the railing then turned to their oars. Sixty tonnes of wood and metal surged out into the currents as the captain called the timing.

Shouts chased after them as the soldiers reached the shore, but they faded quickly as the river drew the galley downstream. The Perfugian recruits clung to whatever they could as the ship lurched, swinging to the south, before turning more slowly to face upriver. Groans came from the sailors as they began to row against the current.

Erika nodded her satisfaction. She had told no one the exact location of her ancient site, but the captain knew to drop them several leagues upstream. Still unsure whether she'd done the right thing, she looked back at Cara. Finally, the full weight of Romaine's words struck her. This woman had been *alone* in Calafe?

The new information forced a reappraisal of the woman. Anyone who could survive a winter in the wilderness, let alone in Tangata territory, was surely a force to be reckoned with. Her heartbeat quickened as she realised the woman could be an asset. Perhaps Cara even knew something of their destination.

Erika was already reaching for the map in her satchel before she thought better of it. It would not be prudent to speak of their destination in front of the captain and his sailors—who knew where else Gemaho might have agents? Better to wait and talk with Cara and the Calafe warrior privately.

Moving to the bow of the ship, she eyed the way ahead. The waters of the Illmoor raced past, the galley surging with each beat of the sailors' oars. There was a mist today, a heavy, clinging cloud that tasted of winter, and ahead the river vanished into the white. There was no seeing what lay beyond; all she could do was trust the captain knew where to go.

"Nervous?"

Erika started as the Calafe warrior appeared alongside her. His eyes were distant, focused as hers had been on the drifting mist, as though he could already see the lands that awaited them. A scowl crossed her face.

"None of your business, Calafe."

"My name is Romaine," he replied, though his gaze did not flicker.

"What?"

This time he turned towards her. Their eyes met and Erika swallowed despite herself. There was a darkness in those steel-blue orbs, a silent grief, an awful anger that promised retribution.

"It is traditional to call a man by his name," he said, voice not rising above a murmur.

Erika opened her mouth but the retort died on her tongue. He was right. Alone of all the soldiers in Fogmore, this man had volunteered to join her expedition. He was risking his life to help her—the least she could do was treat him with respect. She let out a long breath, swallowing her pride.

"My apologies, Romaine," she said, inclining her head. "I am thankful for your help."

A grim smile appeared on the warrior's face. "Thank me when we make it safely back to Flumeer. For now, I'd be happier to know what exactly that gauntlet of yours can do."

It was Erika's turn to smile. "On that, you will have to trust me, Romaine," she replied. "Let it be enough to know its effects are... unpleasant for those who cross me."

Romaine raised an eyebrow at that, but to her surprise he did not press the matter. His eyes returned to the mist. "Can't say I trust such magic," he murmured, "but after that last attack…I have a feeling we're going to need every weapon we can get on the other side."

Instinctively, Erika followed his gaze. The brave words of a few moments before turned to dust on her tongue as the mists began to lift. Dark trees appeared to the starboard of the ship, fog still clinging to their twisted branches.

Calafe waited.

❧ 20 ❧

THE WARRIOR

The forest was silent as Romaine guided his horse carefully between the trees, taking care to avoid the deep drifts beneath the trunks. There was no path here and with the tall pines stretching up around them, Romaine was navigating by instinct. At least the Archivist's map had been detailed—they were making for a plateau in the foothills. The area was beyond their usual scouting routes, but Romaine hoped it might be far enough east to avoid any Tangatan forces marching north.

He marked a tree with a cross as he rode past, then glanced back to check on Travis. They had decided it would be best if he and Cara did not scout together. Someone needed to ride ahead to check for ambushes and ensure the way was passable, but not the both of them. This way if the worst happened, the main party would still have a guide to get them back to Flumeer. Romaine had asked Travis to join him on Cara's horse instead, to be a runner between the groups should they encounter the Tangata.

The recruit offered a nod and Romaine returned his gaze to the way ahead. If the horses were struggling with the snow, he didn't like to think how Lukys and the other recruits were managing. Marching through the snow, in the dead of winter, was not an enviable task.

At least there had been no sign of Tangata tracks so far. That could not last. A party of forty men and women could not go unnoticed forever. The Archivist was bargaining on their force being too large for a Tangata pair to challenge. The beasts would need time to gather more of their fellows to tackle the Perfugians. With luck, they would be long gone from Calafe before then.

At least, that was the hope.

The *thump* of snow falling came from off to their right. The hiss of inhaled breath followed from Travis, and even Romaine tensed, gaze sweeping the undergrowth. After a moment he shook himself and shared a grin with Travis. The recruit smiled back, though it did not reach his eyes. Romaine couldn't blame him. The Perfugian was in unknown territory now.

Even Romaine was struggling to find the usual peace he felt at returning to his homeland. The heady scent of pines was all around and the familiar trees stretched above, untouched by the axes of man. Gone was the cloying stench of smoke and human waste, the incessant pounding of hammers and clashing of practice weapons. This was his home, heavy with the silence of winter…

And yet…he felt something had changed. There was an edge to the air now, one Romaine had not felt before, not even when fleeing the Tangata on his last visit.

The two rode on, what little they could see of the sun through the canopy stretching higher into the sky, but still the source of Romaine's anxiety escaped him. Finally the trees began to thin, pines giving way to spruce and hemlock, and eventually beech. As the sun dipped back towards the horizon, clouds appeared to obscure the sky, and Romaine guessed it would snow again that night.

Thankfully he knew of an abandoned village slightly higher in the foothills. Now that the trees had thinned, he could use the mountain peaks for navigation, and tugging on his reins, he adjusted their path. The village would not be as far as the Archivist had wished to reach on their first day, but with the snow growing thicker, Romaine doubted the recruits could keep pace with her schedule anyway.

He and Travis reached the village several hours before dusk. Here the forest had been cleared to make way for stone cottages. Though there were only a dozen in total, each had been built from rocks of different sizes, likely taken from a nearby stream. The stones had been placed together like a jigsaw to form a whole, and mortar added later to make them whole.

The place had been abandoned less than a year before, but already signs of deterioration had set in. The thatched roofs of several had collapsed beneath the weight of snow, and saplings now grew amongst the stones, as the forest sought to reclaim what had been taken.

With Lukys and the others still some hours away, they dismounted and set about making the place ready. In the end, eight of the cottages were habitable, though Romaine had Travis climb up and dislodge the snow from atop several. Then they set about collecting firewood. They would not risk the smoke during the day, but once the sun set, the flames could be hidden inside one of the buildings.

"It's strange," Travis said when they finally stopped to rest.

They were seated on a stone bench outside one of the cottages, and rummaging in his saddlebag for the beef jerky, Romaine almost missed what the recruit had said. Finally finding the right package, he drew it out and tossed Travis a piece before claiming a strip of his own. He took a bite before looking at his companion, one eyebrow raised.

"What's strange?"

Travis shrugged, then grinned. "It's just this place," he replied, "it almost looks…*normal*. I thought the Calafe were nomadic."

Romaine snorted. "That's what the Flumeerens think as well," he grunted, then tore another bite from his jerky. "It was always more a general dislike of cities," he answered at last. "Places like Fogmore and Charcity and Mildeth, they fight to keep nature out, to separate humanity from the land that bore us. Though, there *are* many of us who prefer a life in the forests."

"And this?" Travis asked, gesturing to the cottages.

Romaine snorted. "Winter houses," he replied. "Even for us, the winter is no time to be walking around in the forest."

"Oh really?" the recruit asked sarcastically. "You should have said something earlier—I *never* would have come had I known."

Despite himself, Romaine chuckled. "This is nothing yet," he said, gesturing to the nearby trees. "Once we get onto the plateaus, the winds blow straight off the mountains. There'll be no shelter our last night, not unless we get lucky and find the Archivist's ancient site quickly." He paused. "Which seems unlikely, given it hasn't been discovered in a millennia."

"Half a millennia," Travis replied absently, then when Romaine raised his eyebrows, continued: "At least, that's what they teach us in the academy: that The Fall took place five centuries ago."

"Useful," Romaine said wryly.

"It would make the Gods slightly less ancient than some would have us believe," he replied, though his tone made it clear he was sceptical. He paused, then glanced his way, eyes shining. "Have you ever seen them?"

"Who, a God?"

Travis nodded, though given his nature, Romaine still wasn't entirely sure he wasn't joking.

"Where would I have a seen a God, lad?"

"Up there!" he exclaimed, pointing. Through the treetops Romaine could still make out the highest peaks of the mountains. "That's where they're meant to live, right? I always thought the Calafe must have some secret knowledge of them, living so close."

"Afraid not," Romaine replied, though Travis's words sent a tremor racing down his spine. "The Mountains of the Gods are forbidden, even to the Flumeeren and Gemahan. No one goes there—or at least, no one that does ever returns." He frowned. "Isn't it the same way, with the ancient sites you've found in Perfugia?"

Travis shrugged. "Yeah, but those are different. The Gods left those. Besides, we fear those places…we're taught that the Gods didn't want to *cause* The Fall. It was an aftereffect of their magic, when they tried to destroy the Tangata."

"They failed," Romaine replied, then shrugged. "Though I suppose the reason hardly matters, after all this time."

"It matters to me," Travis murmured, his tone changing, becoming serious. His eyes drifted to the mountains. "I've always been fascinated by them."

Romaine grunted. "Perhaps you should talk with the Archivist."

"Perhaps I will," he replied, "though…I think Erika is only interested in their magic, rather than the Gods themselves." He fell silent.

"There are rumours," Romaine offered after a moment, "legends, from those who claim to have seen the Gods."

"Really?" Travis asked quickly. "What do they look like?"

Romaine sighed, already regretting speaking up. "There are some who claim they're giants," he rumbled, "that they look like us, with human features, but standing as tall as the great redwoods of southern Calafe."

Travis snorted, the excitement draining from him somewhat. "Seems unlikely. I've seen sketches of these ancient sites the Archivist is so interested in. Some of the tunnels could barely fit a human."

"True." Romaine smiled despite himself. "Though perhaps their magic allows them to change shape."

The recruit nodded, and after a moment, Romaine continued.

"Others claim the Gods exist now only as spirits. That they retreated from the physical world after The Fall, in shame for what they had unleashed. More still claim they soar high above, up amongst the clouds, watching us even now."

Travis glanced upwards at his words, as though they might even now catch a glimpse of the Divine. Then a sheepish smile appeared on his lips and his gaze returned to Romaine.

"Our priests say the same," he replied.

"Who knows, lad?" Romaine waved a hand. "I haven't seen them. Though…I find it hard to believe they're watching. Not with the Tangata invading our lands, murdering…families, innocents."

The smile slipped from Travis's lips. "Maybe…maybe they fear using their magic again, lest they bring about another Fall?"

"Another few years like the last, and humanity will be doomed anyway." Romaine shook his head. "The Flumeerens believe the Tangata are a test, to show whether we are worthy of the Gods' return." He forced himself to laugh. "Trust them to find something divine in the act of war."

Travis said nothing at that, and he saw the man's eyes had returned to the mountains. Romaine let out a sigh, unwilling to stomp any further on the man's dreams. Let the Perfugian recruits pray for deliverance. It could hardly hurt.

"So," he said, deciding at last to change the subject. "Has anything happened between you and Cara yet?"

"*What!*" Travis exclaimed, head swinging around so fast it must have given him whiplash.

Romaine chuckled but did not elaborate further.

"I…what…" he trailed off, his cheeks growing bright. A sheepish look crossed his face. "No. Ah…who else knows?"

"Relax," Romaine replied, still grinning. "I don't think anyone else has guessed. Too busy worrying about the Tangata, no doubt."

Travis nodded, though he still seemed worried. Finally he stood and began to pace up and down in front of the building.

"That's it isn't it?" he said at last. "We have bigger things to worry about. I shouldn't be getting distracted by…things!"

Romaine suppressed another bout of laughter. "Ah lad, you've got a lot to learn."

Travis scowled. "I didn't see a Calafe wife back in Fogmore."

Ice gripped Romaine's chest at his words and he sucked in a breath, struggling to control a rush of rage. Exhaling slowly, he forced aside the pain.

"That's…personal," he said softly.

Travis looked up sharply and his eyes widened at the sight of Romaine's face. He opened his mouth to speak, but Romaine spoke over the top of him:

"Look lad, it's never the right time, okay?"

The recruit hesitated, but after a long moment, he nodded. Silence fell between them once more, and Romaine leaned back against the stone wall of the cottage, eyes on the sky. The clouds were growing darker. It would start to snow soon, and with night approaching, he hoped Lukys and the others were close.

As though summoned by the thought, the distant whinny of a horse carried to them on the breeze. Letting out a long sigh, Romaine levered himself to his feet and glanced down at Travis.

"Coming?"

Travis started as though he'd been caught unawares. A frown twisted his lips as he glanced at the trees, and his shoulders slumped.

"It's just…I failed, you know?" he murmured, slowly coming to his feet. "At literally *everything*."

"Forget the past, lad," Romaine sighed. "We've all failed at… something. That's no bad thing—so long as you learn from it. And from where I sit, you've done well these last weeks."

"If you say so…" Travis trailed off, then laughed. "Ah well, she probably wouldn't go for a city boy like me anyway."

"You'll never know unless you ask," Romaine replied, stepping past the man. "Now come on, they'll be tired from the trek."

He started down the slope towards the path they'd taken. Already movement was visible amongst the trees. Stones crunched a moment later as Travis followed. A smile touched his lips. The man had a good heart—

Romaine stumbled as realisation struck him; he suddenly knew what was off, the edge he'd felt ever since crossing the Illmoor. It wasn't something that had changed in Calafe at all.

It was him.

Always before when he'd come on these scouting trips, it had been with Flumeeren soldiers. Strangers. He didn't care whether they lived or died.

"Godsdamnit," he whispered to the winds.

This time, he cared.

21

THE RECRUIT

Lukys marched at the head of the column for much of their first day. Cara walked at his side, helping to pick out the marks Romaine and Travis had made for them to follow, though she said little. Returning to Calafe seemed to have left her lost for words. Lukys didn't press her—after all, how would he react in her situation? He could hardly imagine Perfugia falling, let alone returning after his land had been claimed by the enemy.

Unfortunately, the conversation was little better with the one who came behind them. So far, the Archivist had shown little interest in anyone but Romaine and, briefly, Cara. As for the rest of them…Lukys had spent enough time around the noble born in Perfugia to sense when someone thought herself above him.

As the day stretched on, the silence began to weigh on Lukys. Occasionally, he wandered back down the line of recruits, checking on their progress. Speaking with the others at least helped to dissolve some of the burden that grew in those silent hours.

It seemed to help the other Perfugians too. Despite their brave words the day before, many marched with their heads down, while others stared at the trees to either side of the thin trail, open fear on their faces. When he addressed them, they would look at him in fright, as though he were announcing the Tangata were upon them. Then their eyes would show recognition and their shoulders would relax, and they would nod and comment about the snow or their boots or the blasted Archivist sitting on her horse.

Lukys did his best to encourage them, though at times he felt it was more for himself than the others. In Romaine's absence and the Archivist's lack of interest in anyone but herself, he felt almost responsible for his fellow Perfugians. There was a voice in his head, whispering that he should have done more back in Fogmore, should have convinced them all to train together.

At midday he called a stop. That was probably the Archivist's responsibility, but she didn't seem interested, and several of the recruits looked close to dropping on their feet. Groans whispered through the trees as men and women lowered themselves to the ground and took out packages of food.

It disheartened Lukys to see their exhaustion. Despite the snow, the trek had been easy compared to their overland hike through Flumeer. The ground had climbed gently so far from the river, but from the path Romaine had outlined before setting out, soon they would start into the foothills. How would his fellow Perfugians manage that climb if they struggled on the flat?

Unfortunately, it wasn't long before the Archivist grew impatient and they were forced to continue. With their late departure, Erika was eager to press on and recover lost time. Never mind that she rode a horse while the rest of them walked.

They set off with Lukys still in the lead, Cara and the Archivist close behind. It wasn't long, though, before Lukys dropped back again, standing to the side while the others continued. Cara lingered though, amber eyes watching him.

"You worry for them," she murmured.

Lukys shrugged. "Maybe." They started walking again.

Cara frowned. "They're not your responsibility."

"No," Lukys sighed. "Maybe I'm not doing it for them though."

The woman's frown only deepened at that and Lukys continued before she could speak, "Maybe I'm just trying to convince myself of something."

"Convince yourself of what?"

"I'm not sure," Lukys replied, then grinned. "I'll let you know when I figure it out. Go on, I'm going to talk with some of the others."

He waved her on and turned to wait for the rest of the column. Cara lingered, but after a moment she nodded and hurried to catch up with the Archivist.

"Bradbury, how's your legs?" Lukys commented as he fell into step with another of the recruits.

It was a moment before his new companion responded. "What?"

Lukys forced a smile and tried again. "Your legs, man! How are they?" he said, adopting a false bravado. "Mine feel as though they're about to fall off."

Bradbury stared at Lukys for a long moment, then returned his eyes to the road. "They're fine."

A sigh escaped Lukys's lips. Clearly this wasn't working. He needed to jerk the recruits out of this stupor that had come over them since entering Calafe.

"Shame we can't just give up, hey?" he continued. "Seems as nice a place as any to set camp, but what do I know. Good thing we've got Romaine, he'll know the best place to stop. This forest is probably infested with wolves or something!"

"Wolves!" Bradbury gasped. Eyes wide, he glanced around, as though the beasts might be creeping up on him at that very moment. "There are *wolves* in this forest?"

"Ahhhh." Lukys cursed inwardly at the fear in the man's face. "Maybe, but don't worry, don't you remember biology class? Wolves don't bother humans."

"That's not what the old tales say!"

"The old tales say a lot of things." Lukys slapped the man on the back. "Remember that one claiming the Calafe are part Tangata? Well, you've met Romaine, right? Does he look like one of those beasts to you?"

"I...no..." The recruit trailed off, before adding, "Though he *is* ferocious."

Lukys forced a laugh. "And he's on our side," he said. "Something to be thankful for, right? And look, the trees are beginning to thin, you can even see the mountains! I'm sure it won't be long before we catch up with Travis and the old Calafe."

With that he gave Bradbury a final nod and strode back up the line. Approaching the front of the column, he saw the Archivist had dismounted and was taking a turn at walking. Even more surprising, Cara sat on her horse, a large piece of paper held out before her.

"You see the red star?" Erika was saying.

"Where did you get this?" Cara murmured, eyes wide as she stared at the unfurled paper.

"One of the ancient sites," the Archivist replied. "Do you recognise the area?" Her voice took on an excited tone.

Drawing closer, Lukys saw that the paper Cara held was in fact a map. His heartbeat quickened as he realized this must be the relic the Archivist had discovered, the one directing them to the undiscovered site of the Gods. Lukys still loathed the thought of stepping foot in those ancient tunnels, of desecrating what had once been a sacred place of the Gods…

Sacred, secret, death.

…a shiver ran down Lukys's spine. The Archivist said that reclaiming the magic of the Gods was the only way to save humanity…but Lukys hadn't missed the glint in the woman's eyes when she spoke of that magic. She wanted more than just protection; she wanted *power*. His gaze was drawn to the gauntlet on her hand and he swallowed. Rumours had swirled amongst the recruits as to what it was, but Lukys knew. Romaine had told him.

It was another artefact, one with true magic. A weapon.

"It is…close to my home," Cara said hesitantly. "Though…I do not know the terrain well."

At least Cara was talking again. She seemed fascinated by the Archivist, though Lukys couldn't see why. Perhaps it was the novelty of meeting a Flumeeren aristocrat, or the woman's study of the Gods. Either way, the interest had not seemed to be reciprocated until now.

"May I see?" Lukys asked as he joined Cara on the other side of the horse from the Archivist.

"Why?" Erika asked sharply. She grasped the reins, as though suddenly fearing Cara would flee.

Lukys raised an eyebrow. "I don't know the terrain. It would be good to know what to expect if we're to protect you, Archivist."

The woman stared at him across the horse, as though if she looked long enough, she might read his mind. Finally, she shrugged and gestured her permission.

"Careful," Cara murmured. Dismounting, she handed it over to him. "It's…old."

"No kidding," Lukys replied as he took it from her hands.

He unfurled the map as he walked, taking care to keep one eye on the uneven ground. It surprised him to see that colours filled the paper, greens and browns and blues and whites and many more. A quick glance suggested what he held was more painting than map. Certainly it was nothing like the charts back in the academy. Those were all black lines and empty spaces on yellowed pages.

As he inspected the mixtures of colours, landmarks started to leap at him from the page. There, a large mass of green and white set apart from the rest, surrounded by blue. He could not read the names on the map, but it had to be Perfugia. He followed the coast-line south, amazed at the detail the ancients had captured, until he found a great river. Its position had shifted, but it could only be the Illmoor. Further inland and to the south, he found the red star the Archivist had mentioned.

"This is where we're going?" he asked.

Stepping back into the saddle of her horse, the Archivist ignored him, but Cara leaned closer.

"Yes, I…think it is a part of the foothills." She frowned, brow furrowing. "That dark green, I think that means it was forest, but there are no trees there now."

"I see," Lukys murmured, his eyes continuing. "Then these here must be the Mountains of the Gods?"

"I…" Cara hesitated, glancing at Lukys then up at the Archivist. Swallowing, she nodded. "I think so."

"Yes, it has to be," he continued excitedly, pointing to white and grey blotches on the paper. "You see these lines? They circle around the white spots—those must be the peaks. The closer they come together, the steeper the slope. They're called—"

"Contours," the Archivist interrupted from her horse.

Lukys glanced at her. "We learnt about them at the Perfugian academy. But…" He hesitated, glancing back at the map. "I've never seen any so detailed." Then he frowned, noticing something else. There was another red star. "And this…there's another site, in the Mountains of the Gods themselves."

No, no, no!

On her horse, Erika chuckled. "You look like you've seen a ghost, Perfugian."

"I…but…" He swallowed. "If this is truly a map of their sacred sites, you realise…"

"*No!*" Cara exclaimed unexpectedly. Before he could react, she snatched the map from his hands.

"*Careful,*" Erika hissed, swinging her horse in front of them. "The boy is right, that star could be the home of the Gods *themselves!*" She dropped from the saddle and almost stumbled. Cursing, she caught Cara by the arm. "Gods, woman, I did not think the Calafe so superstitious."

A tremor shook Cara as she clutched the map to her jacket. Even Lukys found himself shaking. If what the Archivist suspected was true…*Gods*, surely that was blasphemous knowledge? To know where the Gods themselves lived…

"But it's *forbidden!*" Cara whispered.

"Definitely not a good idea," Lukys said at the same time.

"Oh, calm down," Erika said, rolling her eyes. "We're not actually *going* there. The queen has prohibited even speaking of it." She paused, then muttered another curse. "I should have known better than to show you the map. Quick, give it back." Lips pursed, she held out her hand to Cara.

The woman bit her lip, glancing to Lukys then back to the Archivist. Finally she nodded and handed over the map. Erika rolled it back up and slid it into a metal cylinder before placing it in her knapsack. A grin touched her lips as she looked at them again.

"Our superstitions never cease to amaze me," she murmured. "Don't you see? The Gods *left* this for us to find. It is an invitation. They *want* us to come to them." As she spoke, she lifted her gauntleted hand and clenched it into a fist. "Though of course, only the worthy will be welcomed."

A faint light seeped from the woven steel.

It turned Lukys's insides to ice.

22

THE WARRIOR

Romaine groaned as he lowered himself onto the wall at the edge of the village and watched the recruits going about organising their camp—although there wasn't much organisation to be seen. A watch had been set to keep eyes on the forest, but otherwise the Perfugians were doing a poor job of dividing up the eight habitable cottages between them.

Given that the general had put him in charge, Romaine probably should have taken more responsibility, but his mind was occupied. On other scouting trips, he had rarely gone a day without glimpsing signs of the Tangata. That was why they'd spent so little time this side of the Illmoor. So far though, there hadn't been a whisper, not even a boot print in the snow.

After the attack on Fogmore, he'd half expected these forests to be crawling with Tangata. Yet now they found northern Calafe empty. The enemy's tactics often seemed incomprehensible, but this was stranger still. The assault, though made up of at least a dozen Tangata, had never stood a chance of taking the city. Curtis had assumed it had been a precursor, a probe before a greater force attempted the crossing.

Now, though…could the attack have been punitive? Romaine and the scouts had killed two of their number…but no, the Tangata were prone to rages, but they rarely threw lives away on hopeless causes.

Romaine found himself shaking his head. He could make no sense of it. And that worried him.

Movement came from nearby, and Romaine looked up to see Cara approaching. The frown on her face was a mirror of Romaine's own, and he couldn't help but smile at the sight.

"Why the sad face, lass?" he asked as she walked up.

Cara started at his voice, then gave a shrug. Romaine gestured for her to join him on the wall.

"I thought you'd be happy, being back here. This is what you wanted, isn't it?"

"I…coming back is not what I imagined." She rolled her shoulders, eyes turning to the sky. "I never expected…" A sheepish smile tugged at her lips. "To make friends."

A lump lodged in Romaine's throat as she echoed his earlier thoughts, but he pushed it aside. "You're still young, lass," he replied. "Nothing wrong with making a few friends."

Cara sighed, shifting slightly on the wall. It had been constructed in the same manner as the cottages, rocks fitted one on top of the other, though no mortar had been used here. It made finding a comfortable position difficult, and Cara spent a long moment wiggling before settling again.

"I…I have to go, Romaine," she whispered.

"What?" His heart gave a painful throb. "Go *where?*"

"I told you," she murmured, still looking at the sky, anywhere but at him, it seemed. "I have to…find my family."

"You're sure…" He trailed off, not wanting to finish the sentence, but it had to be said. "You're sure they're still alive, Cara?"

She shrugged, not saying anything, but he could see the darkness in her eyes. She didn't know. Maybe she even thought them dead. But until she saw, until she knew for sure…a spark of hope would live on. Romaine knew that feeling well. For too long he had clung to it, like a man clutching to a jagged ledge, knowing it could not save him, and yet…unable to let go.

Living torture.

"I understand," he said at last.

"Why am I not surprised!" Romaine looked up to see Travis approaching.

The recruit whistled as he walked; of all the Perfugians, he alone seemed to be unaffected by their predicament. At least outwardly. Romaine's heart twisted as he recalled their earlier conversation about Cara.

"Leave it to the Calafe to skirt work," Travis continued as he reached them, grinning. "Where do I sign up?"

Romaine grunted. "When you lose your kingdom, we'll talk."

"I…ah…sure…"

The recruit trailed off, looking awkward, and Romaine laughed. "Come and sit, lad," he said, gesturing to the wall.

A smile lit Cara's face as Travis sat beside her, though now Romaine did not miss the edge of sadness that crinkled the corners of her eyes. He sighed. The lad deserved to know…

"So when will you go?" he murmured softly, looking at Cara, "Looking for your family, I mean."

Cara stiffened at his words and she flashed him a glare that could have melted stone. Beside her, Travis looked from Romaine to Cara, a frown twisting his lips.

"You're leaving?"

Biting her lip, Cara looked at the young man, and nodded. "I have to," she said. "My family…I can't stay with you."

"I…see." Travis swallowed, his Adam's apple bobbing up and down. "Of course…"

He trailed off, and an uncomfortable silence fell between them. Romaine cursed inwardly. It had needed to be done, but he should have let Cara broach the subject. After a few minutes, Travis let out a sigh and rose.

"Well…I'd better see if the others need any help," he said, rising. He flashed a smile, though even to Romaine it seemed forced, then wandered back towards the village.

Flashing Romaine another glare, Cara leapt to her feet and chased after him. She did not glance back.

Letting out a sigh, Romaine rose and set off along the waist-high-wall that marked the perimeter of the village. The sun had set and he wanted to check on the lookouts he'd set before it grew completely dark. All were where he had left them.

He found the last standing nervously watching the forest, spear and shield held tight to her chest. Recognising her as one of those who had been training with him, he waved her over.

"Go find yourself some food, lass," he said. "I'll take the watch."

"Are you sure?" she asked, though her expression revealed her eagerness to be away from the trees.

Romaine nodded. "Go, I could use the quiet."

She left, leaving him alone with the night. Letting out a groan, Romaine took her place on the wall, his joints popping. Cara would get over her anger, if she did not leave immediately. She'd said the ancient site was close to her home; he hoped that meant she would stick around at least another day.

Overhead, moonlight touched the sky, setting the distant mountains aglow. They hulked like giants on the horizon, reminding him of the stories he'd told Travis. Perhaps that was the true source of the Calafe legends. Had their ancestors after The Fall come to see those hulking peaks as Gods, passing down tales until modern men viewed them as the birthplace of the Divine?

He almost preferred the idea. For if the Gods truly roamed those remote peaks, how could he not but hate them? It had been their magic, stolen or otherwise, that had given birth to the Tangata. Yet if the legends were true, instead of aiding humanity, the Gods had cast them down, abandoning them to the darkness.

"We lit the fire where you said," came Lukys's voice from the darkness. A second later the recruit appeared, face lit by the cold light of the moon. He held out a bowl made from bark, something Romaine and Travis had prepared before their arrival. "Gruel?"

Romaine nodded his thanks, then took a spoonful and almost spat it back out. It was saltier than jerky. Managing to swallow the mouthful, he set the bowl aside.

"Travis…isn't much of a cook," Lukys said. He hesitated, standing in the darkness, eyes on the trees. "Cara…told us."

"Is she okay?" Romaine asked, turning his eyes towards the trees.

Lukys shrugged and took a seat beside him. "She's fine. Travis will be alright," he hesitated, flicking a glance in Romaine's direction. "It's the rest of them I'm worried about. I tried to encourage them today, keep their spirits up. I don't think it helped much."

Romaine grunted. "They don't need mothering, lad," he said. Reaching up, he took the axe from its sheath on his back and held it up. Its twin blades shone in the moonlight. "They're not children;

you can't tell them everything is going to be alright. They know it's not. Chances are, some of us are going to die before this journey is done."

"Then what do I do?" Lukys whispered. "They're terrified, on the verge of giving up. How do I hold them together?"

A sigh slipped from Romaine's lips. Lukys was taking too much on his shoulders, but then…what else could he do? Romaine couldn't do everything by himself. Someone had to step up.

Taking a firmer grip on his axe, Romaine drove its twin points into the earth. Lukys flinched, but did not look away as their eyes met.

"Show them your strength," Romaine said quietly. "When everything is dark, soldiers need to believe in their commanders— even if they don't believe in themselves."

Lukys swallowed, his eyes wide in the darkness, but finally he nodded. "I understand," he murmured. "I'll do my best."

"That's all anyone can ask, lad," Romaine replied, his heart swelling as he saw the resolve in the other man's eyes.

An image flickered into his mind, of another boy, eyes staring up from a bed of snow. He clenched his fist closed around the hilt of his axe, trying to keep the pain from his face.

"You want me to take over the watch?" Lukys asked.

Romaine raised an eyebrow at the young Perfugian. "You think I'm too old to look out for a few Tangata?"

A wry grin appeared on Lukys's lips as he stood. "Just being polite," he replied, "but since you're apparently happy to sit here in the cold, I think I'll go see if our second cooks any better." He raised a hand in farewell, then turned and disappeared into the darkness.

And Romaine was left alone with his pain.

23

THE RECRUIT

Mountains in a grey sky.
A blood-red moon.
Stark slopes of rock.
Screaming in the earth.
Desperation, despair, lost.
Then…hope!
Life!
A flash, then an image, not like the others…
Colourful, blue and green and white and grey.
Lines of black.
A star of red.
Life!

Lukys gasped as he jerked awake, sitting bolt upright. Curses came from alongside him as the two recruits he shared the tent with mumbled in their sleeping rolls, though neither woke.

Clutching at his chest, Lukys strained to see in the darkness, but no light penetrated the heavy canvas. The sun had not yet risen, and finally he lay back against the hard ground, trying to force his mind to calm. The dream was already fading, though it had seemed so vivid, almost real. He could not have said why, but it left him feeling disturbed. It must have been his exhaustion.

They had marched hard their second day, leaving behind the forest and moving into foothills. Despite the lack of trees, there the going had become harder, as the recruits were forced to scramble up slopes of loose gravel. Even the flatter sections were inundated with spiked shrubs that would catch at their clothing and tear their skin, until they were forced to use knives to cut their way free.

It would have been even worse if not for Romaine's scouting. Travis had ridden with the Calafe again, though at times the column had caught them as they backtracked from a false slope. Thankfully, their efforts kept the rest of them from hiking up the wrong hills; otherwise, Lukys doubted there would have been a single Perfugian on his feet by the end of the day. There had been a collective groan of relief when they'd finally spied Romaine and Travis waiting for them at a notch in the hillside.

Romaine said they would reach the Archivist's plateau by dusk the following day. Though it was half a day behind the Archivist's schedule, Lukys was just glad they still hadn't encountered any of the Tangata.

Finally realising he wasn't going back to sleep, Lukys stifled a moan and slipped out of his bedroll. Unbuttoning the tent flap, he pulled on his boots and stood, closing things again behind him. Then he went searching for one of the lookouts.

The night was clear, though the air was so cold it hurt to breathe. He shivered as he saw the moon overhead, recalling the scarlet globe from his dreams, though here it remained a brilliant silver. It illuminated the dusting of snow on the ground, left over from the fall they'd had the night they'd stayed in the village.

Though Romaine had chosen the campsite for its shelter, a light wind still blew through the valley, raising goosebumps on Lukys's neck. He pulled his fur cloak tighter around himself, then froze as a noise carried to him on the breeze. Suddenly alert, he scanned the hillside around the tent, but in the darkness, it was difficult to tell rock from enemy.

Movement flickered in the shadows. Lukys was about to cry out a warning when the sound came again. Voices. The hairs on his neck stood on end. The Tangata did not speak, but who would be out here in the night? Heart racing, he crept through the lines of canvas tents, eyes fixed on the point he'd seen movement.

"Lukys?"

He started as a whisper came from nearby, reaching for the

dagger on his belt. His hand was on the hilt when he realised it was only Cara. Letting out a long breath, he released the blade. For a moment he thought she'd been the speaker, then the whisper of voices came on the breeze again.

"*Quiet*," he hissed, eyes returning to the hillside. Had they heard her? Stepping closer, he raised a finger to his lips. "What are you doing out here?"

Her eyes widened. "I…couldn't sleep?"

Lukys frowned. "Are you leavin…"

He trailed off as the whispers came again. This time Cara heard them too and swung around, eyes fixed on the darkness. "What are they doing up there?"

"They?"

"Some of your recruits," she replied softly.

Squinting into the night, Lukys cursed, still unable to spot the speakers. "I don't know," he murmured, "but we'd better find out. Come on."

He started forward, crouched low to the ground and taking care not to disturb the loose stones as he moved. Cara followed, her step so light he had to keep checking to know where she was. The voices came from further up the valley, on the slope that sheltered the camp from the mountain winds.

There was meant to be a scout posted nearby, but they found the position empty. Lukys cursed. If they couldn't even trust the other Perfugians to keep watch…

"…only a…of em."

Lukys froze as the voices grew louder, allowing him to recognise several scattered words. Beside him, Cara froze, casting an uncertain glance in his direction. He bid her to wait. Blood pounded in his ears as he strained to hear the rest of the conversation.

"…you seen…that axe…"

Still unable to make out all the words, Lukys crept closer, trying to make sense of them.

"Better than the Tangata!" a man exclaimed, far louder than the others.

Whispers hissed in the night as others quieted him, then silence. Lukys held his breath as he sensed movement above, then a flash of white as someone peered out from behind a boulder and looked down the slope. Crouching lower amongst the rocks, Lukys prayed for Cara to do the same. He wasn't sure what the recruits above were planning yet, but it couldn't be anything good.

A moment later the recruit retreated and the conversation resumed.

"You know they're out here," the last speaker continued in a softer tone. "We've been lucky so far, but how long is that going to last? Sooner or later the beasts will find us. I don't want to be around when they do."

"I dunno…" another argued. This time Lukys recognised the speaker—Bradbury. "You think we can survive without them? The Tangata aren't the only things in these woods, you know…"

Another of the recruits laughed. "You still on about them wolves, Bradbury?"

"We have to go," the first voice repeated.

"What about the Archivist? If she makes it back, we'll be branded as traitors."

"Then we make sure none of them make it back."

Silence answered the speaker's words. Below, Lukys's heart pounded against his chest. He shared a glance with Cara. Her eyes were wide, shining in the moonlight, and he swallowed. They were talking about a mutiny, though from here he could not tell how many.

"We say the Tangata attacked," the speaker continued. The other's silence seemed to have made him bold. "No one will question it. You heard the general, he already thinks this is a fool's errand. Mark my words, he'll be thankful any of us returned!"

Lukys's shock turned slowly to anger. How dare they! Romaine had volunteered to come, to protect them all, yet these recruits planned to murder him. He clenched his fists, though he knew he could not risk a confrontation. With only his knife and Cara for support, he'd be quickly overwhelmed.

He rose and slipped back towards the camp. If they could raise the alarm, the traitors would not have a chance to enact their plan—

The moon slipped behind a cloud, plunging the night into utter black. He cursed, stumbling on the uneven ground…

Crack.

His foot struck a rock, sending it tumbling down the slope. Lukys froze where he stood, praying the darkness would shield him…but then the moon reappeared overhead, casting its silver light across the valley.

"*There!*"

Stones rattled above as shadows raced towards him. Stomach twisting in knots, Lukys looked in the direction of camp. They'd come farther than he'd thought. No way he'd make it before the recruits overtook him. He looked at Cara.

"Go warn Romaine," he murmured.

Cara glanced at the approaching shadows, eyes wide, face pale in the moonlight. For a second it seemed she would do as he said. But shuddering, she pulled her cloak tighter around herself and faced the traitors. Lukys nodded. It was probably too late for her to escape anyway.

The traitors slowed as they approached. There were a dozen of them, each armed with their spears, though they didn't wear armour. They spread out around him, weapons at the ready.

"Lukys," Bradbury gasped, his weapon held awkwardly to his chest.

"Of course." Another recruit pushed past the man, a sneer on his lips. It was a moment before Lukys recalled his name—Dyge. "Little bastard, always sticking his nose in other people's business."

Lukys scanned the ring of Perfugians, noting those who seemed doubtful, others who looked ready to run him through. Dale stood amongst the circle, though for once he did not appear to be the ringleader. Drawing in a breath, Lukys faced Dyge.

"Quite the commotion you lot are making out here," he said softly, fighting for calm. "Think you'd best return to your tents, before you catch your death."

"Is that a threat, peasant?" Dyge snarled, stalking forward until they stood face-to-face.

Lukys did not flinch away. "It's a cold night," he said, spreading his hands. "Anyone with half a brain should know to be in his bed."

Whispers came from around the circle as those who had looked uncertain shared glances.

His foe only growled and grabbed Lukys by the front of his

shirt. "What's the matter?" Dyge laughed. "No Calafe warrior to come to your rescue?"

Lukys calmly looked from the man's hands to his eyes, though inwardly his heart was racing. His hand crept to his belt as he spoke. "Release me."

"Like The Fall," Dyge snapped. Then he grinned, the gesture a cold, hungry look. "You know, I think you were right. In this cold, you might just catch your dea—"

He broke off as Lukys pressed the point of his knife into the man's groin. Dyge's mouth opened but Lukys pushed the knife harder.

Death, death, death.

"I suggest," Lukys said again, "that you return to your tent."

"I…" Dyge swallowed, then nodded eagerly. "Yes, you're right. I think I'll do that." He released Lukys's shirt and raised his hands, gesturing at the knife.

Lukys lingered, holding the man's gaze before finally drawing back. Dyge licked his lips, still appearing nervous, while Lukys turned to look at the others.

"We're all afraid, remember," he said, "but our only hope is to stay together. Alone, we don't stand a chance out here."

The others said nothing, unable to meet his eyes, and Lukys nodded his satisfaction. In silence he shared a glance with Cara, then led her towards a gap in the circle.

"I'd rather die alone than stand with the likes of you," Dyge's voice came from behind them.

Die, die, die.

Lukys spun, knife still in hand, but his foe now held a spear. The razor-sharp point flashed for Lukys's throat…

…and was knocked aside as another recruit leapt to his aid. A roar of anger came from Dyge, but before he could bring his weapon around to attack again, the newcomer slammed the tip of his spear into the man's chest.

A stunned look appeared in Dyge's eyes as he looked up at the recruit that had stabbed him.

"Da…Dale?"

Blood burst from his lips as Dale yanked back his spear, allowing the traitor to slump to the ground. He stepped back, eyes still on the body, spear clutched at the ready. Lukys could only stare at the man, unable to believe it had been *Dale* who had come to his rescue.

Finally Dale lowered his spear. He still did not look at Lukys, but instead turned to face the circle of recruits. They stared back at him, open fear on their faces.

"Dyge was a fool," he said softly, "and if any of you think the same as him, you're fools as well. None of us would last a day out here without the Calafe. The Tangata would have you by suppertime."

"The Tangata will have us anyway," Bradbury said, looking despondent.

"Maybe," Dale replied. Finally he looked at Lukys. "But I'd rather die with honour than as a traitor."

"Dyge was the only deserter here," Lukys said, his voice hard. He ignored the others who'd looked ready to murder him—they could not fight them all. "Go back to your beds and speak no more of this."

The eyes of several flickered to Dyge's body, and Lukys caught a glimpse of anger there. But it faded as they looked again at Lukys and Dale and Cara, giving way to resignation. Without further word, they collected up their spears and started off towards the camp.

Lukys let out a long breath as he watched them go, and allowed the mask to slip. He swallowed, legs suddenly trembling as he realised how close he'd come to death.

"Thank you," he said, offering a hesitant smile to Dale.

The young noble grunted. "Don't take it personally," he replied. "Like you said, doesn't matter if we're friends or enemies. We need to stick together this side of the Illmoor." With that he turned and followed the others, leaving Lukys standing alone with Cara.

They stood there a while, saying nothing. Lukys stared out into the darkness, replaying the moment again and again. Inevitably, his gaze was drawn to the body of Dyge. He'd underestimated the man —but had it been his hatred, or his desperation? A shiver ran down his spine and he forced himself to look away.

"I'm sorry," Cara whispered, drawing Lukys's gaze.

She stood with her arms wrapped around herself, eyes staring into the distance, tears streaking her cheeks. Surprised, he shook his head.

"Sorry for what?"

"I should have stopped him," Cara whispered. Her amber eyes flickered to Dyge's body, shining in the moonlight. A shudder went through her. "So much…blood."

Blood, blood, blood.

"Hey, it's not your fault," Lukys exclaimed, stepping close and opening his arms to hug her.

She flinched away, eyes wide, and he remembered her fear of being touched.

"Sorry," he said, turning his hands palm out. Then he smiled. "But I'm okay."

Cara watched him for a long while before responding with a nod. "Okay." She yawned, stretching her arms, before a grin appeared on her face. "Guess we'd better head back to camp then." She gestured at the mountain slopes around them. "Who knows what else is out roaming in the moonlight?"

Lukys started as his dream came rushing back to him, the scarlet moon, the shadows rushing across a barren slope, the thumping of blood in his ears.

Not seeming to notice, Cara started off towards the camp. Lukys followed after a moment's hesitation, though his mind was elsewhere, lingering on the dream, on that moon. The same moon that hung above them, though without the red…

…he glanced back towards where Dyge lay, though in the darkness he could no longer make out the body.

Nor the blood that now stained the rocks.

24

THE ARCHIVIST

I mpatient to be going, Erika had the Perfugians break camp in the dark so they could be on the road at dawn. She was surprised there had been no complaints, though there had been a sullen mood about the soldiers as they set off. Too bad; they were already half a day behind schedule—she'd wanted the afternoon to explore the area, hopefully find the unknown entrance.

Perhaps if the recruits increased their pace, they might still reach the site with daylight to spare. She sought out the young man who seemed to take on the role of officer while the Calafe was absent. What was his name…Lukys! She spotted him marching at the front as usual and edged her horse alongside him.

"Lukys," she said, drawing his attention. Eyes ringed by shadow glanced at her from the road, and she hesitated a moment before continuing: "Your soldiers need to pick up the pace. I want to reach our destination before we lose the light."

A groan came from behind her, but Erika ignored the other recruits.

An extended moment passed before Lukys shook his head. "No," he said, and returned his eyes to the road.

"What…" Erika's mouth fell open, shocked at the man's disobedience. *She* was in charge here, not this upstart of a soldier. Clenching her fist, she took control of her emotions. "That was not a question, recruit," she said, voice cold now.

"I know," the man replied, eyes fixed straight ahead.

"Then just what do you think you're doing?" Erika hissed, losing control despite her best efforts.

"Keeping us all alive," came the response. He glanced in her direction. "With all due respect, *Archivist,* you don't have a clue."

"How dare—"

"I dare!" the recruit snapped, swinging on her. She flinched in the saddle and tried to pull away, but he snatched the reins, bringing the horse to a stop. Angry eyes glared up at her. "I dare, because if you push them any harder, we'll have a mutiny on our hands." He sucked in a breath, and seemed to calm somewhat. Releasing the reins, he stepped back. "If you didn't notice, we're already a man short today."

He started off again, leaving Erika sitting stunned on her horse. Cursing, she shook herself and kicked the beast after him.

"What do you mean, a mutiny?" she hissed.

"It's taken care of," Lukys replied, eyes ignoring her again.

Erika swore beneath her breath, but decided it best not to press the man. Suddenly, she wished Romaine had not ridden so far ahead. Clutching her fist, she sought out the power of the gauntlet, feeling its warmth as it began to glow. She let out a long breath, the pressure in her chest relenting a little. It came racing back as she remembered the forty-odd soldiers marching behind her. Even with the magic of the Gods, she could not fight them all.

"Are you okay, Erika?" Cara asked, approaching on Erika's left.

"I'm fine," she said shortly. Clutching her reins close, Erika tried to quell her racing heart.

Laughter came from the Calafe girl. "You look like you woke up on the wrong side of the tent." She leaned closer in a conspiratorial manner, eyes dancing. "Or just found out about the excitement in the night."

"I…" Erika glanced sharply at the woman. "You were there."

Cara only shrugged and began to whistle.

Erika opened her mouth, then decided it was best to forget about the whole thing. She couldn't cope with the strangeness of these people. The Perfugian spoke of a missing man and walked as though he carried a boulder on his shoulders, and meanwhile the Calafe woman…whistled?

No wonder Erika's mother had decided to return to Flumeer after her father had died. If all the Calafe were as strange as Cara, or stoic as Romaine…not to mention the boredom of life in this wild, untamed world. Erika couldn't understand how anyone could live in a village such as the one they'd camped in for the night, so far from the pleasures of civilisation.

Sure, she had enjoyed that life as a child, when the forests and mountains had been an unending land of adventure…but children were easily entertained. A true Flumeeren could never have been happy with such an existence.

The weather warmed as the day passed on, melting the last of the snow from the slopes—and turning the ground to mud. To Erika's frustration, their progress slowed further, though she decided to keep her mouth shut for the moment. By the time the column stopped to lunch, they had barely covered five miles.

Erika was just dismounting when a distant sound carried down from the slope they were about to traverse. Lukys was on his feet in an instant, swinging the shield from his pack and holding his spear at the ready. A moment later the noise resolved into hoofbeats as a rider topped the crest of the nearby hill.

The man, Travis, riding hard.

"Perfugians, at the ready," Lukys bellowed.

The rattling of steel came from behind them as the recruits clambered to their feet and clutched at their weapons. Some even seemed to know what to do with them.

Heart racing, Erika eyed the crest of the hill, reins clutched tightly in one fist. Travis was racing down the slope towards them, seemingly uncaring of the uneven ground. There was no sign of Romaine. She cursed beneath her breath. Had the Tangata finally appeared?

Movement came from the top and Erika released a breath as the Calafe warrior appeared. His axe remained undrawn and he was riding slower than the recruit. She took it as a good sign and edged her horse forward alongside Lukys.

"What is it, recruit?" she called as the woman rode up.

"Travis, are you okay?" Lukys asked at the same time.

The man's face was pale as he pulled to a stop, his horse drenched in sweat. They must have ridden hard and for some distance. Blood thundered in Erika's ears and she wanted to scream as the man sucked in great lungfuls of air.

"Tangata!" he gasped finally.

Erika's blood ran cold.

No, no, no.

It couldn't end like this, not when they were so close, just a few hours from triumph. The secrets of the Gods, of their magic, she could almost *feel* it, pulsing in her fingertips…

…she started as the others looked at her, foreheads creased in concern. Light pulsed from her fist and she realized the magic of the gauntlet had arisen unbidden. Ice touched her chest and she forced herself to exhale. The light faded slowly.

No harm done, she thought, hoping her face did not show her shock. Out loud, she said:

"How many?"

The man swallowed as he met Erika's gaze. "Twenty, at least."

Gasps came from behind Erika and she gritted her teeth. Twenty was an army, far too many for one regiment, even had they been properly trained. A curse slipped from her lips before she controlled herself.

"Where?"

"Heading towards us," the recruit said shortly. "They don't seem to know we're here, but…we're right in their path."

Erika cursed again, though the pounding of hooves as Romaine rode up covered the words. She looked to the Calafe warrior, hoping against hope he would refute the recruit's claims.

"You can put those away," he said as he dismounted, looking past Erika to the recruits formed up behind her. "We're not in danger—yet. They've set camp for the day."

"What is your assessment, Romaine?" Erika said, remaining in her saddle.

"The Tangata are ahead of us," he said as though their path was clear. "Too many for us to fight. Thankfully we were downwind. The horses sensed them before we did and we weren't seen. But they're definitely heading in this direction."

"We have to turn back!" called a voice from the recruits behind Erika. Others rose in agreement. She ignored them, fixing her eyes on Romaine, waiting for him to continue.

The warrior spread his hands. "I'm sorry, Archivist. We have to turn back, and quickly, or there'll be no avoiding crossing their path."

"Unacceptable," Erika snapped, no longer bothering to contain her anger. "The fate of humanity is at stake. We must press on, whatever the cost."

"The cost will be your life," Romaine replied bluntly.

A shudder went through Erika at his words, and suddenly she was back in the throne room, standing before the queen, subjected to her displeasure.

Do not fail me.

Erika didn't need to ask what would happen if she returned without new treasures. The queen had been promised the magic of the Gods and she would have it—even if it meant cutting the gauntlet from Erika's corpse.

No one else had moved at Romaine's words. They all looked to her, waiting for her to speak, to accept her fate.

"The cost of failure will be my life regardless, Romaine," she said softly, forcing herself to meet the warrior's eyes. "So I will go on, alone if needs be. Maybe I can slip by them, though without you, I doubt it." She hesitated, before adding: "You and I both know how it would look to General Curtis should you return without me."

A moment of silence answered her words, followed by the angry buzz of voices. Erika's heart pounded hard in her chest but she held the Calafe's gaze, determined not to be the first to break.

"Are you truly so selfish," he whispered, without a trace of anger in his voice, "that you would sacrifice us all for your folly?"

Erika lifted her chin, defiant. "I…" She hesitated, the words stumbling on her tongue before she recovered her composure. "For the fate of humanity, I refuse to turn back."

Romaine shook his head. Stepping from the path they had been following, he slumped onto a boulder. Erika was shocked to see the despair in the man's eyes. The Perfugians fell silent as they saw the hero who had led them this far bowed low. A cold wind blew across the mountainside, sending shivers down Erika's spine, but still she did not retreat.

"What if just a few of us cut through the hills?" a voice said from alongside Erika.

She started as the recruit, Lukys, stepped into her path. There was a determined glint in the man's eyes as he faced her, spear held firmly in hand, head high. Where Romaine looked ready to give up, somehow this recruit still radiated strength.

"What are you suggesting?" she asked, intrigued.

"Romaine is right; the entire regiment cannot continue unnoticed. When the Tangata continue in this direction, they'll pick up our tracks and follow. Whatever we do, it will be a race to reach the Illmoor before they catch us." He drew in a breath before continuing. "But they might miss a few of us if we split from the rest and took another trail to reach the site."

"Another trail?" Erika pressed, heart throbbing painfully in her chest. Could there really be another way?

Lukys gestured up the mountain. They'd been cutting across the hillside, making for the pass Romaine and Travis had returned from not long ago. "We've been following the easier passages through the hills," the Perfugian continued, "but what if we cut straight over the mountain?"

Glancing up the slope, Erika wondered if such a thing was even possible. These foothills were mere shadows of the Mountains that loomed beyond, but the slope Lukys had indicated was still steep, and covered in loose gravel. It would be a terrible, dangerous climb. The horses certainly could not pass that way. And even if they reached the top, there was no telling what else awaited. The way down might prove impassable.

She glanced at Romaine, waiting to see what the warrior would say, but Cara spoke up instead: "There is a path down the other side."

Erika's breath caught in her throat as she spun to face the woman. "Truly?" she gasped. "You've been that way before?"

Cara hesitated. Her eyes flickered in her face as she bit her lip. "I've seen it from afar," she said at last. "A path between the cliffs—steep, but passable. I think."

"Then we try it," Erika said, turning to Romaine.

The warrior looked back at her, eyes still hard, and she saw now his anger. He hated her for making him consider this option, for making them take this risk. She didn't care. They had a chance!

"Very well," he said, rising. "Let's be about it then." Turning, he cast his gaze over the column of recruits. "Travis, do you think you could find the way back to the trees?"

The man hesitated, but after a moment he nodded. "I think so."

"Good. You'll take the horses and lead the recruits back to the Illmoor. Leave everything behind you don't need and don't stop except for sleep; once the Tangata find your scent, you can be sure they won't. Once you reach the river, signal the other side. The forts all know to look for us. Don't wait; hopefully the Tangata don't notice our scent, but if they do, we're dead."

Travis hesitated, but after a moment he nodded. Drawing in a breath, Romaine turned to the other recruits.

"Lukys, Cara…" He paused, eyeing the Perfugians lined up across the hillside. The recruits shifted nervously on their feet. "Dale and Groner," he named two of the recruits Erika didn't recognise, "you're with us."

Erika was surprised when the two stepped forward immediately. Romaine had chosen well, but there was another problem. She swung on the Calafe.

"We need more," she said quickly. "To bring back what we find."

"No," Romaine rumbled. "You see that slope, those rocks? A single misplaced step could start a small avalanche. Six will make enough noise as it is; any more would doom us. If the Tangata have scouts out, we'll likely fail anyway. No, you'll have to make do with the six of us."

Erika swallowed, but it was clear there would be no arguing the point. She nodded, and Romaine turned to the others.

"We need to move quickly as well," he said, addressing those that would continue. "Empty out your packs. We'll bring two tents and enough food for three days. Rope, the Archivists tools, nothing more. Whatever space is left we'll need for these artefacts of the Archivists."

They were ready before Erika had finished processing his words. Still reeling from the sudden turn of events, she stepped from the saddle and found her legs trembling. Sucking in a breath, she recovered her knapsack, then looked at the slope again. Loose rocks stretched up at least 600 feet before disappearing over a lip. She swallowed. Could she truly climb that?

"Good luck." The scout, Travis, said from amongst those recruits who were to return.

"Same to you," Lukys replied, and they embraced.

Erika looked away again, feeling inexplicably guilty. Angrily, she forced the emotion aside. There was no room for sentimentality on this journey, not with the fate of humanity in the balance—not to mention the queen's expectations. Letting out a breath, she faced the Calafe warrior.

"Let's be off then," she said shortly. "I'd rather not still be standing here when night falls."

ॐ 25 ॐ

THE RECRUIT

I t was growing dark by the time Lukys and the others reached the top of the slope. Lukys, Cara and Romaine had taken the climb in their stride, but the other Perfugians had struggled, and at points the Archivist had needed their aid to continue. Without her horse, she did not complain about their slow pace at all now.

Thankfully the night was clear, the ground lit by the growing moon, and knowing time was short, they pressed on. High above the forests, ice lay in patches amongst the stones and a cold wind blew across the slope, cutting through even the heaviest of furs.

Romaine took the lead, twin-bladed axe hanging from his broad shoulders. Lukys and the other Perfugians carried spears and their shields strapped to their packs, while Cara had refused a weapon. The Archivist didn't seem to need any but her magic gauntlet.

The sight of the Calafe warrior standing tall in the darkness was reassuring, though Lukys couldn't quite banish the memory of Romaine sitting slumped beside the trail, defeated. The despair that had flickered in the man's eyes…

No.

He wouldn't think of that. Instead, Lukys turned his mind to the landscape. In the moonlight, stark cliffs rose around them, surfaces glistening with ice. Fortunately, the slope had led into a canyon between the rocks. The ground still continued higher as they walked, but more gently now, other than a few sections where jagged boulders blocked the way. In those places they were forced to climb, fingers seeking out cracks in the stone to pull themselves up.

They did their best to keep silent, but at times the very terrain seemed to be working against them. The smallest of rocks dislodged would send dozens of others careening down the slope, and with the canyon walls amplifying the sound, Lukys was sure the Tangata must hear them eventually. Already he was beginning to regret speaking up, though what other options had there been?

Thankfully, Romaine seemed confident that the beasts would not start off until closer to midnight. If they could cross the crest of the hill before then, they would be safe—unless the beasts picked up their trail.

Even so, Lukys couldn't help but jump at every tumbling rock, every shadow and whisper of movement from behind them. In the frigid darkness, it was easy to imagine the creatures stalking the group. The night was their world, after all. Lukys and his friends were only visitors.

He flicked glances at the Archivist as they climbed, wondering what drove the woman, why she had staked so much upon this mission. Did she truly think recovering the magic of the Gods was so important? She clenched and unclenched her fist as she walked, a faint light flickering from her gauntlet. Lukys shivered and looked away.

No, there had to be another way to defeat the Tangata. Surely using the magic of the Gods could only lead them down the same path as ages past, to a repetition of the mistakes that had caused the entire world to fall.

But it was not his place to make those decisions.

His boot caught on another rock and he suppressed a curse as it went scattering away. Thankfully no others were dislodged. It took a moment for him to realise the slope had changed. They were heading down. Movement came from nearby as Cara came along-side him.

"I hope this path of yours is close," he said.

Cara glanced at him, then up at the sky, as though she could read their position from the stars. Her lips pursed. "I don't know."

A sigh slipped from Lukys's lips. "Doesn't matter," he said, "I just hope the Archivist can make it."

Cara glanced back at where Erika was falling behind again. "She's stronger than she looks," she replied.

"You like her, don't you?" Lukys asked.

"She's different," the woman replied with a shrug, then grinned. "You all are."

Despite himself, Lukys smiled. He watched as Cara strode ahead. She moved with more confidence and grace than the rest of them combined, each step barely disturbing the loose rocks on which she strode. Long gone were the days when she'd clutched her broken arm to her chest. How long ago had that been now? No more than a month. The Calafe healed quickly.

They marched on, the ground growing steeper again, though now that they climbed downwards Lukys had to be careful again about where he put his feet. Every mistake sent rocks tumbling down the slope towards the others. The sharper their descent became, the more the danger grew, until finally they were forced to take turns moving down each stretch of the canyon.

Exhaustion weighed heavily on Lukys's shoulders as the night grew late. They stopped for a time to rest, though on the steep slope it was impossible to pitch the tents, and with the threat of the Tangata lurking in the background, they were soon moving again.

Eventually the moon dropped below the clifftops, plunging the canyon into darkness. A moment later, light flashed on the canyon floor as Erika raised her hand. Her gauntlet blazed a brilliant white as she took the lead, outstretched hand guiding the way.

Finally they found themselves standing atop a broad cliff, looking down upon a plateau some six hundred feet below. The Mountains of the Gods loomed overhead, their icy peaks lit by the first hint of dawn. Below, the plateau remained in darkness.

From where they stood, Lukys could see no hint of a path down the escarpment. Indeed, it looked almost sheer. But Cara was insistent, bidding them wait before starting off along the clifftop, her poise making the perilous walk look easy. She returned before long, and led them across to a narrow gap where a section of the mountain had broken away. The rubble left behind provided a steep but not quite sheer, way down to the plateau.

"After you, Calafe," Dale said softly, glancing nervously at Cara.

Her teeth flashed in the light of Erika's gauntlet as she grinned back. "Just try to keep up."

Lukys's heart lurched in his chest as she leapt from the edge. The others cried out, but to all of their surprise, she landed easily on the steep slope. Stones shifted beneath her weight but did not send her tumbling into the darkness. She slid several feet before coming to a stop at the edge of Erika's light. Her face was flushed as she looked back at them.

"Almost like flying," she said, grinning at them. "Are you coming?"

Everyone turned to look at the Archivist. She would need to go next, to light the way for the rest of them. Drawing in a breath, she followed Cara over the edge, making it look far more difficult than the young Calafe had. Rocks tumbled into the darkness with her every step, the sound of their fall echoing from the cliffs.

As Lukys started after her, he saw now why Romaine had insisted on so few. Even with just the six of them they were making far too much noise. Surely anyone—or anything—out on the plateau would hear the falling stones and investigate. At least the Tangata were behind them.

The light on the horizon grew as they continued down, the sun appearing slowly above the peaks, until finally Erika was able to dismiss her gauntlet's magic. Watching her as the glow died, Lukys wondered where the power came from. Sweat drenched the woman's face and she was pale in the dawn light, but that could easily be exhaustion from the night's climb.

As they neared the bottom, Lukys spotted movement out on the plateau. His heart palpitated, and a moment later he saw a dozen heads lift from the alpine tussock. Standing on four legs and covered in grey and orange wool, the strange long-necked creatures watched the group of humans descending towards the plateau. With their slow-blinking eyes and lazy smiles, they were apparently unconcerned.

"Guanaco," Romaine explained as they stopped on an outcropping of rock that gave them a place to sit. "They usually keep to the higher peaks. It was rare to see them, when we inhabited this land..." He trailed off, blue eyes on the distant creatures. "My people consider it good luck to cross the creatures on a journey."

Lukys shivered as he glanced at Romaine. It was easy to forget sometimes that this rugged, untouched land had once belonged to his people.

"They farm them, in the higher pastures of Flumeer," the Archivist said. Her voice seemed sad.

"Bad luck to cage a creature that has set eyes upon the Gods," was all Romaine said.

He rose and started off again. Now that they were close to the bottom, the way was easier and they made good time. Lukys kept one eye on the slope high above as they walked, seeking sign of anything that might be following them.

The earth was dry beneath his boots as he walked, the rocks stained scarlet and orange. Looking at the tussock growing upon the plateau, Lukys wondered how it survived, how anything could live in such a barren environment. Even the last of the snow and ice dried away as they reached the bottom and moved out onto the flat.

The Guanaco finally wandered away at their approach, making for the distant snow-capped peaks. A light breeze blew through the valley and drifted up the slope they had just descended. If the Tangata *had* followed their group, the creatures had their scent now.

"This is it," the Archivist whispered. She looked from the map clutched in her hand to the broad plateau. "It's here, somewhere. Waiting for me."

Lukys swallowed at the glint he caught in the woman's eyes, recalling his earlier assessment of Erika. Whatever the Archivist claimed, she hadn't come all this way just to save humanity. There was a reward in this for her, one that had driven her to risk near certain death.

Just get on with it, he thought to himself.

The sooner they found the ancient site, the sooner they could leave. He still feared the magic of the Gods, and what might happen when they stepped foot in such a sacred place. But the wrath of the Gods seemed an unlikely possibility compared to the ever-present threat of the Tangata.

Lukys flinched as a sudden, brilliant light swept across the plateau. For a second he thought their very presence there had somehow angered the Gods, before realising it was only the sun finally topping the last mountain peak. He glanced around sheepishly and was glad to see no one had noticed his reaction. Letting out a breath, he closed his eyes, basking in the warmth of a new day.

"We'll have to spread out." The Archivist's voice drew him back to their present danger. "Divide the plateau up into sections. Look for anything that looks unnatural, rock formations that are too smooth or horizontal, sections of ground that are too flat."

For once they did as the woman bid. There was no point in arguing, and she was right—they could cover more ground separately. It wasn't like they could fight the Tangata if they appeared anyway. In fact, being apart meant if one was attacked, the others might at least have a chance to escape.

Small consolation if Lukys was the one to be caught.

The alpine grass grew surprisingly tall here, not so high that it obscured their view of any approaching creatures, but enough that it made searching for unnatural rock formations difficult. Lukys could only see the ground within a few yards of where he stood. An hour passed as they made their slow way across the plateau, then another, until Lukys found he was watching the path they had taken down the mountain more than he was looking for the entrance.

If the Tangata had found their tracks, how long would it take—

"*No!*"

Lukys swung around as a scream carried across the tussock grass, high pitched and brimming with agony. Someone was dying, under attack…but how had the Tangata come upon them unnoticed?

The scream had come from Erika. She stood a dozen yards from him, face pale, twisted into a mask of horror. The scream came again, seemingly drawn from the depths of her soul, as though someone had taken a hot poker and stabbed it through her belly.

She stood alone.

Then suddenly she darted across the plateau—and disappeared.

THE WARRIOR

Romaine cursed as the Archivist started to run, then swore as she vanished, seemingly into the earth itself. He froze, trying to process what he'd seen. The tussock grew up tall here, obscuring the ground. Starting after her, he lifted the axe from his shoulders as he went. Weapon extended, he approached the area where the woman had vanished…

…and cursed again.

"Blasted woman!" he shouted, coming to a stop.

In front of him, the earth had been torn apart, exposed soil and broken rock cast in all directions. At its centre was a shaft of sheer rock, six by eight feet wide. A steel ladder disappeared into the darkness. The Archivist had already vanished into the black.

Shouts came from around him as the others approached. Romaine clutched his axe tight, cursing the Archivist with every expletive he knew. Had she lost her mind? It was clear the Tangata had discovered the site ahead of her. What if more were waiting below, left behind by the group they had seen the day before? There was no other explanation for her actions.

"How did the Tangata find it?" Lukys whispered as he staggered up to the hole.

"They're good at finding underground places," Romaine grunted.

It was true, the Tangata preferred these dark spaces—but there was no way they could have known this was here. Not unless somebody had told them…

"What do we do?" Cara murmured as she approached.

"We get The Fall out of here," Dale croaked, his face pale.

Ignoring them, Romaine crouched beside the broken earth. The Tangata had made a mess of the site around the shaft, trampling back and forwards through the dirt. There was no way of knowing their numbers.

"Nobody move," he murmured as the last recruit, Groner, arrived.

A glare ensured they would obey. Romaine stepped carefully away from the entrance and circled the exposed area. It didn't take long to locate the path the Tangata had taken to reach the site—a broad stretch of tussock had been trampled beneath their boots. There he knelt again, trying to determine how many had passed through. Fresh dirt had been trodden into the flattened grass, confirming his suspicions that the group had left. There was still no telling whether any remained.

Romaine sat back on his haunches. "They left," he said, more to himself than the others. "It was probably the group we encountered. But…why would they leave?"

"Erika needs our help." Cara interrupted his musings. "She's… all alone down there."

"That was her choice," Lukys replied.

"The Tangata are gone," she replied, meeting each of their eyes.

Romaine let out a sigh, then nodded. Coming to his feet, he marched back to where the others waited, shields now clutched in hand, spears pointed at the silent shaft.

"Stand down," he grunted, gesturing over his shoulder at the tracks. "The Tangata already left. Come on, we'd better go fetch the woman."

The others exhaled loudly as they lowered their weapons, the tension that had built amongst them draining away. Lukys shook his head, face paler than normal as he turned to Romaine.

"Do we have to?"

Romaine forced a laugh but did not reply. Sheathing his axe, he stepped past the others and approached the shaft. Despite his reassurances, he was not sure what might wait for them in the dark.

None of this made sense. *How* had the Tangata known to come here?

A faint glow was visible far below—the Archivist's gauntlet. He hoped.

"Dale, the torches," he said softly.

The recruit handed his spear to Groner and swung the pack from his back. He searched inside for a moment before coming back out with the torch. Once it was lit, he held it out for Romaine.

Drawing in a breath, Romaine took one last look at the sun. Then he grasped the flaming torch and swung over the side of the shaft. An icy cold wrapped around him as he started down the ladder. Holding the torch made the task difficult, but it was not his first time climbing one-handed.

Rung by rung, he made his way down into the depths of the earth. With the flames shining in his eyes, he could no longer make out Erika's light, while those who came after him blacked out the surface. Soon there was only the darkness, only stone walls pressing in, the cold steel beneath his fingers. It seemed the shaft must go on and on, all the way down to the source of the world.

Until finally, it ended.

The sound of his boot striking stone seemed impossibly loud in the darkness. Romaine grunted, surprised to find solid earth rather than another rung. Holding the torch away from himself, he checked to see whether he had truly reached the bottom.

Firelight illuminated a wide chamber, its walls, ceilings and floor all carved from the same plain grey stone of the shaft. There was something abnormal about that stone, an unnatural smoothness and lack of patterns within the rock, as though it had been formed by magic rather than ordinary forces.

His light also illuminated three tunnels leading from the chamber. A heavy layer of dust covered the ground, revealing the footprints of those who had passed before. There were dozens, though all had taken the same tunnel, and returned from the same direction. It seemed the Tangata had known where they were going.

The Archivist had vanished, though the faintest glow revealed she'd followed the same path as the creatures. Did she realise the Tangata had left, or was she simply insane? Either way, Romaine was done with the woman's games. She had endangered everyone by coming down here.

Romaine should never have contemplated this plan. He should have ignored her pleas and bound her in chains, carried her all the way to the Illmoor, if necessary. Anything but this mad plan.

Scuffling noises came from above and Romaine stepped away from the shaft as the others dropped into the chamber—first Dale, then Lukys and Cara, with Groner bringing up the rear. They had tied their spears to their packs with strips of rope, and quickly set about freeing them. Drawing his axe again, Romaine moved into the mouth of the main tunnel to see what waited for them.

Shadows danced in the flickering light. This was no place for living things. Abandoned by the Gods and the ancient humans who had once worked alongside them; now it was home only to the dead.

Or so Romaine prayed.

They started down the strange tunnel, surrounded by those smooth walls, following the footprints of the creatures who sought to kill them. Romaine tried to count their numbers, but the prints criss-crossed and overlaid one another. Though he did notice those leading back towards the entrance were less defined, the strides longer. Had the creatures left in a rush?

A million other questions leapt at him, but there were no answers. They could not return without the Archivist. Romaine had no plans to be labelled a mutineer

Ahead the tunnel split in two, but again the footprints only led in one direction. The glow of the Archivists light still shone, brighter now. They were closing the distance. Axe still held in hand, Romaine picked up the pace.

This new tunnel was lined with doorways, seemingly cut from the strange stone itself, though inside most were plain and empty. These the Tangata had ignored, their attention seemingly fixed on some distant goal.

A few, though, the creatures had entered. In these chambers, Romaine was surprised to find the remains of ancient devices scattered about the room, objects of metal and precious glass and other unidentifiable materials, all smashed to pieces against the unforgiving floor.

"What The Fall?" Lukys whispered, stepping up beside him.

Romaine shook his head. "Let's find the Archivist," he said. "Nothing about this place make sense."

They continued. The deeper they ventured, the more stale the air became, the harder to breathe. There was a dryness to it, a faint sweetness too, though amongst the other scents it seemed foul, like a field of flowers gone rotten. The light ahead continued to grow, vanishing at times as the Archivist disappeared into different chambers. Romaine did not call out. He was sure the Tangata must have departed now...

...so why did he still feel they were not alone?

He did not have long to wait for the answer. As they passed around a bend in the tunnel, a terrible smell touched their nostrils. They didn't encounter the source until several doorways further down the tunnel. Within the chamber, Romaine could see liquid and broken glass covering the floor—and something else. White flesh reflected the light of the torch. The stench was so strong Romaine would have done anything not to enter. But he had to know.

Taking a cloth from his pocket, he held it to his nose and stepped inside. Lukys and Cara followed, while the others remained without. Holding the torch high, Romaine suppressed a shudder.

Three naked bodies lay on the floor, human in form, though so far gone as to be almost unrecognisable. Their flesh was like wax, twisted, melted, and strange lumps grew from their arms and legs and backs.

Glass crunched beneath his boots as he moved closer, heart pounding in his ears. Three circular platforms of solid steel stood in the centre of the chamber, just an inch from the ground. Jagged pieces of glass still stuck out from the edges.

"They were...preserved," Lukys said quietly. "The glass must have formed cylinders, with the liquid and bodies inside, some chymical..." he hesitated. "Why would the Tangata break them?"

"Death," Cara whispered, eyes wide, face pale.

Lukys looked at her sharply, as though she had said something profound. Ignoring them, Romaine held his breath and knelt beside one of the bodies. Carefully, he lifted its eyelids. Even in its decomposing state, he could see the iris had been grey.

"Tangata," he croaked, rising and backing away.

"The original traitors," Dale's voice came from the doorway.

"Then why are they still here?" Lukys asked.

Romaine shook his head. "I don't care." He retreated to the doorway. "Let's find the Archivist, *now*."

"What did the Tangata come here for?" Lukys whispered as they started down the corridor again. Erika's light had drawn further away while they'd been stopped.

"We…should leave this place," Cara said, voice so low Romaine hardly heard her.

He glanced at her. "What about Erika?"

Her lip trembled as she stared back. For a moment he thought she was going to bolt, but instead she nodded, resolve returning to her eyes.

They passed more chambers, most—thankfully—empty. In a few, they found other broken things, and in one, two empty cylinders of glass. Romaine paused in the doorway of this one, shocked at their size. Not even the crafters in New Nihelm, once famed for their glassblowing, could have managed anything half as large.

Finally the light ahead grew still. It seemed the Archivist had reached the end of the tunnel. They picked up their pace once more, eager to find the woman and begone from that terrible place.

Crash.

Romaine flinched as the sound of something breaking carried down the tunnel. He glanced at the others, then they were running, racing towards the soft glow ahead. The light quickly grew brighter, until it lit the hallway ahead of them, seemingly too bright for the Archivist's gauntlet. Looking ahead, Romaine saw the source: a brilliant white emerging from one of chambers.

He staggered to a stop in the entrance, axe thrust out ahead of him, torch clutched tight, though it was no longer needed. The light was blinding, and he squinted into the chamber, trying to see what waited. Slowly the room took shape.

Erika stood a few feet away, head bowed and arms limp at her side. No light came from her gauntlet—instead, it emerged from a dozen crystals lining the wall. Romaine shuddered at the magic, but the other contents of the chamber were far more pressing. He stepped up beside the Archivist, scanning the bodies that lay nearby for signs of life.

Unlike before, these were no ancient, persevered things. Men and women in plain-spun clothes lay scattered about the floor, throats torn out, limbs separated from bodies. Blood pooled around them and eyes stared sightlessly into the brilliant light of the crystals.

Grey eyes.

A shudder ran down Romaine's spine as he looked on the dead Tangata. Five of them. Impossible. What could possibly have done this to *five* Tangata?

His eyes were drawn to the rear of the room. Two more of those strange massive cylinders had stood there, and these too had been shattered by the Tangata. Except here, *light* shone from crystals set into the steel bases, the same as those on the wall.

Somehow, the magic of the Gods remained in this room, indifferent to the countless passage of centuries.

Light glinted from the liquid spilled across the stone, but Romaine's heart lurched in his chest as he realised something was missing.

The bodies. Where are the bodies from the broken cylinders?

"We need to *go*," came Cara's voice from the doorway, high-pitched, panicked. Ready to flee.

Romaine nodded, reaching for the Archivist.

"They were looking for them," Erika whispered, still staring at the dead Tangata. "How did they know they were here?"

"Archivist—" Romaine cut off as a scream came from the corridor.

Lukys, Cara and Dale scrambled into the chamber, then spun to face the doorway, spears raised. Groner followed them—then crumpled to the ground, blood seeping from a terrible wound in the back of his skull.

An unfamiliar stepped into the light. Fluid dripped from the things naked body as it moved into the chamber. Another followed, making a pair, one male, the other female.

Grey eyes swept the room, terrifying, mad, intelligent.

Tangata.

Or something else?

Romaine hefted his axe and stepped towards the creatures. Shards of glass crunched beneath his boots as he sought the rage that had saved him so many times, that had given him the strength to defeat so many of these creatures. For once it did not come.

He glanced at the bodies on the floor. Dead Tangata. Nothing could have killed so many, not in such brutal fashion. At least, nothing living.

Looking at the creatures in the doorway once more, he saw them for what they were. Not Tangata, but something new—or very, very old.

The originals; those ancients who had betrayed the Gods to gain their power.

Preserved here, hidden away from the world, asleep, waiting.

A terrible fear touched Romaine as he faced the beasts. They could not be allowed to leave this place. If they could so easily destroy the Tangata, nothing would stop them if they escaped into the world.

With a roar, Romaine rushed them, axe raised to slice the beasts in half—

Breath exploded between Romaine's teeth as a fist struck him like a club to the chest. Stars flickering across his vision, he staggered backwards, folded in two, unable to breathe. He looked up to find the male of the pair standing over him. He hadn't even seen it move.

Cries came from the others as they reacted, Dale leaping back, Lukys thrusting out with his spear, Erika raising her magic gauntlet.

The female was faster than all of them. Lukys was thrown aside, spear snapped in two, and Dale crumpled, his weapon clattering to the ground. Light flashed from the Archivist's gauntlet—then the beast was upon her. A scream echoed from the walls as a blow sent the woman tumbling backwards across the chamber.

No, no, no!

Romaine strained to recover his breath; it felt as though he were inhaling through a swamp reed. Fighting through the pain, he struggled to straighten, to fall into a fighting stance, to lift his axe. The creatures moved so fast, it couldn't be possible, couldn't be…

Two pairs of grey eyes turned to watch him. He gasped as the male suddenly came face-to-face with him, then tried to swing his blade. A hand caught the shaft, halting the blow as one might bat

aside a fly. Moans came from around the room as the others struggled to recover, but in that moment, Romaine saw the truth.

None of them were leaving this place alive.

The knowledge granted him a strange sense of calm. After all
this time evading death, finally it had come for him. There was no
fighting it this time. These creatures were a force of nature, born of
the Gods themselves, beyond any mortal man to resist. He had only
to open his arms and embrace his fate…

No.

Romaine tensed, pushing back against the creature's strength. If
he was to die, he would take this monster with him. He could feel
the creature resisting, its power unmatched, but…

Romaine relaxed, then swung out with his spare hand, aiming a
blow for the creature's throat. His change of tact threw the thing
off-balance, giving him an opening—

A scream tore from Romaine's throat as pain erupted from his
arm. He staggered back, gaping at the blood now spurting from his
wrist. His left hand was…gone. The axe slid from his still-working
hand and struck the ground with a *clang.*

His hand was gone!

He stared at his foe in horror.

The monster smiled.

❧ 27 ❧

THE RECRUIT

Danger, *death, death!*

The words pounded on the inside of Lukys's skull like a drum, robbing him of thought, of action. He watched in sheer terror as Romaine stood alone against the Tangata, so overwhelmed he could not move, not even when the female leapt at him, splintering his spear in two.

Even to his inexperienced eye, he knew there was something different about these two. The dead Tangata lay all around, and he knew instinctively they'd been killed by the creatures now battling against Romaine. Why they would do such a thing he could not say, but he knew now why Perfugian legends warned against disturbing these ancient places.

The Gods may have departed, but their magic, their creations, remained.

And they were terrible.

Lukys gaped as his mentor staggered back from the monster, his left hand…*gone!* A groan came from Romaine as the axe slipped from his fingers and he clutched at the severed limb, all the fight gone from him. Laughter whispered from the narrow walls as the monster stepped after him.

Rage ignited in Lukys's chest. He still held his shattered spear. Tossing aside the useless end, he took a two-handed grip of what remained to him, steel tip aimed at the monster's chest.

"All of us together!" Lukys bellowed, trying to bring their broken remnants together. "Like Romaine taught us!"

A flicker of shadow, air hissing between his teeth—then pain.

Lukys belatedly crumpled in two as the female attacked, her fist slamming into his stomach. Unable to breathe, he crumpled to the stone, vision flickering. Too late he realised they'd never stood a chance, that these…things had only been toying with them.

A grin twisted the male's face as it picked up the fallen spear. Terrible silver eyes examined the weapon, then turned on Lukys. It lifted the blade…

And disappeared.

Or rather, the creature was *flung* across the room by a tempest of copper hair and grey furs.

Lukys watched in horror as Cara and the male struck the ground and rolled. Steel glinted in his friend's hands, but a dagger was no match for these things, no match for their strength—

Blood spurted across the stones as Cara leapt to her feet, her knife left behind, impaled in the male's throat. It thrashed against the floor, hands clutched desperately at the wound, but there was no stemming the gushing of blood and in seconds it grew limp, lying still amidst the broken glass and swirling liquids.

Across the room, the female stared at its mate for a long moment, silver eyes wide, registering disbelief. Then they narrowed, and a terrible growl echoed from its throat. The pounding began again in Lukys's skull as it faced Cara, though now it seemed there were twin beats…

Death, life. Death, life. Death, life.

"Cara, run—" Lukys tried to warn her, but his words came too late.

Faster than his eyes could track, the beast charged at his friend, teeth bared, naked limbs flashing, roars echoing in the narrow chambers.

Cara leapt to meet it.

Lukys's fear gave way to shock as he watched, stunned, as the two fought their way across the room. It…wasn't possible, but Cara matched the beast blow for blow, each movement little more than a blur. No human could move so fast—not even the Tangata were as quick.

Snarls filled the chamber as the two exchanged strikes, inhuman, wild cries echoing from the ceilings. Staring at the two, Lukys tried to reconcile the woman he had known these last weeks, his friend, with the creature that stood before him now. Blood covered her face and clothing, so that she seemed more animalistic than even the beast she had fought.

Lukys winced as a blow caught Cara in the shoulder, sending her backwards, but he made no move to help her. Whatever was happening…he couldn't understand what was going on, how his friend had transformed. What they were seeing, it was not possible.

Cara straightened with a snarl, auburn hair tangled, obscuring her face. The ancient Tangata came at her again, but this time Cara was quicker, her fist colliding with the female's head, sending it whipping backwards.

Deathlife, deathlife, deathlife.

Straining to think through the chaos, Lukys's eyes swept the room. Dale was down on one knee. He still clutched a spear, but his face was pale, eyes wide as he watched the two creatures circle one another. A body slumped nearby was the Archivist, but whether she was unconscious or dead, her magic could not help them against this thing.

Then there was Romaine.

The axeman had managed to regain his feet, though he'd left the massive axe on the floor beside him. The colour had left his tanned features. Blood stained the floor around the Calafe—a lot of blood. The sight shook Lukys from his daze, and he darted to the axeman's side

"Romaine," he said, grasping the man's shoulder.

The axeman glanced at him, but his eyes showed no sign of recognition. "Can't let them leave," he was muttering beneath his breath.

Lukys cursed. At least the Calafe had retained enough sense to clutch a rag to his wound—but a glance at the severed limb told Lukys it would need more than that to stem the bleeding. Quickly, he dragged the belt from his trousers and pulled it tight around the axeman's forearm. Romaine hardly seemed to register the makeshift tourniquet. Like everyone else, his eyes were fixed on the battle.

Death, death, death.

A scream rang from the walls and Lukys spun in time to see Cara catch her foe by the arm. Blood flowed as she wrenched, sending the creature to its knees. An answering shriek echoed from the walls, but it ended in a gurgle as Cara's fingers lashed out, tearing through flesh and cartilage and bone.

The creature fell to the floor, dead beside its mate.

Silence fell like a blanket over the chamber as Lukys and the others stared at the body, watching as the blood pulsing from its wounds slowed, then ceased. As one, they turned their gaze on Cara.

The grey eyes of a Tangata stared back at them, mad, enraged. Despite everything he'd seen, Lukys flinched. It was as though Cara herself had reached into his chest and wrenched out his heart.

Death, death, death.

"You're one of them," he whispered, eyes burning.

They had been betrayed. Somehow, the Tangata had created one who could walk amongst humans without being noticed, a Tangata without their telltale eyes. One who could speak, who could pretend, who could even adapt their mannerisms. But now she had revealed herself...

"Lukys, no…" Cara whispered.

She blinked, and the animal vanished, the grey receding from her irises, replaced by the usual amber. In seconds, it was no longer a Tangata who stood before them, but the human he had known all these weeks, the sweet young woman he had met on the walls of Fogmore. She stared at him, eyes wide and filled with fear. There was no sign of the fury of just moments before.

"Yes."

Somehow Romaine had moved without Lukys's notice. The Calafe now stood near the entrance to the chamber. Shoulders drooping, face grey from lost blood, he held his axe before him like a sword. Pain shone from his eyes, and though blood still seeped from his severed hand, Lukys sensed it was the agony of betrayal he saw.

"Romaine," Cara whispered, holding out a hand. "Your hand—"

"You're one of them," the axeman repeated Lukys's earlier words. He staggered forward, though it seemed his legs could hardly hold his weight now. "You've betrayed us…why?"

Cara retreated from Romaine, shaking her head. "No, no, no," she whispered as she looked this way and that, seeking to escape. Her eyes met Lukys's, and he could almost hear her pleading.

Help me, Lukys!

Lukys was still trying to process what he'd seen. Cara had… saved them…but she was one of the Tangata…why would she help them? His eyes were drawn to the clothed bodies, those of the modern Tangata. A cold hand gripped his heart. She had avenged them, her fellow Tangata, those who had fallen earlier to these creatures.

He clenched his fists, steeling himself against pity. She had deceived them all, had tricked them, played them as fools for weeks. This was only another manipulation, a testing on their emotions, to try and recover her act. Romaine had already seen it. No, they couldn't afford mercy, not now, not after seeing the power this new Tangata held in her hands. If they could stop her…

"Dale, get up," Lukys hissed, stepping sideways to place Cara in the middle of the three of them. His foot brushed the broken spear and he swept it into his hands.

Across the room, Dale came slowly to his feet. His face registered shock rather than pain. He hadn't known Cara as they had, wouldn't feel the same depth of betrayal. Lukys and Romaine and Travis had opened themselves to her, to the monster that lurked in their midst. Spear held extended, Dale crept closer to the Tangatan traitor.

"Please," Cara murmured, swinging to Romaine again. "I never wanted to hurt anyone."

The blood covering her heavy coat said otherwise. Lukys held his broken weapon higher, though it seemed inadequate after witnessing Cara's disposal of the two creatures. He tightened his grip. It would be enough. It had to be.

"Lukys…" She tried him again. Tears shone in her amber eyes as she extended a hand. "Please, you know…"

Please, please, please.

The sight of her tears froze Lukys in place. Blood pounded in his ears as their eyes locked, and he could almost hear, could almost believe….

No, no, no.

The scraping of leather against stone gave Romaine away. Spinning, Cara leapt back from the Calafe as his axe swept down, narrowly avoiding the terrible blades. A scream echoed from the walls—not of rage, but grief.

"Romaine!" Cara cried, but the Calafe warrior was beyond listening.

Teeth bared, eyes shimmering, axe clenched in his one good hand, he advanced. Lukys watched on, unable to move. In his mind, he saw again the creatures attacking, the awful battle, the blood…

The broken spear shook in his hand as he lifted it, then lowered it once more, trapped in a cycle of indecision.

"You don't have to be afraid," Cara gasped, hands raised to Romaine. "Please, I—"

"Enough!" Romaine bellowed.

The razor tips of his axe came up, the weapon flashing for Cara's skull. Again she leapt back, and Romaine staggered. Agony contorted his face and Lukys could hardly believe the man stayed on his feet. Any normal man would have passed out from the pain, let alone loss of blood.

Please, please, please.

Lukys stifled a moan and raised a hand to his forehead. His skull ached as though someone were banging on it with a club. Another roar drew his attention back to the conflict as Dale tried a clumsy thrust with his spear. Cara evaded it easily, but…

She was standing directly before Lukys now. Back turned, she didn't seem to remember he was there…or hadn't realised her evasion had brought her so close.

He swallowed, the spear trembling in his fingers. Across the room, Romaine met his eyes. Axe raised, the Calafe started forward again, drawing Cara's attention.

Lukys stared at Cara's back, at her unprotected spine. He imagined driving the point of his spear through that soft flesh, imagined hearing his friend's final cries, the last breath rattling from her chest…

She's not your friend!

There was no doubt. He had seen her, had seen those horrible grey eyes, sensed the violence in her soul. She was one of them, one of the Tangata, living amongst them, a spy, a traitor. A dangerous new breed, a monster that must be destroyed.

So why did this seem so wrong?

Please!

Lukys's heart throbbed. He had to act now. Cara was so close, he could have reached out and touched her, though she hated that.

Why?

It seemed an odd phobia, for one of *them*.

He shook himself. There was no time for doubt. Again he met Romaine's eyes. Silently he lifted the broken spear.

And brought it down on the back of Cara's skull.

28

THE ARCHIVIST

Erika sat watching as the light slowly grew between the distant peaks. Mist formed in front of her face each time she exhaled, and the air was so cold it hurt just to breathe. Her head ached from the blow she had received in the caverns and it still hurt to walk on her left leg.

She hardly cared.

The battle was two days past now. She could remember only flashes. A contorted face. Grey eyes in the darkness. A flash of white. Agony.

Then staggering through an endless tunnel, supported by a faceless man in blue. Climbing, hand over hand, up and up, metal rungs —then rocks. Feet slipping in gravel.

Sleep.

The first she'd truly wakened was the next day, when the sun had found her exposed on the mountainside. That had been yesterday morning.

Watching the sun rise now, she lifted her hand and squeezed. Light ignited between her fingers. Just a few days ago, the sight had given her a thrill, filled her with a feeling of power. Today, it did nothing to shift her despair.

Down in that darkness, her magic had proven useless. Before the might of the Gods, she had been powerless, knocked unconscious before she'd ever had a chance to use the power.

Worse still, she had failed.

Lukys was leading them back towards Flumeer, back to the rest of their regiment and the safety of the Illmoor. But what did that matter to Erika? Once again, her expedition had proven fruitless. The queen had warned of the consequences if she returned empty-handed…

If only she had reached the tunnels before the Tangata. Who knew what priceless artefacts the creatures had destroyed in their rage? No, that had not been rage, but a methodical destruction. Her Archivist's mind wanted to know why. But apparently not even the Tangata had expected to find those ancient monsters…

Erika shuddered, her mind recoiling from that memory. It was a relief when the images faded back into darkness, though the fuzziness of her thoughts could not hide the truth from her. She was ruined, betrayed yet again.

Her eyes were drawn to where the treacherous spy lay. She was bound hand and foot by heavy rope, her mouth gagged in case she tried to call for help. Dale also sat nearby for good measure, their one good spear at the ready. Erika still wasn't sure why they'd kept her alive. Lukys had apparently struck her hard in the head with the blunt end of his spear, then stopped Romaine from slaying her where she lay.

He thought they needed to know how the Tangata had learned to speak, and whether there were others.

Erika didn't care.

Movement came from the shadow of a nearby boulder, but it was only Romaine. He blinked as the brightness of the rising sun touched his face, then rolled over to present his back to the light.

Erika shivered as she glimpsed his stump. It was swathed in cloth, but she'd seen the ruin the creature had left of it the night before, when Lukys had changed the bandages. They'd used the burning torch to cauterise it, down there in the darkness. It had stopped the bleeding and saved the man's life.

Not that the warrior seemed interested in living any longer. Whether it was the loss of his hand, or the girl's betrayal, Romaine had hardly spoken a word since leaving the caverns. His depression made Erika seem joyful by comparison; it was as though his entire world had ended down there in the darkness.

Soon the others began to stir, first Lukys, then Dale, and finally Cara. The woman—no, the beast—had obeyed their every instruction since awakening, though Erika often glimpsed tears in the thing's eyes as they walked. If Cara thought her act would soften their hearts, she was sorely mistaken.

Romaine was last to rise. They had lost many of their possessions in the caverns, including most of their food. They had eaten the last of their supplies the night before. The Calafe started off without saying a word, leaving the rest of them standing there in silence.

"He'll be okay," Lukys said finally, glancing at the others. Erika and Dale said nothing, and after a moment, Lukys held his hand out to the other recruit. "Pass the spear," he murmured, "I'll guard her through the morning."

They started off, though the going was slow with Cara between them. The rope tying her legs was long enough that she could walk in short steps, though if she tried to run it would quickly become entangled. On the uneven rocks, it caught frequently anyway, sending her stumbling forward until she recovered or fell. With her arms bound behind her back, she often ended up on her face.

Even so, she did not struggle or say a word as the day progressed. Lukys followed behind her, spear held ready to run her through if she tried to escape. Exhaustion hung over them like a shroud, but at least the snow had held off, and soon they were back amongst the trees. The only hope that kept them going was the thought of reaching the Illmoor, of the hot food and safety that awaited them on the other side.

Erika paid little attention to her surroundings as they marched. Despite her hunger, despite her haste in the day's past, she cared little for whether they reached the camp or not. What did it matter whether she died out here, or by the queen's hand back in the capital? That day in the throne room seemed an age ago now; even that last night in Fogmore, spent enraged at the general's deceit, was a distant memory.

Anger touched her again. Could this venture have ended differently had she been accompanied by *true* soldiers? If she'd delayed, waiting for orders from the queen for Curtis to provide her with better men?

Such folly.

Maybe if Lukys and Dale—the only ones lucid after the attack —had allowed them to linger in the caverns, Erika might have found something that had survived the Tangata's methodical destruction. But by the time she'd recovered her wits, they'd already been far away.

They reached the abandoned village as the sun was setting, though walking at the rear of the group, Erika didn't realise until she saw the first of the cottages. The sight came as a relief—at least they might be able to risk a fire, even if there was nothing left to eat. And it meant there was less than a day's walk to the Illmoor.

Then she saw the bodies.

A fiery rope looped its way around her stomach. She staggered, seeing first one, then another, then…more. Choking, she stumbled on, igniting the light of her gauntlet, ready to strike. A shadow shifted in the darkness and she cried out, lifting her fist. The light illuminated Lukys's face and she sagged, the fight fleeing her in a rush.

"Lukys!" she gasped. "What happened here?"

"The Tangata," Lukys said, his voice cold, face registering no emotion. These had been his friends, but the past two days had taken something from all of them, robbed them of their innocence. "Come, this way."

Erika did as she was bid, too tired to resist, to ask questions. Bodies lay scattered in the path and alleyways between the buildings. In the growing dark, Erika could see no sign of their wounds. They might have been sleeping, had it not been for the awful stillness that lay over the place.

Lukys led her through the village to one of the cottages—the one she'd slept in, Erika recalled. Within they found Romaine slumped against the wall, Dale standing alongside him. Cara had been banished to the corner, her bonds tightened so she could not so much as stand. Erika clenched her fist at the sight of the woman, struggling to contain her rage.

"What happened here?" she asked again.

The Calafe said nothing, only sat staring at the floor. Shivering, Erika turned to the Perfugians.

"The Tangata caught them," Dale whispered. His eyes were haunted, the tip of his spear trembling.

Lukys paced the cottage, glancing from Dale to Romaine. "They're not all here," he muttered. "There's only…a dozen. I can't find Travis. Tomorrow, we'll search for tracks."

"They're gone," Romaine croaked, though he did not look up. Blood showed on his bandages but no one had moved to change them yet.

"We don't know that," Lukys said resolutely, crouching alongside the axeman.

"*They're gone!*" Romaine screamed. He lurched to his feet and Lukys flinched away. But Romaine ignored the recruit and staggered towards Cara. "You killed them all!"

The woman, the creature, Cara, did not move. She lay staring up at Romaine, helpless before his rage. Slowly she shook her head.

"It wasn't me, Romaine," she croaked, voice breaking. "Please, you have to belie—"

Her plea was cut short as Romaine slammed a boot into her stomach. Crying out, she curled into a ball, though with her arms bound behind her back, she had no way of protecting herself. The warrior drew back, preparing to throw another kick, but Lukys stepped between the axeman and the prisoner.

"*Romaine,*" he hissed, hands extended, "that's enough."

Erika raised an eyebrow at the recruit's gall. Despite his lost hand, Romaine stood head and shoulders above the Perfugian. In a moment of passion, he might have struck Lukys down, but instead the Calafe hesitated, staring at the man before him. Lukys looked back, open grief—and anger—shining from his eyes.

"My friends are *not* gone, Romaine," he hissed, though even to Erika it seemed a plea. "Travis, the others, they're alive. They're out there somewhere, either taken or on the run. I will *not* give up on them."

Silence answered the recruit's words, until finally Romaine shook his head. "Perhaps if they fled towards the river…" He trailed off, eyes distant, as though his mind was someplace else. "But even if they made the Illmoor…will the general send a ship? With so many Tangata in the area, they would risk being ambushed, overrun."

"You're saying we may be trapped here," Erika whispered.

Silence fell over the group as each contemplated their likely fate. Erika's thoughts turned once again to her failure. She couldn't understand how the Tangata had even known the site was there. It had lain undiscovered for hundreds of years; yet the beasts had reached it just a day ahead of them. Surely that could not be coincidence.

Her eyes were drawn to where Cara lay. The beast had seen the map, had known the location of the site. But Cara had been with them night and day. Could she possess some other way of communicating with the other Tangata?

Slowly Erika rose to her feet. It was past time their prisoner answered some questions.

"You betrayed us," she said, stepping towards the inert creature. "Somehow, you alerted your brethren to our destination."

Cara didn't respond, only lay looking up at her, amber eyes shining in the light of her gauntlet…

…Erika paused, glancing at her hand. The magic had ignited once more, unbidden. Her eyes were drawn back to the prisoner. Rage throbbed in her skull, mixing with the pain of her injuries. She didn't know how, but she *knew* the beast had betrayed the location of the site to the Tangata. How she longed to hear the treacherous creature scream.

A growl built in Erika's throat and before the others could react, she lifted the gauntleted fist and opened her hand. Light flashed as the magic responded. A scream tore from the traitor as light spilt from Erika's fingers, though a second later it was silenced. Mouth still stretched wide, Cara arced against the ground, unable to breathe, to so much as cry out as the power of the Gods claimed her. Erika may have found herself useless in the caverns beneath the earth, but she could at least still do this, could still take her revenge.

Other than the unnatural light, there was no visible sign that the gauntlet did anything. But its effect on the traitor was clear. Veins stood out on Cara's neck as she strained against her bindings, but even she apparently had her limits—or perhaps the magic stole away her strength.

The tiniest of squeaks came from the girl as Erika stepped closer, bathing Cara in the light of her gauntlet, determined to see her pain, to drink upon her agony. Blood began to run from the girl's nose and her eyes bulged. Romaine stood nearby, but the axeman made no move to stop Erika, only watched on, eyes dark even in the light of the gauntlet.

Then a hand grabbed Erika by the arm and pulled her back. The light from her gauntlet went out. She spun, snarling as she found Lukys standing behind her. A sob came from the corner as Cara collapsed against the dirt.

"Why did you stop me?" Erika snarled, raising her fist. She kept it clenched, the power controlled, though it would be so easy…

"I will *not* see her tortured," Lukys said, eyes shining.

"She betrayed us, doomed us all!" Erika shot back. "She deserves it."

"Maybe," Lukys said. His shoulders slumped and for a second, he seemed to hesitate. Then he shook his head. "No, I won't become like them."

"We should kill her," Romaine murmured.

Erika glanced at the warrior, surprised by the suggestion. The man stood over Cara, staring down at her. A knife had appeared in his hand.

"Romaine, don't…" Lukys murmured.

The Calafe warrior glanced at the recruit, then back at Cara. "She's dangerous."

"She may be our only bargaining chip," the recruit replied. "If we cannot evade the Tangata. And she has information. We need to know more about…what she is."

For a long moment, it seemed the Calafe wouldn't listen. But finally he nodded. Retreating to the side of the cottage, he slumped to the ground and leaned against the wall. Silence fell once more between them, though soft sobs still came from the corner. Erika clenched and unclenched her fist, still feeling the need to unleash her anger, her rage. But she found no support in the eyes of Dale or Romaine; it seemed Lukys had won the argument for now. Slowly she relaxed, and a wave of exhaustion swept over her.

"Why do you hate them so much?"

Erika started as Cara's voice whispered through the cottage. The four of them turned to stare at the captive, but Cara had eyes only for Romaine. At first, it seemed the warrior had not heard her words, but finally his head lifted, blue eyes glinting as they fixed on the creature who had betrayed them.

"You took everything from me," Romaine whispered.

Erika glanced at the others, but no one moved to silence the traitor, and voice breaking, Cara spoke again:

"I'm sorry they took Calafe from you."

"Calafe?" Romaine asked, his voice growing bitter. "What do I care for *Calafe*? Our kingdoms are a falsehood, a lie created to unite us against one another, so the people will not question their rulers. No, I hated you long before our king fell in the south."

Erika flinched at the mention of that first, terrible battle ten years before. How long had it been…?

"Then *why*?" Cara interrupted her thoughts.

The room was silent now, all eyes fixed on the Calafe. Erika found herself holding her breath as she watched the broken man, and it seemed the room grew a little darker, as though the moon itself hid from his pain.

"I had a cottage like this once," Romaine murmured. His eyes had a distant look; he didn't seem to be talking to anyone now. "In the southern forests. Small, far from the city, safe. A peaceful place built by my wife and I, to raise our son." His eyes flickered, focusing on Cara. "Until you took them from me."

The moment stretched out as they watched the man that had carried them so far. Then Lukys stepped forward and crouched beside him. "I never knew," the recruit murmured, placing a hand on the warrior's shoulder. "Romaine, I'm so sorry."

"Now you understand," the Calafe whispered, eyes flickering back to where Cara lay. "What is a kingdom, beside family, beside friends, beside the people we love?" He trailed off, his Adam's apple bobbing. "When the Tangata broke the truce, when they first invaded southern Calafe…" His eyes closed, the lines on his face growing deeper. "They took everything, left me with nothing but a hole, a void in my soul that I can never fill."

Erika shivered. His story sounded all too familiar, though for her…it had been her father the Tangata had slain. Left with nothing, her mother had fled back to her homeland, before the true war came.

Romaine's voice broke as he continued: "I would do anything

for another day with them—one more hour," he continued, "but that can never be, not until the end comes." His eyes passed around the room, and Erika shivered as his gaze touched her. "And so I fight, seeking death." He lifted his ruined hand. "But still it evades me."

"You can't die." To Erika's surprise, it was Cara who spoke.

Romaine's eyes showed no emotion as he looked at her. "Why not?" he whispered, voice bitter. "Your kind have left me with nothing else."

"All life is precious," Cara whispered.

The axeman stared at her until she lowered her gaze, then shook his head. "Wise words, from a traitor." He turned towards Lukys. "In the morning, you will leave me here. I have nothing left to give this world."

"No," Lukys replied, still crouched beside the axeman. He held up a finger when the Calafe looked set to argue. "We're not leaving anyone behind, end of story." He hesitated. "And you still have us, Romaine. You saved me, helped me when no one else would. Let me do the same for you."

The warrior stared at the Perfugian for a long while, but finally he nodded. A tear streaked down his bearded cheek but otherwise he said nothing. Drawing in a breath, Lukys rose and faced the rest of the room.

"Anyone else have something to add?" he murmured. No one spoke, and after a moment he nodded. "Then tomorrow we march for the Illmoor. And pray to the Gods that we find Travis and the Gods already there."

❧ 29 ☙

THE RECRUIT

Lukys sat in the middle of the abandoned town, staring into the distance, remembering his first night in this haunted land. Just a few short days ago, and yet everything had changed. Back then, his biggest concern had been ensuring there wasn't a mutiny amongst the other recruits.

Now those recruits were dead or gone, his mentor broken, and his friend…a traitor.

Cara.

A cold breeze blew through the empty window frames and he shuddered. How many nights now since they'd last had a fire, since he'd been warm? The night they'd slept in this abandoned place? They didn't dare light one now, not with the Tangata likely close. Besides, he didn't want to see what the fire would reveal—the faces of the dead, still lying where they had fallen.

They're not all gone.

Travis and the others were still out there, they *had* to be, surely… but there was no way to know, no time to search for them. The Tangata were close, he could *feel* it. They could not remain on this side of the Illmoor much longer without being detected.

Then there was Cara. Dale had volunteered to take the first shift guarding her, saying he wouldn't sleep anyway. Lukys was little different. Would any of them ever have a full night's sleep again,

226

after what they'd seen down in the darkness. Just the memory of those…things sent shivers down his spine.

And Cara had fought them, killed them. Had she truly done so only to save herself, to avenge the Tangata the monsters had killed, or…

To save her friends?

No, no, no.

Lukys shook his head, banishing the thought. He had seen the grey eyes, seen the terrible, animalistic rage. There was no questioning it—Cara was one of them.

The enemy.

He shivered, remembering how she'd looked as the Archivist unleashed her magic, hearing again her scream. Despite her betrayal, he could not bear to see such pain in the eyes of someone who'd been his friend.

Lukys cursed. Sleep wasn't going to come. Letting out a sigh, he rose. Picking up the spear he'd taken from one of the fallen recruits, he moved outside. The night was clear, the moon nearly full now. Using its silver light, he made his way through the village, averting his gaze from the bodies still lying in the streets. He'd wanted to move them, to do something to honour his fallen comrades, but doing so would give them away should the Tangata return to this place. And they were still a full day's march from the Illmoor.

Finally he found himself approaching the building they'd placed Cara in for the night. It was the smallest of the cottages, little larger than a woodshed, but with only one entrance and no windows, it made an adequate prison.

Movement came from the doorway and Lukys nodded a greeting as Dale stepped into the moonlight.

"Lukys," his former rival said, then glanced at the sky and frowned. "It's not your shift yet."

Lukys shrugged. "Can't sleep either." He leaned against the wall of the building.

Dale watched him for a moment, but soon resumed his post in the doorway. They stood like that for a while, their breaths misting in the darkness, listening to the wind as it whistled through the broken roofs.

"Why?" Lukys said suddenly, stepping back into the street and facing Dale.

"Why what?" Dale asked quietly.

"Why did we fight, Dale?" he replied after a time, struggling to focus on just a single mystery in his life. "I never did anything to you."

For a long while, Dale said nothing, only stood staring at the moon. "It seems like an age ago now, doesn't it?" he said finally. "The games of children." Then he shook his head. "You never had to do anything but be who you are."

"What?"

"You're a better man than me, Lukys," came the reply. When Lukys only frowned, Dale chuckled. "You don't know what it's like, to be the son of someone important. I was *expected* to be great, to become a knight, or a politician."

"What has that got to do with me?"

"Because I failed," Dale said, as though that explained everything. "I thought the frontier would be the making of me." He snorted. "What a lie that turned out to be. And then, in the moment of our greatest shame, it was *you* who stepped up. *You*, the son of a peasant, a nobody, who proved we might yet make something of ourselves."

Lukys started, then snorted. "You mean during that first attack? I didn't prove anything. I was so terrified I could barely hold my spear straight."

"You led us, Lukys," Dale murmured. "Just as you've been leading us ever since we crossed the Illmoor."

"I…" Lukys trailed off, frowning.

Had he truly become their leader? He'd tried to be brave, to stand strong as Romaine had told him. But…it had only been an act, hadn't it? Surely Dale and the others had seen through his charade?

"It's okay," Dale said, a wry grin twisting his lips. "I've accepted my place. If not for you, I think we would have all died down in those caverns. I'm glad to call you my officer, Lukys."

Lukys opened his mouth, then closed it, struggling to swallow the emotion that welled in his throat.

"Thank you," he managed at last. "And for what it's worth,

you're not a failure, Dale. You saved my life, that night in the mountains. And you did not flee when those…creatures attacked."

Dale laughed. "Maybe you're rubbing off on me."

Lukys smiled, but his joy was fleeting. Dale was but one of many concerns. His eyes were drawn to the darkness beyond the doorway. "I need to talk to her."

Glancing inside, Dale shuddered. "I know." He looked back at Lukys. "She saved us. Why?"

"It's time I asked her."

Dale watched him for a long moment, as though judging whether Lukys was ready for that confrontation. Finally, he nodded. "Then I'll stretch my legs." He walked away without looking back, leaving the entrance to Cara's prison unguarded.

Letting out a breath Lukys hadn't realised he'd been holding, he stepped inside before his nerves betrayed him. The floor of this cottage was dirt, but hard and dry beneath his boots. At first, he could see nothing in the dark, but as his eyes resolved, he found a pair of amber globes staring back at him. Cara took shape as she awkwardly pushed herself up off the ground, putting her back to the wall. They had stoppered her mouth again, but her eyes said everything.

Friend…

Her amber gaze bore into Lukys's soul, until finally he strode forward and pulled down the strip of cloth they'd used to silence her.

"The creatures you killed," he said, stepping back. "Why did you do it? To avenge your brethren?"

"No," Cara whispered, her voice hoarse.

"Then why?"

"To save you," she replied, "to save my friends."

Lukys choked, a lump lodging in his throat. He struggled on.

"How can we be friends?" he hissed. "You lied to us!"

"I never lied."

"I saw your eyes. They changed. You were…*are* a monster."

Cara flinched at the word. "Is that what you see me as now?" she asked, and he could hear the pain in her voice. "A monster?"

"You're one of them."

"Maybe the Tangata are not the monsters you think."

"Why do you still insist you're not one of them?" Lukys asked.

"Because I'm not," Cara whispered.

Truth, lies. Truth, lies.

Lukys shook his head, struggling to think. "It doesn't matter what you say." He looked away. "We saw the truth. No human could do what you did." Letting out a breath, he faced her once more. "They're going to kill you, if we ever reach Flumeer. But not before they make you talk."

"Yes, I know what…your people are capable of." She shuddered, not meeting Lukys's eyes. "I thought…I thought you were better than them."

"Than who?"

"Please, Lukys," Cara whispered, ignoring his question. Her amber eyes caught his. "I never wanted to hurt anyone. Please, you have to help me…"

"I wish I could," he murmured, surprised to find he meant it.

Help, help, help.

Pain shone from Cara's eyes as he rose, but she said not a word. Nor did she turn away, and he forced his eyes closed, unable to look into those terrible depths any longer. Silently he hardened his heart.

"But I can't." Stepping forward, he shoved the gag back into place. "You are my enemy."

With that, he turned and walked away.

❦ 30 ❦

THE ARCHIVIST

Standing on the banks of the Illmoor, Erika wondered if she had ever experienced such a bittersweet moment. Somehow, they had made it. Despite signs of the Tangata all through the forest, despite Romaine's injuries and their treacherous prisoner in tow, they had reached the border of Flumeer.

There had been no sign of the other Perfugians on the way but…Erika had little hope any still survived.

No, all that left to be seen now was whether the cursed general would send the ship.

Lukys stood alongside her, a red flag hanging from his spear tip, waving in what she presumed was some predetermined signal for the watchers on the other side. They weren't at the rendezvous point and were a day late, but with forts placed at regular intervals along the Illmoor and regular patrols on the opposite banks, surely someone would spot them.

Thankfully the day was clear, and though the light was fading fast, Erika could just make out the distant shapes on the opposite banks. So close, even a simple rowboat would have been enough to carry them safely across. But all such vessels had been taken or destroyed long ago, when northern Calafe had been evacuated.

So far, there'd been no visible response. She flashed a nervous glance at the trees. In the forest, she'd at least felt protected, concealed by the dense vegetation. It didn't feel safe, standing out here on the riverbanks, exposed. She wondered if that was the Calafe in her.

No, Erika had left that part of herself behind long ago. This past week had proven it. These endless forests, the jagged mountains —they were no longer her home. Perhaps they never had been, though many times as an adolescent, she'd longed to return.

Facing the waters once more, another realisation struck her. Despite its vast wealth and luxuries, despite all her work to climb the echelons of its society, Flumeer was not her home either.

So where did that leave her?

"What was that?" Lukys gasped beside her.

Blinking, Erika looked from him then back to the distant banks. Light flashed, once, twice, three times. From such a distance, it was difficult to identify the source, but she thought there might be something…

"Three means yes!" Lukys exclaimed, dragging her into a hug in his excitement. After his sombre mood of the last few days, she was surprised to see his sudden levity. "We're almost saved!"

Erika swallowed, wishing she could share in his joy. So close to salvation, and yet Flumeer offered her no true freedom. The queen's words rang in her mind, their threat, and Erika suppressed a shudder.

For the first time in weeks, she thought again of the stranger that had accosted her camp, to the offer from the King of Gemaho. She still had the map. There were other sites that had not yet been explored, even…even that remote site in the Mountains of the Gods.

But could she trust the Gemaho, after what they'd done?

Did she have a choice?

Movement came from the shadows as Lukys waved to the others. Cara appeared first, struggling to walk with her bindings, followed by Dale, then Romaine bringing up the rear. The axeman seemed to have stirred from his grief now, though he still walked with his head down, bandaged arm clutched to his chest. No doubt it would take time for him to come to terms with the injury.

So few.

A shiver ran down Erika's spine at the thought, and guilt twisted at her heart. So many souls lost, all because of her ambition.

No, because of her! She thought, glaring at Cara.

Her anger flared, though it was short-lived. Treachery might have brought about the failure of her expedition, but it had always been madness to come here. The Perfugians deserved better than what the general had given them, than where she'd led them.

"They're out there, Archivist," Lukys said beside her, as though reading her mind. His eyes were on the trees.

"We'll find out soon enough," Erika whispered.

She started as a bugle cry carried across the Illmoor. Hairs stood up on the back of her neck and she swung back towards the water, wondering why the Flumeerens would sound a horn. If there were any Tangata in the area, it was bound to draw their attention.

Her heart lurched in sudden understanding, and she spun to face the trees. Shapes darted amongst the shadows, then the Tangata emerged, one by one, until five stood at the edge of the forest. They did not move to attack immediately, though the grey eyes watched the humans with terrifying intensity.

No, they're not watching us! Erika realised, following their gaze to where Cara stood bound.

Romaine and Dale were already pushing the girl to the ground and fastening her bindings. Then they strode forward to join them, though the Calafe would surely struggle to wield his axe with one hand. And that was if he could ignore the pain from his severed hand.

Catching movement from the corner of her eye, she swung back as one of the beasts suddenly rushed them. Instinctively, Erika's arm came up, the magic spilling from her palm, lighting the growing darkness. The Tangata staggered as the light fell upon it, its headward rush faltering. A scream echoed in the twilight as it collapsed, thrashing against the damp ground.

"Kill it!" Erika screamed as another leapt towards her, forcing her to divert the magic.

Too late, Lukys and Dale responded. Lifting shields and spears, they charged the fallen creature. Snarling, the beast clambered to its feet and leapt away, carrying it out of range of Erika's magic. The second had only made a feint, coming close enough to draw her attention, but not enough to suffer from her power.

Erika cursed beneath her breath. Even after all these weeks, she didn't know enough about the gauntlet—how far its magic stretched, how long it took to kill. She should have tested it long ago, despite its potentially fatal effects.

Lukys and Dale joined shields and extended their spears, then moved between Erika and the Tangata. It was a brave gesture, though futile—without her magic, they couldn't hope to resist the creature's strength. Heart pounding, she stepped forward so she stood beside them. Romaine joined on their other side a moment later.

"I'll do my best to keep them back," she whispered, "if you can kill the ones that drop…"

The Tangata watched them from across the clearing. Erika's magic seemed to give them doubt, though that could not hold them back long. If they attacked all at once, she and the two recruits would be overwhelmed. Maybe if…

Screaming their rage, the Tangata rushed them. They moved with a deadly grace, seeming to slide across the earth rather than run, though even amidst her terror, Erika noted they were far slower than the creatures they had awakened beneath the earth. What about the passage of time had so weakened them, made them more…human?

Then the beasts were upon them, and there was no more time to think. Raising her gauntlet, Erika drew on its power and swung her hand in an arc. A brief touch would not be enough to seriously harm any one of them, but she hoped to at least slow them for the soldiers to fight.

Her hunch was proven correct, as each of the beasts reeled beneath the magic light, momentarily stunned. Seeing their opening, Lukys and Dale roared and leapt forward as one, targeting the beast at the centre of the Tangata line. Their spears flashed out, catching their foe in the chest and throat just as it recovered.

Shock showed on the beast's face, and snarling, it reached for the spears that had impaled it. But Lukys and Dale were already retreating, dragging back their weapons and presenting their shields to the enemy. The injured Tangata made to follow, but only managed a step before blood loss dragged it down. The remaining four retreated out of range of Erika's magic, their movements cautious now.

"If we could do that four more times…" Lukys said lightly, though he did not smile and his eyes did not leave the remaining creatures.

"Time to trade Cara for our lives, you think?" Dale asked.

"No," Lukys said.

Erika might have argued, but at that moment the Tangata attacked again. This time two angled directly for her, moving with terrifying speed. She had only enough time to direct her magic against one of the beasts. It collapsed with a scream of agony, while the other kept on, eyes locked on Erika, fingers raised to tear out her throat…

Dale and Lukys leapt between her and the beast, and a sharp *thunk* followed as it struck their raised shields. A groan came from Lukys as he staggered back, but Dale remained standing, and with a thrust of his shield he threw the beast back. Straightening, Lukys lanced out with his spear, catching the Tangata a blow to the hip.

Howling, the beast retreated, blood running down its side. Screams came from its companion, still pinned by Erika's magic, but Dale silenced them with a thrust of his spear.

A cry from their left reminded Erika of the remaining Tangata. Gasping, she swung the gauntlet towards the sound. Fatigue struck her as she summoned the magic once more, and she staggered, but thankfully the threat had passed for the moment.

Romaine crouched nearby, shoulders heaving, great axe buried in the chest of a dead Tangata. The second was retreating with its fellow, a knife embedded in its shoulder. Shocked, Erika stood gaping at the Calafe warrior, unable to believe her eyes. Injured and alone, he had fought off *two* of the Tangata?

Then she saw the blood seeping through his shirt, and knew the skirmish had not been without cost.

A *thunk* came from nearby as something hard struck the ground. Lukys still stood beside Dale, eyes on the remaining Tangata, but he had let his shield fall. She saw with shock it had been split in two by the last attack. Ignoring the loss, Lukys took a two-handed grip on his spear, then shared a glance with Dale. The second recruit tossed aside his spear and gripping his shield, stepped up beside Lukys.

"Romaine, get back to the shore," Lukys hissed as the recruits moved to put themselves between the axeman and the remaining Tangata.

Erika followed them, though her vision swam with the movement. Her eyes were drawn to the gauntlet, and she saw now how its glow had dimmed. She'd used too much of its magic, too quickly. Again she cursed her lack of experience. Would it kill her, drain all her strength, if she continued using it?

Coming to a stop alongside the axeman, Erika fought to clear her mind, to bring back the magic. The gauntlet brightened somewhat. She prayed it would be enough. Beside her, she could hear the rattling of the axeman's breath. She didn't need to look beneath his shirt to know the injury was bad.

"Can you walk, Calafe?" she hissed, eyes still on the Tangata.

A groan whispered from the axeman, then movement came from alongside her as he staggered to his feet. Somehow he had managed to drag his axe from the Tangata corpse, though he didn't seem to be strong enough to lift it any higher. Blood dripped from the steel tips.

"Must…fight," he rasped.

"Get to the riverbank, soldier," Erika snapped, flashing him a glare.

Romaine grunted. "Don't take…orders…from you."

"By The Fall, you're stubborn," Erika gasped. She grabbed him by the arm and shook him. "But by the blood of my father, *your Gods-cursed king*, you will obey!"

"Your…father?" the warrior mumbled. His eyes were bloodshot, face growing pale. He swayed on his feet, managing to look confused. "That's…what?"

"Let's discuss it over tea sometime, shall we?" she snapped. "*Go!*"

Finally, miraculously, he obeyed. Erika watched him as he staggered away, and couldn't help but think how like her father the man was—or perhaps it was all Calafe men. Stubborn, proud to a fault. Determined to stand their ground no matter the cost. Maybe if her father hadn't been so foolish, he might have survived, might have returned from that disastrous southern campaign…

She shook herself, returning attention to the Tangata pair. What did it matter to her? Erika's mother had only ever been the man's courtesan. They would have been sent away eventually, regardless. His death had only hastened their fall from grace.

"You okay, Archivist?" Lukys said, glancing over his shoulder. "Don't think we can defeat these two without your magic."

"Thought you were superstitious, soldier?" she snapped.

Regardless, she looked again at the gauntlet. Its light had died again, and silently she ignited its glow, then stepped up on Dale's other side. Somehow, he would have to protect them both with his broken shield. A low growl sounded from across the clearing as the Tangata approached again, slowly now, testing their own resolve. They flinched as she raised her gauntlet, eyes drawn to the device, but they did not stop.

Then their foes split apart, one sliding to their left, the other two the right. Erika shared a glance with the two recruits.

"You take the one to the left," she whispered.

Lukys and Dale nodded and she turned away, attention focused on her enemy, the female of the pair. She clenched her fist and was satisfied to see the light grow brighter. A smile touched her face. It seemed at least some of her energy was returning. Lengthening her stance, she beckoned the creature forward.

Smiling back, it raised a fist.

Too late, Erika noticed the rock it held. Snarling, it hurled the projectile at her head. Instinctively, Erika raised her spare hand. A sharp *crack* followed as the rock struck her wrist and a scream tore from her lips. Red flashed across her vision and the magic died. She staggered back, and for a moment, pain washed away all thought, all reason.

Her senses returned.

Fighting through the pain, Erika forced her eyes open, just in time to see the Tangata leap. Adrenaline swept through her as she raised the gauntlet. Light burned in the gloom and a bloodcurdling scream rent the air as her magic struck the beast.

But the Tangata was already airborne, and though her power drained it of reason, she could not avoid the blow it struck as they collided. The weight of its impact drove the breath from her lungs and toppled them both into the mud.

The magic flickered out again.

Howls came from alongside Erika as the Tangata thrashed, free of her magic's grasp but momentarily disorientated. Its fingers reached for her, trying to stop Erika from summoning the power again.

Gasping, yet unable to inhale more than a whisper, Erika scrambled away. Her vision spun and pain seared up her broken arm, threatening to steal away her consciousness. Cries seemed to come from all around her, but she could no longer tell which direction was the forest, which was the river.

Air brushed against her neck and instinctively Erika threw herself to the side. A boot slammed into the mud where she had lain and she clambered backwards, staring up at the Tangata. Red streaked its eyes and its face twisted as it started towards her again, yellowed teeth bared.

Erika screamed and opened her fist, directing everything she had left at the beast. Its shriek mirrored her own as the power struck. The Tangata staggered back, clutching its ears, shaking its head in violent convolutions, as though something horrible were trying to drill through its skull.

Erika did not relent. Pushing herself to her knees, she kept the gauntlet poised, bathing her foe in its ghostly light, until finally the Tangata collapsed and lay still.

Gasping for breath, she sat back on her haunches and looked around, expecting to see the final Tangata approaching. Instead, she was shocked to find Lukys and Dale still standing, though the beast they faced had retreated once more, apparently deciding it could not face the three of them.

"The ship!"

A cry came from Romaine behind them, and Erika spun to see the white sails of a ship rearing overhead. A *thud* came from the riverbank as a plank slammed into the earth. Soldiers stood at the railings, shields and spears at the ready. Her heart soared to see them.

But they did not advance.

Erika frowned as she realised they were not coming to their aid. The soldiers were only going to defend the vessel. If those on the shore wanted rescuing, they would need to reach the ship themselves.

Following her orders, Romaine was already staggering towards the ship, Cara somehow swung over one shoulder. But the ship had landed some thirty yards downriver. They needed time, needed to ensure that the last Tangata did not pick them off as they retreated.

Heart pounding, Erika came to her feet and faced the beast. Dale and Lukys still stood strong, but the two were little more than boys. They wouldn't even be here, fighting for their lives, if not for her.

Light ignited in the palm of her hand.

"Get to the ship," she said softly. "I'll hold it off."

31

THE RECRUIT

Blood pounded in Lukys's skull as he watched the last Tangata. He still couldn't believe they were alive, that they had managed to defeat *four* of the things. Sure, the Archivist's magic had helped, but still…

He risked a glance over his shoulder. Romaine was staggering towards the ship, but his injuries and Cara's struggling hampered him. Lukys glimpsed the desperation in her eyes as she looked at the last Tangata. He shook his head—how had he ever thought of her as a friend?

"Get to the ship," the Archivist said suddenly, striding past them. "I'll hold it off."

"What?" Lukys asked, swinging on her. "Not a chance, Erika. We stand against it together."

"Together," Dale agreed, joining them.

Death, death, death.

The Tangata's eyes narrowed as it looked past them to where Romaine was nearing the ship. Lukys could see the longing in its eyes. For whatever reason, these creatures wanted Cara back. Well, they couldn't have her. She would answer for her crimes against humanity.

A growl came from their foe as it started towards them. Lukys realised it was trying to put the two recruits between itself and the Archivist's magic. He stepped sideward to join with Dale, while

Erika shifted to the right so that they stood apart. Whether the Tangata attacked Dale and Lukys, or the Archivist, it would be exposing its back to someone.

Lukys didn't allow it the chance.

"Now!" he hissed.

Dale responded immediately, and they surged forward together. Lukys aimed his spear for the creature's chest, hoping to run it through. The Tangata were hardy and such a wound might not prove fatal, but it would at least slow the beast long enough for them to escape.

A rumble came from the Tangata as it leapt to meet them. Apparently, it had no misgivings about tackling two humans—it was the Archivist's magic it feared. Its hands snatched for the spear and almost caught it, forcing Lukys to retreat half a step. Snarling, it chased after him, but Dale blocked its path, thrusting out with the steel brim of his shield.

The blow connected with the Tangata's forehead, staggering it for a brief second, and Lukys attacked again, this time aiming for its throat. At the last second it twisted, avoiding the blow, though the spear tip still scored a mark on its arm.

Its hand swept down again, and this time it managed to catch the haft of Lukys's spear. Before he could react, the Tangata pushed back, driving the butt of the spear hard into his chest. Breath exploded between his teeth and Lukys felt something go *crack*. He stumbled, struggling to keep his feet, even as the spear slipped from his fingers.

Looking up, he saw the Tangata leap—then Dale was there, shield slamming into the creature and hurling it aside.

Death, death, death.

Dale leapt back as the beast swung on him. A smile spread across its lips as it saw he was unarmed. Snarling, it started towards him.

Pain radiating from his chest, Lukys wanted nothing more than to lie down and surrender to the release of oblivion. But the *thunk* of flesh striking wood drew him back to his feet. Dale was retreating from the beast's fury, his shield now splintered and broken, useless. A sound like laughter came from the Tangata as it advanced.

Seeing his spear lying nearby, Lukys swept it up and followed them. But the pain from his chest slowed him and he couldn't keep a moan from escaping his lips. The creature swung at the noise, eyes widening to see him back on his feet. Then the smile returned and it drew itself up, preparing to spring…

…and collapsed to the ground as the Archivist finally managed to unleash her magic.

Face gaunt, glowing hand extended towards the creature, she advanced past Dale. A tremor shook her, then a second. Realising she was close to collapse, Lukys staggered forward and drove his spear through the creature's chest.

Silence.

Unable to believe they had truly won, Lukys stood gasping for breath, spear still clutched tight. Staring at the dead thing at his feet, he found himself unable to look away. With its eyes closed, the thing could have been human, might have been a young man little older than Lukys.

If he had not been cursed by the Gods.

Finally Lukys tore himself away. Dale had slumped to the ground nearby, face pale as he sucked in great lungfuls of air, though he seemed unharmed. The Archivist met his gaze and offered a nod, her face grim. They had won—but what did it matter, when so many others had been lost?

Stop, stop, stop.

Silence had fallen over the riverbank, and looking back at the Illmoor, he saw that Romaine had made it onboard with Cara. Despite their victory, his heart sank. They had succeeded, but he still could not shake his sadness. They would have to hand Cara over to the general. It just didn't seem…right.

"Lukys!"

His gaze was drawn back to the ship as a voice carried to them on the breeze. He frowned. Why…were the soldiers pulling up the gangplank? The danger had passed, hadn't it?

Spinning towards the forest, Lukys watched in horror as more Tangata emerged from the trees. Dozens at least—more even, as he glimpsed movement further into the shadows. The hope that had swelled his chest evaporated. An army. Too many to fight, even with the soldiers on the ship.

The creatures advanced in a line, and now he could see the fury in their eyes as they watched the escaping vessel. Aboard the ship, Romaine stood at the railings, his face contorted with grief. Tightening his grip on the spear, Lukys offered the axeman a final nod.

Then he turned to face the Tangata.

Movement came from nearby as Dale and Erika joined him. The Perfugian had reclaimed his spear, but without a shield between them, and exhausted as they were, they stood no chance.

Not that they ever had, against what marched towards them.

Only the Gods could save them now.

32

THE WARRIOR

Romaine staggered up the gangway, forcing Cara before him, his breath coming in painful gasps. The Tangata had struck him hard enough to break bones and he could taste blood in his mouth. Liquid burned in his chest, dragging at his strength, adding to the agony of his arm. He continued on, though he could not have said why.

Hadn't he wanted to die?

Reaching the deck of the ship, he stepped from the gangplank and almost crashed to the floor. As it was, he fell to one knee, desperately straining for a breath he could not quite find. Men shifted around him, Flumeeren soldiers taking up positions along the railings. The vessel bobbed against the river currents, shifting in its berth…

Groaning, Romaine forced himself to his feet. Somehow he made it to the railing, but it was already too late. The ship was pulling away from the shore, though three figures still stood in the clearing, their shoulders slumped in exhaustion.

"What are you doing?" Romaine tried to shout, but the words came out more as a croak. He swung on the nearest soldier and grabbed desperately at his coat. "We can't leave them."

The man shook him off. "We don't have a choice, Calafe," he said. There was no anger in his voice. He only pointed back at the shore.

Still struggling to regain the breath he'd lost from speaking, Romaine followed the gesture. Despair wrapped its icy hands around his stomach as he saw the reason for the soldiers' fear.

Tangata. More than had been seen in months. Several raced towards the ship, but when it became clear they would not catch it, they turned back, leaving the three lonely figures surrounded.

"No," Romaine whispered.

Something died inside him as Lukys met his gaze from across the waters. The recruit gave a simple nod, then turned away, spear raised to the hoard.

No, no, no, not again!

Helpless, Romaine could hardly bear to watch as the Tangata closed on his stranded companions. But neither could he turn away. He owed them that much. Abandoned and left behind, the least he and the other soldiers could do was witness their final stand, to tell the world of their courage.

"*No!*" a voice screamed from amongst the ranks of soldiers.

Romaine spun at the sound, recognising Cara's voice. Had she gotten free? His vision blurred at his sudden movement, but he forced himself to search the deck, determined she would not escape. Not after everything they'd been through to bring her to justice.

Two of the soldiers were trying to get a handle on his former friend, but even bound, Cara was proving to be a handful. Thrashing on the deck, she had somehow managed to dislodge her gag. Another scream tore from her throat as she kicked out with both feet, catching one of the soldiers in the chest and hurling him across the ship. Shouts came from others as they were struck by the falling man.

Agony wrapped its thorny tendrils around Romaine's heart as he watched the woman struggle. Lukys had made them spare her, had said they would trade the traitor's life for their own if it came to it. Instead, Lukys had sacrificed his own life to save this creature.

A tremor shook him as the familiar rage ignited in his chest. Reaching up with his good hand, he drew his axe. Despite the pain and exhaustion, the weapon felt right in his hand. He stepped towards where Cara still lay struggling. Another kick sent a second soldier flying. Someone should have done this long ago.

She froze when she saw him approaching, axe in hand, and her eyes widened.

"Are you going to kill me?" she whispered.

Romaine swallowed. Those eyes, that voice. Somehow, this young woman had found a place in his heart he'd thought long dead. Steeling himself, he clenched his fist tighter around the haft of his axe. Nausea wrapped around his stomach at the thought of what he must do, of plunging his terrible blade through her chest...

"No," he croaked, opening his eyes. The axe slipped from his fingers, the twin points striking the deck and lodging in the timbers. He shook his head. "I can't."

"Then free me!" Cara shrieked, struggling to sit up. "I can save them!"

Romaine frowned at her words, unable to understand. "Save them?" he murmured.

"Please!" Cara gasped again, still struggling at her bonds. There was something about the way she lay that seemed wrong, the way her arms pressed against her back as she fought to free herself. "Oh please, quick, Romaine, if you ever cared for me at all, *let me go!*"

"Why?" Romaine whispered. Taking hold of the shaft of his axe, he dragged it from the timbers and stepped towards her. "What are you going to do?"

Amber eyes met his. "Trust me."

For some reason, he did.

Falling to his knees, he turned her so she was facedown and carefully sliced the cords that bound her arms, then her legs. Dropping the axe, he stepped away, the last of his strength gone. Even as he watched her come to her feet, Romaine sensed he had made the wrong decision, doomed them all with his foolishness. Cara was Tangata. She would slaughter them all.

But what did he care?

Cara rose slowly, fists clenched, a growl building at the back of her throat. Around the ship, several soldiers retreated a step, though they did not know what it was they faced. Only Romaine knew the doom he had unleashed.

He did not flinch as the grey eyes met his. The terrible rage of the Tangata stood amongst them, but he was past caring. Let her slaughter them all—

Cara winked.

What?

Before he could react, she was sprinting towards him. Powerful legs sent her bounding across the deck, past soldiers and sailors, over the twisted ropes and canvas that had tripped her just a few short months before, when he'd first brought her to Flumeer. Romaine flinched, yet Cara's eyes were fixed not on him but the distant shore. Tearing the heavy winter coat from her shoulders, she bounded onto the railing, and leapt…

…and flew!

Romaine froze where he stood, unable to believe what he was seeing. Out across the waters, great wings spread from Cara's back, auburn feathers sweeping down, sending her soaring…*upwards!* It wasn't possible, couldn't be…

Suddenly everything clicked into place.

Cara had spoken the truth—she wasn't Tangata.

She was a *God!*

Falling to his knees, Romaine watched the winged woman race through the sky. Sharp intakes of breath came from others as realisation struck them, then they too were falling to the wooden boards, struck down by awe—and terror. Had they truly tried to restrain one of the Divine, set hands upon a *God?*" Prayers whispered across the decks, begging for forgiveness, for salvation.

Romaine could not tear his eyes away from his friend. The wings that had hidden beneath her coat for so long beat down again, stretching wide across the waters, ten, twenty, thirty feet. Each stroke sent her soaring upwards, higher and higher above the swirling waters, towards the distant riverbanks.

Romaine's fear came rushing back as his eyes fell upon the shore, where Lukys and the others still stood surrounded. Thankfully, the Tangata had frozen at Cara's appearance. There was a hunger in their eyes as they watched her approach, and Romaine remembered then how she had drawn the others' attention. What did the Tangata want with one of the Gods?

Several of the creatures seemed to realise she was coming for the humans in their midst. Crying their fury, they rushed at Lukys and the others. Several went down as the Archivist's gauntlet flashed, but there were too many even for her magic. She threw herself aside as a Tangata leapt, avoiding its outstretched fingers, then disappeared into the throng.

Lukys thrust out with his spear, trying to bring a creature down, but it batted aside the blow and swung on him. Romaine's heart palpitated in his chest as the beasts closed on his friends. Without shields or room to manoeuvre, they didn't stand a chance. His eyes returned to Cara, but not even the sight of her auburn wings slicing the sky could bring him hope. Even if she had the power to face so many Tangata, his friends would be slaughtered before she could reach them.

Cries came from the shore and he watched as first Dale, then Lukys, had the spears torn from their grasp. Before they could retreat, the Tangata were upon them. Romaine held his breath, waiting for the slaughter, but instead the beasts only caught the men and held them fast.

Nearby, a cluster of the creatures had gathered around where Erika had fallen, but now they suddenly leapt back. The Archivist struggled to her feet, light pulsing from her gauntlet as she directed it at any Tangata that grew close. Step by step, she retreated towards the river. The rattling laughter of the Tangata carried across the waters as they followed her. The creatures were toying with their prey.

Then with a scream and a flash of red and gold, Cara arrived. Descending from the heavens, she struck the Tangata with the fury of a storm. With fist and boot and wing, she hurled the creatures from their feet. The breath caught in Romaine's throat as she fought her way towards his friends.

But few of those that Cara struck stayed down. With so many aligned against her, the Goddess had no time to strike mortal blows, and growling, the Tangata clambered back to their feet. As the fallen returned to the battle, their greater numbers pressed her back. Cries came from Cara as they grasped at her wings, tearing at the auburn feathers.

Ice formed in Romaine's stomach as he realised why the Tangata had spared Lukys and the others. With the humans dead, Cara would have retreated, but so long as they lived…

Chaos descended upon the shores of the Illmoor as the Tangata besieged Cara, seeking to use their numbers to bring her down, to overwhelm her. But the Goddess refused to be caught. She moved through the beasts like a whirlwind, a wing sweeping out to strike one aside, a fist taking another in the chest, boot striking yet a third in the face as she bounded clear of the rest.

But there was no safe ground upon which to land. As she hovered, another of the Tangata leapt, colliding with her back and knocking the Goddess from the air. The breath caught in Romaine's stomach as the Tangata converged on where she had fallen, but a second later Cara was back on her feet. Blood now streamed from a cut above her eye, and snarling, she tossed the creature that had downed her at her nearest foe, sending both crashing to the mud.

Despite himself, Romaine was impressed with how she fought. In the caverns, against those unspeakable creatures, she had been a wild animal, all untamed fury. Now, Cara fought with precision and control. That was all that kept her alive against the hordes.

Even so, it was clear the Goddess could not prevail alone, not against so many. She was already beginning to slow, her divine strength worn down by weight of numbers. Just like the soldiers of Flumeer, the Tangata worked together against her, attacking whenever her back was turned, launching themselves at her wings, her legs, seeking to drag her down.

Romaine's heart beat faster as he realised the pattern of their attacks—they weren't trying to kill her; they were trying to take her captive.

Why?

As he watched, Cara caught a blow to the chest. It sent her staggering back, and losing her footing, she sank to one knee. The Tangata were on her in a second, rushing in a group to attack together. But the wings she had hidden all this time snapped open, striking two hard enough to knock them from their feet. Cara surged into the gap, catching the third of her assailants by the throat. Before the others could come upon her, she hurled the beast face-first into the ground. This time the Tangata did not get back up.

But the others would not allow Cara to catch her breath. They pressed closer, robbing her of space to manoeuvre, to evade their blows. She staggered as more attacks caught her, but there was nowhere left to retreat.

Then a voice carried to Romaine's ears from across the waters, a distant, feeble cry of desperation. A familiar voice.

"Cara, *run!*"

Romaine's insides froze over as he found Lukys amidst the mob, still held fast by the Tangata. He still fought, struggling to break the creature's hold, but there was no escaping the Tangata. His mouth opened wide as he cried out again.

"*Please, save yourself!*"

"No!"

Screaming, Cara laid into the creatures around her. They leapt back from her fury, apparently happy for the Goddess to expend her energy. In frustration, Cara charged them, trying to break through to the others, but she was flagging now. Hands grabbed at her wings, her arms, her legs. She fought them off, but still more came on. Step by step, she was forced back from the captives.

A shriek tore from Cara's throat, and Romaine heard the despair in her cry. The Tangata retreated, expecting another assault, but with a whirl of feathers, Cara spun and hurled herself into the air. A beat of her wings carried her over the heads of the nearest Tangata, to where a diminutive figure lay forgotten. Before those nearby could react, Cara had the Archivist over her shoulder.

Too late the Tangata realised what was happening. They raced at her, howling their fury, but with a giant beat of her auburn wings, Cara hurtled skywards.

Kneeling on the deck of the ship, Romaine watched her come, his heart in a vice, the hope of a few moments before crumbling to ruin. He looked again at the riverbanks. The Tangata dragged Lukys and Dale forward and held them there, taunting the humans floating offshore, daring them to return. But there would be no rescue now.

There was a heavy *thunk* as Cara landed on the ship, followed by a cry as Erika staggered away from her. Face pale, the Archivist crumpled to the ground and began to sob. Romaine and the other soldiers ignored her. Aboard that ship, not a soul had eyes for anyone but the Goddess standing in their midst. Just a few minutes before, they had tried to restrain this creature. Would she now take her retribution?

Cara did not even look at them. The auburn wings drooped,

then folded behind her back as she tucked them away. A shudder shook her and amber eyes searched the deck, finally settling on Romaine. He swallowed at the grief there, a mirror of his own. She took a step towards him, lip quivering, a single tear upon her cheek.

"Romaine," she croaked. "I'm so sorry."

33

THE ARCHIVIST

Erika sat at the bow of the ship. Her entire body shook as she watched the shore grow closer, the lights of Fogmore a lantern in the darkness. She dared not look back to where the Goddess sat in the aft. It felt as though her entire foundation had shifted, as though every part of her world had changed in the last few hours.

The Gods were real!

A God had saved her!

This changed everything. Though she had always *believed*, she had never…known.

Her eyes fixed on the approaching shore and she tried to focus her mind. In the chaos of battle, she had forgotten about her other troubles, but now they came rushing back. General Curtis would want answers. Erika had found nothing but death in the caverns, and they still did not know what had become of the other recruits. It seemed certain they were dead, though…where then were the rest of the bodies?

And what if there were more of those terrible creatures that the Tangata had woken? Was that why the Tangata had been seeking them? Did they think of those ancient monsters as *their* Gods? Would they seek out more of them, now that the secret had been uncovered?

Despite herself, Erika's gaze was drawn to the aft of the ship once more, to where Cara crouched alone on a crate. Not even

Romaine, not even her magic, could stand against those monsters. The Gods alone could defeat them. Humanity needed their aid, to discover the source of their power. Could an emissary be sent into the Mountains of the Gods to seek them out?

Excitement touched her at the thought, before reality dragged her back down. Regardless of Cara's revelation, Erika had failed. The queen would have no more use of her now, other than prying the magic gauntlet from her corpse.

Erika could not allow it.

Her mind worked quickly, another possibility opening itself to her. Gemaho bordered the Mountains of the Gods. Solaris wasn't far from the hidden site on her map, as the bird flew. And travelling from east of the mountains, they wouldn't have the Tangata to contend with.

The only difficulty would be smuggling Cara out from under the noses of Queen Amina and her general. They would not allow her to leave Flumeer, and certainly not to go to their eastern rival. Nor would Cara leave without the Calafe warrior.

Romaine himself had lost consciousness shortly after they had begun the journey downriver. Erika was surprised that he'd been able to resist the pain of his wounds as long as he had. She swore, at times the Calafe did not seem entirely human himself. The ship's medic was tending to him, but it was obvious the warrior would not be leaving Fogmore for some time.

Erika did not have the luxury of time on her hands. She could not wait for him…

She shook herself, irritated to realise she'd grown to like the man's company. But just because he knew of her heritage now, didn't mean she could trust him. After all, his people had already betrayed Erika and her mother once, hounding them out of the kingdom after her father's death. No, it was time she left the last traces of her past behind.

Looking out across the deck, she clenched her fist, but did not summon the power of the gauntlet. Her entire body ached as though she'd been riding for days and she dared not waste what remained of her strength.

Stones crunched and the ship shook beneath her. Erika's head jerked up as she realised they'd already reached Fogmore. The voyage had passed unnoticed while she'd dreamed. Her doom was already at hand.

No. She forced her mind into action. *The general cannot touch you; it's the queen you must fear. There is still time yet.*

Exhaling, she rose unsteadily to her feet and turned to where the gangplank was being lowered. She started to find Cara standing directly behind her. The young Goddess's eyes had returned to their usual amber. They were wide, anxious. The Tangata had torn strips in her tunic and she sported a black eye where a blow had caught her unaware, but otherwise she appeared unharmed from the battle.

"Are…are you okay, Erika?" Cara whispered.

As she spoke, her wings lifted a little from her back, giving Erika another glimpse of the auburn feathers. The sight summoned memories of their flight across the river, the water flashing past far below, the screams of the Tangata still ringing in her ears.

Erika banished the image and focused on Cara's words. "I'm okay," she replied, bowing her head in respect. "Thank you for rescuing me, Oh Great One."

Red crept into Cara's cheeks at the words and she quickly looked away. "Please don't call me that," she croaked. "I'm…not what you think."

Erika hesitated, before offering another nod. Whatever the girl asked, it would be difficult to think of her as anything but Divine now. Though…it was clear Cara also was not immortal. Her arm *had* been broken the first time they'd met. She could be hurt—by the Tangata, and by Erika's gauntlet. Why was that?

Questions for another time. For now, she pushed aside her confusion, bit back the pain of her broken arm, and forced herself to smile. A plan was coming to her, though she would not survive for long without the Goddess on her side.

"Very well," she said, trying to keep her voice even. "Well, would you accompany me to shore? I am still somewhat…weak from the magic."

Cara licked her lips, eyes flickering to the distant shores of the Illmoor. Though darkness had fallen, Erika had the distinct feeling the Goddess could see the other side perfectly.

"Poor Lukys," Cara whispered.

"You did everything you could," Erika murmured, placing a hand on the young woman's shoulders.

Cara did not react—confirming at least one of Erika's suspicions. The Goddess had never been afraid of touch—only of someone feeling the wings beneath her heavy cloak.

Gently, Erika led Cara towards the gangplank. It felt strange, offering comfort to this creature, to a literal God. But…there was something distinctly human about Cara's pain, about her grief. And perhaps it created an opportunity.

Most of the soldiers had already disembarked. Word would have already reached the city of the God they had brought back from the south. Fogmore would be abuzz with rumour. Dozens had already appeared on the shores, ignoring the obvious danger of the Tangata that they had left behind on the other shore. Whispers rose from the crowd as Erika stepped onto the plank, but it was not the Archivist they had come to see.

Gasps spread through the gathering as Cara followed. Her wings lifted at the sound, half-unfurling. An involuntary reflex, Erika guessed, after the way the Goddess had tried to go unnoticed for so long. The crowd drew back as they reached the shore. And who could blame them? The Gods were remembered not just with deference, but fear. After all, they were responsible for The Fall.

"My lord…Goddess…Saviour!"

The whispers grew louder as they stood there, and Cara pressed close to the Archivist. She shuddered as a feather brushed her arm, and had to suppress a scream. There was something unnatural about those wings. They reminded her far too much of the Tangata.

That…will take some getting used to.

"Soldiers, at your stations!" The hairs on the back of Erika's neck stood on end as a voice bellowed from the top of the slope. General Curtis came marching through the ranks of men and women, his face a carefully controlled mask. "Get these civilians back into the city—there are Tangata about this night."

He came to a stop before Erika and the Goddess while around them the soldiers leapt to obey. Erika drew herself up as he stood regarding her, resisting the urge to shrink before the rage that glinted in his eyes.

"General," she said, offering a polite nod.

"The Perfugian recruits?" he asked curtly.

Guilt stoppered Erika's lips, but finally she managed to blurt out a single word: "Gone."

"And the magic of the Gods?"

"Lost."

He gave a curt nod. "As expected." His eyes flickered to Cara, taking in the auburn wings. His jaw clenched, though to his credit, he showed no other reaction. "Great One," he murmured, bowing. "The gates of Fogmore lie open to you."

Cara's cheeks brightened and she lowered her eyes. Seeing her opportunity, Erika spoke into the silence. "The Great One is somewhat…unaccustomed to human scrutiny. She will accompany me to my quarters."

The general's eyes flickered in her direction. "My orders were to take you into custody, should your endeavour prove fruitless." Erika's heart lurched, but the general drew in a breath and continued: "But…I am certain the queen would not wish to go against Her Divinity." He faced Cara once more. "I hope that you might break your fast with us come the morning, Great One."

Cara flicked an uncertain glance at Erika before offering a nod. Suppressing a smile, Erika linked arms with the Goddess and led her up the slope.

"What about Romaine?" Cara whispered as they walked.

"I'm sure his wounds are already being tended to," Erika reassured her. The Calafe had been one of the first off the ship, carried on a stretcher. "We can visit him in the morning."

That seemed to reassure the Goddess, and they continued up the path. The gates opened before them and Erika strode through without looking back. Let the general worry about the Tangata; she had other concerns now. She led the Goddess through the streets, steadfastly ignoring the stares of the crowd as they passed.

She was pleased to find her quarters still empty. Hastily constructed from timber boards, it wasn't much better than the abandoned cottages back in Calafe. But at least it was private, and would give her the chance to question the Goddess, to figure out her next move.

Pulling open the door, she held it for Cara. "Come on in. You'll be safe from the stares here. At least until morning."

Cara hesitated on the threshold, eyes wide, cheeks a bright red, but finally she stepped inside. Erika swung the door closed behind them, plunging the room into darkness. Throwing the latch to keep out unwanted visitors, she hesitated, then decided she had strength enough to summon the magic. The soft light of her gauntlet lit the room.

"So, you survived."

Erika almost leapt out of her boots as a voice spoke from the shadows. Beside her, Cara gave a shrill cry and leapt sideways, wings snapping open. Something went *crash* in the gloom—the potted plant beside her window. Heart racing, Erika raised her fist, and a brilliant light cast back the darkness.

The stranger from Gemaho sat at her table, one leg crossed over the other, fingers drumming against the table. A sheathed sword lay beside the woman, as though to say she was not there to fight, though Erika was sure she would have other weapons at her disposal.

Still struggling to catch her breath, Erika lowered her fist. "I am," she said softly, then paused, before adding: "No thanks to the queen."

A smile tugged at the woman's lips. "So I heard." She uncrossed her legs and stood. "So your quest failed?"

Erika hesitated, heart thudding painfully in her chest. She found herself holding her breath, unsure how to proceed. Glancing to the side, she saw that Cara was watching her, wings spread wide, ready to flee.

Forcing a smile, Erika raised her hand. "It's okay, Cara," she said softly, seeking to reassure the Goddess. "She's with me."

The girl said nothing, though her wings retracted an inch. Releasing her breath, Erika faced the Gemaho spy once more.

"Not entirely," she said in answer to the question. She gestured at Cara. "As you can see, other discoveries were made."

"My king knew you were resourceful." her visitor said with a smile. "And what of our offer?"

"I accept," Erika said at once. "I will go with you to Gemaho."

"Excellent." The stranger's eyes flickered to Cara. "And your...friend?"

"Gemaho?" Cara whispered, looking to Erika. "But they're your…enemies, aren't they?"

"Not anymore," Erika said soothingly.

"But Romaine," the woman continued, frowning. "We can't leave him, not after…" Tears formed in her eyes as she trailed off.

"My king will require a demonstration of your goodwill, Archivist," the woman said softly.

Erika sighed. This wasn't how it was meant to go. But nor could she ignore the general's words on the shore of the Illmoor. The queen had already condemned her. She might have fooled them for now, with her claim of friendship to the Goddess, but that could not last. One way or another, the queen would find a way of disposing of Erika, and taking the magic for herself.

She could not go to Gemaho empty handed. That left only one option.

Sucking in a breath, Erika spun and brought up her gauntlet. Realisation showed in Cara's eyes and she opened her mouth to cry out, but Erika didn't give her the chance. The magic struck and the scream died in Cara's throat. With a flash of light, she fell to the ground, and knew no more.

❧ 34 ❧

THE RECRUIT

Lukys watched with a mixture of relief and despair as the winged Goddess that was Cara threw the Archivist over one shoulder and took to the sky. His heart soared, glad at least someone had escaped. The joy was short lived as the remaining Tangata turned towards them. Terror rose to take its place.

The others had escaped.

But their nightmare had only just begun.

Rage burned in the eyes of the Tangata. He realised now it had been Cara the creatures had wanted all along. But there was no time to consider what significance the Gods had to the monsters.

Fight, live, kill.

Drums sounded in Lukys's mind as the creatures crowded them. Beside him, Dale still fought to break free of his captor, but Lukys stood frozen, overwhelmed by the horde of grey eyes watching him.

Suddenly the Tangata released them. Lukys staggered as the hands holding him vanished, swaying on his feet. Before he could look around, a fist struck him in the stomach, driving the breath from his lungs. He doubled over, gasping, even as he heard the *thump* of Dale striking the ground alongside him. Eyes watering, he tried to straighten, but a second blow slammed into his back.

He screamed as the ground rose to meet him, the broken bones grinding in his chest. Pain wrapped itself around his body as a boot struck him in the side, hurling him sideways. From somewhere nearby, another voice cried out, but Dale was lost amidst a forest of flashing limbs.

Fight, kill. Fight, kill!

Another boot caught Lukys in the side of the head and stars flashed across his vision. He tried to roll away, but the creatures were all around. Falling on his back, he cried out, begging for mercy, but another blow slammed into his stomach, stealing away the last of his breath.

He collapsed to the ground, vision growing dark. Overhead, a sea of faces spun, mouths twisted in anger, yellowed teeth bared, murder in grey eyes.

Kill, kill, kill!

Lukys opened his mouth to cry out, but all he could manage was a whisper. The Tangata retreated slightly, and for a second he thought they were showing mercy. Then one amongst them stepped forward. Sunlight flashed and even through his fading vision, Lukys glimpsed the spearpoint in its hands.

Desperately, he tried to scramble away, but now iron hands grasped him by the arms and legs, pinning him down. A cry came from nearby as others did the same with Dale. Then all Lukys could do was watch as the beast raised the spear overhead.

Death, death, death…

NO!

Lukys wasn't sure whether he screamed the word or thought it. Only thought it, surely, for he still had not recovered his breath. Yet the creatures around him reared back as though they'd been stung, as if he had suddenly turned into something foreign, something dangerous.

Grey eyes stared down at him, and though their mouths did not move, suddenly it was as though there were a hundred voices screaming in Lukys's mind, so many he could not make out a single word—though he sensed their rage, their confusion.

All at once the voices cut off. Movement came from amongst the crowd as a new creature appeared, a female. It moved to stand over him, eyes narrowed. The silence in Lukys's head was practically deafening as the female knelt. He flinched as a hand reached out, expecting death to follow, but the Tangata only traced a finger across his face, touching his nose, his cheeks, his lips. He lay there in terror, hardly daring to even breathe as she inspected him.

Finally she sat back, though her eyes never left him. He realised then how strange her eyes were—still the grey of the Tangata, but somehow deeper, as though this creature carried a great weight on its shoulders. She inspected him for a moment longer. Then a voice spoke in his mind.

Who are you?

AARON HODGES

WRATH OF THE FORGOTTEN

DESCENDANTS OF THE FALL

PROLOGUE
THE SOLDIER

Lukys stumbled through the night, his feet catching on unseen obstructions, eyes straining to pierce the gloom. His chest ached from the blow he'd taken just hours earlier and the chainmail vest weighed heavily on his shoulders, but he kept on. He had no choice. Cords bound his hands tight behind his back, and another was looped around his neck, constricting whenever he slowed, his captors urging him on. Grunts came from behind as his fellow captive, Dale, struggled to keep pace.

Briefly, light shone from overhead and Lukys's eyes were drawn to a gap in the canopy. A sliver of the moon appeared between the branches. Then it was gone, the forest returning to darkness—but not before he glimpsed the movement all around them. Their captors. The Tangata.

Lukys shuddered at being surrounded by the creatures. Cruel and inhuman, they had no problem seeing in the dark. It was one of their many powers, stolen from the Gods in ages past and inherited down through the generations. For decades the Tangata had waged war against humanity, destroying all who came against them. And now he was their prisoner.

He still struggled to understand how it had come to pass. He'd arrived on the frontier with his fellow Perfugians, thinking he was to become a soldier. Reality had crushed those aspirations. Untrained and terrified, the Perfugian recruits had been ordered into battle that first day. Against the superhuman strength of the Tangata, they'd never stood a chance.

Yet Lukys had survived. Survived because of Romaine, the ferocious warrior of Calafe. Even amongst other soldiers, the man was an enigma. Wielding a great battle axe, he had stood alone against one of the creatures, and won. Lukys had never heard of such a feat —the professors of his academy learning asserted that just one Tangata possessed the strength of three human soldiers.

After the battle, Lukys had sought out the warrior and begged for his help. Reluctantly, Romaine had agreed to train him—and eventually over half the surviving Perfugian recruits had joined them. They'd fought together, learned together, had almost thought themselves true soldiers.

Until this disastrous expedition. Now his fellow Perfugians were dead, all except he and Dale. The two of them should have been slaughtered as well, cut down on the banks of the Illmoor River, but something had given the creatures pause. Something had changed their minds.

Something about Lukys.

A tremor slid down Lukys's spine as his eyes fixed on the creature that led them. Long, curly brown hair suggested it was one of the females of the species, though they were just as strong as the males. Lukys had no doubt she could tear him in half should the desire take her. She had not said a word through the night. The Tangata did not speak. Or so they'd thought…

Move…further east…catch them…

Around him, the forest was silent, the movements of the Tangata abnormally quiet. But in Lukys's mind…words whispered, mixing and churning against one another like the rumblings of a packed crowd. Unintelligible, yet unmistakable for what they were:

The thoughts of the Tangata.

Lukys didn't know why he could hear them—he hadn't even recognised the voices for what they were until that confrontation on the banks of Illmoor. Not until one of the creatures had spoken directly into his mind.

Who are you?

Ice filled Lukys's belly at the memory. The Tangata had seemed as confused as Lukys about his ability. That alone had saved them.

But how long could this deferment of their execution last? How long before the beasts grew tired of their human captors, and put them down? Lukys had no illusions as to what awaited them.

Unless they could escape. Cautiously, he glanced back, seeking out Dale in the darkness. Until recently the two had been rivals, but they'd formed a mutual respect during this fateful expedition. Fighting together, they had slain several of the Tangata, in itself a miracle. Perhaps they could—

A flicker of moonlight sliced through the night, momentarily revealing Dale's face. Bruises purpled his cheek and had almost swollen his eyes closed, while a trail of blood ran from his mouth. The creatures had beaten them both before discovering Lukys's talent, but Dale had received the worst of their anger.

A soft wheezing came from Dale's throat and with his eyes on the ground, he didn't notice the attention. Quickly, Lukys returned his gaze to the way ahead, all thoughts of escape fleeing his mind. Dale could barely walk, there was no way they could outrun the Tangata, even if they somehow managed to break free.

Despair wrapped its thorny tendrils around his heart and began to squeeze. In his mind he heard new whispers, not of the Tangata now but his own, commanding him to give up, to sit down and surrender to his fate.

Yet he stumbled on, legs burning, chest screaming, driven by some tiny, determined part of him to reach the morning, to survive the night. The Tangata were not immortal; they *could* be defeated. All Lukys could do was wait, and hope.

Almost imperceptibly, the light began to grow, the sounds of the night retreating. Focused on the rhythm of the march, Lukys didn't notice at first. Eventually though, he began to make out shapes on the ground before him, tree roots and fallen branches, rocks and the footprints of creatures that walked before him.

Blinking, he lifted his head and felt a tingle of triumph. The red light of dawn now filtered through the winter forest. The Tangata had kept to the lowlands—that much he knew from the gentle terrain they had traversed—and the canopy was low above their heads, empty branches reaching for them like claws. The sky was clearly visible, though grey clouds stretched out as far as the eye could see.

Lukys was no woodsman, but there was only one direction the creatures could be taking them—south, towards those unknown regions beyond the broken Agzor Fortress, to the ancestral homeland of the Tangata.

The thought twisted his bowels into knots. They were passing now through the fallen kingdom of Calafe. Just six months ago, with their armies broken, the last of its people had fled north into Flumeer. Only the Tangata roamed these lands now. But at least they still bore the echoes of that lost civilisation. What would they find in the Tangatan homeland, unknown to humanity for centuries?

Their captors did not stop with the emergence of the day, and though the light made the going easier, Lukys could feel his final reserves of strength dwindling. The last weeks had taken their toll and now he desperately needed rest. Dale could hardly be any better. Yet still the female who led them continued, her brethren slipping through the forest in their silent manner.

"How much farther?"

The words slipped from Lukys in a desperate gasp. Even as he spoke them, he stumbled, his weakened legs tripping on a rock that protruded from the hard ground. With his hands bound he was unable to steady himself, and he slumped to one knee. The rope tightened around his neck, but thankfully the Tangata had stopped at the sound.

Slowly she turned, and Lukys felt a bolt of fear as solid grey eyes fell upon him. Those eyes were the mark of the Tangata, the only outward difference to a human. Yet they meant everything. In those eyes, Lukys could see his death.

Not long now, human.

Lukys's skin crawled as the voice whispered directly into his mind. The whispers around them remained indistinct, but this creature's words were crisp, clear. Their presence in his innermost thoughts felt like a violation, and he wondered what else the Tangata might be capable of. Could the monster before him read his mind? Was she doing it even now? He swallowed, staring into those cold eyes, but seeing no signs of emotion.

Finally he nodded and carefully pulled himself back to his feet.

The Tangata regarded him for a long moment, then turned and started off again. A tug on the rope urged Lukys to follow.

"It's useless," a voice gasped from behind him, "I…can't keep up…sorry, Lukys."

"Don't give up," Lukys hissed, glancing back at Dale. "We're almost there."

A frown touched his friend's forehead. "What?" he rasped. "How…do you know?"

"I…" Lukys hesitated.

He hadn't told the other recruit about the whispers. What would Dale think if he discovered Lukys could *hear* the enemy? It seemed…treacherous, blasphemous even. No, better he keep it a secret for now, until he learnt more about this new ability.

"They can't run forever," he said instead. "Even the Tangata have to rest."

Despair shone from Dale's eyes, but after a long moment, he nodded and lowered his head. Lukys breathed a sigh of relief as the man continued walking. He didn't know what the creatures had in store for them, but the thought of being left alone with the beasts… it didn't bear thinking about.

Lukys stumbled as the rope around his neck suddenly went slack. He looked up, surprised to find that the female Tangata had come to a stop. Her silver eyes were watching him again, and he quickly looked away, unable to hold that eerie gaze. Movement came from nearby as the others emerged from the trees.

Rest. The voice seemed cold in his mind, like a ghostly breath upon his neck. *We will stay here a time.*

He forced himself to meet the female's gaze. No more words were forthcoming, and after a drawn-out moment, Lukys turned to Dale.

"I think we're stopping here."

The recruit didn't wait for confirmation. He slumped to the ground and leaned against a nearby tree trunk, a moan slipping from his mouth. Lukys longed to join him, but instead he turned to inspect their surroundings.

The forest had thinned here, the canopy opening to grant them a view of the nearby hills. What Lukys saw confirmed his suspicions from the night. They were moving through one of the southern passageways—long, flat valleys that ran for hundreds of miles, so straight that some claimed they'd been carved from the earth by the Gods themselves. There were some in Flumeer as well—Lukys and his fellow Perfugians had taken one on their journey to the frontier. But that passageway had ended some fifty miles from the town of Fogmore, forcing them to climb the foothills to reach their destination.

There was no sign of an end to this passageway, though. Stark cliffs stretched away into the distance, their tops covered by a scattering of deciduous forest. Standing amidst the grandeur of that landscape, Lukys could understand how some had come to associate them with the Gods. Many were the legends of the Divine beings that had brought about The Fall, that terrible darkness that had almost destroyed humanity centuries ago. The Gods had vanished during that time, retreating into the forbidden mountains, it was said. Never to be seen again.

Until now. Until the battle for the Illmoor.

A smile crossed Lukys's lips as he pictured his friend Cara soaring above the river, wings spread wide, auburn feathers shining in the dying light of day.

A Goddess, hidden amongst them.

She had fallen upon the Tangata with vengeance, tearing through their ranks, hurling them aside with wing and fist and boot. More than a few of Lukys's captors sported bruises from that encounter, and he wondered what they thought of the Divine being that had appeared amongst them. Did the Tangata know what Cara was, what it was they had fought?

The whispers continued in Lukys's mind and he tried to focus, to draw sense from the chorus, but the words remained a jumbled puzzle, nonsensical.

He shook his head, spirits deflating once more. In the end, not even a Goddess had been enough to save them. Cara had been driven back by sheer numbers, and while she'd managed to rescue the Archivist, she could not save them all.

Dale and Lukys had been left behind.

His gaze fell to Dale again. Bruised and broken, the man had slipped into a doze. Watching him sleep, Lukys could hardly imagine this was the same arrogant noble born who had mocked

Lukys on the journey south from Mildeth. The weeks of strife had changed him—had changed them both. Blood and dirt stained their uniforms to the point where the Perfugian blue was barely recognisable, yet Lukys felt more a soldier now than he ever had north of the River Illmoor.

A shame those new skills hadn't mattered, in the end. They had been defeated all the same.

Come, human.

Lukys started as their captor's voice spoke into his mind once more. Swinging around, he was surprised to find the female standing directly behind him. Somehow, he managed not to shrink away.

"Already?" he hissed softly, struggling to contain his anger. He gestured at Dale. "He can barely stand."

The Tangata's grey eyes flickered toward Dale, then returned to Lukys. *He can stay,* came her reply.

"Stay?" Lukys muttered. Suspicion touched him and clenching his fists, he stood his ground. "I won't let you harm him."

The female crooked her head to the side, eyes unchanged, unreadable. *The other…will not be harmed,* she said finally. *You are wanted.*

"Wanted by who?" Lukys asked, his voice trembling despite himself.

A face burst into Lukys's mind in response: of himself lying on the shores of the Illmoor, a Tangata raising a blade above his head. In that instant, he sensed this was their leader. Lukys didn't need to question further to know who wanted him.

"What does he want?" he whispered finally.

A knife appeared in his captor's hands. He flinched at the sight of it—though of course, she needed no weapon to kill him. Before he could pull away, the blade flashed out, severing the rope that had connected him to Dale. He staggered, but a firm tug on the cord around his neck prevented him from falling. His breath was stolen away as she hauled him back up, bringing his eyes level with hers.

Come!

Lukys went.

THE FALLEN

Consciousness came slowly to Romaine. It began as an ember on the forest floor, slowly growing brighter, greater, until suddenly it burst asunder, pressing back the darkness. He fought to stay, but the pull was irresistible, and slowly he was drawn back into the cold, unforgiving light. Back to the pain.

An ache radiated through his chest as he opened his eyes, revealing a rough wooden ceiling above. He quickly closed them again as a pounding began in his skull and stifled a groan, though none of those aches compared to the searing heat that engulfed his left hand.

Or rather, his missing left hand.

Images flickered through his mind and he saw again the creature as it attacked, the terrible grey eyes staring out from an all-too-human face. The thing might even have *been* human once, but there was nothing natural about the way it had moved in those caverns beneath the earth. Nothing normal about the strength it had wielded, about the way it had broken him.

Shuddering, Romaine pushed aside the memories and drew another breath. It hurt a little less this time. The scent of burning coal carried to his nostrils and he realised someone had lit the brazier. Exhaling, he forced his eyes open once more and struggled to sit up. The ache in his chest turned to a lancing pain, but if he didn't move too quickly it seemed manageable.

He gritted his teeth as his head swam and stars flashed across his eyes. When his vision finally cleared, Romaine was surprised to find himself in his own cabin. His wounds couldn't be as bad as he'd feared if they hadn't kept him in the infirmary. Then again, he supposed a medic could do little for broken ribs or severed hands.

His gaze passed over the cabin, though the space was hardly worthy of the name. His bed was pressed up against the wall opposite the entrance, and there were few furnishings besides the brazier in the corner and the clothes chest tucked against the wall. He didn't need anything more than that, between taking his meals in the soldiers' mess hall and the occasional visit to the communal bathhouse. Indeed, the cabin was more than a simple soldier could normally expect. While those of other nations were bunked in barracks of fifty, the last soldier of Calafe slept alone.

Grief washed over him like a wave, threatening to overwhelm him. He had set off on an expedition in search of hidden ruins, of a place abandoned by the Gods. Tunnels dug beneath the earth, sealed away for millennium, their secrets with them. But the site was in enemy territory, in lands that had once belonged to his people. Romaine hadn't expected to return. He had gone to protect the men and women he had mentored, Perfugian recruits who had stood little chance of surviving without his guidance.

How fitting, then, that he should now find himself back here. Alone.

Romaine scrunched his eyes closed, struggling to contain the pain, the sorrow. He had failed them all—Lukys, Travis, Dale and so many others—failed to protect them, to save them. Now they were all gone, slain by the Tangata, their corpses left for the scavengers.

Was he cursed to forever suffer this grief, to watch everyone he cared for perish, while he lived on? Even his family had been taken from him, so long ago now, yet the wound still felt fresh. The memory of his son lying dead in the snow, of his wife's silent corpse, haunted him to this day. They too he had lost to the Tangata, the first of many he had loved. After a decade of war, Romaine was tired of counting the bodies.

At least there was still Cara.

Regret touched him as he thought of the young woman. *She*

might have saved the others, might have saved them all, if only he had not been so blinded by his hatred. He'd thought her a spy, one of the Tangata that had learned to camouflage itself amongst humanity. They'd all seen her eyes in those awful tunnels, seen the grey madness of the enemy lurking there.

But they'd been wrong.

Cara wasn't Tangata at all, nor even human. She was a God.

Driven by desperation, she had revealed herself on the banks of the Illmoor River. The sight of her soaring across the muddied waters, auburn wings spread wide, was one Romaine would remember until his dying days.

He could hardly believe it now, that one of the Divine had hidden amongst them, had spoken with them, befriended them. The Gods were mythical beings, their true nature long since hidden beneath rumour and legend. To think of one living amongst humanity…it changed everything.

Yet even Cara's power was limited. Alone, she had fought to rescue their friends. But it had not been enough to stem the tide of Tangata that had swarmed across the banks of the Illmoor. In the end she had been forced to retreat, able only to save the Queen's Archivist, Erika. The others…

Romaine scrunched his eyes closed and levered himself to his feet. The agony returned to his chest, but it seemed preferable now to the pain of his loss. He staggered to the trunk at the foot of his bed and retrieved a fresh tunic—the one he still wore was stained with blood. It was a struggle to pull it over his broad shoulders with only one hand. So strange, how he could feel it still. If he closed his eyes, he could swear his fingers were there...

But no, better he face reality. There was only the ruined stump now. The thought filled him with dread, and his gaze was drawn to the great-axe that had been left propped against the head of his bed. He reached for it, then paused.

The axe was a two-handed weapon. Desperation had allowed him to wield it against the Tangata in defence of his friends, but even then, only by luck had he survived the encounter. No, it would be the height of arrogance to continue carrying it into battle. His hand returned to his side and he clenched it into a fist. He would need to find a new weapon.

In the meantime, Romaine turned his attention back to dressing himself, pulling on a fresh pair of pants and a belt. The simple manoeuvre left him panting, the pain in his chest robbing him of strength. But he managed it before slumping back to the bed, gasping.

The murmur of voices came from outside as the citizens of Fogmore woke to begin their days, and the squeak of boards from overhead announced that his neighbours had risen. Romaine let out a sigh, struggling to beat back the despair. What was the point of leaving his bed? If not for Erika, he would have lain down and died back on the banks of the Illmoor. He would have finally been free. Now he wondered what madness had taken him, that he had listened to the woman.

She had claimed to be the daughter of his fallen king. Even now, the thought made his stomach flutter. The Calafe king had been slain in the first battle against the Tangata, when he'd led an allied army deep into enemy territory. It was said the enemy had taken him by surprise, decimating the Calafe forces before the Flumeeren warrior queen had come to their aid. That had been the beginning of the end for his people.

Maybe that was why, through the pain and fatigue, he had accepted Erika's claim so readily. But in the cold light of day, her assertion seemed farcical.

The voices in the street were growing louder, and letting out a sigh, Romaine rose from the bed. He took a moment to gather his strength, then staggered to the door and slipped into his boots. Deciding the laces were beyond him, he pushed out into the street instead. A cold breeze greeted him, a reminder that winter had not yet released its grip on the land. Ducking his head beneath the doorway, Romaine stepped outside.

A light snow was falling, though the passage of people had already crushed it into the muddy streets. Clouds hid the sun above, but from the faintness of the light Romaine knew it still to be early. He pulled the door closed and started down the three wooden steps that led to street level, taking care not to slip on any ice and injure himself further.

"Romaine!"

He had just placed his boot into the puddle at the bottom of the stairs when a voice cut through the crowd. A moment later, he glimpsed the scout Lorene moving towards him down the street. The man had not accompanied the Perfugians south with Romaine, but he was probably one of the few Flumeeren soldiers he knew beyond a casual acquaintance.

Relieved for an excuse to rest, Romaine sat on the bottom stair. More than a few of the passersby flashed him strange looks as they went about their business, but Romaine ignored them, his attention instead on the approaching scout. There was a sense of controlled urgency about the man. He was puffing by the time he stopped in front of Romaine and his cheeks were a bright red, as though he'd run the entire way. Even so, he still had time to frown as he looked Romaine up and down.

"The medics said you'd be in bed for a week," Lorene commented.

"Fast healer, lad," Romaine grunted, though his head was swimming. "Something you came to tell me?"

Lorene hesitated, seeming to doubt himself for a moment. He swallowed, jaw tight. It obviously wasn't good news. Romaine wondered what fresh agony the world had in store for him.

"It's Cara…ah, the Goddess," Lorene croaked. "She's gone. We think the Archivist took her."

❧ 2 ☙

THE FUGITIVE

E rika sat in the front of the sailboat, watching how the mist curled around the bow, how it clung to the swirling waters. The white tendrils hid the night sky, concealed everything but for a sparse foot around them. It also hid them. Just as well—with their pursuers out in force, the fugitives needed every advantage they could get. Even now she could hear the voices on the river, the distant calls of the Flumeeren hunters, seeking their prize.

They would not have her.

It was the second night since she had fled the town of Fogmore, aided by the mysterious Gemaho spy. Her gaze was drawn to where the woman sat at the back of the boat, hand on the tiller. Erika didn't even know the woman's name—only that she'd been sent by the King of Gemaho. Why the man would want to help her, Erika couldn't understand, though…

Her eyes fell to the vessel's third occupant: the woman lying chained at Erika's feet. At first glance, Cara might have been mistaken for human. Copper hair hung across her shoulders and the amber eyes that looked out from her narrow face were far from the Tangatan grey. Her clothes were plain, grey and red, borrowed from their Flumeeren hosts.

But even in the darkness, there was one stark difference between Cara and a human, one that marked her as one of the Divine.

Wings.

Swathed in auburn feathers, they sprouted from somewhere near the middle of Cara's back. At this moment they were furled around the young Goddess and bound in chains for good measure —along with her arms and legs. Thankfully, they seemed to be enough to hold her. Erika didn't want to find out what the Goddess would do to them if she ever got free.

Shivering, Erika's gaze returned to the mists, and she found herself wondering what she was doing there. She was an Archivist, a student of history, of the Gods that had vanished after casting down the world. She should be asking Cara questions, seeking answers to the mysteries that had plagued humanity for centuries. Not locking her up, not making her their enemy.

Yet, what choice did she have?

She had lost everything in that disastrous venture south: her reputation, her position in the Flumeeren court, her chance to stand side by side with the nobility. All because of General Curtis's betrayal, because he had sent her Perfugian recruits instead of real soldiers. The queen had promised penance should she fail. Erika wasn't about to allow the general's incompetence to cost her life. So when the King of Gemaho had offered her a lifeline, she had grasped it with both hands.

She would do whatever it took to survive.

Even if that meant betraying a God.

Erika's insides twisted and her gaze was drawn back to Cara. She winced as their eyes met and she saw the rage flickering in those amber depths. That look promised revenge. Instinctively, Erika found herself flexing her right hand, on which she wore a gauntlet crafted from impossibly fine wires of an unknown metal. It had fused to her very flesh when she'd first put it on and she had been unable to remove it since.

Light blossomed around her knuckles as she clenched the fist. The gauntlet held incredible magic, power enough to strike down the Gods themselves. It was with this that she had captured Cara, taking the Goddess by surprise. A violent, unholy act.

Just a few weeks ago, it would have been unthinkable to Erika. Yet she had done it with hardly a thought. Now she sat sailing through the night, fleeing the kingdom that had supported her for over a decade, intent on delivering the Goddess into the hands of their enemies. Never mind that the Gemaho King had tried to take her life just a few weeks before, or that Cara had rescued her from the Tangata, that she had been Erika's friend.

A shudder racked her and she allowed her hand to relax. The light died and she found herself looking into Cara's eyes again. Now she saw the pain beneath the Goddess's anger. All of Erika's excuses, all her justifications, withered beneath that look.

Finally she looked away, unable to meet the accusation in her former friend's eyes. If the Goddess wanted to live amongst humans, it was time she was taught this lesson. It was one Erika had learnt well as a child. Don't trust, don't allow others to get close. To do so was to invite betrayal. Others were only worth as much as they could benefit you.

And Cara…well, she was the key to a secret world, to powers unknown, ones even greater than the gauntlet. First though, they had to escape the lands of Flumeer.

"Get down," a voice hissed from the back of the boat.

Immediately, Erika slipped from the bench and crouched alongside Cara. Behind, her companion ducked beneath the gunwale. In the darkness, Erika could see little of the woman from Gemaho. Whispers carried through the night and Erika squinted, trying to pierce the mist, seeking the source. An orange light flickered into life and the breath caught in her throat. Another ship was drifting somewhere out on the river.

Fortunately they had kept to the northern shore. The hunters loomed farther out in the currents, though as Erika watched, the light from their ship seemed to grow. She looked back as their boat shifted direction. Her silent companion had her hands on the tiller, directing them towards the shore. There was a *thud* as the bow pressed up onto the mud, barely audible over the whispers of the breeze.

Erika held her breath, eyes on the glow of their pursuers. It continued to grow closer. Silently, she tightened her fist, preparing to summon the power. Then she hesitated, glancing at the gauntlet, wondering. She had come to rely on its magic since finding it in that hidden chamber, come to thrill in its power.

Erika's heart thundered in her ears as she looked on her metallic fist. She had made so many mistakes these past weeks, had hurt so many people. Shouldn't she care? A tremor shook her as she recalled the creatures they had encountered in the caverns beneath the earth, driven mad by the magic they had stolen. Could the same be happening to her?

The gauntlet drew on her own energies—she had discovered as much on the banks of the Illmoor, when its exertion had all but drained away her life force. But she would have known if it was changing her, if it was making her like…those things in the dark. Wouldn't she?

Releasing a breath Erika hadn't realised she'd been holding, she unclenched her fist, allowing the light to die. What was she thinking, anyway? The gauntlet's magic was only useful in close quarters. Her hunters would know that—their archers would pepper her with arrows long before they came close enough for Erika to use the power.

"Make sure the girl is quiet."

Erika frowned as the spy's words drew her back to the present. Her companion never addressed Cara as a God. It seemed blasphemous, though of course, the Gemaho were not known to be a Godly people. Still, with the wings just…hanging there, Erika would have thought they'd be enough to convert the most studious of disbelievers.

Even so, she shifted closer to Cara and made sure her gag was firmly in place. The Goddess squawked in protest, but the cloth muffled the sound and it was easily lost in the lapping of water against the hull. Turning back to the spy, Erika nodded that their… passenger was secure…

…and noticed the light still growing brighter in the mist beyond their white sail. Her heart thudded painfully against her chest and instinctively she clutched a hand to Cara's shoulder, pressing gently. Erika's own strength could never harm the Goddess, but with her gauntleted fist, the threat was clear and Cara ceased to struggle.

At the rear of the boat, her companion cursed softy and reached into a pack. Erika expected the spy to draw out a weapon, but instead her hand emerged with a smooth sphere of glass. Silently, the woman held up the object, a frown wrinkling the plain features of her face.

Erika's gaze was drawn to the sphere as it began to glow. A cry started in her throat—the light would give them away—but immediately the glow faded, becoming muted, the orb itself fuzzy and indistinct. Abruptly, it vanished—and the woman's hand with it, as though they had been drawn into some other dimension. The spy did not react, only raised a finger to her lips as the effect expanded outwards, swallowing her arm, then the woman herself entirely.

Clutching at the Goddess lying alongside her, Erika fought not to scream as the strange magic crept across the boat towards them. Within seconds, half the boat had been consumed, until finally she could take it no longer. Stifling a cry, Erika scrambled up, preparing to throw herself over the side before the magic claimed her as well.

"Don't move," a voice hissed from the emptiness where the spy had crouched a moment earlier.

Erika's mouth fell open and she froze. The magic reached her before she could recover from the confusion, and she watched in horrified fascination as it swallowed her leg. Beside her, Cara blinked out, even as the power continued up her waist, her chest, her throat. Silently she sucked in a breath, as though that might save her from being wiped from existence…

Darkness followed as the magic enclosed her, and for a moment Erika thought it was over, that the power had claimed her. Then the black fell away, and she found herself clinging again to the sides of the sailboat. Cara lay alongside her, while the spy sat nearby, finger still to her lips.

Erika's racing heart began to subside. She looked around, seeking their pursuers, and found herself surrounded by a bubble of light. It was as though they had been encased in a snow globe, the plaything of some giant. The outside world could barely be seen through its glow. Surely their pursuers must see it?

But recalling again how the spy and boat had vanished before her eyes, Erika realised that the globe had simply rendered them invisible from without. Her gaze was drawn to the orb still clutched in the hands of her companion. Its crystal surface was aglow, seemingly a reflection of the magic that surrounded them. Somehow, this object concealed them.

They sat in silence, listening for the telltale whispers of their pursuers. Breathing deeply, Erika strained her ears for hint of their approach, for sign they had been spotted. The acrid scent of burning pitch carried to her nose and she caught the occasional whisper, of voices on the breeze, the squeak of boards beneath boots, waves lapping upon a wooden hull, but the hunters came no closer, and slowly even those soft noises faded away.

Silence returned to the night, and finally the Gemaho spy released her grip on the globe. Its light died away and the greater orb vanished, returning them to the world. Erika watched as the woman put the object away. It had to be another artefact from the Gods.

They waited a few minutes more before the spy resumed her station at the tiller and directed them out into the currents.

"Where did you find that?" Erika whispered as the wind filled their sails.

The woman shrugged. "You are not the only one who searches for remnants from before The Fall, Archivist," she replied.

Erika nodded, resuming her seat at the bow. "Why don't you use it all the time?"

The woman frowned as she looked up from the rudder. "Have you not discovered the limitations of your own artefact, Archivist?"

"Ah," Erika nodded. "It draws from your own strength?"

The spy obviously didn't deign the question worthy of reply, for her lips remained pursed closed, eyes on the swirling mists. Erika let out a sigh, following her gaze, wondering at the situation she had gotten herself into. She had only this unnamed woman's word that she could trust the king.

"My name is Erika, by the way," she murmured after a time, then: "What should I call you?

Before, Erika had rarely bothered with names. Those worthy of her respect already knew her name, and she knew theirs. Those of lesser rank used the title "Archivist." It was the same with all those who participated in the dance of power amongst the Flumeeren nobility. But after betraying the queen and fleeing her adopted nation, it no longer seemed quite...right.

The spy did not reply immediately, and Erika sighed, returning her gaze to the darkness. It was going to be a long trip to Gemaho—

"You may call me Maisie," her companion finally whispered. "And I suggest you get some sleep. We cannot travel during the daylight. I will need someone to keep watch while I rest, or it will be a long three days to the Fortress Illmoor."

THE SOLDIER

The Tangatan leader stood in the centre of the clearing, its back turned towards Lukys, gaze lifted to the cliffs hemming the valley. Long white hair hung across its broad shoulders and like most Tangata, its only weapon was a dagger worn on its belt. A plain tunic and cotton leggings would have suggested a simple upbringing amongst humans, but was normal attire for the Tangata. Indeed, with its stiff posture and hands clasped behind its back, there was an almost noble bearing about this individual.

Lukys hesitated at the sight of the lone figure, glancing back at his Tangatan escort, but she said nothing. She had freed him of his bonds and now watched on with an expectant look. Taking his cue, Lukys swallowed and stepped into the clearing. Sunlight washed across his face and he felt his fears dissipate. Lifting his head to the sky, he drew strength from its warmth, the night's chill banished in an instant.

A flicker at the edge of his vision drew Lukys's gaze back to the Tangatan leader. He swallowed as he found the creature now watching him, grey eyes seemingly darker despite the daylight. He'd never paid attention to the differences between individual Tangata, but there was something distinctive about the creature before him, an aura of power, of invincibility, that set his knees shaking.

Human. The voice was louder than those of the guards, than the whispers of the others. Lukys grated his teeth, struggling to hold himself in place, to fight the urge to flee. *It is time we spoke.*

Lukys shuddered, but he was slowly getting used to the voices, and he straightened. "I am a soldier of Perfugia," he said shortly, hoping the creature was unaware of their true reputation, "and you will get nothing from me."

Perfugia? Laughter whispered in Lukys's ears as the creature paced a circle around him. His courage wilted beneath that appraisal and he found himself shrinking, as though to escape his captor's scrutiny. But there was no escaping the words in his mind. *Ah yes, I see the blue beneath the filth. A fitting addition.*

Lukys flinched as the creature came to a stop before him. Its face was just a few inches from his own. A sickly smile twisted its lips as it leaned closer.

Tell me, human, how does it feel to be betrayed by your own kind?

A lump lodged in Lukys's throat and he knew he was exposed, his every secret laid bare beneath this monster's gaze. It knew he was a failure, that the Sovereigns of Perfugia sent the worst of their people to the frontier to die, rather than consume precious resources. His gaze dropped to the forest flaw.

"My name is Lukys." It felt important to speak the words, to remind himself that he was no longer the naïve man who had arrived in Fogmore all those weeks ago. He had made something of himself since those first days, had stood against the Tangata and creatures far worse. Straightening, he looked again at the Tangata. Suddenly his captor no longer seemed quite so intimidating. "What do you want, beast?"

A scowl crossed the creature's face. *Respect, human.* The words rumbled in his mind and he glimpsed the anger in those terrible grey eyes. *I am called Adonis. You would do well to remember the name.*

An icy breeze blew across Lukys's neck as the creature turned away, hands clasped behind its back once more. Lukys opened his mouth, then closed it, struggling to string together a sentence in his mind.

"My apologies," he said, finally managing to approximate something resembling words. "I...didn't realise you used names."

Laughter rasped from the creature's throat as it swung on him, causing Lukys to flinch.

How little you humans think of us, its voice whispered in his mind.

Lukys clenched his fists and met the creature's gaze. He could see the loathing there, the hatred. "Why didn't you kill me?" he asked abruptly.

The Tangatan leader did not reply immediately. It stood watching him with those cold eyes, thin lips pursed, long white hair waving gently in a breeze. Anger touched Lukys as he suffered that piercing gaze, and he found himself stepping forward.

"You killed my friends," he snarled, the fiery heat in his stomach giving him courage. "Slaughtered them, so why spare us? Why go to the trouble of dragging us all this way?"

Still the creature did not reply, only stood staring at him, unblinking. The rage left Lukys as quickly as it had appeared and he found himself retreating a step, a sudden terror sweeping through his veins. The Tangatan leader slowly shook its head.

So…archaic, your kind. Its voice sounded amused. *Screaming your thoughts for all the world to hear.*

It advanced a step and Lukys tried to retreat further. A hand like iron caught him by the arm—he'd forgotten the female still stood nearby. Unable to break her grasp, he stood fixed in place while the leader approached.

Perhaps we are toying with you. Is that not what you humans do, when you take our people captive? It paused, still eyeing him, head bent slightly to the side. *Or is it for some other purpose? Tell me, Lukys of Perfugia, what is the fate of my brothers and sisters you take beyond these lands?*

"I…" Lukys trailed off.

He'd never seen the captives Adonis spoke of—Perfugia did not keep Tangatan captives. But he had read of such practices at the academy. The creatures were extraordinarily difficult to take alive, but human armies had on occasion been known to subdue a Tangata enough to be captured.

Initially, the Flumeeren physicians had hoped to discover the secrets of Tangatan physiology from those captives. But in ten years, they'd made little progress, and eventually the prisoners had been put to other uses…

Images flickered into Lukys's mind, sketches he had glimpsed in his textbooks, of Tangata in cages at the Flumeeren court, of beasts with arms and legs severed, of creatures tormented by their human gaolers. Lukys had thought little of the images at the time—after all, the Tangata were a distant threat to remote Perfugia, an inhuman enemy that occasionally called for them to send soldiers to the frontier...

A soft growl was the only warning Lukys had before Adonis caught him by the throat. He gasped, but the sound was abruptly cut off as the Tangata lifted him into the air. Desperate, Lukys kicked out. His boot connected with the creature's chest, but Adonis took no notice.

And you call us the monsters! Adonis's voice practically screamed into his mind.

The grip around Lukys's throat tightened, fingers digging into his flesh. He would have screamed if he could have drawn in enough breath. Instead, all he could manage was a pitiful squawk. Strength fading, he clasped at Adonis's fingers, trying to pry them loose, but there was no fighting this creature. Darkness circled his vision and the strength began to fade from his limbs. His mouth opened and closed, straining for even a wisp of oxygen.

Adonis! a voice cried in his mind.

Then suddenly Lukys was soaring through the air. He cried out, still aware enough to half curl into a ball before he struck the ground. The impact robbed him of whatever breath remained in his lungs. Dark spots danced across his eyes as he wheezed, gasping, until finally his chest filled.

Rolling onto his side, Lukys sucked in great lungfuls of the chill morning air, hardly able to believe he was alive. When he finally looked around, he was surprised to find the female Tangata standing across from Adonis. No sounds passed between the two, and yet... Lukys heard snatches of their voices. He closed his eyes, trying to concentrate through the pain, to draw meaning from the whispers...

Need...future...assignment...

Groaning, Lukys slumped back against the ground. It was no good. He could understand nothing from the snippets. It seemed he could only make out full sentences if the creatures directed their thoughts at him. He wondered why the female had interfered— Adonis was clearly her superior. It seemed they needed him for something...but what, Lukys couldn't begin to understand.

Bastard, he thought, looking again at Adonis.

Across the clearing, the Tangatan leader's head whipped around, the silver eyes fixing on Lukys. A wicked grin appeared on the creature's face and suddenly it was stalking towards him. Lukys tried to scramble away, but Adonis was faster still, and before Lukys could stand he was clutching him by the front of the shirt and hauling him to his feet.

So you can *Speak!* the creature exclaimed. There was triumph in the creature's words as they sounded in Lukys's mind. *You're the one we've been hearing.*

Lukys struggled to break free of the Tangata's grip, and to his surprise, Adonis released him. He staggered, then slowly backed away. "What are you talking about?" he croaked, throat still in agony.

You're different, Lukys. The Tangata's words chased after him. *We can Hear you. We've been hearing you for weeks.*

What? Lukys whispered in his mind, staring at the creature, unable to believe…

We thought it was the Anahera at first, Adonis continued, though Lukys did not recognise the name. *But no, even young, she would not be so unschooled.*

"What are you talking about?" Lukys said aloud, rejecting that inner dialogue. It felt unnatural, projecting a thought for this creature to hear.

Laughter answered the question. *How little your species understands of our power,* the Tangata said eventually. Then Adonis leaned in close. *Did you not wonder how we discovered your intrusion into our territory, how we found the hidden Birthing Grounds?*

Lukys shook his head, but unbidden, memories flickered into his mind, of the strange dreams he'd experienced ever since arriving in Fogmore. He'd had another of the nightmares that night in the mountains, the night before the Tangata had found them…

"No…" he said. "It's not possible."

It had been him all along. The Archivist had accused Cara of betraying them, before they'd learned her true identity. But Lukys had seen the map, had known where the Archivist was leading them, the location of the ancient site of the Gods. Unknowingly, Lukys has betrayed them all.

He sank to his knees, thinking again of the bodies they'd found in the abandoned settlement. His fellow Perfugians, betrayed by his careless mind, dead because of him.

I should thank you, Adonis continued, and Lukys could hear the disdain in his words. *We have worked long to keep the secrets of the ancient world from humanity. Had we not arrived first, I shudder to think what new magics might have fallen into human hands. Though it was a shame the Old Ones were…lost.*

Adonis's words ended up abruptly, and Lukys thought he caught a flicker of something in the creature's eyes. Fear? A shiver touched him as he recalled what had waited in those tunnels beneath the earth. The Tangata that had arrived before them had woken something—the "Old Ones" Adonis spoke of. It seemed even the Tangata feared the creatures.

"What are they?" he asked.

A darkness crept across Adonis's face and he quickly looked away. The clearing fell still, and Lukys knelt, waiting, wondering…

The last hope of the Tangata.

The words were so quiet Lukys wasn't sure whether Adonis had meant for him to hear them. He did not respond, and after a moment the Tangata shook himself. Drawing in a breath, he turned to where the female still stood watching.

Put him back with the other one. The order was directed at the female, but it seemed the Tangata were able to make their thoughts heard to more than one listener, should they wish. *The Matriarch will wish to question him further. Perhaps together we can find the source of his ability.*

With that, Adonis clasped his hands behind his back and turned away. Lukys shivered. The action was unnervingly similar to a nobleman dismissing a servant. Shaking his head, he rose as the female approached. Keeping her eyes averted from Adonis, she took his hands and bound them again, thankfully in front of him this time.

She started to lead him away, but Adonis spoke again before they reached the edge of the clearing.

Sophia. Lukys's escort froze at the name, her head slowly turning to look back. The Tangatan leader stood staring after them. *Your insolence has not gone unnoticed.*

The female Tangata swallowed. *Yes, Adonis.*

Then they were retreating, the female leading him back into the trees. Lukys found himself staring at her back, remembering how she had interfered, stopped Adonis from killing him.

"Sophia…" he said suddenly. Ahead, the Tangata froze, spinning to look at him, eyes wide. Lukys spoke into the silence: "That's your name?"

Light filtered through the canopy overhead, revealing the confusion on his captor's face. Seeing such a human emotion made it easier to ignore those terrible grey eyes, and Lukys found himself taking note of her other features. A small scar marked her cheek, accented by copper skin tanned in the southern summers. Twigs and branches tangled in her ash-brown hair and dirt streaked her plain-spun tunic and leggings, though she was probably cleaner than Lukys after his weeks in the wilderness.

Yes, her reply came finally, a frown still creasing her forehead.

"Why did you save me?" Lukys blurted out before he lost his nerve.

The Tangata leaned her head to the side. *You killed my partner,* she replied, her frown deepening. *You are mine.*

❧ 4 ❧

THE FUGITIVE

Exhaustion weighed heavily on Erika's shoulders as the soldier led them through the narrow corridor. Wide windows on the wall opened to the dawn, granting her a view of the shadowed gorge beyond the ramparts of the Illmoor Fortress. After three nights of sailing in darkness, they had chased the rising sun to arrive before the daylight. She could see it even now, its orange glow just appearing on the distant cliffs.

It almost felt strange, to be on her feet as daylight approached. They had spent their days in hiding, the boat pulled in amongst tall reeds that dotted the shallows of the Illmoor. Each day she had lain waiting in that boat for their pursuers to catch them, for the arrows to find her, to strike her down.

Now she was finally safe from the queen's reach. All that remained to be seen was whether the King of Gemaho would keep to his word. She prayed it was so. Walking the corridors of the Illmoor Fortress, she was in his power now.

Guards had met them on the shore outside the fortress, crossbows trained on their little sailboat. Thankfully, they had lowered the weapons when they'd seen Maisie. With the guards help they had been able to lift Cara from the boat with minimal effort. By then they'd covered her wings with a heavy fur coat, thinking it better not to announce her presence to all the world.

Finally they were led into a high-ceilinged room lit by brass chandeliers and furnished with white velvet sofas and tables of glass and steel. The lavish sight brought relief for Erika—she'd half-feared they were being led to the dungeons. The sensation was immediately followed by one of discomfort. Her only bath for the last two weeks had been an unplanned dip in the river water. She had long since ceased to detect her own scent, but with her hair stiff with mud and clothes stained brown, she had no illusions about the current state of her appearance.

She turned to the guards to ask about a private chamber to bathe, but they were already vanishing into the corridor. The door swung closed behind them with a distinct *thunk* that suggested a locking bar had been slid into place on the other side. She looked at Maisie, but the woman seemed unconcerned. Cara, on the other hand, smirked.

"Looks like we're both prisoners now," Cara muttered. Her chains clinked as she wandered across to one of the sofas and slumped into its cushions.

Erika winced as dirt from the Goddess's clothes left streaks of dirt on the velvet. "I don't think our host will appreciate you ruining—"

"Bitch," Cara interrupted. The scowl the Goddess wore suggested she knew exactly what she was doing.

Letting out a sigh, Erika turned away. She'd tried various times during the journey to explain herself, but Cara had remained stubbornly silent, deaf to anything Erika said. The only constant were the looks of hatred the little Goddess sent every time Erika looked her way.

"I wouldn't worry about it," Maisie added, reclining into one of the sofas herself. "Nguyen tends not to care about such things."

"Is he here, you think?" Erika asked. She cast an eye over the sofas, before muttering a curse and falling into the nearest one. She was too exhausted to remain on her feet for a second longer.

"I sent a bird from Fogmore before we left," the spy replied. "I doubt he'll have waited in Solaris for what I promised him."

Erika narrowed her eyes at the woman's words. What *had* Maisie promised the king? Did the spy intend to betray her and claim

Erika's offerings as her own? She clenched her fist and felt the pulsing of the gauntlet's magic. If Maisie did betray her, she would find her lifespan measured in minutes rather than years…

Angrily, Erika shook her head, banishing the thought. Despite her chosen discipline, Maisie had been a surprisingly pleasant travelling companion—at least compared to Cara's open animosity. They had developed a system to sleep and keep watch, and the woman had even shown Erika a little about what it took to navigate the swirling currents of the Illmoor. Not enough that she could sail unsupervised, but at least it had taken Erika's mind off the constant threat of the hunters.

Still though, if the king was in the fortress, *where* was he? Surely he'd been summoned as soon as the guards recognised Maisie? A frown wrinkling her forehead, Erika glanced at the door, impatient—

She flinched as her eyes fell upon a man standing in the doorway. Somehow, he'd opened the door and entered without them noticing. No, without *Erika* noticing—there was a knowing grin on Maisie's face as she watched Erika's reaction, and she caught a snort from Cara. Chuckling, the man stepped into the room, allowing the door to close behind him.

"Greetings," he said, spreading his arms. "Maisie, I have had searchers out watching for you. The river is crawling with Flumeer. I was beginning to fear they might exceed even your talent for concealment."

A smile crossed the spy's lips as she rose and gave a short bow. "Gladly, that day has not yet come, Nguyen."

Erika swallowed as she looked from the spy to the newcomer. Nguyen, King of Gemaho. Though he wore no crown or other indication of his position, there was a presence to the man, a power in the sea-green eyes that watched her from across the room. Age had added white streaks to the short-cropped brown hair and his clothes were plain, if expertly tailored. A short sword hung from his belt and he wore leather riding gloves. Had their arrival interrupted other plans the king might have had for the morning?

Her stomach twisted uncomfortably as the king turned his gaze on her, and she stood in silence, suffering his inspection. This man was regarded as a traitor by the Calafe, for he had abandoned the alliance after the disastrous southern campaign. Without Gemaho soldiers to aid them, the lands of Calafe had fallen all the quicker to the Tangata. Erika supposed she should hate him for that—after all, Calafe was her native homeland.

But then, the Calafe had turned their back on Erika's family after the king—her father—had fallen. By birth, she should have been a princess, honoured amongst the Calafe nobility. Instead the council had named her mother the king's paramour, and sent them from New Nihelm in exile.

Why should Erika care whether this man had betrayed the Calafe, when they had done the same to her?

"So this is Queen Amina's famed Archivist," the king said finally.

Erika offered a short bow. "Thank you for inviting me to your kingdom, Your Majesty," she replied.

The king wrinkled his forehead. "It was the least I could do for the daughter of an old friend."

For a moment, Erika didn't understand the man's words. Her heart twisted in her chest and her mouth suddenly felt dry. She swallowed, struggling for words, as the stoic expression she had cultivated amongst the Flumeeren nobility slipped. There was only one man alive who knew the identify of her father, and she had left him in an infirmary bed back in Fogmore. Surely Romaine hadn't told anyone…

"I…what?" she croaked.

The king chuckled. "I came to know King Micah quite well during our campaign in the south," the king replied. "It pained me when he…fell in that last battle. It was some years before I learned what had become of his family. I have followed your progress with interest over the last years."

Erika clenched her fists, struggling to contain her sudden anger. "I suppose that's why your man tried to have me killed," she grated.

The smile slipped from the king's lips. "A regrettable miscommunication," he replied. "I was most relieved to learn you had survived."

"And was it also a 'regrettable miscommunication' when you abandoned my people to the Tangata?" Erika spat, taking a step towards the king. In her anger, her earlier thoughts were thrust aside.

Arms clasped behind his back, the king stood regarding her for a long moment. Then he sighed. "I have made many mistakes over the last decade—first among them leading my soldiers against the Tangata. I argued against the invasion, but in the end, I allowed myself to be convinced." He shook his head. "We were fools to poke the hornet's nest. Thousands of lives were lost in the south, and for what? Our forces were so depleted that we couldn't even defend our own lands."

"You didn't even try to defend Calafe," Erika hissed.

"It pains me, what has befallen Micah's nation," the king replied, "but the sand upon the shore cannot hold back the tides. What we witnessed in the south…" He swallowed, and there was a tightness to his voice as he continued. "The Tangata cannot be stopped, not over open land. Once the Agzor Fortress fell, Calafe was already lost."

Erika opened her mouth, then closed it as she saw the pain lurking in the king's eyes. The anger slipped from her like water through a sieve. He might have only been acting—he was a king after all—but something about the way he spoke about her father, of Calafe, Erika found herself believing him.

"What's done is done," she said finally. "Regardless of the past, it seems you are now the lesser of two evils, Your Majesty." She bowed her head, projecting defeat. It would not hurt for this man to underestimate her. "The Flumeeren Queen is mad—she would do anything to gain the magic I hold."

To her surprise, Nguyen laughed. "The courts of Flumeer have trained you well, Princess." Erika started at the title—only her father had ever called her that—but the man continued before she could reply. "You do not need to flatter me, nor belittle my rivals. I imagine Amina and I are much alike. We both seek to protect our nations, to keep our peoples safe from enemies. Though, I'll admit our approaches tend to differ somewhat."

Erika frowned and glanced at Maisie, struggling to piece together the meaning behind the king's words, but the spy only shrugged. On the other couch, Cara still sat glaring at the two of them. The king had not yet addressed the Goddess, and for herself,

Cara had been remarkably quiet for the duration of the conversation. Almost as though—

Click.

A cry burst from Erika's lips as the steel cuffs slid from the Goddess's wrists. With a flicker of movement she was on her feet. The jacket kept her from spreading her wings and chains still bound her legs, but the shimmer in her eyes suggested they would not hinder her.

In panic, Erika lifted her gauntleted hand and the magic ignited in her fingertips. Its power thrummed in her ears and she felt that familiar rush, the feeling of ecstasy that promised she could destroy her enemies…

…a gasp tore from Erika and she staggered, closing her fist, smothering the magic.

What was that?

A growl returned her attention to Cara. A snarl twisted the Goddess's face and before anyone could react, she leapt for the king, fingers outstretched…

…only to slam down into one of the glass tables, all momentum stolen from her spring. A scream tore from Cara's throat as she smashed through the glass, sending shards tumbling across the floor. Then the cry cut off, though her mouth was still stretched wide, the veins of her throat bulging against her skin. Glass cut her flesh as she thrashed amongst the remnants of the table, as though she were in some great agony…

Erika's gaze dropped to her gauntlet, but the light remained dim, its power subdued. It was not she that had struck down the Goddess.

"I see you're getting better with the gauntlet's power," Maisie said as she stepped around the ruin of the table.

Turning, Erika took in the king's outstretched left hand. But he didn't wear a gauntlet, only the leather riding gloves…the breath hissed from Erika's throat as she realised what he'd done. He hadn't been going for a ride—the gloves were to conceal the ancient artefact he wore, a mirror of her own.

Smiling gently, the king finally lowered his hand and Cara slumped amongst the glass, her breath coming in ragged gasps. Despite herself, Erika felt a rush of guilt at the Goddess's treatment.

This wasn't right. Cara had been her friend, had saved her life. And this was how she repaid her?

"An interesting weapon, don't you think?" the king said conversationally as he stepped up alongside Erika to regard the crumpled Goddess. "I take it this is the fabled creature that was seen soaring over the waters of the Illmoor?"

Erika swallowed. "Goddess," she rasped, then belatedly added: "Her name is Cara."

"Does it speak?" the king asked.

A muffled snarl came from Cara as she pushed herself to her hands and knees. "Yes," she spat.

The king raised his gauntlet, his smile unchanged. "Well that's an improvement on the Tangata at least."

Breath hissed between Cara's teeth as she looked at the king. "You humans really know nothing about who you fight, do you?"

"Little enough," Nguyen agreed, surprisingly jovial for someone that had just been attacked by a God. "Was there a gap in our knowledge you would like to fill in for us?"

Cara sat back on her haunches. "I'm sure your ignorance could fill the endless miles between the earth and our moon," she muttered. She shifted her shoulders, then winced and glanced at the king. "Am I allowed to stretch, or are you going to smite me again, oh mighty king?"

Nguyen chuckled as he stepped back and gestured for her to stand. Cara climbed to her feet, obviously wary. Slowly, hesitantly, she pulled the jacket from her shoulders.

The king inhaled sharply as wings stretched across the room. Joints creaked and a moan of relief slipped from Cara's throat. The auburn feathers shone in the light of the chandelier and even Erika found herself retreating a step. Belatedly the king raised his gauntlet, but this time Cara made no move to attack. Instead, she closed her eyes and her face softened, obviously relieved to finally be free of the jacket's confinement.

Erika swallowed, still not quite able to process the sight. A feather had come free with the jacket, and it drifted across the room, coming to rest at her feet. It was almost a foot long and half as broad as her hand. Instinctively she crouched and picked it up, turning it in her fingers. In the days since fleeing Fogmore, her fear had been such that her mind had not lingered on the Goddess, but looking at the feather in her hand, the implications of what she'd done finally began to catch up with her.

Across the room, Cara opened her eyes and saw that they were all staring. Red tinged her cheeks and the wings quickly retracted against her back. Her gaze fell to the floor.

"You really have no idea how uncomfortable that thing is…" she muttered, gesturing at the jacket.

Erika swallowed, unable to summon the words. She figured the sight of Cara's fully unfurled wings tended to have that effect on people. Beside her, though, the king chuckled.

"So this is what you westerners call a God?" he asked. Hands clasped behind his back, he began to circle the room, as though to appraise Cara from every angle.

"What would you call her?" Erika asked, a frown curling her lips. She'd known the Gemaho were not the religious sort, but… surely not even they could maintain their disbelief with the winged Goddess standing before them.

"You know I can hear you, right?" Cara muttered, crossing her arms. A twitch tugged at her cheek.

"My apologies, of course," the king replied politely, as though he hadn't just sent the Goddess crashing through a glass table. He came to a stop before Cara. "It would seem we now have a simple way of answering our greatest theological questions. So…what do you call yourselves?"

Cara hesitated, mouth parted as though to speak. She bit her lips. "We call ourselves the Anahera."

Erika frowned, turning the word over in her mind. Of course the Gods would have their own name for themselves.

"And you are Gods?"

Cara answered the question with a shrug. "What is a God?"

The king nodded, as though her words had actually been an answer, then turned to Erika. "I suppose it is a matter of perspective," he said, gesturing with the hand that wore the gauntlet. "Surely whoever created these artefacts were Gods, and yet, why would they grant the devices power over themselves?"

"The Tangata were born from their magic," Erika said, quoting the legends. "Perhaps the gauntlets were crafted to fight the creatures."

"It could have been so." The king nodded along to Erika's logic. "But, what of this situation we find ourselves in? Cara is now my prisoner. Are your Gods truly so feeble as to be taken hostage by their own creations?"

"Still standing here," Cara muttered.

Looking from Cara to the king, Erika could only shake her head. "There is much I do not understand," she replied.

Her gaze lingered on Cara. The Goddess had relaxed her wings a little, allowing the auburn feathers to stretch out on either side of her. Her eyes were fixed on a point between Erika and the King, but Erika could see the tightness in her jaw, the way she clenched and unclenched her fists. Suddenly the Goddess turned and their eyes met.

Erika shivered as she looked into Cara's amber gaze and found herself transported back to those caverns beneath the earth. Her memory of that time was still hazy—she'd been struck in the head by one of the creatures—but one image stood out in sharp relief.

Cara covered in the blood, the unstoppable creatures dead at her feet, grey eyes piercing the darkness.

Silently Erika swallowed and looked away. Whatever the king said, she sensed that if Cara had really wanted them dead, no chains or weapon on this earth could stop her. Which begged the question: why had she allowed them to come this far?

"Regardless, it seems the good Anahera is to be my guest for a time," the king was saying. "I have had accommodations prepared. I hope you find them suitable. Erika, we shall arrange another meeting once you've rested—I understand there is a map in your possession that has been the source of much interest. For now, though, I must leave you. It seems I will soon have unwelcome guests on my doorstep."

"What's this?" Maisie asked, her head coming up.

Nguyen offered a grim smile. "It seems Cara's arrival and subsequent departure from Fogmore has stirred up quite the firestorm. The queen is on the march."

Erika's heart lurched at his words and she opened her mouth to demand more details, but already the king was striding away, vanishing through the doorway. A thundering sounded in Erika's ears as several servants stepped into the room. She hardly heard what they said. Her gaze fell to the gauntlet she still wore on her hand, and she heard again the last words the queen had spoken to her.

Do not fail me, Archivist. One way or another, I will have that magic.

5

THE FALLEN

Romaine staggered up the steps of the general's quarters, the effort less now than it had been a week ago. That knowledge offered him little comfort. Failure weighed heavily on his shoulders as he reached the door. It opened before he could grasp the handle, a guard within nodding a greeting. A second stood beyond, spear resting casually against his shoulder. These were uncertain times and the general was taking no risks with his safety.

Pain sliced Romaine's chest as he stepped inside and his boot caught on the doorstep. He thrust out his ruined arm to catch himself, and bit back a scream as it struck the doorframe. Belatedly he used his right hand to regain his balance. Teeth clenched, he paused on the threshold, ignoring the stares of the two guards. Stars danced across his vision but he dragged in great lungfuls of air, and eventually they passed.

"Can I…ah, help you with your coat, sir?" the guard who held the door asked awkwardly.

"I'm no damned officer," Romaine snapped, drawing himself up. "And by the Fall, I can take off my own coat."

Just as it had for the past week, it took Romaine a good minute to drag the heavy furs from his shoulders. By the time he hung the coat on a hook, he was panting again, and he cursed this newfound weakness. He had always been a quick healer, but then, he'd never had injuries like these. The loss of his hand was not something one simply *recovered* from. A short sword now hung from his belt, but even that was a façade. He still wasn't strong enough to even practice with the blade.

It dragged at him, to feel so weak. Each day he woke to the whisper of voices, telling him to surrender, to give in to his weakness.

And each day, Cara's face flickered into his mind, and he would force himself to his feet.

He had failed Lukys and the Perfugians, had failed his comrades and his wife, even his own son. He would not fail the Goddess.

Finally recovering his breath, he nodded to the guards and started down the corridor. These visits had become his daily habit, the only thing he felt he could do in his weakened state. Little enough, but it was a start, gave him a reason to leave his house each day.

The general's quarters were in one of Fogmore's original buildings and therefore was better built than the barracks and mess halls, which soldiers had hastily erected to accommodate the standing army now needed to defend the frontier. Panelled walls kept out the worst of the winter drafts and warmth radiated through the corridor from the brazier he knew would be burning in the general's office. Despite his age, General Curtis was renowned as a leader who did not back down from a hard day's work—but neither was he a man to suffer unnecessary discomforts.

Muffled voices carried from adjoining rooms as Romaine strode the length of the hall, the various secretaries and quartermasters of the army already at work. Curtis had not come to be general of the allied armies only for his prowess on the battlefield; it was his administration that kept the mammoth machine of the Flumeeren army running smoothly.

Romaine found the man himself sitting behind his desk, head craned over a stack of papers. Later in the day the general would be amongst the men, overseeing the installation of new defences and checking weapons and armour, or watching battle manoeuvres in the central square. Many questioned why a man so far above the rank and file would bother himself with such trivialities, but those did not understand the nature of soldiers. By working alongside the common soldiers, Curtis had gained a respect few generals could imagine. They would obey his orders without question, trusting he would not send them into danger needlessly.

Unless you were Perfugian, of course.

Anger flared in Romaine's stomach. Despite his respect for the man, there was no denying Curtis had sent Romaine's friends to their deaths. But he kept his anger on a short leash. There was nothing he could do for Lukys and the others now. They slept the endless sleep. But he could still help Cara.

"There has still been no news of the Goddess, Calafe," Curtis said, not looking up from his papers.

The man's dismissive attitude earned another flare of anger from Romaine. He strode to the desk and placed his palm on the papers. His fingers left a streak of dirt on the white.

"Do you not care?" he hissed.

The general looked up with a sigh. "She is a Goddess, Romaine," he said. "If she did not wish to go with the Archivist—"

"She would not have left willingly," Romaine snapped, "not without telling me. You did not see her, after we lost Lukys…"

How could he explain to this man that last look she had given him on the ship? The shared sorrow they had felt, at failing to save their friends. Goddess or no, Cara had been distinctly *human* in that moment, vulnerable, overwhelmed.

"Calm, Romaine," the general murmured, leaning back in his seat. "You were delirious on the river. We cannot pretend to know the mind of a God, the reasons why she came to us, nor why she left."

"She left because the blasted Archivist took her!"

Romaine hammered his fist onto the table to emphasis his point, but the effort only served to steal the breath from him, and instead he was left bent in two, gasping while the general watched on.

"Think rationally," the general said finally, entwining his hands. "We have had scouts out all week. If they had left the city by land or river, we would know of it. Only the Goddess herself could have stolen them away in such secrecy."

Romaine scrunched his eyes closed. The general's calm words made a certain sense, but Romaine knew the truth was different. It was just too convenient that the Archivist would disappear rather than face the consequences of her failure in the south. And Erika had disappeared with the one figure who could answer her questions about the past, about the Gods and their magic. No, something had happened between Cara and Erika. He just needed to—

"The man is right, Curtis," a voice from the corridor interrupted his thoughts. He swung around as a woman entered the office. "It pains me to admit it, but my Archivist has betrayed us. Yesterday, they passed beneath the walls of the Illmoor Fortress."

Romaine stood gaping as the woman crossed the room. Head held high and arms clasped behind her back, she walked with a cool confidence. She spoke with a Flumeeren accent, and in a kingdom whose women generally did not march to war, she wore chainmail armour stained scarlet. A sword hung from her belt and she carried a full-faced helm under one arm. Golden wires had been fused to the crown of the helmet, marking her as—

"Your Majesty!" the general exclaimed, stumbling to his feet. "What…how…I did not receive word of your coming?"

A smile appeared on Queen Amina's lips as she paused beside the general's desk. "You thought I would remain in Mildeth when the Gods walk the land again?" she asked, one eyebrow arching towards locks of almond hair.

"I…" Curtis trailed off, seemingly lost for words.

Amina *tisked*. "Though, imagine my disappointment when I learned you had *lost* one of the Divine."

Curtis swallowed visibly, but he quickly pulled himself together. "We believed she had left of her own accord, travelling with your Archivist, Your Majesty."

"I did not take you for a fool, Curtis." The queen's words were like acid. "Were your orders not to take the woman into custody the second she returned?"

"I…yes, Your Majesty, but…she said…" He withered beneath the monarch's glare.

"She said what?" the queen asked. "That you should ignore your queen's orders? You disappoint me, General." The queen paced to the rear of the office, where several medals hung on display. "After so many years of service, I had thought you knew me better. I ordered you to seize the Archivist for one simple reason: she has betrayed us to a foreign king."

Romaine's heart lurched at Amina's words and for a moment he thought she spoke of his own king, the man Erika had claimed as her father. But no, if she had passed into the Illmoor Fortress, Erika was heading east. The queen was speaking of Nguyen, king of the Gemaho.

"I suspected something was amiss when she claimed to have survived an attack by one of Nguyen's spies," the queen went on, once more facing Curtis. "That man is many things, but careless is not one of them. It seemed unlikely one of his agents could fail to best a simple Archivist. But I deemed it an acceptable risk, sending her south to retrieve artefacts of the Gods, knowing you would be here to detain her when she returned." There was a stringent pause as the queen eyed Curtis. "It seems in that regard, I was wrong."

The general bowed his head. "I have failed you, my queen."

"Yes." The queen's eyes shifted, focusing on Romaine. "It would seem this Calafe has more sense than my own general."

Romaine inclined his head as a show of respect, though he did not bow. She was not his queen.

Amusement danced in the woman's eyes at the gesture.

"Regardless, it seems the time has finally come to confront our eastern neighbours."

Hope flared in Romaine's stomach at the queen's words, while behind the desk, the general started.

"What?" he blurted out, then seeming to remember his manners, added: "Your Majesty, the frontier cannot afford the troops for a second campaign…"

"Of course not, General," the queen replied, "though I trust you will continue defending our lands against the scourge of the Tangata while I am otherwise occupied."

The general hesitated. "Your Majesty?"

The queen gave a throaty chuckle. "Thankfully, the Gods have blessed me with great foresight," she replied. Turning, she gestured in the direction of the town. "I did not leave Mildeth alone. The Queen's Guard marched with me, five thousand of our finest soldiers. By their might, I will finally claim retribution against the Gemaho for turning their back on our alliance."

A long silence followed the queen's proclamation. Romaine could see the indecision in the eyes of the general, the doubt. It was clear Curtis did not think it prudent to start a war against Gemaho while the Tangata still threatened the frontier. Despite Cara's abduction, Romaine was inclined to agree. Yet if this was the only way of getting her back…

"Your Majesty," Curtis said, clearing his throat, "I must advise against—"

"Your concern is noted, General," Queen Amina replied, her voice cold, "but you would do well to trust more in your queen. Just as I trust that you will defend these shores to the last man."

The general hesitated for another long moment, but finally he nodded. "I will, Your Majesty. You have my oath."

"Very good, General," the queen said. She turned her eyes on Romaine. "And what of you, Calafe?" she murmured. "What path will you take?"

"Your Majesty?" he asked, eyebrows drawing into a frown. He clenched his one good hand, though it only served to remind him of the missing one. Surely she couldn't be asking…

"The Gemaho have assaulted the personage of our Gods," Queen Amina mused. "It is my understanding you are familiar with her Divinity. I would have your aid on this journey, Calafe, if you wish it."

Romaine swallowed. "I would march through the fires of hell itself for Cara, Your Majesty."

The queen nodded. "As would I, Calafe," she replied. Then she smiled, and Romaine saw in her emerald eyes an anger, a rage that could only come from betrayal. "Besides," she added, "the good Archivist has something of mine I would like back."

❧   6   ❧

THE SOLDIER

New Nihelm.

Standing on a hilltop, Lukys looked across the valley to where two great rivers came together on their long journey from mountains to ocean. At the point where they converged, an island had formed amidst the swirling waters. It was there the Calafe had built their only city.

Lukys had never seen anything like it. New Nihelm's rustic beauty equalled even that of Ashura, the ancient capital of his own kingdom. Yet unlike its rival capitals, this city had no walls, no spiralling guard towers or fortifications. New Nihelm had only been founded a hundred years before, long after the warring tribes of humanity had settled into kingdoms. Its creation had been constrained only by its architect's imagination.

Instead of walls, walkways led around much of the island's circumference, set atop the breakwaters that protected the inner reaches of the city from the river's wrath. Beyond, great domes of platinum and silver dotted the city, rising above the slate rooftops of the common buildings. And higher even than the domes, spires sliced the skyline, their gold and marble materials shining in the morning sun, forming a jagged pattern that seemed to mirror the mountains rising to the east.

The daylight slowly illuminated the shadowy streets, revealing a broad, tree-lined avenue that ran from one side of the city to the other, connecting with the northern and southern bridges that were the island's only physical connection to the mainland.

Lukys could only shake his head. He had not expected to find such a wonder amidst the vast wilderness of Calafe. They had been a nomadic people even before the Tangata came, only settling in stone cottages during the worst of the winter months. All except the inhabitants of New Nihelm, it seemed.

Movement on the hillside drew Lukys's attention back to the present. Dale came alongside him and they shared a glance. A week had passed as they marched south, always in darkness, so long that Lukys had begun to feel he were a creature of the night himself. At least the journey had allowed time for their bruises to heal, and some life to return to his friend's face.

"You think this is where they've been leading us?" the larger man asked, his hazel eyes drifting to the city.

Lukys shrugged, rolling his aching shoulders. The Tangata had granted them more freedom since that first night, only binding them when it came time to sleep. That did not mean they went unguarded. A flicker in the corner of his eye revealed Sophia hovering nearby. He shuddered, haunted by her words from a week before.

He had killed her mate. He should have realised it earlier—the creatures usually came in pairs. Now it was only a matter of time before she took her revenge.

Swallowing, he forced his thoughts back to Dale and the city below.

"Romaine said the city was destroyed," he said as they started down the hillside, shepherded along by their Tangatan captors. "Why would they have spared it?"

Neither had an answer, and silence resumed between them. Lukys could feel the exhaustion dragging at him, a creeping fatigue that called for him to sleep, but he fought it off. He had no desire to draw their captors' wrath—at least, not any more than he already had.

He hadn't told Dale of his conversation with the Tangatan leader. That would have required revealing the truth about his newfound ability. Guilt still hung about Lukys's shoulders at the role he had inadvertently played in bringing the Tangata down upon them.

About the role he had played in their comrades' deaths.

Adonis had not called him again to speak, and for that Lukys was grateful. Though the Tangatan leader held a certain…civility about himself, he had proven no less vicious than the others Lukys had encountered in battle. It was as though a beast lurked in every one of the species, chained in some, set loose in others, but always there, waiting for its opportunity to strike.

It was only a short journey from the hills to the floodplains of the Selman basin, though the bridge to New Nihelm was another mile downstream. They had left the denser northern forests behind a day ago and the land before them now was of verdant grass, the open fields dotted with wandering herds of sheep and goats.

Several of the creatures grazing near the riverbanks raised curious heads at the group's approach, but soon returned to their meal. They wore thick coats of wool, untouched for a season by the shearers of men, and Lukys felt a touch of pity for them come the summer. If left unshorn for much longer, their coats would become so heavy as to make them slow runners, easy prey for predators.

Or did the Tangata already know this? He glanced at Sophia and her companions, recalling then that most of the species wore clothing spun from wool. How had humanity come to be so ignorant of their enemy, that they had not even questioned where the creatures found their clothing?

The Tangata leading their group reached the riverbanks and turned towards the west, where the bridge beckoned. Looking into the waters swirling below, Lukys was shocked to see they were crystal clear. After spending so long around the Illmoor, he had come to assume all mainland rivers must be murky and polluted. But then, the Illmoor ran for hundreds of miles through Gemaho before reaching Flumeer. Turning his gaze to the mountains rising to the east, Lukys could see no break in their endless peaks; the waterways of Calafe must run directly off those snow-capped summits.

Looking ahead, Lukys was surprised to see a slow trickle of people moving across the bridge. The sight brought a frown to his face, but it wasn't until they got closer that he began to recognise the smooth, balanced movements of the Tangata. He shared another glance with Dale, but neither said a word. So it was true: the Tangata had taken up residence in the husk of Calafe society. New Nihelm was their destination.

What are they doing here? he wondered, watching as the creatures left the bridge and started into the surrounding pastures.

You think us such savages, human. Lukys started as a voice whispered into his mind. Jerking around, he found their ever-present guard watching him from nearby. Sophia. *Why should we not desire a place of safety for our people to shelter?*

Lukys swallowed, unnerved that Sophia had heard his thoughts. He quickly turned his eyes ahead again before Dale noticed. What else could she hear—and how could he prevent the creatures from listening? He knew it was possible; otherwise he would hear more than just muffled rumblings from the other Tangata. Unfortunately, he doubted any of the creatures would be willing to instruct him.

I'm sorry. He tried to broadcast the words to where Sophia walked. *I am…ignorant of your kind.*

A rumble that might have been laughter—or a growl—whispered in his mind, but Sophia did not reply. He swallowed, her words from that first morning returning to him again. Just now though, she did not seem angry or vengeful, and Lukys decided to press his luck.

But…why here? he tried again, pushing the words from him in the direction of the Tangata.

To his surprise, Sophia leapt as though someone had just grabbed her by the shoulder. Landing in a close approximation of the fighting stance Romaine had taught him just a few months past, she swung around, eyes wide, teeth bared.

Lukys froze midstride, while Dale leapt backwards away from their guard and raised his fists.

"What the—" He bit back the words as the other creatures turned towards them.

Thankfully, Sophia had been walking a few paces ahead; otherwise Lukys feared she might have struck him. With the strength each of the Tangata possessed, such a blow could easily have proven fatal.

There was a moment's tension before Sophia lowered her hands. Dale quickly did the same, his eyes on the surrounding creatures.

Slowly the others relaxed, and finally one of the other Tangata gave a grunt, indicating they were to move on.

Letting out a long breath, Lukys obeyed, though as he fell into step alongside Dale, he flicked a glance at Sophia. She was still watching him, and for a moment their eyes met.

You do not need to shout, her words whispered gently in his mind.

Despite the danger of his situation, Lukys felt his cheeks grow warm. He quickly dropped his eyes to the river, focusing on the rocks that shimmered beneath the surface rather than his mortification. Shout? He barely knew how to speak this way!

It is strange for us too, hearing a human Speak, Sophia's words chased after him. There was a pause before she continued. *There is a beauty in this place, even for our people. The Matriarch saw no reason not to make use of it.*

Her words inspired a dozen more questions in Lukys's mind, but before he could formulate a sentence, Dale shifted closer to him.

"What was that about, you think?" the other recruit hissed, looking in Sophia's direction.

Lukys shook his head, struggling to shift back to a verbal conversation. "Something startled her," he offered finally. "We're lucky she didn't tear our throats out."

That seemed enough for Dale and he let the topic drop.

I would not have harmed you, human. There was a touch of humour to Sophia's words now.

Frowning, Lukys glanced in her direction. He was about to mention to her something of their words in the forest, but at the last moment thought better of it. There seemed to be little point in reminding the creature of her loss. Instead, he offered an observation.

My name is Lukys, he tried, reaching out more gently with his mind now.

Yes, it is. Her voice turned cold again, and Lukys swallowed as silence fell across his mind.

It was a strange sensation, having a conversation all in his mind —almost like he were talking to himself. He wondered how the Tangata did it, how they distinguished their own thoughts from those of their fellow Tangata. Sophia's voice had a distinct tone to it, but often the whispers he heard coming from the others were indistinguishable from his own inner musings.

Finally they reached the bridge spanning the Shelman River. It stretched some six hundred feet to the distant island, built from great blocks of granite that plunged down into the swirling waters. Bricks had been laid to protect the structure from the endless traffic, but these had been worn smooth over the decades, and twin ruts in the centre revealed the gradual erosion left by the wagons.

There were no wagons now, though. The few Tangata leaving the city were on foot, many carrying great packs upon their backs. Lukys expected them to stop and stare at the human prisoners Adonis had brought to the city, but instead the passersby paid them little attention.

Halfway across the bridge, the polished stone turned abruptly to wood. Lukys paused, eyeing the ragged section of planks spanning a gap between the granite blocks. He guessed the allied forces of humanity must have blown this section of the bridge to protect their retreat to the north. The Tangata had evidently lacked either the skill or the patience to repair the damage with stone.

Sophia and the other Tangata continued across the patched section without hesitation, leaving Lukys with no choice but to follow. The boards groaned as they took his weight, but thankfully held, and a moment later he returned to the bricked path.

They continued, reaching the shores of the island and passing onto the broad avenue that split the city in two. Lukys was surprised to find the street awash with colour. Trees lined the avenue, pink blossoms sprouting from their wiry branches, their petals swirling at every breeze and filling the air with the sweet scent of flowers.

More than that, though, the buildings themselves were each a display of individuality. Just like in the border city of Fogmore, the Calafe had built their city of wood. But the similarities ended there. Where Fogmore appeared to have been thrown together overnight, New Nihelm had been built with care, the wooden beams and panels of every building fitted together with precision.

Each house had also been painted in different colours from its neighbours. Façades of red and yellow and blue and green led away down the street, creating a vibrant, picturesque image of a city united by its differences.

Sadness touched Lukys at the thought, as he remembered that the families who had so lovingly crafted the image were gone, forced from their homes by the threat of the Tangata.

The sun was lifting higher into the sky, bringing with it more of New Nihelm's new Tangatan occupants. They moved about the paved streets much the same as the citizens of his own city back in Perfugia, though they were not half so numerous. It would have been easy to forget the creatures around him weren't human.

Easy, but for the fact they lived in a city stolen from its rightful owners. It had not been the Tangata who had thought to build their city upon this island. It had not been their skill that had crafted such beautiful homes, nor their hardship that had maintained it for a century. No, the only thing built by the Tangata on this entire island were the wooden boards they had used to span the broken bridge.

Everything else they had stolen from the Calafe.

Eventually, their captors led them off the main avenue into the smaller streets that crisscrossed the island. There they began to see further signs of life—vendors standing behind stalls, groups of Tangata on street corners, and still others carrying great packs of goods on their backs. Only…Lukys could not help feeling there was a strangeness to it all, an unnaturalness that hung about the city.

It was a while before he could put a finger on the abnormality.

It was the silence.

In every city, every town he had ever visited, there was a constant buzz, a distant rumbling of wagons and beating of hammers, of voices, of life. With the Tangata in New Nihelm, there was none of that.

They crossed a number of bridges spanning smaller watercourses, though these were broad, arcing things that lifted several yards higher than the surrounding streets. Crossing them, Lukys began to realise New Nihelm was not one island at all, but many, divided by canals that crisscrossed the city. At the edge of each channel, stone foundations were revealed, plunged deep into the mud and hidden by the structures that had been built atop them.

Anger touched Lukys as he was again reminded of the effort the Calafe had put into the construction of their city, only to have it stolen away. He found himself glaring at the creatures they passed in the streets, wishing there was something he could do, some magical way of restoring to Romaine's people what was rightfully theirs—

Lukys froze as he caught a glimpse of a figure amongst the Tangata gathered around a nearby fruit stall. Frowning, he came to a stop, watching them, aware there was something different about this group. Sophia and the other guards did not immediately realise his absence, and silently he stepped towards the stand. Two males and a female stood perusing the vegetables on display. In another time, he might have wondered at the oddity of the monsters from his nightmares out shopping, but something about the female's movement had caught his attention.

Struck by a sudden suspicion, Lukys darted forward and reached out to grasp the woman by the shoulder. A belated cry came from behind him as Sophia finally realised his absence, but she was too late. Crying out, the female he'd accosted spun, hands raised in fright, eyes wide.

Eyes of a brilliant sea green.

The woman was human.

THE FALLEN

The Illmoor Fortress was five days ride from Fogmore, though the queen lingered a day in the riverside town to prepare supplies before pushing on. Her Guard rode large destriers bred for war, their iron-shod hooves capable of caving in the skulls of even the most ferocious of the foes. Behind them came the supply wagons, though many would be left in the smaller forts that lined the shores of the Illmoor, restocking them for the coming months of conflict against the Tangata.

Romaine himself rode a smaller mare, for which he was thankful. The destriers might make great warhorses, but their thumping gait would have been agony for his injuries. Even with the smoother strides of the mare, Romaine was aching by the time the sun set on the first day. It was a relief when he finally topped a rise and found the vanguard setting camp on the floodplains below.

Tugging on his reins, he drew the mare to a stop and watched the preparations. Still far from Gemaho, there was little chance of an attack by Nguyen's soldiers. Indeed, if they were lucky the man might not yet know of their advance.

As for the Tangata…an attack seemed unlikely, but with the Illmoor River less than a mile from their position, nothing could be guaranteed. The soldiers below were certainly taking no chances. There were no trees available for a stockade wall, but a defensive ditch and embankment were already nearing completion.

The thumping of hooves came from below and a moment later a rider topped the rise and approached Romaine.

"Have to admit, those Royal Guards sure are an efficient sort."

Lorene wore a broad grin on his youthful face as he pulled his mount to a stop alongside Romaine's. He'd volunteered for the expedition when the queen had asked for scouts to help navigate the journey east. There were no roads or passageways in these parts, and so close to the river it would have been easy for the queen's forces to become bogged in the marshland. The seemingly solid ground in the open pastures had a habit of sinking beneath the weight of horses, so it paid to have scouts along who knew the territory.

Romaine only grunted and swung from his saddle. He would walk the rest of the way down the hill—his body could use the stretch. Grinning at some unspoken joke, Lorene did the same, and together they started down the hill.

Romaine did his best to keep the pain of his injuries from his face, but it was difficult to ignore the searing that touched his chest with each step. How much longer until he healed? Days, weeks, months? Despair swelled in his throat and he struggled to push it back down. What good was he to anyone, let alone a Goddess, if he couldn't even walk without pain?

"You think she's really going to attack the Gemaho?" Lorene asked as they threaded their way down the hillside. There was a path that wound around in a gentler manner, passable for the wagons, but they had opted for the more direct route.

Romaine flicked a glance at the man but said nothing for the moment, keeping his attention focused on the ground beneath his feet. The grassy slope fell steeply to the campsite and they were doing their best to zigzag the horses down. The mare snorted and tugged at her reins but otherwise followed Romaine without question. No doubt she was relieved at the break from his weight upon her back.

"You know, you didn't need to join us," Romaine said, skirting the man's question, then muffled a curse as a patch of earth slid beneath his boot.

These hills had once been covered in forest, much the same as his own homeland across the distant waters, but for the last decade the banks this side of the Illmoor had been progressively burned away. The Flumeeren soldiers had feared the Tangata would use the forests as cover to pass their defensive lines and attack settlements further inland. Now though, the land lay exposed, and many hill-sides were slowly crumbling beneath the forces of erosion.

"I know," Lorene replied with a shrug. "It's just…it didn't feel right, staying behind last time. I should have gone with you lot when you went south."

"If you had, there'd be one more corpse lying in the forests of my homeland."

"Maybe," Lorene said, a self-deprecating grin appearing on his lips, "or might be I could have helped. Can't know now, can we?" His eyes turned ahead, to the distant mountains. A sharp V between the soaring peaks marked the valley through which the Illmoor passed. Beyond, the plateaus of Gemaho waited. "But at least I can still help the lass."

Romaine chuckled at that. "Can hardly call her a lass now, you know."

Lorene grinned. "Nah, maybe that's the real reason I'm coming. Didn't get a chance to see her before her untimely departure. Wouldn't mind a glimpse though. Something to tell the grandkids about, you know?"

"The Gemaho might have something to say about that."

"Ain't that the truth."

They fell silent at that, each pointedly turning his eyes from the distant mountains. Before anyone could reach the plateaus of Gemaho, they first had to pass the granite walls of the Illmoor Fortress. And the defenders wouldn't let the queen's army pass without a fight.

Reaching the bottom of the hill, Lorene nodded a farewell and mounted up again to set off around the perimeter of the camp. Romaine watched him go, then led his horse on through a gap that had been left in the fortifications for the arriving army.

With no tasks of his own to occupy him, Romaine wandered through the camp. The vanguard had staked out areas for the army's tents, which would soon arrive in the wagons. Watching the men work, Romaine found himself thinking of the coming conflict. Again, doubt touched him. The Tangata were massing beyond the

Illmoor. With an attack imminent, was now really time for the queen to start a war between the kingdoms of man, the first in more than a generation?

Yet…neither could Romaine bring himself to disagree with the queen's decision. After all, it was his only chance of rescuing Cara. And perhaps the dispute could be ended without bloodshed. After all, surely the King of Gemaho did not intend to hold one of the *Gods* against her will. The eastern peoples were not known for their devotion, but not even they could deny Cara's divinity.

Though Romaine had to admit, he still hadn't entirely come around to that truth. It seemed impossible the innocent young woman that had spent so many weeks at his side was one of the Divine. What had a God been doing here anyway, sparring with the Perfugians, eating with the other soldiers in the mess hall, even befriending Romaine? But then, that was the way of the Gods, was it not, that mere mortals could not understand their motives?

Shaking his head, Romaine returned his attention to his surroundings. The queen had been riding with the vanguard and now he saw her ahead, supervising the last touches on the camp fortifications. Romaine's horse gave a soft whinny, announcing his approach. A smile lit the woman's face and she waved a greeting.

"Romaine, come, join me," she called. "I trust the ride was comfortable?"

Romaine nodded. Thankfully, Amina did not call him out on the lie, though he feared the truth was written on his face.

"What do you think?" she asked, gesturing to the men at work.

Romaine cast a professional eye over the fortifications. The ditch was a good four feet deep, the mound rising behind it almost the same. Enough to stop the most determined of cavalry charges, but against the Tangata…the creatures could easily leap the width of the trench, and a mound of dirt was not likely to slow them.

Turning to the queen, he shrugged. "Good work."

A smile tugged at the queen's lips and there was a hint of laughter in her eyes as she drew him away from the working men. "You may speak truthfully with me, Calafe," she said. "You think such measures inadequate against the threat of the Tangata?"

Romaine glanced over his shoulder at the soldiers. They were out of earshot now, but several had broken away to follow the queen. Her personal guard. Shaking his head, he regarded the woman.

"You are no fool, Your Majesty," Romaine replied. "And the fortifications will at least provide a line for your men to hold, should the Tangata strike. But…if the creatures were to attack in any force, there is little a mound of dirt will do to stop them."

The queen nodded and they continued away from the boundaries of the camp, heading towards the centre. The supply wagons had arrived now and many were hard at work setting the tents for the night. One of the queen's grooms approached as they walked, eyes on Romaine's horse. He handed over the reins with reluctance—a man should always care for his own horse.

"You are right, of course," the queen said as the groom led his mare away, "but a leader must think not only of the day at hand, but those to come. Would you believe I had my soldiers perform this ritual every night we spent camped between Mildeth and Fogmore?"

Romaine frowned. There would have been little risk of attack by man or Tangata in those lands. "No wonder you travelled so slowly."

The queen gave a throaty chuckle. "Of course, without such precautions, we might have reached the city a day sooner." She gestured to the soldiers moving past. "However, in a matter of days, we will be faced not by Tangata, but men. My soldiers must be ready to repel any attack. I thought it prudent that they have some practice at setting a war camp before we marched into enemy territory."

"You truly think it will come to that?"

"This is war, Romaine. I discount no possibility when it comes to my enemies. Especially one so wily as King Nguyen."

She came to a stop at that, and Romaine realised they were now standing in front of a canvas tent at least five times the size of the others that were being set up around the campsite. Two of the queen's personal guard already stood outside, spears held upright, eyes fixed on Romaine.

Romaine shook his head. "What does that man want with Cara?" he murmured, more to himself than the queen.

"There are several possibilities that come to mind," the queen mused. "However, I had hoped you might shine some light on the subject. You knew the Goddess best. Would you join me for a drink, Calafe?"

For a moment, Romaine was tempted to turn the woman down. His chest was aching something fierce and he wanted little more than to lie down and sleep a dozen hours. But...one did not simply turn down a request from the Queen of Flumeer. Muffling a sigh, he nodded, and the queen led the way inside. Ignoring the hostility of her guards, Romaine followed.

Within, the tent was more luxurious than he had expected for a woman who wore a full suit of armour. But then, he supposed even a warrior queen needed a few indulgences. The floor of the tent had been lined with stone tiles and Romaine quickly did his best to wipe the mud from his boots in the doorway. Warmth greeted him as he stepped inside, drawing his attention to a brazier set in the corner. Several plain wooden chairs had been set there, while beyond a feathered mattress lay on a slate bed.

Surprised they had managed to fit so much into the supply wagons, Romaine returned his gaze to the queen.

"Take a seat, Calafe," she said, gesturing to the chairs beside the brazier. "Perhaps the warmth will ease your injuries."

The warmth was only adding to Romaine's weariness, but he did as he was bid while the queen moved to a cabinet set beside the bed. She joined him shortly though, proffering a glass of amber liquid. Accepting the drink, Romaine sniffed gingerly before raising an eyebrow.

"Calafe gold?" he murmured. It had been almost a decade since he'd last drunk the wine. One of the first attacks by the Tangata had burned the grapes on their southern vines.

"Of course," the queen replied, lifting a glass of her own in salute. She leaned forward then, the glow of a lantern setting her emerald eyes alight. "So, tell me of her, Romaine. What was it like to sup with the Divine?"

Romaine found himself unable to hold the queen's gaze. Instead, he took a sip of the wine, and instantly found himself carried away to another time, one lit with sunshine and love and hope, to days spent with his wife and son, before the Tangata had stolen everything away. He sighed as the images faded, to be replaced by one of Cara, sitting in the plaza of Fogmore, lit by the winter sun.

"In many ways, she was just like us," he murmured. "A little strange, innocent, but I doubt we would have ever realised her true identity if not for the creatures we found in the caverns."

He clenched imaginary fingers at the mention of the beasts, a shudder running down his spine. His memory of the time beneath the earth was foggy—he'd lost a lot of blood—but he could still recall the faces of those ancient creatures with terrifying clarity.

"I have read your report," the queen murmured, pursing her lips. "The Goddess fought them off?"

Romaine nodded. "Her eyes turned grey, just like the Tangata—and those…other things. We believed it meant she was one of them. The creatures had slain several of the Tangata and we thought the sight had enraged her." The words were bitter in his mouth, for that had been the first of many mistakes he'd made in the south. "It wasn't until…the river that I realised who she truly was."

"A shame," the queen murmured, "though understandable, given the eyes. They were amber normally, no?"

"Yes," Romaine replied. It seemed the queen had done her research well. "Those creatures, Your Majesty, I've never seen the like. If there are more of them…" He swallowed, lifting his left arm instinctively, and the queen's eyes were drawn to the bandaged stump. Despite her calm demeanour, she shivered and rubbed her own wrist. Ignoring the gesture, Romaine went on: "Let's just say, we could not have defeated them without Cara's help. She fought like nothing I have ever seen, killed them with hardly a thought."

As he spoke the words, Romaine was drawn back to the battle on the banks of the Illmoor. The way Cara had fought against the Tangata had been utterly different to the conflict in the tunnels of the Gods. In the darkness, her eyes had been mad, her blows wild, sickeningly strong. Beside the river though, she had fought with a cool precision and skill, and the Tangata she had downed had not been slain.

"Such a wonder, that the Gods allowed their magic to fall into the hands of humanity. No wonder it drove those sorry souls you discovered in the depths mad."

"Mankind is not meant to wield such power," Romaine murmured in agreement.

The queen only smiled. "It does lead me to wonder how Erika has wielded her magic gauntlet for so long. Tell me, did you notice a change in her, during your time south of the Illmoor?"

Romaine hesitated, recalling for an instant the way Erika had tortured Cara with the magic, when she'd thought the woman responsible for her ill fortune. That had been before they'd discovered Cara's true identity, when they'd thought her a Tangatan spy, but even so, her actions had been vicious, vindictive…

…but then again, after discovering the Perfugian recruits butchered, Romaine had not acted much differently. Finally, he shook his head.

"No, not that I noticed."

"A pity," Amina mused, "though I suppose when we recover the artefact, her experimentation will serve me well." She chuckled. "I admit, that was one of the reasons I permitted her mad expedition. The magic needed testing before I claimed it for my own."

"That 'mad expedition' claimed the lives of my friends," Romaine replied, struggling to keep the anger from his voice.

The queen looked up at that, her eyes widening with surprise. "The Perfugians, of course," she said after a moment. "Their loss was…regrettable."

Romaine ground his teeth, but said nothing. It was not his place to criticise the Flumeeren monarch, however much her decisions angered him. Instead, he found himself staring at the open grate of the brazier. The occasional *pop* came from the burning coals.

"You think me cold," the queen said after a time. "I cannot deny it. The skill is one I have perfected much over the years, that ability to weigh my decisions without thought to personal sentiment. But then, that is the burden of a monarch."

"Not to care for the people you rule?" Romaine asked, unable to keep the words to himself any longer.

"To focus on what creates the greatest good for my people, that which will protect the greatest number of lives."

Silence fell at her words and Romaine couldn't help but feel a touch of guilt. He said nothing, though. The queen might be forced to justify the death of dozens, or even hundreds, in protection of her nation, but he could not. Would not.

"I suppose she told you of the map?" the queen asked finally. "A shame I listened to her paranoia." She snorted. "No doubt my rival king will be delighted to know the Archivist escaped with the only copy."

"I saw the map." Romaine hesitated. "I do not recall much of its details."

"Nor I, sadly," the queen replied. "Though there was one site…"

"The home of the Gods?" Romaine nodded, recalling the scarlet star that had marked the secret location, deep in the mountains east of Calafe. "Something a man isn't likely to forget."

"Yes, it would be quite the discovery," the queen said, turning her head in the direction of those distant peaks. "I fear that is the reason Nguyen chooses now to act against me."

"You cannot think he would be so bold as to break the prohibition?" No human had set foot in the Mountains of the Gods for centuries—or at least, none that had lived to tell the story.

The queen's eyes remained distant, even as she spoke. "It is one of several eventualities I am considering," she mused. Then she blinked, returning her gaze to Romaine. "Assuming your Goddess is her prisoner, where do you think the Archivist would go, should she be given the choice?"

Romaine hesitated, remembering the fervent glint that had come over Erika's gaze when she spoke of the Gods and their power. A shiver ran down his spine as he realised the truth.

"If she were desperate enough…" He swallowed. "If the king allowed it, you're right, she would make for the home of the Gods. There are no other sites left to explore, other than a handful deep in the southern territories of the Tangata."

Amina sighed. "Yes, that is as I thought." She shook her head. "No matter. With luck, we will have both the Goddess and my Archivist returned before the king can make his move."

Romaine's stomach twisted, though he wasn't sure it was for the hope of Cara's return, or the prospect of an approaching war between the kingdoms. Before he could find the words to reply, movement came from the entrance to the tent, and a man appeared between the flaps.

"Amina," the newcomer said informally, then hesitated at the sight of the two of them by the brazier. "Didn't realise you had company."

A frown touched Romaine's forehead as the man stepped closer to the light. His clothes were mud-stained and there was a weariness about his face that spoke of a long journey. He wore a rough-spun cotton tunic rather than the red uniform of a Flumeeren soldier. The guards outside must have recognised him though, for they had admitted him without commotion, despite the longsword he wore at his waist. The handle of a crossbow also hung over his right shoulder. A broad grin split the man's face as he looked from the queen to Romaine, though he did not speak whatever unseemly thoughts might have generated it.

"Yasin," the queen said in greeting, rising from her chair. "I hadn't thought you would arrive until morning."

"We rode for three days straight after I got your message, my lady," Yasin replied, falling into a half-bow that seemed more mocking than respectful.

Romaine's frown deepened and he found himself reaching for the hilt of his own sword. The newcomer did not miss the movement. He straightened, feet slipping into a defensive stance, though his hands did not stray near his blade. Romaine froze, shifting his gaze to the man's face. He still wore the mocking grin, but there was a hardness to the sky-green eyes now. Whatever the man's outward appearance, this Yasin was a warrior.

Silence hung over the tent as the two regarded each other, until the queen stepped between them.

"Enough of that," she snorted, waving a hand. "Romaine, this is Yasin, captain of my…private security. Yasin, this is Romaine, soldier of Calafe."

The two warriors eyed each other for a moment longer, before Romaine finally nodded and took his hand from the sword hilt. A trickle of despair touched him as he realised how little good the weapon would have done him anyway. The weapon was unfamiliar in his hand. Even his greater size and reach would not have meant much against an expert swordsman—and Romaine had no doubt the queen only employed the best. Silently, he resolved to start practicing from that night onward.

"Thank you for the drink, Your Majesty," Romaine said finally, "it was a rare treat. But I will bid you goodnight. My injuries still bother me, and I must rest if I am to be any use to you in the coming days."

The queen smiled. "Of course, Calafe, rest well."

Nodding his thanks, Romaine strode past the two and out into the night—though not before he caught a soft snort of laughter from Yasin. Anger flared in Romaine's stomach but he ignored the man. He was in no position to fight the man, or any other. No, he needed to regain his strength, and his skill.

Clenching his fist, he breathed in the night air. Then he strode into the night, seeking Lorene. If the man truly wanted to redeem himself for not travelling south, he could volunteer as Romaine's sparring partner.

❦ 8 ❦

THE SOLDIER

Fear shone in the woman's eyes as she tore herself free of Lukys and retreated. Before he had a chance to question her, a hand of iron grasped him by the arm and dragged him away. He stumbled, almost falling, before straightening to find himself face-to-face with Sophia.

What are you doing? her voice hissed into his mind.

Seeing her anger, Lukys tried to shrink away. She held him fast, looking for all the world like she was about to take the revenge he had been anticipating these last days.

"She's…human!" he gasped, panic forcing the words from his mouth before he could stop them.

Sophia hesitated, a frown furrowing her brow. Behind her, Dale was struggling with one of the other Tangatan guards, but he froze at Lukys's words.

"What?" he gasped, twisting to try and see past Lukys and Sophia.

But the woman and the Tangata that had been with her had already fled. Lukys's heart pounded in his ears as he locked eyes with Sophia.

"What was she doing here?" he hissed, yanking at the arm that held him. To his surprise, she released him. He paused, drawing in a breath. "What are *we* doing here?"

Dale looked confused by the outburst, but Lukys paid him no

attention. Glancing beyond his fellow recruit, he scanned the other Tangata moving about the streets, squeezing their way past the roadblock their group had formed across half the avenue. With the sun now streaming down between the rooftops, it was easy to see their eyes, to recognise the eerie greyness—

There!

A man walked by, hazel eyes focused on the path ahead. Then another, this one a woman with brown eyes. Humans. There were humans in New Nihelm, in a city of Tangata. And suddenly he thought he knew why he and Dale were there.

"They're slaves," he croaked.

"Wha—" Dale broke off as the other guards gripped him by the arms and started dragging him down the street.

Lukys turned his gaze on Sophia, waiting for her to do the same with him. But she made no move to grab him again, only gestured in the direction the others had taken Dale.

Come, Lukys, she said. *You will not find your answers here.*

Swallowing, Lukys considered trying to run. But even if he could evade Sophia's lightning reactions, where would he go? The Tangata were everywhere; they would catch him before he made it a block. Finally he let out a long breath and nodded. Sophia took hold of his arm again and led him along the street.

They soon caught up with Dale and the other guards. His friend had given up his struggles, though a look of relief appeared in his eyes when he saw Lukys. Released from their guards, they fell into step together, though now Sophia and the others hardly gave them a foot of breathing space.

They must have covered another half a mile after that. Lukys paid more attention to the faces of those they passed this time, and soon spotted more of the strange, human citizens of the city. He didn't try to contact any of these others, and for their part, the humans kept their eyes downcast, averted from the fresh prisoners being marched past.

Finally they found themselves at the edge of the island again, though this time in the western reaches. There they passed beyond a low flood wall, out into a broad plaza of ash-stained tiles. The river bordered the opened space to north and south, while directly across the plaza from where they had entered stood a single building in the shape of a pyramid.

Lukys's heart throbbed as he recognised it as a Basilica to The Fall. Stretching from the swirling waters to either side, the sloped granite walls loomed over the plaza, seeming to have a presence of their own. Most older cities had at least one of the structures, built in the early days of civilisation as appeasement to the Gods that had brought the darkness down upon them. Today few believed the temples had placated anything, and so it was surprising to find one in a city as young as New Nihelm. He supposed that living in the shadow of the Mountains of the Gods, the Calafe might have erred on the side of caution when it came to inciting Divine Wrath.

Regardless, the Tangata seemed to have found a use for the structure, for a large group waited outside the polished gold and brass doors. The rest of their party was already halfway across the plaza, Adonis in the lead, and at a push from Sophia, Dale and Lukys started after them.

As they neared the basilica, Lukys saw that the group standing outside the doors was similarly streaked in mud and filth. He frowned, wondering whether another group of Tangata had also returned from the wilderness. The gentle buzz of conversation carried to them on the breeze...

Lukys's heart lurched as he realised the group was speaking out loud. They were humans, others captured by the Tangata and brought to the city as prisoners. But where would the Tangata have found so many humans this side of the river...

...he glimpsed a face in the group. His mouth fell open—then he was rushing forward, leaping past Sophia, Dale only a step behind. He recognised that face, these people, those filthy blue uniforms.

"Travis!" he bellowed.

Travis's eyes widened in shock, before a grin split his face. Stepping away from the rest of the Perfugians, he opened his arms and dragged Lukys into a hug. Lukys gasped as the bigger man crushed the air from his lungs, but there was laughter on his lips as they broke apart.

"What are you doing here?" he gasped, still gaping at the sight of his friend alive.

The rest of the Perfugian recruits gathered nearby, though they were not so bold as to approach Lukys as Travis had. Their numbers had been reduced to just fifteen including Lukys and Dale, just a fraction of the fifty men and women that had arrived on the frontier just a few short months ago. But still a far cry more than he'd feared.

"Where else would I be?" Travis replied with a grin.

His beard had grown out in the two weeks that had passed since they'd seen each other. Between his dishevelled uniform and the grime covering his face, he had seen better days. Footsteps came from behind them and Travis offered Dale a nod as his fellow noble born approached.

Beyond, Sophia and the rest of their escort didn't seem overly concerned by their reunion, though they did not take their eyes off the group of humans. Adonis had already reached the Tangata that had been guarding the Perfugian recruits and now seemed to be waiting for something.

"We...found the village," Lukys said finally, recalling the moment he'd stumbled into the cluster of abandoned buildings and seen the bodies of his comrades.

Travis's face darkened and a scowl twisted his lips as he glanced at the nearby Tangata. "We were so close." He shook his head, looking away. The village had been less than a day's march from the safety of the Illmoor. Drawing in a breath, Travis went on: "There were too many to fight, but we stood our ground anyway. Only...after the first clash, with a dozen of us dead on the ground, the bastards just stood there, watching. Eventually one of us threw down their spear. Rest of us followed. Guess we figured it was worth trying to surrender." He shrugged. "So here we are."

Tears touched Lukys's eyes, and without speaking he dragged his friend into another hug.

"I'm glad you're here," he said as they broke apart.

A grim smile appeared on Travis's face as his gaze swept the plaza. "And the others?" he asked softly.

"We lost Groner," Lukys said, feeling guilty that he'd hardly thought of the man since that terrible time in the tunnels beneath the earth. "Romaine lost his hand, but the others are fine. They got away." He hesitated, thinking about Cara. Travis didn't know what she was. "We, ah, have a lot to catch up on."

Beside them, Dale snorted. "That's an understatement."

Travis exhaled hard, relief momentarily showing on his face, though there was still confusion in his eyes.

Lukys shook his head. "Later," he said, looking past Travis and the other Perfugians to where Adonis and most of the Tangata had gathered before the polished doors. "What's happening here?"

"Your guess is as good as mine," Travis replied with a shrug. "We arrived in the night. They put us in some building until the morning, then brought us here." He shivered, and Lukys glimpsed the fear his friend was hiding behind the calm façade. "Isn't it creepy?" His eyes were fixed on Adonis's group. "They never make a sound, yet they're communicating."

"It's that damned magic they stole from the Gods," Dale answered, his face hardening. "I wonder if that's why Cara came, to take it back?"

"What?" Travis said, his eyebrows knitting together in a frown.

"Ah…" Dale trailed off, turning to Lukys for help.

Lukys swallowed. "Err…you know how Cara was always wearing her furs, even inside?"

Travis nodded, though his eyes showed he didn't know where Lukys was going with the subject.

"Well…you see…it turns out she was hiding something…"

"She's got bloody wings!" Dale exclaimed.

Lukys suppressed a groan. "It's true," he said to Travis's confusion. "She's one of them, one of the Gods."

Before Lukys's eyes, the colour drained from his friend's face. "Wh…what?" Travis's mouth opened and closed, but no further words came out.

"Easy, man," Dale said gently, patting Travis on the back.

Lukys nodded and was about to speak further when he felt another presence brush against his mind.

Lukys.

A shiver ran down his spine and he turned to find Adonis approaching, Sophia at his side. Behind him, his friends froze, and even the murmurs of the other recruits faded to silence. Lukys swallowed as he looked into the eyes of the senior Tangata, remembering his rage back in the clearing. He'd hoped Adonis was done with him.

Come with us, Lukys. Sophia's voice was softer than the senior Tangata's, but it was clear the instructions were not optional.

He swallowed as the two came to a halt before him. He hesitated, waiting several moments before turning to his friends.

"I…I think they want me to go with them," he rasped, still unsure about how to tell them of his ability.

Sophia caught him by the arm before the others could respond, and Lukys was dragged away. Travis and Dale watched after him, lips downcast, eyes haunted. They looked for all the world like they had just attended his funeral.

Swallowing, Lukys forced his eyes ahead. *What are you going to do with us?* he asked, trying to direct the question at Adonis.

That is for the Matriarch to decide.

He offered no further explanation. Lukys allowed himself to be shepherded past the other recruits towards the polished doors of the basilica. They swung open as two of the Tangatan guards entered first, revealing darkness beyond. Swallowing, Lukys took one last glance at the sunlit sky before the black swallowed him up.

Bright spots danced across his vision as the doors closed again behind them, and he blinked, struggling to pierce the gloom. Movement flickered somewhere within, betrayed by the gentle whisper of clothing, of leather boots upon stone.

A gentle push from behind urged Lukys forward. He staggered, and glancing around, he managed to pick Sophia's face from the shadows. Swallowing, he obeyed her silent command, taking tentative steps on the smooth floor, afraid the ground might drop out from under him at any movement.

Slowly his eyes adjusted, and he began to make out shadows around the room. Light from above led his gaze to tiny windows set at the point of the pyramid high overhead. Returning his eyes to the ground, the room began to take shape from the dark.

The basilica had only one enormous chamber, its inward sloping walls leading up to that single point above. Amidst the shadows, he could see no other entrances or inner rooms, not unless they were hidden behind the altar of the Gods.

Set upon a dais raised some four feet above floor level, a giant slab of marble dominated the room. Otherwise the place was unadorned, though as Lukys took another step, he caught a shimmer from the base of the dais. He frowned, moving closer, and realised the dais was situated in the centre of a great pool of water. It seemed to be flowing slowly around the stone, though a glance at the walls did not reveal a source.

Movement drew Lukys's eyes back to the altar, and a figure stepped forward. Rustling came from around the room as all the Tangata knelt and pressed foreheads to stone. Before he could ask what was going on, Sophia gripped him by the shoulder and pressed him down. He cried out, legs weakened from the endless march south giving way beneath her strength, forcing him to his knees.

Quiet! Sophia hissed in his mind.

There was a sense of urgency in her voice, and Lukys bit back his cry, heart suddenly racing. Turning to face the altar, he stared at the figure that had appeared there, trying to make out her features through the gloom. Swathed in long robes, she could only be the Matriarch that Adonis had spoken of. She stepped closer, and the light from above fell across her face.

The breath hissed from Lukys's lips as he looked on the aged face. He had never seen an older Tangata before—those they fought were always young, their appearance that of humans in their twenties. This creature though, her face was more wrinkles than skin, and her hair was a pale grey, drained of its colour by the countless passage of years. Her hands were speckled with age spots, and her eyes…Lukys swallowed. They were pure white. Without the grey of the Tangata, he might have thought her human…yet there was something about her manner, about the way she stood, that left Lukys in no doubt as to what she was. And those eyes were looking directly at him.

Adonis, what have you brought me?

9

THE FUGITIVE

Sitting on the pillowed bed, Erika stared down at the intricate lattice of metal fibres that covered her hand. It clung to her flesh, so close she could run her hand from gauntlet to her arm and hardly feel the difference. The strange metal was even warm to the touch, as though it had become a part of her, feeding off her energies.

Without thinking, she clenched her fist and felt the familiar thrum of its magic. The soft glow bathed her face, radiating a new heat now, one that promised power, promised glory. She shivered and released it once more, and the sensation faded. Disgust replaced it, clogging her throat, and she thought of all the terrible things she had done with this gauntlet.

Ibran, her assistant turned traitor, deafened, blind, abandoned in the darkness.

The Tangatan prisoner in Amina's court, screaming its agony.

Cara, writhing beneath the gauntlet's power, begging for her mercy.

Standing suddenly, Erika strode to the window and looked out over the rooftops of the fortress proper. It had been five days since their arrival, and she had only seen the king one other time, a brief visit in which she'd handed over the map showing the hidden locations of ruins that had once been occupied by the Gods. Little good it had proven—there was but one site inside the bounds of Gemaho, and it had apparently been discovered years ago.

The remaining stars were beyond their reach, mostly hidden deep in the south, in lands that had been claimed by the Tangata generations ago. All but for the one marked high in the Mountains of the Gods. But not even Nguyen seemed interested in that venture. The Gemaho might not be religious, but even they avoided those forbidden peaks.

Letting out a sigh, Erika turned from the window and began to pace. The inactivity was starting to grate on her, and the knowledge that Queen Amina was approaching had not helped at all. The woman was vicious, her resolve hard as iron. She would stop at nothing to get what she wanted.

And she wanted the magic that had fused with Erika's arm— even if it meant cutting it from her corpse.

The room the king had placed her in was large and well-adorned, with furniture crafted of pinewood and lit by chandeliers of silver and brass. She had been forced to share the accommodations with Maisie, but thankfully the spy was rarely there—her bed had not even been slept in last night. Cara had been taken to separate quarters; Erika had not seen the Goddess since.

Slumping back to her bed, she found herself staring at the gauntlet once more, wondering again at its power. The king's words about how it worked on Cara had stayed with her. It had proven an effective weapon against the Tangata, but it still seemed strange that the Gods—or the Anahera, as Cara had called them—would create a weapon that could be used so easily against them.

Did that mean it had been created by somebody else?

A cold breeze blew across Erika's neck. She had used the magic so recklessly these last weeks, with hardly a thought to the consequences. The Tangata had been changed by the magic they had stolen, and she wondered now if the same could happen to her. But…it *hadn't* harmed her, hadn't changed her.

Had it?

No, surely not, or the king would not use its power so freely. Unless he too did not understand the power he wielded. How had he come by another of the artefacts anyway?

Erika shook her head and scrunched her eyes closed. Questions upon questions. In her mind she recalled the way the king had struck Cara down. He had acted quickly, without hesitation, without even knowing Cara's identity. A vicious act, without mercy.

A *click* drew Erika's attention to the entrance as Maisie entered. Rings circled the woman's eyes and there was mud on her leggings, as though she had spent the night wading through the marshland beyond the walls of the fortress. Erika raised an eyebrow as the spy crossed the room and dropped onto the other bed.

"I take it these nightly disappearances aren't to see some secret lover?" she asked, trying to be friendly.

The Gemaho woman grunted. "Afraid not." Letting out a groan, she sat up and eyed Erika from across the room. "Your queen is drawing close."

A vice closed around Erika's throat at the woman's words and it was a moment before she managed to reply. "She's heading here?"

"With an army," Maisie confirmed.

Fear drove Erika to her feet. She paced the room again, fists clenched, warmth radiating through her body…

She froze, her eyes falling to the gauntlet. Light shone from the metallic fibres and she realised she'd summoned its magic again without thinking. Letting out a slow breath, she relaxed her hand and the magic died.

"How long do we have?" she asked quietly.

"Less than a day."

"*A day!*" Erika cried.

She swung around, panic gripping her…but there was no escaping the Queen of Flumeer. A moan built in her throat and she clutched her hands to her hair. What had she been thinking? Better that she had thrown herself upon Amina's mercy than betray such a woman. She would get no clemency now.

"Oh, calm down," Maisie snorted, lying back on the bed. "You're safe here, or had you forgotten? A *fortress* lies between us and the woman. Her army could hurl itself upon the walls of the Illmoor Fortress for a decade and never come a step closer to taking you."

"You don't know her like I do," Erika argued, though she ceased her pacing. Drawing in a breath, she sought calm. "The woman is devious."

"And you think Gemaho has survived all these years because Nguyen is not? Believe me, he has been three steps ahead of Amina for years."

The breath hissed from Erika's nose as she exhaled sharply, but she did not argue further. There was little point. She slumped back to her bed.

"Sorry," she murmured. "It's just…I've never felt so lost. None of this makes sense. Even this magic…I think it's doing something to me."

"Oh?" Maisie asked, leaning forward on the bed. "Why would you think that?"

Erika shook her head. "I don't know." She made a gesture, as though to dismiss her concerns. "Though…maybe you can help. The orb you have, the king's gauntlet…how long have you had them?"

Maisie eyed her for a long moment, as if weighing up whether that was information they could trust Erika with. In the end though, she must have proven herself worthy, for the woman let out a sigh.

"Two years," she replied. "We found them in our only ancient site, far to the east. There was a sealed room, much like the one you discovered in Flumeer, I hear. It held several artefacts, though only Nguyen's gauntlet and my orb retain any power."

Erika nodded. "And the king…he hasn't changed, having the gauntlet for so long?"

"Not to my knowledge," the spy replied with a smile.

Despite herself, Erika let out a sigh, relieved. If the king hadn't changed after using the gauntlet after two years, then…she frowned, glancing again at Maisie. She too wielded one of the artefacts of the Gods; could that have altered her perception of the king?

Angrily Erika shook her head. She was being paranoid, wasn't she? Surely Cara would have said something about the gauntlet earlier, if it could corrupt them. But then, the Goddess had rarely offered information freely…

"I need to see Cara," Erika said suddenly, coming to her feet. "It's time I asked her some more questions."

"Ah…" The woman hesitated. "I don't think she's taking visitors right now."

Erika narrowed her eyes, suddenly suspicious. She should have checked on Cara days ago, but she'd been preoccupied with the queen and her own magical dilemmas. Now something about the spy's behaviour set her suspicions aflame.

"Where is she?" Erika demanded.

Maisie sighed. "She's safe…and secure."

"You put her in a cell, didn't you?"

"Well, we could hardly leave her in those chains after she got the first pair off, could we?" Maisie argued.

"I want to see her."

Air hissed between the spy's teeth as she exhaled, but after a moment she nodded. "Come on."

Maisie led her through the long corridors of the fortress until they came to a narrow stairwell of cold granite, leading down into the depths beneath the keep. Erika hesitated as the spy took a torch from its bracket, memories of other underground tunnels flickering into her mind.

"You ready?" the spy asked, raising an eyebrow.

Erika nodded quickly and they started down into the darkness. Maisie's torch lit a bubble of light around them, but watching the flames flicker, Erika couldn't help but think how easily they might be extinguished. Then the darkness would claim them. A shiver ran down her spine and she clenched her fist, reaching for the magic, before stopping herself.

The stairwell ended in a narrow corridor lined with the iron bars of several cells. It stretched only a few yards—apparently Fort Illmoor hadn't had a great need for jail cells until now. Maisie led her past several empty cells before coming to a stop at the last one. She held up the torch and glanced at Erika.

"Well…ask your questions."

The breath caught in Erika's throat as the flames illuminated the room beyond the bars. It held no furniture but for a steel-framed cot bolted to the stones and a bucket placed in the corner. There were no windows or other exits, though movement came from the corner as a rat squawked at the light, disappearing into a hole between the bricks.

Erika's gaze was drawn to the bed, where a figure sat, knees pulled up to her chest. Dirt-stained wings hung limp across the bed, though Erika was surprised to see the cuts the Goddess had suffered from the king's attack already appeared to have healed. Slowly, Cara lifted her head, her amber eyes glinting in the lantern light.

"So you finally decided to come," she said as their eyes met.

A lump lodged in Erika's throat and she quickly dropped her gaze, unable to face that accusation, that anger. How far had she fallen, that it had come to this? She had seen her friend, the Goddess that had saved her life, imprisoned, locked away, all to save herself.

"I was meant to go home, you know," Cara's voice whispered through the bars. "That night in the mountains, before I led you to your precious hidden site. I was meant to go *home*."

"I'm sorry," Erika rasped, and her vision blurred. She turned to Maisie. "You can't leave her like this. It's not right. She's a *God!*"

"One of your Gods, not mine," Maisie said, but her face flickered as she spoke the words, as though she found herself doubting them. Her fingers played with the hilt of her sword as she glanced into the cell. "Besides, it's not my call."

"That's right—it's mine, Princess."

Erika swung around as the king's voice carried down the corridor. He appeared a moment later on the granite stairwell, his way lit by the unnatural glow of his gauntlet. Apparently, he had decided not to wear the riding gloves today.

"She doesn't deserve to be treated this way," Erika argued, taking a step towards him. "Whatever you think she is, Cara has done nothing wrong."

"She did try to attack me," Nguyen replied as he strode up. "I'd say imprisonment is a fairly light punishment for assaulting a monarch, wouldn't you?"

A growl came from inside the cell and Erika only shook her head. "You cannot be serious—"

The king waved a hand, cutting her off. "Calm yourself, Princess," he said, still using the moniker, much to Erika's annoyance. He moved to stand before the bars of the cell. "The good Anahera has proven...difficult, but these are only temporary accommodations, while I have been making...other arrangements."

"Other arrangements?" Erika asked as Cara's words echoed her question from inside the cell.

Nguyen chuckled. "All in good time," he replied, then offered a bow to the Goddess. "For now, I am afraid I must steal your visitors, Cara. There is something pressing we must attend to."

"Oh?" Maisie asked as the king turned away from the cell. Within, Cara had sat up and was watching them closely.

"Yes, I am afraid things are coming to a head rather faster than I had forecast," he said, looking from the spy to Erika. "The queen has arrived. There is to be a meet. With luck, I can forestall an attack long enough for my preparations to be completed."

"You're going to *talk* with her?" Erika hissed.

She clenched her fist, realising suddenly how precarious her situation was. The king already had a gauntlet of his own. With Cara and the map, there was little reason for him to protect her—not when the choice was between peace and a terrible war. Being the daughter of a dead king certainly wasn't going to save her.

The king's eyes glinted in the light of his magic. "You're afraid I will betray you?" he asked, as though he had read Erika's thoughts.

Erika swallowed. "Are you?"

Nguyen grinned. "On the contrary, princess. I was hoping you might help me."

10
THE SOLDIER

Adonis, what have you brought me?

Adonis had dropped to his knees with the other Tangata, but now he stood.

An anomaly, Matriarch, he replied, apparently making no efforts to shield his words from Lukys. *This human possesses the ability to Speak, and to Hear.*

Is that so, human? Milky eyes turned on Lukys. *You can Hear us?*

Lukys flinched—this time the Matriarch's voice was far louder in his mind, as though all her will had suddenly focused upon him. The creature lifted its eyebrows at his reaction.

So it's true. Her attention returned to Adonis. *An anomaly indeed. How did you make such a discovery?*

Chance, Matriarch, came Adonis's response. *He was broadcasting when we pursued the Anahera into human territory.* He hesitated. *She may have a connection with this human. She revealed herself trying to free him.*

Pieces fell into place in Lukys's mind at Adonis's words. The Anahera were the Tangata's name for the Gods. His blood ran cold as he realised the truth. His first day on the frontier, the Tangata had attacked, slaying dozens and suffering heavy losses themselves. But that had also been the night Romaine had arrived with the injured Cara. He frowned, staring at Adonis. Did the Tangata really hate the Gods so much that they had pursued Cara across the river, even thrown away so many of their own lives for a chance to slay her?

So the Anahera are finally returning to the world, the Matriarch mused. *Perhaps there is hope yet.* Her eyes shifted back to Lukys, and again the strength of her voice redoubled. *Tell me, human, what interest do the Anahera have in humanity?*

Lukys's skin crawled at the power of her words, though this time he thought he managed to keep the reaction from his face. Suppressing a shudder, he made to climb to his feet. A hand from Sophia stopped him until the Matriarch nodded her permission.

"The Goddess is a friend to my people," he said out loud, the words echoing in the silent chamber, "and she will come for us."

Laughter rasped around the room as the Matriarch shuffled to the edge of the dais. *Goddess?* A smile curled her lips. *Yes, of course, humans are such superstitious creatures.*

There was a flicker of movement, and suddenly the Matriarch was leaping forward, clearing the pool of water in a single bound and landing beside Lukys. He cried out and tried to retreat, but a wrinkled hand caught him by the shirt and dragged him back.

Tell me, human, are you truly a friend to the Anahera?

"I…" Lukys swallowed, suddenly finding himself trapped in that awful gaze, in those bleached white eyes.

Words abandoned him, but images flickered through his mind, memories of Fogmore, of time spent with Cara and Travis and Romaine. Good times, gone now, swept away by the madness of the Archivist's expedition.

So you speak the truth, the Matriarch murmured, and Lukys shuddered as he realised she had seen the memories. Then she sighed, and released him. *Still, it must be a faint hope that she would come to this place of her enemies.*

Lukys swallowed as she swung away from him, his entire body trembling. Had she simply read his mind, or had he been broadcasting those memories? Swallowing, he forced the fears away. He had to be strong.

"What do you want with us?" he asked, taking a step towards her.

A hand caught him before he could take another. He muffled a curse as Sophia dragged him back to where the other Tangata stood, though the Matriarch paid him no attention now.

I understand there are other humans without, Adonis? she asked, moving to stand before him.

Yes, Matriarch, he replied. *We brought fifteen for assignment.*

So many, the Matriarch mused. *And have you chosen one of your own?*

Adonis hesitated, but finally he shook his head. Lukys frowned at the exchange, but the Matriarch continued.

You are of the third generation, Adonis, she reproached him. *The last of my true progeny. You cannot delay forever, however distasteful you consider the chore.* Then she sighed and waved a hand. *But let that be a matter for another day. Tell me, how did so many come into your possession?*

Adonis's eyes flickered to where Lukys stood before returning to the Matriarch. *The humans led an expedition into our territory,* he said, his mental voice dropping to a murmur.

An expedition? To what ends?

Adonis swallowed visibly. *They had discovered another of our Birthing Grounds. Thankfully, the human's broadcasts forewarned us. We arrived first.*

Good. Perhaps now the humans will respect our territory, she paused. *And what did you discover there?*

The Old Ones, Matriarch, he whispered.

His words were met with a stunned silence. Watching the Matriarch's face, Lukys thought he glimpsed something there...of wonder, or hope? The thought sent a tremor down his spine as he remembered the creatures Adonis spoke of, the so-called "Old Ones." He could still recall the madness in their eyes, the bloodlust. They had slain even the Tangata that had woken them.

Suddenly he realised that words were no longer flowing through his mind, and looking up he saw the eyes of Adonis and the Matriarch on him. Adonis licked his lips, glancing uncertainly at his leader.

The human is right, he said finally. *The centuries had destroyed their minds. We fled before the creatures killed us all.*

Is that so? The Matriarch took a step towards Lukys, her eyes boring into him once more. *And how did the humans know where to look for this Birthing Ground?*

We do not know, Matriarch, Adonis replied.

The milky eyes did not leave Lukys. *Well, human?*

Lukys shivered, an image of the Archivist's map rising unbidden in his mind. Desperately he tried to press it back down, to hide it away. Laughter rasped from the aged creature as she stepped closer.

He resists me. Her whispers reverberated through Lukys's mind. *Let us see your strength then, human.*

A sudden, searing pain blinded Lukys at her words. In that instant, he felt as though his very being were being washed away, and in the distance he heard a voice crying out, agony ringing in his ears. The strength went from his legs and he sank to the ground. For a second the cold stones offered relief—but then another wave broke upon his soul, and the map he had glimpsed just once sprang to life in his mind.

Coloured lines and stars and circles appeared before his inner eyes, each depicting some real-life feature of the world in which they lived—mountains and forests and rivers and so much more. Inevitably his eyes were drawn to a scattering of scarlet stars spread throughout the kingdoms. The ancient sites of the Gods, what the Tangata had called their Birthing Grounds.

Lukys's pain vanished as quickly as it had appeared. Letting out a cry of relief, he slumped against the ground, sobbing softly into the granite floor. He knew, in that moment he had betrayed his people. The secrets of that map were important in a way none of them had ever realised, not until they'd stepped foot in those dark tunnels and discovered the Old Ones waiting.

Ahhh, so there is a map! Despite his misery, Lukys could not keep out the words of the Matriarch. *It shows all of our Birthing Grounds, even those long forgotten.*

There are others? Adonis asked, his mental voice betraying his excitement.

Several… Lukys looked up as the Matriarch hesitated, and saw a frown creasing her face. *Even…could it be…the home of the Anahera?*

Truly? Adonis hissed. *Then there is a chance—*

No, the Matriarch interrupted. *I have seen your memories; our people are not prepared for a confrontation with the Anahera, not yet.*

Then let us forge an accord! Adonis cried. *Surely they must understand our plight—*

Guard your thoughts, Adonis, the Matriarch interrupted, flicking a glance at Lukys. Adonis swallowed visibly at the creature's admonishment, and Lukys wondered what he had been about to reveal. After a moment, the Matriarch went on: *No, the risk is too great. The Anahera are as likely to slaughter us as treat with us. But…there is another Birthing Ground yet to uncover. Perhaps…*

Matriarch…is that wise?

An icy feeling spread through Lukys's gut—fear. But not his own. Images flickered through his mind as he stared at Adonis, of bloodshed and death and vicious creatures screaming in the darkness. Adonis too feared the Old Ones.

We must take the risk, she said, dismissing his objections. *Go, Adonis. If you will not take an assignment, then this is your task. Take five of our finest warrior pairs and find this final Birthing Ground. If the Old Ones slumber there, wake them, and do your best to bring them back to us.*

The map welled in Lukys's mind again, but this time it came not from him, but the Matriarch—she was projecting it to Adonis. He found his focus drawn to one of the scarlet stars he'd paid little attention to. There, far in the south, deep in the ancestral lands of the Tangata, on an island not far off the coast.

"No," he whispered, finally struggling to rise. His heart hammered in his chest and he held out a hand. "No, you can't, those creatures, they're insane!"

But it was already too late, as Adonis bowed his head and left the chamber. Alone before the Matriarch, he swallowed as her eyes fixed back on him.

We do as we must, human, she spoke into his mind.

You can't control them, Lukys replied, so desperate now that he cast the thought at her, and all the memories of bloodshed and death he had taken from that dark place beneath the earth. *They'll kill us all.*

The Matriarch remained unbending. *So be it,* came her reply. *Better the world burn than have my children go whimpering into extinction.*

Lukys shook his head, wishing he could somehow convince this strange creature, but already she seemed to have dismissed him. Then movement came from alongside him. He looked around in time to see Sophia approaching. He'd almost forgotten she was there.

Matriarch? she murmured, her head bowing slightly in deferment.

The Matriarch started at her words, seemingly surprised at her interference. *Yes, my child?*

I wish to claim my assignment.

The Matriarch's frown deepened and the pale eyes looked Sophia up and down. *You are of the fifth generation?* She paused, only going on when Sophia nodded. *You are still young, child. There may be time for you yet.*

My partner was slain, Sophia replied. Suddenly her grey eyes fixed on Lukys. His blood ran cold as she continued: *Slain by this human.*

Blood pulsed in his ears and he longed to flee. But there was nowhere for him to run, nowhere he could escape Sophia's gaze. So instead he stood fixed in place, knees trembling, and waited for his fate to be decided.

Ahhh, the Matriarch murmured, joining Sophia now. *Are you sure, my child?*

Yes, Sophia replied, turning again to Lukys. *The human slew many of my generation. He will be a good assignment.*

There was a long pause before the Matriarch spoke again, and all the while her eyes watched Lukys. He could feel them drilling into his soul, the touch of her mind upon his, and finally he was forced to look away.

Very well, my child, the Matriarch said finally. *He is yours—though beware, the Anahera may yet come for him.*

Then we will deal with her, Sophia replied, bowing her head deferentially. *Thank you, Matriarch.*

Lukys swallowed as footsteps approached. Fear and anger warred within him as Sophia moved forward. He would not be made a slave, would not surrender to these creatures, his will crushed so he only served them. Silently he steeled himself.

Then his eyes met Sophia's, and he felt something brush against his mind. His emotions faded as she stepped up before him, grey eyes piercing him just as the Matriarch's had. The resolve he'd felt just moments before drained away like a plug had been pulled in his core. And her voice whispered in his mind.

Now you truly are mine, Lukys.

❧ II ❧

THE FALLEN

Standing atop the river terrace, Romaine let out a long breath as he looked across at the Illmoor Fortress. Curtain walls of stark granite swept out from the cliffs, the blocks seeming more an extension of the mountains themselves than a manmade structure. Watch towers marked the ramparts at intervals, their twisted rooftops flying the yellow of Gemaho.

Their approach would have been noted days ago and now hundreds of soldiers stood atop those walls, armour shining in the noon sun. Looking on the men and women who opposed them, Romaine was reminded again of the madness of it all, that humanity should war upon itself while the Tangata still threatened their very existence. Not that he would be involved in much of the fighting. He had been training in the sword with Lorene and his injuries were healing well, but he would be little use in a pitched battle.

Pushing the thought aside, Romaine continued his appraisal of the enemy fortress. Away to the right, the waters of the Illmoor River had narrowed until they were just half a mile wide. The currents rushed between the twisted peaks of the Mountains of the Gods—and beneath the broad walls of the fortress. An incredible feat of engineering had erected a bridge of stone above the rushing waters as an extension of the curtain walls. Iron grates between the support pillars prevented the passage of ship or swimmers, and could be raised during storms or to allow debris to be removed. Only in the centre of the river were ships allowed to pass through a giant portcullis—at least during peacetimes.

The walls continued on the southern banks of the river, ensuring none could pass unnoticed into the lands of Gemaho. Other than the water portcullis, the only way through was the land gate— massive doors of heavy oak bolted by steel. Without ships for an aquatic assault, it was there that the queen would launch her attack.

Silently, Romaine turned his gaze to the floodplains before the fortress, where the queen's army had formed up, shields and spear tips glinting in the noonday sun. Behind the formation, others were hard at work preparing the camp fortifications. Romaine was again impressed by the speed at which they were securing the position. Unlike some of the irregulars he'd fought alongside on the frontier, the Queen's Guard were professional soldiers, and each knew his role.

Dozens had already paced out a perimeter for the camp and were now directing men with shovels where to prepare the defensive ditch. Others were preparing latrines downwind from the main camp, while still more went about setting the tents and organising the now-empty supply wagons into a second defensive perimeter. All the while, a squadron of archers stood in reserve.

Within an hour the camp would be set. Shaking his head, Romaine spurred his horse down the hill in search of the queen.

He found her amongst the soldiers standing in formation, her banner fluttering overhead, as though daring the Gemaho forces to attack. Sitting on her great destrier, garbed in the scarlet armour of the Flumeeren royalty, Romaine could imagine for a moment how it must have looked when she had led the charge against the Tangata in the disastrous southern campaign.

A smile lit her face as she turned and saw his approach. "Calafe, we've been waiting for you. Are you ready?"

Romaine frowned as he drew his horse to a stop alongside the queen. On her other side, Yasin grinned, though the gesture was mocking. Ignoring the silent taunt, Romaine rested his hand on the pommel of his saddle.

"Ready for what?"

"There is to be a truce for discussion. I plan to demand the

Goddess's return. Given your affiliation with her Divinity, I thought you might wish to attend the meet."

Romaine hesitated, flicking a glance at the towering walls, but there didn't seem to be any activity atop the ramparts to indicate an attack was eminent. So instead he nodded, and the queen kicked her horse forward. Romaine followed. The ranks of scarlet soldiers split ahead of them, while a squadron of guards formed up behind the queen's delegation. Leaving behind the shelter of her army, they rode some hundred yards towards the fortress before pulling their horses to a stop. There they waited.

It wasn't long before the gates to the fortress creaked open to emit a column of riders. The queen's soldiers tensed, but Romaine was thankful to see their opposites numbered the same as their own party. They approached at a slow trot, finally drawing up a dozen yards from the queen and Romaine.

"King Nguyen," the queen said as one of the riders heeled his horse forward a step. "I had not expected you to welcome me personally to your kingdom."

A grin appeared on the rider's face and still in the saddle, he offered a mocking bow. "Of course, my lady," Nguyen replied. "When I learned of your movements I made for the Illmoor with all haste. I would be a poor king indeed if I did not offer greeting to a neighbour who comes to visit."

"Ay, poor indeed," the queen said, her voice as frigid as the snow-capped peaks towering above. "Though no more poorly than sending thieves behind a neighbour's back."

"Thieves, my lady?" the king said, feigning horror. "What has become of the world that such suspicions enter between friends?"

"The Gemaho have not been friends to Flumeer for a decade," the queen snapped.

She edged her horse forward and the soldiers behind the king reached for their swords. One, though, flinched at the queen's advance. Romaine frowned as he looked past the king to the soldier…

…only the rider wasn't a soldier at all. It was Erika, the queen's former Archivist. The one who had taken Cara.

"*You!*" he hissed, pointing a finger at the woman. He kicked his horse forward, but several of the king's soldiers drew between him and the opposing party. Teeth bared, Romaine bellowed a challenge. "What have you done with Cara?"

Blood hammered in his ears as he looked past the soldiers at Erika. The Archivist's face had grown pale at his challenge, but now her features smoothed as she quickly masked her emotions. Nearby, the king smiled.

"Ah, so I see you have met my new Archivist," he said with a laugh.

Watching at Erika sitting amongst the Gemaho, Romaine felt himself a fool. She had convinced him to trust her, to believe she was the long-lost princess of Calafe, but it had all been a ploy, a way to escape the clutches of the queen.

"So you admit to the crime," the queen snarled.

Behind the king, Erika tensed, but Nguyen laughed and gestured her forward. The woman hesitated, but one of the soldiers prodded the backside of her horse, and with a nicker it trotted forward until she sat alongside the king. His face hardened as he turned and regarded the queen once more.

"I am here because a foreign monarch has camped an army on my doorstep," he said, and now his voice had lost all humour. "Gemaho does not take kindly to threats against our sovereignty. I would ask you to remove this army from my border, lest blood is once again spilt between the kingdoms of man."

The queen sneered at his words. "So now the cowardly king concerns himself with the kingdoms of man," she spat. Clutching her reins, she stared across the field at the enemy king. "Surrender the thief, and the Goddess Cara, and perhaps I will consider leaving your pitiful walls standing."

Nguyen stared back at them, his expression kept carefully masked. Beside him, however, Erika was a picture of terror, her carefully crafted persona shattered by the queen's threats. Romaine couldn't help but feel a touch of satisfaction as he watched her squirm. He cast his eyes over the other soldiers, but there was no sign of Cara. He clenched a fist and swallowed another outburst.

"I am afraid the Calafe princess has requested my asylum," the king said finally. "In respect for my fallen brother king, that is a pact I will not break."

Romaine's heart lurched at the king's words—not least because this was the man who had abandoned his nation to its doom. Teeth clenched, he looked from Nguyen to Erika. Did the man truly believe her claim, or was he using it as a political tool, a weapon he could wield against the queen?

"What nonsense is this?" the queen hissed, her eyes flicking from the king to Erika. "The bitch is no princess."

Mock surprise showed on the king's face. "You did not know?" he gasped, then *tisked*. "Amina, I am disappointed. I thought your spies were better than that."

The queen narrowed her eyes and a strained silence followed. Romaine guessed that Amina was weighing the king's words, trying to decipher whether he spoke the truth. Erika's potential royalty might mean little, or her appearance could stir up unrest amongst the hundreds of Calafe refugees camped outside her capital.

"You may keep the Archivist," Amina said finally, though her voice was strained. "It is the artefact she uncovered which concerns me. Her expeditions were funded by Flumeeren coin—the gauntlet belongs to me."

"The gauntlet?" the king murmured. Then his eyebrows lifted as though he had suddenly remembered something, and he pulled off one of his riding gloves. A gauntlet of silver steel was revealed beneath. "You mean this?"

For just a second, the queen's mask cracked, and Romaine saw the terrible rage simmering beneath the surface. Around him, her guards recoiled, hands tightening on spears and swords, but the king only held up the gauntleted hand. His eyes glinted in the sunlight.

"I'll admit, it is an interesting trinket."

"The Archivist had no right to gift it to you. It belongs to me," the queen hissed through clenched teeth.

"Is that so?" the king mused.

He chuckled, and with his free hand he grasped the gauntlet around his wrist. There was a muffled *hiss*, as of steam from a kettle, and even in the bright daylight the metal began to glow. Then something went *click* and he slid the gauntlet from his hand.

"Take it," he said, tossing it across the open ground. It struck the ground before the queen with a heavy thud. "Its power did not...sit right with me anyway," he added with a smile.

The queen stared at him for a long moment before turning her eyes to the gauntlet. Romaine swallowed as he glimpsed the greed there. He had seen what that gauntlet was capable of, the power it held. In the span of a second it could reduce grown men to agony, could knock even the Tangata from their feet.

The queen indicated for Yasin to collect the artefact. Eyes never leaving the enemy, the man dismounted and claimed the weapon, then handed it to Amina. She took it reverently, though not without another glance at the king.

Still sitting on his horse, Nguyen spread his hands. "So, we have peace then?"

The queen's eyes narrowed. "What of the Goddess?" she asked. "She was taken against her will. Flumeer will not stand idle while you assault the personage of the Divine."

The king chuckled. "I would have thought your Gods better able to protect themselves," he replied. He waved a hand, as though to dismiss Amina's concerns. "I will speak with the Goddess, though I believe she has already made arrangements for her future."

"Liar," Romaine snapped, the king's words finally pushing him beyond the bounds of reason. "You took Cara against her will."

"You must be Romaine." The king smiled as their eyes met. "Good to finally make your acquaintance. I have heard much of the last soldier of Calafe. Cara was most concerned for your health."

Romaine was forced to bite back a rude retort as the queen raised her hand. "My army will not be leaving while Her Divine Personage remains your prisoner, Nguyen."

The king let out a sigh. "Then it seems we are at an impasse."

Amina's eyes were hard as stone as she stared him down. "I know the Divine was brought here in chains by the woman who stands beside you, Nguyen," she grated. A growl rumbled from Romaine's chest at her words, but the queen went on: "I will not stand for it. Grant the Goddess her freedom by the morrow, or the bloodshed that follows will be on your hands."

With that, the queen turned her horse and started back towards the camp. For a moment, Romaine sat on his own horse, staring at Erika. The Archivist shrank beneath his gaze, before she finally broke and tugged on her reins, turning away. Shaking his head at her cowardice, Romaine went after the queen.

"—really his daughter?" He caught the queen's words as he approached.

Riding alongside her, Yasin shrugged. "Was a long time ago, but it could be true. Hair is the right colour."

"Romaine," the queen said as he came alongside her, "what do you think?"

"She claimed the same to me on the banks of the Illmoor," he grunted.

Amina cursed. "Nguyen is no fool. If he says it's true, more than likely he's right."

"Does it change things?" Yasin asked.

The queen did not reply immediately. Her eyes had fallen to the gauntlet she held across her saddle pommel. "What game is he playing, giving it up so easily?" she murmured. Then she shook her head and looked at Yasin, as though finally hearing his question. "No," she replied. "I don't believe so."

"Then I'll have my men ready by nightfall," Yasin replied.

"What's this about?" Romaine asked softly.

"Nguyen has been a step ahead of me since all of this began," the queen replied, "but no more. This time, I know what he's planning to do next."

"How?" Romaine breathed.

"Because it's what I would do." A grin spread across the queen's face. "Are you ready for a rescue mission, Calafe?"

Romaine swallowed, clenching the reins in his fist. "Anything for Cara."

The queen nodded. Then her eyes returned to the gauntlet, and she held it up to the light. A twitch tugged at her cheek, but then she seemed to steel herself, and in one fluid movement, she slid her hand into the ancient artefact. Light burst from the shimmering links as she clenched her fist.

"Good," she breathed, "because it's time we took back the initiative."

$\mathscr{X}$ 12 $\mathscr{X}$

THE SOLDIER

Lukys woke to darkness. For a moment he felt panic, that the nightmares of his sleep had somehow followed him to the real world. His heart hammered in his chest and he cried out, fumbling desperately at the black, and was rewarded by slamming his hands into something solid. Pain lanced through his fingers and he cursed, rolling away—

Thump.

The breath hissed from Lukys's lungs as he toppled off the ledge on which he'd been lying and slammed into the ground. He lay there groaning for a moment, memories slowly returning to him.

After his encounter with the Matriarch, Sophia had led him to the back of the basilica. There an opening hidden behind the dais had revealed a staircase leading down into the earth. Below, they'd discovered a seemingly endless corridor leading away into the depths of the earth, lined by iron doors.

A prison.

Sophia had not spoken as she locked him in his cell, leaving him alone in this awful darkness. Lukys had spent the hours since pondering his fate. Why had Sophia locked him in this place, if he was to be her slave? What was a prison even doing hidden beneath the Calafe's Basilica to the Fall?

Eventually Lukys had fallen asleep on the low bench that lined the walls, though there was no way of telling for how long. Time did not seem to move in this dark place. He found himself wondering what had happened to Dale and Travis and all the others. Had they too been locked in this awful place? He'd tried yelling through the heavy iron door, but from the way his voice echoed in the tiny space, he guessed little noise escaped.

A shiver ran down his spine as he began to wonder how long he would be kept here. How much time would it take before he went mad in the absolute black, robbed of all sense of time, of hope? He had found a crevasse of water in his first moments within the cell, but his stomach was already starting to rumble. Would they feed him, or was starvation part of his punishment?

Lukys…

Lukys yelped and almost fell off the bench as Sophia's voice whispered in his mind. He swung around, half expecting to find that the Tangata had snuck into his cell. But that was impossible—the first thing he'd done was run his hands around the walls in hope of finding another way out, and there'd been nothing. Slowly he turned towards the door. She was outside.

"What do you want?" he snapped, then cursed as his words echoed within the cell.

She must have heard him though, for laughter whispered into his thoughts. *Careful, you'll wake the dead with such noise.* She paused, before adding: *This would seem a good opportunity to practice Speaking…Lukys.*

The hairs on the back of his neck lifted at her words. *The dead?*

That's better. There was amusement in Sophia's inner voice. *It's said that many of our ancestors perished in places such as this, in the time before The Fall. Perhaps their spirits do haunt these corridors.*

The Tangata believe in spirits? Lukys frowned; even after a week with the creatures, he hadn't contemplated the thought they might have a concept of an afterlife. A dozen questions rose unbidden in his mind, but he brushed them off. Now was not the time for scholarship. *What is this place, then?*

Another of our Birthing Grounds. The Calafe tried to cover it up, but my people are good at sniffing out secrets.

Lukys nodded to himself, recalling how the Tangata had managed to locate the entrance to the other ancient site, despite it lying buried in an empty plateau.

Why did you bring me here?

There was a pause before Sophia replied. *We have been assigned,* she said finally, as though that explained everything.

Frustration touched Lukys and he crossed to the door, placing his head against the cold metal. "But what does that *mean?*" he hissed out loud, trying to cast the thought through the iron at the same time.

I told you—it means you are mine, Lukys. There was a pause.

Lukys's skin crawled at her words. *So that's it, then,* he murmured, turning away from the door, his heart suddenly racing. *You're going to lock me here in the dark forever, taunt me and torture me, all because I killed your partner?*

His words were followed by a long silence and he closed his eyes, thinking she'd left him again. Panic touched him and he realised he didn't want to be alone down here, trapped, starving, lost. Better he had someone's company, even if it *was* only to punish him.

A sudden *clang* came from the door as Sophia drew back the locking mechanism. Lukys leapt as a soft light spilled into his cell, first just a fine crack where the door opened, then growing larger to reveal a lantern. He swallowed as Sophia entered the cell, retreating the rest of the way to the rear of his little prison. But she made no move towards him, only watched him for a moment with those terrifying eyes, then sat herself on the bench. She placed the lantern down beside her.

I do not seek to hurt you, Lukys.

For a moment, Lukys did not understand the words she'd spoken into his mind. He blinked, hesitating. *What?*

I fought alongside Zachariah for many years, Sophia murmured. *But such bonds are…complicated for our people.*

Lukys frowned, the pounding of blood in his ears fading slightly at the calmness of Sophia's words. He hesitated, glancing at his hands, recalling the conversation that had passed between Sophia and the Matriarch. In his fear, he hadn't really taken in the words, but now he found himself wondering…

"The Matriarch told Adonis to take his best warrior pairs," he said finally.

Sophia nodded. *When we come of age, my people are partnered with another of our generation. We are required to serve five years as warriors, to ensure the safety of our people from…humanity.*

"Then…he wasn't your mate?" Lukys asked.

Mate? Still you think of us as animals, Lukys!

"No!" he gasped, raising his palms in a gesture of peace.

He hesitated when he saw the grin on her lips, and a peal of laughter rang through the cell. His racing heart slowed as he watched the Tangata. What was this creature playing at? Slowly he lowered himself down onto the bench opposite her.

We were many things, Sophia said finally. She leaned forward, her eyes fixing on him once more. *But…our time together was coming to an end.*

Lukys swallowed. "You…don't seem…overly bothered by his death."

To his surprise, Sophia looked away at that. He thought he might have glimpsed a touch of red to her cheeks, but in the flickering lantern light he could not be sure.

Zachariah was…passionate. She glanced at him. *He loathed your kind, and joyed in his…role as a warrior. Alas, I never felt that same passion.*

"Oh…" Lukys hesitated. "Well, I for one am thankful that you haven't torn me limb from limb."

The hint of a smile appeared on Sophia's lips, surprisingly feminine. *It was lucky you sparked Adonis's curiosity,* she replied. *He is another who…dislikes your kind's role in our society.*

Her words gave Lukys pause and he found himself looking away, eyes caught in the lantern light. He savoured the orange glow, even as its brightness caused stars to dance across his vision. Despite everything Sophia had told him, there was still one thing he did not understand.

What am I doing here, Sophia? he murmured, reaching out with his mind.

A sigh slipped from the Tangata's lips but she did not answer. Lukys forced himself to look at her again and was surprised to find her watching him. He swallowed. The sight of those grey eyes still terrified him, caused something primal in him to cry out.

"Am I to be your slave?" he asked at last, unable to keep the despair from his voice.

No. Sophia rose abruptly. She walked to where the iron door still stood open and for a moment he thought she would depart. But she swung back, fists clenched, lips pursed tight together. She shook her head. *This isn't how it is meant to go.*

"And how is it *meant* to go?" Lukys snapped, anger rising in the face of Sophia's disappointment. He found himself on his feet. "Was I meant to just bow down to you, submit to my new overlord? Is that what humanity is to become, if you conquer our world? Your playthings?"

We do not want your world, Sophia replied.

You took this one! Lukys hurled the words at her. *This city belonged to my friend's people once. You stole it from the Calafe, slaughtered their families, drove them from their lands. Now you make slaves of those who were left behind.*

They are not slaves! Sophia snarled into his mind.

She stepped towards him, teeth bared, her whole body trembling. Lukys was suddenly reminded of what he faced. For a moment he'd managed to convince himself he spoke to another human, to forget what she was. Now that realisation came rushing back and he retreated from her fury.

Sophia's eyes widened at his movement and the anger drained from her face. Silently she took a step back from him, and he thought he saw something in her eyes…terror, revulsion? Then she shook her head.

They are not slaves, Lukys, she repeated. *All chose their fate, chose to live amongst us.*

Lukys clenched his fists. "Then I am free to leave?"

Air hissed between Sophia's teeth and she looked away. *You cannot,* she replied finally. *You have seen too much.*

"Then I am your prisoner," Lukys stated.

A sigh slipped from the Tangata's lips. *I cannot force you to accept our assignment, Lukys.* Her voice came as a murmur, as though she barely dared to speak. *But neither can I release you, not until you swear yourself to me. The Matriarch would not stand for it.*

So you're to be my jailor? he spat back.

Sophia's eyes narrowed. *If that is how you wish to view it.* She turned and strode to the door. *I will return tomorrow, and every day after.* She pushed open the iron door and picked up the lantern from the bench.

Panic touched Lukys at the sight of the light being taken. "Wait!" he gasped.

Grey eyes turned on him. *What?*

Lukys hesitated, unsure of what to say. The thought of lingering in the darkness for another day, for all his remaining days, made his entire body shake. Yet he could not surrender his freedom so easily. He thought again of Travis and Dale and the other recruits.

What of my friends? he asked finally. *What has become of them?*

Silence lingered in his mind, then: *A few have already sworn themselves to their assignments,* Sophia admitted finally. *Most…still resist, as you do.*

Reassured that at least his friends had not been butchered, Lukys nodded. Sophia might have been lying, but somehow he didn't think so. Speaking mind to mind, he sensed it must be difficult to tell a falsehood.

"Thank you," he murmured.

Sophia only turned away, preparing to leave, and Lukys's stomach twisted again with fear.

Wait! He hesitated. *Can…you leave the light?*

Looking over her shoulder, Sophia regarded him for a moment. Then in silence she set the lantern on the bench beside the door and slipped out. The door clanged shut. And he was alone in the silence.

❧ 13 ❧

THE FUGITIVE

Panic ate at Erika as she lay awake in her bed, staring up at the hidden ceiling. Darkness clung to the room and the only sound to break the silence was her own breathing. Maisie was gone again, off completing some task or another for the king, no doubt. But despite the tranquillity of the night, Erika found sleep would not come.

She could not stop picturing the queen, could not stop seeing the hatred in her eyes, the promise for vengeance. Princess of Calafe or not, the woman wanted her dead. And what Amina wanted had a habit of coming true. Would she send Romaine to take his revenge?

No, it would be a true killer, someone well prepared to strike another down in cold blood. Immediately the face of the other man who had ridden alongside the queen leapt to Erika's mind. There had been a darkness in that man's eyes, and something else…a familiarity, as though Erika knew him from somewhere. But Erika could not quite put her finger on it.

Grinding her teeth, she sat up suddenly and threw off her covers. Rising, she crossed to the window and looked out at the silent vista. Stars shone in a cloudless sky, but the moon was hidden behind the mountains that bounded the fortress. Somewhere in the distance, though, between the stark cliffs of the canyon, she glimpsed the faintest of glows.

Dawn was already approaching. She shook her head, returning to her bed, though she did not bother to close her eyes. Instead, Erika turned her mind to the king and his actions. Why had he given up the gauntlet to his enemy? Had he truly thought to buy peace with the queen—or was there something more nefarious in his actions?

Erika's eyes were drawn to her own gauntlet. In the darkness, the faintest shimmer of light could be seen amongst the metallic fibres, though she had not unleashed its power in days. Was there some danger to that glow, some effect of the magic she did not understand? Regardless, she needed it now. It was her only protection should the queen's killers come for her.

Her heart twisted as she turned her thoughts to Cara. How badly she had repaid her friend's kindness, to allow her to be imprisoned, locked away like a common criminal. Teeth clenched, she lurched from the bed and threw on a tunic and coat, then boots. It was time she began making up for her mistakes.

Erika was just starting for the door when it swung open. A lantern carved the darkness and she raised a hand and squinted against its brilliance.

"Oh good, you're up," came Maisie's voice from the doorway. "Grab your things, the king wants us away before dawn."

"What are you talking about?" Erika gasped.

"We're leaving," Maisie replied, as though it made perfect sense. She turned away as Erika's vision began to adjust to the light.

"What?" Erika repeated. Her heart hammered in her chest as she looked around the room, but her only possession was a small day pack. Scooping it up, she followed the spy out into the corridor. There, though, she hesitated. "What about Cara?" she said softly. "I'm not going anywhere until I know the Goddess is no longer locked in that cell."

Maisie paused at that, one eyebrow arcing towards her fringe. "Oh, so now you've developed a conscience, have you?" She chuckled and swung away. "Don't worry about it, Cara is coming with us."

Erika opened her mouth, then closed it. She'd already made herself look ignorant enough. Recovering her composure, she strode after the Gemaho woman. A cocoon of light spread out from the lantern Maisie held, shielding them from the night's darkness, though Erika caught glimpses of the approaching dawn through the windows they passed.

"So where are we going?" she asked finally.

"Here," Maisie replied, pressing a steel tube into her hands without breaking stride. "We're going to the home of your Gods."

Distracted by the object she'd been handed, Erika didn't immediately understand the significance of the spy's words. Removing the top of the tube, she drew out an aged piece of paper, before quickly replacing it in the protective cylinder. She didn't need to unfurl it to know what it was—the map she had recovered, the one she'd given to the king…

"Wait, what did you say—"

Erika's words were cut off as her foot caught on a wrinkle in the carpet. Crying out, she lurched forward, arms windmilling, until a hand from Maisie settled her upright once more. Cursing, she looked at the woman.

"You can't be serious?" she gasped, abandoning all attempts at keeping her cool.

The spy laughed and continued down the corridor. Erika hurried to catch up. It wasn't like she hadn't considered the idea. Ever since she'd seen that distant star marked in the Mountains of the Gods, she had wondered. But it was forbidden to enter those mountains. Now that they knew the Gods truly dwelled there, what they were capable of, surely such an expedition was suicide.

"Can't say I'm too thrilled with the plan," Maisie said matter-of-factly as they turned down a set of stairs that led towards the river, "but *Nguyen* is serious, and therefore, so am I."

The stairwell opened out onto a series of berths nestled in the space behind the bridge wall. Several ships of varying sizes were currently docked, though at this hour the only movement came from a large galley further down the jetty. Beyond, Erika glimpsed an arcing dike of boulders that stretched out into the river, sheltering the port from the currents.

"Maisie, Erika, I'm glad you made it," Nguyen greeted as they approached the vessel.

Erika came to a stop alongside the king. Taking a moment to gather her thoughts, she glanced at the ship the man had prepared for them. It looked much the same as the galley that had once taken her across the Illmoor to Calafe, though the mast currently bore no sail. With the wind blowing down the canyon from Gemaho, the sailors would have to use the oars until they passed beyond the sheer cliffs.

From there she could imagine the path they would take from the map she held in her hand—sail south through the plateaus until they reached the valley that would lead them up into the icy peaks, up to the ancient site marked by a scarlet star. It was madness, though…Erika couldn't help but feel a thrill of exhilaration. What fresh wonders must await in the home of the Gods themselves?

"Excited, Princess?" the king asked, though his eyes were on the preparations.

Erika swallowed. "I'm…not sure we'll be greeted warmly," she replied.

"No, I imagine not. These Anahera have distanced themselves from human civilisation for centuries. They are unlikely to welcome uninvited guests."

"Then why…" Erika trailed off as she glimpsed a new figure approaching along the jetty.

Cara still wore iron manacles on her wrists and ankles, but it looked like she'd at least been allowed to bathe and change her clothes. A heavy cloak of wolf fur hung around her shoulders, concealing her wings, and her copper hair had been tied back in a ponytail. She also still wore her familiar scowl, and a troop of some twenty soldiers followed behind, swords and spears held at the ready. Apparently they had been told to treat this prisoner with extreme caution.

"Welcome, Your Divinity," the king said, adopting a cheerful smile. "I trust the facilities were to your liking?"

Cara's scowl deepened as she stopped before them. "Where were all the 'Your Divinities' when you had me thrown in your dungeon?"

"Ancient history," the king replied, dismissing the complaint.

"It was happening up until an hour ago."

"Yes, well," the king continued, apparently unperturbed. "I do hope that we might put the past behind us."

The Goddess folded her arms—or as best as she could with the heavy manacles. "How about I knock you out first and stuff you into a cargo hold for a week. Then maybe we can talk."

"A rather unproductive proposal, I would say." Nguyen smiled. "I would much rather learn more about the Anahera."

Cara narrowed her eyes. "I will talk no more of my people."

"Yes, yes, you've made that quite clear," Nguyen replied. "Only, if you must know, I am growing quite desperate. The threat of the Tangata grows ever closer, and now the Flumeeren queen brings an army against me. I have a need for allies."

"The Flumeer are here?" Cara's head perked up. "Is Romaine with them? Is he okay?"

Erika snorted. "Seemed fine to me when he was threatening my life."

Cara flashed her a glare but the king interrupted before the Goddess could say anything else.

"Yes, yes, the Calafe is quite fine, though I fear that Amina has her claws in him now. We were discussing how you might aid me, Your Divinity."

Cara snorted again and lifted her hands, giving the chains a rattle. "Why don't you take these off, and I'll think about smiting these enemies of yours."

The king sighed. "It is not your powers I require," he replied. "Though your cooperation would no doubt be of great aid. I seek to contact your people, the Anahera, to ask for *their* aid."

The Goddess stilled at his words, her eyes taking on a look of surprise. "You can't."

"I must," Nguyen said, then gestured to the ship. "The sailors will take you as far as the river allows, the soldiers the rest of the way into the mountains."

"*You can't*," Cara repeated, taking a step towards the king.

Swords rattled against shields as the soldiers behind her advanced, but Nguyen raised a hand to stop them. The Goddess's amber eyes never left him.

"They'll…stop you," she croaked.

"Ahh, but my dear Cara, we have *you*," the king replied, eyes shining. "I am sure the Anahera will welcome the return of one of their own."

Cara's shoulders slumped at that and she looked away. "You don't understand," the Goddess grated between clenched teeth.

Erika swallowed. There was no missing the anger in Cara's voice. How much longer would she endure such treatment? The king wore his riding gloves, no doubt to hide that he had given away his power, and the gauntlet still hung heavy on her own arm, but…it would be a long journey. Erika didn't savour the thought of being alone with an angry Goddess high in those icy mountains.

But the king was right: humanity needed allies, and Gods or no, the Gods alone had the power to defeat the Tangata. Their strength and magic would be a substantial advantage to whichever kingdom won them as allies.

"Well, I suppose it's time the three of you set off," the king announced, bringing his hands together in a clap that made them all jump.

"You're not coming?" Erika asked, surprised.

The king chuckled. "Much as I would enjoy the adventure, I have a kingdom to run." He gestured towards the wall. "Not to mention your old mentor to handle—"

As though summoned by his words, a horn sounded in the distance. A frown touched the king's forehead and together all eyes on the dock turned towards the walls. Another blast of the horn sounded, closer this time, followed by a faint roar, as of a thousand voices crying out as one.

Crack!

The stone shook beneath Erika's feet and she swung around, as though expecting some giant to come charging towards them. The king only shook his head.

"It seems Amina is early," he said, turning to Erika with a grim smile. "Time for you to get moving then, Princess. Fate of the world and all. Best of luck."

With a final wave, he turned and strode away. Erika stood for a moment staring at the towering walls, until Maisie grasped her by the arm and dragged her aboard the ship. Cara followed, trailed by the soldiers, and moments later they were adrift in the currents of the Illmoor, each stroke of the oars sending them ever closer to the legendary home of the Gods.

And the screams of the dying chased after them.

❦ 14 ❦

THE FALLEN

Whooorl.

Romaine came to a halt as the sound of horns carried up the slope. His gaze was drawn past the plunging drop just a few feet from where he stood, down to where the walls of the fortress stretched across the valley. They looked smaller from his vantage point, the soldiers upon its ramparts like beetles in their shining armour.

Beyond the walls, a second swarm of beetles raced across the open ground, covering the green grass in black. The horn sounded again and moments later the cry of a thousand voices raised in unison reached them on the mountainside.

"I take it back," Lorene murmured, standing just behind him. "Going south might have been safer."

Romaine did not reply, as the first screams began from below. He forced himself to look away. It felt wrong, to see humans fighting against humans, while the threat of the Tangata loomed so close, less than an hours boat ride away. From their vantage point he could see the wild lands of Calafe, stretching almost to the walls of the fortress. It might be the last glimpse he ever got of his homeland.

"Come on, you two," Yasin's voice came from ahead. "Amina's guards can only distract them so much. We're exposed out here."

Below, the clash of weapons began as the first of the Flumeeren soldiers scaled their ladders and reached the ramparts. Shaking himself free of his misgivings, Romaine shared a final glance with Lorene before continuing. Seemingly determined to finally set eyes upon Cara and her wings, the man had volunteered to join them on this mad journey, though neither he nor Romaine knew where it would take them.

Along with Romaine and Lorene, Yasin had brought another thirty men, though none were of the calibre that Romaine had come to expect of the Queen's Guard. Rugged and unkempt, if not for their polished weapons and armour, Romaine might have guessed them to be brigands or mercenaries. As it was, from the scars most sported, it was clear they were veterans of some sort.

Yasin took the lead once more, leading them along a goat track high above the Fortress Illmoor. From below, Romaine would not have thought it possible to traverse these rugged cliffs. Indeed, the trail was not without risk. Not only were they exposed should any of the defenders decide to look up, but a single misstep would see them plummet hundreds of feet to the rocks below.

No wonder they hadn't started this section of the trail until the sun had begun to rise. Thankfully the queen had timed her distraction well, and with their weapons and armour covered by cloth to prevent them reflecting the sun, Romaine prayed their passage would go unnoticed. If not…well, then no doubt Nguyen would have a welcoming party waiting for them.

Romaine tightened his fist at the thought. He was still practising the sword with Lorene and the queen had gifted him a shield which could be strapped to his left arm rather than held. But the chest injury still hindered him and his progress had been slow. He needed more time to regain his former skill—time he did not have.

At least he was healed enough not to slow their progress. Yasin did not seem overly happy to have them along, but Amina had insisted. They needed someone Cara knew if they were to rescue her out from under the Archivist's nose, though Romaine still hadn't been filled in on the details of that plan.

Their journey continued, winding along the tops of cliffs and across treacherous slopes. All the while, the battle raged on. When the queen had first mentioned this trail, Romaine had wondered why she didn't send a larger force to attack the fortress from behind. Afterall, the Illmoor Fortress had only been designed to defend against a foreign aggressor. Now he understood. It would be a miracle if they passed unnoticed and without incident—a greater force would be spotted in minutes.

Entering the centre of the pass, Romaine wondered at the queen's boldness. Nguyen's soldiers were well-armed and taking a terrible toll on those attempting to reach the ramparts. The bloodshed was terrible to behold. It seemed a terrible price to pay for a distraction. And all for what? To save one woman.

Or to save a God?

The distinction was still muddled in Romaine's mind, his memories of Cara seemingly split into two people. There was the Goddess he had seen on the shores of the Illmoor, wings spread, eyes burning with untold power. But there was also the sweet, innocent young woman he had known in Fogmore. That woman felt far more real to Romaine, his memories of the days they'd spent training together, the sharp smiles and her flitting romance with the recruit Travis crystal clear. Despite the importance of the Goddess, it was that Cara he searched for, that Cara he sought to rescue.

An hour passed quickly in their desperate race across the mountainside, up spires of rock and down into twisted gulleys, their passage all the time punctuated by the distant shrieks of weapons clashing, the howls of the dying. Romaine kept his eyes on the trail, thankful that Yasin seemed to know his way. It made him wonder how many times the man had crossed this way, what other undertakings he might have performed in the lands of the Gemaho.

Though whatever disreputable actions the queen might have taken against the kingdom, Romaine couldn't help but think it was justice. The king's cowardice in abandoning the alliance had left Calafe exposed, their armies too weak to withstand the Tangatan assault. As their kingdom inexorably fell to the creatures, Romaine and his comrades had often cursed the man's name.

What sort of king hid behind his walls while the rest of the world burned, while his former allies fought and died in the name of freedom?

Such cravenness could only bring fate down upon such a man—and his kingdom, too. Romaine prayed to the Gods above that he would live to see the day.

Finally they moved beyond the sheer cliffs into deeper grooves in the mountainside. Pillars of stone rose around them, shielding the company from view of those below. The path also widened, allowing Lorene and Romaine to walk abreast. The normally cheerful scout wore a grim expression as they started the climb down towards the lands of Gemaho.

"You okay, lad?" Romaine grunted.

The scout flashed Romaine a glance. "That battle seemed far too bloody for a distraction," he said after a while. "What is Queen Amina thinking, committing so many of our soldiers to an assault on Gemaho?" He gestured towards the south. "Has she forgotten the Tangata are still out there?"

Romaine said nothing for a while, though the scout was voicing the same concerns that had plagued him these last days. Finally he shook his head.

"Best not to question the scheming of monarchs," he murmured, though he could see his words did not mean much to the soldier. After all, it was Lorene's countrymen who were dying below.

"You really think we can find her?" the scout said after a time. "I doubt the king would be so foolish as to keep her in the fortress."

Romaine grimaced, recalling Nguyen's words from their meeting. "No," he replied, eyeing the men who went ahead of them. "But I have a feeling the queen is relying on that."

A frown touched Lorene's forehead as he followed Romaine's gaze. "Who are they?" he said softly, so the words would not carry to Yasin or the others. "Seems strange to send a bunch of mercenaries on a mission of such importance."

"They're not mercenaries," Romaine replied. "Yasin is far too comfortable with the queen. And despite their appearance, they're just a little too professional about all this business."

Lorene nodded. "You're probably right." Then he smiled. "Ah well, least we're not marching with a bunch of sellswords who'd turn on us the second old Nguyen offered a bigger pile of gold."

Romaine grunted his agreement, but did not voice his own concerns. Yasin's men might not be mercenaries, but the ease with which they'd taken to this assignment suggested they were far from regular soldiers. He suspected Yasin and the others were the people she sent when she needed something carried out in secret.

As they continued down the mountainside, Yasin slowed, allowing others to take the lead and falling into step alongside Romaine. While his sword and armour had been covered by cloth for the crossing, the crossbow was mostly wood and so hung from its usual strap across his back.

"How's the hand, Calafe?" he asked with a grin.

Romaine gritted his teeth but ignored the not-so-subtle gibe. "As well as it's going to get," he replied, doing his best to keep the dislike from his voice, then quickly changing the subject. "What is your plan for infiltrating the fortress, once we leave the mountains?"

"The fortress?" the soldier said, a look of surprise crossing his face. Then he snorted. "We won't find your Goddess lass inside those granite walls. Old Nguyen started making preparations to move her soon as he learned Amina was coming."

Romaine nodded at the confirmation of his earlier suspicions. "Then what are we doing?"

Yasin chuckled. "All in good time, Calafe," he replied. "Amina is more than a match for the old Gemaho bastard. We already know where they're taking her, we just have to catch up!"

"And how will we do that?" Lorene cut in, his voice light. "Seems to me the Nguyen wouldn't be so foolish as to send the Goddess by foot, when he's got such a nice river on hand."

All trace of mirth left Yasin's face as he turned his gaze on the scout. "Do you think your queen an idiot, soldier?"

"I..." Lorene trailed off beneath Yasin's glare, perhaps sensing what Romaine had that first night he'd met the strange warrior. The knowledge that he was staring into the eyes of a killer. Swallowing, the scout tried again. "Do you have a ship tucked away in some magic pocket we don't know about?"

The joke fell flat in the emptiness of Yasin's stare. Lorene clamped his mouth shut, glancing at Romaine.

"The man's got a point," Romaine commented.

He did not flinch as the warrior turned on him, and after a moment a smile cracked Yasin's face.

"By the Gods, your training buddy is jumpy, Calafe!" he laughed. Beside them, Lorene frowned, but Yasin only chuckled and gestured to the way ahead. "You'll see when we reach the ground."

With that he set off ahead once more, leaving them to trail behind the group.

Lorene watched the man go, his jaw clenched, forehead still marked by frown lines. "I'm not sure I like that man," he remarked finally.

Romaine sighed. "I'm not sure we're meant to, lad," he replied. "Doesn't matter though, so long as they help us get Cara back."

The scout nodded, though the expression on his face suggested he wasn't convinced. They continued after the others, winding their slow way down towards ground level.

While the most dangerous part of the crossing needed to be completed in daylight, they had climbed much of the mountainside in the night and so it was only several hours more before they neared the bottom of the gorge.

Only once was their journey interrupted, as movement in a nearby gully sent them all scattering for cover. The action sent loose rocks tumbling down the mountainside, disturbing the group of Guanaco that had been hidden in the shadows. The long-necked creatures leapt nimbly across the trail, disappearing into a nearby ravine, knocking hardly a stone out of place.

Yasin and the other soldiers cursed the creatures, but in the tradition of the Calafe, Romaine took them as a sign of good luck. Covered in heavy wool with long ears and beady eyes, the Guanaco were considered the flock of the Gods. Their presence before a long journey was meant to herald good fortune, though that had not entirely been true the last time he'd crossed paths with the creatures. That had been just hours before they'd unearthed the monsters beneath the earth, to which he'd lost his hand—and almost his life.

After that, Yasin called a stop and they waited there for the sun to finally set behind the distant peaks. With the twisting ravines falling into deep shadow, they continued for another hour until they finally reached the floor of the canyon.

There, Yasin led the way confidently across the narrow flood-plains, following the gentle whispering of the Illmoor River. By then the darkness was complete, with only the faint glimmer of the emerging stars to light the way. Romaine almost tripped several times as they made their way downriver, and his irritation with Yasin grew with each passing hour.

Finally, the sound of the river changed, and he heard the tell-tale squeak of wooden boards shifting on water from ahead. His heart picked up and he strained to pierce the night, seeking out the ship he was sure must be waiting for them. By then he hardly cared how the queen might have gotten word to her informants, nor even that she apparently had enough connections in Gemaho to procure them a ride.

The ship emerged slowly from the gloom, its features mostly obscured by the darkness, though he could see the movement of sailors upon its upper deck. Lorene inhaled sharply alongside him and he flashed the scout a grin.

"Looks like they had a ship in their pocket after all."

The scout only shook his head, and together they picked up the pace, eager to catch Yasin and his men before they decided to leave the pair of them behind. Broad sails stretched high above them, and dozens of oars poked from the gunwales, lifting Romaine's heart. For the first time in weeks, he felt a touch of hope. His gaze was drawn to the east, to that distant, unknown land of Gemaho. Somewhere out there, Cara was waiting for him.

I'm coming, he whispered to the universe.

THE SOLDIER

Lukys passed a week in his cell—or at least a week by his best approximation. Without any hints from the outside, Sophia's daily visits were his only measure of time. He said nothing during those occasions, though Sophia spoke sometimes, talking of the goings on in the city above. Lukys could do nothing to prevent the whispers from entering his mind, and so he would sit in silence, staring into the distance, determined not to acknowledge her presence.

But even Lukys's anger could not last forever—particularly when the Tangata was his only source of light and food and water. The food was mostly fish, trout and salmon caught in the crystal waters of the surrounding rivers, along with tubers and the occasional helping of red meat. In fact, he had to admit the food was far better than anything the Flumeerens had ever fed him.

That thought ate at him during those long hours beneath the earth. What reason did he have to be loyal to humanity? Had his own kind not failed him at every turn? The Flumeerens had refused to train him, to prepare him in any way for the battles to come, had even sent him on the suicide mission that had ended in his capture. Even the Sovereigns that claimed to rule Perfugia for the good of all had betrayed him, ordering him to the frontier to die.

Yet despite Sophia's apparent kindness, he could not submit himself to the Tangata. After all, they too were guilty of terrible deeds, of driving the Calafe from their lands. Even before the war began, they had raided the Calafe southlands. No, to give in to the Tangata would be to betray everything and everyone he had ever known. And yet...

...gave us a long chase. It might have escaped had it made the river, but its heart gave out.

Lukys blinked, pulling himself back to the present. Sophia sat across from him, lips pursed, eyes on the wall as she recounted the story of a stag the Tangata had brought down that night. Apparently she had been assigned to a hunting pack. Lukys's attention was drawn to the wooden plate she had brought for him, where half the venison lay uneaten.

"Has Adonis returned?" he asked suddenly.

His sudden communication shocked the Tangata so much that she half leapt off the bench. Gasping, Sophia sat upright for a moment, hand on her heart. It was the first time he'd said anything since that first day in the cell.

What? came her voice to his mind.

Adonis, Lukys repeated, looking her in the eye. *The Matriarch sent him to seek the Old Ones. Was he...successful?*

Sophia stared at him, as though suspicious he had come up with some secret plan to escape. Finally, though, she shook her head.

No, he has not returned. The Birthing Ground is many days' journey from here, even for a Tangata.

Lukys nodded. "Good," he murmured, turning away for a moment. "Were you...with him, when they woke the others?"

Images flickered into his mind by way of response, memories that were not his own. He found himself looking at two giant cylinders filled with liquid, lit from below by magical lights of purest white. Within each of the cylinders, two seemingly human figures stood suspended, eyes closed, their bodies somehow sustained for centuries by the magic of the Gods.

Shuddering, Lukys tore his mind from the horror. "A simple 'yes' would have been sufficient," he said softly.

Sophia nodded and rose. She began to pace the cell, moving with the graceful, balanced posture he had only ever seen amongst the Tangata. Well, the Tangata...and Cara. Jealousy touched him as he watched Sophia's movements. He had spent weeks with Romaine training to improve his balance, to give himself a fighting chance when the Tangata came. He'd improved slightly, but Sophia moved with a natural fluidity he could only ever dream of.

I know you can't understand it, but what Adonis does is necessary, Sophia said at last, though Lukys could still sense the fear radiating from her.

He only nodded by way of answer—it was clear that the Tangata would divulge the true reason they were seeking the Old Ones. After a moment, Sophia sat once more beside him.

So, you're speaking again?

Lukys sighed. Sophia sat with one leg propped up on the bench, elbow leaning against her bent knee, chin in her hand. She arced an eyebrow, obviously expecting a reply.

Lukys rolled his eyes. Carefully he picked a piece of venison from his plate and began to chew. It was cold as always, but the rumbling in his stomach hardly cared. *Was* he speaking again? There seemed little point in his silence now. He wasn't going anywhere regardless.

"I guess so," he muttered finally, flashing her a glare, "but it changes nothing."

Very well. Despite his hard words, a smile tugged at the Tangata's lips. *Though you should know, the last of your friends have now sworn to their assignments.*

A chill touched Lukys and for the first time, he felt truly alone in that cell. He was the last one, the only Perfugian that still refused to accept his new place in the world. How could the others have given in so quickly? Unless Sophia was lying, trying to convince him to do the same. But there was a ring of truth to the Tangata's words, and he shivered, unconsciously hugging his arms to his chest.

Are you okay, Lukys? Sophia whispered, concern showing on her face.

He shook his head. *I'm glad you did not kill them.* The words slid from his mind. *It…is more than my people would have offered your kind.*

A visible shudder shook Sophia and he caught a wave of revulsion from her. *Yes, I saw what you showed Adonis.*

Showed him? It was a moment before Lukys realized what she meant. Of course Adonis had seen images of the Tangatan captives in his mind—Lukys had known nothing of his strange skill that day in the clearing. He swallowed. *I am sorry you had to see that. We…do not all support such atrocities. My own kingdom does not take Tangatan prisoners.*

*Perfugia…*The word slipped from Sophia like a sigh. *The kingdom beyond the great sea. It amazes me, the distant lands humanity has reached in the short years since The Fall.*

Lukys looked down at that. *They say we were founded by those who sought to flee the wars that humans once fought amongst themselves.*

Sophia's eyebrows lifted in surprise. *Your kind wage war amongst yourselves?*

The Tangata do not? Lukys asked. When Sophia only shook her head, he sighed. *They say the first century after The Fall was terrible. What little knowledge we had of the days before was lost to the darkness. I guess I can't blame my ancestors, for fleeing that.*

A smile touched Sophia's lips. *What are they like, your people? We know little of distant Perfugia.*

We are a…practical people, he replied without thinking. *Our children are taken from their families at eight, to be raised in an academy.*

Shock registered on Sophia's face as she reeled back. *Why would they do such a thing?*

Lukys shrugged, though he was surprised at the strength of her reaction. *To ensure all are given an equal opportunity in life…though it doesn't entirely work that way in practice. The noble born are still favoured by the professors, receive better accommodations. Only a handful were so unlucky as to be chosen in our cohort of recruits.*

Is it not an honour to fight for your people? Sophia asked, her head tilted to the side.

Lukys snorted. *That is what we thought, until we reached the frontier,* he replied. He looked at her and let out a heavy breath. *Myself and the others here with me were chosen because our leaders judged us failures. We served no purpose in their perfect society, so we were sent here, untrained, to fulfil their quota of soldiers on the frontline.*

That is…terrible. Sophia seemed at a loss for words.

As I said, we are a practical people.

Sophia looked away. *The Tangata are also practical. There was a time when we too sent away our weakest, to preserve the strength of our species. It did not work.*

Lukys swallowed. *Maybe my people could learn from the Tangata.*

He was surprised by the smile that lit up Sophia's face. *Perhaps one day,* was all she said, then: *You are getting better at Speaking.*

What? Lukys started as he suddenly realised they'd conducted the entire conversation in their minds. His cheeks warmed. *I guess I am.*

Silence fell for a while then, and Lukys found his mind turning to his friends once more. Had they truly abandoned their loyalty to humanity so easily? Or had they simply realised their loyalty had been misplaced? He wished he could speak with them. Maybe then he would understand.

Sophia, he said after a time. *Is…possessing a slave truly so important to your people?*

Sophia winced. *I…wish you would not use that term. As I said, we do not force your people into assignments. Neither do we treat them poorly. Your friends are happy with their new lives.*

I wish I could believe you, Lukys sighed.

He flinched as Sophia stood suddenly, lifting an arm to defend himself, but the Tangata only stood there, eyes shining in the light of the lantern.

Maybe I can show you.

Lukys frowned. *I thought you said I could not leave…*

I will tell the Matriarch you have sworn yourself to me.

You would…lie to your leader? Lukys asked, regarding Sophia with a frown.

*Yes…*Sophia hesitated. *But…this would require you to trust me.*

Lukys might have laughed. Trust one of the Tangata? And yet… the prospect of leaving his cage, of seeing daylight again, was tempting. Could he so easily dismiss a lifetime of mistrust for her kind?

His eyes were drawn again to his plate. He had almost finished the venison now, and the tubers had vanished as their conversation went on. There was a warm, satisfied feeling in his stomach. He had only felt such contentment once in Fogmore, when Romaine had insisted they eat with him in the main soldier's mess hall. Every other night, the gruel they'd been given might as well have been river water for all the nutrition it had held.

"I trust you." He spoke the words before he could change his mind.

And Sophia smiled.

❧ 16 ❧

THE FUGITIVE

"I don't understand why you're doing this," Cara hissed as Erika settled down alongside her.

The Archivist let out a sigh. The sun was just beginning to lift above the endless plateau to the east and the sailors were preparing the ship to sail. They had anchored for the night in a broader section of river where the currents were sluggish, but everyone was eager to depart, the memory of screaming soldiers and clashing of weapons still fresh in their minds.

Not that the queen could have taken the Illmoor Fortress so easily. Not once in centuries had its walls been breached. It was just…better to be prudent when Amina was involved. The warrior queen had a reputation for achieving the impossible.

Shivering, Erika focused her attention on the Goddess. She still wore her manacles, though this pair had apparently been permanently welded shut to ensure she did not pick the lock again.

"Humanity is desperate, Cara," Erika said after a moment. "Surely you've seen that?"

They were sitting on the benches on either side of the raised bow, Erika's customary position when setting sail. She enjoyed the feeling of journey it brought, of heading off to explore unknown lands, to discover fresh secrets of the ancient world. It was the elation of discovery that had led her to become an Archivist in the first place.

"And you think my people will help when you show up on their doorstep with their daughter in chains?" Cara asked pointedly.

Erika sighed. "What have we got left to lose?" she replied. "You won't help us, won't show us the way. So we have to use you as a bargaining chip."

"You don't *have* to do anything, Erika," Cara said, turning away. "You chose to attack me, to kidnap me, to give me to the king. All of this is by your own choice."

"The queen wanted me dead," Erika rasped, though the words seemed inadequate now, and she found her gaze drawn again to the gauntlet encasing her hand.

"Maybe you deserve it," Cara snapped.

Erika found herself nodding. "Maybe," she replied.

Silence answered her reply. When she finally looked up, Erika found the Goddess staring at her, lips turned down in a frown.

"I'm sorry," Erika croaked finally. "None of this makes sense to me, Cara. Ever since I uncovered this gauntlet, since I discovered that map, it feels as though I've been cast adrift. I'm barely keeping my head above the water—and now the tide is coming in."

Cara said nothing, only stared back at her, amber eyes unreadable. Erika let out a sigh and rested her head back against the bulwark. Above, the sky was an endless blue, barely marked by a single cloud.

"Why are you here, Cara?" she whispered finally.

"Good question," the Goddess replied archly. "I think I mentioned something about a kidnapping…"

"I meant, why has a God returned to the lands of humanity?"

The Goddess did not reply immediately, and when she did speak, the words were whispered: "It was…an accident." Erika looked sharply at Cara and was surprised to see her cheeks had coloured. "I'm not meant to be here," she added, her voice becoming hoarse.

"What?" Erika asked. "How is that possible?"

Cara shrugged. "I'm, err…somewhat of a rebel." The Goddess offered a sheepish smile. "We aren't allowed to leave the mountains, according to the Elders, but…" She trailed off, a tinge of anger appearing in her eyes. "I mean, how would you feel, being able to soar through the clouds, go wherever you want…but not having the freedom to do it?"

"I…ah, the Elders?"

Cara scowled. "My family, you might say…" She hesitated. "It's not like I haven't done it before," she mumbled. "Only this time…"

"You were attacked by the Tangata," Erika surmised, remembering Romaine's story. "He said…you had a broken arm?" She frowned. "But…you fought off dozens of the Tangata on the Illmoor. How could two have done anything to hurt you, even with your injury?"

"It wasn't just my arm that was broken," Cara replied, her face losing some of its colour. "I…fell." A shudder ran through the diminutive figure. "That's never happened before."

"You fell?" Erika asked softly.

"There was a snowstorm," Cara answered shortly, then paused before going on: "I was caught in it on the way home, it drove me out of the sky. Before I knew how low I was…the tree came out of nowhere! My wing…" Her voice grew taut, as though she were remembering some terrible pain. "I almost passed out from the pain. And then those Tangata caught my scent."

Erika shook her head. "That doesn't make any sense; why would the Tangata follow you? Why stay in Fogmore? Why come with us to Calafe?"

"I stayed because they were kind," Cara whispered. "Because I wanted to help Romaine and Lukys and all the others. Because I wanted to help *you*."

The intensity in Cara's voice forced Erika to look away. Her gaze fell upon the sailors moving below, on the soldiers as they lounged about the deck, the packs of supplies and weapons. The sight reminded her briefly of her other expedition under Flumeeren rule, the miserly supplies and poorly trained recruits that had been sent to protect her. There could be no comparison to the preparations Nguyen had made for her, to the bearded veterans that would march with them.

But…could she trust them? Lukys and the Perfugians might not have been the most skilled of warriors, but they had been earnest, without a bone of treachery in their bodies. And Romaine, Cara— they had volunteered to come, despite the danger. These men and women, how far would their loyalty to the king stretch, when faced with the dangers in the Mountains of the Gods?

"I think they're desperate as well," Cara said suddenly.

Frowning, Erika looked across at the Goddess, but her gaze was on the open plateaus. "Who's desperate?"

"The Tangata," Cara replied, meeting Erika's eyes now.

"The Tangata?" Erika shook her head. "Desperate? I doubt that. They've enjoyed a decade of victories against our forces, taken an entire kingdom from the hands of humanity. What do they have to be desperate about?"

"I don't know," the Goddess said, "but I could sense it in their voices when they chased me, when they tried to capture me on the banks of the Illmoor."

Erika blinked. There was a lot to unpack in the Goddess's statement. "Their voices?" she started, before adding: "They were trying to capture you?"

Cara smiled. "You know, for an intellectual, you're not the most observant." She hesitated, before continuing. "They're afraid of something, the Tangata."

"Fear?" Erika snorted at that. "You think that was fear?"

The Goddess stared back at her, those amber eyes seemingly aglow in the morning light. Finally Erika swallowed and changed the subject. "Why would they want to capture you?"

The way the Tangata had launched themselves at Cara, it had not seemed like the creatures were interested in taking the Goddess prisoner. And yet…there *had* been a moment when Cara had been knocked to the ground, pinned beneath a horde of the creatures. Surely then one of the creatures could have managed a fatal blow…

"I don't know," Cara replied with a shrug. "There is much about their people I do not understand."

"Maybe they wanted to capture your magic?" Erika suggested. After all, that was how the Tangata had first been born.

"My magic?" Cara looked at her blankly. "Whatever…power I have, they could not take it. I don't think."

Erika let out a long breath, turning her memories of the battle over again in her mind, trying to piece together the clues. But recalling the fight, another thought occurred to her.

"Why didn't you kill them?" she asked, running her hand over the metallic links of her gauntlet. "I didn't think much of it at the time…but the Tangata you struck all got back up."

Cara bit her lip, suddenly looking nervous. Rubbing her shoulder, she looked away, and Erika didn't think she was going to answer.

"My people…do not kill," Cara croaked finally.

"What?" Erika frowned. "But you killed those…things in the caverns."

A visible shudder shook Cara and she hugged her knees to her chest. "Please…don't remind me."

Erika was about to press the matter when she noticed Cara's face had lost all colour. Whatever had happened in the caverns of the Gods, it had shaken Cara just as much as Erika and the others. At least Cara's claim helped Erika make sense of why she hadn't tried to kill them at the earliest opportunity.

Letting out a sigh, she let the subject drop. Silence fell between them, and finally Erika rose. "You'll stay here?"

The hardness returned to Cara's eyes as she looked up. "Not like I have any choice."

Erika's stomach twisted, but there was no correcting the situation now. Without anything else to offer, she left Cara where she sat. The ship rocked beneath Erika's feet as she crossed the deck, searching for Maisie, finding her at the tiller with the captain. Sails cracked overhead as she wandered towards them, the ship surprisingly steady beneath her feet. But then, the river was smooth today, with hardly a ripple to impede their passage.

Maisie waved as she saw Erika approaching and stepped away from the captain, nodding her thanks, then beckoned Erika across to the railings. Joining her, Erika leaned against the bulwark and looked out across the empty plains. The lands of Gemaho were said to be as large as the other three kingdoms combined. Without the threat of the Tangata, it was difficult to imagine how such a kingdom had united beneath a single ruler—and had remained that way down through the centuries.

"Why are we doing this?" Erika said suddenly. Regardless of her assertions to Cara, she still found herself doubting their path, not sure whether what they did was best for humanity, or if it was for her own personal gain.

The spy flashed her a glance. "The world is changing, Erika," she murmured, her words so soft as to be barely audible over the cursing of the sailors. "Magic has fallen again into the hands of mankind and ancient creatures walk the earth. A new age is approaching for humanity."

"Assuming we survive," Erika snorted.

"We're a resilient species," Maisie replied. "Here in Gemaho, we have watched the war from afar, read the reports. You think you're losing, but each battle costs the Tangata more in blood. Ten years ago, when the war first began, we lost five soldiers for every Tangata we slew. Nowadays the number is down to three."

Erika frowned; she hadn't heard that piece of information. What would cause such a change? She supposed it made sense; over ten years, humanity had come to learn the enemy's tactics. But even so, Maisie's numbers still meant they were significantly outmatched. "That doesn't mean we can defeat them," she argued.

"Perhaps not yet," the spy mused. "Regardless, it is the magic of the Gods that will determine our future. Imagine a hundred soldiers equipped with gauntlets like yours, or an army wielding orbs like mine, able to march under a blanket of invisibility."

Erika looked self-consciously at her gauntlet. "It would be an edge," she admitted. "That was why I went looking for their magic in the first place. But do you think the Gods will just *give* us such weapons?"

Maisie shrugged. "I do not know." She looked at Erika then, and her face was grim. "But I *do* know that whoever is first to gain their power will do more than just defeat the Tangata. Whoever controls that magic, controls the world."

A shiver ran down Erika's spine. "Then why would Nguyen give away his gauntlet?"

A smile tugged at Maisie's lips. "Nguyen is cunning; he knows how it will play with the queen's mind. And besides, one device will not change either kingdom's fate."

Erika eyed the woman, wondering how much truth there was to her words. "And what of Nguyen? Do you believe the king is worthy of the power you would place in his hands?"

All sense of mirth slipped from the spy's face as she looked at

Erika. "Would you prefer the power fell into the hands of your queen?"

"Of course not," Erika said, pursing her lips.

Maisie nodded, turning her eyes to the water passing below. "He's a practical man, Nguyen. He does what he must, but he is never cruel or vindictive." She sighed. "And there is a kindness in him that few ever see."

Erika snorted.

"You don't believe me?" Maisie murmured. "I don't blame you —he hides it well." She hesitated, the breeze whistling through the rigging overhead. "I was a street rat once," Maisie said, her voice so soft Erika almost missed her words. "Years ago, before the war began. Belonged to one of the gangs in the capital. I was just a child. Nguyen found me, saved me. Even trusted me with his magic."

The spy looked at Erika then, and she glimpsed something in her eyes, something beyond the respect or even loyalty she professed. Love, perhaps? Maisie looked away again quickly, as though realising she had revealed something secret. Her hands tightened on the bulwark, her knuckles turning pale.

"Eventually, you'll have to make a choice, Erika," she said softly.

"I thought I already had."

The spy laughed. "You chose Nguyen out of self-interest. One day, though, you'll have to choose someone to put your faith in, without regard for what they can give you. Regardless of what it might cost."

With that, the spy pushed away from the railings. Offering Erika a nod, she wandered away. Alone now with her thoughts, Erika stared down at the swirling currents, and wondered when her life had become so complicated.

17

THE TANGATA

Adonis sucked in a lungful of air as the wave swept towards him. A second later the white waters washed over his head, plunging him into the swirling depths. With a powerful kick he fought the currents, struggling to rise to the surface. Sound came rushing back as he burst again into open air and dragged in another breath.

The water lifted him as the next wave rushed past and he scanned the way ahead, desperate for a glimpse of the island. Surely it couldn't be far now. Through the surging harbour he thought he caught a flash of rock, but it was difficult to make out, still so far, so far…

Forward!

He kicked out again, sending silent encouragement to his brothers and sisters. They would make it—they were Tangata after all, not some weak humans to fail against the raging of mother earth. The storm might hurl its strength against them, but the Tangata would endure, just as they had for centuries.

Roaring against the swirling clouds above, Adonis fought on, and was finally rewarded with a view of the island. Sheer cliffs rose from the seas ahead, stretching high above, a small ledge of shore beckoning them on.

Still so far, though. They probably should have waited out the storm, Adonis knew. The Matriarch's need was urgent, but while he and his warrior pairs could survive the crossing, they needed their strength for what lay ahead. Adonis had not forgotten what had transpired in the last Birthing Ground they had uncovered. The unbridled rage of the Old Ones had been terrifying to behold. Whatever the Matriarch said, he could not dismiss his reservations about her plan.

The Old Ones were not Tangata, not as they had been since The Fall. They were something else, something that might save his species—or perhaps might doom them all.

Exhaustion weighed heavily on Adonis by the time he finally pulled himself ashore, the pain of endless hours spent on the move. He had pushed his brethren hard to reach this remote outpost, travelling day and night at a pace that would have broken lesser creatures. But Adonis was of the third generation, and those warrior pairs he had chosen were of the fourth. They relished the challenge.

It pained him to learn this Birthing Ground had been here all along, hidden in the Tangata's own territory. Their plight would have ended long ago had they uncovered the Old Ones sooner.

But he was getting ahead of himself. Despite the Matriarch's hopes and his own fears, it was unlikely anything remained of this place. The Birthing Ground might have gone undiscovered all these years, but that did not mean the Old Ones slumbered here too. The ones they had woken in northern Calafe could have been the last…

Despite his orders, Adonis felt himself hoping that was true.

One by one, his warrior pairs emerged from the waters. Adonis had lost his own partner years ago, but had resisted swearing himself to an assignment. The thought of spending so much time amongst humans made his skin crawl. The creatures were loud and undisciplined, and the images he'd glimpsed in the mind of Lukys only added to his distaste. Unfortunately, the Matriarch would not tolerate his disobedience much longer, despite his parentage.

Not unless he found another way.

In silence, he and his followers left the sandy shores. Each of his five pairs carried a great hammer between them—they would need the tools should they find the entrance sealed. Behind them, the ocean continued to rage, the crack of thunder echoing from the nearby cliffs. Sand gave way to gravel beneath their feet and ahead,

Adonis's sharpened vision spotted a goat track leading up between the escarpments.

Adonis picked up his pace, making for the track. He did not know where on the island they would find the entrance to the Birthing Ground, but the view from up high would give them somewhere to start.

The others followed, their inner voices silenced. This was holy ground, one of the hidden sites from which their ancestors were said to have first emerged. He could sense their doubts. Some had been with him when they'd freed the Old Ones before. They had witnessed the madness in the eyes of those creatures, had experienced the same feeling of powerlessness as their fellows were slaughtered. Against the Old Ones, his people might as well have been humans, for all their powers aided them.

Adonis slowed as they reached the top of the track, taking a moment to recover his breath as he scanned the area atop the cliffs. Before him the ground flattened out into a plateau of unnaturally smooth stone—a sure sign that one of the ancient sites had once occupied this island. The hairs on the back of Adonis's neck tingled at the sight. There could be no doubt now.

Spread out, he ordered as the others joined him. *Seek the entrance.*

They moved quickly, fanning out across the plateau, scanning the stone for some clue of an entrance into hidden tunnels. It didn't take them long.

Here.

Adonis joined the pair that had called the discovery. Dirt and moss had built up through the years, but the harsh winds blowing across the island had kept them from completely covering the unnatural rock. At first glance the spot where the two stood looked no different from the rest of the plateau, but a closer inspection revealed there was a slight mound here, circular in shape.

Crouching, Adonis scraped aside the moss for a better look at the rock beneath. It was rougher than the rest of the plateau, and the rain and wind had carved rivulets across the surface. He looked at the Tangata who held the hammers.

Break it.

They set to the task, the harsh crash of steel against stone ringing across the plateau. Adonis left them to their work and wandered back to the clifftops. No evidence remained of what had been here before The Fall and his people had not visited this place before. The Tangata might be capable of defeating the waters, but they did not needlessly hurl themselves into the murky depths either.

Beyond the shores of the island, the storm was finally breaking. It had come upon them quickly and now seemed intent on departing with the same speed. The winds would linger—they rarely ceased on this part of the coast. It made him wonder why the humans had once built a city here, of all places.

Standing atop the high cliffs, Adonis looked across the waters to where the ruins of the original Nihelm stood. Jagged spires of iron lay rusting on the distant shores and blackened stones formed great mounds. He suspected the fallen city's existence had been lost from the records of humanity—certainly those humans assigned in New Nihelm never spoke of it. Even the Tangata knew little of that broken place. The time of their awakening was recalled only in the mind of the Matriarch now, passed down from her forebearers. But one thing was known: the Tangatan homeland had once belonged to humanity.

Some claimed those early days had been peaceful, that the Tangata and humanity had lived together in harmony. Adonis doubted such claims. The humans feared that which was different from themselves—especially when those others threatened their supposed superiority amongst the species of the earth. Tangata were faster, stronger, *better*. How could humanity *not* loathe them?

Besides, humanity had shown time and again they could not be trusted. Their invasion of the Tangatan homeland ten years ago had slaughtered thousands of innocents. Only the Matriarch's harsh retaliation had prevented further losses and driven back the enemy forces.

That victory had seemed to herald the fall of humanity as a danger to his people. Even the Matriarch spoke now of maintaining the peace, of leaving the humans to live beyond the great river.

But Adonis feared the war had only just begun. Humanity had proven surprisingly resilient. Despite their inferiority, they fought with a frightening ferocity. And after ten years of war, their numbers seemed untouched, as though the more soldiers they lost, the more their pairs produced.

Meanwhile, the Tangata dwindled, their strength shrinking with each passing year.

No, the Matriarch was wrong in that regard. There could never be peace with such creatures. Their fear, their anger, their *greed* had proven such aspirations mere delusions. He had no doubt what the creatures would do if they ever realised the Tangata's weakness. His people would be hunted down, slaughtered like animals.

Or worse, put in cages to be tortured, as the human had shown him.

I will burn their civilisation to the ground before I allow them to destroy us.

But for that they needed to renew their power, fresh blood to restore the Tangata to their former greatness. The Matriarch was right, the Anahera would not aid them. That left only the Old Ones.

Adonis, a voice sounded in his mind. *The entrance is open.*

Despite his resolution, Adonis felt a thrill of fear. Angrily he brushed it aside. Whether the Old Ones slumbered below or not, he would face them with courage. Humans allowed terror to control them; he was Tangata.

Smiling, he crossed back to where the others waited. Their strength had made short work of the mound of stone, and a hole now lay open to the howling wind. Darkness beckoned beyond.

Adonis leapt without hesitation.

18

THE FUGITIVE

Three days passed before Erika and the others finally disembarked from the ship. By then Erika was more than a little fatigued by the endless hours of inactivity, of sitting in the bow and staring into the distance.

Unlike the ever-varying landscapes of Flumeer and Calafe, Gemaho never seemed to change. Beyond the Mountains of the Gods, endless plains stretched onwards to the horizon, their pastures stained brown by the warm spring sun, and not even the golden crops offered much in the realm of contrast. There were no forests to speak of, hardly any trees at all. While grasslands and rainforests flourished beneath the heavy rains of the west coast, here the very air seemed dry, a strange phenomenon, considering how far they had travelled on the broad waters of the Illmoor.

Now standing on the banks of the river and looking up at the towering peaks, Erika wasn't surprised to see they offered little more in the way of variety. Here the farmlands of Gemaho ended, to be replaced with a low, almost grey scrub, the rocky soils lying exposed beneath. A stream trickled down from the valley in which they stood and a few taller bushes grew along its path, though even these barely came to her breast, and their leaves were short and stunted, their branches dotted with thorns.

Shouldering her pack, Erika glanced at Cara. The Goddess's mood hadn't improved much during the three-day journey, probably something to do with the shackles she still wore. At least she had shown no outward signs of resistance, other than her reticence to speak of their final destination. Beyond the Goddess, the last of their soldiers had disembarked from the gangplank, allowing the vessel to pull away. The sailors were to continue upriver to Vanror, where they would collect supplies for the war effort then return to the Illmoor Fortress, hopefully picking them up on the way past.

If we're still alive by then.

"Ready?" Erika asked, forcing a smile as she looked again at Cara.

The Goddess held up her manacles and glared at her. Letting out a sigh, Erika gestured for the Goddess to go ahead. The chains on her legs were not so tight as to hinder her ability to walk. Several of the king's soldiers had already started up the valley, scouting the way ahead, while those remaining spread out around Cara and Erika, their eyes alert for trouble. Only one man lingered near the shore, but upon seeing their departure, he brought up the rear behind Erika.

As they started off, Erika found herself wondering at the men and women the king had sent with them. From her conversations over the past few days, she had come to realize they knew little of Cara's true identity—only that she was dangerous. They hadn't asked any question, though from their whispers Erika surmised they thought Cara to be some new kind of Tangata, just as she and Romaine had believed all that time ago.

More surprisingly, the soldiers didn't seem concerned about their expedition into the Mountains of the Gods. Erika wasn't sure what to think of such loyalty—did it speak of a king who earned his followers' faith, or a man that did not suffer disobedience?

Shaking her head, she set her mind back to the trail. Reaching the home of the Gods was her most pressing concern. The going was easy for those first few hours, the trail sloping gently upwards. But soon they reached the first of the foothills, hills of scarlet rock rising around them, and the way became steeper. Sparse vegetation marked the slopes and the gentle bubbling of the stream grew louder as the waters picked up pace, racing over ever larger rocks.

A chill wind blew down the valley, but as the sun approached its zenith, Erika found herself beginning to sweat. For a time, undoing the buttons of her jacket relieved the heat, but the next time they stopped to rest, the cold quickly found its way back. The warmth drained from her body at a frightening speed and while Erika refastened the buttons, even when they started off again, she never regained the lost heat.

Cara herself seemed little bothered by the trek, despite the hinderance of her shackles. Where Erika slipped and stumbled on the loose rocks scattered across the slopes, the Goddess nimbly picked her way up the path. Again Erika found herself wondering at the Goddess, why she came along with them. Even if her people were forbidden to kill, surely Cara was powerful enough that she could have escaped by now. Could it be she *wanted* to be here?

Night found them camped on the shores of a small mountain lake, its waters no more than a few hundred yards wide. The stream had led them there, up between the ever-narrowing slopes of the winding valley, and now stark cliffs hemmed them in on either side. They had been forced to clamber over boulders for the last hour, the remains of a landslide that in ages past had filled the valley.

Though spring was already underway, the days were still short and darkness came quickly to the mountains in Gemaho, the sun stolen away by the walls of stone rising around them. With the dark, the cold came in earnest, and Erika huddled close to their fire, glad for the ring of boulders surrounding them that provided shelter from the wind. There hadn't been enough room for the entire party, and half the soldiers had set a second camp close by. The whisper of laughter came from the other camp.

Listening to that distant mirth, feeling the warmth of the flames on her face, Erika thought again how different this journey was from her last. In Calafe they had been moving through enemy territory, never knowing when the Tangata might stumble upon them, whether their lives would be measured in days or even hours. Now though, despite the significance of this expedition, despite what might await them, Erika could almost convince herself to relax.

Almost—but not quite. Her gaze was drawn to where Cara crouched nearby and her heart twanged. Seeing the sadness in the Goddess's eyes, she quickly looked away. The fire was beginning to burn low. She rose, then crossed to the pile of wood the soldiers had gathered from beneath the scraggly trees that grew alongside the lake. Adding a stick to the flames, she watched as tongues of fire licked their way up the offering.

The soldiers nearby paid her no attention and Maisie had vanished a little while ago, probably to scout their surroundings or check on the other camp. Letting out a long breath, Erika moved to where Cara sat and lowered herself down.

"How was your food?" she asked quietly. The soldiers had cooked a stew using dried meat and grains they'd taken from their packs. It didn't compare to the meals she'd been provided in the fortress, but then, she wasn't sure what the Goddess had been fed in her cell.

To her surprise, an audible rumble came from Cara's stomach, though the Goddess only shrugged. Back to one of the boulders and her knees drawn up to her chest, she kept her gaze on the flames.

Erika frowned, studying Cara's face. She'd eaten as much as any of them, but perhaps that wasn't enough for one of the Anahera. Rising, she found the pot the soldiers had set aside. There was still enough for another serving inside. Taking the handle and a spare spoon, she returned to Cara's side and held out the pot.

Cara eyed Erika for a moment before taking her offering. She settled herself back down as the Goddess ate, though after leaning against the stone for a few minutes, Erika began to feel the cold seeping through her heavy furs. Apparently Cara's wings gave her a little more insulation—or perhaps she was simply unaffected by the cold. These mountains were her home, after all.

Pulling herself off the boulder, Erika hugged her knees to stay upright and looked again at the Goddess. The stew was disappearing rapidly, giving her the distinct impression she'd been right about Cara's metabolism.

After a moment, the Goddess flashed her a glance. "You know, for a species who claims it's rude to stare, humans sure do it a lot."

Erika's cheek warned at the remonstration. "Sorry," she said, "we're not exactly used to having one of our own Gods amongst us."

Cara's amber eyes were aglow in the firelight. "Sorry?" She grimaced. "Another word that has no meaning for your kind." Her brow furrowed. "They really mean nothing to you, do they? Your words. You say whatever you like and it doesn't matter to you, the falsehoods. There is no honour, no fairness amongst your kind."

"I…" Erika hesitated, caught off-guard by the directness of the Goddess's attack.

A dozen excuses rose in her mind, that she hadn't lied, that she regretted the things she'd done, but…there Cara sat, dragged halfway across the world against her will, hands and ankles still bound in chains. Erika could apologise all she liked, but Cara was right: what did it matter if she continued doing the very thing she was apologising for?

"You're right," Erika whispered finally, choking on the words. Her vision blurred as tears formed in her eyes. "It wasn't fair of me to treat you like this." She blinked then, forcing herself to harden. "But our world, it isn't fair, Cara. I don't expect a God to understand, but humanity is only what our environment has forced us to be. When I was young, my future was stolen from me. I have spent every day since fighting to win it back. For years I worked to earn a place in the queen's court, but in a matter of days that too was stolen away. I'm not sorry for doing what I needed to save my life."

The last words left her mouth in a rush, giving way to silence. Cara still watched her, though to Erika's eyes it seemed her expression had softened somewhat, as if the outburst had helped her finally understand something. Letting out a long breath, Erika swallowed the last of her emotion.

"As I said," she added finally, "I wouldn't expect you to understand. You're a God."

Cara shrugged. "So you say," she started, looking uncertain. "But you're wrong. I do understand. At least a little." She raised her eyes to the sky, and in that moment, she looked more like a young woman than she'd ever looked a Goddess. "You say you lost everything, but at least you once had freedom. That's something I've never tasted before. At least, not until Romaine found me in that forest." A tear streaked her cheek. "I'm not even sure…not sure how my people will receive my return. It is a terrible crime for us to leave the mountains, let alone reveal ourselves to humanity. But after so many decades—"

"*Decades?*" Erika interrupted, eyes widening.

The hint of a smile tugged at Cara's cheeks. "How old do you think I am, Archivist?"

Erika opened her mouth, then closed it again, unwilling to take a guess, though she would have said a human of Cara's looks couldn't be older than twenty.

Cara chuckled. "I would be close to fifty in your years, though amongst the Anahera I am still but a child."

Erika shivered. She shouldn't have been surprised that Cara was older than she looked. She was a Goddess after all, with the strength to hurl a man across a room as though he weighed no more than a few pounds. And wings. Yet it was still disconcerting, to look on the face of a teenager and know the soul within had seen fifty years of life.

"My night flights, they were my little show of rebellion." Cara's eyes danced as she spoke. "Is it still called the rebellious teen years? It seemed so harmless, flying from the mountains in the night. That is, until that storm. God, I was so *stupid*."

"We all make mistakes, Cara," Erika said, feeling more than a little strange to be comforting a being twice her age. How did new Gods even come into existence? Yet another question she would like to ask, though perhaps another time would be more appropriate.

Cara sighed but said nothing, and Erika settled back against the boulder. There had been few clouds during the day and now the night sky was an open tapestry of light, an orchestra of stars stretching overhead into infinity.

"I won't run." Erika's head jerked up as Cara spoke again and she found the Goddess watching her. She frowned, not understanding, and the Goddess elaborated: "If you freed me, I wouldn't fly away."

"You know I can't trust you," Erika whispered.

"I know," Cara said, nodding sadly. "You're too accustomed to falsehoods. But my people, the Anahera, we do not lie. I don't expect a human to understand that." She smiled wryly. "But it's the truth."

Erika swallowed, and in her mind, she saw again a vision of Cara in flight, swooping down to pluck her from the clutches of the Tangata. How poorly she had repaid that deed. Her words now about the unfairness of the world seemed hollow, and to her surprise she found herself rising. Light lit her gauntlet as she reached for the shackles that bound the Goddess, but at the last moment she hesitated, a thought occurring to her.

"But you lied to Romaine, when you said you were Calafe."

Red tinged Cara's cheeks. "I...never actually *said* I was Calafe," she mumbled. "I just...never corrected anyone when they assumed..."

Laughter burst from Erika at the Goddess's words and she shook her head. "Now who is accustomed to falsehoods?"

Even so, she reached again for the shackles. She'd never used the gauntlet in such a way, but it felt right, to use it for at least one good deed. Not quite knowing what she was doing, she took the shackles between her fingers and squeezed. Magic lit the metallic fibres and she focused on directing it into the steel chains.

There was a flash as the gauntlet brightened, followed a sharp *crack*. Steel rang against rock as the locking mechanisms failed in both shackles and they fell from Cara's wrists. Erika blinked, surprised it had worked so well, then glanced at the Goddess. When Cara made no move to attack, she turned her attention to the ankle chains.

Those too fell away and Erika backed away, waiting to see how Cara would react. The Goddess rose slowly, pulling the jacket from her shoulders. Freed of their confines, her wings spread wide with a sharp *crack* of feathers. Gasps came from the soldiers on the other side of the fire, but Erika kept her eyes on the Goddess, wondering if she had been wrong.

"I trust you, Cara," Erika whispered finally. "I'm sorry I didn't earlier."

Before Cara could react, movement came from the shadows nearby and Maisie appeared between the boulders. The spy paused when she saw them both on their feet, then her eyes were drawn to the chains lying beside Cara. A frown wrinkled her forehead.

"Well, that seems like a bad idea," she murmured.

Without saying anything further, she moved to the fire and sat. The cooking pot lay nearby and Maisie reached for it, moving as though to place it over the flames once more, before pausing. Turning, she scowled at the two of them.

"Someone want to explain what happened to my dinner?"

Erika blinked, then glanced at Cara. The Goddess's eyes widened and she adapted an innocent look. "I think the Archivist ate it," she said. "Terribly greedy, that one."

She crossed to the fire and sat herself by the flames. Beyond, the soldiers still sat gaping at her, but Cara ignored them, turning her eyes to Maisie instead.

"If you *are* going to cook more, though, count me in." A rumble came from the Goddess's stomach. "I'm *starving*."

19

THE FALLEN

The light was fading as Yasin directed their ship ashore, the sun dipping towards the mountains towering to the west. Watching the peaks turn scarlet, Romaine couldn't help but think how strange it was to find himself this side of the mythical mountains. They stretched up overhead, at once the familiar points he had known all his life, yet also different, the stark slopes and escarpments leading to a snowline that was unfamiliar to him.

And how different they were. Where in Calafe, pine and fir trees would have stretched from the river almost to the snow, here in Gemaho the foothills were practically bare, rolling and elongated where those in his homeland were jagged.

Aboard the ship, the sailors hurried to prepare for their disembarking, eager to be rid of Yasin and his soldiers. Throughout the journey, it had become clear their presence did not sit well with all the crew. Romaine couldn't blame them—just a few days ago, Flumeer had declared war on their kingdom. The queen's power could only buy so much loyalty. He wondered whether these sailors would report their passage to the king when they reached the next port—or if prudence would win out. After all, every Gemaho sailor on the ship had committed treason by granting them passage. Romaine doubted Nguyen was the kind of king to forgive such a transgression, however hard they might try to redeem themselves.

Shouldering his pack and readjusting the sword on his belt,

Romaine followed the others down the gangplank. The weight hung heavy on his shoulders and there was still an ache in his chest, but three days of rest on the ship had helped to ease the pain. His injuries were healing.

Romaine hesitated as he reached the shore, taking a moment to look around. Why had they chosen here to come ashore? There had been no obvious signs of another ship disembarking here, and in the dying light it was impossible to tell whether others had passed this way recently.

He looked up as the crunch of footsteps announced Yasin's approach. "I won't be able to track them in the darkness," Romaine said softly. The moon had been growing larger these last nights, but it would not be enough to find footprints in the rocky earth. "Even if this is the right place…"

Yasin laughed. "Don't sweat it, Calafe," he said, slapping Romaine on the shoulder. "I know where we're going."

Romaine frowned, but at a gesture from Yasin, the others in their group were already forming up. Anger touched him at being so easily dismissed, but he said nothing. Lorene came alongside him as the leader took his place at the front.

"What do you make of that?" he asked quietly, eyes on the man.

Clenching his fists, one phantom, the other real, Romaine tried to repress his rage. "I told the queen back in camp that Erika would eventually seek out the home of the Gods." His gaze lifted to the mountains, where the last of the day still lit the icy peaks. "Could she have another copy of the map after all?"

A grimace touched the scout's face. "You know, I signed up to *save* a Goddess—not trespass in their homeland." He hesitated, eyes flickering in Romaine's direction. "You sure about this, Romaine?"

Romaine sighed. "Amina's the only one who gives a Fall whether Cara lives," he said. "I trust her…" He glanced at the smaller man. "I have to."

The scout hesitated, then gave a quick nod. "Better hurry up then, before they leave us behind."

Without another word, the two started up the valley after Yasin's crew. Now that they were off the ship and deep in enemy territory, Romaine had strapped the queen's shield to his arm and kept his hand close to the pommel of his sword. Each evening when the ship had pulled ashore, he and Lorene had practiced with the blade, and despite his injuries, he was beginning to feel more confident with the weapon. He might be of use to Cara yet.

Even so, he was surprised by how quickly his body began to ache as they started up the valley. The daylong climb through the mountains around the Illmoor Fortress had been a trial in the extreme, the sheer slopes they had scaled to reach the goat track requiring short, sharp bursts of exertion. Here though, the long valleys of Gemaho provided a different kind of challenge. The ground might be less steep, but the slow, endless rise of the earth beneath their feet was no less draining. And the darkness made it all the worse.

Without vegetation to bind the soil, the loose rocks were a constant threat. Thankfully his leather boots protected him from twisting an ankle, but more than once the treacherous stones almost sent him crashing to the ground. Lighter on his feet, Lorene seemed to be having a better time of it, but several amongst Yasin's men were even larger than Romaine. Their grunts of discomfort kept the two company through the night, but otherwise the soldiers paid them little attention.

Romaine was happy with the silence. He had grown to enjoy it over the last ten years, to welcome the whistling of the wind through branches, to cherish the gentle bubbling of a stream, the hoot of a distant owl. The Perfugians had offered him companionship, a break from the stillness, but in truth he enjoyed it.

Eventually, however, the silence led his mind to thoughts of Cara. If they were truly on her trail, the Goddess could be as little as a day ahead of them. His heart raced at the thought and for the next half hour, the way felt a little easier.

They continued up the valley, shadowing the stream as it wound its way between the stones. Their quarry had no doubt followed its path for the ready source of water—it must be scarce in these parched hills. Just breathing the air this side of the mountains left Romaine's mouth as dry as the dusty stones.

Yasin led them on through the night, undaunted by the gloom. After three days on the ship, his men were reckless, eager to be on their way. Like their dark-eyed leader, these were fighting men, killers in search of prey.

Romaine still couldn't understand how they were able to track Cara and her captors in the darkness. The moonlight was enough to pick out the largest of the rocks on the valley floor, but Romaine struggled to make out the footprints of even his companions. How could Yasin track the passage of those who had passed hours, or even days, before?

Picking up his pace, Romaine overtook several of his companions, leaving Lorene to trail behind as he sought Yasin. He found the man still in the lead, picking his way up a slope dotted by ragged boulders the size of small dogs. Coming alongside the man in the gloom, he nodded a greeting.

"How far behind are we?" he asked, trying to find some clue as to how they were tracking their quarry.

"What am I, Calafe, a magician?" Yasin asked with a laugh.

Romaine scowled. "You seem to know where they're heading."

Yasin grinned at that. "Curious about Amina's secret, are you?" he murmured. Then he flicked Romaine a glance, and his eyes narrowed in the moonlight. "Or is it the Goddess that's got you so worked up?"

"Just professional curiosity," Romaine said with a shrug. "I grew up near these mountains, though on the other side. Even in daylight I would have struggled to follow a trail on these stones."

"You Calafe are far too practical, you know that?" Yasin replied with a shake of his head. "So focused on what's in front of your face that you miss the bigger picture." He snorted. "Maybe that's why you're basically extinct."

Romaine scowled, grinding his teeth together in an effort to keep the curses from tumbling from his mouth. Instead, he swallowed his anger and shrugged. Let the brute mock, so long as he led them to Cara.

"Perhaps you can show me the error of my ways," he replied, though he failed to keep the hard note from his voice.

Yasin only grinned. "Nah, where's the fun in that?" he chuckled, then returning his eyes to the path, he strode ahead. "Relax, big man. We can't be more than half a day behind the bastards."

Romaine frowned and was about to press the matter further when they topped the rise and found themselves on the shores of a small lake. Yasin hesitated, his eyes sweeping their surroundings, and the faint scent of smoke carried to Romaine's nostrils. The breath caught in his throat and his hand dropped to the hilt of his blade, but there was no sign of movement in the nearby boulders.

Yasin was still searching for something, but focusing on the ashen smell. Though the wind was only blowing lightly at that moment, he knew how violent mountain gales could turn. If he'd been making camp on these shores, those boulders would have provided the perfect shelter.

The stench of smoke grew stronger with each step, and fist tensed, Romaine entered the cluster of rocks. Lorene found him there a few minutes later, crouched alongside the remains of a fire.

"So we're on the right track," the scout said as he approached, looking grim. "Suppose that almost makes the trespassing acceptable, right?"

Romaine only grunted, his mind on the discovery. Whoever was accompanying Cara obviously had not suspected they were being followed, for they'd made no attempt to hide their campsite. What were they doing here anyway? Why would Nguyen have taken Cara hostage, only to send her into these mountains with his soldiers?

It had to be the Archivist's doing. Had she promised the king God magic, as she had all those weeks ago to Queen Amina? Perhaps that was why the man had so easily yielded the gauntlet—if Nguyen thought he would soon have the full power of the Gods at his back, its magic must seem trivial.

But no, it still made no sense that he would surrender it to an enemy. And it left unexplained how Erika planned to win the magic of the Gods. Did she expect them to greet her with open arms when she turned up on their doorstep with one of their own in chains?

He touched a palm to the ashes. They were cold, and given their quarry's apparent lack of concern for their pursuit, it seemed unlikely they would have marched through the night.

"More than a day," he muttered to Lorene.

"What?" the scout asked with a frown.

Romaine shook his head and rose as Yasin stepped into the ring of boulders. "They're further ahead than you thought."

A scowl crossed the man's face, though he shrugged off the criticism. "It'll be less by the time the sun rises," he countered.

A few grumbles came from the shadows behind the man, but

they cut off as Yasin flashed a glare over his shoulder. Romaine made to join them, when a glint of moonlight reflected off something lying amongst the boulders nearby. Turning from Lorene and the others, he crossed to the gap between the stones and lifted a pair of shackles.

"What have you got there, Calafe?" Yasin questioned. When Romaine did not immediately reply, he shouldered past Lorene to get a closer look.

Romaine's attention was fixed on the chains, and he ignored Yasin as the warrior stepped up alongside him. Unless Erika had dragged more than one prisoner into these remote mountains, they could only have belonged to Cara. But there was no sign of a breakage in the steel. Someone had unlocked them, had freed the Goddess. What did that mean?

He passed a quick eye over the campsite, seeking signs of disturbance, for some indication that Cara had fought her way to freedom. There was nothing. Finally he shook his head and handed the shackles to the queen's man.

"What do you make of this?" he asked, eyeing Yasin closely.

He turned the shackles in his hands, but the night's gloom hid whatever reaction his eyes might have revealed.

"So your little Goddess got loose," Yasin said finally. A smile tugged at his lips as he glanced around the campsite. "No bodies though. I wonder how Nguyen's soldiers regained control of Her Divinity."

Romaine raised an eyebrow. From what he'd seen of Cara in action, he doubted any number of human soldiers would be able to contain her. But at least the shackles finally confirmed once and for all that the Archivist *had* taken Cara against her will. He clenched his fist at the thought of the hateful woman. Erika would pay for what she'd done.

True to Yasin's word, they pushed hard through the rest of the night, pausing only to pull fresh food from their packs. Weighed down by his injuries, Romaine found himself dropping to the back of the line once more, though Lorene kept him company. His mind continued to return to the chains he'd found, to the Goddess and Erika and the king's soldiers. Was Cara still a prisoner, or had she somehow gained the Archivist's trust?

But there would be no answers, not until they finally caught their adversaries. Only then would the truth be revealed.

Throughout the night, Romaine found no more hint of their quarry's passage, though Yasin still seemed confident in his ability to track Erika and the Gemaho soldiers. Only as the first hint of light appeared on the distant horizon did the man begin to slow. Reaching the top of another slope, he squinted, scanning the rocky ground ahead before finally choosing a direction.

Romaine paused as he reached the spot where Yasin had hesitated, feigning the need to catch his breath—though after the slope they'd just traversed, it wasn't much of an act. Ahead, the others continued along a ridge where the way was gentler, while Lorene came to a stop nearby, a grin breaking through the unkept beard that had appeared on his face over the last weeks.

"Getting old, Romaine?" he asked.

Grunting, Romaine ignored the jibe, his eyes turning instead to the east. Looking back across the plains of Gemaho, he was again reminded of the strangeness of where he found himself. Flat land, perfect for farming, stretched out as far as the eye could see, to that distant rising sun.

Even the sight of the sun on the eastern horizon was a novel sensation. In Calafe, the sun's glow appeared behind the Mountains of the Gods hours before it broke their twisted peaks, leaving the land in shadow for much of the dawn. But here the light was already racing across the land towards them, casting back the last of the dark. Shaking his head, he turned his attention back to the trail…

…and caught a glint of something amidst the rocks. He frowned, hesitating in place, even as Lorene started to move off. The forbidden mountains rose ahead of them, capped by glacial peaks, but it was not those mountains that had drawn his attention.

Stepping from the trail, he knelt beside a boulder. A small X marked the rock, glowing with some phosphorescence in the shadow. But even as he leaned closer, there was a flash as the sun finally reached them, and the X vanished.

"You alright, Romaine?" Lorene called back to him.

Romaine remained kneeling for a moment, staring at the spot where the X had disappeared. Blood thumped in his ears as he turned the discovery over in his mind. It might have been created by some natural phenomenon, an algae or fungus that grew here in the mountains, yet…then surely it would have been elsewhere?

No, it had been no natural marking. This was the same spot where Yasin had hesitated, as though looking for something. Something to mark the way for them, perhaps?

Swallowing, Romaine returned to his feet and waved a hand to Lorene that he was okay. Ahead, the light of the rising sun had reached Yasin and the others, who appeared to be downing packs and setting camp for the day.

The sight confirmed Romaine's suspicions. Someone was leaving markers for them to follow, ones that could only be seen in darkness. They couldn't continue now, for Yasin would not be able to track their quarry. There was a spy in Erka's party.

20

THE SOLDIER

Stepping from the darkness of the basilica, Lukys squinted as the sudden brilliance of sunlight greeted his freedom. After so long beneath the ground it was all but blinding. Within moments, tears were streaming down his face. He embraced them.

A warm breeze touched his cheeks. Though winter had hardly just past, it was warmer in the south and the taste of spring was already in the air.

Finally his vision began to clear and he found himself staring across the plaza, empty now, his companions long since taken to their new…homes? He glanced sidelong at Sophia, wondering what had become of his friends, where he was to be taken now. Another day had passed before the Matriarch had granted his freedom and Lukys had spent much of that time wondering at his decision, whether he'd made the right choice. His acceptance had come quickly after the long silence—though of course, he hadn't truly sworn himself to Sophia.

Had he?

Sophia said nothing, only stood watching him, a look of concern creasing her forehead, as though even now she worried what he might do.

But Lukys had made his decision, down there in the darkness. He had resolved to trust the strange Tangata with her earnest expression, and that was what he would do. For better or worse.

So he offered Sophia a smile and nodded for her to lead the way. A smile of her own appeared on Sophia's face and she started off across the plaza without looking back. Drawing in a deep breath, Lukys followed her into the city.

It was still early, but dozens of Tangata already thronged the streets, moving about their business in the graceful manner in which they completed all tasks. Morning mist clung to the city, making it difficult to spot the humans amongst the wanderers, though if Lukys paid attention he saw them. Assigned humans apparently made up some ten percent of New Nihelm's population.

Despite the presence of his fellow humans, it felt odd to walk so freely amongst the Tangata. There were no guards now, no bonds or watchful eyes. Only Sophia and that gentle smile.

Did the Tangata truly trust their human slaves so easily? What was to keep them from attempting an escape, even after swearing themselves to their assignment? Though even as the thought came to him, Lukys realised the futility of such an action. Where would they go? The Tangata were faster and stronger, better in the wilderness than even the Calafe. It would not take long for the creatures to hunt down an escaped human. Lukys had no doubts as to what would happen then.

The numbers on the street swelled as they made their way deeper into the city, though they still numbered nowhere near the crowds in human cities such as Mildeth or Ashura. He found himself scanning those who passed them, practicing spotting his human comrades.

His lips twisted into a frown as he glimpsed something strange amongst the crowd. Distracted, his foot caught on a loose cobble and he stumbled, barely catching himself before he fell. Something that sounded distinctly like laughter touched his mind and he scowled to see the eyes of several Tangata upon him. They looked away as he met their gaze, but the whispers continued. These creatures did not know he could hear them.

Shaking himself, Lukys attempted to close his thoughts to the sound and focused on what he'd seen. Sophia had come to a stop nearby, but she said nothing as he searched the pedestrians moving around them. For a moment he thought the group might have already passed on…

There! Lukys stared as the two children wandered past. Their grey eyes were fixed on the curb beneath their feet, arms stretched out wide, and they trailed behind an adult, trying to keep up as they balanced on the stone lip.

"What the hell…" Lukys muttered.

He started after them, but Sophia stepped between him and the youngsters.

What are you doing?

I've never seen Tangatan children before, he admitted.

The sight shattered the last remnants of the lie he'd been taught his entire life. Watching the boy and girl wander past, playing on the street as any human child might have done…it was impossible to resolve with the image of the Tangatan savage, of monsters that sought nothing but the extinction of humanity.

Did you think we grew on trees? Sophia asked, one eyebrow raised.

Lukys shook his head. The two had fallen off the curb and were now leaping from cobble to cobble, obviously trying to keep from stepping on the cracks. Their minder had noticed the delay and turned back to collect them. His eyes were a light blue.

"You trust us with your children?" he whispered.

The amusement vanished from Sophia's face. *Come,* she said, taking him by the arm. *We're almost there.*

Lukys allowed himself to be led away, though not without a sense of confusion at Sophia's reaction. Why did she want him away from the children? He kept an eye out for others as they continued, but after a few more turns, they found themselves in quieter streets. Here, the vibrant colours of the buildings did not change—or rather, they continued to change with every building they passed, and Lukys found himself wondering again at the beauty created by Calafe's spirit of individuality.

Where exactly are we going? Lukys asked finally.

There was a strange look about Sophia as she glanced at him. *Our new home.*

Before he could question her further, she came to a stop in the street. Lukys paused beside her, realising they stood before a set of open wooden gates. A narrow corridor beyond led into what appeared to be small courtyard. The buildings here were only two stories high and even with the day still young, he could see the space was lit by sun.

"Here?" he asked.

Sophia nodded and took his hand. He flinched at the intimate touch, though her hand was surprisingly warm, and flashed her a sharp look.

Together, remember? she murmured.

Lukys detected a sad undertone to her voice, as though his resistance to her touch hurt her. But she was right. The Matriarch, the Tangata, everyone in this city believed he had sworn himself to her. He needed to play the part. Swallowing, he accepted her hand and he gave her fingers a squeeze, trying to reassure her. Sophia seemed to take the action as acceptance, and led the way through the open gates.

Inside the courtyard, a single tree stretched up above the low roofs, its wiry branches brightened by the same pink blossoms that had lined the main avenue through the city. Someone must sweep the cobbles within the court regularly though, for the stones were free of both blossoms and dirt. To their right a set of polished wooden stairs led up to a terrace that ringed the courtyard. Doors to inner rooms led from both the terrace and the lower floors, and Lukys guessed each must belong to a different household.

Wooden tables and benches had been placed out in the courtyard and several figures were already seated there, steaming mugs lifted to their lips. A sharp pressure tightened around Lukys's chest as he caught the distinct northern twang of Perfugian accents amidst the group's chatter. He let out a heavy breath as he recognised several faces, his last reservations fading. Sophia hadn't been lying. His friends were alive.

Heart racing, he started towards them. Several spotted Lukys as he approached and soon the entire group were clapping him on the back and welcoming him to the yard. Despite himself, Lukys found himself laughing, grinning alongside his friends. Travis appeared, dragging him into another bearhug, then Dale was gripping his hand.

After so long alone in the darkness, it felt surreal to suddenly be surrounded by people, by his friends. Somehow he'd expected them to be changed somehow, broken by their own time in isolation, their wills crushed by Tangatan captors. But the smiles on his fellow recruits' faces seemed…genuine. They were happy, just as Sophia had said. It was more than any of them had experienced in Fogmore.

He spotted Sophia standing at the edge of the group, her arms folded, watching him. Their eyes met and he offered a tentative smile. She nodded back, and her voice whispered in his mind.

I told you.

"So you finally decided to join us!" Travis said, drawing Lukys's attention back to the bulky recruit.

"I…guess so," Lukys said, managing a smile. Despite his friends' apparent happiness, it was overwhelming, being amongst them again.

"Glad you finally saw the light," Dale said with an approving nod.

"Yeah…"

Lukys was surprised to find Dale in such a bright mood. In a way, he'd expected that of Travis, as he always seemed to find the silver lining in any given situation. But Dale…he was a true noble born, proud and aloof. It had taken him weeks just to accept Lukys as his equal. And he had loathed the Tangata. Now he smiled and laughed while one stood watching from just a few feet away?

"Care for a coffee?" Travis offered, gesturing to the tables. "I'm sure Isabella can rustle you up a mug. She does tend to burn it, unfortunately, but it's still better than that river water they used to feed us in Fogmore."

"Coffee?" Lukys frowned. Where had the creatures gotten coffee? "Isabella?"

Dale gave Travis a punch in the shoulder. "Slow your boots, the man's just walked in." He grinned at Lukys. "Relax, Lukys. You look like you're about to have an aneurysm. Why don't you take your lass upstairs? She was here last night, she knows which door is yours. We can swap stories later…" For a moment, Dale faltered. "I…already told them what happened in the north."

Still in a bit of a daze, Lukys nodded, finding Sophia still standing nearby. It didn't seem like she was going to join them, so he took Dale's advice and bid his comrades goodbye. There was obviously more he needed to know about their situation—best he find out from Sophia rather than being caught in a lie by his own friends.

They seem happy, he noted as he re-joined her.

She raised her eyebrows. *You seem surprised.*

Lukys shrugged, deciding it was best not to explain himself. He watched as the recruits returned to their table.

Why keep us together? he asked.

This new life can be…difficult for new assignments, Sophia replied. *The Matriarch has found your kind are able to make the adjustment easier with company from their former lives. It gives them a sense of normality.*

Lukys nodded. *And what of their Tangata?* he asked. *Shouldn't they be here with their new…assignments?*

They have already bonded, Sophia said, looking away.

Again he sensed the sadness in her words. What was the importance of these assignments that the Tangata seemed to covet? His resistance was clearly a source of disappointment, if not pain, for Sophia. He wished he could understand why.

When he didn't respond, Sophia started towards the stairwell, leading them up onto the terrace. It felt surreal to walk along the squeaking boards, listening to the voices of his comrades whispering up from below, to feel the sun upon his face. Ahead, Sophia stopped at a door and turned the copper doorknob. It opened without resistance—apparently there was no need for locks here.

She disappeared inside, but Lukys hesitated in the doorway. This all seemed so *normal*, as though he had somehow stepped into another world, one where the war between Tangata and humanity had never existed.

But it was a lie. He could feel it in his soul, a wrongness about it all, even in the way Sophia looked at him—as though she were looking for something in his eyes. He lingered on the terrace, watching as she turned back to him, and for a moment he wondered if he should run. Sure, he wouldn't make the front gates, and yet…

…wouldn't that be better than betraying his people?

A shiver ran down his spine as he remembered the Tangatan children. There'd been no children in Fogmore—they'd all fled with their families, heading north in search of safety. Only the soldiers and those who supplied them had remained. Yet here…the children played freely in the streets, and humans and Tangata mingled openly, without hatred or strife. Could it really be so easy?

Are you coming? Sophia's voice whispered in his mind.

Lukys swallowed as he looked into those grey eyes. Then he nodded and stepped into the house.

For some reason, he'd expected to find the inside somehow different, as though everything before had only been an illusion to get him here. But it wasn't like the Tangata needed to scheme—Sophia could have forced him here with one arm tied behind her back. So he shouldn't have been surprised to find the inside of the house as normal as the courtyard outside.

He stood in a small, undecorated foyer that opened out into a plain dining room. Sophia had paused in the foyer to remove her boots and after a moment's hesitation, Lukys did the same. In Fogmore, the mud had been so bad most had given up keeping it from their dwellings. Strange that the Tangata should have a greater sense of cleanliness than the militaristic Flumeerens.

Now in socks, Lukys moved into the dining room. A mahogany table was in the centre, while a cabinet of fine porcelain plates stood in the corner. Silver cutlery glinted from a shorter cabinet, and there was no small amount of other finery, lamps and carved wooden animals and teapots. The sight made Lukys lift his eyebrows—were they to have dinner parties in the future?

But no, it had probably belonged to the place's former owner. No doubt they had left in a rush—or perhaps they'd been killed when the Tangata had taken the city.

The thought shook Lukys from his stupor. Hardening his heart, he allowed Sophia to lead him through the rest of the apartment. They passed from the dining room through a second living space, this time furnished with a plain sofa and coffee table, an unlit fireplace stacked with wood in the corner.

A rich scent hung in the air, and as they passed through the room, Lukys spied the kitchen through another door. He hesitated, then diverted from Sophia's tour. In the kitchen he found an iron coal stove and a simple dining table. Warmth radiated from the stove, as though it had been recently used. His eyes were drawn to the wooden board set on the table, where a loaf of bread was cooling.

Lukys… Sophia's voice called to him.

He turned in the doorway, finding her standing behind him. "Did you…bake that?" he asked.

To his surprise, the Tangata's cheeks turned red. *It was…an experiment.*

Lukys couldn't help it—he laughed. A grin split his face as he watched the inhuman creature that had haunted his nightmares for so long grow brighter. Had he *actually* found himself in some parallel reality? It seemed the only explanation.

Finally he managed to catch his breath, though his smile remained. *It smells good,* he offered. *Can I try some?*

The Tangata's eyebrows lifted in surprise and she seemed to hesitate. Then she swallowed, glancing away. *Yes…but not yet. There's something you need to see…first.*

Lukys frowned at the tone of her voice, but she was already moving away. There was only one other door that adjoined the second living room. Sophia crossed to stand before it, then hesitated, glancing at him one last time.

Come.

She disappeared within.

Letting out a sigh, Lukys followed. He stepped into the last room and found her standing in the far corner, eyes on the floor, feet scuffing the wooden boards. His frown deepened as he crossed to her, but he only made it a few feet before the contents of the room drew his attention. He froze.

Stumbling to a stop, Lukys stared at the bed. A duvet of white silk shone in the light from the windows and half a dozen pillows had been stacked against the oaken headboard. There was not a hint of straw on the floor as was common in the dormitories of Perfugia and Flumeer, suggesting a mattress stuffed of fur or feathers. It was far more luxurious than any bed he had ever seen in his life.

There was also only one.

I'm sorry, Sophia's voice spoke into his mind. Her cheeks were even brighter than a few moments earlier.

Lukys could only stand there gaping, the wheels of his mind still churning, struggling to place the pieces of the puzzle together.

"What is this?" he whispered.

There was a long silence before Sophia answered.

You trusted me with your life, she said softly. He was surprised to see her eyes were shining. *Now I must trust you with a secret the Tangata have kept from your people for generations.*

❄ 21 ❄

THE FALLEN

A fire glowed in the valley below.

Crouched amongst the rocks, Romaine looked down at the campsite. The light had appeared suddenly as they marched through the night, appearing beyond the boulders that filled the valley floor. Yasin had called a halt immediately and they had backtracked far enough to ensure they would not run afoul of any scouts that might be patrolling the area. Then they had scaled the escarpment at the edge of the valley to gain a vantage point over Erika's people.

Now looking down at the flickering fire, Romaine could hardly believe the chase was at an end. It had taken another two nights—longer perhaps than Yasin would have preferred—but finally Cara's rescue was at hand. Shadows flickered close to the flames and he found himself wondering which was the Goddess, which was Erika. The gloom made it impossible to discern one person from another.

In truth, the queen's spy had made their task easy. Romaine had said nothing of his discovery to the others, but the following nights he'd paid greater attention to Yasin's actions, and had soon begun to spot more of the phosphorescent X's himself. He wondered at the person who dared to commit such treason against his kingdom, to gift his loyalty to a foreign sovereign.

Or perhaps their unknown benefactor was simply one of the few believers amongst the Gemaho, one who renounced their king's blasphemy.

Regardless, it wouldn't be long now before the spy's identity was revealed and Cara freed. A lump rose in his throat at the thought of seeing the little Goddess again. They had hardly spoken a word to each other after the disaster on the Illmoor. It had been too much, the pain of his injuries, of their loss. Lukys and Travis and all the other Perfugians, gone in an instant. The two of them left alone to grieve. Even then, at least they might have had each other, if not for Erika…

"We'll make camp here," Yasin said, interrupting his train of thought. The warrior rose and retreated from the edge of the valley.

"Why not take them now?" Romaine questioned. "There can't be more than twenty." Yasin's own fighters numbered some thirty. "If we attack under the cover of darkness, by surprise, they're like to surrender with barely a fight."

"Is that so, Calafe?" Yasin asked as the others gathered close. A smile tugged at the man's face as he glanced at Romaine's hand and raised an eyebrow. "Suppose you'll be leading the charge?"

Romaine scowled. The queen's man had grown progressively more dismissive of Romaine and Lorene over the past days, as though he blamed them for their quarry's continuing evasiveness. That was at an end now though, and grinding his teeth, Romaine gestured back towards the valley.

"Did you have a better plan?"

The warrior smirked. "I prefer not to go barrelling into a fight blind, Calafe," he replied with a smirk. "First I'm going to scout their camp and see what we're up against."

"And risk stumbling into one of their scouts in the dark?" Romaine argued.

Yasin stepped in close and narrowed his eyes. "What's your rush, man?" he asked softly. "Are you so eager to rescue your precious Goddess? These are Nguyen's soldiers we're talking about. He might not have our queen's nuance, but the man's not a fool. I won't throw my men's lives away by rushing into a trap, though I'm starting to see what went wrong with those sorry Perfugians you led into Calafe."

Romaine almost struck the man. Red flashed across his vision and he dropped a hand to the hilt of his sword. Yasin didn't react. Dark eyes regarded Romaine and a smile touched the warrior's lips. There was no hint of fear in his posture, no concern for the man he faced, though Romaine towered over him.

Swallowing his anger, Romaine shook his head. "You're right," he admitted finally. "Scouting won't hurt—if we're careful. I'll come with you—"

"No," Yasin cut him off. "You and your friend will stay here."

Romaine stared at the man for a long moment. "Yasin, I know the mountains," he argued, trying to keep an even temper. "In the dark, on these slopes, even a single rock knocked loose could ruin everything."

"Then I guess I'd better not knock over any rocks," Yasin said. Dismissing Romaine with a wave, he turned to his followers. "Set the camp. I'll be back within the hour."

He disappeared in the direction of the valley. Romaine watched him go, still smouldering. If the man alerted Erika and her soldiers to their presence it would ruin everything. They had the Gemaho outnumbered, but their quarry could even that advantage if they had time to reach defensible terrain.

"You know, I'm beginning to think he doesn't like us," Lorene commented as the other men began unpacking their sleeping rolls.

Romaine grunted. "There's something more to this," he said, then glanced in the direction of Yasin's followers. They were out of earshot now, engaged in their own conversations. He looked back at Lorene. "I think he has a spy in the Gemaho camp."

Lorene raised his eyebrows. "And how do you know that?"

"They've been leaving markers for us," Romaine replied. "That's why Yasin was only able to track them at night."

"And you didn't think to tell me this earlier?" Lorene scowled, gesturing in the direction Yasin had taken. "Here I was beginning to think the man must have some secret magic!" He hesitated. "You think he's gone to meet his contact then?"

"Could be," Romaine mused. "Though that would risk alerting the others." He shook his head. "The excuse he gave doesn't make any sense either—if this was all a trap set by Nguyen, surely the spy would have warned us."

Lorene sighed. "You know, I'm beginning to miss the days when all I had to worry about were superhuman creatures thirsty for my blood. Simpler times, you know?"

Romaine rolled his eyes. "No one forced you to come."

"Yeah, I'm seriously beginning to question my past self's decision-making abilities." He paused, then shrugged. "Ah well. We going after him then?"

A grin crossed Romaine's lips as he glanced at the others. Just like the past few days when they'd set camp, Yasin's men paid them no attention. He gave a short nod and silently the two of them slipped away into the darkness. Together they crept back to where they'd spied on the Gemaho.

"How do we find him?" Lorene whispered as they paused at the edge of the valley.

"Not sure," Romaine replied, looking down at the burning fire.

He felt a sudden urge to ignore Yasin entirely and head for those flames, to draw his sword and rush the camp, to free Cara from whatever bondage Erika had placed her under. His fist tightened on the hilt of his sword and he drew in a breath. Pain dug at his chest, less now but still there. No, he couldn't rescue Cara alone. But he could at least find out what Yasin was up to.

Exhaling, he started down into the valley, heart beating hard against his ribs. In the darkness, they had to take extra care of the uneven ground, but over the past few nights both had come to perfect the art of stealth. The earth was steep, but there were sections where sheer rock rather than gravel allowed them to move without sound, though having only one hand made it difficult for Romaine to grip the stone.

The light below grew brighter as they continued down the slope, but Romaine had a feeling Yasin would not go too close to the camp. There had to be a reason he was out here. Maybe Lorene was right and he was meeting with their spy. Romaine was still trying to work out the why.

Straining his ears, Romaine caught the first murmur of voices from ahead. The Gemaho were still awake despite the late hour and the cold, though with a fire to warm them they would be far more comfortable than the queen's men.

"What was that?" Lorene whispered, reaching out to catch Romaine by the arm.

Romaine frowned, but before he could reply, he caught another set of whispers—from their left this time. Away from the Gemaho camp, farther up the valley. Following his instincts, Romaine diverted towards the sound. As they moved, the sound of the camp fell away, but the other whispers rose and Romaine slowed, struggling to make out the words over the soft whistling of the wind.

Finally a flicker of movement came from ahead, revealed by the growing moon. Romaine froze, lifting a hand for Lorene to do the same, before crouching and slinking forward into the shelter of a nearby boulder.

"…didn't tell me she was a *God!*" an unfamiliar voice hissed in the night.

"Enough," Yasin replied. "You already wasted enough time responding to my signal."

"Shouldn't have come at all," the spy hissed. "She's a *God*—"

There was an audible *thump* as something hard connected with flesh, followed by strained gasping. Romaine imagined the spy bent in two, struggling to breathe through winded lungs. Why he objected to Cara being a Goddess was still not clear. Romaine shared a glance with Lorene, and carefully they crept closer.

"Listen here, you little bastard," Yasin's voice came again. "Queen Amina doesn't care about your superstitions. You'll do what you're told."

The wheezing continued for another moment before the voice rose in soft defiance. "Please…"

The crunch of stones beneath boots followed as one of the men shifted his feet, though this time there was no sound of blows being exchanged.

"Look, lad," Yasin said, sounding reasonable again. "I understand. You've found yourself caught up in the workings of monarchs and Gods. I'm trying to help you, but you need to do your part."

"But I don't *want* any part of this!" the spy gasped.

An audible sigh came from Yasin. "You should try not to think so much, you could catch your death." There was a long pause at the threat. Romaine glanced at Lorene, but Yasin went on before either could speak. "Or perhaps you think the Goddess will save you?" Yasin chuckled. "She is not all-powerful, my friend, nor all-knowing. Perhaps she could save you from me, if I chose to spare your life just now. But if I do not return, things will go poorly for your wife and daughter. I hear the queen sent old Skheller to accompany em. Just between you and me, the man's not particularly sane. Certainly not someone *I* would like minding my loved ones."

Romaine's blood turned to ice at Yasin's words. Their spy was not loyal to the queen at all. Her people had gotten to his family, were threatening to harm them if he didn't obey. Images flickered in his mind, of his wife's face, pale in death, of his son lying frozen in the snow. Slowly his hand dropped to his sword hilt. Steel hissed on leather as he dragged the blade free.

"*Romaine,*" Lorene hissed as he stepped from the boulders, "Romaine, wait!"

It was already too late. At the movement, Yasin had spun to face them. His eyes narrowed as he saw the blade in Romaine's hand.

"That's enough, Yasin," he said quietly. Footsteps came from behind him as Lorene followed, though Romaine didn't risk a glance back. Yasin had his crossbow in hand, a steel bolt loaded in place. A second man dressed in the dull yellow of Gemaho stood beside the queen's man, eyes wide in fright. The two stood close together on the slope, though behind them the earth abruptly fell away, the moonlight rocks turning to empty darkness.

"Calafe," Yasin said softly. "What are you doing out here?"

"Let the man go," Romaine said coldly, hand tight around his sword hilt. "He's done his part."

Stones crunched as Lorene moved alongside him. He too held naked steel in his hand. Yasin's eyes flickered to the scout before returning to Romaine.

"Relax, the both of you," Yasin replied, gesturing with the crossbow. "Our good friend here is just helping us out with your little Goddess. He's going make sure she doesn't get hurt amidst all the bloodshed."

Beside him, the spy seemed to pale at Yasin's words. Romaine took another step towards them.

"I said, *let him go*," he repeated. "I'll not work with anyone who threatens a child." He lifted the shield strapped to his left arm and slid into a fighting stance.

"Just do what he says, Yasin," Lorene said softly. "No one needs to get hurt here."

The queen's man chuckled at that. "Is that so?" he asked. Then the smile slid from his lips. "And by what right do you command me to do anything, Flumeeren? I am here on the orders of Queen Amina. *Your* queen, last I checked. Or are you declaring yourself a traitor, soldier?

Lorene faltered, then bared his teeth. "I stand with Romaine."

A strained silence followed as the three of them stood facing one another. The helpless spy shrank away from the conflict, but Romaine only tightened his grip on the sword. He knew Yasin's kind. The man was a killer—he would not back down from a fight—

"Oh, very well," Yasin said suddenly. Letting out a sigh, he lowered the crossbow. "Have it your way."

Romaine blinked, still staring at the man, unable to understand his sudden capitulation. He glanced at Lorene, but the scout seemed just as confused by the sudden turn of events.

Twang.

Before either of them could react, a crossbow bolt materialised in Lorene's chest. The man staggered slightly at the impact, his eyes falling to the projectile. A frown crossed his forehead and belatedly he lifted a hand to the arrow, as though confused as to how it had gotten there. Before he could touch it, though, the strength fled his legs and he crumpled to the ground without a sound.

For a second, Romaine stood staring at the body of his friend. Lorene didn't move, didn't speak, didn't even groan. He just lay against the stone, sword still clutched in a pale hand.

Laughter carried across the slope to Romaine. "You just going to stand there for me, Calafe?" The question was followed by the slow racketing sound of the crossbow being reloaded.

A scream tore from Romaine's throat and suddenly he was rushing across the broken stones, sword raised, eyes fixed on the killer. He might have lost his hand, but he was still Calafe. He would not allow his friend to die unavenged.

Yasin grinned as Romaine rushed towards him. Without time to finish reloading the crossbow, he tossed it aside and dragged his sword from its scabbard.

"That a boy," he hissed. "Let's see whether the last soldier of Calafe has any fight left in him."

Romaine's answer was to attack. Muscles rippling across his shoulders, he sent a wild swing slashing for his foe's face. Laughing, Yasin leapt aside, landing easily on the loose stone. His own blade flashed out and Romaine recoiled—though not before the sharp steel opened a cut on his forearm.

"You know, I told the queen," Yasin murmured, stalking sideways, putting himself on even footing above Romaine. "I told her you were the wrong man for this job. Too sentimental, I said. She was hopeful, though, seemed to think you could bring the Goddess to our side."

Romaine barely heard him. His mind was on Lorene, lying dead on the mountainside, slain because he'd cared, because he'd wanted to help a friend. Grief swamped Romaine but he pressed it down. On the slope above, Yasin snared down at him, but Romaine fought to calm his rage. He no longer had his axe, was no longer the warrior he'd once been. If he was to defeat the queen's personal killer, he needed to be smart.

"It's a shame really…" Yasin was still talking. He slid sideways on the slope, seeking an advantage over Romaine. The Calafe retreated a step, eyeing his foe's feet. On the treacherous ground, a single misstep could gift him the opening he needed. "Our inside man here tells me your Goddess friend has gotten right and cosy with the Gemaho. Just as Amina feared."

The words cut through Romaine's rage. "What?"

The man grinned. "Your little Goddess has betrayed us, Calafe," he sneered. "No choice now but to put her down. Best thing for everyone, if you ask me. Can't have Gods going around pretending they're people. Especially if they side with our enemies."

Romaine tightened his grip around the hilt of his sword and tried to ignore Yasin's words. The man could do nothing to harm Cara. She was a God, beyond his power to touch. Wasn't she? Despite his faith, doubt assailed him. Hadn't she suffered beneath Erika's gauntlet, hadn't the Tangata bruised her, stopped her? What would a crossbow bolt, delivered from the darkness, do to Cara?

He gritted his teeth, forcing himself to focus on the battle at hand. Yasin would never have the chance to harm his friend. Drawing in a breath, Romaine sought calm, allowing the man's words to wash over him.

Yasin sighed when his taunts failed to bring a response, then without warning he surged forward, sword lancing for Romaine's throat. Moonlight flashed from the blade as Romaine skipped back, his shield barely lifting in time to deflect the blow.

Overhead, a cloud slipped across the moon, and Romaine cursed as the world was plunged into darkness. Pain radiated from the slice on his arm and he retreated another step, swinging wildly to deter any attack. To his surprise, the blade connected with a soft *thud*, though he hadn't put much power behind the blow.

Light returned as the cloud passed and he watched as Yasin staggered back, clutching his arm. Blood seeped through his jacket, but it didn't appear to be a bad cut. Cursing, the queen's man released the wound and hefted his sword.

"You'll pay for that one."

Yasin leapt to the attack and Romaine gasped as a blow slipped beneath his guard. The short sword slammed across his chest and only his chainmail prevented it from penetrating. Even so, agony exploded from his injured ribs, and groaning, he staggered back, trying to lift his shield to deflect another blow.

To his surprise, Yasin did not follow. Instead, he smiled. "I'll admit, you put up a better fight than I expected, Calafe. But it's time for this to end."

Before Romaine could respond, Yasin lurched forward. Lifting his blade, Romaine tried to counter the attack, but the warrior's blow was only a feint, and instead Yasin lashed out with his boot. The kick caught Romaine square in the chest and he cried out as the pain redoubled. He staggered backwards, but his foot slipped as the gravel began to give way beneath him.

Too late Romaine realised he'd been manipulated. In his rage at Lorene's death and in the darkness cast by the cloud, he'd allowed Yasin to direct the battle, swapping their positions. Now he stood at the edge of the ravine he'd spotted earlier. A cry on his lips, he struggled to regain his balance, to claw his way back from the edge.

Laughing, Yasin stepped forward and shoved him hard in the chest.

And Romaine fell into the darkness.

The sun dropped below the rooftop, casting the courtyard into shadow. Lukys snarled as he spun the stave, slashing it down into the face of an invisible enemy, then stepping back and throwing up a block to deflect a riposte. Air hissed around the wooden staff with each thrust. Had there really been anyone in the path of his blows they would have broken bones. As it was, Lukys only spun, continuing through the drill Romaine had taught him back in Fogmore.

He had asked Sophia for the stave after their conversation. It had been a surprise when she'd actually brought one, though the guilt in her eyes told him why. It had no spear tip, of course, making it useless as a weapon against the Tangata. But that wasn't the point.

He needed a distraction, something to take his mind off their conversation, about the truth…

The Tangata are nearly infertile.

Memory of Sophia's words whispered in his mind and gasping, Lukys leapt, launching an attack that would have impaled his enemy. His feet shifted smoothly through the stances his mentor had spent so long drilling into him. It felt good to be moving through the patterns again, to feel his body fall into the familiar rhythms.

Less and less of our pairings can produce children.

He fought on, teeth bared, spinning and slicing, desperate to fend off the unseen enemies, to forget the words that whispered in his mind. A thrust stabbed one foe through the heart, a kick hurled his corpse away, freeing the imaginary blade.

The Tangata are a dying race, Lukys.

A growl slipped from his lips as he moved forward in a series of thrusts, overhand blows, and blocks.

That is why we must take human partners. The pairings are more… favourable. Without them, our species would have died out a generation ago.

Now Lukys began to retreat, his hands moving farther apart on the stave and lifting high, then low, driving his opponent's blade into the cobbles. A kick from his boot sent the imaginary assailant flying backwards.

Zachariah and I, we were a fifth-generation pair—that is, there are five human ancestors in each of our lines.

Grinding his teeth, Lukys's hands tightened on the spear, his knuckles turning white. His breath came in gasps as he paused, spear held parallel to the ground, elbows bent. Slowly he straightened his arms upwards, as though straining to push away an enemy blade.

Sometimes, a child is possible in such couplings. But after five years…

Despite the cool evening breeze, sweat soaked his back. His heart thundered in his ears. Panting, he staggered to a stop. The staff slipped from his fingers, clattering to the cobbles. He blinked drops of perspiration from his eyes, slowly becoming aware of the crowd that had gathered around him. A sigh slipped from his lips as he struggled to recover his breath.

I can sleep in the living room.

The conversation had ended there. Still in a state of shock, he'd asked her for the staff not long afterward. She'd left the compound then, off to hunt deer or maybe pick coffee beans, or whatever she and the other Tangata did during the day. It was his fellow Perfugian recruits who watched him now. Talking to them was the last thing he wanted to do right now, but it didn't look like he was going to have the option not to. He had to keep up the pretence of happiness.

"What was that all about?" Travis asked as he approached, Dale just a step behind.

The other Perfugians wandered over to the tables, most taking seats while a few fetched drinks from their houses. With night falling over the city, coffee looked to have been swapped for ale.

Lukys focused on his two friends. "Felt like I needed to move after all that time in the cell," he offered. "Besides, it's good to practice. No point forgetting everything Romaine taught us."

A grin twisted at Travis's lips. "I suppose. Seems a bit much like hard work to me."

Lukys only shrugged. "Doesn't hurt to be prepared though, right?"

Dale frowned, then clapped Lukys on the shoulder. "I know it's hard to let go. We gave so much of ourselves to the cause. But we're safe here, Lukys. No one's sending us to our deaths, ordering us into the frontlines. I doubt we'll have to ever fight again."

"And thank the Gods for that," Travis added with emphasis. He shivered. "I especially don't miss the cold!"

Eyeing his friends, Lukys found himself nodding to their words. He might not understand the speed at which their attitudes had changed, but he could appreciate their reasoning. Flumeer and Perfugia both had betrayed them, treating them like playthings, to be cast away when their entertainment ran out. Yet amongst the Tangata they had found acceptance, even appreciation, for their presence.

Though…looking at Travis, he wanted to ask him about Cara. Travis had fallen hard for the Goddess, and while he hadn't known her true identity at the time, she…had seemed to reciprocate the feeling. Had he so quickly given up on the object of his desire?

Movement came from the street beyond the open gates and Lukys watched several Tangata entering the courtyard.

"I suppose it *is* good exercise, though," Travis said. He grinned, though his eyes were on the approaching Tangata. "Gods know, I need to keep up my strength."

That is why we must take human partners.

Lukys's cheeks burned as two females broke off from the group and approached them. Smiles lit Dale and Travis's faces. No words passed between them—they still could not hear the Tangata apparently—but soon they were wandering away with their assignments. Swallowing, Lukys tried to dismiss the nausea in his stomach.

Footsteps sounded behind him. *Lukys…*

Ice spread through his veins as he found Sophia standing behind him. He opened his mouth, then closed it again. What could he say to her after their conversation that morning?

Maybe we'd better go inside? she murmured, looking surprisingly hesitant as she stood there.

Swallowing, he nodded, and together they crossed to the stairwell. Laughter carried up from the courtyard as they slipped into their apartment and Lukys's cheeks warmed again. They found themselves standing in the living room, staring at one another from across the coffee table.

I'll make some tea, Sophia said abruptly, then spun and disappeared into the kitchen.

Closing his eyes for a moment, Lukys slumped onto the sofa. What was he going to do? He had agreed to this arrangement to escape his cell, but he had not accepted this new life as the others had. How could he? Despite all the revelations, the realisation that the Tangata were not so different…it was still wrong. Wasn't it?

Movement came from the doorway to the kitchen as Sophia reappeared holding two steaming mugs. She hesitated, then crossed quickly and placed one of the teas on the table before Lukys.

Peppermint, she said, stepping aside. *For the anxiety.* She paused. *May I sit?*

Letting out a sigh, Lukys nodded. The sofa was big enough for the two of them. Picking up the cup, he breathed in the steam, then took a sip. The pounding in his head retreated a little and he managed a smile.

"Thank you," he murmured, eyes in his mug.

An uncomfortable silence fell over the living room. Lukys watched as a few pieces of green leaves bobbed to the surface of his cup. It was one of the ceramics from the cabinet that stood nearby. He noticed the teapot was missing from the set as well. When had she taken them?

"Sophia, I don't know what to think of any of this," he said at last.

I'm sorry, she replied, and he noticed she didn't seem able to look at him either.

The others, my friends, they don't know…the real reason they're here?

Sophia shook her head, and Lukys let out a sigh. He'd thought as much, but it was best to be sure before he accidentally blurted out any secrets. It meant he was likely the only human alive who knew the Tangata's secret.

What is it that you want, Lukys? Sophia's voice whispered in his mind. *What is it you fight for?*

Lukys looked at her sharply. "For humanity…" He trailed off, a lump lodging in his throat and he slumped into the sofa. Absently he took another sip of the tea, wondering at the question. How could he *not* fight for humanity?

And yet, what had his fellow man ever done for him? Other than Romaine, the only friends he'd ever had in this world were sitting outside enjoying the cool evening air. And they had sided with the Tangata.

"I don't know what I fight for anymore," he said finally. "I've only ever known what they taught us in the academy, but that was all lies. I'm lost."

They were silent for a while then, though it was pensive. There was a depth to Sophia's expression now, her eyes lost in the distance, as though she were contemplating the secrets of the universe.

I never wanted to be a warrior, Sophia said at last. *I did it for my people, to protect the weaker amongst us. But I am tired of killing for duty.*

Lukys nodded. He recalled the last Tangata he had slain on the banks of the Illmoor. It had hardly been older than himself. Lukys recalled the fear he'd glimpsed in the creature's eyes before the final blow. Maybe that had been Zachariah. He would never ask.

I want children, Lukys. His heart clenched and he struggled to look at her as she continued: *To bring life to this world, instead of death.*

The truth shone from her eyes, could be seen in the earnestness of her smile. For just a second he wondered what that would be like, to give himself to this strange creature. A shiver ran down his spine and he stood up suddenly.

"I can't," he gasped, heart suddenly racing.

Sophia stared at him for just a moment, those solid grey eyes wide, then looked away.

I think you must have Tangatan blood, you know.

Lukys started at her words. "What?"

She still couldn't look at him, but was instead inspecting the blue flower pattern on her cup. *It's the only explanation for your talent. It's why I chose you.*

That's impossible! he shouted in his mind, but still she did not look at him.

It's not…unheard of, she murmured. *Those of the seventh and younger generations, many are born with human eyes. They practically* are *human. They sometimes went to live amongst the Calafe, before the war.*

He shook his head. "How would they have gotten to Perfugia?"

Sophia shrugged, but there were no answers this time. Lukys swallowed, his mind turning over her words. It wasn't possible, was it? Perfugia was hundreds of miles away from the Tangatan homeland. How would one of the creatures, even one who appeared human, have reached the distant island? And yet…if not the Tangata, where *had* his ability come from?

There were still so many questions, but he wouldn't find the answers this night. Letting out a long breath, he looked towards the bedroom.

"I'm…going to sleep," he said, his voice strained.

Still Sophia did not look at him. *I'll sleep here.*

There was no missing the sadness in her voice. It tugged at Lukys, but he steeled his heart and nodded. *Goodnight.*

He strode through the open door and closed it softly behind him. Then he was alone, looking down at that soft bed, the empty covers, the pillows plumped and stacked lovingly against the headboard. Tears stung his eyes and he slumped onto the cushioned mattress.

It was just all too strange.

❦ 23 ❦
THE TANGATA

Adonis stood in the unnatural glow of the magic lights and gazed upon the Old One. His heart was racing, fear setting his every sense on edge, images of blood and gore flashing through his mind.

The Matriarch had been right. They had found one, alive, still slumbering in a magic sleep. The creature hung before them in the giant glass cylinder, suspended by the liquids within, her bare body cast in a red glow by the illumination rising from below. A slight hum filled the room, like the distant buzzing of bees, but otherwise the Birthing Ground was silent, as though the very earth held its breath, waiting for what came next.

A shiver ran through Adonis as he looked upon his ancestor. The red light felt almost a warning, as though whoever had left the creature here had feared someone might one day try to wake her, and was sending him a warning.

But Adonis could not heed their council. The female hanging suspended before him represented the hope of his entire race, their last chance to restore strength to future generations. From her would spring a new first generation of Tangata, their powers, their strength restored. Then humanity would quiver before the might of his people.

If she was sane.

His skin crawled but Adonis fought to suppress the sensation and held out his hand for a hammer. There was no point lingering, delaying that which must be done. Breath held, he stepped forward and hefted the tool. But as he approached the cylinder, his doubt came rushing back, and he hesitated, hammer raised to strike.

Was this the right thing to do, the right decision for his people, for the world?

What do I care about the world if it belongs to humanity?

He brought the hammer down.

A *crash* shattered the peace of the Birthing Ground as the glass caved outwards, the pressure of the liquid within sending the cylinder's contents spilling across the ground. Adonis leapt aside as the body followed. Not the most dignified reawakening for his ancestor, but the Tangata did not know enough about the magic of this place to free her any other way.

Retreating to stand with his sisters and brothers, Adonis watched as the Old One slowly woke. He kept the hammer clutched tight at his side as he waited, watching for the first hint of madness, for a clue that the endless passage of time had stolen her sanity. If he struck fast enough, perhaps he could avert disaster…

A hiss whispered through the chamber as the Old One took her first breath. Lying naked amidst the broken glass and strangely gelatinous liquid, blonde hair plastered against her skull, she sucked in great lungfuls of air. Her skin was drained, turned an unhealthy grey, almost translucent, though as Adonis watched, colour reappeared in her cheeks, life returning. The hammer shook in his hands; the window to act was quickly closing. But he did nothing. Slowly the Old One's head lifted, and her eyes fell upon them.

A soft growl rasped from her throat as she rose, and despite himself, Adonis took a step backwards. The terrible eyes flickered in his direction. They were the eyes of the Tangata, pure grey, pupils dilated by the light, but in those depths he saw none of the intelligence of his people. The madness was upon this creature, the berserker rage that sometimes came upon them in battle.

He tensed, sensing what the creature was about to do, and lifted the hammer.

There was a rush of movement, a harsh *thud*. Beside Adonis, his brother Tangata died.

A cry echoed through the chamber as the Tangata leapt back

from their companion, weapons held at the ready, but the female did not pay them any attention. Instead, she held their dying brother by the top of his skull, his feet an inch above the floor. Blood still pulsed from his throat, but as Adonis watched, it slowed to a trickle, the last of his brother's life fled.

Lips curled back in a snarl, the Old One leaned in close, as though to inspect her victim. Whatever she'd expected to find, apparently their brother was found wanting. With a flick of her wrist, she sent him toppling sideways. And the grey eyes turned once more to the living.

A cry escaped Adonis's throat, one of rage and frustration, of the knowledge that he and his comrades had made a terrible mistake. Hammer clutched in one hand, he moved towards the Old One.

She was faster. Another of his Tangata cried out and Adonis watched, helpless, as his sister crumpled, a terrible hole torn through her chest. Laughter whispered from the Old One as she stood over the body, blood dripping from her fingers.

Stop her! Adonis screamed, and his brethren charged.

They died one by one, the Old One dancing between them like a fox amongst the chickens, dropping them at will. Adonis's hammer blows failed to touch her and even his enhanced vision struggled to follow the speed of her movements.

Aghast, Adonis found himself retreating from the carnage. He watched in horror as the best of the fourth generation were butchered like humans. It took the Old One just moments to finish his warrior pairs, though the last she lingered with, feinting, toying, as though she enjoyed watching his fear, his pain. Finally, with a cry of defiance, the Tangata leapt, hammer raised in a desperate strike. She struck him with a backhanded blow so powerful he was flung backwards into the broken cylinder, impaling him on the giant shards of glass.

Then she turned her insane eyes on Adonis. Something in their icy depths seemed to understand he would not fight her, and a smile touched her lips.

Adonis shivered as she approached him, her naked figure covered in the blood of his companions. He knew now how great their error had been. This creature cared not for the Tangata. It cared only for death. This creature would see the world burn.

Death, death, death.

The words pounded in his skull and Adonis found himself taking a step back. Faster than thought, the Old One was there, her fingers closing upon his throat like an iron vice. He cried out, but a squeeze stole the sound away as her fingernails clamped upon his windpipe. Desperately he tried to break her hold, to tear himself loose, but for the first time in his life, Adonis's strength failed him in the face of a greater foe. The hammer was still in his hand and awkwardly he tried to swing it for her face. She caught him with her spare hand.

Death, death, death.

The fist tightened around his throat, but through his agony, Adonis finally recognised the whispers for what they were. Gasping, he thrust out with his mind.

Stop, please!

The Old One let out a cry, and releasing him, she leapt back, teeth bared, eyes wide. Adonis collapsed to the ground and gasped in great breaths of the stale air. The creature's scent was strong now that she was free of her liquid cocoon and he found his head swirling. But eventually fresh oxygen restored strength to his failing body and his mind cleared.

Slowly, Adonis drew himself back to his feet. His eyes were drawn to the bodies of his brethren. They lay all about him, their blood staining the cold stone. He quickly looked away, looking at the Old One once more. Why had she stopped? She hadn't hesitated to strike a mortal blow against the others.

She made no move to attack now, only stood watching, as though she were waiting for something…

What…are…you?

Adonis leapt back as the words reverberated in his skull. The Old One's voice was so loud she was practically screaming into his mind.

So strong!

He drew in a breath, then sent his thoughts out towards the creature.

We are your descendants, Old One, he said, his gaze drawn again to the dead. His heart twisted at the loss, but he forced his mind to focus. The grey eyes still watched him. *Centuries have passed since you began your slumber. We came to wake you, to free you from your chains.*

The Old One regarded him in silence. The strange liquid still dripped from her naked body, mingling with the blood of his brethren. Adonis clenched his fists as he suffered her gaze, wondering what it must have been like, to slumber for so long, to wake in a foreign world. No wonder she was insane…

Show me. She spoke in a softer tone this time, with more control, though the words still pierced Adonis to his very core.

He bowed in response, and silently he summoned memories of these past years—of the terrible force of humanity that had invaded their homeland, slaughtering children and innocents, of the Tangatan counterattack, the years of battle and death as wave upon wave of humanity came against them. Each time the Tangata had emerged victorious, yet still the enemy fought on, and all the while the Tangatan numbers dwindled, their strength fading.

Finally he saw again that last battle on the banks of the Illmoor, the humans they had taken—and the Anahera that had come against them, wings spread in the wind. The Old One started at this image, a frown creasing her forehead.

Adonis let the images fade. *You see?*

There was a long pause before the Old One replied: *These… Anahera, they are your enemy?*

Adonis hesitated. The Anahera had not been seen in centuries —a single one did not mean they had joined the war on the side of humanity. And yet…there was a glow in the Old One's eyes as she watched him, and swallowing, he nodded.

So it would seem.

The Old One took a step towards him and Adonis flinched, still expecting to be struck down. But she only reached out a hand, gentle now, as though fearing she might harm him unintentionally.

What is your name, child?

A shiver ran down his spine at the creature's words and for a second he felt an inexplicable desire to flee. He could feel the weight of her mind pressing against his, the power behind her words. It was almost like…

He shook his head as the thought trailed away to nothing. *I am Adonis.*

The Old One nodded. *You may call me…Maya.* Her smile grew as she traced a finger down the curve of his jaw. *Fear not, child. I will see our enemies burn like the forest before an inferno.*

❦ 24 ❦

THE FUGITIVE

It was a few days before the soldiers finally began adjusting to the sight of Cara and her wings. To her credit, the Goddess hadn't taken to the skies in that time, though Erika sensed this was more to assuage her worries than their companions' benefit. Even so, Cara's actions still felt incomprehensible. The Goddess had still made her disapproval about their destination clear, refusing to give the slightest hint as to whether they were on the right path. Yet she had also kept her word.

If Erika had been in the Goddess's shoes, with wings and the freedom of the sky beckoning, she would have fled at the first opportunity. But then, that was the point, wasn't it? Erika was only human, not a fifty-year-old Goddess in the body of a twenty-year-old with wings. She couldn't possibly hope to understand the forces that bound the Anahera.

At least the Gemaho had not been *completely* struck dumb by Cara's wings, unlike their Flumeeren counterparts. Nguyen's soldiers might have been stunned by the sight, but they hadn't fallen to their knees in awe, and their shock had mostly passed quickly. There were only a few now who still lost their ability to speak in Cara's presence.

Which was fortunate, as the going had become progressively more difficult with each passing day. While the snow line seemed higher this side of the mountains, the valleys they traversed had become progressively steeper, the terrain more and more difficult. And as they neared the soaring peaks, Erika found each inhalation brought less energy, as though however hard she tried, she could not quite fill her lungs. By the end of each day, her temples were pounding, and despite the warmth of the sun overhead, she found herself trembling whenever they stopped for more than a few minutes.

Dawn, on their fifth day since disembarking the ship, found them waking in a broad, U-shaped valley, snow-capped peaks towering all around them. Despite the cold, Erika rose from her sleeping bag touched by excitement. If her guess was correct, the home of the Anahera was close.

Shadow still clung to the valley as she pushed aside the canvas tent flap and stepped into the open. Several of the soldiers were already up and busy repacking their tents for the day's journey. Erika was relieved their presence had spared her from carrying the heavy things.

A moan came from inside her tent and a few moments later Cara's face appeared, tangled copper hair hanging across her face. Erika might have trusted the Goddess not to harm them, but it had still seemed prudent to keep her close in the night.

"Arg, Erika, the sun's not even up." Cara muttered as she crawled through the flap. "You know, if you're going to drag me back to my parents, you could at least let me sleep in a little."

One of her wings caught in the canvas and the Goddess cursed and had to contract the limb before she could pass. The movement dislodged several of her feathers and a gust of wind sent them swirling away. Absently, Erika snatched one from the air. The things still amazed her, their length, the depth of their colour. Shaking her head, she released it again. Despite her growing familiarity with the Goddess, the sight of those wings still sent a shiver down her spine at times.

Ignoring Cara's complaints, she turned towards the remains of last night's fire, only to find another of the soldiers standing there, eyes wide as he watched Cara finish clambering from the tent. Erika sighed—this was one of the few Gemaho who still hadn't overcome his awe for the Goddess. Knowing it would be some time before he recovered his wits, she stepped around him and approached the ring of stones they'd placed there for seating.

Lowering herself onto her rock from the night before, Erika was relieved to see someone had already lit the fire for the morning. Stretching out her hands, she let the heat wash over her. Her eyes drifted to the way ahead.

Gravel slopes rose away from them, turning to sheer cliffs a few hundred yards up the valley, becoming a narrowing gorge that twisted out of sight. There was no way of telling whether the canyon would end in a dead end. Where they sat, they could still climb from the valley and continue along the ridge instead, but Erika didn't relish the thought of climbing those treacherous slopes. If only Cara had been willing to take to the skies and scout the way ahead, she could have told them which was the best option.

Still muttering to herself, Cara lowered herself onto a rock nearby. Apparently recovered from his shock, the soldier stepped past her to attend to the fire, before pulling a pot from a nearby pack and placing it over the flames. Oats and a generous helping of water from an oilskin followed with a soft *hiss*.

Erika watched the man with amusement—he seemed to be studiously trying not to stare at Cara. Across the flames, the Goddess wrinkled her nose as she watched him, then rose and crossed to where the soldier was working, her footsteps silent on the loose stones.

"Arg, is there a reason for humanity's obsession with oatmeal?" she asked, pouting slightly. Beside her, the soldier yelped as he finally noticed her presence at his shoulder, but Cara only went on: "I can't imagine why you find it so appealing, it's basically just grey mush."

"I…I…sorry, Your Divinity!" the improvised cook gasped. He fumbled at the pot and almost dropped it into the flames.

"You should be!" Cara exclaimed, leaning forward and fixing him with a glare.

The man yelped and almost tripped over himself. Erika rolled her eyes. Just as the soldiers had become accustomed to her presence, the Goddess had grown used to their staring. In fact, now she seemed to take a certain amount of amusement from their awe.

"Oatmeal is perfectly acceptable, soldier," Erika said before Cara made the poor man any more mortified. She turned her gaze on the Goddess. "If you'd ever made it to Mildeth, I'd have shown you a real breakfast."

Erika immediately regretted opening her mouth as Cara's face darkened.

"A shame," was all the Goddess said, but the conversation died after that, and they waited in silence for the soldier to finish preparing the breakfast.

"Here, Archivist," the man said finally, offering her a bowl of freshly poured oatmeal.

Nodding her thanks, Erika accepted the offering. She held her tongue when she saw it was just as unappetising as Cara had claimed. The man collected another bowl and turned his back from them to scoop another portion from the pot—or probably two, knowing Cara's appetite—before bowing low and passing it to Cara. She took it with a smile.

"Thank you."

The man hesitated, still looking nervous, before he finally blurted out: "Are you really a God?"

A smile touched Cara's lips and she crooked her head to the side, eyeing the man. "What do *you* think?"

"I..." The man swallowed visibly. "You...you have wings."

Cara glanced over her shoulders and gasped. "You're right!" The feathered limbs lifted slightly with her mock surprise. "What does it mean?!"

The soldier swallowed again, shaking his head, looking at the ground. "I don't know. We...I...didn't believe...not like they do in the west. I don't...know what to think."

Erika chuckled to herself as she watched the exchange, but at the man's last words Cara's shoulders drooped and she looked away.

"Maybe I'm not sure what I am either," she said at last.

The soldier stared at her for a moment, then finally he nodded, seemingly satisfied. He let out a long breath. "Enjoy your meal."

He moved away at that, and Erika returned her attention to her oatmeal. To the man's credit, he'd added dried apple and raisins. They gave a little flavour to her first bite. She ate slowly as the soldiers moved about, preparing for the day's march, until Maisie finally appeared from her tent. Erika waved the spy over.

"Enjoying the meal?" Maisie asked as she approached, nodding a greeting to Cara.

Her mouth full of oatmeal, the Goddess didn't reply, and the spy chuckled. Turning to Erika, she raised an eyebrow in question. The spy didn't need to speak for Erika to understand her question.

"I think we're in the right place," she said, then reached into her satchel and drew out her map. "See these," she said, pointing to the twin white spots on either side of the red star marking what they thought was the home of the Gods. She nodded to the peaks rising either on side of the valley.

The spy leaned closer, eyes wide. "We're almost there?" she asked, scanning the map. Then her head whipped around to focus on Cara and she repeated the question: "We're almost there?"

Cara looked up from her meal, scowled, but said nothing. Silently she scooped the last morsel from the wooden bowl and placed it in her mouth, then exaggerated chewing motions.

Erika rolled her eyes. "Ignore her," she replied. "She won't tell us anything useful."

Maisie nodded. "But you're sure?"

"I am."

"Excellent!" Maisie exclaimed. "Then what are we sitting here for? Let's go find the city of your Gods!"

Despite herself, Erika's heart throbbed at the thought. Stifling a groan, she levered herself to her feet and looked at Cara. "Well, are you going to sulk? Or join us?"

Cara rolled her eyes, but after a moment she set aside her bowl and made to stand. She managed to rise halfway to her feet, but suddenly seemed to lose her balance and pitched forward. Erika's hand snatched out and caught the Goddess by the arm, steadying her.

"Are you alright?" she asked with a frown.

Cara nodded. She released Erika's arm and tried to take a step, but immediately swung off-balance and staggered sideways instead. This time Erika wasn't fast enough to catch her, and the Goddess slumped to her hands and knees beside the fire. Her wings flared outwards, the twelve feet of feathered limbs forcing everyone back.

"Cara?" Erika hissed, suddenly concerned. "What's wrong?"

A moan rumbled from the Goddess. "I...don't feel so well," Cara croaked, even as she tried to push herself back to her feet.

This time her legs gave way completely and she pitched face-first into the rocks. Pale fingers clawed at the stones as Cara twisted on her side. Her eyes were wide, pupils dilated, becoming huge black circles amidst the amber depths. They darted around in her skull as she looked up at Erika.

"Why is it getting dark?" Cara whispered.

Heart clenched, Erika reached for the Goddess, but before she could reassure her, Cara's back suddenly arched, a scream tearing from her throat. She started to thrash, arms and legs and wings hurling stones, forcing everyone back. Another cry rattled from her throat before she stilled, on hands and knees now, sucking in great mouthfuls of air.

"Erika…" Cara's voice was barely a whisper now. "Something's…not right."

The Goddess's face was a terrible grey when she looked up and sweat beaded her brow. Erika moved quickly, kneeling beside Cara and placing a hand on her shoulder, but the act seemed to offer little reassurance. With a final moan, Cara crumpled back to the stones.

"What's happening to her?" Maisie whispered.

Swallowing, Erika glanced at the spy. She was about to say that she had no idea, when her eyes alighted on the breakfast bowl lying nearby. A sudden suspicion touched Erika and she swung around, searching the faces of the gathered soldiers. All stared at the Goddess with looks of confusion—all except one.

The young man that had served their breakfast stood at the rear of the soldiers, eyes wide, his face pale. He stared in horror at where the Goddess had fallen, a soft keening sounding from the back of his throat.

Without thinking, Erika leapt to her feet and rushed the man. The man cried out and tried to flee, but her hand was already coming up, the gauntlet bursting into life. Her victim screamed as his legs crumpled beneath him.

Enraged, Erika stalked towards the fallen man, palm extending, magic still pulsing from her gauntlet. On the ground, the soldier thrashed, mouth wide, veins bulging from the flesh of his throat. Reaching the thrashing body, Erika did not relent. Teeth bared, vision stained red, she thrilled in his suffering. He must have slipped poison into Cara's food when they hadn't been looking. Now he would pay…

"Erika!" Maisie snapped, catching her by the arm and dragging it away from her victim.

The soldier collapsed to the stones, gasping as though his lungs had just been released from a vice. Shaking herself free of her anger, Erika looked at Maisie, then the soldier. Blood ran from his nose, ears, and nostrils, turning his face to a scarlet mess. He lay on the ground moaning, unable to move, to see, probably even to hear. A few moments longer, and he would have succumbed to her magic.

A lump lodged in Erika's throat as a sudden horror touched her. It had been so long since she'd used the magic, she'd almost forgotten the thrill of its power, the call to use it against her enemies.

"I'm sorry." A whisper rasped from the man's throat. "I'm sorry, I'm sorry, I'm sorry. Please!"

Looking at his pitiful form, listening to his pleas, Erika felt her anger rising again, but Maisie moved faster. A knife appeared in her hand and she crouched beside the soldier and placed the dagger against this throat.

"What did you do?" she hissed.

"I'm sorry," the man repeated. He blinked, as though struggling to clear something from his vision, but the whites of his eyes had been stained red with blood. He would likely never see again. "The queen...she made me."

Erika's heart turned to ice at the man's words. The queen? She couldn't possibly be here, could she?

Before any of them could question the man further, a horn sounded from above. Swinging around, Erika watched as thirty men leapt over the ridge above and raced down the slope towards them.

❧ 25 ❧

THE SOLDIER

Lukys sat in the courtyard looking up at the starless sky, a pint of ale before him, the laughter of his friends all around. He joined in with them every now and then, if only to keep up appearances. Watching their merriment, it occurred to him that he was no longer their leader, that the authority he'd built as Romaine's right-hand man had slipped away as he sat alone in the darkness. Lukys found he did not miss it.

A week had fled like the snow before the breath of spring. He and the other recruits had been put to work, though that was often no more than sitting on the riverbanks with a fishing pole.

The most strenuous of activity came when they cleared the buildings yet to be occupied by the Tangata. Thankfully any dead had been removed from the city long ago, but many houses were worse for wear after close to a year of unoccupancy. Coal stoves had cracked with the invasion of winter's cold and had to be removed, while vines were busy invading through cracks and windows. At times the Perfugians were even asked to attempt basic repairs on shutters and rooftops. Then they would be joined by groups of Tangata who watched their actions with interest, Lukys assumed to learn from their human captives.

If that was the case, though, they were sorely disappointed, as the recruits had few such skills. They hadn't been sent to the front-line to die because they'd been useful to Perfugian society.

Maybe that was why his friends laughed now, why their smiles seemed so genuine—they had finally found a place in society, even if it was amongst the strangest of people. They even seemed able to communicate with their Tangata through notes and actions, despite their obvious limitations.

Watching his friends embrace their new life, their new lovers, it left Lukys feeling excluded, as if there was something wrong with his resistance to Sophia. It wasn't that he did not find her attractive, in a lithe, Tangatan manner, or even that he did not like her. She had surprised him with her sweetness. The image of her baking bread each morning was such a sharp contrast to the monsters he'd always imagined the Tangata to be…

…perhaps that was the source of his reservations—not that he did not find her attractive, but that he *did*. She had taken him captive, stolen away his freedom. Human or Tangata, he should *loathe* her.

Instead, he found himself lying awake each night, tossing and turning in the giant bed, thinking of Sophia sleeping alone on the sofa. Of the pain he glimpsed in her eyes each morning when he found her with her bread.

It was galling.

"You're looking grim."

Lukys looked up as Travis sat across the table from him. Most of the others had been washing up after their afternoon on the river-banks and Lukys had been enjoying the peace in the courtyard. He forced a smile.

"Didn't catch anything today."

His friend chuckled. "Fish not biting? Ah well, rest day tomorrow, no point stewing over it." He lifted his mug and clinked it against Lukys's.

They drank and Travis laughed again, then gestured around the courtyard. "Who knew our damned Sovereigns were hiding this from us all this time?"

"You think they knew?" Lukys asked, surprised.

Travis's eyebrows lifted into his mop of light brown hair—there were certainly no barbers in New Nihelm. "You think they didn't?"

Lukys's eyes drifted over the groups of Tangata standing nearby. "I don't know what to think anymore," he mused.

His friend said nothing at that, and when he looked back at Travis, he found the other man's gaze fixed on him. He swallowed, worried he might have given away his secret, but after a moment the Perfugian waved a hand.

"Ain't that the truth," he said, then leaned across the table. "So, what's it like?"

"Huh?" Lukys asked, mug halfway to his lips.

"Being able to hear them," Travis explained.

Lukys quickly dropped his eyes to the table. That was one secret he had been unable to keep. The other Tangata had soon learned of his ability from Sophia, and often came to him when they wanted to convey something to their partners. It seemed a novelty to them, to be able to communicate with Travis and the others without using notes. For Lukys, it was slightly mortifying.

"I…" he stammered, unsure how to progress. "It's…different."

"I bet." Travis wore a grin from ear to ear. "Especially at night. I can only imagine the thoughts running through Isabella's mind sometimes."

Warmth flushed Lukys's face but thankfully he was spared any further conversation about his love life by the arrival of voices at the gates of the compound. He frowned, turning in his seat to see several men and women approaching, carrying straw baskets.

"Hello to the compound!" the first of the new arrivals called, the southern twang in his accent announcing him as Calafe. "We heard there were some new arrivals, how are y'all settling in?"

The Perfugians stood around the courtyard as the group approached, frowns revealing their confusion. So far they hadn't had much interaction with the other humans in the city. But the frowns soon turned to grins as the newcomers revealed the contents of their baskets.

"Y'all hungry?" A woman asked, approaching their table.

"Damn right!" Travis exclaimed, rising to look into the basket. He jabbed a thumb in Lukys's direction. "This one didn't catch us anything for dinner."

Lukys flashed Travis a scowl, but nodded his thanks as the woman passed him something wrapped in a cloth. She took a seat alongside Travis as Lukys unwrapped the offering, revealing a small pastry pie within.

"It's venison," the woman explained, taking out one of her own. Uncovering the pie as Lukys had done, she proceeded to take a bite while holding the bottom half in the cloth.

Raising an eyebrow, Lukys shared a glance with Travis, then attempted to mimic their new companion's actions. The pastry was still hot, and taking a bite, he was surprised to find chunks of meat and gravy inside. It dripped down the side of the flaking pastry, but thankfully the cloth kept it from scalding his fingers.

"So Perfugians, right?" the woman asked as they ate. "We don't get many of your kind here. Must be quite the story."

Lukys glanced at the woman, thinking it must be the same with her. These were Calafe—this had been their city, before the Tangata had come. He wanted to ask her what they thought about this new life, their new masters. But that would have given him away.

"You're dammed right about that," Dale said, interrupting Lukys's thoughts as he appeared alongside them.

He'd gotten a pie of his own from another of the Calafe, and sitting beside Lukys, he started to tell the tale of how they'd found themselves captives of the Tangata. Travis interrupted now and then with his own witty remarks, but Lukys found himself tuning out their words.

Their expedition with the Archivist seemed like another life now, a different reality. Had he met Sophia back then, he would have run her through with his spear. Now, though…

Lukys started as a single note of music rang through the courtyard. Swinging around, he saw that one of the newcomers had taken out a lute. Eyes fixed on the instrument, the woman paid the rest of the courtyard no attention, only strummed the instrument again, starting into a song—soft at first, but quickly building in volume. Each strum of the strings reverberated from the wooden walls of the courtyard.

A harmonica soon joined her, then a violin, as others took instruments from their baskets and began to play. The Perfugians remained at their benches, a look of wonder in their eyes as voices rose to greet the night. It was an old song, beginning in the darkness of The Fall, when death had stalked the land and even the Tangata had hidden far beneath the earth.

Then the pace increased. Hope appeared in the tone of the

singers, as light returned to the world. Swept away by the music, Lukys sat with his eyes closed, imagining those ancient days when the only worries of mankind had been their own follies. The early tribes had warred upon one another, until finally alliances had been formed. Kingdoms had risen from the ashes, binding the people together and restoring civilisation. But even then, the wars had continued, as each kingdom strove for supremacy.

Only the threat of the Tangata had finally united them.

What was left of that alliance now? Calafe had fallen and Gemaho had retreated, seeking refuge behind the mountains. Even Perfugia shirked its responsibilities, sending only their rejects, their unwanted to fight against the Tangata. Flumeer alone fought on.

Lukys opened his eyes as he sensed movement nearby. A female Tangata now stood beside Travis—Isabella. Her grey eyes shone in the lanternlight as she ran a hand through his friend's long hair. Lukys noticed then that the others had returned as well. He found himself looking around for Sophia.

Lukys.

Lukys started as a voice spoke into his mind. He looked back at Isabella, finding her eyes on him.

Yes? he asked tentatively.

She glanced at Travis. *Could you tell him I would like to dance?*

Oh! Lukys lifted his eyebrows, surprised by the request. He hadn't realised the creatures even knew what dancing was. Smiling, he shifted his gaze to Travis. *She wants to dance.*

Travis grinned and standing, he offered a hand to Isabella. "Hey, would you like to dance?"

Isabella was still watching Lukys, a frown creasing her forehead, but after a moment she smiled. The two moved into the open space in the middle of the courtyard. Lukys watched as Travis drew his partner close.

They began to dance, cautiously at first, moving slowly in time with the music. The bulky recruit appeared clumsy beside the Tangata's fluid grace, yet the smile Isabella wore seemed genuine. The music washed over the two, carrying them away across the cobbles.

Lukys found himself wondering where the Tangata had learned such things. Legends claimed they'd been little more than animals when they'd first emerged from beneath the earth. Had those too been lies? Or had their species evolved through the centuries?

"I wonder where Travis got that idea," Dale commented.

Frowning, Lukys turned to his companion, but at that moment the man's partner appeared. He rose without prompting and the two followed Travis and Isabella out into the middle of the courtyard. The couple danced freely now, in tune with one another's bodies, sliding through the steps with a refinement the recruits had never managed with Romaine's drills.

One by one, others rose to join the dancers, bringing the courtyard to life. The Calafe woman that had given them the pies rose to join one of the guitarists, leaving Lukys alone on his bench. Sitting there, he could almost begin to see the magic of the place, the peace his friends had found with these strange creatures. Some struggled more than others, moving through the steps with difficulty, but their Tangatan partners didn't seem to mind; indeed, they wore patient smiles on their faces.

Lukys shook his head as he watched the dancers. Then he frowned, his thoughts drawn back to what Dale had said. Why had the man been confused about Travis's actions? Lukys had told his friend that Isabella wanted to dance…hadn't he?

They seem happy.

Lukys looked around as Sophia's voice interrupted his thoughts, finding the Tangata standing beside him. For once, her arrival did not startle him. It seemed right that she was here, and at first he did not reply, only sat looking at her.

Sophia's eyes were dark in the starlight, her hair cascading down around her shoulders, sharp cheekbones adding an elegance to her face that Lukys had rarely seen amongst humans. She had changed into a satin dress, the fabric of purest black, clinging to her athletic frame, highlighting her slim waist, and…other things.

Suddenly Lukys's throat was dry. Heart pounding, he felt as though he were seeing Sophia for the first time. He had treated her poorly these past days, ignoring her for the most part, staying away. Now though…

Rising, Lukys offered his hand. *Would you like to dance?*

Sophia's eyes grew wide and to his surprise, she dropped her gaze. *You don't have to do that.*

I want to.

He took her hand before she could argue further. She didn't resist as he drew her towards the other dancers, though he sensed her trepidation.

Are you sure? she asked as the music picked up pace, sending the dancers spiralling around them.

Lukys nodded, and the hint of a smile touched her lips. Silently, she stepped closer and Lukys placed his hand on her hip, so that their bodies were just inches apart. A spark shot through his body, a thrilling, surging sensation that set his every nerve alight.

I'm dancing with a Tangata.

Sophia's smile broadened and he realised she'd heard him. Silently she placed a hand on his chest. He shivered at the touch. They began moving to the music. Lukys was no dancer, but he found the steps came more easily to him now than during his days at the academy, and he realised this wasn't much different from the fighting patterns Romaine had taught him atop the walls of Fogmore. His feet, accustomed to maintaining his balance now, moved naturally through the steps.

With their minds in tune, he found Sophia moving almost before he did, matching him stride for stride. Together they spun through the courtyard, bodies pressed close, breaths mingling, the rest of the couples forgotten, until Lukys felt it was just the two of them, alone in the courtyard. For just a moment, he allowed himself to be carried away by the music, drawn in by the shimmer in Sophia's eyes, the magic of the moonlight shining down from overhead.

His mind pounded with a distant beat, matching the pulse of the music. Belatedly, he realised it was the voices of the other Tangata, the racing of their minds, the murmurs of their silent voices to the music of the Calafe.

How can I hear you all? Lukys asked, looking at Sophia.

Her eyes were only an inch from his, her lips so close he could feel the warmth of her breath on his cheek.

I told you, her reply came hesitantly, *or perhaps…perhaps humanity is evolving?*

Perhaps…

Concern showed in Sophia's eyes as she watched him. It pained Lukys to see it, and without thinking he pressed his lips to hers. She flinched in his arms, but a moment later he felt her relax, and then she was kissing him back, her lips parting, the warmth of her mouth mingling with his.

Lukys found himself grinning as he drew back and saw the shock on Sophia's face.

That was…unexpected, she murmured.

He didn't reply, only held her in his arms, turning her through the steps of the waltz. She was right—he'd surprised even himself. But maybe he was done ignoring his own logic, done fighting the inevitable. The music was fading now, and he realised belatedly that they were the last couple in the courtyard. The others had vanished into their apartments, to their rooms…

Lukys's heart started to race as he looked into Sophia's eyes. His hand tightened around hers as he found himself imagining what it would be like to share that grand bed with this strange woman, to look into those strange eyes as they…

The thought was interrupted as a distant thumping sounded in his mind. It began like the distant whispers of the Tangata, but quickly rose in pitch, until it seemed it would force all other thoughts from his mind. The smile fell from Sophia's lips, and he knew she was hearing the chanting too. Slowly the words took shape.

Death, death, death.

The hairs on his neck tingled as though a cold breeze had blown through the courtyard. The chant was already growing to a crescendo, the words practically shouted now, like the banging of drums, a call to war. And he knew then that he'd heard this same chant before, deep in the tunnels under the earth, in the Birthing Grounds of the Tangata.

The Old Ones.

His blood ran cold as he looked at Sophia. "They're here."

❧ 26 ❧

THE FALLEN

Pain engulfed Romaine as he reached out with his one hand and gripped the rock.

One, two, three.

Groaning, he heaved himself halfway onto the ledge, then using his injured arm to lodge himself there, then shifted his hand so he could push himself up the rest of the way. His feet found fresh purchase and gasping, he looked up, seeking his next handhold.

The brightening sky still seemed so far away. The crack that marked the mouth of the ravine might as well have been a hundred miles off. He would never make it, certainly not before Yasin…

One step at a time.

Determined, Romaine reached out again, hauling himself up, planting himself in place with his elbow, then pushing up the rest of the way. He was lucky—the ravine was not as steep as it had looked from above. The ground sloped at maybe a sixty degree angle. With his body pressed to the stone, he had just enough purchase to hold himself in place. If it had been a sheer cliff, he'd never have climbed out.

But then, the fall probably would have killed him, and he wouldn't have been around to worry about whether he could escape. He wouldn't still feel the pain of his loss, of seeing yet another friend murdered, wouldn't have felt the agony of his own failures. Despair hung around his shoulders like an anchor, threatening to drag him back into the depths, whispering for him to let go, to surrender.

Just a little farther.

He would not give up. He would not let Cara down. She was all he had left.

Hours before, Romaine had awoken in darkness, surprised to find himself alive, though his body ached as though he'd taken a dozen beatings. Thankfully his sword had been lying nearby, and while the shield Amina had gifted him was dented, its strappings had survived the fall. If he made it out of this hole, Romaine would need both. Yasin would not go quietly.

He'll kill you anyway.

Thrusting aside thoughts of defeat, Romaine continued, climbing up and up, until finally he found himself rolling over the lip of the ravine, free. Sunlight touched his face, searing his eyes, waking him from his despair. Romaine blinked, then pushed himself up. A familiar collection of boulders dotted the site around him.

Lorene still lay where he had fallen. A groan tearing from his lips, Romaine crawled to his friend. Blood stained the dirt beneath him, but otherwise Lorene could have been sleeping. There was a peacefulness to his face, if one ignored the bolt still embedded in his chest.

Romaine scrunched his eyes closed, struggling to contain his grief. Only one thing kept him from lying down beside his friend and waiting for death to find him.

Cara.

He came to his feet. His legs felt weak, unsteady, but at least he hadn't broken anything in the fall. His eyes were drawn to the sky and he saw that the sun was still low on the distant horizon. Erika and the others would just be preparing to depart. If Yasin had not ordered an attack in the night, there might yet be hope to warn them

Fist clenched, Romaine started towards the campsite, but as he cleared the ring of boulders, a distant sound carried to his ears. He hesitated, heart hammering in his chest. It sounded almost like…

Romaine started to run. The clashing of steel and the screams of men grew louder as he cleared the last of the boulders and started down the slope. The valley twisted away from him, hiding the Gemaho campsite from view, but they couldn't be far. Pushing beyond his pain, Romaine increased his pace.

Ahead, the basin twisted and at last he spotted movement, still a few hundred yards away. Men swarmed around across the valley floor, where flashes of yellow revealed the Gemaho soldiers, desperately trying to defend themselves.

Gathering his strength, Romaine drew his sword. Pain swamped him. He knew he could not change the outcome of the battle. Yet still he pushed on, past the doubt, past the agony. In that moment, it didn't matter if he succeeded, only that he tried, just as Cara had tried to save their friends, back on the shores of the Illmoor.

Stones crunched beneath his boots but none of Yasin's men noticed his approach above the roar of battle. He saw one of the defenders go down, then another, and pressed on. The Gemaho seemed to be gathered around a cluster of boulders, but there was no sign of Cara, or even Erika. Had something happened to them?

There was no turning back now. The remaining Gemaho were outnumbered, but where Yasin's men attacked with cold fury, they met them with a cool proficiency. Even so, the thugs that had accompanied Romaine on the journey from Flumeer were taking a heavy toll. The Gemaho would not last much longer.

Then Romaine noticed something strange. As one of the Flumeeren warriors attacked, he staggered as though struck by something invisible. Before he could recover, a Gemaho sword took him in the throat. Narrowing his eyes, Romaine saw it happen again to another soldier. Realisation followed and he searched the thrashing bodies for a glimpse of Erika. There was still no sign of her amongst the defenders, but he was sure it had to be her magic. It gave him a flash of hope, though he couldn't understand how she had tricked the queen. Had Nguyen given her an imitation gauntlet?

Romaine was growing close now, and as the bodies of Yasin's fighters piled up, he finally caught a glimpse of the man himself. Yasin stood at the rear of his soldiers, crossbow in hand. As Romaine watched, he calmly fired over the heads of his men into the Gemaho ranks, taking a man in the shoulder. Drawing another bolt from the quiver at his side, he began to reload.

Rage touched Romaine and for a moment he longed to throw

himself at the cursed warrior. But what would that achieve? He had already failed to defeat Yasin once. In his injured state, he wouldn't stand a chance now. No, he had to find Cara, to protect her. She was all that mattered.

Where would she be? He had expected to see her somewhere below, but there was no sign of the winged Goddess. Could it be that she'd never been with the group in the first place? Romaine's stride faltered and he almost crumpled at the thought. But no, Yasin's spy had talked about the Goddess. So where was she?

Ahead, one of the Flumeerens glanced back and finally saw Romaine approaching. His eyes widened in shock and gritting his teeth, Romaine put on a burst of speed. Caught between the Gemaho soldiers and Romaine, the man hesitated. It was enough, and dropping his shoulder, Romaine slammed into the man's chest, hurling him back into his fellows.

The Flumeerens staggered away from their comrade while on the hillside above Yasin himself cried out in rage. Ignoring them all, Romaine waved his sword and leapt past the Flumeerens, making for the Gemaho line. The yellow garbed soldiers drew together, weapons raised, but before they could strike a voice called out from somewhere behind them.

"Don't!"

Erika appeared—not from the boulders but seemingly thin air. Romaine started, so shocked by her materialisation he almost forgot about the armed men around him. But instinct carried him forward and as the Gemaho responded to the Archivist's orders and parted, he joined them in the line. Spinning, he raised sword and shield, prepared for the inevitable charge.

Steel shrieked on steel as a crossbow bolt struck his shield and embedded there. Thankfully, its razor tip missed the flesh of his arm. Romaine's eyes were drawn to the hillside where Yasin still stood, calmly reloading the weapon. Gritting his teeth, Romaine prayed for the ability to strike the man down, but already the Flumeerens he'd scattered were forming up again.

The Gemaho gathered to either side of Romaine, more than one flicking him bewildered glances, but he ignored them, his attention fixed on the Flumeeren, on Yasin above. Their eyes met and the man sneered, but then the Flumeer were upon him and Romaine had time only for the battle.

A shudder jarred his arm as his shield deflected a sword. Pain tore at his chest and Romaine's knees buckled. Silently he reached within, drawing on his last reserve of strength, and surged forward, short sword stabbing low. Trapped between his fellow Flumeerens, his foe had no room to manoeuvre and Romaine's blow took him in the stomach. Blood burst from the wound as Romaine tore back his blade and retreated to his position amongst the Gemaho.

Another of Yasin's men stepped in to fill the gap and the battle raged on. Despite his early success, Romaine found the others who came against him far more wily, and slowed by his wounds, he struggled to fend them off. Luckily, blows that would have killed him were diverted as attackers stumbled—due to Erika's magic no doubt, though the woman had vanished again.

Yet even with the Archivist's magic, the Gemaho were being pressed back, their numbers whittled down by the relentless assault of Yasin's warriors. Caught off-guard, the ground they defended offered no advantages, and too many had fallen in the first minutes. And Yasin's arrows continued to do their damage, though he hadn't managed to strike at Romaine again.

"Romaine!" Erika's voice rose above the clash of weapons, drawing Romaine's attention. "We need you."

Unable to turn his back from the enemy, Romaine stepped back from the frontline, allowing the Gemaho to close ranks around him. Only then did he glance back, though he kept an eye out for more of Yasin's arrows. There was no sign of the Archivist though, and puffing, he was about to return to the fight when something grasped him by the arm.

"Quickly!"

Romaine flinched as Erika's voice spoke from empty air. The pressure on his arm tugged him towards the boulders, and still shocked by whatever new magic she was wielding, he allowed himself to be drawn away.

There was a flash of light, and then suddenly the Archivist was standing before him. Despite their inherent danger, the rage Romaine had been nurturing over the past weeks boiled to the surface. This was the woman who had betrayed him who had kidnapped Cara and sold her loyalty to a foreign nation. His fist tightened around the hilt of his sword and he clenched his jaw, fighting the urge to drive the blade through her chest.

"Cara needs you," the Archivist hissed.

The words cut through Romaine's anger like a knife. He lowered his sword, heart racing. Erika's lips were pursed and there was fear in her eyes. Blood was beginning to seep through a bandage wrapped around her upper arm, though she didn't seem to notice. Light glowed from the gauntlet she wore on her arm, and Romaine frowned, still wondering how she had fooled the queen. But there was no time for questions now. Only one thing mattered.

"Where is she?" he growled.

Erika glanced at him, and she hesitated as their eyes met. Romaine wondered if it was guilt he saw in her eyes, but she quickly broke away, nodding towards the cluster of boulders the soldiers were protecting.

"In there," she said.

Movement came from the shadows and a second woman stepped out from behind a boulder. She held a globe of brilliant white in one hand, though there was no source of fire. Magic, like Erika's, he presumed. For the first time, he looked around, noticing the dome that enclosed the area before the boulders. Beyond, the soldiers still fought, but they looked indistinct now, as though viewed through a film. Putting the connections together in his mind, he faced the newcomer.

"How are you doing that?" he asked.

The woman only raised an eyebrow. "Is that really what you want to talk about right now?"

Romaine shook his head, and stepping past him, Erika gestured into the boulders. "Come on, Maisie is hiding us, but she won't last much longer." She hesitated, looking over her shoulder. "And neither will they."

With that Erika slipped into the shadows. Casting a final glance at the Gemaho soldiers himself, Romaine followed. He felt a pang of guilt at abandoning them, but there was nothing he could do to save them.

The Archivist didn't ask how he'd come to be there. She had probably guessed he'd come with the Flumeerens. Nor did Romaine hurl accusations. There seemed little point when they might all be just minutes from death.

They didn't have to go far before Erika came to a stop again. Romaine froze as he saw the figure lying propped against a nearby boulder. Cara's auburn wings lay limp in the dust and her copper hair stood out in stark relief against her pallid skin. With each inhalation, her eyelids fluttered. She appeared to be unconscious, but as he took a step towards her, she spoke:

"Romaine..." Her voice was like sandpaper, and his name was followed by a soft groan, lines wrinkling her forehead. "I thought...I smelt you."

A sob tore from Romaine and in a second he was at her side, drawing her into a hug. "I thought I'd lost you," he murmured.

Pained laughter rasped from the Goddess. "How...?"

"We'll talk about it later, lass," Romaine murmured.

He'd never seen her like this, not even when he'd found her injured and alone in Calafe, when the pain of her broken bones had caused her to pass out. Swallowing, he looked at Erika.

"What happened to her?"

Erika shook her head. "She was poisoned."

❧ 27 ❧

THE TANGATA

New Nihelm.

For some reason, Adonis was surprised to find himself looking down upon the city. When he'd left, a part of him had been convinced he would never return, that the Old Ones would slay him when they woke. Looking at Maya standing beside him, he could hardly remember why he'd feared such a thing.

Wearing the clothing of Adonis's fallen sister, Maya's slender figure was covered now, though he had come to know it in intimate detail this last week. She had invited him to lie with her their first night, pinning him to the stone. She seemed to delight in his weakness, in her power over his body…his mind.

He could feel her touch on his consciousness now, like the constant beating of a drum, though he could never quite make out the words she whispered. It no longer seemed important.

New Nihelm lay spread out beneath them, its lights glittering on the surrounding waters, waiting. It had taken them just a week to return. They had moved faster without his fallen brethren, and Adonis had found himself the slower of the pair. It did not bother him. He was only thankful she had chosen him.

Maya's long blonde hair swirled in the breeze as she turned to look on him, dark grey eyes aglow by the rising moon. *Your city reeks of humanity, Adonis.*

Adonis bowed his head. *Yes,* he replied deferentially, *we have spoken of the Tangata's weakness. We need them.*

No longer, Maya whispered, running a hand across his cheek. *Come, it is time your Matriarch and I spoke.*

Her gaze returned to the city and despite himself, Adonis shivered. Maya was everything the Matriarch had hoped for—powerful, intelligent, *sane.* An opportunity to sever themselves from the humans altogether.

Silently, he followed her down the hillside. The southern bridge beckoned and Maya strode across without hesitation, unchallenged. Only as they approached the island did two shadows appear to bar the way.

Who goes there?

The words seemed mere whispers in Adonis's mind after so many days spent with Maya. The Old One advanced on them, her stride unchecked by their warning, and Adonis hurried to catch her before blood was spilt.

Adonis, he called. He didn't recognise the guards, but they would know him. There weren't many of the third generation left now. *We have returned from the south.*

Confusion shone on the guards' faces as Maya finally drew to a stop before them. Their eyes flickered from her to Adonis.

Where are the others?

Adonis shook his head. *They were lost.*

How—

You guard these shores, child? Maya's voice interrupted, so strong each of the guards leapt back half a foot.

A long silence followed as they stood staring at the Old One. Understanding seemed to dawn in their eyes and they straightened, bowing their heads in respect.

Yes…Old One, the one who had been speaking replied.

Good, Maya rasped. Her gaze lifted to stare down the broad avenue that stretched across the island. *And there are others…to the north?* When the two nodded, she stepped closer, placing a hand on the first's chest. *Better. Go to your brethren in the north. Tell them that none may leave the city this night. Then return to your post.*

I… the Tangata's eyes flickered in Adonis's direction. He gave a slight nod, and the Tangata repeated the gesture to the Old One.

Releasing him, Maya stepped back. The guard seemed to take a moment to gather his composure, then he spun and started down the avenue, running with the long, bounding stride of the Tangata. Maya turned her gaze upon the second of the guards.

You know your duty, child? she whispered.

The Tangata nodded eagerly. Maya left him as he was and with Adonis they started down the avenue after the first of the guards, though they soon turned onto lesser streets. They made their way quickly through the moonlit avenues, over bridges and between the blossoming trees, making for the grand basilica the humans had raised to honour their so-called Gods.

The thought sparked an image in Adonis's mind and he saw again the Anahera as it soared towards him, wings flared, teeth bared. With the memory came anger. The Anahera could have aided the Tangata, could have stood alongside them against the disease that was humanity. Instead, they had sided with the enemy.

He shook his head. The Anahera would pay dearly for their betrayal, but that revenge would have to wait. The creatures were too powerful—first the Tangata must regain their strength.

The sound of voices came from some of the buildings they passed, and at these Maya would pause, eyes shimmering in the lanternlight. Adonis could sense her anger, that her descendants had fallen so low. But she never made a move towards the revellers, and finally they neared to the basilica.

Crossing the open plaza, they found the great doors of the temple barred. Guards of the fourth generation stood to either side, eyeing their approach, though they bowed their heads in respect when they recognised Adonis.

We must see the Matriarch, he called to them. *Our greatest hope has been realised.*

Grey eyes turned to inspect Maya. She said nothing beneath their appraisal but met their gaze with a soft smile. To Adonis's inner ears, it seemed the pounding in his skull increased in notch. A flicker crossed the guards' faces.

Old One, they whispered, any hints of defiance evaporating beneath her piercing stare.

The Matriarch, Maya's voice all but thundered in the silent square.

The guards leapt to obey, thrusting open the great doors to admit them. Maya strode through, once again leaving Adonis scrambling to keep up. The familiar darkness greeted him within, though it made little difference to his vision. An aged figure moved upon the dais as the Old One strode across the chamber.

Adonis, my child, what have you brought me? The Matriarch rasped into his mind as they came to a stop before the pool that surrounded the upper dais. He was surprised at its softness—always before her voice had rung with power. Now it seemed but a whisper beside the thundering of Maya's words.

He fell to his knees all the same. *Matriarch,* he called, *I bring you Maya, of the Old Ones.*

Whispers spread through Adonis's mind as movement flickered at the edges of the chamber. Beside him, Maya said nothing, though her eyes flickered towards the unseen guards.

So it's true. Clothing rustled as the Matriarch leapt from the dais to land before them. She inclined her head to Maya. *Welcome to New Nihelm, Old One. You have no idea my joy at your emergence.*

Maya leaned her head to the side, regarding the Matriarch with those deep, dark eyes. *And how* did *you find my prison?*

The Matriarch smiled. *A human who came to us. He bore a map of the Birthing Grounds from which the Tangata sprung. Yours was the last.*

Silence answered the Matriarch's words as Maya paced. *And why did you seek me?*

Our people are dying, unable to produce offspring without a human partner, the Matriarch responded. *And so our powers fade with each generation. But if we were to merge our line with yours, we could begin to rebuild, to create a new generation of Tangata.*

Maya did not immediately reply to the Matriarch's words. Her gaze fell upon Adonis, still knelt upon the floor beside them. A frown touched her face.

Why does he kneel? she murmured, though even at a whisper her words had the strength to make the lesser generations flinch.

The lines on the Matriarch's face deepened as she frowned. *Kneel?* She glanced at Adonis, then gestured for him to rise. *It is a gesture of respect, Old One.*

I see. There was a long pause as she regarded the Matriarch. *Then...kneel.*

Shock registered on the Matriarch's face and even Adonis lifted his head in surprise.

I am the Matriarch. The response was slow in coming. *This is my city, the Tangata my people. I bow to no one.*

Cold grey eyes watched her for a long moment, then Maya smiled. *Of course.*

Turning away, she paced to the edge of the chamber where the guards stood watching. She started her way around the circumference of the chamber, eyes on the dark alcoves in which the Tangata hid. Adonis and the Matriarch watched as she disappeared behind the dais.

Such grandeur, Maya's words carried to their minds. *All of it, crafted by the strength of your Tangata?*

She reappeared, rounding the chamber, drawing the eyes of the guards. Doubt showed in the Matriarch's face as she watched the Old One's return.

Crafted by humanity, she admitted hesitantly as Maya returned to stand before her. *Taken from them as spoils of war. It will be the foundation on which we build our own civilisation.*

*Civilisation…*Maya seemed to roll the word in her mind as she appraised the Matriarch. *And…what of the humans who live amongst you?*

To Adonis, the Matriarch seemed to shrink before Maya's presence. *The assigned are carefully controlled.*

A frown touched Adonis's forehead and he stared at the leader that had guided the Tangata for so many decades. Her power, her cunning and strength of resolve had held his people together when the threat of humanity might otherwise have broken them. They owed her for that, honoured her for it, and yet…

…Adonis saw none of that strength now. Instead, a creature withered by age stood in place of the Matriarch, her will crushed by the endless warring, the relentless threat of the enemy. Where before there had been awe, now Adonis felt only disdain.

Controlled? Maya smiled and looked around the hall. To Adonis, it seemed her eyes fell upon every one of the guards. *Their stench is everywhere, even in this place that you claim as your seat of power.* Her eyes returned to the Matriarch. *I ask you, do you seek to defeat your enemy…or* become *them?*

A snarl crossed the Matriarch's lips and she stepped in close to

Maya. Her eyes burned as they faced one another, and for a moment the strength of the Matriarch's voice matched that of the Old One.

Everything I have ever done was for the survival of my people!

Maya did not react to the words, though a flicker of movement went around the chamber as the Tangatan guards flinched at the force of her voice.

Survival? Adonis found himself replying, his voice taking on a bitter tone. *Is that what you call this? Living amongst the hovels of our enemy, forced into bondship with them, to breed with them?*

There was no choice! the Matriarch spat back. She turned her strength on him now, but bolstered by the rhythmic pounding of Maya in his mind, Adonis endured. Faced by his defiance, she seemed to wither and her voice took on a desperate tone. *Please, Adonis, my child, you were ever my champion.*

Adonis shuddered as he felt two minds pressing upon his consciousness. But in the end there was no contest. He stepped up to Maya's side.

He is your champion no longer, Maya replied.

The Matriarch retreated a step, her pale eyes taking on a panicked look. She swung around, searching the shadows, her movements betraying her desperation.

My children, guard yourselves! she cried to the guards hidden in the wings. *Before—*

One by one, the guards emerged from the shadows. Their eyes were focused not on the Matriarch, but Maya. Advancing until they stood in a circle around the three of them, the Tangata fell to their knees.

For a long moment the Matriarch stared at them, shoulders slumped, one hand extended as though to lift them back to their feet. Then slowly she faced Maya, and for the first time, fear registered in her eyes. Adonis watched on, impassive, as Maya laid a hand on the Matriarch's shoulder.

You have allowed humanity to claim this world, the Old One said softly, almost apologetically. *Allowed them to infect our own people, to bring the Tangata to the brink of extinction.*

A tremor shook the Matriarch and her pure white eyes fixed on

Maya's face. A single tear slid down the lines of her cheek, but she did not retreat from the Old One's gaze.

It is you who will lead my children to extinction, Old One, she replied, her voice little more than a croak now.

A heavy silence hung over the chamber; and then Maya spoke: "Your time has come to an end, Matriarch."

With a sharp, jerking movement, she snapped the Matriarch's neck. The *crack* of breaking bones sounded like a klaxon in the empty basilica, so loud that even Adonis flinched. He watched as the light faded from her eyes, and felt an inexplicable thrill of terror. This was the leader who his people had followed for decades, who had led them to victory after victory against humanity. Without thinking, he took a step towards her.

But already she was falling, crumpling to the ground, lying still against the stones. Her pale eyes stared up at him and for a second, guilt clamped around his heart, stilling his breath.

Then he turned and found Maya watching him, and the feeling receded, replaced by the glory of victory. Maya smiled, then turned to his brother and sister Tangata.

Rise, my children. Her words lifted them back to their feet, reborn beneath the power of the Old Ones. *No longer will you go quietly to your destruction. Today, a new age dawns for the Tangata.*

What do you wish of us, Old One? the guards called back. There was desperation in their eyes. They were of the fourth generation, eager to please, subservient to one so far above them.

A smile crept across Maya's lips as she looked towards the doors, her grey eyes seeming to take in the city beyond.

Bring me the humans, she commanded. *It is time for a cleansing.*

28

THE SOLDIER

Bring me the humans, the Old One's mental voice carried from across the plaza. *It is time for a cleansing.*

Lukys's heart thundered in his ears as he listened to the words. At his urging, he and Sophia had tracked the pounding of the Old One's thoughts across the city. Even hidden in the shadows on the other side of the plaza from the basilica, they had easily heard her from within—though the others' voices had been fainter.

Now they stood beside the river and watched as silhouettes raced past—the Matriarch's guards, off to do their new master's bidding. Thankfully they did not look left or right as they disappeared into the streets of New Nihelm. Silence returned to the night. It would not last. Whatever safety he and his friends had found here, it was at an end.

His whole body trembling, he looked at Sophia. *What are we going to do?*

Run! she hissed.

There was fear in Sophia's eyes, bordering on panic. Lukys could hardly blame her. He had felt the Matriarch's power, her strength. And the Old One had slaughtered her, had claimed her guards, even Adonis, as her champions. The thought gave him pause and he wondered at the creature's power. But there was no time to linger.

I can't leave the others, Lukys replied, taking her hand in his. *Please, you have to help us, Sophia.*

Sophia's grey eyes were large in the moonlight, but after a moment, she nodded. In silence they turned and raced away, desperate to reach the compound before the Tangata did. As they ran, Lukys scanned the way ahead, fearful they would encounter the Matriarch's guards—but the streets remained dark, empty.

After several blocks, though, he began to hear sounds behind them. Doors slammed and masses of boots struck pavements as the city woke. A distant buzz touched his mind and he felt the tingle of annoyance broadcasted by the collective minds of the Tangata. The odd voice carried through the night as well. Lukys did not look back, though in his mind he pictured Tangata and their human partners forced from their houses, corralled into the streets.

Shame touched Lukys as he contemplated the fate of his fellow humans. But there was nothing he could do for them. It was already too late. He couldn't fight the Old One; he couldn't even fight the Tangata—at least not unarmed.

Sophia! he cried, his stride slowing. *We need weapons.*

His partner glanced over her shoulder, then drew to a stop. Concern showed on her face.

Lukys…

Please, Sophia, he insisted. *We don't stand a chance without them.*

Still Sophia hesitated. He could sense her doubt. What he asked was a betrayal of her people, to arm the very enemies they had waged war against for a decade. And yet…he had seen the Tangata's affection for their human partners. Looking at Sophia…Lukys thought he could almost understand his friends' decision, almost accept.

"We're not your enemies, Sophia," he whispered. He looked back then, eyes lifting to the spire of the basilica. "That thing…that thing is the enemy of all of us."

He looked back at Sophia, wanting to say more, but the words didn't come. Still, he was surprised to find a smile on her lips. She nodded.

This way. There's an old storage building close by, many of the weapons found in the city after its fall were placed there.

Weaving through unfamiliar streets, it took them only minutes to reach their new destination. Unlike most buildings in New Nihelm, this one was of stone, though thankfully the door was still wood. It gave way beneath a single blow from Sophia, unleashing a wave of dust and forcing Lukys to stifle a sneeze.

Pulling his shirt over his face, he moved with Sophia into the darkness. It took several long minutes before he found what he wanted—a bundle of spears tied together by twine. He took one from the pile and immediately his heart began to calm. It felt good to hold a weapon again, to feel like his fate was in his own hands again.

Unfortunately, there was no armour—and time was quickly evaporating. If the Tangatan guards arrived at the compound before they did, this would all be for nothing. He reached for the bundle, but Sophia was faster. Hefting the spears onto her shoulder as though they weighed no more than a sack of feathers, she nodded for the door.

Outside, he let her take the lead again, still unsure of himself in the dark streets of New Nihelm. The moon had shifted overhead, the night stretching on, and he swallowed. Even if they escaped the city, the Tangata would come for them. What then? They could not outrun these creatures.

Despair touched him, but he forced it down. One step at a time. First, he needed to convince his companions that they must flee. After the comfortable weeks they'd spent in New Nihelm, even that task could prove difficult, even with Sophia's support.

They found the doors to the compound standing open, though where they'd left the courtyard empty, now dozens of tired faces stood around the tables. It was clear from their faces that they'd heard the sounds of alarm from elsewhere in the city.

"Lukys?" Frowning, Travis stepped up to greet him. "Where have you been?" The recruit's eyes were immediately drawn to the spear in Lukys's hands. "Where did you get *that?*"

Sister, several of the Tangata present spoke at the same time, moving toward Sophia. *Why is your human armed?*

Lukys and Sophia shared a glance. "The Matriarch is dead," Lukys said to them all. Whispers assailed his mind as the Tangata cried out, demanding answers, but he pressed them down and continued: "She was slain by an Old One. She calls herself Maya.

Adonis is with her. The creature intends to rule over the Tangata." His eyes slid to Travis and the others. "And cleanse the humans from amongst them."

Silence fell suddenly over the group and Lukys nodded, gesturing to Sophia. "Quickly, take a spear and gather supplies for the road. We need to be gone before the creature's followers reach us…" He trailed off as he saw the group was no longer watching him.

Their eyes were on the gate to the compound. His stomach twisted as a voice whispered into his mind.

My dear human, Adonis said softly. *I hope you aren't trying to leave us. Maya was so looking forward to meeting you. There is so much you could tell us of our enemies.*

Heart hammering in his chest, Lukys turned to face the Tangata. Adonis stood in the entrance to the compound, arms clasped behind his back. His eyes narrowed as he stepped into the courtyard, taking in the gathered recruits and their Tangatan partners, before settling on Lukys and Sophia. A tightness crossed Adonis's face as he saw the spear in Lukys's hands.

Sister, he murmured, turning to Sophia. *Have you betrayed us?*

Sophia wilted beneath that terrible gaze. *I—*

Adonis surged forward before she could finish speaking, his hand flashing out, catching her by the throat. A cry sounded in Lukys's mind and he raised his spear, but a backhanded blow from Adonis sent him staggering backwards. A silence settled over the courtyard as the others shrank back from the Tangata's rage.

Teeth bared, Adonis lifted Sophia into the air. *You would betray your own kind for these…these swine?*

Terror swept over Lukys as he watched his partner struggling to break Adonis's grip, but she was as helpless in his grasp as any human would be. Her mouth opened and closed, gasping for breath, but no sound came out. With a sneer of contempt, Adonis tossed her aside, sending her crashing into one of the tables. The heavy wood cracked beneath the impact and she slumped amongst the ruins, unmoving.

"*No!*" Lukys screamed.

Smiling, Adonis faced him. Their eyes met and Lukys froze. Death reflected from those icy depths, its promise pounding against his mind, assaulting his consciousness. A gasp escaped his throat but words, thought, abandoned him. Tears burned in his eyes as he sank to his knees, but still he could not look away, not even to seek out where Sophia had fallen. Whispers of movement came from around the courtyard as the others followed, Tangata and human alike.

Brothers, sisters, Adonis called, arms spread as he turned those terrible eyes on the Tangata. *The Old Ones have returned. They have cast down our tyrannous Matriarch. No longer will we bow to humanity, allowing them to live among us as equals.*

Out from under his direct gaze, Lukys felt as though he could breathe again. His heart pounded in his ears as he watched the Tangatan leader. Anger touched him, but it was like a spark amongst damp tinder, unable to catch. How could he go up against this creature if even Sophia could not match him? He was like a fly, trapped in the spider's web. Nowhere to hide, nowhere to run; he could only wait for death to finally find him…

His gaze travelled to the other Tangata. They bowed their heads to Adonis's words. The spark in his core flickered, burning brighter. How could they kneel there and accept the death of their leader so easily? How could they sit and do nothing when this creature would condemn their human partners to death? Had Lukys only imagined the fondness he'd seen in their eyes, the love?

Then he frowned as he noticed how Travis and Isabella held hands as they knelt. Tears shone on the Tangata's face. Looking past them, he saw the same grief in the eyes of others. He ground his teeth. Why did they not act? There were a dozen of them—surely Adonis could not defeat so many at once, whatever his generational advantages…

Lukys's frown deepened as the despair swelled once again. What did it matter if they fought? They were doomed regardless. They would never escape the city now, never make it to safety, make it home…

The thought trailed away as Lukys's gaze settled on his spear tip. In that moment, he was transported back to that desperate battle beside the Illmoor. He had been terrified then as well. There'd been no denying the death that awaited them, no escaping it. And yet he had stood strong and faced the Tangata with courage. He had not lost heart then.

So why would he now?

His head lifted as the pieces of the puzzle clicked into place. Movement came from the corner of his eyes. His heart throbbed as he saw Sophia on her knees. Blood streaked a trail from her lip and a bruise swelled on her forehead, but she was alive.

Hope.

Lukys clutched at the thought as he fixed his gaze on Adonis. Here was the reason the other Tangata did not act. Somehow, Adonis controlled them, controlled his despair. He had noticed Sophia now and his laughter whispered on the breeze.

Still alive then, sister?

You can't do this, she whispered, seemingly unable to regain her feet. *It's forbidden.*

Forbidden by your treacherous Matriarch. Adonis shook his head, sweeping a hand across those gathered in the courtyard. *But no longer. All will have a part to play in the coming conquest, but no longer will we constrain ourselves on behalf of the weak. A new age dawns for the Tangata, one ruled by the strong!*

Lukys's heart was pounding so hard against his ribs he feared it might explode. The fear returned as Adonis turned on him once more, but now he knew its source. Closing his eyes, he endured, clinging to that memory beside the Illmoor, to the feel of the spear in his hands, to the presence of his friends at his side, to the sight of Cara soaring across the swirling waters.

"Adonis," he found himself saying.

Silence fell across the courtyard and opening his eyes, he found the Tangata watching him. His breath caught in his throat and for a moment he could not think, could do nothing but stare into those deadly eyes.

Hope.

Lukys swallowed. "You said the Old One wants me?" he rasped. A frown twisted the Tangata's features. When he did not reply, Lukys continued: "I will…go freely," he choked out. "If you spare them."

Lukys, no! Sophia's voice shouted in his mind. Sobbing, she tried to stand, but could not seem to gather her feet.

Adonis laughed. *You think you have a choice, human?*

The cold eyes bored into Lukys and he gasped as his entire

body began to tremble. The spear slipped from his fingers, clattering to the cobbles. Desperately, he tried to stand, but wave upon wave of emotion broke upon him, of desolation, of anguish, cast at him by the creature he faced. His gaze fell to the bricks beneath his knees.

Hope.

Footsteps approached, soft in the darkness. *No, human, your weakness betrays you, betrays all your kind. Betrays even our lesser generation. No wonder so many of the fifth fell to your blade. No wonder they wilted before the Anahera. But no longer.*

Lukys gasped, hardly able to breathe, to think. All he could hear were the words, that pounding in his skull, the awful doom approaching on soft feet. He could not fight this thing, could not endure. He could only fall.

Hope.

With Maya, we will forge a new world. The Tangata will be restored in all their glory. None can prevent it, not humanity, not even the Anahera.

The footsteps stopped beside him and Lukys looked up. A silhouette towered overhead, blacking out the stars, the moon—though beyond he could see Sophia struggling, arm outstretched, a desperate grief in her eyes.

Hope.

Lukys met Adonis's steely gaze.

Are you ready to meet your doom, human?

His fingers closed around the wooden haft lying beside him.

"My name is Lukys," he hissed.

Adonis's eyes widened as the spear tip slammed into his chest. His hands came up, but Lukys did not relent, driving the blade deeper, screaming his rage, until the point burst from his enemy's back. A growl came from Adonis's throat and the terrible eyes fixed on Lukys, but skewered by the spear, they no longer seemed to hold any power.

A cry bubbling from his throat, Adonis stumbled back, tearing the weapon from Lukys's hands. Gasping, he clutched at the spear, fingers curling around the wooden haft. Another scream echoed through the courtyard as he began to pull.

Heart pounding in his chest, Lukys watched as the Tangata drew the bloody spear from his body and tossed it aside. Grey eyes fixed again on Lukys, but as Adonis took a step, his knees buckled and he crumpled face-first to the cobbles.

A groan slipped from Lukys's lips as he looked at the fallen Tangata. His own legs shook as he tried to take a step. A wave of exhaustion swept over him then, and suddenly he found himself slumped against the bricks. Whispers came from the others and a moment later a hand touched his shoulder.

Lukys.

He flinched away from the voice, looking up to find the bruised and battered Sophia crouching beside him. His insides twisted as he looked into her eyes. How could such honest eyes have lied so easily? All this time, she'd hidden the true secret of the Tangata, of the power they possessed. The power that Adonis had used so easily to subdue them.

She reached for him again, but he shrank away, and a frown creased her purpled forehead. "Lukys, what's wrong?"

Tears burned in his eyes as he looked at her, seeing her pain, and a lump lodged in his throat. He swallowed it down, forcing himself to speak the words.

"Stay away from me."

29

THE FUGITIVE

"There was a spy," Erika said.

"He was a pawn," Romaine replied. The Calafe was still crouched beside Cara. "The queen had his family abducted, forced him to leave markers for us to follow you. Where is he?"

Erika's heart twisted and she looked away, her eyes falling to the soft glow of the gauntlet. "Dead," she whispered. He'd passed before they could drag him into the shelter of the rocks, succumbing to whatever internal damage her magic had done.

Romaine cursed, but Maisie spoke before he could reprimand them. "He didn't know what kind of poison it was anyway."

"Didn't you hear me?" Romaine snapped. "He didn't want to be here."

"None of us *want* to be here, Calafe," Maisie replied coolly. "But we each made our choices."

Romaine fell silent at the Gemaho's words and Erika did not miss the grimace that touched the warrior's face. She glanced towards the sounds of fighting. The men that had attacked might not be wearing Flumeeren colours, but the archer who led them had been with Amina back at the Illmoor Fortress. The same man she'd found so familiar, though she still could not remember from where.

"Can't you stop them with your magic?" Romaine asked from the ground.

Erika shook herself from her stupor and scowled. "Oh yes, I

hadn't thought of that," she hissed. The anger left her as quickly as it had come. "I've done what I can, using Maisie's magic to hide me, but your *friend* with the crossbow figured us out." She lifted a hand to the bandage Maisie had wrapped around her arm. Thankfully, the arrow had only grazed her.

"Then what's the plan?" the warrior growled.

Erika and Maisie exchanged a glance, before looking back at the warrior. "The city of the Gods is close, we think," Erika whispered, gesturing at Cara. "If anyone can save her, surely it's her people."

Romaine was silent for a moment. "What about those men out there?"

"I can conceal us long enough to get away," Maisie replied.

"I wasn't talking about Yasin's men," Romaine said, glaring at the spy.

Maisie sighed. "We cannot save them, Calafe. At least they will die knowing they were protecting a Goddess. Maybe that will give them some comfort."

"I'm sure they'd prefer not to die at all," the Calafe snapped, but Erika could see the defeat in his eyes.

Silently, she looked Romaine up and down, noting the bruises on his face, the wounds and his missing hand. He'd fought well against the Flumeerens, but...

"Can you carry Cara?" she asked softly. "She's...heavier than she looks."

"I heard that," muttered Cara. But even as Erika smiled, the whisper turned to a moan and she coughed, sending blood splattering across the rocks.

Romaine nodded, but he hesitated as he reached for the Goddess. "Can you...do something about your wings, Cara?" he asked. "I don't want to damage them."

The Goddess didn't reply, but her face tightened, and the auburn wings contracted slightly. She only managed to half fold them before her strength gave out.

Erika swallowed, tears springing to her eyes at the sight of Cara in such pain. She moved alongside Romaine and they shared a look. Something passed between them, and together they rolled the Goddess onto her side.

It was the first time Erika had taken a closer look at her wings.

They sprouted from either side of Cara's spine, though lower on her back than she'd thought, stretching upwards then folding back down to allow them to fold flat. At some point Cara had cut an extra hole in her shirt, almost like a third sleeve, to allow them freedom.

"Her jacket," Romaine grunted.

Erika nodded. Her jacket could cover her wings and hold them in place while they carried her. She looked to Maisie, and taking a breath, the woman vanished. Erika hadn't even realised she'd let the illusion drop, though it made sense. Amongst the boulders they couldn't be seen from the outside, and the Gemaho spy needed to conserve her strength.

Romaine still crouched beside her, but neither spoke as they waited, their eyes on the way leading back to the battle. The clash of distant weapons and the screams of the dying filled the silence, and Erika wondered how much time they had now. Without her magic, how much longer could the brave men and women of Gemaho last?

The thought made her shiver and her eyes fell again to the gauntlet. It had felt good to use its power again, to strike down men who came to kill her. And yet…she shuddered as she recalled the young man groaning at her feet. He'd betrayed them, had left breadcrumbs for the queen's soldiers to follow, had poisoned Cara.

Now Romaine claimed that he'd only done it all to save his family.

She clenched her fist, watching as the light of her gauntlet pulsed. Had he truly deserved death? A shudder ran through her, but before she could consider the matter further, Maisie sprung from empty air beside them. Romaine flinched but Maisie only tossed them the jacket.

"Quickly," she hissed. "Nguyen's soldiers won't last much longer."

Erika nodded, and as Romaine held Cara on her side, she carefully folded the auburn wings tighter against the Anahera's back. Cara whimpered at the movement, a trickle of blood running from her mouth, but she no longer spoke. Surely it was sacrilege to touch such talismans of the Divine, but Erika had already done much worse. If the Gods intended to condemn her, this would be the least of her crimes. With Romaine's help, she managed to get

Cara's arms into the jacket, covering the wings and holding them in place.

Then she looked at the Calafe. "Can you do this?"

Romaine only grunted. Sheathing his sword, he scooped his one good hand around Cara and hefted her onto his shoulder. When they were sure the Goddess was secure, Erika drew in a breath and raised her gauntlet. She no longer trusted its power, but there was no choice now. They would need every advantage they had to survive what was to come.

She turned to Maisie. "You ready?"

The woman nodded grimly and raised her sphere, unleashing a flash of brilliance. A moment later they were cast into that odd light again, the outside reduced to a shimmering other world.

"Stay close," Maisie said as she turned towards the battle. "The area of influence needs to be small if we're to sneak past the soldiers."

Together they crept back towards the battle. Light shone through from the outside, but it seemed unnatural, changed by whatever magic Maisie's talisman cast. Ahead, they could see the soldiers that had travelled with them all this way.

Suddenly, Erika was struck by a terrible sense of déjà vu. She staggered, and the others glanced at her. She ignored them, a moan building in her throat. There were less than ten of the Gemaho left now. So many dead. As she watched, another fell, his head almost severed from his shoulders by the vicious swing of an enemy axe. The others retreated another step, seeking to plug the gap left by his death, but the Flumeeren men continued to press forward.

She scrunched her eyes closed, overwhelmed. It was happening again—innocent men dying because of her folly. She shuddered, faces running through her mind, of the men and women she had failed, too many to name.

The last was a face she had tried hard to forget, to push from her mind, his loss too painful to remember. Her father, the man that had raised Erika to be a princess, who had shielded her from the evils of the world, who had protected her. If only she could have protected him in return.

"*Erika!*" Romaine's voice cut through her pain. Their eyes met and understanding passed between them. "You can't save them," the Calafe said softly. "But you can still save *her*."

She nodded, forcing her grief to the side. Space had appeared to either side of the defenders now, but the enemy had been enraged by their defiance, and rather than seeking to encircle the Gemaho soldiers, they continued to attack from the front, determined to destroy them.

But this also created space for Erika and the others to escape. Staying close to Maisie, they snuck past the battling soldiers. Erika felt a coward, watching those brave souls fight to the death while she fled. But then, wasn't that what she had always been, ever since that day she and her mother had fled Flumeer?

A coward.

Never again.

Clearing the line of soldiers, they started away from the battle. Looking back, Erika was shocked by the toll the Gemaho had taken on their attackers. Half the Flumeeren number had fallen, and while only a handful of Gemaho fought on, the battle had been far closer than she'd thought. Even the Flumeeren archer seemed to have disappeared. Maybe if they'd stayed...

Another Gemaho soldier fell, run through by a long sword. His comrades tried to retreat, but the Flumeeren men fell upon them, forcing them back against the boulders, though not before yet another died screaming.

Quickly Erika looked away. It was over. The remaining few might fight on a little longer, but there would be no victory. Erika could only hope the Flumeerens would be unable to track them, now they'd lost their spy. She hurried after Romaine, heading up the slope, up the narrow canyon, and prayed it led to salvation.

Slowly the canyon twisted away from the campsite, hiding them from sight of the soldiers below. There was a soft *pop* as Maisie released the magic, and the globe that had covered them vanished. Suddenly the sun was shining full upon them. The return of its heat was so shocking that Erika swung around, half-expecting a fresh wave of soldiers to fall upon them. There was no one, though. Hopefully their pursuers would take a long time to figure out how they'd escaped.

Facing ahead again, Erika found Maisie slumped on her hands and knees. The spy's face was pale as she looked at them.

"Might have…pushed myself a little too far," she murmured, looking down the valley. "Think I bought you enough time."

Anger touched Erika as she saw the defeat in the woman's eyes. She strode forward, stones crunching beneath her boots. "Get up," she snapped.

Maisie shook her head. "Don't have the—"

She broke off as Erika slapped her across the face. "No," she said, then offered her hand. "We're going on together, got it?"

The spy's eyes had widened at the blow and now she stared up at Erika, as though not quite sure what to do.

"I'd do what she says," Romaine grunted from beside them. "She's a princess, after all—used to getting what she wants."

Maisie looked at the Calafe, still looking dazed, but finally she took Erika's offered hand and allowed herself to be pulled back to her feet. Looping the woman's arm across her shoulder, Erika took some of her weight, then nodded her thanks to Romaine.

The warrior said nothing, only started up the slope once more, Cara still hung across his back. The Goddess's eyes remained closed, and her face was grey as death. Erika's heart twisted at the sight. Would they make it in time? Could Cara's people even help with her ailment?

Of course they can, they're Gods!

But there was a voice whispering to her, her Archivist's mind, asking if that was really true. Being weak to magic or the Tangata was one thing—both came from the Gods. But poison? She looked at Cara again, heart twisting, stomach in knots. Surely a God should be immune to something as benign as poison?

She thrust the thought away. It did her no good now, not while danger still lurked, while they were still so far from help or rescue. One thing was without doubt—Cara's people *were* out here. Gods or no, they would help Cara. They would protect them from the queen's soldiers.

If they let you in…

Erika cursed and started after Romaine, dragging Maisie with her. They continued up the gorge, though its walls grew narrower with each bend in its winding depths. Erika began to wonder if they'd chosen the wrong path after all—if the canyon did not open out soon, they risked striking a dead end. Yet the ground was still lifting beneath their feet, and looking around she thought that the cliffs looked shorter. Or perhaps that was just hopeful thinking. There was no going back now.

After a time Maisie seemed to recover some of her strength and was able to walk unaided—much to Erika's relief. Romaine, on the other hand, lagged farther and farther behind, struggling with his burden. Erika wished she could aid him, but there was nothing either of them could do besides rely on the big Calafe's strength—they'd already tried.

Eventually though, Erika saw that she'd been right. The cliffs were shortening as they climbed, until finally they were barely twice their height. In places they might have even climbed free. They were so close now, Erika could sense it, could almost feel the secret calling to her, waiting to be uncovered. The city of the Gods was here somewhere.

The crunch of footsteps from ahead suddenly ceased and Erika looked up, surprised that Maisie had come to a halt. Then she realised the spy had stopped because the mountain had come to an end. While the cliffs still rose to either side of them, the slope beyond Maisie vanished, starting back down into a fresh valley. Could this be it?

Blood pounded in Erika's ears as she staggered towards the spy. Maisie hadn't said a word, but her eyes were fixed on the land beyond, as though…as though there was something *there!*

Romaine reached the crest a second before Erika, but he too remained silent, only came to a stop, eyes fixed on the unknown beyond. Erika scrambled her way up the last few feet and straightened at the top. Holding her breath, she looked down at the valley beyond…

And frowned.

An empty scree slope stretched away beyond them, down into a broad valley between the icy peaks. But that was not what the others were looking at. There in the centre of the valley, a squat, square building rose from the barren mountainside. Shaped of the same smooth grey rock she'd encountered in other sacred sites, it was massive, ringing a large yard in its centre. But other than its size, it seemed so…plain.

Erika didn't know what she'd been expecting from this sacred place hidden away in the forbidden Mountains of the Gods, but the structure below certainly hadn't been it.

"Welcome to my home." Cara's voice was bitter as she laughed into Romaine's shoulder.

Erika turned to the Goddess, but a movement from across the slope drew her attention instead. Stones came crashing down from above, then a dark figure dropped from the cliff, striking the ground with a crash. The man straightened, a smile on his lips, crossbow pointed at Erika's chest.

"If you'd be so good as to lower the gauntlet, Archivist," the man said, "I think it's about time we had a little chat."

30

THE SOLDIER

Racing through the streets of New Nihelm, Lukys wondered how he could have ever been so blind. The others ran around him, Tangata loping along in stride with their human partners. Travis, Dale, all the others, they didn't know, couldn't see.

But then, how could they?

The Tangata were playing with their minds.

His stomach twisted as memories flickered before his eyes—of the Matriarch towering over him, drawing the map from his mind; of Sophia's daily visits, the slow whittling down of his will. No wonder his friends had given in so quickly. They couldn't distinguish the creatures' whispers from their own thoughts, couldn't resist as he had.

They had been brainwashed, their minds manipulated until they thought they loved the creatures who ran alongside them.

How could he not have seen it sooner?

Grinding his teeth, Lukys forced his mind to the task at hand. Sophia's betrayal would have to wait—now he needed to concentrate on escaping the city. Ahead, the others had slowed as they approached a corner. Beyond, lanterns lit the main avenue across the city. So far they had kept to backroads, avoiding the whispers of Tangata and humans heading through the city, making for the basilica. Guilt touched Lukys as he thought of his fellow humans, prisoner to their Tangatan partners, being led to their deaths. There was nothing he could do for those poor souls.

But he might yet save his friends.

If they'd reached the main avenue, they must be near the bridge. He slunk forward, ignoring Sophia as he passed her and coming to a stop just before the corner where Travis stood waiting.

"Guards," the recruit hissed.

Lukys cursed. They were at the southern edge of the city. He'd thought they might outthink the Tangata's new leader by taking the least likely escape route, but apparently the Old One was taking no chances in letting anyone out of the city. He leaned out for a glimpse of his own and spotted the two guards watching the entrance to the bridge.

There was no way their group of thirty-odd humans and Tangata were leaving unnoticed. They might have fought their way past, but the noise would attract attention and point their eventual pursuers in the direction they'd taken. They needed to escape without anyone knowing which way they had gone.

Dozens of eyes watched him as he glanced back, some frightened, others simply confused. The Perfugian recruits had gathered what food and clothing they could from the compound and now carried them in bundles they'd made of sheets from their apartments. With spring beginning, Lukys hoped they could scavenge more on the road, or perhaps bring down a deer with one of their spears, but first they had to escape.

His gaze switched to the unreadable eyes of the Tangata. A shudder ran down his spine and he wondered how he could have ever come to trust these creatures. He didn't want them with him, but there'd been no choice, not with the others still convinced of their love for their Tangatan partners.

"What now?" Dale asked, creeping forward.

He held his spear tight in one hand. Most of the recruits were similarly armed, and Lukys was momentarily tempted to cast caution aside and rush the bridge. Night was passing quickly and it was only a matter of time before Adonis's body was found. Then the pursuit would begin in earnest. They needed to be a long way from New Nihelm by then.

Lukys pushed down the temptation to attack. The others were

looking at him to save them. How quickly he had become their leader again. He couldn't let them down now.

There were only two ways out of the city, two bridges. If there were guards here, there would be others at the northern bridge. There had to be another way.

Could they swim? The river was broad and the current swift, but coming from an island nation, Perfugians were decent swimmers—and used to the cold. It would be dangerous in the darkness. He eyed the others, wondering if anyone had ideas to offer. Instead, he glimpsed Sophia moving towards him.

"We swim," he said quickly. He looked at Travis but the recruit only raised an eyebrow. Lukys sighed. "We need somewhere we can enter the water without being seen."

Travis only raised an eyebrow.

"Trust me," Lukys said.

I know a place, Sophia offered, coming to a stop beside them.

A bolt of rage struck Lukys as he looked at her. Their dance, their kiss...they seemed a million years ago already, a lifetime. Silently he pushed his anger down. At least she could be trusted to help them escape. After Adonis's death, none of these Tangata had a place in New Nihelm any longer. He gave her a curt nod.

There was no missing the hurt in Sophia's eyes as she looked at him. Lukys still hadn't told her he knew. How would she react? Would she try to control him again, to manipulate him, to wash away his doubts with her power?

"Show us," he said shortly.

Sophia's jaw tightened and without a word she turned away, striding back the way they had come. Lukys gestured for his friends to follow her, even as he felt a flare of distrust. He pushed it down. She and the others had tried to fight Adonis; they could at least be trusted this far. Couldn't they?

They retreated several blocks before cutting into an alleyway leading back towards the river. Lukys frowned as he realised they were upriver of the bridge. There was no way they could fight the current. That meant they would be washed straight back to where the guards were waiting...

...except the guards weren't watching the water. An idea started to form in his head.

The place Sophia knew turned out to have been an old water-front restaurant. By the polished mahogany furnishings and crystal chandeliers, Lukys thought it had probably been an expensive place to eat once, frequented by the wealthy of Calafe society. Apparently, the Tangata hadn't been so easily impressed, for a thick layer of dust now covered every surface.

Sophia led them through a room stacked with dining tables waiting for patrons that would never return, to where a small jetty stretched out into the river. Lukys was relieved to see the nearby buildings were dark, leaving the river to reflect the faint glint of moonlight.

Boards creaked as Dale stepped onto the jetty. He froze, but no movement came from the surrounding buildings, and they were a good quarter mile upriver from the bridge now. Not even Tangatan guards would hear the noise from such a distance.

Beneath the planks, the dark waters of the Shelman River swept past, shimmering in the starlight. Lukys glanced back at the others, wondering how they would cope with such a crossing. There was no way any of them could fight the current, but if his plan worked, that wouldn't matter.

Exhaling, he looked out across the river, but even by the light of the half moon, he could barely see beyond the jetty. In those currents, there would be no knowing whether they were making progress. They could be ten feet from the other side and not know it until their feet struck rock. And the icy waters would quickly drain their strength. It would be a dangerous crossing, even for the best of swimmers.

Hopefully they wouldn't need to swim the entire crossing.

"We're going to use the bridge," he said, his words carrying in the silence of the night. "Once you're in the water, kick out as far as you can, but don't fight the current. Eventually the river will carry you beneath the bridge. When that happens, grab for the support pillars. Use them to cross the rest of the way. Hopefully we'll be far enough out into the river that the guards won't hear us.

The Perfugians stared back at him, fear shining in their eyes. He cursed inwardly, suddenly doubting himself. Could they do this? Surely there was another way to escape, some plan that didn't risk them all perishing in the icy waters…

Travis stepped forward and clapped Lukys on the shoulder. "Let's do it."

Moving past Lukys, he took hold of a ladder at the end of the jetty and slid over the side. Isabella followed him, her eyes catching Lukys's. He suppressed a shudder, but said nothing. The Tangata were powerful swimmers, capable of crossing even the broad expanse of the Illmoor. Perhaps they could help their partners survive what was to come.

"Hurry The Fall up." Travis's voice came from below. "The water's bloody freezing."

"Go," Lukys whispered. "Wait for us on the other side."

His words seemed to break some spell that had been cast over the rest of the recruits. Dale followed and one by one they stepped past him, jaws clenched, eyes fixed on that distant, invisible shore. Freedom. Finally only Lukys stood on the jetty—until a figure stepped from the shadows, and he realised Sophia had not yet entered the water. A lump lodged in his throat as the Tangata approached.

Lukys, she whispered. He tried to turn away, but she caught him by the arm. *Lukys, please, what's wrong?*

He looked at her and saw the pain in those pure grey eyes, the fear. He swallowed, seeing again their dance, the soft music whispering in his ears, their kiss. His heart throbbed and he could almost taste her lips, feel her breath against his cheek…

His stomach twisted as another image came to him, of Adonis towering over them, his mind crushing them down. Anger returned and he tore his arm loose.

"You know," he spat.

Her eyes slid closed and he could see the truth on her face, so much more open than the other Tangata, as though she could not help but reveal her true emotions to him. He ground his teeth, fists clenched, wishing…for what?

I can explain, she whispered, reaching out an arm.

He stepped back. "Explain what, Sophia?" he asked, voice bitter. "That you've been manipulating us all along, controlling us? Is that what you can explain?"

No! she cried, a tear streaking her cheek. *That's not how it works, not how we use our Voices!*

"No?" Lukys growled. "Are you telling me you and your brethren were *happy* to bow to him, to allow him to murder us?"

I… Sophia trailed off, her eyes wide. Then she hung her head, and Lukys sensed shame rolling off her. *What Adonis did, feeding our despair, using our fears to subdue us, it was forbidden.*

And yet each of you has done the same to us.

We haven't, Sophia hissed, matching his gaze now. *At least, not as he did. We can only…encourage what is already there—trust, appreciation, happiness, joy. That is why not all assignments are…successful.*

Encourage? Lukys asked. He looked away. *And what have you encouraged in me?*

Nothing, Sophia murmured. She stepped towards him, placing her hand on his arm again. He shuddered, but this time he did not pull away. *Don't you see, Lukys? Your Voice, it's…stronger than mine. That was why you could resist Adonis, why the humans follow you. I could never have encouraged you, nor manipulated you as you claim. I could only wait for you to see me as I truly am—rather than the monsters from your history books.*

Lukys's heart throbbed at her words, and yet…how could he believe them? After everything she had lied about, everything the Tangata had concealed from them, the trust was gone. He looked at her, at the woman he had spent so much time with these last weeks, and felt only a coldness in his core.

And the others? Lukys asked, his inner voice bitter.

Sophia shook her head. *What they feel is real, Lukys,* the Tangata replied. *Their partners only helped them see the truth…faster. Please, Lukys… you have to see—*

"No," Lukys whispered. He swallowed, glancing back at her. "I don't. I'm sorry, Sophia. You're right, I can see you're not the monsters we thought. But…this is wrong. I can't trust you."

With that he turned and stepped to the edge of the dock. The dark waters rushed past below, silent, the others disappeared into the night. He let out a long breath, blood thundering in his ears, and fought the urge to turn back, to embrace the warmth he had found in this strange city. Clenching his fists, he leapt.

And plunged into the icy depths.

31

THE FALLEN

Romaine froze as Yasin's voice whispered across the pass. Cara weighed heavily on his shoulders and exhaustion had wormed its way deep into his soul. His legs ached from the ascent and his head was pounding. He was at the end of his endurance, but he turned to face the man who had tried to kill him.

Wearing a smug grin, the Flumeeren pointed his crossbow at Erika. He was obviously well aware of the powers contained in her gauntlet.

"Take it off," Yasin growled, his finger wrapped around the trigger. "Now, like old Nguyen did before."

Breath held, Romaine glanced at Erika. He had seen her down Tangata from as far away as Yasin stood from her. She could do it now—if she had the courage. It was almost certain that Yasin would be able to fire before the magic incapacitated him, but at least then he and Maisie would have a chance to stop the queen's man.

No, even without the crossbow, he's more than my match.

Romaine's shoulders fell as he realised they would all die here. Erika must have known it as well, for she reached up and pressed her thumb to the gauntlet around her wrist. There was a soft *hiss* as the relic released, before it dropped to the ground with a gentle ring of metal chains.

"Good, good," the rogue laughed. His beady eyes turned on

Romaine. "Why don't you put the Goddess down now, Calafe? I'm sure the burden couldn't have been easy, carrying her all this way."

The hairs on Romaine's neck stood on end as he stared Yasin down. In his mind, he saw again and again the image of Lorene falling, crossbow bolt in his chest. He clenched his fist, straining for something—anything—that might allow him to fight back. But there was nothing.

Cara whimpered as he lowered her slowly to the stones. Then he rose and stepped in front of her.

"Why are you doing this?" he growled.

"Why, *I* haven't done anything." Yasin laughed and spread his hands. Romaine tensed as the bow was lowered, but on the uneven slope he would never reach the man fast enough. "It was the villainous Gemaho who kidnapped the daughter of the Gods. The noble queen of Flumeer tried to save her, but alas, we only arrived in time to take vengeance."

Romaine bared his teeth. "I won't let you harm her."

"Yasin…" A murmur from Erika drew their attention. She still stood beside her fallen gauntlet, but now her eyes narrowed as she stared at the man. "Why do I know that name?"

"You can't stop me, Calafe," Yasin continued, ignoring the Archivist. "I do as Amina commands. I'm sure you would have done the same for your king, if the fool hadn't gotten himself killed."

A sharp intake of breath came from Erika, but this time Yasin kept his attention fixed on Romaine. The man seemed to have decided he was the most dangerous of the three. If only he knew how Romaine's entire body ached, he might have reconsidered.

"You're one of Amina's spies," Maisie said. Stones shifted as she moved to the side, as though trying to divert his attention.

Yasin laughed at that. "Spy, soldier, cutthroat." He shrugged. "I have the honour of being whatever my queen requires of me." He flicked a knowing glance at the woman. "I hear you have some experience in that regard…it's Maisie, no?"

Maisie sneered. "You're little more than a common thug, Yasin."

"No, no, no," Erika staggered forward a step, breaking into the conversation. She pointed an accusing finger at Yasin. "I *know* you!"

The smile slipped from the cutthroat's face. "Ah, so you finally recognise me, Princess."

"You were a friend of my father."

"For a learned woman, you took a long time to make that connection." Yasin smirked. "I guess gullibility runs in the family."

Romaine's blood ran cold at the man's words. "What is he saying?" he asked, looking from Yasin to Erika in disbelief.

She shook her head. "It's not possible," she whispered. "You... you rode south with him. You're...dead!"

"Ay." Yasin turned the crossbow on Erika. "Now I can see the resemblance. That open-mouth surprise, that disbelief. Your father looked much the same when I drove my blade through his chest."

"*No!*" Erika screamed.

A ringing sounded in Romaine's ears as he stared at Yasin, trying to understand, to pry meaning from his words. He had killed Erika's father, the Calafe king. *His king.* But that wasn't possible. King Micah had ridden south with the allied armies, to destroy the threat of the Tangata once and for all. It had been the beasts that had slain him...

...but then why would the queen's own cutthroat have been friends to the Calafe king? Not unless...

"She betrayed us," Romaine whispered, but Erika drowned out his words.

"*You killed my father!*" Erika screamed. She started towards the killer, but Yasin lifted the crossbow and she froze.

"Now, now, Princess." He tisked. "I'd rather not have to kill you. The queen was rather excited by the prospect of welcoming you back to her court."

Fists clenched, Erika's entire body was trembling. "Why?" she hissed.

The rogue raised an eyebrow. "Why? Why else?" he asked, looking from the Archivist to Romaine. "Calafe lies shattered, Gemaho grasps at empty straws for its survival, and Perfugia withdraws more and more from the workings of the continent. Meanwhile, Flumeer is resurgent. All because of that disastrous campaign."

"But the Tangata," Romaine growled, clenching his fist. In that moment he wanted nothing more than to reach out and throttle the man. "Surely the queen couldn't have thought..." He trailed off, unable to complete the sentence.

"The thoughts of the lion rarely make sense to the sheep," Yasin replied. "Who would think the death of a king could lead to the fall of his nation. Yet here we are."

"She cannot hope to fight the Tangata alone."

Yasin's face hardened. "The beasts are cursed by the Gods. They are destined for extinction." There was a coldness to his eyes as he glanced at Maisie. "As are the Gemaho, when the Gods learn of the depravity that took place here."

The three of them fell silent, staring into the eyes of the killer. Then to Romaine's surprise, stones crunched behind him. He glanced back, and watched in horror as Cara pulled herself to her feet. Her face a motley grey, she took a trembling step towards Yasin.

"The Anahera will not help you," she croaked, her voice barely audible above the wind whistling through the pass.

"Of course they will," Yasin said easily. "They just need the proper motivation."

The crossbow came up. A gasp came from Maisie. Erika screamed.

Romaine was already moving.

The bolt took him full in the chest, just as it had for Lorene. For the briefest of seconds, he felt nothing, only a rush of triumph, that he had stopped the arrow meant for Cara, that he had succeeded.

Then the pain struck, a searing, burning agony. It blossomed in his lungs and spread outwards like the tendrils of a rose, tearing and rending through his body, through his very being.

He staggered, then slumped to one knee as the strength went from his legs. Somewhere, someone was screaming, but he could barely hear them over the pounding in his ears. His vision swam and suddenly he was lying on the cold stones, staring up at Yasin. The man looked surprised, as though he couldn't quite believe what Romaine had done. Before he could reload his crossbow, a blurred figure attacked with sword in hand, and the two danced out of Romaine's field of vision.

The tear-streaked face of Cara replaced them as she fell to her knees beside him. She reached out a hand and her lips moved, but Romaine could no longer hear what she said. The agony was still growing, threatening to sweep him away on its irresistible tide. But he couldn't let go yet—not until he knew she was safe.

"Run!" he tried to gasp, though he couldn't know whether the word actually left his mouth.

Romaine! Inexplicably, Cara's voice spoke into his mind, a keening, howling sound that pained him beyond even the arrow in his chest. *Romaine, please, no!*

Tears burned in Romaine's eyes and somehow he lifted a hand, grasping at her jacket, desperate for her to flee, but his lips no longer seemed to work. He spoke them in his mind instead, a desperate prayer to the Goddess crouched beside him.

Cara, please, you have to run!

32

THE SOLDIER

Lukys gasped as his head broke the surface. A pounding began in his skull and he struggled to inhale, the sheer cold pressing on his chest, making each breath a battle. He swung around, trying to find his bearings. Lights drifted past him, away to his right—houses occupied by the Tangata. The currents were carrying him downriver fast. He needed to make it farther from the shore before he reached the bridge, lest the guards notice his passage.

Turning, he kicked out. His boots slipped on the currents, making the going difficult, and his clothing threatened to drag him down. At least the spear he held helped to keep him afloat. Teeth chattering, he focused on the darkness ahead, seeking some sign of the others, of the distant bank, of the bridge, but there was only the soft glint of the waters around him.

His body grew numb, the icy waters drawing away the last of his heat. Pain stabbed at his calves as he struggled on. At least he didn't carry any of their supplies like the Tangata. How had the creatures managed to cross the Illmoor? Its waters were twice as wide as these. Already he could feel his strength fading, his desperate gasps unable to sustain him.

Time crept by, the moon high above, the whispers of the river the only sound in his world. Soon, Lukys began to wonder if he had somehow missed the bridge. Surely it should not be taking so long to encounter it. Fatigue crept through his limbs, slowing his strokes, and he found himself glancing back, struggling to judge how far he'd come.

Something large loomed in the darkness, blocking out the moonlight. He gasped, realising the bridge was upon him. In the pitch-black, he grabbed desperately for a pillar. But its surface was smooth, cloaked in algae, and his fingers slipped. He cried out as the currents swept him between the pillars. Unable to see, he thrashed out with the spear, hoping to catch it on something, anything that would keep him from being dragged past the bridge—

Lukys lurched to a stop as something caught his spear, almost jolting it from his grasp. Water rushed around him and gritting his teeth, he held desperately to the weapon as he was dragged into a sheltered nook behind one of the columns. A hand went around his waist, pulling him in the rest of the way, until he found himself pressed against a warm body.

Grey eyes glinted in the darkness as Sophia held him close, keeping him from being sucked back into the river. Lukys swallowed, a shiver running through him, though he wasn't sure whether it was from the cold or her closeness. He opened his mouth to thank her, but amidst the shadows she raised a finger to her lips, then pointed to the stones above.

Lukys's heart lurched as he caught the soft tread of feet from overhead. He swallowed back the words he'd been about to speak. The steps grew closer, and he sensed the distant whisper of voices in his mind, still faint, but growing closer. He clutched at Sophia, her warmth bringing him back to life, and prayed the guards hadn't—

I heard something, a voice announced, clear now. *I swear.*

He felt Sophia tense against him, could feel her heart racing in pace with his own. There was no sign of the other recruits—hopefully they were already across, out of sight, free. Lukys closed his eyes and waited. There was nothing else they could do.

There's nothing out here, another replied. *You really think someone got past us?*

You really want to face that Old One if they did?

A pause. *Should we check the other side?*

The whispers in Lukys's mind grew louder as they neared. Beneath the bridge, they could not be seen, but Lukys's heart quickened at their words. If they crossed to the southern banks, there would be no missing the Perfugian recruits that had gone ahead.

He frowned as an idea came to him and he looked again at Sophia, turning her earlier words over in his mind. What had she said…that they could *encourage* emotions in others? Did that include the Tangata? She'd said he was stronger, that his Voice carried more force—could he use that? Had he already?

Silently, Lukys stretched out his mind to the guards, trying to take care not to broadcast his own fear. He was still too new at this, too inexperienced. Surely this was too dangerous…

…but no, he couldn't allow the guards to reach the far shore. One glimpse of the recruits would doom them all.

He touched their minds, gently, softly, brushing against their thoughts. He sensed their worry, their fear of failure, broadcast for the world to hear. But deeper, he sensed the fiery confidence of the Tangata, the belief in their strength. He mimicked those thoughts himself, trying to augment, to reassure the two creatures there was nothing there.

No, the first said finally. *Nothing got passed us. Come on, I don't want to be caught away from our post.*

Lukys released a breath he hadn't realised he'd been holding as the footsteps retreated, moving quickly back towards the city. Sophia's eyes found him in the darkness, but she said nothing, and after a moment Lukys looked away.

They continued across the river, the cold now so ingrained in Lukys's bones that he could barely feel his extremities. If they spent much longer in the water, he feared discovery would be the least of their worries. He tried to pick up his pace, moving through the currents by pushing off one pillar with his feet and grasping desperately at the next as it came within reach, using the spear to find them in the darkness. In some places, though, the pillars were missing, and here it took all Lukys's energy just to keep from being swept away. On two occasions, Sophia had to grasp his spear and drag him back to safety. He prayed to the Gods that Travis and the others had managed to cross safely.

Lukys's frozen mind barely registered their arrival on the distant shore. He stumbled from the river, water coursing from his clothes. Shadows flickered ahead as first Travis, then Dale stepped from the darkness and embraced him. A tremor shook Lukys, but his friends were just as cold as he was. After a moment they broke apart and Lukys slumped to the sandy shore.

It was the worst thing he could have done. Now that he'd stopped moving, the tremors redoubled until his teeth were chattering so loudly he feared the guards might still hear him all the way from the city. He looked around as Sophia strode from the water. Their eyes met and he opened his mouth to thank her, but could not get the words out.

Get up, she said, the words a command. *If you don't move, you'll die.*

Lukys hesitated at the coldness to her tone, but finally he nodded and dragged himself off the sand. He almost went to her, but fought the urge. They stood beside the bridge, its shadow stretching away into the dark, only to reappear in the distance where lanterns burned at the entrance of the city. He wondered how long it would take the Old One to discover their absence.

Still shaking, he turned his gaze from the river to the shoreline. His fellow Perfugians stood there in various states of wakefulness. It looked like all had survived the crossing, no doubt aided by their Tangatan partners. The creatures themselves stood alongside the recruits, keeping them moving, keeping them warm. A pang of longing touched him, that he could experience that same closeness, but he shook it off. His friends still didn't know what had been done to them.

That could wait. They needed to be away from this place.

"Where to?" Travis asked as the recruit caught his gaze.

Lukys shook his head, trying to force his frozen mind into action. His gaze lifted to the east. The first hints of morning silhouetted the Mountains of the Gods. He swallowed, images of Cara soaring towards him across the Illmoor appearing in his mind. Somewhere in those peaks, her family lived, their location marked by the map he held in his head. If they could reach that hidden site…

He turned back to his comrades, taking in their sodden state. Half appeared to have lost their spears in the currents, and only the supplies carried by the Tangata had made the crossing. Their clothing was thin, suited to the milder climates of the south, and in the endless wilderness of Calafe there would be no finding anything better. Without proper cloaks and furs, they wouldn't last a night in those snow-capped peaks.

His heart sinking, he returned his gaze to the river. The currents swept past, making their endless journey down through lowland Calafe, to the coast, to the ocean. They had made it to the southern shore, the least likely place the Tangata would look for them, but they would need to cross again eventually if they wanted to journey north. But what then? Hundreds of miles lay between here and the questionable safety of Flumeer—and all of it territory claimed by the Tangata.

He shook his head. They would never make it.

"Let's go," he said, trying to keep the despair from his voice. They needed to move or they wouldn't even last the day.

We must walk in the water, Sophia's voice drifted through his thoughts. *The older generations might track us by your scent.*

Lukys gritted his teeth, but nodded. "Back in the water," he said to the recruits. "We go downriver."

Several flashed him strange looks, but they were soon marching west away from the bridge, boots squelching with each step. Thankfully the water was shallow this side of the Shelman, the stones firm beneath their feet. They made good progress, though Lukys could feel the cold eating at his legs. Despite the risk, they would need to light a fire when they finally stopped, or risk frostbite.

They pressed on through the darkness, making it a mile downstream before finally leaving the water. From there they continued west, threading their way through the light shrub that grew along the riverbank.

Despite their progress, Lukys could feel his spirits falling with each step. He still didn't know where they could go, whether they should cross the river again. All he knew was they had to keep moving. But were they only delaying the inevitable? Even if they reached Flumeer, how long could the nation stand? Against the power of the Old One, of the Tangata, the human armies that defended the banks of the Illmoor seemed pitiful by comparison.

A sense of hopelessness crept into his thoughts and he found his shoulders slumping, his steps slowing in the darkness. What was the point of fighting on when all hope was lost?

He started as light appeared in the darkness, illuminating the ground beneath his feet. Stumbling to a stop, he swung around, almost surprised to see the sun lifting out from behind those towering mountains. Again he felt the urge to seek the distant peaks. Perhaps there he would find answers—about Sophia and the other Tangatan partners, about the Old Ones, about his own strange ability.

But that path was barred to him. Yet the sight still lifted him, reminded him there were still greater forces at play in the world, counters to the power of the Old One. Cara would stand against them, Romaine as well. They had already defeated the creatures once, down in the bowels of the earth. They could do it again.

No, Lukys needed to focus on his own survival, on the survival of his Perfugian companions. Let the queens and Gods and the Tangata wage their war; Lukys only needed to save the few brave souls that had dared to follow him this far. He would see them safely home.

His eyes lifted to the river and he thought again of its endless journey, down to the distant ocean, and his heart quickened as a thought came to him. He turned, seeking out Sophia. His heart clenched as he found her nearby, ashy hair lit by the rising sun. She had stayed close, his own personal guardian—

He shook off the thought, concentrating on the task at hand.

Sophia, he murmured, keeping their conversation private for now. She looked around, eyes lifting in surprise, and he quickly went on. *You know these lands. What lies at the mouth of the river?*

The Tangata's eyebrows knitted together and it was a moment before she responded. *Sand,* she replied, *and…there is a small fishing village, I believe.*

Lukys's heart quickened, and nodding to her, he strode ahead. They would stop soon, to rest and recover, to dry out their soaked clothing, but for now a fresh determination set him alight. He knew where they needed to go now, difficult as the journey might be. There was only one place left in the kingdoms of man that might grant them safe harbour, one place that could withstand whatever fate befell the rest of humanity. One place where he might find answers.

We're going home.

33

THE FUGITIVE

Erika watched as Romaine slumped to the ground, his eyes fluttering closed. The Goddess clutched desperately at his chest, but the Calafe did not move.

Grief touched Erika as she looked on the dying man, but the loss barely registered beside her anguish, beside her rage at the man Yasin. Nearby, Maisie had drawn her blade and was battling furiously with the Flumeeren cutthroat. Silently Erika crouched, her fingers closing around the gauntlet she'd dropped.

Lifting it to her hand, she made to put it back on, then froze. Blood pounded in her ears as she looked on the source of the magic she had wielded these past months. Fear touched her as she recalled the ecstasy she had felt at its use, the power it had granted her. She longed for that power, and yet…if she put it back on, would she ever have the strength to remove it again?

A *thump* from nearby diverted her attention back to the warring pair in time to see Maisie's blade go skittering across the gravels. The spy herself staggered back clutching her arm. Blood soaked her fingers as she tripped over the uneven ground and collapsed against the stones.

It was now or never. Closing her eyes, she moved her hand towards the gauntlet.

Then she flinched as a terrible keening sound erupted through the pass. Her eyes snapped open and she watched as Cara strode past, her eyes fixed on the Flumeeren killer.

Eyes stained grey, eyes the colour of death.

The keening turned to a terrible growl as auburn wings snapped wide. Cara no longer looked on the verge of death. She looked as she had in the tunnels of the Gods, fighting those ancient creatures.

Like a monster herself, the Tangata reborn.

And her gaze was fixed on Yasin.

"What the…" Yasin began, then broke off as Cara continued towards him.

Realising his danger, the cutthroat leapt for his crossbow. Erika's heart lurched in her chest and she looked at Cara, but the Goddess made no move to stop him. Snatching up the weapon, Yasin hesitated, seeming confused at Cara's hesitation. But he didn't hesitate for long, and quickly he wound back the crossbow and dropped a bolt into place. Looking more confident now, he pointed it at Cara.

"Now, where were we?" He smiled again, though this time it seemed forced.

Cara only tilted her head to the side, as though perplexed by the human's actions. A snarl tore from Yasin and a sharp *twang* followed as the crossbow discharged. Erika cried out as Cara seemed to *shift*, but a blink later, and the winged Goddess was still standing. Only now she held a crossbow bolt in one outstretched hand.

What?

The terrible growl rumbled through the pass again. Then the Goddess was stalking towards Yasin, and her grey eyes promised death.

Cursing, Yasin threw aside the crossbow and drew his sword. "Come on then, bitch," he hissed. "Let's see if Gods bleed."

A smile spread across Cara's lips. Erika shuddered as she looked into the Goddess's eyes. There was a madness in those grey depths. This was not the woman she had come to know over the last weeks, the Goddess who had spoken of unbreakable promises and peace. Cara had become something else entirely. And all her attention was fixed on Yasin.

Screaming, Yasin leapt at Cara, sword flashing for her throat. The attack came suddenly, without warning, and despite herself Erika flinched. Cara only watched him come, that same sickly smile on her lips, until at the last moment she twisted, becoming a blur, and the sword cut empty air.

Carried forward by his momentum, Yasin found himself standing alongside the Goddess, sword pointing in the wrong direction. Snarling, he swung again, and this time Cara was forced to move, ducking beneath a wild sweep of his blade. She straightened almost instantly as Yasin stumbled past, her cold grey eyes still watching him, mocking him.

Yasin roared as he spun and stabbed out again. This time, Cara's hand flashed down, catching the Flumeeren by the wrist. Cursing, he tried to pull himself free, but Cara didn't seem to notice his efforts. She looked into his eyes, then her grip tightened. And the rogue started to scream.

Erika's hair stood on end as the sharp *crack* of breaking bones carried to her ears. Steel clashed against rock as the sword tumbled from the man's fingers. Then suddenly he was free, released from the Goddess's grip. He stumbled away, hand held up before him, and Erika choked, her stomach roiling.

His wrist was bent where Cara had held him, a shard of bone jabbing from the flesh. A moan rattled from Yasin as he stared at the mangled limb, but adrenaline must have swamped the pain, for as Cara moved again he screamed, and dropping his left hand to his belt, he drew a dagger. Face twisted in agony, he drew back his hand to hurl the blade.

Cara moved faster still, her wings beating down, sending her hurtling forward. Before Yasin knew what was happening she was upon him, his left arm now in her grasp. The cold smile spread as he cried out, a plea on his lips…

…it turned to a shriek as she wrenched. Another *crunch* echoed through the canyon.

Yasin staggered back from Cara, dagger on the ground, mangled arms held before him. His screams were constant now. Erika could hardly bare to watch, though this was the man who had killed her father, who had cast her entire life into the void. The murderer's face was pale and tears ran from his eyes as he retreated from Cara, shaking his head, pleading.

The Goddess stalked after him, and with a mortal cry, Yasin turned to flee.

Like a cat with a mouse, Cara pounced. She moved with a languid confidence now, of a predator that knew its prey could not escape. Her boot flashed out, catching the Flumeeren in the side of his knee. Another *crack* punctuated the blow.

Yasin slammed into the rocks, his cries breaking off as the impact drove the breath from his lungs. Cara stood over him, wings spread, icy eyes watching him. She was still smiling. A desperate moan came from the man as he finally caught his breath. It turned to sobs as he looked up and saw the Goddess.

"Please, Gods, no—"

She broke his other leg.

Unable to bear it any longer, Erika looked away. A shudder ran down her spine as her gaze fell on the gauntlet. It was still in her hand, but the thought of putting it on now turned her insides to liquid. If this was what the magic of the Gods could do to the peaceful, good-humoured woman she had known, what would it do to her?

A sudden silence fell across the canyon as Yasin's final scream was cut off. Erika flinched, and looking up, she noticed Maisie. There was fear in the eyes of the spy. Steeling herself, Erika looked for her friend…and stifled a scream as she found Cara standing just a few feet away.

Blood covered the Goddess's tunic, still dripped from her hands. The scream again built in Erika's throat as she looked into Cara's grey eyes and saw the madness there, the thirst for blood. A snarl rumbled from the Goddess's chest as she bared her teeth and stepped towards her.

"Cara…"

The voice was so soft, Erika barely caught it on the wind, but the Goddess heard. Her head whipped around as though she'd been struck, grey eyes fixing on the crumpled figure in the mouth of the pass. Romaine had not moved from where he'd fallen, and Erika swallowed at the sight of blood staining the rock beneath him.

Glancing at the Goddess, Erika watched as Cara blinked. Once, twice, three times. Then the grey was gone, the amber returned. Tears spilt down her cheeks as she cried out. In a second she was at the Calafe's side, crouching beside him, reaching for the bolt that still protruded from his chest.

"Don't," Romaine breathed.

"Romaine," Cara whispered, hand still outstretched, voice filled with pain.

Erika moved closer, her own vision blurring at the sight of the fallen Calafe warrior.

"Is it…done?" the man croaked, trying to lift his head.

A moan built in Cara's throat as she looked at where the mangled remains of Yasin lay. Erika could see her horror—and something else. Terror at what she'd done? Quickly Erika moved alongside them, crouching on Romaine's other side.

"He's gone, Romaine," she murmured. "We're safe."

"Good," Romaine whispered. "Good."

"Romaine, no…" Cara sobbed, grasping at his shirt, Yasin's blood mingling with the Calafe's. "No, please don't, you saved me, you can't…"

"Ah, little one," Romaine replied. He reached up with a trembling hand, touching it to her face. "Don't cry. I couldn't…let him hurt you. Couldn't fail…anyone else. Ahh…but that hurts…"

"My people, they'll help you," Cara gasped. "We're so close, just don't go, please, promise me."

A smile touched Romaine's face, but his eyes no longer seemed to see them. "No, little one," he whispered. "No, not…this time. They're…waiting for me."

Air whispered from his throat in a long, unending sigh. Erika crouched alongside him, waiting for the next whisper of breath. It never came. The keening sounded in Cara's throat again, but this time she only threw herself against the warrior's chest. Muffled sobs sounded as she hugged him and Erika looked away, grief touching her as well.

She sat back on her haunches, unable to believe the warrior was really gone. They had survived the creatures of the earth together, withstood the assault of the Tangata, escaped the soldiers of Flumeer. After so much, he had seemed invincible, able to overcome any obstacle.

Now he was dead.

The last warrior of Calafe, her final connection with a past she had tried for half her life to bury.

Or perhaps not. Looking down at the face of the warrior, she was reminded of all those lost refugees of Calafe camped outside the Flumeeren capital. She had looked down upon those sorry men and women, condemned them for their weakness, judged them for failing to rise above the destruction of their nation.

But the truth was, Erika was the one who had failed. The queen was a tyrant, had schemed and plotted to murder her father, to see Calafe fall, all so Flumeer could rise from the ashes of their kingdom. And Erika had served her. The thought was like bile in her mouth.

Slowly she rose and turned to look down upon the valley below. The squat building still awaited them. The secrets of the Gods, of her gauntlet. Drawing in a breath, she took a step towards the valley.

A sharp *crack* from overhead brought her to a halt and she swung around, thinking it must be Maisie. But the spy's eyes were on the sky. The hairs on the back of Erika's neck stood on end as she followed the direction of the woman's gaze in time to glimpse a flash of green and blue. Then something solid slammed into the ground nearby, sending a shower of stones flying outwards from the figure that had landed. Two more followed as the first straightened.

The breath caught in Erika's throat as she looked upon the Gods. Two were male with wings of emerald and sapphire feathers, stretched wide for all to see. The last female bore wings of purest white, an angel from the heavens. The sight robbed Erika of her courage and she slumped to her knees, unable to tear her gaze from their glory.

Beside her, finally Cara moved. Releasing Romaine, she rose. A tremor shook her body as she cast one last look at the fallen Calafe, then she stepped past him to face the three Gods.

"Hello, brother," she whispered.

The first of the Gods stepped towards her, emerald wings lifting in response. Eyes the colour of flames inspected the little Goddess, before darting to the bodies of Romaine and Yasin. Upon sighting the fallen cutthroat, his jaw tightened and he returned his gaze to Cara. A look of pain crossed his face as he shook his head.

"Ah, sister," he whispered. "What have you done?"

EPILOGUE
THE TANGATA

Adonis gasped as consciousness returned in a sudden flash of agony. He groaned, struggling to suck a breath into lungs that felt as though they were drowning. Tasting blood in his mouth, he rolled onto his side and spat it out. It didn't help. He clenched his fists, struggling against the pain, against the call of unconsciousness.

So you live.

A shiver ran down Adonis's spine and looking around, he found Maya standing nearby. The stony eyes pierced him as she crossed the courtyard and stopped beside him.

Where is the human? she asked, crouching.

Adonis swallowed, trying to draw back his memories. There was a warning in the Old One's voice. She would not tolerate failure. He had to be strong. Gathering himself, he pulled himself to his knees. Agony threatened to swallow him and a trickle of hot liquid ran down his chest. Gritting his teeth, he pressed a hand to his wound to slow the bleeding.

Gone, he replied, meeting her gaze.

Maya did not offer him a hand, though her eyes remained on him, as though waiting. Clenching his fists, Adonis forced himself to his feet. Pain radiated from the wound. The spear had punctured his left lung, but thankfully missed his spine. Again he felt the drowning sensation and for a second his vision spun. He held on, clinging to consciousness until it cleared. He was of the third generation; he would not allow a mere human to strike him down.

And yet it had. How? Adonis gritted his teeth. He would be sure to ask the human when he caught it.

A smile twisted Maya's lips at the sight of him standing and she reached out to stroke his cheek. Adonis sighed, some of the pain receding at her touch.

It will not get far, he breathed. *I will hunt the human down, bring it back for you.*

No, Maya replied softly.

She took his hand then and led him from the courtyard, out into the street. The sun had risen unnoticed as he slept, and now it shone brightly in a cloudless sky. In the distance, the snow-capped peaks shimmered in the morning light.

Show me again my enemy, Maya's voice whispered into his mind.

Unbidden, Adonis found himself back on the banks of the Illmoor, watching as the Anahera fought her way through his warrior pairs. She had batted them away like mere children at first, wings and feet and fists making short work of the fifth generation Tangata. Yet after each blow, his warriors had risen and come for her again, fighting on until eventually even the Anahera's strength had faded.

She does not kill, Maya's voice whispered over the scene, and Adonis again found himself standing in the streets of New Nihelm. The Old One looked at him, eyes alight with bloodlust. *My enemies have grown soft.*

Adonis swallowed as he found himself trapped in that steely gaze. *What do you wish of me, my love?*

Laughter rasped from Maya's throat as her eyes returned to the mountains.

It is time we brought war to the Gods of man.

AARON HODGES

AGE OF GODS

DESCENDANTS OF THE FALL

PROLOGUE

Nicolas screamed as an explosion shook the world, hurling him to the ground. Flames rushed overhead, scorching, violent. They vanished as quickly as they had appeared, leaving only the stench of smoke burning in his nostrils, choking his lungs. Gasping, he forced himself back to his feet.

Screams came from around him as fellow soldiers fled in every direction, all semblance of order lost in the face of an unstoppable enemy. The battlements of Fort Illmoor loomed above, its great blocks of stone torn apart, leaving a hole the width of several houses. Soldiers dressed in red poured through the breach, swords held high as they fell upon Nicolas's comrades.

Another explosion rocked the fortress, though now it came from farther off, as the enemy catapults turned their terrible weapons on a new section of wall. Gasping, Nicolas stumbled in the opposite direction from the soldiers. Black smoke obscured his vision and he struggled to distinguish friend from foe, to find a path to safety. Somewhere above, a horn sounded the retreat, though few defenders were still standing their ground against the terror of the enemy.

Even as he fled, Nicolas struggled to understand how this could have happened. The Gemaho had thought themselves secure behind their giant walls. The Illmoor Fortress had never fallen.

Against man and Tangata both, it had stood strong through the centuries. Not even the Flumeeren queen could defy its might.

How wrong they'd been.

Forcing his way through the press of men, Nicolas cursed his king for a fool. Nguyen should have given up the false Goddess, should have surrendered the Calafe princess—whatever it took to appease the mad queen.

Instead, the Gemaho king had goaded Queen Amina, rebuffing her demands.

Now the full strength of Flumeer came against his kingdom.

And Gemaho would fall.

The screams of the dying chased after Nicolas as he picked his way through the rubble. What new power the Flumeerens had discovered, he could not begin to comprehend—only that it was terrible, destructive, unstoppable. The first explosion had blown blocks of granite the size of horses a dozen yards across the inner grounds of the fortress. Nicolas shuddered to think what had become of the soldiers manning those ramparts.

A roar came from nearby and he swung around as a group of soldiers emerged from the smoke. Red and yellow battled furiously as the melee converged on Nicolas. Cursing, he dragged his sword from its scabbard and leapt at the nearest of the red-garbed soldiers, desperate to cut a path to safety.

The blow connected, slicing through the enemy's unprotected forearm and lodging in bone. As the man screamed, Nicolas tore his weapon free, then stabbed the soldier through the chest. He fell, but another was already stepping forward to take his place.

Nicolas grunted as the enemy's sword slipped beneath his guard and struck him in the chest. The chainmail vest he wore *crunched* with the impact, absorbing most of the blow, though the air was still driven from his lungs. He staggered, struggling to breathe, and swung his blade in a clumsy arc to fend off a second attack.

The enemy soldier parried the attack with a contemptuous swipe of his sword, then stepped in close, blade aimed for Nicolas's throat. Before the blow could fall, a woman in yellow appeared alongside him. Her short sword leapt to meet the enemy's, and steel rang on steel as the weapons clashed. Carried forward by his own momentum, the enemy staggered, and the woman's blade buried itself in his throat.

Blood gushed from the wound as the woman freed her blade, allowing the enemy to crumple. The Gemaho woman flicked a glance at Nicolas as he straightened. Silently he nodded his thanks. She vanished back into the melee before a word could pass between them.

Finding himself at the edge of the chaos, Nicolas took a moment to take stock. An opening between the blocks of granite beckoned, leading away towards the docks. If a resistance could be mounted, he would find it there. He staggered between the chunks of stone—

Boom.

A terrible force struck Nicolas in the back and flung him from his feet. The bricked ground rushed up to meet him and this time Nicolas felt something go *crack* beneath his chainmail. Pain sliced his chest, even as the air turned to fire, his inhaled breath burning, searing…

…the flames vanished, leaving again the cloying smoke, the scorched stone, the moans of the dying. Ears ringing, Nicolas forced himself to move. To stay still was to die. His vision spun as he regained his feet, but even as stars danced across his eyes, he found himself looking upon a sight of horror.

One of the enemy's explosive projectiles had landed a dozen yards behind, where his fellow soldiers had still been battling with the enemy. The explosion had torn through friend and foe alike, leaving them scattered in pieces across the bricked yard. Some still moved, clawing at the ground, their screams just now becoming audible over the ringing in his ears. The woman that had saved him was dead. Only the great blocks of granite had protected Nicolas from the same fate.

Stifling a moan at his own pain, Nicolas stumbled on. A part of him yearned to turn and make a final stand, to die facing the enemy with courage. Yet his duty was clear, even now that the trumpets had fallen silent. If Gemaho was to survive, some needed to escape, to regroup, to warn the cities. The fortress was lost—there was nothing he could do to change that. But he could still serve his nation.

A staircase beckoned, leading down from the plateau upon

which the walls had been built. Relieved, Nicolas started down, his body aching, chainmail torn and twisted by the blows that had struck him. Blood was trickling down his side, though he could not feel the wound. Perhaps he was already dead, his body yet to realise it. He'd heard tales of soldiers that fought on with mortal wounds, driven by adrenaline, until they finally dropped dead.

Nicolas thrust the thought aside as the staircase twisted, the port coming into view below. Sails rose from the murky waters of the river and he glimpsed dozens of his comrades already gathered on the pier—those who had escaped ahead of him. They were struggling to board the galleys docked in the river, their only chance for escape.

There was surprisingly little panic, and Nicolas continued down the stone stairs, trying to estimate the numbers below. Between those still on the pier and the others already aboard, there had to be at least a thousand. More than he'd dared hope, after the disaster above. Perhaps there might yet be a chance for resistance.

He forced his weary body on.

Then his eyes alighted on the flag flown high atop the largest ship. He paused in his stumbling, grasping desperately at the stone railing, straining to see, to know whether it was true…

Yes!

Despite his earlier reservations, Nicolas's heart soared at the sight of his king standing on the gunwales of the warship. Whatever Nguyen's failures, he was the only one who could unite Gemaho against the invaders. Perhaps they might yet repel the mad queen's invasion.

Filled with renewed hope, Nicolas resumed his descent, desperate to reach the safety of his comrades. Normally the pier could have been reached in minutes, but slowed by his injuries, he struggled on, time racing by with each pained step. He could feel his injury now, a dull ache radiating from his ribs, draining the strength from his limbs.

Finally, he reached the stone docks that led along the shore of the Illmoor. A dozen piers already stood empty, but near the end a group of soldiers still waited to board the last of the galleys.

Blood pounded in Nicolas's skull as he struggled towards them, forcing himself to pick up the pace. The pain grew and he clutched at his side, feeling the hot blood soaking his tunic. Dark spots danced across his eyes, but he forced his vision to focus on the king's flag, still flying high above, the last hope of his broken nation.

He was halfway along the pier when a sharp pain tore through his calf. His legs collapsed and he cried out, crashing to the stone. Sprawled on the dock, Nicolas's gaze was drawn to his injured leg, where an arrow now protruded from his flesh. His head swam at the sight, not quite able to believe what he was seeing.

A scream tore from his lips as an agony like red-hot fire swept through his leg. The sound rang from the walls of the fortress, drawing the eyes of his companions on the nearby ships. Shock showed in their faces, before gazes shifted, turning to the stairwell he had just descended.

Nicolas twisted to follow their gaze and glimpsed movement on the stairs. Cries carried from above as a dozen archers appeared. One was already stringing another arrow to his bow, while others raced past him, bounding down the stone steps, eager to place themselves in range of the ships on the river. The rattle of shields being raised came from out on the waters, even as the first arrows flashed towards the king's fleet.

Clenching his jaw against the pain, Nicolas forced himself to hands and knees, then reached down to grasp the wooden shaft piercing his leg. With a sudden wrench, he ripped it free. Despite his best efforts, another scream tore from his throat. Thankfully there were no barbs in the arrowhead, and it came out cleanly. Even so, blood coursed from the wound as he dropped the shaft to the stones.

Nicolas gritted his teeth and began to crawl towards the nearest ship. Dark spots floated across his vision as he watched the last soldiers on the pier fending off arrows from above. Nicolas knew he could not reach them in time. The archers were too close, the Gemaho cause too desperate to delay for one man.

Yet he kept on, eyes on that distant flag, on the soaring eagle on a yellowed background. Nguyen was an honourable man, often seen walking the ramparts of the fortress, joking with the men, enjoying their company. He would not leave a soldier behind.

And so Nicolas crawled on, the darkness growing, vision narrowing until all he could see was the single figure standing atop the gunwale of the king's ship. Hand clutched to a rope for balance, it seemed to Nicolas that the king was watching him, that there was recognition in those green eyes. No, Nguyen would not leave. He was a hero to the people, was going to save them all from the mad queen, from the Tangata…

Nguyen turned away, dropping to the deck of the ship.

Above the soft ringing in his ears, even above the roaring of enemy voices, Nicolas heard the order given:

Set sail!

He crawled on.

In the distance, the last of the ships drifted away from the pier to join the rest of the fleet. Wind filled the great sails of the Gemaho ships and the cries of the sailors carried across the racing waters.

Nicolas continued.

On the waters of the Illmoor, the ships turned slowly, the king out of sight now, though his flagship led the way. Sails cracked as they caught the wind, and shouts came from Nicolas's comrades as they taunted the enemy trapped upon the shores.

Then they began to race away, heading…downstream.

Even through the haze of agony, Nicolas frowned, lifting his head a notch. Gemaho was upriver—downriver was only Flumeer, only the enemy. What was Nguyen thinking?

But already the fleet was nearing the river gates of the fortress, which swung open on their approach. Dark figures swarmed away from the control tower and hurled themselves into the waters, only to catch ropes thrown to them from the galleys. Too late, the Flumeerens realised the Gemaho were escaping. Shouts chased after the departing fleet, but Nguyen was already away, fleeing west.

Abandoning his kingdom to the mad queen.

Despair touched Nicolas then, and he slumped to the stone dock, the last of his will fading. His king had betrayed him—had betrayed them all. The other kingdoms had long accused Nguyen of cowardice, that he had abandoned their alliance in the time of their greatest need. But the people of Gemaho had never believed those claims.

Now the truth lay uncovered for all the world to see.

The patter of approaching boots came from behind. Nicolas didn't lift his head. His death would come by the hands of the Flumeeren archers, but he no longer cared. Instead, he turned his eyes to the mountains above. The snow-capped peaks made even the great walls of the broken fortress seem tiny by comparison. The other kingdoms called them the Mountains of the Gods, and perhaps there was some divine beauty in them. A fitting sight, for a dying man.

The footsteps fell silent, as though a dozen men had suddenly frozen in place. A single pair continued, their tread falling softly on stone, the odd rattle of metal betraying the bearer's armour. Despite himself, Nicolas looked around for a glimpse of his killer.

And found himself looking upon the face of a woman. A strange sight, given that the Flumeerens did not permit women in their armies, but as he looked closer, Nicolas saw the helm the woman carried beneath her arm, the golden wire bound into the steel, forming the impression of a crown. His eyes were drawn to her face, taking in the emerald eyes, the brunette hair woven tight against her scalp, the narrow cheeks and arrogant smile.

Amina, the Queen of Flumeer, stood before him.

"Where has your king gone, soldier?" she asked, crouching beside Nicolas. "Tell me, and I will make your passing quick."

Even through his pain, Nicolas reached for his sword. The queen kicked it away before his hand could close around its hilt. Her steel boot fell upon his wrist.

"I will give you one last chance, soldier," she admonished.

"I would rather burn in your so-called hell than help you," Nicolas spat back.

Amina sighed. "I feared as much."

Nicolas flinched as she raised a fist, but to his surprise, she held no weapon. Instead, a gauntlet covered her hand, its metal threads woven so finely they almost seemed to merge with her flesh. In the full light of day, it shone a soft red…though the light did not seem to be a reflection of the sun.

"Sadly, your resistance matters not. You will tell me everything, by the end."

Baring his teeth, Nicolas made to spit some fresh insult at the woman. Before he could form the words, though, she opened her fist. Light flashed—and then a terrible shriek filled his ears, shearing through the roar of the distant battle, through the distant explosions, until all he could hear was the screeching. It drilled through his eardrums, seemed to slice into his skull itself, to ignite a furnace in his mind.

A scream tore from Nicolas's throat as he clapped his hands to his ears. It made no difference. The flames spread, burning, tearing at his consciousness, until he arced against the stones, until his whole body was aflame, until blood filled his mouth and he could no longer even scream.

Standing over him, the queen leaned closer. He heard her whisper through the briefest lull in the shrieking.

"Tell me, soldier, what is Nguyen planning?"

I

THE HERO

Crouched in the shadows of a pine tree, Lukys looked across the gravel beach to where a row of fishing ships lay stranded on the shore. They could not have been touched by human hands in the year since the kingdom of Calafe had been abandoned, and not for the first time, Lukys wondered whether he had chosen the right course for his companions. Most of the ships looked worse for wear, their sails hanging in tatters from broken rigging, boards of hulls broken by passing storms.

Had he led his friends to disaster? Those ships were their only hope of escaping this land, of evading the Tangatan hunters that might even now be closing in on them. He was surprised they'd made it this far. No human could outrun the Tangata in the wilderness, not with their unnatural endurance, their heightened senses.

A shiver spread down Lukys's spine as he glanced sidelong at the figure crouched alongside him. Sophia. With her curly brown hair and softly tanned skin, she might have been mistaken for human—if not for the entirely grey eyes. Like all members of her species, they were the only distinguishing feature that marked her as different, as Tangata.

But the differences ran far deeper than mere appearances, deeper even than Lukys had realised before their escape. Confronted by the Tangata Adonis, he had felt the full force of the creature's power, its whispers in his mind, the pressure on his emotions, filling him with sheer terror, sending him to his knees.

That was the true power of the Tangata. Beyond their inhuman strength and agility, their supernatural senses, behind the grey eyes, they possessed mental abilities unheard of amongst humanity.

I don't see any guards, Sophia whispered into his mind.

Lukys had long since grown accustomed to her touch on his consciousness—an ability that he alone of his human comrades apparently shared with the Tangata. Only recently had he begun to understand what that truly meant. For it was not just words that Sophia and her brethren could press upon his mind.

They could also touch emotions, manipulate how another Tangata or human felt.

And in doing so, control them.

Lukys's gaze was drawn to his fellow Perfugians, hidden behind him in the undergrowth lining the shore. Dale and Travis crouched on his other side, their Tangatan partners close by. He had rarely seen the partners separated since they'd fled New Nihelm. The terror of the escape, of their battle to survive, seemed to have only strengthened their bond.

Or had the Tangata been influencing them again, pressing on the emotions of his friends?

Anger touched Lukys as he recalled the long days he'd spent in the cells beneath New Nihelm, Sophia his only visitor. He had come to trust her in that time, to believe the Tangata were not the monsters he'd thought them to be.

And all the while her brethren had been manipulating his companions.

With his newfound ability, Lukys alone had been immune—or so Sophia claimed. There was still so much he did not understand, it was difficult to pick the truth from the lies.

For the moment, though, he must focus on the task at hand. Sophia and the others might have manipulated them, but those they'd left behind in New Nihelm were far worse. A new power had taken control of the Tangatan city, an ancient creature from the time before the Fall, when the Gods had cast humanity down for its sins. That Old One had no desire for peace, no wish for union between human and Tangata.

It wanted only death.

Lukys and his comrades had barely escaped with their lives. The other humans in the city, those who had found peace amongst the Tangata, would not have been so lucky.

Where are your people? Lukys directed the thought at Sophia. It was a strange sensation, reaching out with his mind to touch another, but over the last few weeks it had become almost as natural to him as speaking out loud.

A dozen huts of wood and thatch stood amongst the trees across the beach from where they crouched. There was no sign of movement, but Sophia had been sure this village was occupied by Tangata.

They…won't be far, Sophia's response came after a moment's pause.

Lukys's jaw tightened and he struggled to ignore the flutter in his stomach caused by the touch of her voice.

We'll have to move quickly then, he replied, tightening his grip on the spear he carried. The spear Sophia had given him…

He pushed the thought aside and focused his attention on the village. For the most part, the Calafe had been a nomadic people, before the Tangata had forced them from these lands. But for the capital of New Nihelm, their villages tended to be simple constructs, built from local materials. Now the Tangata had taken up residence in these abandoned villages, though fortunately they had not yet filled all of them. The Perfugian recruits had managed to salvage some supplies in another farther upriver: thick furs to protect them from the last of winter's chill, even some tools and knives they could make use of.

They needed only one thing from this place.

A ship.

Lukys gaze was drawn past the rocky shore to where great dunes of sand rose in the distance. They loomed over the river like small mountains, concealing the ocean beyond. Those endless waters offered safety, freedom—but without a ship, they may as well have been beyond the Mountains of the Gods.

Drawing a breath, Lukys tensed and was about to launch himself toward the line of ships when a hand caught him by the shoulder. He flinched away from Sophia's touch, muffling a cry, and glimpsed a flicker of pain in the Tangata's eyes. Guilt touched him, but he crushed it with an iron hand.

What? he growled, glaring at her.

Sophia said nothing, only nodded to the shore. Teeth clenched, Lukys followed her gaze. Movement flickered amongst the huts and he quickly waved the others down. The dense undergrowth of the forest would shield them from view, but one could never be too careful when it came to the Tangata. Fortunately, the breeze was blowing from the dunes, putting them downwind. Even a whiff of human scent would bring the creatures down upon their hiding place.

As Lukys watched, two figures emerged from the huts. They held no tools or weapons, and their clothes were of the same rough-spun cotton that Sophia and the other Tangata wore. They didn't appear alert to the Perfugians' presence, but Lukys held his breath all the same, grip tight around the haft of his spear. These creatures were strong enough to tear him in two, should they wish. The weapon was his only advantage—the Tangata fought with their hands.

The pair wandered down to the shore. The Shelman River was sluggish here, pressed up against the dunes, its currents sapped by the broad plains of Calafe. An estuary had formed in the shelter of the coast, running a mile behind the sand dunes before finally spilling into the ocean.

Lukys watched as the pair crouched in the shallows—one female, the other male. Warrior pairs, humanity had come to call them on the frontlines, though they had not understood their true significance. Lukys knew. It was the great secret of Sophia's, one they had kept from humanity for generations.

The Tangata were almost impotent, rarely able to breed amongst themselves. Their Matriarch had tried to preserve them by partnering youths as they marched to war, in the hope some would produce children. But all too often the efforts had proven futile. That had been the case for Sophia and the others who joined them now. That was why they'd come to be partnered with the Perfugians.

To create the next generation of Tangata.

A splash drew Lukys's attention back to the Tangatan pair. His eyebrows lifted in surprise as he saw that the male now held a shimmering fish above his head. A second later, the female dived, her hand darting out to break the water and clutch at something beneath the surface. Then she too was lifting a fish high.

The two exchanged smiles. From their hiding place, Lukys couldn't sense the thoughts that passed between them.

Gatherers, Sophia's words came to him. *Those who refuse to fight may still partner, but they will not be assigned with a human. If they fail to produce a child together, their lines will come to an end.*

Lukys flicked her a glance, but did not respond to that silent look in her eyes, that longing.

Below, the two left the water and started up the shore with catch in hand. No children appeared from the village as they disappeared into the buildings, and Lukys wondered if that meant their partnership had been unsuccessful.

Shaking off the thought, he turned to Travis. The recruit's usually tidy blonde hair was matted with three days' worth of twigs and dirt streaked his face. His eyes were fixed on the ships below. Travis claimed he knew how to sail, but…

"Are you sure you can sail one of those things?" Lukys asked softly.

"He'd better," Dale muttered from Travis's other side. "Given we're all dead if he can't." At six feet, the man was taller by a good three inches than either of them. His bulk looked awkward crouched amongst the shrubbery, but Lukys had come to rely on the recruits strength these last months.

"You know, I'm starting to see why you lot were sent away," Travis said, his eyes dancing. "We *all* had to learn the basics of sailing, you know."

"You do realise they sent you to the frontlines with us, right?" Dale growled.

Travis waved a hand. "Clearly a mistake was made." He rose to his feet, eyes on the distant ships. "But yes, I think I'll manage." He hesitated, his eyes lowering a fraction, and for the first time Lukys thought he sensed doubt in his friend. "With a bit of help from the others, of course," Travis added at last.

Lukys eyed his friend, wondering just how far the man was over his head. But it was too late for second thoughts now. For better or worse, their path was set. He clapped Travis on the shoulder, then gestured the other Perfugians forward. There were fifteen left, their Tangatan partners making them a party of thirty. Rejects all. Lukys couldn't help but wonder how their people would receive them. What would their Sovereigns think about the reappearance of recruits they'd thought long dead?

Not to mention the Tangata who accompanied them.

No, he couldn't think about that, not yet. First they needed to escape the lands of Calafe. Shaking his head to dislodge the distant worries, Lukys gestured to the line of ships.

"Which one?"

Pursing his lips, Travis studied the gravel shore, though from a hundred yards out Lukys wondered how much his friend could truly tell about their condition. He said nothing though—Travis would only make some joke about having the razor-sharp vision of a Tangata. There was no point questioning him in front of the others.

"The one on the end," Travis said finally as his partner, Isabella, came alongside him. Absently, he placed an arm around her waist as she drew close. "The sail looks to be intact, and I can see some oars on the decks. We'll need them to navigate the estuary."

Lukys nodded, but before he could address the others, Isabella caught his eyes. Her words whispered into his mind:

He is worried, she said softly. *He is not...certain he can do what you are asking.*

Her words gave Lukys pause, though they echoed his own earlier thoughts. He watched her, wondering if she was reading Travis's mind. Sophia had assured him that was impossible, that not even the Old Ones possessed such an ability, but...Sophia had lied to him before. Glancing at Travis, he took in the tightness of his friend's jaw, the way his eyes did not waver from the distant ships. Finally Lukys let out a sigh and returned to Isabella.

Welcome to the human condition, he said softly. *You're right, he doesn't know. We might very well fail to even get the boat off the gravel. But...we'll try it anyway.*

A flicker passed across Isabella's face and when she spoke again, Lukys sensed her fear.

How do you stand it?

Stand what? Lukys asked.

The uncertainty, Isabella's reply came as a whisper, even as she turned from him, her grip tightening around Travis's arm. *The not knowing.*

Lukys frowned. *If no one ever did things they weren't sure would succeed, we'd never do anything new.*

Isabella's eyes widened a fraction and Lukys found himself smiling. This was a side of the Tangata he hadn't seen before. Sophia and the others were always so confident, so self-assured. Even the way they moved—like fluid grace, always in balance—bespoke their confidence. These were creatures capable of running for days, of swimming across the wildest of rivers. At times it seemed there was nothing they *couldn't* do.

He supposed it made sense then, that they would find the prospect of failure disconcerting.

There are others in that village, Sophia interrupted. *Perhaps…they might wish to join us, when they learn what has become of New Nihelm.*

No, Lukys replied sharply, with more force than he'd intended. Sophia flinched, and he drew a breath before continuing. *We can't trust them.*

Can't trust them? Sophia snapped. *Or can't trust me?*

Before he could reply, she spun and slipped away through the others. Lukys cursed silently to himself as he watched her join Dale and his partner, Keria. But Sophia's anger would have to wait. Travis still stood tense beside him, and the other Perfugians were beginning to shift nervously on their feet, awaiting his command. How they'd come to look to him, Lukys could not understand, but he would not let them down now.

"Travis, you and your crew will board the ship and make ready to sail. The rest will work together to push it from the sand. Dale, you're with me." He hesitated, eyeing the others. "Kloe and Warren, you too," he finished, naming two of his best fighters.

Lukys waited for the three to join him before turning back to Travis.

"We'll stand guard, in case those Tangata realise what we're doing."

Silence answered his words, and looking over the group, Lukys could see the fear, the trepidation in their faces. In that moment, he wished he were one of the generals from the history books at the academy, able to give his followers courage with an inspiring speech, to lift their spirits, quell their fears. Instead, all they had was him.

"I know the last few days have been hard," he said softly, "but we're almost there. Just one more push, soldiers."

He met Travis's eyes and the man nodded. The heads of the others seemed to lift a fraction. Jaws clenched and grips tightened on pillaged weapons. Nodding his satisfaction, Lukys raised his own spear and pointed it at the distant ships.

"Let's go find ourselves a ship."

THE EMISSARY

Wind tugged at Erika's hair as she soared upwards. Wings beat down as she left the Mountains of the Gods far below. From so high above, the largest of boulders became no more than pebbles, the raging mountain rivers seemingly reduced to a trickle, the sheer slopes no more than rolling hills. Not even the glacial peaks seemed to tower so high, though they surrounded her still, their chill piercing, even through her thick mountain clothing.

Watching the ground passing below, she allowed herself to embrace the glory of flight, if only for a moment. Blood pounded in her ears and she wondered at the marvels of the earth, the seemingly endless mountains. Soaring so high, the troubles of her world seemed to recede into the silence, leaving only the fluttering of wings, only the cracking of feathers striking the air, the sharp intake of breath.

If only the wings belonged to her.

Her shoulders were already aching where the strong hands held her beneath her arms. The view was worth the pain though, and it was with sadness that she realised they were beginning to descend, as the God holding her aloft angled for the basin below. The racing of her heart slowed as the valley floor approached, the glory of flight fading as her worries returned.

Erika had trespassed on forbidden land, had journeyed farther into the Mountains of the Gods than any human living. She had searched all her life for proof that the Gods still lived, that they might come to the aid of humanity, might save them from destruction at the hands of the Tangata.

Now she had finally found them.

Any other time in her life, she would have been enthralled by the creature that held her. But everything had changed these last few days.

Wind tugged at Erika's blonde hair as her gaze was drawn to where another of the Gods flew. Cara's auburn wings stretched wide as they caught the air, her amber eyes fixed on the ground. Erika had come to know the Goddess well these last few weeks, but she could not read the expression in her friend's eyes now.

It was Cara's appearance that had drawn Erika to this place, all those weeks ago on the River Illmoor, when the Goddess had first revealed herself. Erika had still been an Archivist then, servant to the Queen of Flumeer, a fledgling noble, with fame and fortune written in her future. But that had been before these past few weeks, before she'd failed, before she'd turned her back on the queen.

Before she'd betrayed Cara.

A tremor shook her at the memory of her own treachery, a shame she felt deep in her stomach. How desperate she had been, how contemptible. To avoid retribution for her failures, Erika had attacked the Goddess, taking her prisoner and fleeing for the lands of the Gemaho.

Only nothing had gone as planned. It hadn't taken long for Queen Amina to follow, launching an attack against the very kingdom in which Erika had sought sanctuary. Seeking an ally against his new enemy, the King of Gemaho had sent them into these cold, unforgiving mountains, to the lands of the Anahera, of the Gods. He hoped to earn their friendship by returning Cara to her people.

But even in the Mountains of the Gods, there was no escaping the reach of the Flumeeren Queen. Her assassins had followed them here, setting an ambush that had slain their escort, had almost slain Erika herself. Poisoned by a traitor in their midst, even Cara had been laid low by the queen's assassins.

If not for poor, brave Romaine, they would have all been killed. The last warrior of the Calafe, of her own people, he had been the best of them. He hadn't run away like Erika, hadn't abandoned his kingdom to the Tangata. He had stood to the last against the darkness.

Now because of her he was dead, buried in a shallow grave, left behind in the mountains. Alone.

Erika would never forget his sacrifice, his bravery. No more would she flee her responsibilities, her heritage. When she finally left these mountains, she would seek out her people, the refugees of Calafe, and take up her father's crown. She would lead them back to the light.

She felt a pang in her heart at the thought of her father. His death had come more than a decade ago, and for all that time she had thought it the Tangata who had slain him. Now she knew the truth: the King of the Calafe had fallen to treachery, stabbed in the back by the queen's agents as he led a charge against the Tangata. The Calafe army had been broken that day, the human alliance fractured, weakened. All so Queen Amina could gain ascendancy.

A shudder ran down her spine at the thought. For the better part of a decade, Erika had served her father's killer. The man that had delivered the blow was dead now, struck down by Cara in her rage, but it was Amina who was responsible. She had already succeeded in seeing Calafe destroyed. Now she threatened the lands of the Gemaho. The woman needed to be stopped before all the land fell beneath her heartless rule. There was only one force, one power left who might yet oppose her.

Erika let out a breath as her feet touched down. Released by the God, she sagged to the ground, taking a moment to recover her balance. The Anahera that had carried her said nothing, only strode past to where the City of the Gods waited.

Although now that she had seen it herself, it hardly deserved the title of 'city'. Instead, she found herself standing before an enormous building that dominated the floor of the valley in which they had landed. Smooth walls of the strange grey stone she had come to identify as the material of the Gods stretched some thirty feet above them. There were no windows or embellishing features she could see, though the harsh mountain elements had left their impression, wind and ice opening cracks in the stone.

The erosion came as a surprise to Erika. She had spent her life exploring the ruins left behind from before the Fall, chambers carved beneath the earth by the Gods when they had once lived side by side with humanity. In those places, this same stone had stood untouched by the passage of time.

It was in those chambers that she had first discovered the magic of the Gods. Even as Erika looked upon the city, her thoughts were drawn to the knapsack she carried at her side. Covered in dust and blood, it held the gauntlet she had wielded until today, the secret artefact that had been forgotten to the ages. Only by its power had Erika survived the past months. She had removed it under duress by the queen's assassin, yet now...

...now she had come to distrust that power, to fear it. It was said the ancestors of the Tangata had stolen the magic of Gods—and that the magic had driven them to madness. Erika feared the same corruption had touched her soul, that perhaps her cruelty these past months came not from herself, but from that terrible power. She dared not wield the gauntlet again, dared not risk her soul for its power. Not unless—

The crunch of gravel snapped Erika back to the present. She looked around as Cara landed and folded her wings against her back. The Goddess had discarded the jacket which had covered the auburn feathers for so long—she didn't seem to need it, despite the warmth it provided. The Anahera obviously did not feel the cold as a mortal did, though whether that was a function of their divinity, or their mountain home, Erika did not know.

Certainly, Cara had been vulnerable to the poisons of man, though she seemed to have recovered now. Something had happened back in the pass when she'd confronted Yasin, the queen's assassin. Her rage had been terrifying to behold, a terrible, bestial thing promising only death. Whatever poison that had affected her had been burned away, and Yasin had died horribly. Cara's clothes were still stained with his blood.

Erika shuddered at the memory, for there had been a moment when it seemed Cara would not stop there. For the briefest of seconds, she had thought the Goddess would attack her next, that the bloodshed would not stop until every soul on the mountainside had perished.

But then Romaine had breathed his final words, and the

Goddess had returned to herself, leaving only the grief they all carried now in their hearts.

Another of the Anahera touched down, carrying the third surviving member of their party. Maisie, spy to the Gemaho king, looked unusually pale as the God deposited her on the open ground before the city. She staggered as they landed and almost fell. Erika stepped in to offer a hand when the God that had carried her ignored the spy's disorientation.

"You okay, Maisie?" she whispered.

Maisie nodded and tried to straighten, before deciding better of it and bending over instead. Erika leapt back as she vomited onto the stones. But a moment later the spy straightened once more, wiped her mouth with a sleeve, and forced a smile.

"That was…quite the experience," she managed, though there was still a sickly colour to her face.

Erika grinned in response. Whatever discomfort the spy had experienced, the short flight had been exhilarating. It reminded her of something Cara had mentioned a few days ago, about how she had been forbidden from leaving the mountains, from soaring beyond the range of her home. After just a taste of that magic above, of the freedom, she could understand the Goddess's desire to explore greater expanses.

Turning, she appraised the young Goddess. With long copper hair and amber eyes that seemed to pierce her soul, Cara appeared no older than Erika's own twenty-five years of age—though she'd confessed in the last days to being closer to fifty. Yet despite that, she often acted with the exuberance of an adolescent, and was innocent to the workings of humankind.

Now though, her usual smile was absent, and the sadness in her eyes couldn't help but remind Erika of the comrade they'd been forced to leave behind. Romaine. A lump rose in her throat as she thought of the old warrior, of his struggle to protect those he'd loved. Finally, he had saved one.

A third Anahera landed behind Cara, the one she had called her brother. His wings were a dark emerald, his hair a short-cropped black that reminded Erika of the soldiers in Flumeer. Eyes stained scarlet made her shiver, though there was no animosity in his face.

In fact, concern showed in his gaze whenever he glanced in Cara's direction.

"So you have returned."

A voice, hard and without emotion, cut through Erika's thoughts. She looked around to find the speaker—a new God that had emerged unnoticed from the city. Wings of pure white stretched wide to either side of him, while his dark hair was cropped short, a match to Cara's brother. His amber eyes did not lack anger as he looked upon the intruders in his valley.

Standing alongside the humans, Cara lowered her head in supplication. Erika's heart twisted at the sight of the fiery Goddess bowed low, and silently she reached out to grip her friend's hand. Cara flinched at the touch, glancing at Erika. Her lips tugged upwards, though she didn't quite manage a smile, before returning to the newcomer.

"Hello, Father."

The God said nothing. He stood staring at Cara, seeming to appraise her, taking in the torn and blood-soaked clothing, her filthy feathers and downturned eyes, until finally he blinked, seeming to notice Erika and Maisie for the first time. His lips drew tight as he shook his head.

"I see your recklessness has finally born fruit," he said, his voice like gravel. "Have you doomed us all, my daughter?"

❦ 3 ❦
THE HERO

Lukys sprinted along the shore, gravel slipping beneath his boots, the others racing alongside him, desperate to reach the line of ships before the Tangata noticed their approach. Spear grasped firmly in hand, he kept his eyes on the village as he ran, watching for the first signs of movement. Dale drew slightly ahead, Kloe and Warren just a step behind, the four of them leading the charge.

Then they were beneath the broad hull of the chosen ship. It was smaller than the ships that had been an ever-present feature of the harbour in Ashura, with only a single hull and no cabin atop the deck. They would be exposed to the elements on the long journey north. Lukys hoped the twin masts would at least make for a faster journey.

Grunting from the exertion, Travis rushed past and splashed into the water with hardly a care for the sound he made. Speed was more important than stealth now. So close to the village, the Tangata could not miss their presence on the beach…

Lukys's heart clenched as a figure appeared between the wooden huts. Despite his time living amongst the Tangata in New Nihelm, he couldn't help but feel a familiar terror as the Tangata emerged from the shadows. The reaction was almost innate, beaten into his psyche through his years at the academy, and even before, in those shadowy memories of bedtime tales told by his parents.

Shifting his feet into a fighting stance, he nodded his satisfaction to see Dale and the others readying themselves. Above, more of the creatures had emerged from the village, half a dozen and still growing. Lukys felt a cold breeze upon his neck. Too many. Even the weaker amongst the Tangata were the equivalent of three soldiers on the battlefield.

A shame Sophia and her brethren would not fight, but they had sworn not to go against their own kind. The very idea was anathema to them. And Sophia had told him long ago that she was tired of war, of death. That she wanted something else for her future, to create new life…

Gritting his teeth, Lukys forced the thought from his mind and risked a glance behind. Travis and his crew were already hauling themselves aboard the chosen ship and taking up oars. With the lack of wind, those oars would be needed to negotiate the estuary before they reached the ocean—especially if the Tangata decided to pursue them into the water. In the sluggish current, it would be easy for the creatures to overtake them before they reached the freedom beyond the dunes.

Those not part of Travis's crew gathered around the hull of the ship, preparing to push it into the water when Travis gave the signal. But already Lukys could see something was wrong. Travis was tugging at the ropes hanging from the mast and shaking his head. A moment later he rushed to the bow and waved at them.

"Sails are rotted," his voice carried across the sands.

Lukys cursed. Oars might help to navigate an estuary, but they would struggle in the open oceans without sails.

"Try another!" he called back, grimacing.

There was a moment's pause as the men and women with Travis exchanged glances—then they were leaping from the gunwales. Water splashed around them as they raced to another vessel. Most carried oars with them and some rope bails—hopefully they would make up for any shortages on the other vessel.

But it was obvious they would not have the ship afloat before the Tangata reached them now. Gathering himself, Lukys faced the enemy and gestured his comrades closer. Unconsciously, he reached out to them with his mind as he did with Sophia, seeking to reassure, to grant them courage. It might have been his imagination, but Dale and the others seemed to stand a little straighter.

Above them, a dozen Tangata had now gathered at the edges of the village, grey eyes locked on the Perfugians who dared intrude on their territory. A flicker of fear passed through Lukys as several started forward, but he clenched his teeth and resisted its call. He couldn't afford weakness, not now, not with the lives of his friends on the line.

Lukys. Sophia's voice called to him from where she stood preparing to push the ship from the shore. *Lukys, please, do not—*

Tightening his fists around the haft of his spear, Lukys pushed the words aside. He couldn't afford the distraction of Sophia just now. Just the thought of her, of her deceptions, set his anger alight. How could she have manipulated him so, betrayed his trust, convinced him of her innocence? Now she thought to repair their connection, to pretend they could be like the others. That they could be happy…

He clenched his jaw as rage filled him, set his body to trembling. Instinctively he reached out with his mind for the enemy, for a hint of what was to come. For a moment he sensed fear, confusion, then…a shudder touched Lukys, a red-hot heat, like his own rage reflected back at him. He could almost hear the snarls of their inner voices as the pair atop the beachhead started towards them. Stones crunched as they approached the four recruits aligned against them.

The pounding in Lukys's mind redoubled, his rage taking hold. Images flickered through his mind, of other battles, of the Tangata that had come against him, that had fallen to his blade, their blood staining the earth, their souls cast forever into darkness…

With a roar, the Tangata charged.

Snarling, Lukys leapt to meet them, Dale at his side. Lacking the customary shields Romaine had trained them to wield alongside their spears, they needed to work together now more than ever if they were to hold back the creatures.

Fortunately, the two leaders had drawn ahead of the rest. Stepping in unison, Lukys and Dale moved to intercept the female, while Kloe and Warren lowered their spears against the male.

Teeth bared, the first of the Tangata threw itself at Lukys, her anger reverberating from the nearby sand dunes. Lukys stabbed out with his spear, seeking to skewer her on its steel point. Rage showed in the female's stony eyes as she twisted aside, moving with deceptive speed on the soft ground. Lukys flinched as she darted past his blow, struggling to bring his weapon to bear, even as fingers extended like claws slashed for his throat.

Only a thrust from Dale's weapon saved him. Snarling her rage, the Tangata turned away from him, her forearm slamming into the haft of Dale's spear to turn aside the blow. Even so, the razor point slashed her hip, tearing through the faded tunic she wore.

The Tangata's eyes widened as she retreated, reaching down a hand to press against the wound. Her fingers came away stained red, and her brow wrinkled in surprise. Then her eyes flicked up, catching on Dale, and Lukys saw a darkness pass across them. A growl rattled from her throat and Lukys felt the familiar fear swelling in his chest.

The Tangata moved faster than Lukys would have thought possible on the loose gravel, darting around Dale's outstretched spear. Before Lukys could react, the creature slammed into Dale, hurling him back. Metal flashed as the spear spun through the air and the creature hissed. It raised a fist above the Perfugian's face, ready to crush his skull against the stones.

Roaring, Lukys threw himself at the creature. She looked up in time to brush aside his spear, but the momentum behind his charge carried him forward, and now it was his turn to slam his weight against the enemy. Despite her superior strength, the blow still staggered her, forcing her back from his friend.

A moan came from Dale as he struggled to regain his feet, but teeth bared, Lukys focused all his attention on the Tangata. Blood pounded in his skull and he felt a rage in his heart, a hatred for these creatures, for how they had manipulated his friends, how…how Sophia had tricked him, worming her way into his heart.

Across the stones, the Tangata straightened, but now she flinched away from him as though struck. Lukys snarled and advanced, taking advantage of his enemy's weakness. This time when he attacked, the Tangata's movements seemed sluggish. The gravel slipped beneath her feet and she stumbled. Lukys didn't hesitate, and leaping forward, he drove the point of his spear at her chest. Again she twisted, her fist sweeping down to deflect the blow.

This time though it was not enough, and with a sickening *thud*, the spearhead slammed into her thigh.

A scream sounded in Lukys's mind as the Tangata staggered back, tearing the spear free of her leg. Blood stained the gravel as she crumpled against the shore.

Heart pounding in his ears, Lukys raised the weapon again.

Lukys! Sophia's voice cut through his thoughts, thrusting aside his defences. He froze. *Don't!*

Images flashed across his consciousness, of their time in New Nihelm, of the children he'd seen in the streets, of the peace he'd found in that strange city, however briefly. For a second, his rage receded, and he felt a sense of peace, of calm…

Then he saw again the Tangata Adonis, standing in the yard of their compound, felt the creature's mind pressing against his own, the terror Adonis had thrust upon him. And he saw those new emotions for the truth of what they were.

Sophia. Toying with his mind. Again.

Tightening his grip on the spear, Lukys brought it down, driving it through the heart of the Tangatan woman. A distant cry sounded in his mind, but he thrust it away and slammed the doors of his mind shut. Tearing his spear loose, he quickly looked around, and was pleased to see that Warren and Kloe had finished off the second enemy. Dale had regained his feet as well, though he looked unstable.

Still standing at the edge of the village, the other Tangata seemed to have been given pause by the death of their brethren. Sophia had been right—these individuals were not warriors. If they had been, he and the other Perfugians would never have stood a chance.

Shouts came from behind, and Lukys's heart soared as he saw that Travis and his companions had the second ship afloat. Flashing a last glance at the remaining Tangata, Lukys called the retreat. Forming up with Dale and the others, he led them from the shore, though they kept their spears to the enemy in case of another attack.

Lukys gasped as they plunged into the icy waters, though in truth the Shelman River had warmed since their desperate swim to escape New Nihelm. Carefully they waded out to where the rest of their companions waited. Ropes were thrown over the gunwales, and in moments the four of them were clambering aboard their new ship.

Water rushed from Lukys's clothing as he splashed onto the deck. Dale and the others had gone first, and he exchanged a grin with his friend, part joy at their success, part relief—that they had survived yet another encounter with the deadly enemy.

Drawing in a breath, Lukys gathered himself, taking stock of their situation. Travis was already at the tiller, and those he'd chosen as his crew were busy manning oars and preparing the sails. But none of that would matter should the Tangata decided to follow. Steeling himself, Lukys gathered his spear and moved to the gunwale.

But the Tangata had made no move towards the water. Instead, they were gathering around their fallen brethren. More than two dozen stood on the beach now. Silence fell over the shore as several of the Tangata fell to their knees and reached for the lifeless bodies, though Lukys knew they were likely communicating in the wordless way of the Tangata.

You blocked me out.

He looked around as Sophia appeared at the gunwale alongside him. Glimpsing anger in her eyes, he quickly faced the shore again. The ship rocked beneath them, turning slightly as Travis's recruits shifted their oars.

You were trying to stop me, he said finally, keeping his gaze carefully averted from the Tangata beside him.

Back on the shore, a figure moved amongst the huts. Lukys frowned, straining his eyes as he tried to guess how many more of the creatures hid in the village. Were they planning to cut through the forest and head the Perfugians off before they could reach the outlet to the ocean?

I wasn't trying to control you, Sophia replied, her voice touched with emotion. *I was only trying…trying to make you see the truth. To warn you.*

Warn me of what? Lukys snapped, swinging on her. *Warn me that the Tangata you claimed were peaceful were trying to kill me?*

Sophia did not retreat from his anger. Instead, her grey eyes caught his, so human, and yet so eerily different, foreign.

They attacked because you threatened them, Lukys.

"What?" he spoke out loud, a frown crossing his face. "No—"

You did, she snarled. *I told you that my people cannot control you, that it is forbidden.* Her words faded and Sophia looked away. In that pause, Lukys sensed a sadness from her, before she continued. *But the same cannot be said for you.*

Lukys started. *What?*

Sophia's eyes returned to watch him. *Just as you did with the guards as we escaped New Nihelm, your mind touched those of my brethren. I told you before the dangers of broadcasting, but now…*

A sudden dread touched Lukys, a fear for this new ability he possessed. *What did I do?*

Your rage, Sophia whispered, anger showing in her own eyes. *Your…your hatred for us. You broadcast it to the world, Lukys, to those you see as your enemies. You drove them to attack us.*

On the shore, a lone figure emerged from the village. She was smaller than the others, only a child, but she moved with the fluid movement of the Tangata as she ran down the beach. At the last moment, the others saw her approach. Several tried to stop her, but these she evaded. The rest stepped aside, accepting this was something they could not protect her from.

Lukys watched as the child fell to her knees beside the Tangata he had slain.

And a distant cry of anguish carried across the waters.

I told you they were not warriors, Sophia whispered.

❈ 4 ❈

THE FOLLOWER

Standing on the banks of the Shelman River in New Nihelm, Adonis watched as the blindfolded humans edged forward. With their hands bound behind their backs, they were as sheep led to the slaughter. A smile touched his face at the thought. Finally, the humans who had lived so openly amongst the Tangata had assumed their rightful place.

They numbered in the thousands, some who had been assigned Tangatan partners, others who had been born amongst them, several who had even descended from the Tangata themselves, though their eyes had lost their grey, turning to the treacherous hues of humanity. Some amongst them could even still Speak. Adonis could hear their voices in his mind, clearer than the beastly cries of the other humans, though reflecting the same desperation, the same pleas for mercy.

The joy he felt at their doom almost made the agony of his chest wound bearable. But only the capture of the human who had dealt the blow would sate that pain. For now, he would make do with these sorry souls.

Beside him stood Maya, the last of the Old Ones, the ancient ancestors of the Tangata. Her long blonde hair wavered in the breeze and her skin shone in the rising sun, pale from her eternal sleep. He had woken her from that darkness and she had rewarded him with a place at her side. Partnered in body and mind, they would lead the Tangata to a new future.

Under their watchful gaze, there would be no mercy for the humans of New Nihelm.

Only death.

The cold grey eyes of the Old One watched those below, supervising her new subjects. Her lips did not move, but he could *feel* the pounding of her thoughts, the command radiating from her, the power. It was intoxicating, irresistible.

A scream rose above the gurgling of the river, followed by a *splash*. Adonis watched as the crystal waters turned red with tainted blood. Below, the body sank beneath the racing currents and vanished. The waters cleared, returning to crystal clarity, as though the lost soul had never been.

Ready for their next victim.

Death, death, death.

Adonis watched as his sister Tangata staggered back from the bank. Tears streamed down her face and she only managed a few steps before falling to her knees. Throwing back her head, she howled to the rising sun. Two of Maya's guards leapt forward at once, grasping her by the arms and dragging her away. She would join the rest of her brethren, those Tangata who had already cleansed themselves of their human weakness.

Does your wound pain you? The pounding in his mind dimmed as Maya turned her gaze on him. A shiver ran down his spine as she touched a hand to his cheek.

Adonis quickly removed his hand from his wound. It had been stitched and bound in the hours before dawn and would heal quickly, though he'd been fortunate that the human had failed to land a mortal blow. He still could not understand how Lukys had resisted his Voice, where even his own brothers and sisters of the lesser generations had bowed before him.

It is a reminder, he whispered, meeting his partner's eyes. *When next we meet, the human Lukys will know my wrath.*

Maya's smile grew and she returned her gaze to the cleansing. The pounding redoubled in his mind, and his heart throbbed as the next human was led to the riverbanks. The woman was bound and blindfolded like all the others and he could hear her whimpers over the racing waters. She was whispering a name over and over, pleading with her Tangatan partner to tell her what was happening.

But her partner would not answer. There was a glazed look to the Tangata's eyes as he drew the woman forward, forcing her to her knees. Only then did he pause. Hands trembling, he glanced back, finding where Maya stood overseeing the slaughter. The thrumming in Adonis's mind rose to a fever pitch, and then the Tangata was howling, his fist lashing out…

…and another body fell dead into the waters of the Shelman.

It was a mercy, truly, Adonis found himself thinking as the woman sank into the depths. Death had come for her on silent wings, unknown, unexpected. There had been no suffering, no agony at her partner's betrayal. Only a sharp pain, then…nothing.

Not so for Adonis's brother. A howl rose above the babbling of the river as the Tangata fell to his knees. Adonis listened to his grief without pity. What had they expected, these brethren of his, when partnering with ones so weak? Despite their fallen Matriarch's belief that they could coexist, Maya saw the truth. The humans were a disease, an infection that threatened the Tangata with their very existence.

No, there could be no peace between their species. Only death. Only annihilation.

Before the banks of the Shelman, Adonis's brother made as though to leap into the racing waters, to follow his partner into death. The Old One's guards reached him first, hauling him up, dragging him away. In the end, he went without a fight, arms limp, face downcast, tears staining his stone-grey eyes.

Adonis shook his head at his brother Tangata's weakness, but soon it would be cleansed, burned away in the flames of the Old One's campaign. This pain was necessary. The Tangata could no longer turn their backs on their noble past, on the responsibilities of their species. Maya was amongst the first of them to have been born. Uncorrupted by the taint of humanity, she would renew them, guide them to a great victory.

And so Adonis stood with pride, watching as one by one, the human plague that had infected his people was exterminated.

Until finally, he stood alone on the banks of the river with Maya.

Watching the Old One beside him, he couldn't help but wonder what thoughts passed through the mind of one so ancient. Maya had lived through the time of their birth, had lived to see the world Fall, before being locked into an eternal sleep. Had she dreamed through those countless centuries?

Her eyes flickered suddenly, turning to meet his gaze, and he felt the pressure of her mind against his. Smiling, she reached out to cup his cheek.

Thank you, Adonis, for bringing me to my children, she murmured. *Their rebirth will not be without pain, but a great future awaits us, a glory unlike any your Tangata have known.*

Adonis swallowed as a warmth filtered through his consciousness. He recognised the influence of another's Voice, but did not resist.

What future? he asked. *What glory?*

Maya's lips drew back in a grin as she turned towards the city. Her guards had led their people back within the walls, back to the great Basilica that stood at New Nihelm's centre. The wind blew between the wooden buildings, carrying with it the distant cries of grief.

All in good time, my mate, Maya replied, laughter on her lips. *First, we must prepare my children.*

With that, she moved towards the city, towards the distant howling. Adonis hesitated a moment, watching her as she strode towards the empty gates. Despite his wounds, the heat of desire was strong upon him, the need for her touch, for the warmth of her mind against his.

He made to start after her, but something caught his attention and he paused once again. His nose twitched and he glanced down, seeing for the first time the blood staining the grass beneath his feet. The waters had returned to clarity, but the earth still bore marks of the killings that had taken place through the night. The hackles on his neck stirred as he looked upon that blood, as he listened again to the grief of his brethren…

Are you ready, my mate? Maya's voice intruded upon his thoughts, and when he looked up, Adonis saw that she still stood in the entrance to the city. Her grey eyes watched him, far darker than his own, than any Tangata that had been born in decades. *Come, they wait for us.*

Adonis's blood stirred at the heat of her mind and all thought of the dead humans turned to dust in the breeze. Smiling, he strode after her and together they entered the city. Within, the citizens of New Nihelm awaited their new masters.

5

THE EMISSARY

"I see your recklessness has finally born fruit," the God said. "Have you doomed us all, my daughter?"

Erika couldn't help but flinch at the accusation in the God's tone. She found herself shrinking away from the anger in his eyes, even as Cara shrivelled beside her, eyes on the stones at their feet. Erika glanced at the Goddess, waiting for her to reply, to refute the accusation. But the rebellious woman she had come to know had vanished. A submissive Cara stood in her place now, head bowed low, as though waiting for a blade to fall.

Swallowing her own fear, Erika faced the God again. Cara's father towered over the others, stood taller than most humans, in fact. He made no move to conceal his wings. With their broad white feathers stretched wide, they must have spanned at least twenty feet.

Finding his gaze on her, Erika shuddered and dropped her eyes back to the ground.

"Your…Divinity," she stuttered, her training in the queen's court abandoning her. "We…have travelled through war-torn regions and endless mountains to find you, to beg for your aid. The Tangata ravage the earth, bringing destruction—"

"Was it worth it, I wonder?" Cara's father interrupted suddenly. Erika's head jerked up, and she saw that the God's eyes were locked on his daughter. "To corrupt your soul? To bring shame upon your family?" He drew in a breath, and in his words, Erika sensed something beneath the anger. "To betray your people."

"Father…" Cara said, her voice barely rising above a squeak. "Please, they have committed no crimes—"

"And what of your crimes, daughter?" her father snarled. He made a wild gesture at Cara. "Your corruption lies exposed before us all."

Cara shrank before his rage. Erika's stomach twisted at her friend's distress and she glanced around, seeking someone, anyone that would stand up for the youthful Goddess. But Maisie was doing her best to appear invisible, and the other Gods present made no move to intervene. Finally she swallowed, and gathering her courage, Erika stepped between father and daughter.

"Sir, Your Divinity, please," she said, managing to place more force behind her words now.

But her tongue stumbled as those terrible eyes turned upon her once again, fear raising the hackles on her neck. She found herself squeezing her fist, and was surprised when the warmth of her magic did not materialise. Over the past months, she had grown so used to the gauntlet that its power had become second nature. It felt as though a part of her was missing now.

Still, Erika would not back down, and finally she managed to continue: "Your daughter speaks the truth: we mean you no harm. My people would never betray you as the Tangata once did. We seek only your aid against their darkness."

"The Tangata?" the God snorted. "What do we care for those creatures?" He shook his head, his attention returning to Cara. "It is my wayward daughter that concerns the Elders."

Behind Erika, the Goddess seemed to shrink even further, her wings lifting a fraction, as though she might hide beneath their feathers. The God shook his head.

"Your mother was disobedient, but even she in all her recklessness never brought such darkness to our doors. Even she did not break our most basic laws, did not place her own people in danger."

Erika glimpsed a shine to Cara's eyes as a tear spilt down her cheek, but still the Goddess said nothing to refute the reprimand. Anger touched Erika then, that this being could be so cruel, could condemn his daughter for some imagined crime.

"Your Divinity, my friend and I would both be dead if not for—"

"Hugo," the God interrupted, speaking in a tone that brooked no argument. He gestured to Cara's brother and the Anahera immediately stepped forward. "Take Cara to her quarters. The Elders will convene shortly to judge her crimes."

Cara's brother nodded, and flicking them both an apologetic look, he took Cara's hand. She flinched at his touch, looking at him in surprise, but then her shoulders slumped again. She did not speak as Hugo lead her away, but as she walked past Erika, their eyes met.

Erika shivered as she glimpsed the terror in her friend's gaze. She reached for the young Goddess, but already Hugo was leading her away, back towards the building rising from the barren slopes. Then they were gone, disappeared into the City of the Gods.

Erika allowed her hand to fall back to her side. Icy fear slid down her back as she turned to the God, realising she and Maisie were now alone in his presence. He towered above them, his massive frame and wings dwarfing the two humans, and suddenly she wondered if they might be in danger after all. Cara had confessed to them that the Anahera did not kill, but then…the young Goddess *had* killed Yasin. If her father decided to make an exception…

Swallowing, Erika decided to try another tactic. "I—"

"Come," Cara's father said abruptly, then turned and strode towards the door through which Cara had vanished.

Erika and Maisie remained fixed to the spot, staring after the God's departing back. It was a moment before they threw off the shock of the Anahera's abrupt invitation and scurried after him. The walls of the city rose above, taller than Erika had thought when she'd first looked down from the mountain pass above. Though the lack of windows made it difficult to gauge, she guessed the interior must have at least two storeys. The entire building was the size of a small town.

Cara's father was the only God in sight now, and Erika supposed in such a remote location, there was little reason for the Anahera to venture outside. Certainly there was no sign of water or edible vegetation in the rugged valley. Idly, she found herself wondering where they found their food. Her people believed that the strange Guanaco —the long-necked, woolly mammals that wandered these mountains—were the flock of the Gods, but she could not see any of them now, nor a trail in or out of the valley, for that matter. But then with wings to aid them, what need did the Gods have for roads or trails?

It meant that she and Maisie were trapped here, though. There would be no leaving this place without the Gods' permission, even if they could have survived alone and without supplies in the harsh wilderness.

Shivering, she tried to shake the feeling of being trapped, returning her attention to the city. Drawing closer to the entrance, she saw that her first impression had been right, that the entire structure was shaped from the same strange stone she had encountered in the other ancient sites she had uncovered. But the corrosion was worse than she'd first thought, the outer walls pitted and spotted with patches of stone a different colour from the rest. Repair work, she realised…though why had they not used the same material?

The hackles rose on her neck as they neared the entrance. There was something wrong about this place, this old, almost broken structure. Surely the magic of the Gods should have protected their city, should have preserved it as with those other ancient places.

"So this is the City of the Gods?" Maisie mused as they drew to a stop before a pair of metallic doors. "I have to admit, Archivist, I'm a little disappointed."

Erika nudged her, flicking a nervous glance at their chaperon, but Cara's father was already stepping up to the entrance and did not seem to hear the spy's words. She shook her head at Maisie and offered an irritated frown.

The spy replied with a fleeting smile. She still looked pale, and glimpsing a bloodstain on her sleeve, Erika belatedly remembered that she had taken a wound in combat with Yasin. Still, it couldn't be too serious, or the Gemaho woman would not be on her feet. Though…perhaps it explained her pale colour.

A *screech* came from the entrance as Cara's father pushed open the double doors. Erika winced at the noise, and couldn't help but pause after they stepped inside. The doors were shaped from some unknown metal—the same one they had discovered in the ancient caverns. Her people had been unable to even dent it, and indeed here the metal remained untouched by the elements. The doors

546

themselves slid into cavities in the walls rather than swinging on hinges, but here the wear of nature had taken its toll. Dust and stones from the mountain environment had gathered within, inhibiting the opening of the doors.

"Erika," Maisie called from ahead. The spy seemed to have recovered her composure and gestured for Erika to hurry. "Come on, our hosts don't seem the patient sort. You do recall how humans entering these mountains have a habit of never returning, right?"

Erika's heart lurched at the thought and she jogged to catch up. Every kingdom of humanity had learnt to avoid the Mountains of the Gods. Gemaho such as Maisie might disbelieve in the Gods themselves, but even they weren't so foolish as to defy the prohibition.

Within the structure, Erika was greeted by a familiar sight. A corridor of grey stone stretched away from the entrance. Glowing orbs placed in the walls lit its length, though their light was fainter than the other sites in which she had found the magic active. Protected from the elements, the cracks in the stone were fewer than outside, though farther along the corridor, they discovered other features that had not been present in the ancient sites.

Decorations hung from the plain stone: weavings of plants and twine and flowers, and small mosaics created from coloured pebbles, even several carvings of red wood, though there were no forests in these mountains. Did that mean some of the Anahera were permitted to leave their territory, or did such rules only apply to their youths, such as Cara?

They followed Cara's father through the twists and turns in the corridors, and while Erika tried to keep track of the pattern, she was soon lost in the great structure. The pattern of branching corridors and rooms might have been the same as the other sites Erika had visited, but without her map she could not say.

Only the occasional side chamber was barred by a door. The rest stood open, and Erika took the opportunity to glance into each as they passed. A few appeared to be simple sleeping chambers, but Erika was disappointed to find that most were empty.

Finally the God came to a stop in front of one of the few chambers with a door. Pulling it open, he indicated for them to enter. Erika and Maisie exchanged a look, but there was little opportunity to argue. Cara's father had already made his displeasure at their presence evident.

Hesitantly, they stepped inside, and Erika breathed a sigh of relief as they found themselves in a sparsely adorned sleeping chamber. Barely ten feet by ten feet, it contained two beds pressed up against either wall. Each was little more than blankets stuffed with straw or feathers, but at least they would be preferable to sleeping on the rocky ground as she had done the last few weeks.

The room held little else, but even so, Erika turned and bowed to the God.

"Thank you," she said, pleased that her voice was steady now. "Your daughter tells us your people are called the Anahera. What might we call you, Your Divinity?"

A frown wrinkled the God's face as he glared at the two of them, and for a moment Erika thought he would not answer. Then abruptly he waved a hand.

"I am called Farhan, human," he growled.

"I am the Archivist, Erika, and this is Maisie of the Gemaho," Erika replied, keeping a respectful tone. "Might I ask, what do you plan to do with us, Farhan?"

The God's frown deepened. "You should not be here, human," he said. "You will stay in these quarters until the Elders have decided what to do with you."

"And what of your daughter?" Erika pressed, then hesitated. "She...did not lead us here. I discovered a map that revealed the location of your city. Do not blame her for my crime."

Farhan said nothing in response to her words, only stood staring at her, amber eyes burning.

"The Elders will decide my daughter's fate," he said at last.

Then he was gone, the door slamming shut behind him. This one only used a simple hinge, and while the door was of the same strange metal as the outer ones, the hinge appeared to be of normal iron. As it clicked closed, Erika looked at Maisie.

"What now?" she asked.

The spy snorted and fell back onto one of the beds. A cloud of dust billowed out of the pile of blankets and she immediately started to sneeze. By the time she managed to regain control, Erika had hidden her grin.

"What now indeed," Maisie coughed, her eyes still watering. She shook her head and sighed. "Some mess you've gotten us into, Archivist."

Erika frowned. "I thought this was your king's idea."

Maisie laughed. "Monarchs only have good ideas, Erika," she replied. "Didn't your queen teach you that? No, judging by our reception here, this little venture was entirely your doing." She paused. "So, what do we do now?"

❧ 6 ❧

THE HERO

Standing at the railings of the fishing ship, Lukys looked out across the open ocean and tried to pretend his worries did not exist. That the strife he faced, the fear and danger, even the hatred that infected him, all of it might simply float away on the salt-tanged winds. For a while, he almost manged to convince himself there was only the endless water, only the rolling waves and the soft creaking of the ship, the flapping of the hastily-patched sails and the shouts of his comrades as they struggled to recall lessons long since forgotten.

Travis's voice rose occasionally above the others as he shouted out instructions. Lukys was impressed by the way his friend had stepped up since they'd taken control of the vessel. Watching him, he couldn't help but think Travis should have been the one to lead them. The role of sea captain seemed to come naturally to the man.

It was more than Lukys could say for himself. Again, he found himself recalling the Tangata charging down the shore towards him, saw the rage in the female's eyes as she attacked—and her fear as Lukys raised his spear. Heard the child's scream.

Travis would not have lost control, would not have driven the creatures into a frenzy. Travis would not have slain a child's mother.

He screwed his eyes closed, but there was no hiding from the memory. His guilt kept summoning the scene, and each time that cry cut a little deeper. He recalled the look Sophia had given him as they stood at the gunwale, the anger, the hurt in her eyes. Humanity had regarded her kind as monsters for as long as history had been written—yet it was Sophia who wanted to stop the killing, who craved peace, to bring life into the world.

Instead, Lukys had given her only more death.

A shudder shook Lukys and he swung away from the ocean. He would find no lasting peace in those endless depths. Across the little ship, he watched instead as his companions worked. Human and Tangatan pairs toiled side by side, united in hearts and minds, though they could not even truly communicate.

United because the Tangata had manipulated their human assignments into feeling affection, into feeling love for their captors.

Or had they?

Lukys found himself suddenly doubting everything, and he swallowed, seeking out a glimpse of Sophia. He found her near the bow with Keria, Dale's partner, helping to set up a piece of canvas to catch rainwater. The ship had no supplies and though they had some limited food, lack of water would soon force them back to land. With hundreds of miles of Tangatan territory between themselves and their island homeland, every visit ashore would put them at risk. Even an encounter with their own side might prove risky, given they were likely to be accused of desertion, or worse, treason.

As he watched, Sophia finished tying the rope that would hold the canvas in a concave shape. Her head lifted and their eyes met. Her face hardened and she quickly looked away.

"The two of you should talk."

Lukys started as Dale appeared beside him and leaned against the gunwale.

"What?" Lukys frowned at the man.

Dale gestured in Sophia's direction. "It's obvious something's wrong between you," he said, then hesitated before adding: "We can't afford to be divided, Lukys, not when we get to Perfugia. I know it hurt to kill those people on the beach, but we did what we had to. She will understand. Keria does."

Guilt lodged in Lukys's throat—not for the Tangata he had slain now, but for his companions. After New Nihelm, he had delayed telling Dale and the others the truth, about how the Tangata had manipulated them. In the rush of the escape, of fleeing the hunters, there hadn't been time, but now…

"It's…complicated, Dale," he said finally, swallowing hard.

"Love always is," the soldier replied.

Lukys looked sharply in the man's direction. This was his opportunity, his chance to finally reveal the Tangata's deception. Dale had been his enemy once, but over the course of the war he had earned the man's respect, even his friendship. Dale, Travis, all the others, they deserved to know what had been done to them.

"Is it really love we feel?" he whispered.

Dale said nothing, though his eyes drifted to where Sophia stood. Keria had joined her at the gunwale.

"They're not what they say they are," Lukys whispered, the words leaving his lips before he could hold them back.

"I know." Dale smiled.

"No," Lukys said quickly. He shook his head, though his eyes remained on Sophia. "You don't understand. They…the things they can do, what *I* can do, speaking into our minds, it's more than what you think."

"Lukys, *I know*," Dale said softly. Lukys looked at him sharply, and the soldier raised his eyebrows. "You think the rest of us haven't realised there was something strange about how we met, about how we fell for our partners?"

"They're manipulating your emotions," Lukys hissed.

"Yes," Dale replied, "and no." He glanced at Lukys out of the corners of his eyes. "It's strange, our emotions are…heightened around them, enhanced. But I trust her, Keria. Around her, even the bad, even when we fight and I feel anger…even then, I can still feel the good beneath."

"And you don't have a problem with that?"

Dale shrugged, turning his eyes to the distant shore. "Do you remember what it was like at the academy, Lukys? Every moment of our lives was controlled, planned, scheduled. So much pressure, to be better, to excel, to pass." He paused. "Or maybe it was different for you?"

"No," Lukys murmured, memories of sleepless nights flickering through his mind. He might not have been noble born like Dale and Travis, but the pressure had been the same. "I remember."

Dale nodded. "Then we arrived in Fogmore, and I thought things might finally change, that there I could earn myself some respect. Instead, they threw us to the wolves. Even when we survived, we were barely fed, given the most rundown, filthy, cold lodging in town." He sighed. "I was close to giving up. We all were. Except for you. Only you stood up, went looking for help, for someone to train us. You and Romaine, you gave us something to fight for, Lukys. Even if for me that was only saving face."

Lukys shrugged, uncomfortable with the praise, but thankfully Dale went on.

"Then in the dungeons beneath New Nihelm, the despair came for me again. The pain, the hunger. I thought nothing could keep the darkness at bay." A smile touched his lips as he looked over his shoulder at Keria. "Instead, I found happiness, found her. Maybe she pushed on my emotions, but…it was still her kindness that lifted me from the despair."

Lukys swallowed but said nothing. Dale's words echoed his own thoughts during those dark days in the dungeons. He'd come to realise that even as their prisoner, the Tangata had treated him far better than his own kind ever had.

That *Sophia* had treated him far better than anyone else in his life.

He cursed beneath his breath. Beside him, Dale laughed and clapped him on the shoulder. "There we go," he said, flashing a final smile before he moved away to join Travis at the tiller.

Letting out a long sigh, Lukys stepped away from the gunwales and weaved his way across the crowded deck. Sophia was still looking across the waters to the distant horizon. Moving alongside her, he couldn't help but think how tiny they all were, how insignificant their petty squabbles beside the endless expanse of that ocean.

Sophia did not react to his presence, didn't even glance in his direction. Lukys bit his lip, wondering how to begin. She wasn't going to make this easy on him. Struggling for the words he needed, Lukys ran a hand through his hair, watching her out of the corner of his eye. Her figure had narrowed since their escape—the Tangata insisted that the humans eat before they did, and there wasn't always enough to go around. There was a softness to her face beneath the battle-worn edge she showed the world. The wind tugged at her ash-brown hair, tangled from the half-a-week they'd spent on the run. A twig from the forest had caught in one of her locks, and absently he reached out to pluck it free.

She flinched at his touch, withdrawing from him, and his hand fell back to his side.

What do you want, Lukys? Her voice came to him, taut with suppressed anger.

Lukys swallowed, twig still clutched between his fingers. Absently he flicked it over the side, then sank to the deck and leaned back against the gunwale.

I should have listened to you, he whispered to her. *I should have found a way to make peace with those…people.*

He could feel Sophia's eyes on him, but Lukys did not risk a glance, only pulled his knees to his chest and watched as Travis gestured wildly from the tiller, shouting for one of his crew to trim the sails—whatever that meant. He really should have paid more attention to their maritime classes.

There was movement beside him as Sophia joined him, though she left space between them.

And now a child's mother is dead.

Lukys closed his eyes as that awful scream echoed through his mind again. He clenched his jaw, seeing again the fear in the Tangata's eyes as he lifted the spear, heard again Sophia's plea for him to stop.

I'm sorry, he said, though he knew it was not enough.

Silence answered his words. He did not speak again, only leaned his head back against the gunwale and watched as one of the crew struggled to scale the mast, presumably for a better view of the ocean around them. They were trying to keep close to the coast, though not so close they drew the attention of every Tangata in the area.

There has been so much death, Lukys, Sophia's words finally came to him. *You are not the only one who has shed innocent blood. I thought…I thought finding you, with our union, that I might finally leave the nightmares behind. But…*

All I know is death, Lukys finished for her, his voice bitter.

It was true. His assignment to the frontlines had proven his inadequacy in every other facet of life. The Sovereigns of Perfugia had judged him unworthy to even clean the privy of his betters. Only in battle had he excelled, had he found his worth.

No, Sophia replied with surprising force. Lukys started as her hand touched his shoulder. *No, Lukys. You are capable of so much more.* She turned her gaze on the Perfugians and their Tangatan partners. *You united them, lifted them up when they lacked the strength to stand. You ask why Travis does not lead, but you cannot see that he draws his courage from your own.*

Tears stung Lukys's eyes and he shook his head, refuting her words. "My rage will leave them dead, just like that child's mother."

There is a rage in all of us, Lukys, Sophia replied, *in the Tangata. It is the curse of my people.*

Then…how do you control it, keep it from influencing others? He hesitated, thinking of the times he had seen the Tangata enraged, the way they changed, attacking without hesitation or constraint. *From controlling you?*

It was a moment before Sophia replied. *We learn to keep that part of us suppressed,* she said at last, *mostly. During battle, there are some who uncage the beast, but…I dream of a world where such violence is no longer needed.*

And your powers? Lukys added.

Powers… Sophia spoke the word as though she found it strange. *Such an unusual term, for an ability we have from birth. It is much like breathing for us, Lukys, to sense the emotions of others.*

And to influence them?

Sophia hesitated. *You are as a child, Lukys, unschooled. And…your ability is far stronger than any human has a right to—even had you a recent Tangatan forefather.*

Her words brought a frown to Lukys's face. Sophia had said his ability meant there was Tangatan blood in his line, but the claim still rung hollow. How could that be possible, when he came from Perfugia, the one foothold of land the Tangata had never reached? At least, not so far as their history stretched.

Perhaps they would find the answer to that question in Perfugia, though he was not hopeful. Just convincing his fellow Perfugians not to slaughter them on the spot when they discovered the Tangata onboard would be nigh impossible. He couldn't bring himself to think beyond that trial. Though perhaps if he could master this ability…

"Will you teach me?" he whispered, turning to Sophia.

She still sat away from him, but leaning against the gunwale, their faces were close. Her eyes shimmered in the noonday sun, still the strange solid grey of the Tangata, so dark they seemed to absorb the light, though in doing so they grew just a little lighter, more human. Without thinking, he leaned towards her, reaching up to cup her cheek. Her eyelids flickered as his fingers caressed her cheek and silently he moved to kiss her—

No!

Before their lips could meet, Sophia jerked away from him, rearing back. Lukys started, shocked by her rejection as she scrambled to her feet. Now he glimpsed the anger simmering in those grey eyes. Heart pounding, he reached out with his mind, desperate to understand, to know what he had done.

Sophia… he whispered.

Her anger crashed over him like a wave, pounding against his consciousness, and for a second he felt as those Tangata on the beach must have. Then he broke beneath the surface, and an icy cold touched his mind, a freezing sadness…and even deeper, a terrible hurt, pain at his betrayal.

Standing over him, Sophia shrieked, and suddenly Lukys found himself hurtled backwards, torn free of her mind. He gasped, staring up at her, still struggling to process what he had seen, what he had felt. His mouth parted, but her words forced their way into his mind before he could speak.

So arrogant, she spat. *You think you can ignore me, treat me like vermin, and I will simply forgive you?*

I'm sorry! Lukys gasped, coming to his feet and reaching for her. She twisted away from him.

Sorry? Sophia hissed, baring her teeth. A heavy silence stretched out as they faced one another, and reluctantly Lukys allowed his hand to fall. Sophia drew her lips tight, and when she spoke again the anger was gone from her voice. Only sadness remained.

You don't think of us as people, Lukys, she murmured, still watching him with those haunting eyes. *The way you've looked at me these past days…it was like I was some animal that had bitten you.* She swallowed, and he watched as a tear spilt down her cheek. *We're not perfect, Lukys. I should have…should have told you the truth. But…you didn't even give me a chance to explain. Now you ask for my help, try to…try to kiss me?*

He opened his mouth, then closed it again, seeking the words he needed, the ones that would make things right, that would prove his remorse. He could not find them.

We're human, Lukys, she said at last. *Just as human as you or Dale or Travis. Until you realise that…* She trailed off.

With a shake of her head, Sophia turned and walked away.

7

THE EMISSARY

Erika paced up and down between the beds, reaching the wall only to spin on her heel and stride the half-a-dozen steps to the door before turning again. The way she was going, she would wear a groove in the stone floor before they ever saw another of the Anahera. But what else was she meant to do? Farhan had left them here, alone, without a single hint about what was to become of them.

"Gah, how can you just sit there?" she burst out, swinging suddenly on Maisie.

The Gemaho spy lay reclining in the bed she'd claimed, a crystal globe rolling back and forth between her fingers. The orb could have been mistaken for the crystal balls used by fortune tellers at the markets in Mildeth, but Erika knew from experience there was far more to it than met the eye. It was another of the artefacts recovered from the time before the Fall, an item of power like her own disused gauntlet. Contained within was the magic to make them invisible to the eyes of others. Little good that would do them here though, locked in the unadorned room.

Pocketing the orb, Maisie entwined her fingers and looked at Erika. She said nothing, only raised her eyebrows.

Erika growled and did another lap across the room. "What do you think they're going to do with us?"

On her bed, Maisie shrugged. "That probably depends on what they're going to do with Cara."

Erika paused mid-stride. "What do you mean?"

Even as she spoke, she recalled that last look Cara had flashed her when confronted by her father—broken, defeated, terrified. A shiver ran down her spine and she stared at Maisie, waiting for the other woman to reply.

"Well…" Maisie mused. "If she's sentenced to death, chances are we won't be long in following."

Erika started, shocked by the spy's words. She'd thought themselves in danger, trespassing in the forbidden mountains, but Cara? This was her home. Whatever rules she'd broken, surely her father couldn't condone such an extreme recourse.

"No," she said finally, shaking her head. "The Anahera do not kill. Cara said as much, in the mountains…" She trailed off beneath Maisie's unwavering gaze.

The spy raised her eyebrows into her mop of curly black hair, as though to ask whether Erika could really be so naïve.

"I must have knocked my head harder than I thought, back in that canyon," Maisie said finally, her eyes unblinking. "Because I could have *sworn* the 'good Goddess' *tore a man's limbs from his body.*"

Erika shuddered at the reminder of that brutal scene. There had been little left of Yasin by the time Cara had been done with him. Quickly she forced the memory aside. She should be thankful—the man had planned to deliver her to the queen, and the Gods only knew what Amina had planned for her treacherous Archivist.

"You don't think…you don't think that's what Farhan meant, when he accused her of corruption?"

Maisie rolled her eyes. "You know, for someone who dedicated her entire life to studying these Gods of yours, you don't seem to know much about them."

Erika's cheeks grew warm. "I got us here, didn't I?"

"Yes, though personally I prefer to avoid being imprisoned by Divine beings." She paused. "So…do you have a plan yet?"

Erika gritted her teeth and swung away, struggling to recall everything Cara had told her about her people. Two facts stood out stark in her memory—that the Anahera did not kill, and that they did not lie. Yet she had only Cara's word on each—had the Goddess been lying even then?

No, she had seemed sincere when they'd spoken. Erika had put her faith in the youthful Goddess when she'd released her from her bindings. Cara might have betrayed them then, could have torn them apart with her bare hands had she wished.

That meant...

"We need to get out of here," Erika said abruptly.

If Cara had been telling the truth, it meant that what she'd done to Yasin was forbidden in the eyes of her father and the Anaheran Elders.

"About time!" Maisie exclaimed.

Levering herself off the bed, Maisie grabbed her knapsack and moved to the door, where she took something from the bag. Erika frowned, shifting closer to try and decipher what she was doing. But Maisie said nothing, only placed her eye to the keyhole, then lifted her hands. A sliver of metal shone between her fingers and Erika realised what she was planning.

"You think Gods would make a lock a mortal could pick?" she asked, leaning against the wall beside the spy.

Maisie grunted. "Gods? No. Anahera, maybe," was all she said.

Erika rolled her eyes at the woman's casual blasphemy. How Maisie could still disbelieve when the evidence was all around her, Erika couldn't understand. But at this moment, a theological debate seemed the least of their worries, so she kept her silence.

Minutes slipped past, punctuated by the occasional curse from Maisie. The spy had a colourful vocabulary and Erika learned several new words over the next half hour. Absently, she recalled the woman's story of how she'd come to be in the king's employ.

"Did you learn to pick locks on the streets of Mildeth?" she asked, trying to make conversation.

Maisie snorted. There were now three slivers of steel sticking from the lock. "What, they didn't teach you how to pick locks in Archivist school?"

Erika rolled her eyes. "We preferred black powder," she said, then: "Actually, we didn't even *have* locks at the school. What do students have to steal from one another..."

She trailed off as an idea came to her. Maisie didn't appear to be listening anyway. Frowning, Erika thought again of everything Cara had told her, then reaching out, she twisted the door handle. A soft *click* followed as the door to their room swung open. Outside, the corridor was empty. Farhan hadn't even posted a guard.

Still on her knees in the now open doorway, Maisie scowled. "Well that takes the fun out of this."

Erika chuckled. "What purpose would a society that only ever tells the truth have for locks?"

"I'd say it makes them easy picking for a species that lies," Maisie commented, regaining her feet and tucking her tools away.

A smile twitched on Erika's lips and she extended a hand towards the corridor. "Ladies first?"

Maisie's scowl deepened but she took the lead. She kept her magic orb out of sight, and Erika guessed the narrow corridors would make it difficult to evade the Anahera, whether they were invisible or not. The magic created a bubble around its users that concealed everything within, but anyone who stepped into the bubble would immediately see the truth.

And besides, it wouldn't hurt to keep a few secrets of their own. Her hand drifted to her bag and the gauntlet within. She knew its magic could bring down a God—she had used it on Cara herself. Perhaps it was best it remained hidden, at least for now.

Thankfully, the corridors around their rooms appeared empty, and Erika wondered again at the strangeness of the place. Without any clue where to go, they headed in the opposite direction from which they'd entered. They moved slowly at first, taking time to inspect the rooms they passed and to pause before branches in the corridor, wary of Anahera who might be wandering the place.

But all they found were chambers and corridors empty of their inhabitants. As they drew deeper into the building, more and more of the chambers appeared as living quarters. These rooms were warmly decorated, mostly with objects found in nature and shaped by Anaheran hands. The larger of the chambers held as many as half a dozen beds, and Erika found herself imagining entire families sharing a single space together. It was stranger still to find each chamber open, without even doors to provide the inhabitants privacy to those without.

Though she supposed it followed with what Cara had told them, of a people without secrets, with no fear of death or crime. A paradise, just as human records spoke of the days before the Fall, when humans had lived side by side with the Gods. Little wonder humanity's corruption had driven them to these distant mountains. With the power they wielded, the Anahera must have feared humanity would betray them again, would try to steal their magic as the Tangata once had.

Such deliberations did not bode well for Erika and Maisie. She quickly swallowed the lump in her throat. King Nguyen's plan had relied on Cara being welcomed home with open arms—not put to trial for murder…

Quickly Erika forced the thought aside. This was the City of the Gods, a place of wonder and miracles. Whatever their reluctance, when the Anahera learned of the state of the world, of the Tangata rampaging across the land, burning villages and driving humanity to the brink of destruction, surely they would not stand idly by. Surely they would aid the kingdoms—

Bang!

Erika cursed as she walked headlong into Maisie. The Gemaho spy had come to an abrupt halt and was staring at the wall beside them. Erika frowned, but her mouth dropped as she followed the spy's gaze. A painting covered the wall from floor to ceiling, its details perfectly preserved beneath a pane of glass. Glass of such size alone would have been something to wonder at back in Flumeer.

But it was the painting itself that had drawn Maisie's attention. The detail of the image was something to behold—so fine that Erika could not even begin to make out the individual brushstrokes. It didn't seem possible that a human could have the skill to create such a masterpiece, but then, this was the City of the Gods…

…and the image depicted was a scene beyond her wildest imagination. A blue harbour stretched away from the artist's viewpoint, a bridge of deepest red rising from the raging waters, so grand, so enormous it would have put the greatest of human citadels to shame. Beyond the scarlet bridge, brilliant towers of glass rose from rolling hills, far taller than even the greatest works constructed from Perfugian marble, such that only the awesome power of magic could have held them aloft.

A shiver ran down Erika's spine as she stared at the image, as she beheld the true City of the Gods. *This* was what she had expected to find in these lonely peaks, some spectacle of wonder, of impossibility.

"It must be one of the cities lost in the Fall," Erika mused, "but…why have the Gods not built themselves a new heaven here?"

Maisie flashed her a glance and looked like she was about to speak, but then the distant murmur of voices carried to their ears. They hesitated for half a moment before setting off in the direction of the whispers. Erika shivered as they passed more empty chambers, though her mind remained on the image of the city.

They slowed as the voices grew clearer, and Erika sensed they were coming from the next doorway. They approached cautiously, aware they were violating the Anahera's trust, but knowing they could not stand idly by while Cara's fate, and their own, was decided.

They paused a moment outside the room and Erika felt a cold breeze blowing from the opening. She frowned, sharing a glance with Maisie. Voices echoed from beyond the doorway, but they seemed muted, obscured, as though the sound came from a great space.

Erika drew in a breath, then flashing a final glance at the spy, she stepped through the doorway…

…and into an open yard. She blinked at the brightness of the outdoors, and for a moment she did not notice the sudden silence that had fallen. Eyes watering, she struggled as her vision adjusted to the light.

When it finally cleared, she found herself staring across an open space enclosed within the walls of the city. An enormous yard had been left open in the centre of the great building. Around the edges, glass houses stood at intervals. Erika glimpsed vegetation through the great panes, and guessed these must be where the Anahera grew their food.

Otherwise the yard held only dirt and rocks and the occasional snowdrift—and a tall structure of stone rising from its centre. It was there the voices had come from.

At least a hundred of the Anahera were gathered in the centre of the yard and now stood staring in their direction. Each bore wings of every hue and colour, some lifted in fright, others folded neatly against their backs.

Silence had fallen across the yard and Erika couldn't help but shudder as she felt the gaze of the Divine upon her. She swallowed, but there was no chance to turn back now. Flicking one last glance at Maisie, she strode forward in search of Cara and the Elders who would judge them.

The Anahera parted without a word and more of the structure rising from their midst came into view. An enormous altar of granite lay in the centre of the yard, stone monoliths rising from each of its corners, stretching some fifteen feet high. Unlike the rest of the city, the rock for the structure appeared to have come from the surrounding mountains.

As they neared the centre of the yard, Erika finally caught sight of Cara. She knelt in the mud beneath the strange monoliths, her auburn wings drooped low, suffering under the gaze of five Anahera. Each bore the marks of age—lines that wrinkled their faces and hair bleached white, withered limbs, and tired eyes. Even their wings, so glorious in all the Anahera who had gathered in the yard, had lost their lustre, with patches of naked skin showing in the place of feathers.

All, that was, except for the looming figure of Farhan in their centre.

The hackles stood on Erika's neck as she looked from Cara to the Elders, to her father standing amongst them. Outside the city, Farhan had spoken of the Elders as though they were apart from him. Now her blood ran cold as she realised the weight his anger carried. How could Cara have neglected to mention that her own father was amongst the rulers of her people?

Farhan showed no emotion as he watched their approach, and she wondered again at this God. Surely, whatever his anger at Cara's defiance, he could not condemn his own daughter.

"Humans," Farhan growled, stepping from the other Elders to confront them. "You are not welcome here."

A lump lodged in Erika's throat as her heart began to pound. She fought the urge to run, to flee from the power she glimpsed in Farhan's amber eyes, from the towering God before her. Even Maisie beside her took a step back.

But then Erika's gaze was drawn beyond the God to where Cara still knelt in the mud. She had looked up at their approach and her eyes were wide as she stared at the pair of them. A smile touched Erika's lips at the open surprise on her friend's face, and she offered a reassuring nod, before turning to face Farhan.

"We humans have names, Farhan," she said, managing to add iron to her voice. "I am called Erika, as I informed you in our quarters."

For the first time, a frown wrinkled the God's face. She caught a flicker in his eyes as he appraised them, but whatever doubt she had caused, it was quickly replaced by irritation.

"You have trespassed on our lands, corrupted my daughter." He took a step closer to them, his wings lifting to cast the two humans in shade. "Now you come here, uninvited to our private assembly, and demand our attention?" He raised a fist, and Erika couldn't help but imagine an iron hand closing around her throat. "Even our youngest fledglings know to show more respect."

Erika shuddered, trying to still her racing heart, to suppress the sudden desire to throw herself at the feet of this being and beg his forgiveness. Farhan was Divine, God to her people, to herself. What right did she have to stand here and question him?

But that would mean abandoning Cara to her fate, and looking at the terrified Goddess, Erika knew that was something she could not do. Lifting her shoulders, she met Farhan's glare.

"And…what corruption do you speak of?"

The God stood in silence for a long moment, eyes fixed to hers, as though expecting her to melt before his power. But summoning every inch of her court training, Erika resisted the urge to squirm, to subjugate herself before his Divinity. Cara's fate, even their own, might rest in her hands. She would not back down.

"My daughter has spilt the blood of a mortal, an act condemned by the Sacred Founders of the Anahera."

Ice spread through Erika's veins at the coldness of Farhan's words for his daughter. Could he truly be so callous, so heartless? She swallowed, drawing her own mask of nobility about herself, of defiance.

"Very well," she said, advancing a step. "Then I would speak on behalf of my friend."

❦ 8 ❧

THE FOLLOWER

*H**ear me, my children!*
  Adonis's heart swelled as Maya's voice rose above the cries of the Tangata gathered in the square before the Basilica. There was a serenity to her Voice when she spoke, a power far beyond that of their fallen Matriarch. She stood on the steps of the Basilica, arms outstretched towards her children, her mental Voice ringing through the minds of those gathered before her.

Fear not, the darkness has passed, she continued, the inner notes of her Voice swelling to a crescendo, lifting her people, banishing their despair. *No longer will we stand idle. The time of the Tangata has come.*

Thousands had gathered at her command, torn loose from their obligations to their humans. Men and women, old and young packed the streets, and all of them looked to Maya, hanging upon her Voice.

The corruption has been cut from our midst, Maya continued, and for a moment darkness filled Adonis's mind, a hatred, an anger for the creatures that had walked so blatantly amongst them. Rumblings came from the crowd, and he sensed their questions, their confusion, that they had ever allowed such monsters to pretend to be their equals, to be honoured alongside their Tangatan betters.

The future belongs to us, my children, Maya whispered. *Our enemies have grown weak. They war amongst themselves, have grown isolated, divided. They will fall like leaves before the flames. This world, it is ours for the taking.*

Blood pounded in Adonis's ears as she spoke. Long had he petitioned the Matriarch to expand their warrior forces, to lead greater attacks against the human lines, to drive them back into the oceans. She had resisted, believing peace might yet be achieved, that the humans would finally come to see them as equals.

It had been a foolish hope. Humanity in its arrogance could never see another species as peers. But what did it matter now? Adonis had seen the Old One in all her glory, her devastating power. All the armies of humanity could not stand against her, not with the Tangata at her back.

The sobbing had stopped now, as the Tangata of New Nihelm stood and watched their new Matriarch, as they felt her Voice wash over them, calming their minds, sweeping away the grief. A great calm came over the square as every soul waited for her next words.

Today, the Tangata stand united. Today, we all march upon our enemies!

Adonis's head jerked up at the words. Surely Maya could not mean they would leave the city today. Even the Tangata would need time to prepare for a campaign of such size, to gather supplies for the march and survey the enemy formations, even to hunt down what scouts the humans had stolen across the great river.

Nor could all the Tangata of New Nihelm march, however much Adonis might long to see that sight. There were hundreds of aged members amongst their numbers, and as much again children. Those of the lesser generations would struggle with the cold of the northern territories, where winter had yet to release its grip.

But even as he looked from Maya to those gathered in the square, he felt again the pounding in his mind, the desire for vengeance, to finally bring death to the enemies of his people. They had waited long enough, had delayed and obfuscated. No longer. Humanity would finally face retribution for the genocide they had launched against the Tangata all those years ago.

Below him, the Tangata surged from the square, their voices raised in harmony, minds united in a single thought, a single cause.

Death, death, death.

Smiling, Adonis turned to Maya. *What of those who escaped?* he murmured. *The traitors who fled with their humans.*

Maya's eyes danced as she regarded him. Smiling, she stepped closer and placed a hand on his bandage. Adonis struggled to keep the pain from his mind as the muscles of his chest spasmed. Her smile grew and he sensed her consciousness prodding against his.

You desire revenge, my mate? she asked.

Adonis swallowed as the pressure from her hand increased. *Yes, my Matriarch,* he replied, bowing his head. *The human…my pain will not be sated until his body lies dead at my feet.*

Yes…I can feel your rage, Maya replied, stepping closer now, leaving only an inch separating them. Leaning in, she pressed her lips gently to his, and for a moment Adonis's pain was forgotten.

You will have your revenge, my mate, her voice came again, and he felt a rush of ecstasy, *but for now, it must wait. My children, their future, must come first.*

Adonis's heart twisted at her words but then her body was pressing hard against him, her hands shifting their attention, and his concerns were swept away in a surge of lust. A groan hissed from his lips.

Where will you lead us, my Matriarch? he growled, desire burning in his stomach.

For just a second, Maya broke away from him, and he glimpsed a flame burning in her own eyes, a desperate desire, the rage of lost centuries. A sudden chill touched Adonis, though a moment later it was swept away, drowned by the emotions rushing from his mate. Only as they fell to the stone steps did he hear the Old One's reply, the faintest of whispers, a promise of what was to come:

To war.

❀ *9* ❀

THE HERO

Lukys watched in silence as the black clouds raced towards them. The ocean seemed to rise to meet that darkness, white caps bubbling, thrashing, until it seemed they might consume the sky itself. Thunder clapped and for a moment all was turned to a brilliant white.

When the glow faded, Lukys turned from the storm. Onboard the ship, all was chaos. His comrades ran to and fro, clutching at oars and dragging sails into the sky, anything to eke another knot of speed from the little fishing ship.

Lukys already knew it was futile. Even as he caught a glimpse of land in the distance, the oceans rose around them, waves churning the depths to white and cutting off that faint hope. Screams came from the Perfugians as the deck rocked violently beneath them, hurling several from their feet.

The wind followed. Howling down from the sky, it struck the sails with a *boom*. Fabric shrieked and the masts groaned, and for a moment Lukys thought the strength of the storm would plunge them straight to the bottom of the ocean. He staggered towards where Travis stood at the tiller as rain began to fall. Driven by the wind, it slashed at his face like knives, biting where it struck.

"We're not going to make it!" Lukys shouted as he reached Travis.

Fear showed in Travis's eyes as he tore his gaze from the waters ahead. "What do we do?"

Lukys gritted his teeth. What wisdom did he possess that could answer such a question? He forced the doubts aside.

"Whatever we have to," he growled, gesturing to the waters. "Take what shelter we can, ride it out. It's our only chance now."

Travis's face grew pale, but after a moment his jaw hardened and he nodded. Isabella moved alongside him, and they shared a glance. It seemed to Lukys that some unspoken words passed between them, though he knew Travis did not possess his ability. Then Isabella reached out a hand to grip the tiller alongside Travis.

"We'll do our best to see us through," Travis's voice rang through a crash of thunder.

Lukys opened his mouth to order them to take shelter with everyone else before thinking better of it. Instead, he gripped each of them by the shoulder, offering his silent thanks.

Then he turned away and started across the deck, shouting for his comrades to drop oars and take shelter with their Tangatan partners. The storm roared, threatening to steal his words, but some heard and the cry was taken up by others. In moments the Perfugians had released their oars and dropped what ropes still remained in the rigging. They staggered for the bow and gunwales, desperate for something, anything upon which to cling. The Tangata went with them, even their inhuman agility struggling on the sharply-pitching ship.

Lukys cried out as a wave broke over the gunwale. Icy water gushed across the deck, carrying discarded oars and spears with it. Around them, the ocean surged, pitching the tiny vessel back and forth, each wave threatening to finally be the one that drove them into the unknown depths.

As Lukys watched, another wave broke across the railings. Instinctively, he threw himself at the mast, gripping it tight as the water crashed into him. Even so, it almost tore him loose. Drenched to the skin, he clung on as the storm hurled its rage upon them.

A cry carried to his ears. Squinting through the water lashing his face, Lukys caught a glimpse of Warren's face as he was washed across the deck by the waters. There was a crash as he slammed into the gunwale, followed by a sharp *crack*. Before anyone could react, the wooden piles gave way, and the recruit vanished into the swirling currents.

Screams carried across the deck, and a moment later a Tangata plunged after him, hurling herself into the depths. Whether she reached the Perfugian, Lukys would never know. They were gone, and the fishing ship rushed on, another wave looming above.

Glimpsing a rope lying strewn across the deck, Lukys threw himself on a coil and pulled it to him. Gathering it in a loop, he made to tie it around his waist, then hesitated. His eyes were drawn back to the tiller, where Travis and Isabella alone stood against the storm. He sensed those two were the only hope any of them had, that only by their efforts would the ship remain afloat. Looping the rope over his shoulder, Lukys staggered back towards the stern.

He reached his friend just before the next wave struck. It rose above, a mountain upon the ocean. Together they clung to the tiller as Travis directed the little ship towards the peak, defiant. The deck pitched beneath their feet, carrying them up, up, up…

The wave broke as they were halfway up the slope. White water crashed over the ship, engulfing them. For a moment, Lukys knew only darkness, as they were swallowed by the raging waters. Then the chaos receded once more, and he found they were somehow still upright.

With no time to spare, he tied the rope about Travis's waist, then to the tiller. With luck it might save him from being swept away should he fall. He reached for Isabella next, but she waved him away, face taut as she watched the next wave approaching. Nodding, Lukys returned to his friend. Travis's face was grim as he battled the ocean. Lukys could see the terror in his friend's eyes, but thinking of Isabella's warning on the shore, he couldn't help but smile. Whatever Lukys's private doubts, Travis had more than proven himself aboard the ship.

He swung around, surveying the damage the storm had wrought. His remaining countrymen still sheltered beneath the gunwales, but there was no hiding from the storm. Salt stung Lukys's eyes, but he knew he could not rest. These were his people. They had followed him on this mad path, had trusted him to lead them to safety. He would not fail them now, could not.

A cry came from the bow as water broke across the prow.

Lukys's heart lurched as he saw Dale torn from the mast he clung to, the power of the ocean hurling him across the deck. White water surged around him, sweeping towards the hole in the railings left by Warren's fall. Desperately, Dale clutched at the wooden planks—and somehow managed to halt his momentum.

Roaring his fury into the storm's rage, Lukys started across the ship towards his friend. Not a single soul more would be lost to this tempest, not while he lived. He staggered as the ship crashed down the other side of a wave, but managed to keep upright. Dale was not so lucky, the movement dislodging his grip and throwing him sideways, thankfully away from the gaping hole in the railings.

Unfortunately, the mast brought him to an abrupt halt. Lukys winced at the audible *thud* of the impact, and watched as his friend slumped to the deck. Pain showed on Dale's face as he tried to rise, but the blow had damaged something, and he slumped back to the wooden planks.

Lukys continued, even as he searched the ship for Keria. He found Dale's partner at the bow, eyes wide with fear, locked to Dale's slumped form. He knew that expression all too well. It was one of unspeakable terror, one beyond reasoning, the kind that could freeze a soul in place, rendering one unable to move, to act. Adonis had given them all a taste of such fear, back in New Nihelm, but that had been his power. Keria's terror now was real. She would be of no help to Dale, not in that state.

Another wave built beyond the prow and Lukys darted forward. Dale would not survive without aid. The ship pitched beneath them, throwing him off-balance, and he fell to one knee. Desperate, he righted himself, but it was already too late. The wave rushed towards them, thundering down upon the keel…

…in a flash of grey, Sophia crashed into Dale, one arm hugging him tight. Waters surging around them, her other reached for the mast. Her fingers scraped against the heavy oak…

…and missed!

Lukys's heart lurched into his throat as the deck tilted sharpy. Caught in the swirling waters, the two were swept beyond reach of the mast—and towards the gaping hole in the railing.

Without thinking, Lukys dived after them, arm outstretched.

Somehow, his hand found Sophia's. Her fingers locked around his in a crushing grip and he felt a rush of elation—then the weight of his friends yanked him forward, dragging them all towards the raging ocean. In terror, Lukys scrambled for purchase, some hold that would save them from the waters, but there was nothing. The three of them were swept on towards the hole.

Just before they went over, his eyes met Sophia's. In that moment, he saw her panic, her fear. His stomach twisted and in desperation he slammed his fingers into the deck. Their weight tore his nails as they scraped the wood, but it made no difference.

Then suddenly iron fingers were closing around his wrist, jerking him to a stop. The weight of Sophia and Dale almost tore his arm from its socket, but screaming, he clung on to Sophia, to their unknown saviour he couldn't quite glimpse through the raging storm, until finally the last of the water drained away and the ship drew level again.

Coughing, Lukys released Sophia and dragged himself to hands and knees, struggling to catch his breath. Finally he looked up and saw Keria standing over them. Her face was so pale she might have been a spirit, sent by the Gods above to save them.

But no, she was only mortal, only a Tangata, and Lukys watched as she crouched alongside Dale, cradling his injured head in her hands. His eyes were closed and Lukys prayed he was only unconscious. Shaking off his own pain, he forced himself to inspect their surroundings. His stomach lurched as he saw how close they'd come to tumbling through the broken gunwale. Dale's legs were already hanging over the edge. Another second…

"Come on," he rasped, drawing Sophia and Keria's attention. His throat was raw from the salt in the air, but he forced himself to speak out loud. It helped to keep his thoughts focused. The storm still raged around them and any moment now another wave could break across the deck. "We need to get him to safety."

Together they dragged Dale back to the mast, and using another rope torn from the rigging, they bound him in place. There was no time to inspect his injuries, but when Lukys checked his pulse it was strong. That would have to be enough for now. Keria crouched alongside her partner after they'd secured him, holding the man tight. The Tangata still carried the haunted look in her eyes and Lukys couldn't help but wonder what secret strength she'd drawn on to save them. He wished there was something he could do to reassure her, to take away her fear, but all he could do was nod his thanks.

Then, exhausted, barely able to keep himself alert, Lukys crawled his way to where Sophia crouched against the second mast. Her skin was pale from the cold, her clothes soaked, her hair pasted against her scalp. She watched him come, seemingly unable to move, to speak, and Lukys wondered if she'd been injured in the fall.

"Are you okay?" he cried, reaching out to lay a hand on her arm.

Sophia did not move, only tightened her grip around the mast. A shudder shook her, and he saw that her eyes were not focused on him. Their grey depths were fixed on the hole in the railing, on the swirling, icy depths beyond.

Swallowing, Lukys looked around, wondering what to do, but there was no one else. The rest of the Perfugians seemed secure, while at the tiller Travis roared his defiance to the storm, the sound like mad laughter beneath the ringing of thunder. Turning back to Sophia, Lukys swallowed his hesitation and wrapped his arms around her, seeking to warm her, to grant some small comfort amidst the tempest.

There they knelt as the storm raged on, as mother nature hurled all her strength against them, as they waited for the end to come.

And there the sun finally found them as it broke through the clouds. The storm vanished at its appearance, as though banished by its light, by its warmth. The sea grew calm and the wind died away, leaving them to drift at peace.

Lukys found himself blinking, his body stiff, aching with a dozen fresh bruises. Carefully he detached himself from Sophia. As the sun touched her face, she shuddered and the light returned to her eyes. She looked around, frowning to see him so close, as though she had not noticed his presence until that moment. He felt a soft probing upon his mind, a questioning, as though she wasn't quite sure what he was doing. He offered a smile, too exhausted to talk. Then he rose to inspect the aftermath of the storm.

The main mast was now slightly off-kilter, its sail hanging in tatters, while the mast he and Sophia had clung too did not even have remnants. A single oar had been left to them, wedged against the gunwale in the bow.

He was surprised to find Travis still standing, though his friend was sagging against the tiller, though not even that had survived the storm's wrath. At some point the rudder had been torn free from its bracket, leaving only the wooden handle to which Travis clung. Isabella stood alongside him, her arm around his waist, offering her strength. Her eyes met Lukys's, and she nodded.

Lukys swallowed, his throat raw from the salt and the screaming. Bracing himself, he staggered across the deck to where Dale was still bound to the second mast. Keria had remained at his side. She was fumbling desperately at the ropes as Lukys approached, and for a moment he thought the worst. Then an answering moan came from Dale. His head lifted a fraction, words slipping from his lips, too soft for Lukys to hear. Keria cried out and threw herself at Dale, sobbing into his shoulder.

In his mind, Lukys heard her gushing apologies. He helped her with the last of the ropes, then placed a hand on her shoulder.

It's alright, he said softly. *You're both alright.*

Others had not been so lucky. Despite his oath, he could see that some had not survived the disaster. Perhaps twelve Perfugians remained alongside their Tangatan partners. So few. He couldn't help but think back to that first day when they'd arrived in Fogmore, how many faces that had vanished, forever lost.

Anger touched him, at his commanders, his Sovereigns. They had done this to them, had cast aside their lives as though they had no worth, as though they were nothing. Yet he had seen the true strength of these men and women, their courage. They deserved so much more.

The anger faded, though, as he looked beyond the wreckage of their ship, his eyes sweeping the horizons. His heart sank as he took in the endless ocean in all directions and he tried to keep his fear in check, to keep it from broadcasting, from infecting the other Tangata.

They sensed it anyway, and he felt their gazes upon him, heard their unspoken questions. He closed his eyes, not wanting to speak, to tell them the source of his fear.

But there was no hiding the truth now, not from the Tangata.

They were stranded in the middle of the ocean, with no sails or oars or supplies, and no help in sight. He had led them to their doom.

❦ 10 ❦

THE EMISSARY

The Gods were all looking at her—every one of them. Even Cara seemed shocked, as though she couldn't quite believe a human would name her a friend. Sadness touched Erika at the thought. How poorly she had treated Cara over these past months, even after the Goddess had saved her life.

It was finally time to repay that debt.

"As I was saying," Erika managed to say into the silence that had followed her pronouncement. "I would speak for my friend." She cursed inwardly as a tremor betrayed her nerves, but she refused to break from Farhan's stare.

"My daughter has committed an unforgivable crime," the God growled, his words sending a chill down Erika's spine. "There is no need to compound my family's shame by having a human speak on her behalf."

Behind him, Cara's eyes returned to the ground and she slumped where she knelt, her wings draped across the dirt. The sight of the Goddess so subdued lit a fire in Erika's stomach and she bared her teeth.

"Regardless of the shame it might bring you, Farhan, I would defend my friend," she snapped.

Farhan said nothing, only stared at her as though what she had just said was some absurdity.

Taking his silence for permission, Erika pressed on. "Your

577

daughter only killed Yasin in self-defence, in defence of all of us," she argued. "If not for Cara, I would not stand here before you."

"It matters not," Farhan replied, his voice untouched by her plea. "The taking of life is forbidden."

"Even in defence of another? Even if doing nothing means someone you love will die?" She paused, staring up at the towering God, wondering whether to press on. She drew in a breath, knowing it must be said. "Even if it means hundreds of thousands, even millions of lives, will be lost?"

The God did not reply, yet…Erika could see the answer in the coldness of his eyes. Yes, not even to save another could this law of theirs be broken. Not even to save humanity. She swallowed, struggling to comprehend the enormity of what stood before her, to keep the despair from her soul. Balling her fists, she began to shake, to feel herself coming apart.

"All my life," she gasped, her voice close to breaking. "I have been praying for your return. I studied the legends of the past, searched out the secrets of your people, the ruins you left behind, the artefacts, the magic. All in preparation for this day, when I might finally speak with you, might beseech you to return, to save my people. All so that others would not have to go without their fathers, as I have."

She exhaled slowly and her emotion went with it, leaving only an emptiness, a dark despair, devoid of hope.

"Please," she said, unable to summon anything more elegant than the simple plea.

Silence met her words. Farhan stared at her, and Erika couldn't help but think herself as a bug before this being, that at any moment he might decide to crush her beneath his boot. Again she felt a pang of longing for the gauntlet, but she squashed it down and met the God's eyes.

"So naïve," he said quietly. "You know nothing of the Anahera, human. We shaped this world, have already saved it from destruction once. The price was too great. That is why our Sacred Founders forbid interference in your affairs." Slowly he turned to look at his daughter. "That is why we do not kill." For an instant, Erika thought she glimpsed pain in the face of the God, but a second later it was gone, and he continued in the same cold, unyielding tone. "Under threat of de-winging."

"*No!*"

Still knelt in the mud, Cara's head snapped up at her father's words. Terror showed in her amber eyes and her wings lifted from the dirt as she leapt to her feet, as though only now did she think to flee.

The other Anahera were faster. Several that had approached unnoticed darted forward to catch her arms and wings, locking them in grips of iron. Cara screamed and struggled against them, but she fought now against her own kind, and her strength was evenly matched by each of her captors.

Finally she slumped into their grasp, defeated. Tears streamed down the Goddess's face as she looked at her father.

"Father," she rasped in a tone that tore at Erika's heart. "Father, I beg you, don't do this."

"The Elders are in agreement," Farhan said, ignoring his daughter's pleas. Behind him, the elderly Anahera inclined their heads. "All your life, you have ignored the commands of the Founders. No longer can we ignore your wilfulness." He paused then, and again Erika glimpsed a flicker of something in his eyes. "This is for your own good, daughter," he continued finally. "Lest you follow your mother's path."

"No, no, no!" Cara was sobbing, trying to tear her wings from the grasp of her captors. Suddenly the Goddess swung on Erika, and she saw the desperation in her friend's eyes. "Please, Erika, don't let them!"

Erika's heart pounded in her ears as she looked from Cara to her father. "I…" She struggled to find the words to argue, to defy the God before her.

How could he be so callous, so heartless, to stand there and order the mutilation of his own daughter? Yet she saw no give in Farhan's eyes, only a cold determination, an inevitability like the ocean tides to see his sentence passed.

"Please, spare her," she finally managed.

"I have tolerated her dalliances for too long," he said dismissively. "I would not expect your kind to understand." He turned to face his daughter once more. "The guillotine will be prepared over the coming days. The Elders have granted you a week to ready yourself, daughter. Until then, you will be confined to your quarters. Take her there, now," he finished, gesturing to those who held Cara.

Erika watched as Cara was led away through the ranks of Anahera, unable to speak, to so much as move. A knot tied itself around her insides as Erika realised the depth of her failure.

She couldn't help Cara, couldn't save her people. She couldn't even save herself.

"What…what are you going to do with us?" she croaked, no longer able to meet Farhan's eyes.

Silence answered Erika's question. Beside her, Maisie shifted closer, her entire body taut. But after a moment Farhan only shook his head.

"Come with me."

Turning on his heel, he strode through the ranks of the Anahera. They were already beginning to filter from the yard, disappearing into any number of doors lining the walls. Erika frowned as a thought came to her—there were no children present. In fact, Cara would have been one of the youngest.

The squeal of a door opening brought her attention back to Farhan and she drew herself up as he led them from the yard, prepared to make her arguments anew. The Elders had already departed, but they were followed by another of the Anahera this time. Erika drew to a stop as she recognised Hugo, Cara's brother. Before they could speak, though, Farhan reappeared in the doorway. The look in his eyes brooked no disobedience and she hurried forward.

Hugo closed the door behind them as Erika and Maisie found themselves in another antechamber, this one some kind of workplace rather than a living quarters. A bookcase had been placed in one corner, but it was the desk that drew Erika's attention. Made from the same metallic substance as the outer doors, it was covered in an array of unfamiliar objects. Erika's heart started to race at the sight and she thought again of the artefacts discovered in other secret sites, her gauntlet and Maisie's orb. What fresh magic might these objects hold?

Farhan must have seen the look in her eyes, for he stepped between her and the desk, his wings stretching to hide the objects from view. Erika swallowed as she found his gaze upon her and quickly lowered her gaze.

"I…you didn't answer my question, outside," she said lamely.

"My daughter should never have brought you here," he rumbled, as though that was an answer. Erika stared at him, waiting for the rest, and to her surprise, the God turned away. "Now that you have seen our city, you cannot be permitted to leave."

Erika's heart lurched in her chest. She opened her mouth to denounce him, but suddenly her throat was parched and all she could manage was a strange rasping. A shudder shook her as she stared at the God.

"You…you can't," she finally said lamely.

"I am sorry," he replied, and this time he seemed sincere. "You are not the first humans to have reached our haven these last centuries, though you are the first to have been brought by one of our own. But the Elders have made their minds clear. There will be no exceptions."

Words abandoned Erika then and she stood staring at the God, struggling to comprehend the ramifications of his words. They could never leave, were condemned to remain forever in the City of the Gods, locked away high in the mountains, away from civilisation, from their own kind. They would never return to their kingdoms, would never bring word of their discovery back to the realm of man.

She found herself staring at Maisie, wondering what they would do, how they would survive in this inhospitable place for the rest of their lives. There would be no escape. Even if they slipped from the city, there was only barren rock and ice for a hundred miles. The Gods would track them down within a day—if they did not freeze to death first.

"Come on," Maisie said finally, her voice soft, without judgement. She touched a hand to Erika's shoulder. "There's nothing more we can do here. Let's go back to the room."

Erika nodded dumbly, but Farhan spoke before either could move.

"My son, Hugo, will be your guide, until you have…adjusted to our customs."

Erika took that as a reprimand for their breakout. Hugo flashed them what could have been an apologetic look as he held out a hand for them to enter into the corridor. Erika hesitated, looking again at Farhan. Surely there was still something she could say to save them, some plea that might melt his cold heart. But Maisie was already stepping from the room, and realising she had been defeated, Erika followed.

Hugo led them back to their quarters in silence. That suited Erika. In the face of her failure, she was in no mood for conversation. When they reached the room, he gestured them inside and closed the door behind them. Erika didn't need to ask to know he would be waiting outside should they attempt any further excursions.

Slumping to the bed, she looked at Maisie. "I'm sorry," she croaked. "This…this is all my fault."

To her surprise, the spy only shrugged. "Probably." Seating herself across from Erika, she rustled in her bag for a moment, before coming up with a leather-bound book. "Still," she continued, tossing the book to Erika. "We might as well use the time productively."

Erika frowned as she caught the book. It was obviously old, its cover cracked and the papers within so dry they had become brittle. Opening it with caution, she found herself looking upon pages of handwritten script. She looked back at Maisie.

"Where did you get this?"

A smile touched the spy's lips. "I told you they would be easy picking," she replied.

Erika's frown deepened and she looked again at the words on the page. They had faded with the passage of time and had obviously been placed upon the page by someone unused to writing script. The size of the words changed constantly and the author hadn't even kept his lines straight. She flicked to the beginning and read the first line:

What hath we become?

II

THE HERO

They drifted for days without a glimpse of land. Occasionally gulls hovered overhead, circling the empty masts before disappearing back into the endless skies. Travis said that was a good sign. It meant they were still close to the coast—but without any way to navigate or propel the ship, it mattered little.

So they drifted on, carried by the gentle lapping of waves against the hull, by the soft breath of the ocean. No more storms appeared, but exposed on the open deck, the sun beat down upon the Perfugians. The storm had torn through most of their canvas and the little freshwater that remained was quickly consumed. They did their best to ration the food, but even that quickly dwindled. A few of the recruits were now trying to string together fishing lines from the scraps of the sails.

Without water and exposed to the unrelenting sun, Lukys's mouth became as dry as straw, his skin scorched red like a lobster thrown in a pot to boil. An ache began at the base of his skull and grew with each passing day. His eyes throbbed with the constant, unbearable light—yet when the night came, the temperatures would plummet and the sorry crew would find themselves huddling together, desperate for warmth.

And still there was no sign of salvation.

On the fourth day after the storm, Lukys found himself alone in the hull of the ship, curled up against the gunwale, desperately trying to hug a sliver of shade. A terrible silence hung over the ship. Not a soul spoke, not even the Tangata, as each suffered their trial alone. Most remained in pairs, though Lukys didn't know how they could stay so close to one another. His skin was so raw from the sun and salt, it hurt just to brush against the wooden railings.

He looked up as a shadow fell across his legs, finding Sophia standing above him. They had not spoken since the storm, since their argument.

You saved me, she whispered. *Why?*

Lukys frowned at her. *Why would I not?*

She shook her head, glancing away from him. *Because I manipulated you, lied to you.* She paused, and when she went on, he heard the pain in her voice. *Because I'm a monster.*

He jerked at the word, so visceral, and finally he realised the truth, the pain she felt. The way he had treated her, the things he'd said, his anger, his rage, all of it had only served to confirm her own doubts, her own fears. Just as Lukys loathed his own past, that the only thing he'd ever achieved was death, Sophia feared the monster within herself.

Perhaps they were a better match than either of them had realised.

Rising to his feet, Lukys reached out and wrapped his hands around her fingers. *You're not a monster, Sophia,* he said gently. *I never thought that.*

I sensed your hatred, Lukys. She did not meet his eyes, but neither did she pull away from him.

He swallowed. His throat was so raw, he was glad he did not need to speak out loud.

I was angry, he whispered. *I felt betrayed. I didn't know what to think, who to believe.*

He hesitated, turning to stare across the ship, taking in the Perfugians and Tangata huddled together. More hardy than the Perfugians, Sophia's brethren had refused to eat or drink, gifting their rations to their partners. His eyes found Keria seated near the tiller, wrapped in Dale's embrace. He recalled the terror in her eyes as the storm had raged about them. Yet she had come for them, had saved Dale and Sophia and Lukys himself when all else was lost.

Dale was right. Sophia and her brethren were as human as any of them.

But I know now, he said, turning back to Sophia. *You ask why I saved you—but it was you who saved me first, back in that clearing, when Adonis would have killed me.*

For the first time, Sophia's eyes met his. There was surprise there, but Lukys went on before she could respond, fearful of what she might say.

You saw through the nervous recruit, saw past the worst of our species, the terrors in my mind, and still you wanted to know me, to protect me. I…I never thanked you for that.

He thought he glimpsed a hint of red in Sophia's cheeks now as she watched him. For a long while, she said nothing, though her head tilted to the side, as though inspecting him for something. Finally she shrugged and turned away.

Lukys's heart sank, and exhaling, he slid back to the deck of the ship and leaned against the gunwale. His stomach panged, sending a bolt of pain through his side. Dark spots danced across his vision. Like the Tangata, he had set aside his rations for others.

You need to eat, Lukys, Sophia's voice came to him.

He looked up as she crouched alongside him and offered her hand. A piece of jerky lay in her palm. A frown creased his forehead and gently he pushed the food aside.

You eat it, he whispered.

You need it more than me, Lukys, Sophia insisted, *and they need you. It is the responsibility of the strong to protect the weak amongst us.*

Lukys glanced at her. *That is not what Adonis believed,* he replied, remembering how the Tangatan leader had tried to control them, calling them weak.

He'd tried to forget that day, the trembling terror that had come so close to unmanning him. Stronger than all of them, Adonis had pushed the fear upon them, used it to control them. A shudder went through him as he recalled what it had taken to resist, to fight back.

How did he do it? he asked suddenly. *How did he control all of us so easily?*

All of us but you, Sophia replied softly.

Lukys's head jerked up at that, and he saw she was watching him again.

All of us but me, he agreed, then frowned. *How is that possible?*

A sigh slipped from the Tangata's lips and suddenly she was sitting before him, legs crossed, fingers drumming on her knees.

As I said, even untrained, you are stronger than you have any right to be, Lukys.

Lukys swallowed as he was trapped in Sophia's grey eyes. *Then I must learn to control it.*

You must, Sophia agreed.

With a struggle, Lukys tore his gaze from her, looking across the deck instead. *I will ask Isabella to teach me.*

Why?

His head snapped back to where Sophia still sat, unmoving. *What do you mean?*

She rolled her eyes as though the answer were obvious. *I will teach you, Lukys,* she said as though the matter had been decided long ago.

But I thought…

Sophia's brow hardened and Lukys trailed off, swallowing the words. Clearly she had no desire to rehash the past. Instead, he nodded his accord, and a faint smile returned to her lips.

How…how do we begin? he asked after nothing had been said between them for a while.

How should I know? Sophia replied, and her smile grew. *This is like breathing for us, Lukys, the sense of another mind, reading the colours of emotions—*

Wait, the colours of what? Lukys interrupted.

Emotions, Sophia said. *When you look closely, you can see they each have a colour. They are constantly changing, mixing.*

Lukys frowned, thinking back to the bridge in New Nihelm, when he had touched the minds of the Tangatan guards. In his desperation, he had been able to influence them, convince them there was nothing to concern them in the dark waters of the river. Then again in the village, he'd inadvertently broadcast his anger, his rage, into the minds of the Tangata they faced. But he'd never realised there was a colour to those emotions.

Can I…can I see? he asked hesitantly.

After a moment, Sophia inclined her head in agreement. Closing his eyes, Lukys reached out with his consciousness to brush against her mind. Silence fell between them as he concentrated, listening, watching, trying to glimpse the colours she had spoken of. A tingle began in the back of his neck, the hackles lifting as he sensed…something from Sophia, a shimmer of colour amidst the swirling of her thoughts.

He hesitated, lingering, trying to pierce the cloud about her, and slowly colours took shape from the ether. A swirling grey amidst black, hints of pink, but stronger than all that, a deep sapphire, darker even than the ocean that surrounded them. Lukys frowned as he took in the colours, trying to decipher their meaning. They were chaotic, constantly changing, just as Sophia had said, but the blue appeared the most stable. He reached for it with his consciousness, and felt a shudder go through him.

You're afraid, he said softly, his eyes flickering open, *but of what?*

She glanced away from him, and before he could speak again, she rose to her feet. He followed as she leaned against the railing, eyes on the open ocean. Hesitantly, he reached out again, touching his consciousness to hers.

I'm sorry, he spoke with caution, *I did not mean to intrude.*

No, Sophia said, biting her lip. *It's not that. It's…* She glanced sidelong at him, wrinkles creasing her forehead. *I have never…never been on a ship before. At first it was something…different. Now though, after the storm…* She trailed off, and now Lukys glimpsed the fear she had hidden so well in her grey eyes.

You're afraid of the ocean?

Sophia did not reply, only inclined her head.

But…you can swim. Lukys frowned. *Better than any human ever could. Why would you fear it?*

It's endless, her response came sharply, *immense. I could swim—but how far? If I had fallen in that storm…fallen as my sister Tangata did…how long until my strength gave out? I would be…powerless.*

Lukys found himself smiling. Somehow, the fear made Sophia more human, all the more real to him. He wanted to lean in and kiss her, but resisted, knowing that was not what she wanted. Sadness touched him, that he might have ruined something real, but…

We all feel powerless at times, he said softly. He glanced over his shoulder at the rest of their companions. *All of them, they're looking to me to protect them, to save them. It hurts, to know I can do nothing. But…that's what it is to be human—to be helpless before the greater powers in this world.*

I don't like it, Sophia said after a while. *It is not a…sensation that we are familiar with.* She hesitated. *It makes me think of our forgotten ancestors, those who lost their grey eyes, who were sent away on the ocean in exile. What they must have felt, lost on these endless waters, the powerlessness…*

Lukys chuckled despite himself. *I guess being superhuman hasn't put you at too many disadvantages in life.*

A smile flickered on Sophia's face. *I suppose that's true,* she replied, then hesitated, *or it was—until I met you.*

Oh?

Sophia laughed. The sound surprised Lukys—gone was the fear. Instead, he glimpsed a light in her eyes. Reaching out, he caught a glimpse of the swirling colours again. The blue remained, but it had receded, other colours rising to the surface, purples and pinks. Abruptly they vanished and he frowned.

You know, it's rude to pry, Lukys, Sophia said, raising an eyebrow.

Lukys felt his cheeks grow warm at the admonishment, but the Tangata only chuckled and continued with her story:

Yes, none of this is how things were meant to go. Right from that first day in the cells of New Nihelm, I have felt a helplessness I have never known before. While my brothers and sisters found happiness with their assignments, I was forced to sit with you in silence, to suffer your anger, your hatred—when all I wanted was to make you happy. It was…galling.

Strange, Lukys replied with a smile. *I was completely within your power in that cell, yet you were the one who felt helpless?*

Sophia shrugged. *As I've told you, we cannot create emotions that are not already there. I had to wait…* She finished abruptly.

Lukys frowned as she glanced in his direction. *What?*

For a moment, Sophia said nothing. Then she leaned in, her head lifting to meet his, and suddenly she was kissing him. Lukys was so surprised that he almost pulled away. Hadn't she just rejected him, made it clear she could not forgive him for how he had treated her after their escape?

Then Sophia's lips parted and their tongues met, and his worries were washed away by the taste of her, by the feel of her body pressed against his, by the sweetness of her scent. For a moment his senses were overwhelmed, and he found himself carried back to the kiss they had shared all those nights ago in New Nihelm, as they danced to the music of the Calafe. It seemed a hundred years had passed since that night now. Then, Lukys hadn't known yet the true secrets of the Tangata, the power they could wield. He'd been naïve, distrusting. He hadn't known the treasure he held, the sweetness of the creature before him.

Now…now he pulled Sophia tight and breathed her in, savouring every moment. He realised now what his friends had seen so quickly, saw Sophia for the unique individual she was—not Tangata, nor human, but everything in between, with her earnest emotions and a strength all of her own. A person who had dared to dream of something other than death in the midst of a decade long war, a woman who wanted nothing more than an ordinary life. So as the sun dipped towards the horizon, he kissed the strange, wonderful woman that had come to him in the darkness.

And she kissed him back.

Amidst their passion, it was a moment before the two heard the cries from the others. Finally they broke apart, and Lukys spun, thinking the worst had happened, that another storm had finally come upon them, that the winds and waves would soon swallow them up, plunging them to the bottom of the ocean.

Instead, great sails of blue rose from the ocean, marring the horizon. A ship, bearing the colours of Perfugia. Of home.

❧ 12 ❧

THE FOLLOWER

The storm raged around Adonis, the heavy sleet cutting across his vision, the fog closing in. He staggered on, teeth clenched, determined. He would not fail Maya now, would not fall behind. Others marched around him, his brothers and sisters struggling through the storm. Their voices thrummed in his mind, some still strong, urging their comrades to keep faith.

But others were fading, growing weaker as the endless miles ate their strength, as the thick snowbanks and icy chill drained the life from them. Not all possessed the strength of Adonis and the cleaner generations, and these struggled to keep pace against the violence of the spring storm.

It had come upon them with the full fury of the mountains above, its winds howling down through the valley, tearing at the simple clothing of the Tangata with its icy breath, until even the strongest amongst them had begun to struggle.

Except Maya.

With the power of the Old Ones flowing through her veins, she had laughed in the face of the storm. Amidst the grey tempest, her grey eyes had fixed upon the Tangata and bid them to follow.

Fear not, my children, her voice had rasped into their minds, momentarily drowning out the storm. *The raging of this world cannot stop us, will not bow us low. We are…Tangata. We will prevail.*

And so they had continued into the teeth of the tempest. Young and old, strong and weak, every one of the Tangata had followed their Matriarch onwards, clinging to the pounding of her voice in their minds, to the touch of her power, her spirit.

But that had been long hours ago, and now even Adonis could barely sense her mind. She and her guard had drawn ahead and while Adonis longed to follow, he'd found himself lagging instead, held back by the pain radiating from his brethren. They each suffered in silence, but that did not change their aura, the dark greys and blacks of their despair. As the Old One's Voice faded, that darkness only grew.

He tried to encourage them in Maya's place, using his own Voice to lift them, to stir the embers of their rage, their courage, their love for the Matriarch. But even strength was lagging, sapped by the leaching cold, and for once he found his power insufficient.

Soon they began to fall. He found the first lying across his path, her body draped across a snowdrift. Adonis reached for her with his mind, to seek the life within, but death had already claimed her. The snow was beginning to cover her face, and after a moment he turned away, continuing his endless march.

They came more often after that, one after another lying dead where they had fallen, left behind by brethren too weak to offer anything but gentle goodbyes. Despair rang through the forest, the voices of the Tangata crying out for their lost brothers and sisters, even fear for their own lives grew within.

Adonis renewed his efforts to lift them, to add flames to the dying embers of their souls. The few others of his generation had drawn far ahead now; even those of the fourth and fifth were out of sight. It was the youth that lagged, those born in recent decades, the sixth and seventh generations, more human than Tangata.

Yet weak as they might be, their eyes remained grey, and their Voices still rang in his head. They were Tangata still, his people. Their former Matriarch had preached that the responsibility of the strong was to protect the weak. Adonis had scoffed at her philosophies, fuming at the humans that had come to live amongst them. Surely if such weakness was allowed to thrive, they would soon outnumber the strong. What would become of his people once there was no one left to defend them?

Now though, watching his people die one by one, he found

himself doubting his own convictions. Those who fell were weak, and yet…what might be lost with each of the fallen, what knowledge and skills?

Soon he began to find the dead in groups. They had tried to huddle together, to unite in order to preserve the whole, just as the Tangata had since the calamity of the Fall. Yet against the power of the storm, not even that had been enough.

Then he saw the first of the children.

She lay with one of the fallen groups. They had placed her in the centre, using their own bodies to shelter her, to protect that precious gift that was the life of his people. Ice clung to the child's face and her skin had long since turned blue, her life stolen away by the cold, just as it had her parents.

Adonis crouched alongside the group for a long time, listening to the screaming of the wind. Its icy breath tore at his flesh, seeking the warmth at his core, to snuff it out as it had that of the precious child.

But it would not take him. It could not. He was Tangata, strong, enduring. The raging of the storm would not be the end of him as it had been for these sorry souls.

Finally Adonis found himself rising to his feet. There was something wrong about this, about all of this. Something had changed, ever since the day he had woken the Old One from her slumber. Yet his mind was a tangled web and he could not pierce the mystery, could not place the pieces of this puzzle together.

His gaze travelled back to the child, to her ghostly face. Driven by the wind, the snow was already beginning to cover her body. He closed his eyes, taking a moment to memorize her features, to remember what had become of the child in the snow.

❧ 13 ❧

THE EMISSARY

The Guanaco did doth appear this present day. It doest outdoith goat, and tis wool might preserve us. But death cometh upon the land. May those houses of glass provide this winter, or I feareth we might starve…o how didst it cometh to this?

Erika sighed and started flicking forward through the journal. It had been written in some old dialect, by someone she assumed was one of the Anahera—perhaps even one of the Sacred Founders that Farhan had spoken of. It was a struggle just to read, though some of the older works from the library of Archivists had been written in a similar manner.

But the early pages at least spoke of little and less: of empty days and long nights, of dark winters and burning summers. She wondered if the writer was describing The Fall from the perspective of the Gods. If so, his experience had been altogether different from what few legends humanity kept from that time, of ages lost to darkness and destruction.

Finding a fresh entry, she began to read again.

I didst see those folk this present day, creeping from a cave. The Fall didst not taketh all. I should be'est relieved, but I findeth mine own despair only swells with the rising of the sun. Those folk we did doth warn, could hath changed. After all those folk didst commit, the hand wast forced. Though, perhaps there wast another path…

Exhausted, Erika let the diary slip from her fingers and fall to

593

the covers of her bed. Two days had crept past in the cold confines of the city and reading the ancient text was draining. She couldn't help but think there was an irony to her situation, that she had spent most of her life dreaming of this day, when she might stand amongst the Gods and learn their secrets. But now that she was here, she found herself bored.

What was the point of new knowledge, of fresh discoveries, if they could never be shared? So instead she found herself reading the old journal to pass her time. A shame there hadn't been much to write about in these mountains, even during the Fall.

The rest of her time she'd spent exploring the city. Its upper levels had been forbidden to them, but with Hugo as her shadow, she had criss-crossed the lower corridors. The few living quarters she'd found on the ground floor were situated near her and Maisie's room, but the rest of the Anahera she assumed lived above. They seemed to be avoiding the two humans in their midst, and otherwise the lower levels of the City were empty. In her endless hours of investigation, Erika had only found a handful of workrooms like Farhan's, and these were empty.

She made other discoveries though, mostly in the darker nooks, in antechambers barely large enough to fit a single human, let alone the Gods and their wings. Most were empty like the rest of the city, but in a few she found strange boxes filled with orbs of dark glass, like the relics her mother had once collected from old dig sites. As a child she had once managed to make a similar orb emit a flash of light, and so she pocketed one when Hugo was not looking—although the Anahera didn't seem too concerned by her explorations.

Her excitement had been short-lived when she returned to their room, however, as despite her best efforts, she failed to unlock whatever secret power the orb might contain. Not that Erika was sure she wanted to. She still hadn't taken the gauntlet from her knapsack.

Erika's only other discovery was what looked like a prison block deep within the city. She didn't stay long, only enough to see it was empty, the bars and floors dusty with disuse. Even so, the sight sent a tremor down her spine, and from then on she was sure to be thankful for the simple room they had been granted.

While Erika was in their room, Maisie spent much of her time in the corridor with Hugo. Whether the spy had taken a liking to the young Anahera, or she was just seeking another advantage in their trusting nature, Erika hadn't asked. At least she had managed to weasel a few parcels of information from the youth. Hugo had confessed he was only Cara's half-brother—the two shared Farhan as a father—though he would not speak of Cara's mother.

At other times, Erika found herself standing in the corridor studying the painting of the City of the Gods. The owner of the diary had made no mention of that ancient city, nor the incredible powers that had helped raise it. So instead she whittled away the hours by looking upon its likeness. The closer she stared, the more she saw amongst those towering spires. The sleek ships that sailed the raging waters, the shimmering objects that had been caught upon the bridge by the painter—frozen, yet from the circular wheels, Erika guessed they must have been some type of carriage. What magic had driven them without horses?

More than anything though, there was one question that came to burn within her mind, to keep her awake at night. If this was the ancient City of the Gods, then where were the Gods themselves? The skies above the bridge were empty, and what use did beings with wings have for ships and wagons, even ones that moved without horses?

Back in their room, Erika let out a sigh and picked up the journal once more. Perhaps the answers lay somewhere within its pages, though she feared the ancient text might blind her before it gave up its secrets...

"Sleeping well?"

Erika jerked awake as Maisie appeared in the doorway. Hugo stood behind her, and Erika quickly tucked the journal beneath her pillow. The Anahera had not questioned over its absence and Hugo didn't seem overly bothered by her explorations so far, but Erika was quite sure stealing from his father would be against at least one of the commandments left by their Sacred Founders.

"I..." Erika trailed off when she saw the amusement in the spy's eyes.

The door clicked closed on their Anaheran guard, before Maisie threw herself onto her own bed.

"Never thought I'd see you sleeping on the job," she said with a smirk.

"What job?" Erika scowled, then gestured to the room. "This *is* the job, this is everything we'll ever have. Maybe I should ask Hugo if I can have some twine—may as well learn to start knitting now, if this is my retirement."

Maisie said nothing in reply and Erika looked across at her, wondering what the spy was plotting behind those brown eyes. What was she playing at with Hugo? Surely she couldn't hope to turn him against his own people. He might not share the same fanatic beliefs of the Elders, but his loyalty was without question. He had practically hopped to obey every instruction his father had given him.

"Are you done?" Maisie said finally. "As much as I enjoy watching you mope, we're running out of time, Archivist."

"Running out of time? Haven't you been listening—we have all the time in the world!"

"*We* might," Maisie replied, "but *she* doesn't."

Erika's stomach tied itself in a knot at Maisie's words and she quickly looked away. She had spent the last two days trying to forget her disastrous failure, the look Cara had given as she was led away. The despair in her friend's eyes, the terror, had struck Erika to her very core. But…

"There's nothing we can do for her," she whispered.

Again there was silence as Maisie sat staring at her. Then abruptly she shrugged. "Okay," she said, then lay back on the bed and closed her eyes.

Frowning, Erika watched Maisie's chest rise and fall. For all the world she seemed to have fallen straight to sleep. Anger touched Erika as she watched the spy. How could she be so calm, so dismissive of their friend? Cara had saved both their lives back in the valley with Yasin.

"Well, did *you* have a better plan?" she said shortly.

Without moving her head from the pillow, Maisie cracked an eye open. "Why don't you go talk to Hugo?" she replied. "You might find more answers from him than that crumbling book."

Erika scowled. If that was the best advice the spy could offer, Cara was doomed. But Maisie's eye only slid closed again, and after a moment, Erika cursed. She rose from the bed, then crossed to the door and yanked it open.

Outside, Hugo leaned against the wall, his emerald wings drooping to either side of him. His head jerked up at her appearance, and she caught a flicker of excitement in his eyes. It faded though when he realised it was only Erika in place of the Gemaho spy.

"Archivist," he said respectfully. He'd begun to call Erika by her former title after hearing Maisie do so. "Was there something you needed?"

Erika said nothing, only closed the door behind her and leaned against the wall opposite the Anahera. He was one of the few she'd noticed around the city who was younger than Cara, as he was the child of Farhan's new partner. Erika's heart twisted as she recalled Farhan's words about Cara's mother. What had happened, that Farhan should be so fearful of his daughter following in her footsteps? Was that why he was so harsh, why he sought to rob his daughter of her…freedom?

A sob started in Erika's throat at the thought of the young Goddess without her wings. She might have first met Cara as a strange young woman of Calafe, but much had transpired since that day. Erika had come to know Cara the Goddess, who soared through the skies on wings of auburn, who exalted in her life, in her freedom. The thought of what her friend might soon lose…

"Archivist, are you okay?" Hugo asked, his voice hesitant.

Erika looked at him through a mist of tears. The young God shifted on his feet, clearly uncomfortable with her grief. Swallowing, she managed a nod.

"I am sorry, Hugo," she said softly. "I did not mean to impose upon you."

"Why…do you cry?"

"It's just…how is your sister?" she asked.

Hugo frowned and eyed her closely, as though confused or expecting a trap. It was strange how the Gods looked at them, almost as though they were waiting for something terrible to happen. Was that their memory of the human thieves who had stolen their magic all those centuries ago, giving birth to the Tangata?

"Cara is well," Hugo said at last.

"So you've seen her?" Cara said, and her voice cracked. She quickly looked away, wiping a tear from her eye. "Sorry," she whispered. "It's just…I worry for her. She is important to me. She has saved my life more times than I can count these last months. I just want to help her."

"You cannot," Hugo replied in a serious voice, as though she'd just announced a plan to break his sister out of prison. Then he looked away, and when he spoke again, Erika heard a new softness to his voice. "As much as any of us might like to help my poor sister, she…she has written her own fate."

"I know, Farhan has made that clear," Erika said. She had learned enough of Hugo these last days to know he would not go against his father. "But…surely she does not have to face it alone?"

A frown crinkled Hugo's forehead. "What do you mean?"

Erika's eyes returned to the floor. "Nothing…" she said, then: "Only…it seems cruel, to leave her alone, with nothing but her own thoughts for company. Would it not be more…humane to grant her a visit from a friend?"

Hugo hesitated at her words. "For what purpose?"

"So that she would not be alone," Erika replied. She swallowed. "And…perhaps I could help…prepare her for…for a life without her wings. Or has your father forbidden this?"

"No…" Hugo said hesitantly. "Cara is permitted visitors, only… it is not the way of the Anahera to visit the condemned. Only Father has visited her since the assembly."

"Farhan is the one who condemns her," Erika replied. Hesitantly, she reached out and touched a hand to Hugo's. "It is the way of my people to comfort our friends when they face something terrible. Please, would you take me to her?"

"Very well."

Erika was so surprised by his agreement that she already had her next argument half-formed on her lips. Her heart began to race as she swallowed it back and said instead:

"Now?"

He nodded and without further word, he started off down the corridor. Erika glanced at their door, wondering about Maisie, but…this was something she wanted to do herself. Turning, she hurried after the Anahera.

He led her quickly through the twists and turns of the city, passing empty chambers and a few of his fellow Gods. Thankfully none stopped to talk with them, for despite Hugo's assurances, she wasn't certain Farhan would be pleased to learn of her visit with his daughter. Finally they turned up a corridor Erika did not know, where a narrow spiral staircase waited.

Hugo went first and Erika followed close behind, gripping hard to the steel railings. Her heart started to pound as she realised he was leading her into the forbidden second storey of the city. Surely here would be where the Gods hid their secrets, where they kept the magics that had once lifted entire towers of glass into the sky.

But when they emerged onto the second level, Erika was only greeted by another plain grey corridor. Hugo wasted little time leading her through several more hallways, before coming to a stop outside an open entrance. Erika paused beside him. Glancing inside, she was surprised to find a chamber much larger than the others she'd seen below.

Hugo indicated she should enter first, and she stepped hesitantly inside. In the dim light of the magic orbs, she could make out only shadows of the decorations dotting the walls. As she stepped farther into the chamber, she noticed rough patches of stone on the ceiling, stretching in a line from one wall to another. It took her a moment to realise it marked where another wall had once stood.

Other than its size though, the chamber appeared much alike the living quarters she'd seen below, with blankets piled high on a handful of straw beds. They were alone in the room, but Erika guessed this must be the chambers of Hugo's family. Only, where was Cara?

It was a moment before she noticed the door in the far wall. It was the first she'd seen on this level, and as she stepped closer, Erika thought it seemed out of place, its hinges untouched by corrosion.

She turned to Hugo in silent question and he nodded. Swallowing her hesitation, Erika crossed the room and reached for the handle. The mechanism within ground as it twisted, but finally it gave a click as the lock released. The hinges let out a sharp shriek as the door swung open.

Within, a room was revealed unlike any she had seen within the city. Pink paint transformed the plain stone walls, and purple drapes of silk hung from the corners, as though windows hid beyond. The magic orbs still let out the same half-light as the rest of the city, but a lantern had been left lit on a stand in the corner. A pile of books that looked far too modern for a city that had been kept remote from human civilization lay stacked on a bedside table.

Sitting cross-legged on the bed itself, twin amber eyes looked up from an open book.

"Why is it, Erika," Cara said softly as their gaze met, "that ever since I met you, I seem to keep finding myself a prisoner?"

14

THE HERO

Standing aboard the *Brereton*, Lukys watched as the rocky cliffs drew closer. They rose from the waters of the harbour and grew up into mountains, soaring high above. The city of Ashura, capital of Perfugia, lay amongst the narrow foothills between water and sky. Carved from marble dug from the island's bottomless mines, the academy taught it was the most glorious of all the cities of humanity. That was the claim, at least. Having seen New Nihelm and the Flumeeren capital of Mildeth, Lukys now knew such teachings to be false.

There was no snow on the rocky peaks above Ashura, not at this time of year, but that didn't keep Lukys from shivering as a breeze blew across his neck. They were a long way north now, and gone were the long days and warm winds.

This was Perfugia, home. Lukys didn't remember it being so cold.

Watching the cliffs approach, Lukys couldn't help but think this was no longer truly his home, if it ever had been. Ashura might be the city of his childhood, the familiar corridors and classrooms of the academy his upbringing, but he found that memories of this place were entirely lacking joy.

Strange as it seemed, he'd felt more at home for the short time he'd lived in New Nihelm than he ever had in the towering spires of the academy. Sophia's kindness, despite his resistance, was more than his teachers and professors had ever shown him. And his parents…well, he'd been taken from them at eight, as was tradition amongst Perfugians.

He could barely recall their faces now. Had they been told the same lie as Lukys, when he'd been sent south, that their son had been chosen to lay down his life for their nation? Or did they know the truth, that he'd been a failure, banished to die because he could serve no other purpose?

Shivering, he forced his attention to the present, glancing side-long to where the *Brereton's* captain stood at the tiller. They'd been fortunate that the ship was only another fishing vessel and not a warship to take them back to the frontlines. The captain had been suspicious at first of the broken Calafe ship filled with Perfugians. There'd been no point trying to claim they were fishermen, and so Lukys had spun a tale closer to the truth. He'd told the man they were a company of Perfugian soldiers who'd been separated from the rest of their cohort during an expedition south of the Illmoor River. That much was true—but instead of revealing their capture by the Tangata, he'd spoken of their retreat across Calafe until they'd finally reached the coast, where they had managed to steal a ship. Only a sudden storm had kept them from navigating back to a Flumeeren port to re-join the battle.

Thankfully, the man seemed to accept the story.

The identity of Sophia and the other Tangata had been more difficult to conceal. Some quick thinking from Travis had saved them. As the *Brereton* had swept towards their mangled ship, he'd begun grabbing up discarded pieces of sail and handing them out amongst the Tangata. Only when Lukys saw Isabella tying the sash across her eyes did Lukys realise his plan.

When the fishing ship had finally reached them, the sailors found half the ship's passengers lying injured, their eyes burned by the harsh sun, covered now to protect them from further damage. A simple ruse that probably would not have worked, if not for the reputation of the Tangata. Afterall, who would think the mindless beasts who fought against humanity would have the guile to sneak into Perfugia by pretending to be blinded?

At the thought, Lukys glanced at Sophia, unable to conceal a smile. She sat on a stool beside the gunwale, eyes still covered to "protect" against the midday sun. How poorly humanity had treated her kind. If they'd just been willing to talk with their enemies, a decade of war could have been avoided. Instead, they'd treated the Tangata like animals, as monsters to be destroyed, eradicated.

I can't believe, Sophia's voice came to him in the silence of his mind, as though she'd sensed his inspection, *that I finally get to visit Perfugia—and now I don't even get to see it.*

Lukys found himself smiling and he recalled how she'd asked after his homeland, during those first days in New Nihelm.

Don't worry, he whispered back to her, *this is only temporary…*

He trailed off, not wanting to betray his concerns. In truth, when they'd first set off from New Nihelm and he'd chosen Perfugia as their destination, he hadn't expected them to get this far. Reaching the island nation had seemed such an impossible task, and he'd been so angry with Sophia and the Tangata, he hadn't paused to wonder how they would be received. Even aboard their little fishing ship, there'd been greater concerns.

Now though, his negligence was endangering all their lives. Even without the Tangata, Lukys and the others were at risk, should the Sovereigns decide to name them deserters.

No, he said to himself, glancing again at Sophia.

The others were gathered around her, Perfugian recruits and Tangata both. They were all relying on him. He would not fail them now, not when they were so close. One final hurdle, and they would be safe.

He straightened, gripping the railings so tightly his knuckles turned white. He must call on the mercy of the Sovereigns, convince them that the Tangata were not the monsters they'd been led to believe, that they could be allies. Maybe he could present Sophia and her brethren as refugees…

An image flickered into his mind, and he imagined the Royal Guard of Plorsea rushing towards him, spears glistening in the sunlight as they drove them through Isabella's heart, as they impaled Keria, as Sophia cried out for mercy…

No, Lukys growled to himself again.

He would not allow it. He would demand an urgent audience before the Sovereigns. Such a request was far beneath his rank as a recruit, but maybe with his fledgeling powers, he might persuade his betters. He'd spent much of the remaining journey practicing with Sophia, though he had not attempted to push upon any emotions again, not since the disaster at the Tangatan village.

First though, he needed to get Sophia and the others off the ship without being discovered. If the guards on the dock caught even a whiff of the Tangata, a thousand soldiers would descend upon them before he saw the first of the Sovereign's servants.

The city was growing near now, the stone docks stretching out into the harbour, beckoning them home. Gulls cawed overhead and hundreds of ships of all sizes sat docked, sails furled, sleek hulls rising from the calm waters. Perfugia boasted the greatest navy in the world. The fleet had been raised over generations, the envy of the other kingdoms. Successive Sovereigns had each built a dozen ships from the great redwoods that covered the island. Their removal was considered a solemn affair, and they could only be used for the construction of ships. Not for the Perfugians the haphazard wooden constructions they had called 'buildings' in Fogmore.

The sailors of the *Brereton* raced to lower their sails, then quickly extended oars to manoeuvre the final yards to their docking on the jetty. A man leapt from the railings as they drew near, carrying a rope that he quickly looped around a wooden pile. Others followed, and within minutes the *Brereton* was safely berthed.

Lukys drew in a breath. Now came the moment of truth. Fists clenched, he started towards the gangplank being lowered to the pier, but before he could take two steps, the captain intercepted him. The antithesis of the sea captains Lukys had seen elsewhere, the man was tidy and cleanshaven, and so thin Lukys might have knocked him down with a tap.

"Hold it there, lad," the man said as he barred Lukys's path. "Where might you be going?"

"The citadel," Lukys said hesitantly. "I have news of the war for the Sovereigns."

"Might be you do, lad," the captain replied, "but can't let you go ashore without the proper processes." A broad grin split his face, though Lukys read the mistrust behind the man's eyes. Perhaps his story had not been as convincing as he'd thought. "I'm sure your news can wait a few hours yet."

With that, he turned and bounded across the gangplank. Lukys made to follow him, but several of the crew moved between them. Arms bulging with the muscle required to haul fishing nets from the ocean's depths, these were closer to what Lukys had come to expect from seamen. Their stance made it obvious they would not allow Lukys passage without a fight.

Grinding his teeth, he turned from them, mind racing. The Tangata's disguises would not survive detailed inspection. One look at those grey eyes and every man and woman in the harbour would turn against them. He shared a glance with Dale and Travis as he re-joined the others.

"Where's he going in such a hurry?" Travis asked.

"Up to no good, by the looks," Dale answered.

Lukys only grunted his agreement. His eyes were on the shore, where already he could see the captain returning. Only he was no longer alone. Two figures garbed in steel marched at his back, each bearing shining spears of silver and kite shields worn on their backs. Red plumes sprouted from their half-helms, marking them as officers.

But it was the blue armour that made Lukys's blood run cold. These were no ordinary soldiers, but members of the Perfugian Royal Guard, servants to the Sovereigns.

"That's not good," Dale hissed from behind him.

"Get everyone together," Lukys said softly. "I'll do my best to divert their attention from our friends. But…be ready."

He did not elaborate, though he could sense the tension in his friends as they turned to gather the others. At least the sailors had allowed them to keep their weapons, though they both knew that if it came to a fight, their little gang didn't stand a chance. They might no longer be the raw recruits who'd marched south all those months ago, but neither could they fight an entire army.

As the captain approached with the royal guards, the sailors at the gangplank stepped aside. Lukys moved quickly and sprung across, landing on the docks just as the captain marched up. The man stumbled at Lukys's appearance, quickly glancing behind him, as though afraid the guards might have abandoned him.

"Captain!" Lukys exclaimed, forcing a cheery tone to his voice.

"I just wanted to say thank you again for your aid. I don't know what might have become of us if not for your valour."

The man frowned, apparently taken aback by his appearance. Lukys took advantage of his hesitation to turn from the man and address the guards.

"Sirs," he said, drawing himself up and offering a salute. "Cadet Lukys of the Fogmore regiment, at your service."

"I...I..." Beside Lukys, the sea captain stammered, head whipping from Lukys to the guards before he finally recovered his wits. "This is the one who calls himself their leader, sirs."

Ignoring the man, the royal guards moved closer, eyes on Lukys. One a man, the other a woman, both stood a good foot above Lukys and carried about them the aura of a warrior. Unlike those chosen for the frontlines, the royal guard were true soldiers, appointed for their skills in battle. They had positions all across the nation, representing the Sovereigns in all martial matters. But the best of them were selected to defend the Sovereigns themselves; a great honour, considering most Perfugians would never so much as glimpse the faces of those who ruled them.

"You are a long way from your station, recruit," the man said, his voice hard. "What are you doing here?"

Lukys opened his mouth to respond, but the words died on his lips as he looked into the man's eyes and saw the suspicion there. The woman seemed softer, but there was still an edge about her, a glint of danger. He sensed then that simple falsehoods would not convince these two, not unless...

Swallowing his doubt, Lukys squared his shoulders and clasped his hands firmly behind his back. "We were in the battle for the Illmoor, sirs, several months back now. In the chaos, we were separated from our unit and pursued to the coast. There we found a ship and crossed the sea..."

He trailed off as the woman took a step towards him. Suddenly there was only an inch separating them, and he found himself caught in eyes of chestnut. Swallowing, he tried to regain his train of thought, but the woman spoke first.

"An impressive feat," she said, voice quiet despite the noise of the docks. "To have stood against the Tangata, to survive the wild oceans of the west..."

As she trailed off, Lukys caught the glimmer in her eyes and sensed there was a trap to her admiration. Lowering his eyes, he gave the slightest shake of his head.

"I cannot accept such high praise, sir. Our efforts were but the least of what our Sovereigns might have expected of us. I fear had some of your royal guards been present, the enemy would have fallen on the waters of the Illmoor."

The hint of a smile crossed the woman's lips, but beside her, the man only snorted. "Do not think to lick our boots with pretty words, recruit," he growled, stepping past Lukys to survey the ship. "Should your tale prove less than true, I'll not hesitate to see the lot of you strung up as deserters."

"Though if you *are* telling the truth," the woman cut in, "the intelligence you bring of the enemy could prove invaluable. The captain tells us you were stranded on the *Calafe* side of the Illmoor?"

Lukys hesitated before nodding. "Yes, sir."

"And you were pursued?" the woman asked. She stepped past Lukys and the sea captain to join her companion's inspection of those still aboard the vessel. "The sea captain tells us you have injured?"

"Yes," he said quickly, flashing the captain a look. What else had he told these two? "Though their injuries were from the voyage. Those injured by the Tangata...we lost," he finished lamely.

"Ha!" the man replied. "I doubt that pitiable lot ever saw a Tangata in their lives. Look at 'em, bunch of deserters if ever I saw one."

The woman laughed and shared a look with Lukys. "You'll have to forgive Cleo," she said, resting a mailed hand on her colleague's shoulder. "Been stuck on port duty for years—he's spoiling for a promotion."

"Doesn't change facts, Tasha," the guard she'd called Cleo growled. "Something's fishy about this lot."

"Might be the fishing ship," a voice called from above.

Lukys stifled a curse as Travis leaned against the gunwales and waved to them. The last thing he needed just now was the recruit angering the two guards who would decide their fates. Beside him, Cleo scowled while the woman Tasha laughed. A growl rumbling from his throat, the man crossed the dock and thumped up the gangplank. Lukys raced after him.

"What did you say, recruit?" the guard snapped as he came to a stop before Travis.

Eyes wide, the young recruit held up his hands in peace, and Lukys darted forward to intervene.

"This is Travis, our very own sea captain," he said quickly. "It was only by his skill that we navigated the storm. Though, I'll admit, he wrecked just about every inch of sail we had on our little ship."

"Impressive," Tasha said as she joined them. "I didn't realise we sent sailors to the south."

A hint of red tinged Travis's cheeks at her praise, but there was obvious relief in his eyes at the opportunity to change the topic.

"It was nothing, sir," he replied, waving to where Dale had gathered the other members of their group. "I had a good crew."

"Must have been difficult with half of them bloody blind," Cleo snapped.

"Ay, it sounds as you have been through quite the journey, soldier," Tasha said softly, an edge creeping into her voice.

Lukys shifted on his feet, though he thought her tone might have been for Cleo, rather than his companions. The guard seemed to realise it too, for he rolled his eyes and made a dismissive gesture.

"Fine," he muttered, facing Lukys, "let's say I believe your little story. What news do you bring of the foul enemy?"

From across the deck, Lukys sensed a fluttering of emotion from Sophia, quickly stifled. Thankful the royal guards could not sense the Tangatan language, Lukys inclined his head to Cleo.

"The last we saw of them was on the coast, at the village we stole the ship from," he replied.

Cleo nodded, but alongside him, Tasha seemed to lose interest in the conversation. She wandered across to where Travis stood with the others, and Lukys caught the murmur of question, something about compasses and navigation.

"What about the battle?" Cleo growled, leaning closer. "Did you slay many of the Tangata?

"Our company was caught south of the river," he replied, drawing himself up. "The line held, protecting the river, but we were separated from the body of the army." He hesitated. "There is more though, intelligence of grave import we discovered while in enemy territory."

"Well, out with it, recruit," Cleo said, and Lukys caught a glimpse of greed in the man's eyes.

Lukys shook his head. "No," he replied shortly. "This information is too important. I will report to the Sovereigns themselves."

For a moment, the royal guard stared down at Lukys, disbelief twisting his bearded face. Finally he shook his head. "Has the sun addled your wits, recruit?" he growled, advancing a step, so that he towered over Lukys. "I am a soldier of the royal guard, your superior in every way—"

A cry from behind them interrupted Cleo's speech. Lukys spun as a commotion broke out amongst his friends and the disguised Tangata. They scattered away from a blue-garbed figure standing in their midst—Tasha. She held a fist triumphantly above her head, a scrap of cloth grasped between her fingers.

Still struggling to understand what was happening, Lukys saw Sophia next. She stood beside Tasha, struggling to free her arm from the guard's iron grip. Eyes wide, a snarl slipped from her lips as she twisted and finally broke loose. Gasps echoed from around the ship as the attention of the sailors was drawn towards the commotion.

Screams soon followed.

Only then did Lukys realise that Sophia's face was no longer covered. Tasha had torn the cloth loose. Her grey eyes swept the deck and found Lukys, wide with fear.

"Tangata!" Tasha cried, and others immediately took up the call. "Treachery! All arms to the docks!"

15

THE EMISSARY

A lump lodged in Erika's throat as she looked down at the Goddess, at her friend.

Cara had seen better days. Her face was a pallid grey and red stained her eyes, as though she'd spent much of the last few days crying. Her auburn wings hung limp, her feathers ruffled and missing in patches. Erika noted several lying scattered about the room.

Swallowing, Erika stepped into the room and allowed the door to swing closed behind her, locking them both in, and Hugo out.

"Cara, I'm so sorry…"

She trailed off as the Goddess looked away, locks of copper hair falling across her face. "What do you want, Erika?" Cara said shortly.

"I…I was worried about you," Erika croaked, eyes watering at her friend's dejection.

"Sure," Cara replied. "Because you've always been *so* worried about me." Her voice was tainted with bitterness now. She snorted in derision. "Tell the truth, Erika. What's got you so bothered? Are there some more of the Old Ones that need slaying? Or have the Tangata returned? Maybe it's another mysterious assassin from your past who needs taking care of?"

Erika flinched as she saw the accusation in Cara's eyes. Guilt twisted her stomach into knots as she recalled all the things the young Goddess had done for her. She had repaid those kindnesses with mistrust and betrayal. Cara was right to be angry, to hate her. But…

"I swear to you, Cara," she said, taking a step closer to the Goddess. "I'm going to get you out of this."

Cara shook her head, a tear streaking her cheek. "Enough with your lies, Erika," she whispered. Her words no longer held the same bite, as despair replaced anger. "Enough with your false promises. You cannot defy the Elders, cannot deny my father…" Her shoulders slumped and a shudder racked her, as though she were about to shatter right there in front of Erika.

Erika crossed quickly to the bed and sat alongside Cara. "*I will,*" she said, determined, insistent.

Placing her hands on Cara's shoulders, she tried to turn the Goddess towards her. For a moment Cara resisted, but Erika's will was the greater, and eventually she allowed herself to meet Erika's eyes.

"Cara, I swear on my father's memory, *I will not let them take your wings,*" Erika whispered.

Cara stared back, anger in her red-stained eyes. But Erika refused to back down, to look away. She watched as Cara's lip began to tremble, felt the shaking in her friend's body, saw the sheen to her eyes. Then suddenly the damn broke and the Goddess threw her arms around Erika, her sobs vibrating from the walls, her tears hot on Erika's shoulder.

"Please don't let him take them," Cara gasped, her words muffled. "Please, please, please."

Her throat clogged with emotion, Erika said nothing, only held her friend tight, offering her silent comfort. It was a struggle seeing the Goddess in such a state, her will, her courage, broken. This was a being who had stood against Tangata and assassins alike with hardly a flicker of fear.

Finally they broke apart and Cara wiped her eyes, scooting back on the bed to make room for Erika. They sat there in silence for a while, each of them lost in thought, minds wandering from past to future. Erika couldn't begin to imagine how to help her friend, but neither would she turn her back now.

"That man, Yasin, he killed your father."

Erika's head jerked up as Cara spoke into the silence. She opened her mouth, then closed it again, considering her words carefully. Finally she nodded.

"Yes, but it was Queen Amina who was behind the plot to see him dead."

The Goddess said nothing at that, only sat leaning against the wall of her room. With her knees drawn up to her chest, she might have been any other human adolescent, but for the splendour of her wings. That, and the fact she was fifty years of age.

"We never knew what happened to my mother," Cara said finally, her eyes downcast, fixed on the tangled blankets beneath her. "One day she just…didn't come back."

"Your father said she was…like you?" Erika questioned, trying not to probe too much.

Cara shrugged. "It happened when I was young." Her eyes flickered to Erika before returning to the sheets. "When I was just five, I think, still a fledgling."

"Fledgling?"

"We cannot fly until our teens," Cara replied softly. "When we gain our primary feathers. Until then…well, my people are overprotective of our fledglings. My father and the Elders, they would do anything to protect them."

"Is that why there were no children at the assembly?" Erika asked. When Cara only nodded, she went on. "She just disappeared one day?"

"Father says she went out to scavenge beyond our borders," the Goddess replied. "Even then it was forbidden, but…I guess my mother was strong-willed."

"Like her daughter," Erika added. Cara said nothing, but Erika thought she glimpsed the hint of a smile on her friend's face. Swallowing her doubt, she pressed on. "Maybe your mother was right to explore, to go beyond the limits placed on you by these Sacred Founders. The world has changed since their day, grown darker. It could use the Anahera, could use the balance of the Gods."

To her surprise, Cara shook her head. "You don't understand, Erika," she murmured. "None of you do, the darkness inside us…" Cara trailed off, as though she had said too much.

But a memory had flickered into life at the Goddess's words, and

Erika shivered as she recalled what had happened back in the canyon. Romaine's death had driven the Goddess into a frenzy, changed her, transformed her into something…else. A vicious, deadly killer. She had slaughtered the Flumeeren assassin, butchered him. And then there had been her eyes…how they had changed, darkened to become almost…the grey of the Tangata.

"What happened, Cara?" she whispered at last. "Back in the canyon, you changed, didn't you?"

The Goddess quickly looked away, though not before Erika glimpsed the pain on her face. "That was…a flaw," she whispered.

"What do you mean?" Erika pressed.

Cara's eyes slid closed. "A mistake in the makeup of the Anahera."

"A mistake?"

"It makes us dangerous," Cara confirmed. "That's why…that's why we're forbidden from interfering, from killing: the fear we might lose ourselves, that we will succumb to our inner nature, become like…like the Old Ones."

"The Old Ones?" Erika questioned, before connecting the facts. "Those creatures we…discovered in the tunnels?" Cara gave the slightest nod of her head, and Erika swallowed. "What were those things?"

"They were meant to all be gone," Cara whispered, her eyes seeming to stare into some far-off place. "That's what the Founders told us…" She trailed off, her eyes flicking to Erika. "They *are* the ancestors of the Tangata, but unlike their descendants, the Old Ones were mad, deranged. They wanted nothing more than the destruction of humanity."

Erika frowned. "That does not sound so different from the Tangata of today."

"That is because you cannot hear them," Cara replied absently.

"*What?*" Erika asked.

"Oh, right," Cara murmured, shaking her head. "You humans cannot Hear with your minds." She smiled, and Erika glimpsed some of her friend's old mirth. "The Tangata are not monsters, Erika. I tried to tell you before, but you would not listen. They Speak with their minds. Only those with the same ability can hear them."

Erika sat back in her chair with an *oomph*, struggling to process the new information. The Tangata were not simple beasts? How was that possible? All the legends, all the stories, the research by her fellow academics, all of it described them as mindless creatures, driven mad by the powers they had stolen from the Gods. So much of the world relied on that fact, that the enemy were monsters. Surely they could not have been wrong…

But…what if a mistake had been made? Her Archivist's mind began to race at the possibilities created by Cara's revelations. What if the tales had only been true for those ancient ancestors of the past, the Old Ones? What if the Tangata could be reasoned with. Peace between their species might be possible after all…

Then a shiver struck Erika as she recalled the Tangata that had been held captive in the queen's court. It seemed an age ago now, but Erika could still see the look it had given her, before she'd unleashed her magic. There had been despair in its eyes—and hatred. She had not imagined that.

No, humanity could not pretend the atrocities they had committed against the Tangata had never been. Nor would they forgive so easily the excesses of the enemy, the villages destroyed, the innocents of Calafe driven from their land. They had gone too far to find peace now.

Guilt lodged in Erika's throat as she recalled her own part in that darkness, how she had used the gauntlet's magic on the helpless Tangata. She shuddered, clenching the empty fist that had once wielded its power. What terrible things it had made her do…

"You're not wearing the gauntlet," Cara said abruptly.

Erika flinched at her words and looked up, seeing the Goddess's eyes on her empty fist. "I didn't like what it did to me."

"Did to you?" A frown creased Cara's face. "What do you mean?"

"There was a…darkness to that thing, to its power," she said finally. "I could feel it corrupting me, robbing me of something…of my humanity." Casting her eyes to the floor, she slowly unclenched her fist. "I am…afraid that its God magic will change me as it did the Old Ones, that it will make me a monster."

Silence answered her words, and finally Erika looked up. The Goddess sat staring at her, eyes wide, a puzzled look on her face.

Abruptly she burst into laughter.

Erika started, shocked by her friend's reaction. "What?" she snapped angrily. "Your God magic corrupted—"

Cara's laughter rose in pitch and she fell back on the bed, holding her stomach, gasping for air.

"*Oh by the Fall!*" she finally managed.

Erika gritted her teeth, wishing in that instant she had the gauntlet to hand, if only to silence the young Anahera's laughter. Cara shouldn't be laughing at her, not when she was working so hard—

There it was again, the anger. Exhaling, Erika shook her head. "Cara, I know you cannot understand," she said carefully. "You are a God, after all. It is your magic. But there is something about that artefact, it *was* changing me."

A long silence answered Erika's words, and she watched as the laughter died in Cara's eyes. The Anahera sat in silence for a long moment, staring at Erika, as though weighing what she was about to say.

"Erika, it's not our magic," Cara said softly.

"What?" Erika frowned. "What are you talking about, of course—"

"That thing is not of the Anahera," Cara interrupted, then paused, drawing in a breath. "That gauntlet you hold, it is human magic, Erika. It never belonged to us."

❧ 16 ❧

THE FOLLOWER

By the time Adonis finally reached the cave, most of the Tangata were asleep. Or at least those who had survived the storm, who'd had the strength to reach shelter for the night. The rest…

He shivered, recalling the face of the child, frozen in the snow, in death.

Anger touched him. It was one thing for the weak to obey their betters, to bow before the older generations. But for the strong to march them to their deaths, to leave precious children dying in the snow…what was the purpose of such madness, this headlong race through the storm?

Inside the cave, silence prevailed as his brothers and sisters slept fitfully. He found himself counting their number as he crept through their ranks, trying to learn how many they had lost. Yet even those who had reached this simple shelter might not yet wake to see the morrow. Those within lay shivering in groups, their clothing damp, faces pale in the darkness. Not a single fire had been lit.

Thousands had set out from New Nihelm, a host grand enough to sweep away even the largest of humanity's armies. They numbered in the thousands still, Adonis thought, but hundreds had fallen on the way. And the children…

Adonis.

He flinched as her Voice spoke suddenly into his mind, loud, imperious, drowning out his own thoughts. Looking around, he searched for the Old One and found her lounging at the rear of the cave, attended as always by her guards. They were like him, other Tangata of the third generation, those who had once been assigned to protect the old Matriarch.

Like him, they had seen the truth that Maya had shown them: that the Tangata had decayed beneath her rule, becoming subservient, bowing to the whims of their lessers. Unlike Adonis though, they had not lagged during the long journey, had not lingered with the weak and dying.

Adonis, my mate, what became of you? Adonis swallowed as Maya's consciousness pricked at his mind, probing. *Does your wound bother you?*

Adonis reached unconsciously for his chest, but in truth he had hardly noticed its pain during the long trek. Several days had passed now since the humans' escape and despite the damage done by the spear, the wound was healing well. And besides, his pain had been nothing compared to the misery of his brethren around him, to the children…

A sudden warmth swept over Adonis as he found himself looking into the grey depths of Maya's eyes. Fresh energy pulsed in his veins, as though a magic hand had reached out and plucked the exhaustion from him. He knew it was Maya's doing, knew the ecstasy was only an illusion, a spell cast so that his mind would forget his ails, but…he let out a sigh, embracing the warmth, the relief from his grief.

Adonis bowed his head as he approached her, ignoring the eyes of her guards. He wondered if they suspected him of some treachery, *he*, the one who had brought the Old One to them, who had helped to strike down the Matriarch. Or perhaps they thought him weak. He had already allowed the human to strike him, for the traitors to escape. And now he had lagged with those too weak to follow their new leader.

No matter. They were not his Matriarch, not his mate. Only Maya mattered, only her touch, only her power…

Coming to a stop before the Old One, Adonis bowed his head. *I was delayed by our people, my mate,* he said. *By those who had fallen behind.*

Her grey eyes regarded him, her inner thoughts concealed, but after a moment a smile touched her lips.

Your kindness is to be commended, Adonis, she said, stepping forward and placing a hand on his chest. He felt her heat, even through the dampness of his shirt. *But…another might consider this weakness. Why do you waste your strength on those too feeble to serve their Matriarch?*

I… Adonis trailed off beneath her cold gaze. He sensed no anger from her, only a confusion, that he could truly have risked his own strength for those who had fallen behind. *It is not their fault.*

Perhaps. Maya stroked his cheek, her words whispering in his mind. *Neither is it the fault of the parasite, the life it drains from its host. Still, it must be cut out, before its disease threatens the whole.*

Adonis's stomach twisted at her words and the vision came to him once more, of the child in the snow. *There…there were children amongst them.*

Not my children, the Old One replied. She stroked his cheek now, her face close, her breath hot upon his flesh. *Not our children.*

The words reverberated through Adonis as her fingers trailed down his throat, tingling, burning. Suddenly the images in his mind had vanished and he saw only the Old One before him, the power in her eyes, the desire. She had made him her mate the first night after her awakening, but…

…always before, his pairings had ended in disappointment. He had not allowed himself to believe it might be different with Maya. But…he swallowed.

Our…children?

A smile touched the lips of the Old One. It seemed to him there was a danger in that smile, though he could not think why. Her fingers entwined with his as she drew his hand to her stomach.

Their fire burns within me already, she murmured, her eyes locked with his, her mind entwined in his own consciousness. *New children, strong enough to survive this world, to resist even the call of death.*

Now the warmth that swept through Adonis's mind was real, an ecstasy that burned away all his fears, all his doubts. Hope swelled within, a fierce, awesome thing—not just for himself, but for the future of all his people. Their children would be the first born of his generation in decades without the aid of human blood.

A new generation, one revitalised by the power of the Old Ones, a fresh hope for his people.

A growl rumbled from Adonis's chest as he gripped Maya tight, pulling her to him. Heat swept through him as their lips met, banishing the last of the cold. They fell together to the floor of the cave, to the unyielding rock. Cloth tore as they grasped at one another, desperate for the press of flesh, for the heat of one another's bodies.

Adonis gasped when they finally came together, as Maya pushed him down, her strength taking control, a thousandfold his own. His being shuddered as he felt her mind, so vast, so powerful, mingling with his own. Their eyes locked and they moved as one, the last of his doubts burned to ash, until there was only the promise of their future, only the fiery heat of his desire.

Until there was only the Old One.

❧ 17 ❧

THE HERO

"*Tangata! Traitors!*"

The screams echoed across the deck of the *Brereton* as the sailors picked up Tasha's call—followed by the soft hiss of steel on leather as swords were drawn. Lukys's comrades cried out as the royal guard levelled her silver spear, and several darted forward to place themselves between Sophia and the blade.

A growl came from Cleo and Lukys leapt aside as the guard swung at him with a spear, narrowly avoiding the blow. Heart pounding in his chest, Lukys retreated with his comrades. Sailors bearing paddles and rusted blades advanced on them, joining the royal guards.

No, no, no. Lukys shook his head, raising his hands in a desperate sign of peace. This was all wrong. "Please—" he tried, but Cleo thrust out with his spear in a blow that would have disembowelled him had he not leapt aside.

"Enough of your lies, traitor," the man spat as he retreated from a counterattack launched by Dale.

Fists clenched, Lukys swung on the woman, Tasha. "We're not traitors, I swear," he cried. "The Tangata are not the monsters we thought. These with us, they seek only sanctuary!"

"These?" the guard hissed, her blade coming up. "How many of the murderous creatures have you brought upon our peaceful shores?"

Movement came from amongst the ranks of Lukys's friends as Sophia pushed forward, Isabella and Keria at her side, the others too. One by one they removed their blindfolds, revealing eyes as grey as the granite cliffs above. The hiss of inhaled breath came from across the ship as the sailors drew back, and even Cleo shifted closer to Tasha, the sight of a dozen Tangata apparently enough to give even the giant guard pause.

"They won't hurt you!" Lukys said. Drawing on his courage, he took a step towards the guards, hands still raised.

As he spoke, he reached out with his mind, seeking the swirling of their emotions as he had with Sophia. Each was a vortex of rainbow light, but strongest of all was the pulsing yellow, the tang of fear. The fiery red of anger was almost as great, and in desperation he reached for those colours, seeking to sooth them, to lift their other emotions, the purples and blues and pinks, though he could not pause to know their significance.

"They are Tangata," Tasha replied, though there was a pause as her eyes flickered to Cleo, as though in sudden doubt.

Lukys latched onto the opening. "They are just as human as you or I."

For a moment, he thought his words might convince Tasha. Her spear wavered, the tip lowering a fraction as she eyed them, and he sensed a flickering of something—doubt? She looked again at Cleo, though the giant guard wore only the same twisted sneer he'd had since their appearance at the docks.

"Do you know how many of your comrades those creatures have killed?" the man spat, gesturing with his spear at Sophia in a way that left no doubt what he would like to do to her. There was loathing in his eyes as he looked again at Lukys. "And you brought them to our shores."

"Since when do the Sovereigns care for the lives of my comrades?" Lukys bristled, angered despite himself. "They sent us to die, knowing we were untrained, unprepared. If not for the mercy of these Tangata, we *would* be dead. But then, what would you know, sitting here safe in our homeland? Have you ever even *seen* combat?"

Cleo's face turned a mottled red at Lukys's words and gripping his spear with both hands, he started towards Lukys. "By the Fall, I'll show you—"

"Wait," Tasha spoke over the two of them, her voice sharp, barely controlled. Cleo froze, and Tasha fixed her eyes on Lukys. "Why should we believe what you say, when all you have presented us with so far has been lies and deceptions? No…" Her face grew grim as she looked from Lukys to the Tangata. "I think you meant to bring death to our Sovereigns, in vengeance for your perceived mistreatment."

"No, that's not—"

"*Enough!*" Tasha silenced him with a glare.

She turned her eyes to the crew of the *Brereton*. Still armed with their scattering of weapons, they shifted nervously on their feet. Lukys could see their fear. They knew there were not enough of them to defeat so many of the Tangata. But…

…the hairs on Lukys's neck lifted as he saw that seamen from the other ships were gathering on the docks. Many were better armed, having raced to grab weapons when the call of Tangata went out. And farther along the docks, a squadron of soldiers was racing towards them.

"Citizens of Perfugia!" Tasha's voice lifted so that those on the jetty could hear. "These men and women before you have brought peril to our homes, a threat to the lives of our Sovereigns. We must stand against them, must defend our kingdom at all costs. I call on you now to lend me your strength, that we might push these evil creatures back into the oceans from which they have crept."

The rumble of voices spread across the deck of the *Brereton* as the sailors clutched weapons tighter, while others began to leap the narrow gap between the docks and the ship. Grinning, Cleo nodded to his companion and lifted shield and spear.

Lukys allowed his hands to fall to his side as Dale pulled him back into the safety of his friends. Without a spear, he would only get in the way. He found himself standing next to Sophia. Looking into her grey eyes, he sensed her fear, her sadness, but beyond that…acceptance.

It's okay, Lukys, she whispered, reaching out to place a hand on his shoulder. *You tried your best.*

His stomach tied itself into knots. Beyond the lines of his

friends, he heard Cleo bellow a curse, even as Dale closed with him. The shriek of spear striking shield followed, then grunts as Dale leapt back. Without shield or armour, he was badly outmatched by the royal guard.

Lukys found himself clenching his fists as others joined the guard to attack his friends, a rage sweeping over him. Who were these men and women to judge them, to call Lukys and his friends traitors, while they hid on their distant island, untouched by the horrors of war?

Without thinking, he reached out again with his mind, searching for the swirling colours, the pulsing emotions of those who surrounded them. They radiated from the guards and sailors, mixing and mingling, the reds and yellows almost feeding off one another. Watching that vortex of light, Lukys focused on the yellow, gripping their fear tight with his mind.

This time, he sought not to suppress it, not to remove the terror of his enemies. Instead, he fed the sickly yellow, nurtured its glow, until it swelled and grew amongst the men and women facing them, surpassing the red, suppressing all other emotion, until even the yellow succumbed, giving way to pure white, to absolute terror.

Screams rang across the waters of the harbour as men and women fell to their knees, oars and swords and other makeshift weapons clattering to the deck. Several of the sailors turned and threw themselves over the side of the ship, while others simply crumpled, too terrified to even run. Even Cleo, for all his boasting, staggered away from them, face bleached white. None could stand before the terror Lukys had inspired…

…none, that is, except for Tasha.

A frown crossed Lukys face as he saw her standing straight amidst the fallen sailors. Her eyes flickered to her comrade and her lips twitched.

"Get a hold of yourself, Cleo," she said.

"I…I…" the big man struggled, but his tongue could not seem to form words. He staggered back, coming perilously close to the gunwale. In his armour, he would sink like a stone.

"Oh for Fall's sake," she snapped, reaching out and dragging him away from the edge. He struggled against her, until she slapped him hard across the face. Only then did the effects of Lukys's terror seem to lessen. "He's a Melder like us, you idiot," she growled. "Didn't you sense him earlier?"

"I…" A frown creased Cleo's face, and suddenly the colours of his emotions vanished. The rage on the man's face as he swung on Lukys was all too visible though. "The little bastard—"

Tasha struck him again. Cursing, Cleo raised a hand to fend off further blows. "I already locked him out!"

"I know," the guard replied shortly. "Calm yourself." Then she turned towards Lukys and leaned her head to the side.

You're a Melder.

For half a moment, Lukys struggled to process what he'd just heard. Or rather, where the words that had appeared in his head had come from. He stared at the woman, mind whirring as he opened his mouth, then closed it again. She had *Spoken* to him. In his mind. That wasn't possible. The only people who could Speak were the Tangata. Well, the Tangata, and himself…

What did you say? he finally managed, projecting the words recklessly, too shocked for subtlety.

Cleo's head snapped towards him and a scowl twisted his face. *Don't play stupid, traitor. You'll die slowly for what you just did.*

But he made no move towards Lukys, and beside him, Tasha's frown only deepened. Lukys felt a fluttering against his mind, as though a feather were brushing up against his consciousness. Quickly he tried to contain his emotions, to keep her from his secrets.

An untrained Melder, Tasha said at last. *That is…impossible. Why would one of your talent be sent to the frontlines?*

"What does it matter?" Cleo growled, speaking out loud again. "The traitor has chosen his allegiance."

Lukys shook his head, barely able to comprehend what was happening. A human—a *Perfugian Royal Guard*—had spoken to him in his mind. It was one thing to witness Tangata with such power… but hearing the thoughts of his own people, that was something else entirely.

Lukys's influence was beginning to fade from the sailors now and Lukys, Cleo, and Tasha stood in silence as the men and women slowly crawled to their feet. Some regained their weapons, while others simply stood there, staring at the Tangata as though expecting the creatures to tear them apart at any moment.

Forcing his confusion to the rear of his mind, Lukys took a step towards Tasha. Her spear came up, pointing for his throat, but she did not strike. He could still see the anger in her eyes, but there was more there now. Her mind remained closed to him, but it seemed to him that she was as curious about his nature as he was of theirs.

Why have you come here, truly? Her voice came to him again.

Lukys swallowed. *I swear before the Gods above, I am no traitor,* he replied, keeping his voice soft. *These Tangata, they* are *refugees. Something has happened…sir, something that could mean disaster for our people. These Tangata, they're on our side. They want to help us.*

"Want to eat us, more like," Cleo snorted.

We do not eat humans.

If Lukys's ability had surprised the pair, Sophia Speaking shocked them so greatly that Cleo almost dropped his spear again. Their eyes snapped to the Tangata as Sophia approached cautiously, coming to a stop alongside Lukys. He held his breath as their knuckles whitened upon spear hilts, but neither attacked.

Lukys speaks the truth, Sophia continued, inclining her head in what Lukys had come to recognise as a gesture of respect amongst the Tangata. *My people come under a flag of truce.*

The guards' spear tips wavered as Sophia spoke again, as though her Voice meant she might suddenly launch herself at them. A tension hung in the air, as both sides waited for the other to attack, to be the first to draw blood.

Finally Tasha shook her head. *You can Speak,* she said.

Yes, Sophia replied patiently. *As can all my people.* She gestured to the others, and they stepped forward hesitantly. *We have come to you seeking refuge.*

Tasha frowned. *What refuge could Perfugia possibly provide the Tangata…?*

Her words trailed off as she suddenly tensed, and her eyes took on a distant look. Lukys frowned, recognising the look of someone conducting a conversation in their mind. But who? Cleo still stood glaring at them, eyes alert. Silently, he reached out with his mind for some hint of Tasha's intentions, but a second later her eyes flickered back into focus. The tension drained from her and reaching out, she placed a hand on Cleo's spear arm.

"Lower your weapons," she said softly, looking from the big guard to Lukys's company. "It seems you have won yourselves a reprieve."

❧ 18 ❧

THE EMISSARY

The lady hath gone. The others searcheth, but I know those gents shalt not find her. The children mourn, but we didst teacheth them to be stout. There is nay other choice, in this world we didst maketh.

Erika groaned and set the diary down to rest her weary eyes. Turning, she looked out through the window. During her exploration over the last few days, she had finally managed to find what must be one of the only windows in the city. The glass was cracked and somewhat frosted, with fine wires within the panel holding it together, even after all these years. Another remarkable feat of the Gods' magic…

Or was it?

It is human magic, Erika. It never belonged to us…

Erika shuddered as she recalled Cara's words: that the greatest discovery of her lifetime, the weapon she had wielded with ecstasy these past months, the artefact of the Gods she had displayed so proudly in Flumeer…was not of the Gods at all.

It was human.

Swallowing, she returned her attention to the diary, flicking forward through several months' worth of notes. The answers to her questions had to lie somewhere within these pages. She had gotten nothing more out of Cara, even less from Hugo or his father. But this diary, there was a truth here, a detail she was still missing, one that might finally fill in the blank spaces of human history.

Mine own muscles groweth weary, mine own bones frail. I shouldst hath passed from this world long ago. I longeth for yond release, but the power holdeth me to this world. The others hath did find peace, but I remain. Mayhaps I shouldst speak the truth, that others might putteth right mine own crimes…

Erika cursed. The diary's author seemed to grow more cryptic with the passage of each year, his words made all the more unintelligible by the ancient version of their language.

A shiver shook Erika as her gaze was drawn to the gauntlet. It lay on the table beside her, glinting in the magical lights shining overhead, dangerous, threatening…

…or was that all in her imagination?

Cara had explained it was but a tool, that its magic had nothing to do with her anger, or the madness manifested in her kind. Somehow, the Anahera's words rang true, spoke to a reality Erika had suspected all along, however much she might want to resist it.

Because if the gauntlet was human, if it was only a tool, a weapon created to fight the Old Ones, then that meant…

…it meant everything she'd done, her crimes against Cara and those around her, they were of her own doing.

Tearing her eyes from the gauntlet, Erika looked out the window again. Through the tainted glass, she could just make out the great yard in the centre of the city. A storm was raging outside, and every so often a whisper would sneak through the cracked glass, carrying with it the soft breath of ice. Snowdrifts were building quickly against the walls and glass houses. She could barely make out the structure rising from the centre, the four monoliths of stone.

She clenched her fist as a tremor slid down her spine. Today was the day. Hugo had not said how it would be done. He'd been less responsive to their questions since Farhan had learned of her visit with Cara. If calling on his daughter had not been forbidden then, it was now. They had even had a second guard assigned to watch them.

Bang.

Erika jumped as the door to the room flew open and Maisie strode inside. Outside she glimpsed Hugo with a strange look on his face, before Maisie swung the door closed again.

"*There* you are," the spy exclaimed, clearly exasperated.

"Here I am," Erika agreed, irritated despite herself. She'd been trapped in the same quarters with the woman for a week now, and had come to this room to enjoy some peace, however brief. "Were you looking for me?"

The spy slumped into the opposite chair and glanced out the window. "I was," she said, then sighed. "Though I suppose it wouldn't work today, in this weather."

"Huh?" Erika asked.

"You know, I've been thinking, the borders of Calafe can't be *that* far from here. These Gods of yours probably wouldn't expect us to go that way—not towards the Tangata. We could skirt the foothills back to the Illmoor Fortress, avoid any Tangata in the area. We'd be back in the safety of Nguyen's protection in a matter of weeks…"

"What about Cara?" Erika murmured, her eyes on the storm. She had spent all week with the spy brainstorming ways of breaking the young Anahera from her room, but with the two guards watching their every move…

Maisie let out a sigh, and when Erika looked at her, the Gemaho woman did not meet her eyes. "I know I said we should rescue her, but…" she began.

"No," Erika interrupted, coming to her feet.

"Archivist," Maisie said softly, looking up from her seat. "I know how much you care about her, but…" She trailed off, then shook her head. "It's not us they care about, Erika," she continued finally. "Farhan, the Elders, we're a nuisance to them, an inconvenience. It's Cara they're concerned about, the rules she broke. They need to make an example of her, but us…how hard do you think they're really going to search if we disappear?"

"They said we've seen too much…"

"Hundreds of people have seen Cara—the Elders know their existence is no longer secret. It's only a matter of time before others come looking for the City," Maisie replied. Her eyes met Erika's. "We only came here to ask for their aid. If we leave, carry the tale of what we found here, how they have abandoned us…then there is no reason for others to seek them out. Humanity has more pressing concerns to bother themselves with than these mountains."

Erika shook her head. "I can't believe you," she hissed. "What about Cara? We can't just abandon her!"

Maisie let out a sigh. "You know they're her people, don't you?" she asked. "Who are we to interfere in Anaheran business?"

"The Flumeerens were your people too, once," Erika snapped, recalling the spy's childhood on the streets of Mildeth. "That didn't stop Nguyen from 'interfering,' did it?"

"That's different."

"Is it?" she asked, staring the spy down. "Cara is one of *us* now, Maisie. Whether we like it or not."

For a long moment, Maisie said nothing. Then a curse slipped from her lips and she slumped back into the chair.

"What are we meant to do against *Gods?*" She muttered another curse.

"I thought you didn't believe in the Gods?"

The spy made a dismissive gesture. "Gods, Anahera, call them what you will. We cannot fight them, Erika."

A shiver shook Erika and her gaze was drawn again to where the gauntlet lay upon the table. Maisie did not miss the gesture.

"Nguyen wore it for a year, you know," she said softly. "Maybe Cara is right…"

Erika swallowed. She had shared Cara's revelation with the spy, about the true creators of the gauntlet. "Why did he give it away then?" Erika whispered. "Why did he give it to Queen Amina?"

"Always keep your enemies guessing," Maisie replied with a grim smile. "He hoped it might prove enough of a distraction to delay the queen's assault. In this case, I fear the queen had Nguyen's number, given our old pal Yasin."

"So you never noticed him growing…more violent?" Erika whispered.

Maisie hesitated before shaking her head. "No, though he did not use it often," she sighed. "Erika, you know we will need its power, if we're to stand any chance of rescuing her today."

"I know," Erika snapped, more harshly than she'd intended. Reaching out, she clenched her fingers around the fine mesh of the gauntlet. "Don't you think I know? But how…" She trailed off, not wanting to speak the words, but knowing she must. Her eyes slid closed. "If it was really made by us, if it's not what created the Tangata, the Old Ones, that means…that means it was me who did those terrible things."

"They weren't so terrible—"

"I struck down a God, my own friend," Erika interrupted.

"You were trying to escape a mad queen."

"I killed that man back in camp."

"He was a spy."

"Only because his family was threatened," Erika hissed.

"Even so," Maisie replied, and this time she looked Erika in the eye. "He made his choice. We couldn't know his motives—only that he poisoned Cara, that he led the Flumeeren soldiers after us."

Erika fell silent at that, staring out the window. She watched the snow fall, the flakes crystallising upon the glass. The shadow of the stone structure loomed through the storm.

"I abandoned them," she finally whispered, images flashing through her mind, of the refugees milling outside the walls of Mildeth, her own people, condemned to homelessness and poverty by an unforgiving queen. Their nation lost, leaderless. "I condemned them while serving the very woman who betrayed my kingdom. Who betrayed my father."

"Refusing this power will not change the past," Maisie replied. "That would only be giving in to your fear, allowing it to rule you. But perhaps if you face it, you might gain the strength to make a difference, to change the future of your kingdom."

Erika let out a sigh, slumping in her seat. "Maybe," she whispered, still holding the gauntlet in one clenched fist.

Silence fell between them, and Erika found her thoughts drifting. She looked at the journal once more. She was almost at the end now, and idly she flicked through the last few pages, until she found the final verse its author had written.

Tis a weight upon mine own soul. Wast our victory worth the price? Mayhaps this is wherefore I still liveth, still clingeth to life. Beest a wrong to right, though I fear I doth not hast the strength.

A shiver ran down her spine at the words, but before she could contemplate their ancient meaning, the door to the room swung open with a squeal of old hinges. Hugo appeared in the doorway, and quickly Erika slid her bag over the open diary. For a moment she feared he'd seen her stolen property, for he stood staring at them for a long while, jaw clenched, hands shaking.

"It's time," he said abruptly.

The hackles on Erika's neck stood on end and suddenly she found her mouth dry. Beside her, Maisie rose and stepped towards Hugo, placing a hand upon his arm. Erika glimpsed tears in the young Anahera's eyes, but he quickly blinked them back as he struggled to resume his normal stoicism.

"Where?" she whispered.

Hugo nodded to the window, and turning, Erika saw that other silhouettes had joined that of the effigy in the centre of the yard: the Anahera, come to witness the fall of one of their own. She swallowed, looking at Hugo again. His face was drained of colour, but he managed to keep the tears from flowing.

His father would be proud, Erika thought bitterly.

But there was no time for resentment now. The time had come to act. Erika clenched her fist around the gauntlet, the fine mesh digging into her flesh. Maisie was right: without its magic, they could not stand against Farhan. She would fail, and Cara would…

No.

Erika had made a promise.

She slipped the gauntlet over her hand.

THE HERO

Footsteps echoed on stone floors as Lukys and his friends were led through the broad halls of the citadel, though the sound was muffled by the strange architecture of the building. While the sheer white walls of the corridor stretched up some twenty feet to either side, where the ceiling should have begun there was only open sky. He had read of the unusual design during his studies, but never had he imagined visiting himself. It seemed an impractical design in the cold northern climate, but thermal waters from a nearby spring were channelled beneath the floor, keeping the corridors warm on even the coldest of days.

Filthy and unshaven from their long journey, Lukys felt out of place amidst the grandeur of the citadel, as though he were trespassing on holy ground. Even now he was struggling to understand the shift in their circumstances. He couldn't help but think Tasha's sudden change of heart was a trap, a ploy to make them lower their guards and lure them to the slaughter.

But the soldiers of their escort were already more than enough to overwhelm them, even with the Tangata on their side. Sophia and her brethren walked in the centre of their party, their Perfugian partners forming a defensive ring to shield them from the soldiers. Whatever Tasha's assurances, it was clear that the men and women of their escort did not share her mercy—there was no missing the hatred in their eyes as they shot glances at the Tangata. Their minds remained unshielded to Lukys's probing, and he could sense their hatred, a shimmering green consuming them.

So far, only Cleo and Tasha seemed to possess the ability to Speak. Apparently, the powers of a Melder, as the guards had called him, were not so common as to be possessed by the average soldier. But…it still did not explain how *any* of the Perfugians had come to possess the ability of the Tangata.

He flicked a glance at Dale and Travis as they turned a corner and started up a flight of stairs. Neither had heard of the so-called Melders before, despite their noble births. It was clearly a closely-guarded secret, known only to a chosen few. But why?

Shaking himself, Lukys returned his mind to their surroundings. He'd glimpsed several doorways leading from the main corridor now, revealing side chambers of varying uses, most sporting low-hanging ceilings. The passageway itself wound slowly up the hill, running flat across the slope before turning up stairs that led to the next section of flat. Those chambers placed on the downhill sections of the palace displayed great windows of fine glass with glimpses of the harbour.

Finally the corridor came to an end, opening out into a massive amphitheatre. Their escort led them onto an open floor that spanned some fifty yards in diameter. Stands of granite surrounded the perimeter, rising some twenty feet on all sides.

In the direction of the ocean, the stands levelled out into a platform that sat atop the corridor from which they'd just emerged. On the opposite side of the amphitheatre though, the giant steps reached higher, lifting some thirty feet to the balcony of the grand palace. Two thrones of gold and polished marble stood upon the balcony, but for the moment they remained empty.

A ring of statues surrounded the stands, set in pairs and placed at regular intervals. They were the Sovereigns of past generations, their likenesses carved forever in stone to be remembered here, where they had once reigned. Each had ruled as brother and sister, selected by the Sovereigns before them in a manner known only to the rulers themselves.

Lukys looked around as movement came from the edges of the

amphitheatre, and a moment later dozens of guards in blue armour appeared atop the stands. His heart lurched in his chest as they levelled crossbows at the Tangata. Thinking they'd been betrayed, he swung on Tasha where she stood nearby, raising the spear he'd claimed from Travis.

"You said we had a truce!" he cried.

The woman only raised an eyebrow, her face kept carefully blank. "Consider them a precaution."

"Consider yourselves lucky we haven't ordered them to open fire," Cleo growled, his silver spear held tight at his side.

The rest of their escort had put space between themselves and Lukys's friends, leaving only the royal guards standing near. Lukys grated his teeth as he looked from the guards to the balcony, a tingling starting in the back of his neck as he imagined the crossbows aimed at his heart. Once again, his fate rested entirely in the hands of the Sovereigns. He could only pray they would not condemn him again.

"My lieges," Tasha announced, striding towards the stands beneath the palace. The balcony was empty, but Lukys could sense…something from the shadows beyond the broad doorway. "I bring you the Perfugian recruits and the Tangatan intruders, as you commanded."

Lukys lifted his eyebrows at her phrasing, but movement from the shadows beyond the balcony drew his attention to the palace. A guard in blue armour emerged, followed by three others. They marched to the edge of the balcony where the stands led down into the amphitheatre and came to a stop. There they waited, shields and spears shining in the fading light of the day.

His eyes drawn back to the shadows, Lukys held his breath. Despite their danger, despite the threat out on the waters of the harbour, he found himself strangely excited. They were about to set eyes upon the Sovereigns. It was an honour bestowed upon only the most noble of Perfugians. Though for them, that honour might yet prove their doom.

Movement came from the shadows as two figures appeared. Slipping from the darkness of the palace, they separated and moved to seat themselves in the golden thrones. The breath caught in

Lukys's throat as he looked upon the Sovereigns. Clothed in purple silks and wearing silver crowns adorned with sapphires, these were the sacred rulers of Perfugia, the two who would decide whether they all lived or died.

The pair could not have been older than fifteen.

Lukys began to speak, but the words he had been preparing in his mind tripped upon his tongue. Instead, he found himself staring open-mouthed at the Sovereigns, struggling to comprehend what he was seeing. Surely some jest was being played on them. Little was known about the selection of new Sovereigns, but…how could anyone so young hold such a position of power?

Shaking off his shock, Lukys drew himself up. Their age did not matter; the Sovereigns had led Perfugia through the generations, since their people had come to the rugged shores of the northern island. Those first settlers had been refugees from the wars that had gripped humanity since the Fall, sailing the oceans in search of a better world for their children. If only he could convince the two above that Sophia and her people only sought the same, they might finally be safe.

The Sovereigns sat on their thrones for a time, staring in silence at the visitors in their grand amphitheatre. Lukys found their gaze disconcerting, as though they were already judging him. The two did not hold themselves as normal teenagers; there was an aged way to how they sat, a stature far beyond their years.

Despite himself, Lukys wilted beneath that gaze. What right did he have to stand before these two, the rightful leaders of Perfugia, saviours of his people? Who was he but a failed citizen, unworthy of even the most rudimentary position in their glorious society…?

Lukys… He started as Sophia's voice whispered into his mind. Glancing at her, he found her grey eyes wide. *Beware—*

Her voice cut off abruptly as the rustling of clothes carried to them from above. Lukys looked back to the balcony as the Sovereigns stood, moving to stand at the railings. Watching them, Lukys threw off the despairing thoughts. Hadn't he left those doubts behind long ago? He had proven his worth countless times over the last months, fighting across Calafe, defeating Tangata in single combat, escaping the wrath of an Old One.

No, he had no cause to feel shame standing before these two.

636

Glancing again at Sophia, he offered a silent nod. Whatever their judgement said, he was a warrior, a soldier. And he would fight to the end for his people.

"Where have you come from, Melder?"

A hiss escaped from Lukys's throat as the words rang across the courtyard—and his mind. It took a moment before he could piece together the words. The two spoke as one, out loud so that all could hear, but also into his mind, their words thundering in a way that made him shrink from them. He shared a glance with Sophia and saw his own concern reflected back. If the Sovereigns themselves were Melders, how far back did the deception stretch?

Clenching his fists, he took a step towards the balcony, though it did little to narrow the distance to the Sovereigns.

"My name is Lukys," he said, choosing to speak out loud. A gust of wind swept the words from the amphitheatre, sapping them of strength, but he kept on. "And I come from the frontier, from the lands of Calafe." He paused. "Where you sent me to die."

The Sovereigns regarded him in silence, their twin pairs of eyes shimmering in the fading sunlight.

"Many have been sent to die at the hands of the Tangata," their reply came finally. *"It is an honour to give one's life for their kingdom."*

"Not when they die needlessly!" Lukys cried, a rage coming on him as he looked at the teenage Sovereigns. "Not when they are sent untrained. Not when the Tangata themselves do not desire war!"

"The Tangata are blasphemers who betrayed the Gods, monsters who seek the destruction of humanity. All know this," the Sovereigns replied in unison.

Lukys clenched his teeth at their words, preparing to unleash his rage upon them, but a hand on his shoulder gave him pause. A warmth touched his heart as Sophia joined him, though her grey eyes were on the Sovereigns. Following her gaze, he saw that the pair were staring at her.

"Is that not so, Tangata?" They spoke again, and now the words in Lukys's mind were softer, as they directed their question at Sophia.

She bowed her head. *There are some who loathe your kind with a passion,* she replied softly, *some who would see you destroyed. But...there are many others, younger generations who see humanity as equals, as two halves of a whole, incomplete so long as we remain separate.*

"And these youth, they desire peace?" the Sovereigns questioned.

Sophia hesitated, her eyes flickering to Lukys. He faced the pair above.

"If granted the opportunity, many of the Tangata would join us, as Sophia and these others here have," he replied, then hesitated, struggling to put words to what he had seen in New Nihelm.

An image sprung into his mind, of the Old One Maya, as she stood in the basilica in New Nihelm. He blinked, but the image did not fade, and he realised this was a scene he had never seen before. Adonis stood alongside the creature, and as he watched she advanced on his viewpoint. Words were spoken—then the Old One moved in a blur. Blood followed and slowly the image faded to black.

That was the last vision of our Matriarch, Sophia said softly, directing her words to the Sovereigns. *Broadcast to all the Tangata who were nearby in her final moments, to reveal this treachery. Sadly, the others were already in the thrall of the Old One.*

Lukys swallowed and reached out to squeeze her fingers. He had not seen that image as they stood outside the basilica, hadn't realised the horror she had witnessed in her mind. His gaze was drawn back to the Sovereigns and now he saw the doubt that creased their faces. Slowly they retreated to their thrones and sat.

"So the Old Ones have returned," they said at last, voices grim. *"This…changes everything. "*

"Old Ones?" came a voice from behind Lukys. "That sounds ominous."

Lukys spun as a newcomer emerged from the corridor. Dressed in a simple tunic and breeches, he appeared as a common man from the street. Yet no commoner could simply stroll into the court of the Sovereigns, and certainly not with a sword strapped to his belt. And this man carried a bearing about himself that spoke of nobility, as though he were used to others submitting to his every command.

But the royal guards stationed around the amphitheatre clearly had no intention of bowing to him. At his appearance, they sprang to alert, hefting spears and moving quickly to place themselves between the stranger and their Sovereigns.

The man came to a stop as the guards barred his path, though he did not spare them so much as a glance. His gaze remained fixed on the Sovereigns.

"My dear Sovereigns," he said, offering a short bow. "I do apologise for interrupting your court, but it's a matter of some urgency." He paused, a grimace twisting his lips. "I'm afraid Queen Amina has invaded Gemaho."

❦ 20 ❦

THE EMISSARY

Erika shuddered as a gust of wind sent ice and sleet whipping sideways across the open yard. The cold bit at her exposed hand and sliced through her too-thin clothing, and hugging herself tight, she made to clench her fist, to summon the magic of her gauntlet for warmth.

Then she hesitated, glancing at the Anahera who stood gathered around her. They did not know of her power, had not noticed the gauntlet she now wore. Cara and her father were still absent; better she kept the magic secret for now, maintained the element of surprise.

Not that Erika knew what she was going to do—only that she would not stand idly by while her friend was dismembered.

The crowd of Anahera swelled as more arrived from their hidden quarters, though Erika noticed that as before, the children —fledglings, as Cara had called them—were not present. There were several like Hugo, slightly younger than Cara in appearance, but the rest were adults. She shivered to think how many years such beings had seen, if a youth such as Cara had passed fifty years of age.

Inevitably, Erika's gaze was drawn to the monoliths in the centre of the yard. The four towers of stone loomed above, great blocks of stone stretching from the corners of the altar. Their true purpose now lay revealed, as great blades of steel had been placed between each of the towers, forming two terrible guillotines on either side of the altar.

A shudder ran down Erika's spine as she looked upon the terrible device the Gods had crafted to punish their own. Chains lay across the altar, iron manacles awaiting their next victims. Now she was close, Erika could see the dark stains upon the stone, the grooves worn in the altar beneath each steel blade. Remnants of past atrocities. Her stomach twisted at the thought of Cara bound to that cold stone, her wings stretched out, the blades suspended above, waiting…

Tearing her gaze from the awful contraption, Erika focused instead on the object of her anger. Farhan stood nearby, his cold gaze fixed on one of the doorways to the city. Arms clasped behind his back, wings folded neatly behind, he waited with the other Elders, the image of a regal leader.

How Erika hated him. At least Hugo showed some semblance of emotion for his sister, some terror and shame for what was about to be done. But Farhan…Farhan's face could have been carved from stone, his eyes frozen into ice. There was no hint of sadness for the fate of his daughter, no compassion.

Erika grated her teeth, her entire being vibrating with her anger. How could any father commit such a crime against his own daughter? Erika could barely grasp the glory of wings, the freedom of the open sky, but she had seen the wonder of it in Cara's eyes, the joy. To lose that…it would destroy her—

Erika's train of thought was broken as Maisie nudged her in the side.

"What?" Erika hissed, glaring at the spy.

Maisie raised an eyebrow and flicked her eyes downwards. Erika followed her gaze and saw the gauntlet had come to life. Thankfully its glow was muted in the near whiteout conditions of the mountain valley, and quickly she released her fist, allowing it to die. Exhaling, she nodded her thanks at Maisie, even as her own doubts rose again within her. Had the anger been her own? Or had Cara been wrong, and the gauntlet was affecting her again?

No, she thought, returning her eyes to Farhan, *no, this is my own rage. If ever a creature deserved to be hated, it was the parent who fails his child.*

Reassured, she drew herself up, preparing to denounce the God.

Before she could act, a door across the yard slammed open. Her stomach twisted as a pair of Anaheran guards emerged, leading a forlorn figure between them. The gale caught Cara's flaming hair and sent it whipping across her face, and even her auburn feathers lifted at the power in the storm. For a moment it seemed she would be blown off the mountain.

Erika wondered why she did not flee. She had seen the Goddess in flight, knew her speed. She was young—surely she could outrun those who would come after her? But then, what was there for Cara out in the world, now that her identity had been revealed? Erika, humanity, had already betrayed her, had failed her too many times. Perhaps she had come to accept her fate, that there *was* no place in this world for her, for a God who disobeyed her own family, her own laws.

No, Erika whispered to herself, clenching her fist. *She is my friend. I will not let them take her wings.*

Yet she did not move as Cara was led across the square to where the altar awaited. Her heart pounded in her chest as she watched them. The contraption seemed so barbaric, more a creation out of the dark days of the Fall than a tool of the Gods, of those who had created the wonders captured in paint on the walls of their city.

It is human magic, Erika. It never belonged to us.

Erika shuddered as her Archivist's mind began to replay Cara's words, to examine everything she had learned these past weeks, everything she had witnessed, Erika could no longer ignore the question on her mind: what were the Anahera? Yes, Cara's people were glorious, splendid, powerful. But then, so were the Tangata, in their own way. Sleek, balanced, with a grace no human could ever hope to match. They moved as the Anahera did.

Cara sobbed as the guards lay her upon the altar. Chains rattled as her captors forced down her arms and locked them in shackles. She did not fight as the constraints were fixed in place, though Erika noticed her head swinging around, searching the crowd, seeking a friend—seeking Erika.

Erika clenched her fist again, struggling with her anger, looking upon Farhan. How she loathed this God of Gods. Could she defy him, defy the Gods themselves to save her friend?

The hackles rose on Erika's neck as a scream carried across the square. She watched as the guards each took hold of one of Cara's wings, watched as they stretched them across the altar, until her auburn feathers lay exposed to the snow, so beautiful, so frail. Chains rattled as the guards bound them tight to the stone, fixing them in place.

Images flashed through Erika's mind as she imagined the blades falling, their razor-sharp edges slicing through the flesh and bone and feather of the fragile limbs beneath. Not even a God could heal from that…

…or whatever the Anahera were.

Erika found herself turning away from the anguish on Cara's face, looking instead at Maisie. The woman stood nearby, her face a mask, though Erika could sense the tension radiating from the spy. She had never believed in the Gods. Nguyen, the Gemaho leader, had claimed Cara was something else, something like the Tangata.

Something that could be defied, defeated.

"Stop!"

Erika's call shattered the silence of the Anahera, drawing every face towards her as she stepped up to confront Farhan.

"This is wrong," she said, her voice steady now, determined.

Wrong, wrong, wrong.

The words carried more meaning than one. Wrong to commit such a crime. Wrong to have believed in these creatures all these years. Wrong to call them Gods. Her mind struggled to focus, to keep from pondering the implications of her decision—for if the Anahera were not Gods, if they had never been Divine…what did that mean for her life's study, for her purpose, for her people…?

Farhan said nothing, only watched her with those cold eyes. Gritting her teeth, Erika swung on the crowd, seeking someone, anyone who might help her. The Elders stared back, unyielding, but surely not all the Anahera could be so cruel, so heartless as Farhan.

Then she saw Hugo, standing alone, away from the others, his eyes shadowed.

"Hugo!" His head jerked up when she called his name, his eyes showing shock. He retreated half a step, but she would not let him flee, would not let him abandon his sister. "You know this isn't right!" she called, pointing. "That your father is wrong to do this. This cannot be what your Founders wanted for the Anahera, to be hidden away in this place, to live imprisoned by invisible chains, your lives controlled by laws that ceased to have meaning long ago."

Hugo froze, still half-turned to flee, hand raised as though to fend her off. He blinked, slowly turning back towards them, and for a moment she thought he might speak—

"Enough!" Farhan bellowed, drawing the attention of the square back to him. For once his face showed emotion as veins bulged in his forehead. "Enough of your foul temptation, human," he spat, advancing on her. "You have corrupted one of my children already, I will not allow you another!"

He raised his fist as though to strike her and Erika leapt back, her gauntlet coming up instinctively. Light shone upon the silver threads, setting the falling snow aglow. Gasps came from all around as the Anahera drew back, and before her, Farhan froze. Surprise showed in his eyes as he looked upon the gauntlet, but it was quickly masked behind red rage.

"So at last the human shows her true nature," he snarled, baring his teeth—though he did not advance. "The magic of the ancients is born again to be used against us."

Erika quickly lowered her fist, extinguishing the light. "No..." she said, turning to the crowd.

The Anahera stared back at her, fear shining in their eyes.

"You will not stop us from following the path set by our Sacred Founders," Farhan said, and now his voice was soft, implacable.

Turning, he started towards the altar where Cara lay bound. Her eyes widened as he approached and Erika caught the whisper of her voice on the wind, her desperate plea.

"Please, Father, no..."

Erika's heart pounded in her chest and she lifted her hand to strike Farhan down, then froze. There had been something about the way the God had looked at the gauntlet, an expectation. He knew what the gauntlet was, even if he had not known it was in her possession. So why did he turn his back against her now, as though inviting her to use it?

Lowering her arm, Erika darted forward, trying to place herself between father and daughter. As she ran, she spotted Hugo, still standing nearby. He was no longer paying attention to Erika or his father, but instead to Maisie. The spy was speaking to him, but the wind whipped away her words.

Then Erika was standing before the altar, her back to Cara, facing down Farhan's advance. Open rage showed in the eyes of the Anahera as he advanced, and Erika could hear the sobs of her friend from behind, the whispers of the crowd, the hissing of wind through the glass houses.

A calm descended upon her as she clenched her fist, igniting the power of the gauntlet. There was only one option now, one last path left to save her friend, and she sighed as the warmth of the gauntlet's magic bathed her. Cries came from the other Anahera, but this time Farhan did not retreat. Wings spread wide, he bore down upon the frail Archivist.

But Erika did not shrink from him now, did not bow down to this creature of the mountains. No God of hers would commit such an atrocity against his child, against her friend. She raised her hand, clenching her fist tighter, the magic building. The soft crackling of her power sounded across the yard as Erika stood tall against her foe.

And still Farhan came on.

✣ 21 ✣

THE HERO

"King Nguyen," the Sovereigns growled, rising from their thrones. *"What is the meaning of this?"*

Lukys started at their words, spinning to regard the stranger anew. He wore no crown, but his bearing…the greying hair and iron jawline, the piercing emerald eyes…yes, this man was older, more world-weary, but there was a resemblance to the sketches Lukys had studied in the academy. Yet…how had the Gemaho king come to be here, unheralded and alone in the court of the Sovereigns?

Spreading his hands, the king offered the Sovereigns a smile. As he did so, horns began to sound in the distance. Lukys frowned as all eyes turned from the king towards the unseen harbour, upon which towers kept an ever-vigilant watch for sign of attack. But no enemy had ever dared come against their remote island kingdom. Surely it could not have been…

The horn sounded again, a long, shrill note that went on and on. Lukys's blood ran cold as he recognised the signal from his learnings at the academy—the klaxon call to arms, the warning that an enemy had arrived on Perfugia's shores.

"Ah, that will be my fleet," King Nguyen announced, drawing the attention of the amphitheatre back to him. Reaching into his tunic, he drew out a glass and metal object and inspected its surface before returning it to his pocket. "And not a moment too soon!" he announced.

"*Nguyen, what is the meaning of this?*" the Sovereigns snarled again.

They advanced down the stairs from their balcony, hedged by royal guards. Their silver spears were extended towards the king, but he stood calmly beneath their threat, with far more poise than Lukys could have managed under the circumstances. The Sovereigns were practically bubbling with rage—scarlet waves rushed from them in bursts, and Lukys found his own emotions rising in response.

But Nguyen only stared them down as they joined him on the amphitheatre floor. Lukys stared at the man, drawn by the calmness of his aura. This was the king that nearly a decade ago had turned his back on the alliance between the human kingdoms, the man who had doomed Calafe by withdrawing his soldiers and leaving the allies impossibly outnumbered by the Tangata. Now he walked alone into the stronghold of an unfriendly kingdom. Lukys couldn't help but be impressed.

The Sovereigns did not feel the same. Lips drawn back in a snarl, their anger might have been terrifying but for their youthful faces. Even so, Lukys couldn't help but think the king had made a misstep coming to this place.

"My dear Sovereigns, did you not hear me?" Nguyen said with a smile as the Sovereigns reached the amphitheatre floor and came to a stop before him. Though he stood a foot above the two youths, the soldiers that surrounded him made the balance of power clear. "The Queen of Flumeer has betrayed the alliance and attacked the Fortress Illmoor. Even now I fear her armies are pillaging their way across Gemaho. I come seeking Perfugian aid, before her greed consumes us all."

A stunned silence met his words as the Sovereigns stared at the king. Lukys swallowed, shocked at the gall of the man, to beg aid in the name of the alliance he had betrayed. And yet, if what he said was true…Queen Amina had committed an act unheard of in a generation, invading the lands of another human kingdom.

"*You dare come seeking our aid, after you abandoned Calafe in their time of need?*" the Sovereigns replied finally, clearly still struggling to come to grips with the foreign king. "*After you allowed the Tangata to rampage across our neighbour's lands, to slaughter and kill—*"

"Before we start too far down this history lesson," Nguyen interrupted, "Your Majesties do realise there are about a dozen Tangata standing in this very court, yes?"

The Sovereigns started at his words, their heads swinging towards Lukys and the others as though they'd been momentarily forgotten. Lukys might have laughed, if his own life and that of his companions had not also been on the line. He held his breath, wondering at the king's reaction. It seemed not even the sight of a dozen creatures from humanity's darkest nightmares could rattle his composure.

By contrast, for the first time, cracks had appeared in the regal aura of the Sovereigns. "*These Tangata are…exceptions,*" they hissed, eyes still fixed on Sophia and her brethren. "They bring…news of their people, of…an ancient power that threatens all of us."

"It seems this world is becoming clogged with refugees and existential threats," Nguyen replied, grey-streaked eyebrows lifting to crease his forehead as he appraised the Tangata.

Lukys wondered how he could keep so calm—when he'd first encountered the Tangata, it had been all he could manage to keep down his breakfast.

"But then, they say that was why your people first settled on this barren rock, was it not?" he continued, swinging back to the Sovereigns. "To escape the ravages of man and beast." He paused, taking a step closer to the Sovereigns. Steel rattled as their guards moved to intercept him, but after a moment the Sovereigns waved them back. "You condemn me for refusing to participate in a war I no longer believed in, for shielding my people from, yet is that not the principle upon which your nation was founded?"

"*Do not think to turn your cowardice upon us, King Nguyen,*" the Sovereigns snarled. "*We have done our duty to the alliance this last decade. Where Gemaho fled, we have ensured Perfugian steel marched to meet the Tangata wherever they have threatened the lives of humanity.*"

"Yes, yes, yes," the king replied, raising his hands in mock surrender. "I'm sure the children you sent to the slaughter were very noble, but as I said, let us not rehash the past. Alliances change, enemies become friends, and friends enemies. If the Tangata now stand amongst us in peace, we should discuss the true threat to our peoples."

"And who, pray, would that be—if not the man who sails a fleet into our harbour?"

Lukys shivered as the Sovereigns spoke this time, for beneath their words, their tone conveyed their growing rage. It clawed at his mind, threatening to break through his own control. The king stood on unstable ground.

Nguyen seemed to understand the precariousness of his situation, for his face suddenly became serious. "As I have said, Your Majesties, the Flumeeren queen has driven me from my lands. I come here not for conquest, but to beg your aid for my people. Even now, Gemaho burns. And it is my belief Amina will not be content with just the mainland."

There was silence for a moment as the Sovereigns stared at the king. *"We have heard of your provocations against Queen Amina. Tell us, Gemaho King, do the rumours tell it true—did an agent of yours truly creep into her kingdom and assault the personage of our Gods?"*

Lukys started at that, looking from the Sovereigns to the foreign king. "What?" he exclaimed before he could think better of it. "They can't mean…are they talking about Cara?"

The king's eyes widened as he turned towards Lukys, as though seeing him for the first time. "You knew the young Anahera?" Then his brow rose in sudden understanding. "You are Lukys, the Perfugian recruit." His gaze flickered, taking a moment to study the rest of their party. "It appears the rumours of your death were greatly exaggerated."

"Then it's true?" the Sovereigns interrupted, irritation prickling their mental voice. *"You committed blasphemy—"*

"It is not blasphemy to one who does not believe in the Divine," the king interrupted, returning his attention to the dual rulers. "But if you must know, the Anahera—or Goddess, if you prefer—came to no harm under my custody. I only…did what was necessary to ensure she was returned to her people. I fear the same could not have been said had she remained in the care of Amina."

Lukys's heart clenched at the mention of Cara. He hadn't seen her since that day by the river when he'd been captured by the Tangata, since she'd revealed herself as a Goddess. The sight of her soaring above the waters of the Illmoor, auburn wings spread wide, it would stay with him until the end of his days. But if Flumeer and

Gemaho were now at war…could the king be believed as to her fate?

"*You offer us pretty words, Nguyen,*" the Sovereigns replied after a moment, "*but past lies have proven the worth of such platitudes.*"

The king spread his arms and dipped into a half bow. "Then I invite you to verify their truth, Your Majesties," he said with a smile. "Until such a time, might I offer myself as your humble hostage."

"And the fleet in our harbour? I suppose they will remain?"

Nguyen's eyes danced as he stared the Sovereigns down. "Just so."

Red touched the auras of the Sovereigns at his words, but Lukys realised they had little choice but to accept Nguyen's terms. If he was to be believed, a fleet of ships had just sailed into the Ashura harbour. The Perfugian might have more ships, but trapped within the narrow waters, they would be unable to bring their numbers to bear against the assailing force.

The Sovereigns turned away from the king, and for a moment Lukys thought they might throw caution to the wind after all. "*Very well, Gemaho King,*" they said abruptly. "*We will await word from the mainland. In the meantime, I trust you will surrender yourself to our guard.*"

The king bowed his head. "Of course, my dear Sovereigns."

"*Then our business is concluded.*"

With that the Sovereigns turned and began for the steps leading back to their balcony. A pair of guards moved to escort Nguyen from the room. Lukys and the others watched on, their fate still unknown, until finally Lukys could take it no more.

"Your Majesties!" he burst out, swinging from the king to the receding Sovereigns. They paused on the stands, glancing back at them. "What of us? What of the Tangata?"

A strained silence followed his words as the Sovereigns looked from him to Sophia and her brethren. For a moment, something flickered in their eyes, a familiar loathing, a hatred he recognised all too well. Despite his arguments and Sophia's words, despite their shared powers, the Sovereigns still despised the Tangata.

The expression vanished, though it lingered in the faces of the royal guards, like an echo of the Sovereigns' own hidden emotions. Lukys clenched his jaw and balled his hands into fists, preparing himself for their decree. The pair were only a few steps up the stairs towards their balcony—if he was quick, he might reach them before the nearest guard…

"*We will grant you your reprieve.*"

Their response came as such a surprise that Lukys almost fell over himself, one leg already extended towards the steps on which the pair stood. Even the guards seemed surprised by the verdict. Movement came from nearby as Cleo started towards the Sovereigns.

"Your Majesties, you cannot let these animals—"

He broke off as twin pairs of eyes turned in his direction, the words abandoning him. "*Were you asked to speak, soldier?*"

"I only wished to remind—"

"*Enough!*" the Sovereigns boomed, silencing the guard.

Cleo's face turned a mottled red and his mouth opened and closed, but no more words emerged. The Sovereigns continued to glare at him for a long moment, the guard withering beneath the power of their Voice. When they finally turned away, the guard shuddered. Tasha took him by the shoulder, but as she led him away, the guard looked back towards the Tangata. Across the distance, his eyes met Lukys's.

A shudder ran down his spine. He did not need his ability to see the man's hatred, to know it would not end with a command by the Sovereigns. Whatever happened next, he had earned an enemy today.

Then the Sovereigns were gone, leaving Lukys and his friends alone with the guards on the amphitheatre floor. Looking at those surrounding them, at the crossbowmen above, Lukys was touched with despair. He could sense their anger. The abhorrence of his people for the Tangata had been instilled through generations, through childhood tales of bloodshed and slaughter. Could even the blessing of the Sovereigns protect them from such visceral hatred?

"*You and your Tangata will be guarded, confined to your quarters. When this…other matter has been resolved, we will speak more of the Old Ones. Until then, you will have your asylum.*"

The words of the Sovereigns rung from the stands of the amphitheatre, carrying with them a sense of finality, and Lukys knew they had been dismissed. Guards moved forward to escort them, as they had with the king, but Lukys could see the loathing in their eyes as they approached. Looking at the Sovereigns, he felt no relief at their verdict. Their struggle had only just begun.

❧ 22 ❧

THE EMISSARY

"I knew you would betray us," Farhan said as he advanced on Erika. "It is the nature of your kind, to lie, to cheat, to kill."

Erika raised her glowing fist in warning, but the Anahera came on, inexorable, determined. She bared her teeth as the wind howled about them, the raging storm swallowing up the yard, reducing the world to just the two of them.

"No," Erika said, refuting him. "I wish the Anahera no harm. I only do what I must for Cara, to protect my friend."

"She is my daughter!" Farhan snarled, taking another step. His wings beat down, sending snow swirling and adding to the falling sleet. "You know not what you do, the doom you would bring upon us."

"Even so," Erika snarled. "I will not let you have her."

Retreating another step, she flinched as her backside came up against the stone of the altar. Quickly she risked a glance over her shoulder at Cara. The Goddess was struggling now, fighting to break free, but the chains that bound her were clearly intended to withstand the strength of the Anahera.

Erika clenched her fist as she faced Farhan once more, wondering if she could do as she had back in the camp all those nights ago, when she'd used her magic to break Cara's cuffs. If she could get close enough, a few seconds was all she needed.

Abruptly, Hugo stepped between her and Farhan, his eyes wide,

653

wings trembling. Erika flinched, thinking for a moment he had come to stop her. But to her surprise, he raised a hand to Farhan.

"Father, please, do not harm her."

Open shock showed in the Anahera's face as he looked upon his son. Erika opened her mouth to add her words to Hugo's—then paused. The weather was closing in, reducing visibility to just a few yards. With the other Anahera lost to view and Farhan absorbed by the confrontation with his son, this was her chance. Spinning, she leapt upon the altar and scrambled across to Cara.

"Erika," Cara was babbling as Erika reached her. "Erika, I can't, please, don't let him…" She trailed off as Erika placed a hand to her cheek.

"Quiet, I'm getting you out of this, okay?" Erika whispered to the Goddess—whatever she thought of the other Anahera, Cara had long ago proven herself worthy of the title. "Just hold on."

She was surprised to find the Goddess's skin cold to the touch. Tears had streamed down her friend's face, freezing in the cold, and her eyes were red. Clenching her jaw, Erika set to work before the storm drew the last of the warmth from her friend. Through the storm, she could hear Hugo confronting his father, though the wind obscured their words. There was no sign of Maisie. Erika wondered what the spy had said to the young Anahera to convince him to confront his father.

Aware of the great blades of steel teetering above, Erika crawled to the first of the chains that bound her friend and grasped the iron manacle that held Cara's left arm. Her hand began to vibrate as she ignited the gauntlet, and a brilliant glow bathed their faces, then with a sharp *shriek* the metal tore itself apart. A moan came from Cara as she pulled her hand free and Erika's heart soared.

Then a cry came from behind them.

Spinning, Erika looked in time to see Hugo collapsed to the snow, felled by a blow from Farhan. Cursing, she returned her attention to her friend. The chains binding Cara's wings were thicker than the manacles and gritting her teeth, she clenched them tight. A wave of dizziness swept through her as the magic shone, until with another screech of twisting metal Cara's wing came free.

"Archivist!" Somewhere in the snow, Maisie's voice cried a warning.

Thunk.

Erika gasped as something slammed into the altar beside her. For a moment she thought the worst had come to pass, that one of the terrible blades had fallen, robbing Cara of flight forever.

Instead, she found herself staring up at Farhan, his face twisted in rage, his eyes dark…turning darker, stained with grey.

"Human," he growled. "You will pay for your defiance, for corrupting my children, turning them against me."

"I did nothing to your children." Erika bared her teeth as she rose to face him. "It was your own foulness that turned them against you, Farhan."

Before she knew what was happening, Farhan had Erika by the throat. She tried to cry out, to raise the gauntlet, but he tossed her aside as though she were of no more consequence than a mouse before the lion. The storm swallowed up her scream as Erika found herself soaring, the rocky ground rising up to meet her…

Thud.

She struck with a force that drove the breath from her lungs. Light flashed across her vision and for a moment, Erika knew only white. Then the world came rushing back and the taste of blood filled her mouth. Groaning, she pulled herself to her knees and looked up at her foe.

Farhan stood atop the altar, wings spread, face twisted in a mask of rage and sorrow. At his feet, Cara was still trying to tear herself free, the wing Erika had loosed flailing. But with a snarl, Farhan brought his boot down upon the limb, pinning it to the stone. A gasp came from Cara as she beat her fist upon his leg, but Farhan was far stronger, unmovable.

Then broad arms rippling with muscle, he reached up and took hold of one of the blades.

"I will not lose another," he cried. "The will of the Founders will be done."

"Father, please, no!" Cara screamed. She clutched pitifully at his pants now, pleading, in despair.

Farhan did not look at his daughter. His eyes were fixed on Erika, his mouth twisted in a snarl of hatred. She flinched from that look, that rage, as the ropes holding the blade aloft began to vibrate, their threads yielding to the unyielding strength of the Anahera.

Struggling for breath, Erika pulled herself to her feet and summoned her magic. She swayed as the power came. Her strength was running low, but she would not surrender. Farhan had hurled her beyond the range of the magic, and teeth bared, she staggered towards him, fighting back the pain that engulfed her body. Yet even as she moved, Erika knew she would not be in time. The rope was already beginning to give way, the blade creeping down. In seconds it would fall, crushing her friend's freedom, breaking her soul.

Still Erika fought through the howling wind, fist raised, power gathering, desperate for one final chance. She didn't bother with words. The storm had closed in around them anyway, swallowing the watching Anahera, so that it seemed only she and Farhan remained in the square. She wondered what the others thought, why they did not interfere. Surely if Farhan commanded it, they would descend upon her? Yet the Elder Anahera seemed determined to do the deed himself…

Erika hesitated as she glimpsed movement on the altar—then abruptly, Farhan vanished. She froze, mouth falling open as a roar came from empty air. A moment later two figures reappeared, tumbling backwards from the altar. One was Farhan. His wings flailed, but he hit the ground before they could halt his fall.

The other was Maisie. Brown hair swirling, she tumbled from the altar with Farhan, but she landed awkwardly, her leg twisting beneath her. A scream sounded through the storm as she crumpled into a snowbank and lay still.

Heart pounding in her ears, Erika stared at the Gemaho spy. What madness had possessed the woman to use her magic to attack Farhan? Even hidden by the magic of her artefact, surely Maisie couldn't have thought to overcome the Anahera by herself?

A roar sounded from nearby as Farhan surged back to his feet. Wings spread, teeth bared, he started towards the spy, the snarl on his lips promising violence…then froze.

A frown crossed Farhan's face and for a second his eyes took on a distant look. Turning, he looked away from them, up into the swirling storm, as though even now he could see the peaks surrounding the city. His frown deepened.

"What…"

Erika followed his gaze, trying to find what had distracted him, even as she sensed the rumble of other Anaheran voices, raised against the wind and sleet. Something was happening, something the humans could not discern.

Then Erika heard it: a distant reverberation above the wind and snow, already growing louder, more insistent, until she knew it for what it was.

The roar of a thousand voices raised in unison.

"What the Fall…"

"*Tangata,*" Farhan snarled.

23

THE FOLLOWER

Adonis drew in a breath, savouring the crispness of the morning air, the chill of winter's breath. It tugged at his clothing, seeking to steal his warmth…but not even the falling snow could touch the fire at his core, the strength granted to him by hope. There would be a future for his people, a new legacy set by his own children.

That legacy would begin today, with the conquest of their ancient enemy.

The pounding began again in his mind, a dull throbbing, a call to battle. Around him he could sense his fellow Tangata, brothers and sisters all, their minds united. Forgotten were the weak who had fallen behind, lost forever to the sands of time. Each who still remained knew their place, their task for the conflict to come.

Adonis balled his hands into fists as he glanced at his companions, those others who had been honoured by the Old One. Theirs was the assignment of greatest importance, the task upon which Tangatan victory or defeat would rest. If they failed, the sacrifice of his brothers and sisters would be for naught.

Are you ready, my mate?

Adonis's heart pounded in his ears as Maya's call came to him, setting his blood aflame with images of their nights spent entwined, with promises of a new generation of Tangata, more powerful than any seen in centuries.

But that future would not arrive without cost, without sacrifice. Blood must be shed for new life to be born, to ensure the survival of his species.

His stomach stirred as an image flickered into his mind, of the child in the snow, lost despite her parent's own sacrifice. He shivered, seeking to thrust the image aside, but it lingered, refusing to fade.

We are prepared, my Matriarch, he whispered, steeling himself for what was to come.

Then the time has come.

Maya's voice was followed immediately by a rush of adrenaline, by surging, burning anger. Howls rose from the mountainside around Adonis, as the Tangata gathered there responded to the same call to arms.

They had marched hard these past days and nights to reach this place. Now looking down into the valley, Adonis struggled to pierce the falling sleet and snow. Their enemy waited somewhere below, concealed by the growing storm, yet Adonis could sense their minds, buzzing softly amidst the white. Ignorant of what was to come.

The burning within him built, the howls of his brethren growing to a crescendo. Adonis resisted the call to violence. His task would require more than bloodlust, more than sheer ferocity. It would take a refined touch, would necessitate the speed and cunning of the older generations.

He shivered, looking across the slope to where his mate stood, ringed by his brethren, preparing to lead them to war. Her grey eyes were fixed on the valley, as though she could see through the raging of the storm. Perhaps she could—the powers of the Old Ones were far beyond his own, undiluted by generations of human crossings, untouched by the disaster of the Fall.

Tangata, the time has come! Her voice rose above the thrumming in Adonis's mind, and he knew in that moment she spoke to all of them. *Our foes wait below, weak and unaware. Let the power of the Tangata will consume them. Are you ready?*

A roar sounded in Adonis's mind, the raised voices of a thousand Tangata, distorted and unintelligible, twisted by rage.

Then go!

The Tangata screamed again in unison, and then they were

surging down the slopes, a dark wave of movement, rushing over the uneven surface with a speed only the uncanny reflexes of the Tangata could achieve. Adonis and his fellows remained for the moment, watching as their brethren vanished into the cloud, swallowed up by the haunting grey.

But their Voices remained, hurling their fury, their hatred into the valley, to the enemy that awaited them. Adonis shivered, thinking of the terror such a call would bring upon those below, the dread. Would their foes crumble, bowed before the united Voice of the Tangata, as Maya expected? Or would they fight back? Would their terror forge them anew, forewarn them of the danger that came upon them?

It was Adonis and his companions' task to ensure that did not happen, to break the spirit of their foes before a resistance could be mounted, before they could fight back. The battle below, the fury of his brethren, was but a distraction.

Maya still stood on the hillside, watching the valley with those terrible eyes. As though sensing his gaze, she turned to him, a smile touching her lips.

It begins, she murmured. Her hand drifted to her stomach. *Today, we birth a new future for our children.*

Adonis's heart throbbed at her words and he inclined his head. *I will not fail you.*

Then go, she called back. *Crush our enemies. Bring about their despair, so that our children might know freedom.*

A fresh rush of fire wrapped about Adonis, crushing all hesitation, burning away doubt, until all that remained was the call of battle, the promise of Maya's future, and the life that would be born of her womb.

Unleashing a battlecry, Adonis leapt from his perch on the hillside and started down the crumbling rock, down towards the secret valley, the hiding place of their ancient enemy.

To bring war upon the home of the Anahera.

24

THE HERO

They put Lukys in the same room as Sophia.

The decision hardly seemed significant as they stumbled into the chamber and collapsed onto the feathered bed, the days and weeks of exhaustion weighing on them. It was already dark outside, the longest day of his life at an end. His eyes flickered closed and within moments, the lure of sleep carried him away.

He woke to bright sunlight streaming into the room. Blinking, he pushed himself up from the pillow, finding an open window in the opposite wall from them. Unlike the corridors and amphitheatre, the chamber at least had a ceiling to protect them from the elements, and with the thermal waters flowing beneath the floor, it was a strange sensation to awake in Ashura to warmth. At the academy, no resources were wasted heating the dormitories of the students.

Letting out a moan, he sank back to the pillows. The bed was softer than even the luxurious one the Tangata had provided him in New Nihelm. Larger too, though he hardly needed so much space, sleeping alone...

The thought drifted away as he rolled on his side and found Sophia next to him. Her eyes were still closed, and the whisper of her breath tickled his cheek as she snored softly. She had shifted close in the night, and now her scent carried to him, a gentle earthly fragrance, despite their days at sea.

A shiver ran down his spine. Watching her sleep, Lukys was struck again by the softness of her face, the gentle curves of her lips, the occasional snort as she dreamed. How could he ever have imagined the creature beside him a monster, that she was anything but human?

Without thinking, he ran a finger across her cheek. Her eyes flickered open at his touch. A smile creased her lips when she saw him and she gave a quiet groan.

Is it morning already?

Lukys kissed her. It seemed to take Sophia by surprise, just as it had the first time. But she soon melted against him, her lips pressing against his, parting as a moan rasped from the back of her throat. Her tongue swept out to meet his own as he wrapped her in his arms, hugging her tight.

Warmth washed through Lukys as her fingers slid through his hair, drawing him deeper into the kiss, stealing away his breath. A groan of his own built in his soul as he felt her body against his, sensed her desire, her need.

They broke apart for a moment, each gasping for breath, but their lips soon found one another again. Lukys's hands slipped beneath her shirt, pulling it up, forcing them to separate again to lift it over her head. He tossed it aside as Sophia kissed him once more, even as her fingers began working on the buttons of his tunic. Goosebumps rose on his arms as her warm hands slid across his skin, running over his chest, his stomach, then up to his shoulders, pulling, tugging at his shirt, eager.

Taken by a sudden impatience, Lukys tore the tunic from his shoulders. Sophia fell upon him before he could even discard it, her lips moving to his neck, kissing, licking, nibbling at his flesh. A growl rose in his throat and he grasped her by the hips, flipping her so she landed on her back before him.

Despite Sophia's enormous strength, she did not resist, only lay there looking up at him, grey eyes drinking him in, even as he feasted upon the sight of her, upon her naked flesh, lying there, waiting…

He crouched over her, kissing her again, pressing his weight against her, feeling the warmth of her breasts on his chest. Her arms wrapped around him, pulling him tight, and her moans grew more insistent. He resisted, breaking off their kiss, his lips touching her neck, moving slowly to her collar, tasting her soft skin, trailing, circling, until finally she gasped as he kissed her breast.

Lukys!

A smile crossed his lips as she whispered his name, even as he sucked and licked, then moved to the other. Her hands wrapped around his waist, sliding lower, slipping beneath the pants he had been too exhausted to remove the night before. A groan escaped him as her hands slipped beneath the fabric, pulling him down. He looked up from her breasts and saw her mischievous smile, the desire in her eyes.

I want you, Sophia, he whispered to her.

I want you too, Lukys.

They kissed again, hard, passionate, as though that alone would sate the flames burning within. But it was not enough, and they soon slid free of the last of their clothing, leaving them both lying naked upon the bed.

Again he found himself looking into those sweet grey eyes, sensing the warmth there, the passion. Neither moved, even breathed, as they looked upon one another, as though they were waiting for something.

Take me, Lukys.

And he fell upon her, their bodies entwining, minds become one…

Afterwards, they lay gasping in one another's arms, eyes on the ceiling, content to enjoy the silence, the rare peace they had found for themselves. The warmth of the chamber, even as clouds passed before the sun outside, soon had them dozing. They dreamed and woke again, snatching snippets of the sleep that had evaded them for so long—and stealing kisses as well.

Each time Lukys touched Sophia's mind, he sensed a brilliant pink about her, a radiance he wasn't yet ready to contemplate. Though he had no doubt his own mind must be coloured the same.

So far from Calafe, from the threat of the Old One and her followers, Lukys found he was finally able to breathe a little. He knew there were still battles to come, but looking at Sophia as she dozed, he could finally appreciate what he had found. Now he just had to protect it.

They might have the Sovereigns' temporary blessing, but there were other dangers in this city. Cleo was not alone in his loathing for the Tangata—the academy had sown that hatred into the people since long before the latest war. He would need to change their minds, show them the truth about the Tangata, their beauty and intelligence.

But even then, the Old One would not rest. Sooner or later, Maya would come for humanity. She would not stop until every one of their kind was exterminated, until the Tangata dominated the world. With Adonis and his followers at her side, it would take all the kingdoms united to stand against her.

Though if the Gemaho King were to be believed, even that might yet prove impossible.

Focus on what you can change, Sophia's words whispered into his mind as her eyes flickered open.

Lukys smiled and leaned in to kiss her. She was right, of course. They could do nothing about the warring kingdoms or what Maya might be planning in the south. Here, now, there were only the Sovereigns, only the Perfugian citizens to convince of their benevolence.

That brought a thought to his mind. *How could they speak with you?* he murmured. *How could they hear you?*

He was sure that this ability was a large part of why the Sovereigns had accepted the Tangata in the end, why they'd even been granted the honour of an audience. Even the Gemaho King had thought it more prudent to sneak into the citadel, than risk being turned away at the gates. But none of that explained how the Sovereigns and their Guard possessed the abilities of a Melder—as they called them.

There must be Tangatan blood in your people's history, she replied sleepily.

That had been her explanation for his own ability, but it still made little sense to Lukys. His ancestors had come to the island hundreds of years ago to escape the warring tribes of humanity, and had remained isolated ever since. Could a Tangatan ancestor have snuck onto the island unbeknownst to the people? Even then, surely one or two could not explain such a prevalence of Melders.

No, if the ability could be so easily passed on to humans, surely it would have manifested first in the kingdoms with greater proximity to the Tangata.

He shook his head. It was a mystery he intended to solve, but for the moment, he found himself restless. Rising, he crossed to the window and looked out across the city. A rumble of thunder carried across the harbour and he caught a flicker of lightning amidst dark clouds in the distance.

Ashura stretched away below, and he found himself wondering at the view he now enjoyed. It wasn't difficult to pick out the academy, its sandstone walls rising from the otherwise polished marble buildings of the city. The academy had taught duty and austerity, and had been shaped to represent those ideals.

Windowless and glum, most of his life had been spent in its dark confines. The open brightness of the citadel was its opposite in every way. To stand in a room such as this, in the vicinity of the Sovereigns themselves, was something he could never have imagined even a few short months ago.

What are you looking at? Sophia asked, slipping from beneath the sheets. She crossed to where he stood, her movement sensuous as always, fluid, like a cat amongst the grass.

"Just thinking about our problems," Lukys replied.

His gaze continued to where the city curved around the harbour. Half the Perfugian fleet now bobbed on the calm waters, while beyond the yellow sails of the Gemaho blockade seemed to fill the horizon. There could not have been more of them than there were Perfugians, but the other half of their fleet remained docked, unable to join their comrades for fear of collision in the crowded bay. If it came to a battle, the losses on both sides would be terrible.

Then he frowned, noticing a ship passing carefully between the others. It flew the same blue colours as the other Perfugian vessels, but by its broader hull and heavy sails, Lukys realised it was no warship. A trader, perhaps, arrived from the mainland?

Travis might have known, but they'd all been separated as they left the amphitheatre, taken to different accommodations. Lukys wondered now whether they'd been wise to allow it. Apart, there was no way to know what had become of the others. Unless…

A frown touched Lukys's lips as an idea came to him. Back in the throne room, the Sovereigns had mentioned commanding Tasha to bring them to the citadel—yet the royal guard had never left their presence. That meant the Sovereigns must have spoken their orders into Tasha's mind. Lukys hadn't realised that was possible over such a distance.

Closing his eyes, he reached out with his mind. He felt Sophia immediately, and sensed a probing question back from her. Lukys sent a burst of reassurance to her, then turned his attention further afield. Sophia had managed to see what the Matriarch had seen, back in New Nihelm. They'd been some hundred yards from the Basilica, and separated by thick stone walls.

So what were the limits of his own senses? He reached out farther, and immediately encountered another presence, an unfamiliar aura tainted with green. It was still some distance away, but already growing nearer. There was a purpose about the presence, and an image of his own self standing alongside Sophia flickered into his mind.

Shocked at the success of his experiment, Lukys opened his eyes again. For a moment, he felt disorientated, as though he'd truly been separated from his body, but it quickly cleared.

"Someone's coming," he said to Sophia.

By the time the door to their chambers swung open, they were fully clothed and standing in the window, waiting. Tasha frowned as she paused in the doorway, looking from one to the other. Lukys sensed suspicion from her, but after a moment it faded. Thankfully there was no sign of Cleo, though perhaps his absence should have been of more concern. If the boisterous guard was not with Tasha, did that mean he was supervising some of the others?

"You're wanted," Tasha said shortly.

Lukys couldn't help but notice how her face hardened when she looked at Sophia. He suppressed a sigh. If even the most reasonable of the royal guards couldn't bother to conceal their hatred, what chance did he have of winning some to their side?

"By whom?" he asked.

"King Nguyen," the guard replied, then added: "Before you ask, I don't know why. Only that we've been asked to accommodate him."

Lukys hesitated. There was bad blood between Gemaho and the

other nations, but if the king wanted to talk…it meant he might be less prejudiced than the Perfugians at least. He offered Tasha a nod.

"If you're ready then…" She pushed open the door, revealing a dozen regular soldiers outside.

Lukys raised an eyebrow, but the woman ignored him. He shared a glance with Sophia, but she only shrugged and marched from the room without sparing another look at the royal guard. Lukys moved to follow, but as he passed, Tasha grasped him by the arm.

Lukys. He started as her voice whispered into his mind, the words meant only for him. *I have read the reports from Fogmore. You are a brave soldier, worthy of much more than the hand fate dealt you. If you are willing—*

Her words ended abruptly and Lukys glanced at her, wondering at the pause. But her attention was no longer on him. He followed the direction of her gaze, and saw the unmade bed. Their…love-making had left the sheets and pillows in a tangled mess. His cheeks grew warm as he realised what had distracted her.

I am honoured… he started, but her eyes flickered back to him and he couldn't bring himself to finish the words. Gone was the respect he'd glimpsed just a moment ago.

So it seems, she said shortly.

Then she was gone, striding through the open door. Lukys paused a moment, confused by her abrupt change in manner. But her inner mind remained closed to him, and shaking off his doubt, he quickly followed her before they locked him in the room alone.

25

THE FOLLOWER

Adonis howled as one of the Anahera dove towards him, wings furled, feathers rustling as they dove through the hissing sleet. A wooden staff slashed for his head, but he ducked and it missed by inches, the winds sending the Anahera swirling away. Rolling through the snow, he threw a mental curse into the storm as he reared back to his feet, expecting the creature to come for him again. But with the Tangata all around, the Anahera had already picked a fresh target for his wrath.

Whirling, Adonis continued, racing across the torn ground with impossible agility, his companions right behind. Others amongst the Tangata hurled rocks into the sky, striking back against their aerial cousins as they danced in and out of the storm. Whenever one appeared a dozen rocks the size of fists would flash in their direction, though they'd yet to bring one of the Anahera down. They were far more powerful than the Tangata—Adonis remembered well his encounter with one of their kind in the lowlands.

But just as in the lowlands, the Tangata were not without advantages. The Anahera might duck and weave and evade, making them difficult to count, but it was clear the Tangata had them outnumbered. Those few of the creatures that decided to land were swarmed, forced to lay about themselves with staff and wing and foot, just to keep from being overwhelmed. And those of his brethren the Anahera struck did not stay down. They rose to come for their foes again.

The Matriarch was right—the Anahera had grown weak, if not in body, in mind. Had they attacked to kill, the Tangata would have been slaughtered.

Adonis could feel the ecstasy of his brothers and sisters, the pounding of their joy. But Adonis had other duties, and reluctantly he forced his attention from the rush of battle. He could not fail, for even as the Tangata fought valiantly, he knew this was a battle they could not win.

No, they needed something to sway the battle, a way to strike at the heart of their foe, to bring the Anahera low.

A desperate, terrible gamble.

The sounds of battle faded into the storm as Adonis and his fellows crept away from the epicentre. They did not speak, kept their minds shielded now, their emotions carefully in check. For like the Tangata, these enemies could Hear and Speak. And if those within the city were forewarned…

The storm swallowed them up, building to a renewed fury, until even Adonis began to feel its bite, as if it might tear them from the mountain itself. It amazed him, that the Anahera could fly in such chaos, but even so, he could see they were having difficulty. He continued on, senses outstretched, seeking, searching…

There!

From a distance, he sensed a thrumming, pulsing *white*. Fear—so powerful he could almost taste it. His companions sensed it as well, for he caught a flicker of excitement before they regained control. Without a word, they diverted their path, heading now towards the enormous building that filled the valley, towards the fear. Stones crunched beneath their feet, but the noise was swallowed up by the storm. With the world engulfed in white, they had no need to fear being seen or heard. Only sensed.

Walls of plain grey stone emerged from the snow and they paused, scanning the terrain, seeking an entrance. The source of the terror was close now, so potent that the air was practically awash with it.

Adonis wondered at such ill-discipline. Even the youngest of the Tangata learned to control their emotions, to keep from broadcasting to the minds around them. For a moment he was reminded of the human, Lukys, and how his mind had lain open for the world to read. He had drawn the Tangata to him like flies to a corpse.

Maya was right: the Anahera had more in common with their human enemies than the Tangata now. They would have never chosen to ally with his people, never have supported them, helped them. They would see only an enemy to be disposed of. It was better this way, attacking before they could ally with the humans.

Moving along the wall, they finally found a door, heavy and of steel, barring the world without. And unlocked. It opened with a squeal. Adonis could have laughed. Whatever instincts these creatures had once possessed, they had long since succumbed to complacency.

Adonis and his companions slipped into a narrow hallway, pulling the door shut behind them. Within, a faint light lit the empty corridor. Adonis was surprised to see the white globes in the walls, the same as in the place he had uncovered Maya. Only here they were worn and faded, their magic almost spent.

They moved quickly through the place, finding the corridors empty, abandoned. Adonis smiled—the distraction had worked. If guards had been placed here, they were involved in the battle now.

The Tangata threaded their way through the myriad corridors, following a staircase up to a higher level, and all the while the fear grew nearer. Adonis kept his senses alert for sign of the Anahera. Even a single creature might ruin everything, for his ten would fall quickly. Unconsciously he picked up the pace, heart racing, struggling to keep the emotions in check.

Then he paused as a faint scent touched his senses. The others came to a stop behind him, and he felt their confusion. It grew as they too detected the scent, one that should have been foreign in this distant place, so far from the lowlands.

Humans.

So Maya had been right in that as well. The Anahera they had encountered with the humans had not just been chance—they had already sided with one another. The scent was fresh, crisp amidst the lingering stench of the Anahera. The creatures were still here, hidden somewhere in the twisting corridors. His heart began to race and he glanced at his companions, sensing their anger, their hatred.

These were the creatures who had warred against them for years, who had brought destruction to their lands…

What's that?

Who?

They're inside!

Mental voices rose, then shouts that carried down the corridors, pulsing with unconcealed panic. Still distant, but already growing closer.

Adonis cursed, even as his companions' eyes widened, anger giving way to panic. In an instant they were racing down the corridor, making no attempt at caution now. Their footsteps echoed from the cold stone as Adonis focused on their objective. They were close to the source of the fear now. It was the one thing that might save them. They could not outrun the Anahera, could not hide from them here in this city of theirs.

They could only attack.

The fear grew with each footstep, until suddenly he could feel its source, knew it was just ahead, beyond the wall, behind the door ahead of them. With a snarl, Adonis threw himself against it. His heart raced, rage granting him strength, and with a shriek of twisting metal, the door flew from its aged hinges.

Within, voices began to scream.

❋ 26 ❋

THE EMISSARY

The sounds of battle carried from beyond the walls, the distant shrieks of pain, the clash of weapons and thud of blows. Erika shivered, eyes on the sky, expecting one of the Anahera to come tumbling from the clouds at any moment. They were alone now in the yard, the others of the Anahera gone to battle or sent to safety. All but for Farhan.

He stood nearby, forehead creased, his eyes too on the sky. He had ordered his people to arms, to defend their city. Now he listened to their screams through the howling of the storm. Amidst the swirling fog, nothing could be seen but for the occasional flicker as one of the Anahera returned with a report.

Erika shuddered. It sounded as though a thousand enemies had descended upon the City of the Gods. But how was that possible? This place had remained undiscovered for centuries, unknown to human or Tangata. How could the creatures have found their way here? And why now, at the same time as Erika and Maisie? It seemed too great a coincidence to be chance—

"You!"

Erika leapt back as she found Farhan advancing on her. Wings spread wide, he stalked through the storm, his face twisted with fresh rage.

"You did this, didn't you?" he snarled, reaching for her. "Treacherous human, why did you lead them here?"

"It was not us!" Erika replied, stumbling over something on the ground.

She tumbled backwards and crashed into the hard stones. Farhan loomed overhead, but whatever had tripped her drew his attention. Lips drawn back in a snarl, he reached down and plucked Hugo from the ground. The young Anahera blinked, looking disorientated, as though he were just recovering from the blow Farhan had given him earlier.

"Father?" he mumbled, his lips twisted in a frown. "What—"

His eyes widened suddenly, as if he'd just been struck, though this time Farhan had not touched him. He struggled free of his father's grip and swung to stare into the storm.

"Tangata!" he gasped. "Where—"

"Your treacherous humans brought them," Farhan declared, still looming over Erika.

"No—"

Erika's protest was cut short as Farhan surged forward. Still on her hands and knees, there was no escaping him this time. His fist closed around her throat, silencing her cries, and she was hauled helplessly into the air.

"This is what these creatures do, my son," he growled. Erika gaped at him, beating at his wrist with her fists, but it made no difference. "They lie, they steal, they *destroy*."

He was too strong. Erika's vision swum as she struggled to breathe, to inhale, but she could do nothing against the Anahera's power. Already her own strength was waning, drained away by the gauntlet...her eyes widened as she recalled its power, forgotten in her panic. Letting her hand drop, she clenched her fist, gathering its magic.

"It is not your fault they so deceived you," Farhan was saying. "It is their nature, to corrupt that which is pure—"

Now it was the Anahera's turn to cry out. Light flashed from the gauntlet as she directed her palm at Farhan's midsection, releasing its magic. She gasped as Farhan released her, and her legs almost collapsed as she struck the ground. Gulping in great lungfuls of air, Erika managed to catch herself before she fell. Then she straightened, arm still outstretched, and unleashed the full power of the gauntlet on Farhan.

The Anahera staggered back from her, mouth stretched wide in a silent scream, the veins on his neck bulging as he strained against her power. But the gauntlet flashed again, and without a sound he crumpled to the ground, wings and arms and legs thrashing. She advanced on him, lips twisted in a sneer.

"At least I never tried to *mutilate* my own daughter," she snarled.

Erika would have said more, but something solid struck her hard in the chest before she could speak. Hurled backwards by the force of the blow, she felt something go *crack*. Then Erika was tumbling across the ground, rocks tearing at her flesh, light flashing across her eyes.

The altar brought her to an abrupt halt, driving the last of the breath from her lungs. Stars danced across her vision and she strained to take a breath, to comprehend what had happened. Cracking open an eye, she searched for what had struck her.

Through the raging storm, she found Hugo standing over Farhan, helping the Anahera to his feet. The youth had re-joined his father's side. Her heart clenched as they turned towards her, and desperately she tried to push herself up. Agony screamed in her chest as the broken rib shifted, but she could not stop, could not give up.

But neither could she fight any longer. Her strength was almost spent, and the gauntlet's power would not be enough to stop the two of them. Turning, she reached for the lip of the altar and strained to haul herself up. The pain in her chest redoubled and other pains made themselves known, but she managed to flip herself onto the awful chunk of stone.

Cara crouched where Erika had left her, one hand and wing still bound. Her back was turned to Erika as she strained against her bonds, but the metal would not give before even her enormous strength. Erika crawled towards her, gauntlet raised. This she could do, this she could manage. Free Cara, and she would save them all. She had to.

As though hearing her silent plea, Cara turned. Her eyes widened as she saw Erika, surprise showing in their amber depths, but then they flickered, shifting to something behind her. Teeth clenched, Erika twisted on the stone, preparing herself to fend off another attack.

But Farhan and Hugo had not moved. It was not the two Anahera that had drawn Cara's attention. Instead, her eyes were fixed on a door across the yard. Through the swirling storm, Erika glimpsed two figures stumble out into the snow.

Dark laughter carried across the yard the two figures advanced, and Erika saw that one had no wings. And the other…the other was Anahera, but smaller than any she had seen before, barely as tall as Erika's waist. A child.

Terror showed in the girl's blue eyes as the wingless newcomer shepherded her before him. Small wings covered in soft down thrashed against his grasp, but the man refused to release the girl, even as her cries carried through the storm. Erika's heart beast faster as the pair approached, a sense of dread settling in her stomach.

"The fledglings," Cara croaked.

❦ 27 ❦

THE HERO

A fire burned in the king's hearth, crackling gently against the gloom of the fading light. It was wasteful, Lukys couldn't help but think, with the thermal waters warming the tiles beneath their feet. Firewood was a rare commodity in a kingdom that did not cut down its trees, only being collected from what had fallen in the forests. But King Nguyen seemed to appreciate the flames.

Standing in the doorway with Sophia, Lukys stared at the man, waiting for him to announce why they'd been sent for. Instead, the king rose from his chair with a groan and crossed to a table placed near the window. Picking up a decanter, he opened a glass cabinet on the wall and glanced in their direction.

"Whiskey?"

Lukys raised his eyebrows, glancing behind him at Tasha. But the guard only offered a short shake of her head before closing the door behind them, leaving them alone with the king. Letting out a sigh, Lukys watched as the king poured a glass of the amber liquid, trying to decipher his game. If Nguyen was to be believed, this was a man who had lost his kingdom, who had fled to Perfugia with his tail between his legs, his armies broken and defeated.

But the performance he'd given in the court of the Sovereigns had not been that of a defeated man. Had it all been a façade?

Lost in his thoughts, Lukys didn't notice Sophia until she crossed the room and plucked the glass from Nguyen's table. The king's eyebrows lifted into his greying fringe as she raised it to her nose and sniffed, before a smile replaced his surprise. He took several glasses from the cabinet, and poured two extra measures.

You drink whiskey? Lukys asked Sophia as the king offered him a glass.

I'm not sure, she replied with a shrug. She took a tentative sip, and immediately started to cough.

Snorting to cover his laughter, Lukys raised his drink in salute to the king before taking a sip of his own. The whiskey was dry with a sharp smoky taste and burned as he swallowed, though Sophia's cough seemed an overreaction.

Poison? she asked him when she finally recovered, her eyes still watering.

He almost laughed again. *Just alcohol.*

She raised an eyebrow and inspected the glass again, as though expecting it to bite her.

"Fascinating," the king interrupted their silent conversation.

"What?" Lukys asked when the man did not elaborate.

Nguyen gestured at the two of them with his glass. "You're communicating," he said. "Just like Cara said."

"Cara?" Lukys asked. "You said you'd sent her home, to the Mountains of the Gods? What does she have to do with any of this?"

"It was she who told me that the Tangata are not the monsters we thought them to be," he replied. "That they had some way of communicating."

Lukys glanced at Sophia in question, and she inclined her head. *The Anahera also possess the ability to Speak.*

"Apparently, the Gods can Speak in the same way as the Tangata," Lukys translated.

"I see," Nguyen replied. He sank back into his chair and eyed Lukys. "And what of you, young man? What is your part in all this? How can *you* hear the lady speak?"

Sophia started and Lukys flicked her a glance. She stood trembling in place, grey eyes wide and staring at the king, as though he had suddenly transformed into some foreign beast.

What is it? he asked her softly.

She shook her head. *I...no one has ever called me a lady.*

Lukys swallowed, touched by shame, that until just a few days ago he had still thought of her as another species, a creature rather than human. But he knew the truth now, that whatever their differences, the Tangata shared far more in common with humanity than they did differences. He took her hand gently in his.

You are my lady, Sophia, he said, filling his Voice with warmth.

She smiled, her eyes fluttering closed at his touch, and for a moment, images of their morning spent in bed flickered into his mind—

"Fascinating," Nguyen said again, and this time Lukys jumped.

He turned an irritated glare on the king. "We're not some specimens for you to examine."

The man let out a booming laugh. "Your friend Cara said something much the same," he replied. Leaning back in his chair, he entwined his fingers. "So…what makes a man turn traitor to his own species?"

Lukys froze at the man's words, drink half-raised to his lips. The glass shook as anger touched him, but slowly, painstakingly, he raised it the rest of the way and downed the burning liquid. Carefully he placed it back on the table and stared down at the man.

"If I am a traitor, I stand in good company."

The king regarded him in silence. "Again with the accusations?" He waved a hand. "Please, enough with the baseless rumours and past grievances."

"Tell that to my friend Romaine, to his people—the Calafe— and his broken kingdom, to—"

"Your girlfriend?" the king interrupted, one eyebrow raised. He glanced at Sophia. "I'm surprised she hasn't torn out my throat and drank the blood yet."

A growl came from Sophia and she took a threatening step towards him.

Laughter came from Nguyen as he raised his hands. "Peace," he murmured. "I only wished to test a theory." He glanced at Lukys. "Though it shows the consequence of baseless rumours, does it not?"

Lukys stood fixed on the spot, his stomach twisted into a knot by the king's words. Not too long ago, he had stood alongside the fearsome Romaine and fought the Tangata on the shores of the Illmoor.

Those days he had believed in the righteousness of the war, that he was fighting to protect Flumeer and Perfugia, to avenge the fallen Calafe.

What would Romaine say to him now, should they meet again? The man's family had been murdered by the Tangata in the early days of the conflict, his wife and children some of the first victims that had triggered the disastrous invasion of Tangata territory.

But then…Sophia's partner, the Tangata that had fought alongside her for years, who had been her former…lover, he had died at Lukys's own hands, back on the River Illmoor. He swallowed, realising for the first time just how great the void spanned between their two peoples.

"Tell me, my lady," the king said, leaning back in his chair. "What do the Tangata say of our southern campaign, of the invasion we led into your lands ten years past?"

Beside him, Sophia stiffened at his words, and Lukys cast her a quick look, wondering at the reaction. She exhaled sharply, the breath whistling between her teeth, and then abruptly images began to flicker into Lukys's mind, faster than he could process, and yet…

…Lukys was old, his body weary with time, his reflexes slowed, a poor substitute for his youth. Still he thrust the child behind him as the horse raced towards them, steel-tipped lance bearing down, slamming into him, tearing a scream from his lips…

…now he raced across the rolling hills, heart pounding in his young chest as he chased after his parents. His Tangatan father carried his human mother, but even so, he struggled to keep pace. Cries came from behind, and risking a glance back, he saw the village, their home, burning…

…wind swept through his hair as he stood alone on a hill, looking down upon the approaching column. There were a hundred riders, perhaps more—too many. Yet he had to hold, to halt the enemy march long enough for the children to reach the shelter of Nihelm. The Birthing Ground would shield them, wouldn't it? He closed his eyes and sent a prayer for the Old Ones to grant him their strength. The pounding of hooves carried up the hills as the humans spotted them, and he opened his eyes once more, bracing himself for death…

Lukys gasped as he tore himself from the lives and deaths Sophia had shown him, a hundred if they had been a handful. A shudder ran through him as he fought to find himself amidst the images, to shake the feeling of unity, of being one among many.

Sucking in great mouthfuls of air, he glanced at Sophia, wondering at her again, how she could cope with so many lives entangled with her own.

"Well?"

Looking at the king again, Lukys was unable to tell how much time had passed. A moment only, surely? Shaking himself, he straightened.

"I…" He swallowed, his blood still cold at the visions Sophia had shown him. "She says that her people never attacked Calafe, at least not until after the southern campaign. The invasion, it…came as a shock, a breaking of the unspoken truce they had with humanity."

Beside him, a tear streaked Sophia's cheek, and Lukys felt the power of the images she'd shown him again, the pain of a community, of lives attacked, stolen.

"I see," Nguyen replied, his tone uncharacteristically soft. "I am sorry for the intrusion to your grief, my lady, but I must ask, for these are questions I have carried for nigh a decade now. Do your people know why we attacked?"

Sophia gave a sharp shake of her head, and Lukys sensed the anger burning behind those grey eyes.

A sigh slipped from Nguyen's lips. "Calafe settlements were attacked, men and women and children slaughtered. The survivors spoke of Tangata in the night, slaughtering all they came across."

My people would never harm children!

The words reverberated through Lukys's mind as Sophia took a step towards the king, teeth bared. Though he obviously could not hear her words, Nguyen's eyes widened and Lukys caught a glimpse of fear as he raised his hands, as though to fend off her attack.

Tell him, Sophia growled, her voice trembling. *Tell him we would never…*

"The Tangata would not have harmed children," Lukys said softly, as he reached out and drew an arm around Sophia's shoulders. He swallowed, choosing his next words carefully. "I have seen it in New Nihelm…the reverence they hold for youth."

A shiver ran down his spine as he considered the implications. The Tangata had *not* been the first to attack. It had been humanity that had started this war, who had attacked the Tangata unprovoked.

But…who, then, had slain Romaine's family?

"If not the Tangata, then who?" Nguyen mused, echoing Lukys's own questions. Rising to refill his glass, he glanced at the pair of them. "I knew King Micah, before the war. I argued against the southern campaign, but he was insistent, believed we needed to strike decisively to protect Calafe. He convinced me to follow his lead, regretfully. But…perhaps the idea was not his own. Micah was always reckless, boisterous with the drink. Larger than life, like most of his people."

Lukys swallowed as he remembered Romaine and the massive axe the man had carried, the way he had fought. Battle was like breathing for the man. He wondered where Romaine was now, whose side he fought on.

"There were those with influence over Micah, ones whose motives I always questioned…" Nguyen continued, then abruptly shook his head. "Regardless, the past must be put behind us. It was a mistake to attack the Tangata. Witnessing her people charge, the decimation they wrought upon our armies…it convinced me a war could never be won against them. At least, not on open ground." He shuddered, as though recalling those days ten years past.

Lukys frowned at the man, unsure how to continue, and Sophia's words whispered into his mind.

That battle cost my people dearly. Many of the third generation were lost, those who could still partner without humans. Our strength has dwindled ever since.

Knowing her words were only for him, Lukys remained staring at the king. He wondered how the man would react if he learned the true weakness of the Tangata, that they could not replace those of them who fell in battle. At least, not without humanity.

"And what about this?" Nguyen asked, gesturing at the two of them with his glass of whiskey. "I've made a few enquiries since my arrival. Seems there are more than a dozen of you who survived the south. Each bonded with a Tangata. Seems there must be a story there." A smile spread across Nguyen's lips and Lukys could see the calculations turning behind his eyes. This was no ordinary man—he already suspected something of Sophia's secret.

Lukys swallowed, suddenly unable to meet the king's eyes. "As I said before, Sophia and her people are just as human as you or I."

"No doubt, no doubt," the king replied, still smiling. "Yet you cannot deny, it is…peculiar that so many would be bonded."

Lukys shared a look with Sophia, but this time they kept their silence, and the king let out a long sigh. "A shame. Perhaps when I learn the secrets of your abilities, you and I can enjoy a true conversation, my lady."

Sophia's face brightened at his words and the king laughed. "In the meantime, perhaps you could tell me more of why you are here. Your Sovereigns spoke of Old Ones?"

Lukys shivered as he recalled his encounters with the creatures —not just in New Nihelm, but the two they had inadvertently woken on the Archivist's quest to the tunnels of the Gods. That time seemed another life now, but the image of the Old Ones stalking him in the darkness was still etched in his mind.

"You have met Cara," he said softly. Taking control of his doubts, he crossed to the king's table and poured himself and Sophia another glass of the amber spirit. "So you know the Gods are real?"

The king raised an eyebrow at his nerve, but held out his glass to be topped up. "I know there are beings in this world who possess extraordinary abilities," he said, then lifted his glass to Sophia in salute.

Sophia snorted and took a cautious sip of her own drink. *I like this one*, she said into the privacy of his mind.

Lukys looked from one to the other. "Well, Cara and the Tangata are not the only ones with these 'extraordinary abilities.' The ancestors of the Tangata still live. They are far more powerful, but possess none of their…manners. We first discovered them in the ancient site we uncovered in Calafe."

"Yes," the king replied. "My spy briefed me on the situation. Your 'Goddess' slew them."

"Those two, yes," Lukys replied. "The Tangata found another."

Nguyen sat up at that. "You have told the Sovereigns?"

Lukys hesitated. "We were…interrupted by your arrival."

A curse slipped from the king's lips as he rose. "If this is true, I can only pray my envoys to Cara's people were successful. If we cannot match the Tangata in battle, what chance do we have against the monsters that bore them," he paused, glancing at Sophia. "…no offence, my lady."

Sophia inclined her head in acceptance. *You are right, Nguyen,* she said, and Lukys repeated her words. *Not even my people could stand against her…she now rules the Tangata as our new Matriarch.*

Nguyen's face grew grim. "I take it then that you and your friends are less emissaries, more political refugees?"

They nodded and the king's face grew grimmer. "This changes everything. Humanity cannot afford to continue with these petty squabbles. We must unite against this threat. Come."

He moved to the door and pushed it open. Lukys and Sophia made to follow him as he stepped into the corridor, but there he paused, looking around in confusion. It was a moment before Lukys realised what had made him hesitate.

Where are the guards? Sophia whispered into his mind.

Her question was soon answered, as the sound of pounding boots carried down the corridor towards them. A second later, a dozen men charged around the corner at the end of the hall. Most wore the plain uniforms of regular soldiers, but the man in the lead was all too familiar.

"There they are!" Cleo bellowed, pointing with his silver spear. *"Get them!"*

28

THE FOLLOWER

Adonis stumbled as he pushed through the door out into the snow, dragging the child with him. She screamed, her wings beating against his face, and almost managed to dislodge his grip. She was strong, almost stronger than Adonis, but he managed to hold on, digging his fingers deeper into her flesh.

Voices cried out through the storm, and he saw half a dozen faces turned towards him. Surprise changed to open fear as they saw who had come for them, what he had done. His stomach twisted but he would not back down now. Keeping the child firm in hand, he staggered through the snow, lips drawn back in a snarl.

The others had already fallen, knocked down by the few Anahera that had remained with the children. Those same guards followed him even now, emerging from the building, keeping their distance, but eyes alert, waiting for their chance to free the girl.

Adonis would not give them that chance. Only he had been fast enough, quick enough to act. While his comrades had launched themselves bravely against the adult Anahera, Adonis had kept to the plan. The children had scattered at the appearance of the Tangata, separating from their guardians in their panic. In the chaos of beating wings and flailing arms, Adonis had struggled to pick a target.

But he had only needed one.

"Tangata!" a voice called through the snow.

Adonis swung around as an Anahera approached. He was larger than the others, his white wings mingling with the snow, amber eyes fixed on his foe. Baring his teeth, Adonis faced the creature.

Back! he snapped, knowing the creatures could Hear. *Or the child will never join her forebearers in the sky.*

His words had the desired effect and the Anahera paused, uncertainty appearing behind those amber eyes. Adonis allowed himself a smile, though his heart was still racing.

Tell me, Anahera, do you rule here? he whispered to the white-winged creature.

The Anahera bared its teeth. *I am Farhan. I speak for the Elders of the Anahera.*

I will take that for a yes, Adonis replied with a smile.

A scream came from the child and she fought again to break free, begging for Farhan to save her. Cursing, Adonis dragged her back, his hand clamping tight around her wing. She stilled as Adonis squeezed, her cries turned to a whimper as feather's cracked beneath his grip.

"Stop!"

Farhan's command struck Adonis like a hammer and he almost released the child. But there was another Voice thrumming in his mind, distant, yet already growing nearer—Maya. The touch of his mate granted him strength, bolstered him against the command of the creature before him.

I said stay back, he snarled. Another whimper came from the young Anahera as he dug his fingers into flesh. *I will not ask again.*

Farhan did not move, but Adonis could see his fear. The Anahera might outnumber him, but standing in that yard with the child in hand, it was Adonis who had the advantage. These creatures would not risk harm to one of their youths.

Unbidden, an image flickered into Adonis's mind, of a child's face with snow upon her lips, freezing in the snow. A shudder shook Adonis and his grip on the Anahera's wing loosened. What was he doing, threatening a child? It went against his every instinct, and yet…

…words whispered into his mind, Maya's promises of a future, for children of his own. None of that would come to be unless the Tangata emerged victorious this day, and silently he restored his grip on the young Anahera. The fate of his species hung in the balance —he could not turn back now.

"Let her go, Tangata," Farhan growled, his voice low, dangerous. "Let her go, and I will allow your kind to leave this place in peace."

No! Adonis reached for the Anahera's mind. It had a foreignness about it, not so different as the human, but its flavour markedly different from his own brethren. *No, Anahera, not until we have spoken. Not until you have been made to see the truth.*

"What truth?" his foe snapped, broad wings stretching higher, drawing Adonis's gaze.

For a moment, Adonis wondered at those strange limbs, at the glory of these creatures, at their freedom to soar through the open skies. These creatures had the power of the Old Ones, the minds of humanity, wings. They could produce children, renew themselves without growing weaker each generation. They could have conquered the world.

Instead, they sequestered themselves in these mountains, hid themselves away. Such strange creatures.

"You *can* understand it."

Adonis's sensitive hearing caught a whisper from beyond Farhan. He frowned as a figure approached through the snow, arms wrapped tightly about herself. His stomach roiled as he realised that like him, this creature lacked wings. Here was the human he had sensed in the corridors of the city. Snarling, he tightened his grip on the child, alert for a trap.

So you have allied yourselves with the humans, he said softly. *A pity. My Matriarch had hopes for a different outcome.*

A frown crossed the Anahera's face. "You did not come on behalf of Erika's people?" he rumbled, then shook his head, as though to dismiss the question. "Release the fledgling, Tangata. Then we will talk about this truth of yours."

First, call off your warriors, Adonis hissed.

"What is happening?" the human called Erika shouted over the wind.

He noticed she kept her distance from Farhan. Then he noticed the spark of light from her fist. Immediately he pushed the child in front of him, recalling the magic he'd witnessed a human wield in the lowlands. Cries came from the Anahera and Farhan swung on the human.

"Stay back, treacherous human," he snarled. "Have you not done enough already?"

The human flinched away from Farhan, raising her magic fist towards him. Adonis frowned at the exchange. Had he been wrong about the connection between human and Anahera? There seemed to be no affection lost between these two.

Anahera, return to the City, Farhan's mental voice rung suddenly through the storm.

Adonis lifted his eyebrows, surprised with the ease at which the Anaheran leader had capitulated. It might have yet been a trick, but moments later he sensed confusion from his own brethren as the enemy Anahera fell back, disappearing into the swirling clouds. A smile touched his lips as he looked again at Farhan, though he still did not release the child.

One by one, Anahera appeared from the sky to land around them. Confusion showed in the eyes of the human as she retreated towards a strange structure in the centre of the yard, but Farhan said nothing, only stared at Adonis, waiting.

Adonis stared back. Slowly the sounds of battle faded away, until there was only the silence of the storm.

And the soft pulsing of Maya, coming closer.

"It is done, Tangata," Farhan said when the last of the winged creatures had landed. "Release the fledgling."

Adonis stood in silence for a while, watching the Anahera around him, their leader. What were their intentions, these strange, secluded creatures? Why had they suddenly returned to the world. He needed to know, to understand.

All in good time, Adonis whispered finally. *First, tell me, Farhan. Months ago in the lowlands, one of your kind fought against me on the side of humanity. Why?*

"A traitor," Farhan replied, and for a second, Adonis thought he glimpsed something in the creature's eyes. "My daughter," the Anahera added finally, his voice cold. "She will concern you no longer."

Again there was the flicker, the half-glance back towards where the human had retreated. Adonis frowned, following Farhan's gaze to the strange structure rising from the yard. His eyes caught movement there, the human climbing up upon a block of stone. The snow was slowing and he saw something else now, another figure, lying upon an altar.

Ignoring Farhan now, Adonis started towards the monolith, the child still in hand. He narrowed his eyes as he drew close, realising that one of the Anahera had been chained to the stone. One auburn wing flapped free, but the other was still bound tight. The human was crawling across the altar towards her, but the amber eyes of the Anahera were locked on Adonis.

Belatedly, he realised he knew this creature. Farhan had not been wrong—this was the Anahera he had fought at the river, all those months ago

I know you, he murmured, drawing to a stop beside the altar.

"Erika," the creature hissed, and beside her the human spun. Her hand still glowed with magic, but Adonis held the child before him and she did not strike. "Erika," the Anahera bound to the stone said again. "You have to get out of here, you have to leave me."

"*Never,*" the human called Erika hissed. She stood and faced Adonis, though she still dared not unleash her power. "I won't leave you with these monsters."

Adonis raised an eyebrow. Ignoring the human, he looked to the imprisoned Anahera.

We fought once, you and I, Adonis continued conversationally. *Tell me, Anahera, does your father speak the truth? Did you act alone, that day by the river?*

Do not hurt the human, the bound Anahera's words came to him in his mind, raw and untrained.

You do not beg for the child's life like the others? Adonis asked. He gave the girl a little shake to emphasis his point, drawing a scream from her. Nearby, the other Anahera cried out, but a snarl from Adonis kept them from advancing.

"Cara, what is she saying?" the human hissed, her fist growing brighter.

Please, I spared you that day by the river, the Anahera called Cara pled again. *Just leave the humans alone.*

Looking at the human, Adonis shook his head. *Such unpleasantly loud creatures,* he said, then turned to the creature bound in chains. *Would that I could, Cara, but their kind leaves us little choice.*

Abruptly he turned his back on the two and crossed to where Farhan still stood, fists clenched, eyes burning.

I am called Adonis, he said quietly. *I was sent by my Matriarch to treat with the Anahera.*

What is it you want, Tangata? Farhan snapped.

Adonis stared up at Farhan, seeing his rage, a thin veil to his fear. The child—or fledgling as Farhan had called it—was barely moving in his arms now, as though he had already struck her dead. Adonis found himself looking upon her with contempt now, his earlier compassion vanished. No child of the Tangata would have been so submissive. What sheltered upbringings did the fledglings of the Anahera live, to be so weak?

To survive, Farhan, he said at least, turning his eyes upon the Anaheran leader. *To see my people survive the storm that is to come.*

"We are no threat to you," Farhan replied.

No, but the humans are. Adonis turned his gaze on the creature on the altar. The light had gone out in her fist now. He could sense her exhaustion in the slump of her shoulders, but even defeated, the creatures could prove dangerous. That lesson had been taught to him in New Nihelm.

They are a threat to us all, he continued, swinging on Farhan. *You think they will allow your kind to live in these mountains in peace?*

"They cannot reach us here," Farhan grated.

Adonis laughed. *They are a plague upon this world, Farhan. I have seen it. Their greed knows no bounds. They will despoil your most sacred of places, dig up your dead, will bring fire and violence against your people, until you have naught left but ash.*

Silence answered Adonis's words as the amber eyes drilled into him. But finally the Farhan shook its head.

"The Anahera play no part in the wars of human and Tangata," he rumbled, drawing about himself a shroud of resolve, "and only one creature has brought war upon us today. Surrender, Adonis of the Tangata, or you will know the wrath of the Anahera."

Movement came from around the yard as the other Anahera edged closer. Even the child in Adonis's hands seemed to regain some of her fight, as she began to thrash against his hold. Adonis cursed, swinging one way, then another, trying to keep the enemy in sight, to keep them from approaching unnoticed.

"*I thought the Anahera to be lions,*" a voice broke across the clearing, hard, unyielding. The words reverberated in Adonis's mind, reinforced by the powers of the Old Ones.

"*Imagine my disappointment when I woke,*" Maya continued as she approached on soft footsteps. "*To discover they had become sheep, to bow before the human plague.*"

29

THE EMISSARY

Erika watched as the new creature stalked across the yard. The Anahera parted before her, as though this newcomer radiated something venomous, some deadly odour they feared would strike them down. She couldn't sense any outward difference to this new Tangata herself, but Erika couldn't help but shiver as she watched it come. Its eyes might be grey, but they were deeper, darker than the other Tangata.

And she had spoken aloud.

Erika's blood ran cold as she processed the implications, recalling the creatures she had encountered all those months before, the monsters they had awoken in the darkness beneath the earth.

No, this was not a Tangata that stood before her.

It was one of the Old Ones.

Struggling just to breath through her fear, Erika watched as the Old One joined the Tangata who held the Anaheran fledgling. Cara had killed the two they'd woken in the tunnels, so where had this creature come from? And how had she come to stand with the Tangata?

Atop the altar with the wind and sleet hissing down around them, Erika swung on Cara. "What the *hell* is happening?"

Crouched with one hand still shackled, Cara frowned, before understanding dawned in her eyes. "Right, you can't hear them."

The Goddess gave a visible shudder. "Lucky you—she's practically radiating death."

"Radiating death…" Erika shook her head. Extended use of the gauntlet had drained her of energy and she had more work to do yet. Shaking off the dozen questions that came to her mind, she forced her mind to focus. "What do they want?"

A sigh came from the young Anahera. "Your guess is as good as mine," she murmured, then flicked Erika a glance. "Err, don't suppose you've gotten some energy back?" She rattled her chains for emphasis.

Erika's eyes slid closed, but after a moment she nodded. Farhan and the other Anahera were absorbed by the Tangata and their endangered fledgling—punishing Cara seemed the least of their priorities now. Just a little more effort, one last push, surely she could manage that?

Pain from her injuries swept through Erika and she cursed into the howling wind. Then clenched her teeth, she crawled to the second chain and gripped it with the gauntlet.

"Why…didn't they stop it?" she asked as the magic began to gather. It was taking an age, and she wondered what would happen if she pushed too far.

"Adonis?" Cara hesitated. "Father couldn't, not with the fledgling at risk."

Pursing her lips, Erika said nothing. She had seen the pain in the child's eyes, the fear. Her heart went out to the young girl, but…the Tangata were deadly killers. They might not be the monsters humanity had made them out to be, but even so…Farhan had risked everything by calling off his warriors, allowing the Tangata into the city.

"The Old One changes everything though, surely…" Cara was saying.

Before Erika could reply, Farhan's voice rose through the storm, carrying across the yard to where they crouched.

"It's not possible." The Anaheran leader seemed as shocked as his daughter to be confronted by an Old One. "Your kind are extinct…"

The newcomer's face hardened at that, and she advanced until she stood face to face with Farhan.

"And how did that come to pass, Anahera?" she hissed. "When I began the long sleep, it was humanity who wavered, defeated by the last sacrifice of my people, of my own mother." She paused, eyeing the leader of the Anahera. "Yet now I wake to find humanity ascendant, my own children corrupted. Yet here your kind stand, as sickeningly pure as ever."

"The Anahera play no part—"

Farhan broke off as the Old One turned abruptly, marching to where the first Tangata still stood with the fledgling. Movement came from beyond the gathering, and Erika's heart fell into her stomach as more of the creatures filed into the yard—those Tangata who had been warring outside. They looked to number in the hundreds.

Then a high-pitched cry carried across the yard, and Erika watched in horror as the Old One caught the imprisoned fledgling by the wing and dragged her across the ground to where the Anaheran leader waited. The young fought to break free, but the Old One was far stronger than her Tangatan descendants. Faster as well—Erika had learned that in the depths of the earth.

"So this is a child of the Anahera," the Old One muttered, lifting the child by the wing. Beside Erika, Cara winced at the girl's screams. "Even in my day, your kind kept them secret. I can see why, such pitiful creatures."

"Release her, foul beast," Farhan spat, though he still made no move to intervene.

A smile spread across the Old One's lips, a dark, terrifying thing that sent chills running down Erika's spine. "Why don't you make me, Anahera?"

Farhan's jaw clenched so tight Erika could see the tendons standing up on his neck. Even his feathers bristled, so that his wings seemed to almost double in size. For a moment, she thought he would accept the challenge, but...

...that moment stretched out, seconds ticking past, until finally his shoulders slumped.

Laughter answered his defeat. "I came here to bargain, Anahera," the Old One rasped. "To seek an ally in an old rival. I did not expect to find you so craven. Perhaps I should simply take what I desire."

"My people have nothing to give—"

The laughter came again, echoing from the stone walls, a dark cackling that sent tremors to Erika's very core.

"My Tangata, they still value their children, as they did in times past. They are our future, our hope."

"I will destroy you—" Farhan started.

The Old One gave the fledgling a violent shake and she cried out, fingers scrabbling at the snowy gravel. Farhan took a step closer, arm raised, but the Old One was faster. A scream tore from the fledgling as a boot fell upon her wing. The sharp *crack* of breaking bones brought silence to the yard. The eyes of the Old One swept the Anahera. She was outnumbered, outmatched, but Erika could see the ecstasy in her eyes.

"What was I saying?" she murmured. "Oh, yes." Her grey eyes fell to the child once more. She placed a boot upon the fledgling's throat. "My Tangata, they cherish their children, but so too have they learnt the price of weakness. Isn't that right, my mate?"

Beside her, the Tangata stared back at the Old One, then bowed its head in silence.

"Yes, that's right," the Old One continued, looking to Farhan again. "They know that sacrifice is necessary, that sometimes the weak must perish to protect the strong." She crooked her neck. "Have the Anahera learned that lesson, Farhan?"

"*Erika!*" A hiss from Cara drew her attention back to the altar.

Her fist was vibrating with power now, and quickly she gripped the last of the chains in her gauntleted hand. The sharp *shriek* of shattering steel followed, and then Cara was throwing her arms about her. Soft sobs whispered in Erika's ear as she hugged the Goddess back, but there was no more time than that for celebration. Breaking apart, they turned to the confrontation in the yard.

"Please…" Farhan's voice had grown weak. Even Erika could hear his despair. Before the fledgling's pain, he stood helpless. *All* the Anahera stood helpless.

"*Enough!*" the Old One snapped, sneering. "Enough of your pitiful whining. Here is your chance, Farhan, leader of the Anahera. Attack me, prove your courage—but do so in the knowledge that the child will die."

Farhan did not move, and the Old One shook her head. "Ah, my poor cousins, how cruel the passage of time has been for you. But fear not, your saviour has come. I will free you of the burden of your freedom." Her sneer grew wider. "But first, I would have you kneel to your new master."

A growl came from Farhan and alongside Erika, Cara tensed. Before anyone could move, the fledgling began to thrash, her face growing pale as the Old One's boot pressed down. Erika's heart twisted as she saw the panic in the girl's face, streaked now by mud and ice, her mouth open, gasping, struggling to breathe. Clenching her fist, Erika began to rise.

The Anahera gathered in the yard acted first. One by one, they fell to their knees before the Old One. Erika stared, aghast, as the creatures that had been her Gods, the most powerful beings in the world, submitted to the monster in their midst. This couldn't be so, couldn't be happening…

Farhan was the last to kneel. He crumpled suddenly, as though his strength had just given out. Mud and ice cracked as his knees sank into the slush and he said not a word, but Erika could see the despair in his eyes as he looked up at the Old One.

"Release the fledgling," he rasped.

The Old One smiled and removed her boot. The girl gasped, her whole body shuddering, but the creature allowed her no time to catch her breath. Grasping her by the wing, she dragged the fledgling through the slush to where her Tangatan mate waited. She handed the sobbing child to the creature, then returned to Farhan. Smiling, she reached down to stroke his face.

"All in good time, my slave," she murmured. "First you must prove your loyalty." Abruptly the Old One turned, and Erika went cold as those terrible eyes fell on her. "First, we must deal with the human."

Fear swelled in Erika's chest, but she did not flee from the creature. With Cara at her side, they stood atop the altar and watched her approach. The storm was breaking now, the first hint of light appearing overhead. None of the Anahera moved as the creature approached, and Erika had lost track of Maisie in the chaos. With her broken leg, the spy could not have gone far. But even uninjured, what could the Gemaho spy have done against a monster such as this?

"Can you fly?" Erika hissed to Cara as the creature stalked towards them.

Erika glanced at her friend when she did not reply, but Cara's eyes were focused elsewhere—on the face of her father, on Hugo knelt in the mud, on the other Anahera, their heads bowed before the Old One's threats.

"I can't leave them like this," the Goddess whispered.

Erika's stomach twisted and she made to argue, then thought better of it. Reaching out, she took her friend's hands in hers.

"Then we'll face her together," she whispered.

Surprise showed in Cara's eyes, but already Erika was turning away, stepping forward to face the ancient creature that had come to wreak havoc upon all of them. The Old One moved through the mud and snow without haste, a smile on her lips, and death in those terrible eyes. Yet it was not her that Erika focused her attention on, but the Anahera. She searched their faces for some spark, some hope that they might yet rise.

"Is this how the Anahera fall?" she asked, voice soft, rising above the dying of the storm. "Is this what becomes of the Gods of men? For centuries we have prayed to you, longed for your return, that we might together beat back the scourge of the Tangata." Her eyes passed over the collection of faces, but none dared meet her gaze. Not even Farhan. Despair welled in her chest and her eyes burned.

"I believed in you," she whispered.

Laughter was her answer.

Clenching her fist, Erika faced the Old One. She could not hope to defeat a host of Tangata, but perhaps her magic might make a difference against this one. But even as she tried to summon the magic, the strength went from her legs and she cried out, almost falling.

Wings beat the air and then Cara was at her side, lending her strength. Together they faced the enemy, but not even Cara could fight all of the Tangata. As Erika watched, the creatures slid through the ranks of the Anahera, moving to support the Old One, their Matriarch. Swallowing, Erika pressed Cara behind her. It was her the Old One wanted, not Cara.

The creature's cackling grew louder as she approached, but as she reached the foot of the altar, she fell silent and leaned her head to one side. "Gods?" she asked, before looking back at Farhan. "You convinced them that you were their Gods?"

The laughter came again, higher in pitch now, as the Old One threw back her head and howled with true mirth. Erika staggered, shocked by the creature's reaction. Finally the sound faded, and Erika found those terrible eyes upon her again.

"You do not understand why I laugh, do you, human?" the Old One asked, still standing at the foot of the altar.

Erika bared her teeth and raised the gauntlet by way of response. A spark of light lit the metal, only a fraction of its usual fire, but enough to give the Old One pause—or so she hoped.

"I understand well enough," she snarled. "The Anahera are not the Gods of our past."

The Old One chuckled. Then suddenly she leapt, alighting on the side of the altar. Erika flinched back, raising her fist by instinct, but it managed only a flicker before the light died. A wave of dizziness struck her, and suddenly she was looking up at the Old One from her knees.

"Do you know why I came here, human?" the creature asked. "Why I sought out this place, rather than attack humanity?"

Erika could only shake her head, too weak to move, to resist. The Old One's smile grew as she leaned in close.

"Because in my time the Anahera and Tangata were not enemies, human," she rasped. "We were *allies*."

❦ 30 ❦

THE HERO

Roaring, Cleo and his soldiers rushed towards where Lukys stood with the others. A curse came from the king—then he was spinning on his heel and pushing them back into the room, slamming the door closed and throwing the lock.

Heart pounding, Lukys stumbled towards the window, looking from the door to the king.

"What's happening?" he gasped.

The king swung this way and that, searching the room for weapons or an exit, but he paused at Lukys's words.

"It would appear someone has taken it upon themselves to rid Perfugia of our little inconvenience," he said, returning to his search. He winced as something hard struck the door, then added: "That, or your friend out there really doesn't like you."

Lukys swallowed as a sharp *crack* came from the door, one of the wooden panels shattering as an axe appeared through the wood.

I wouldn't discount the second possibility, Sophia said wryly as she came alongside him.

"Cleo's a brute," Lukys said shortly, eyes fixed on the door as it shook beneath another blow. "But I wouldn't have thought him capable of this. And Tasha…" he trailed off, recalling the way she had pulled him aside in the room—and her change in manner when she saw the tangled sheets on the bed.

Bang!

His thoughts were interrupted as the door finally gave way, shattering inwards to emit the first of those outside. Two soldiers forced their way through the broken wood, spears held at the ready.

"What is the meaning of this?" Nguyen bellowed, abandoning his search and swinging towards them.

Cleo shouldered his way past the soldiers, silver spear held in one hand, shield in the other. In the blue steel of the royal guard, he could have been a noble warrior from legend, but the hatred that twisted his face was pure malevolence.

"The beast, her lover, and the traitor king," he snarled. "A match made in hell. The Sovereigns will thank us when you're gone."

At that, he hefted his spear and thrust the razor-sharp tip at Sophia's throat.

Lukys cried out, but moving with Tangatan speed she twisted away and the blade cut only empty air. A snarl rattled from her throat and for a second it seemed as though she would tear Cleo in two. But his comrades pushed forward, their own spears turning on the Tangata in their midst, and Sophia was forced to retreat.

Standing just outside the reach of their blades, Nguyen finally reacted. As one of the guards stepped out of line, the king darted forward and caught his spear with both hands. The man cried out as Nguyen twisted the weapon, then yanked back with all his strength. Taken off-guard, the spear was torn from the man's hands. Reversing the weapon with a speed that belied his greying hair, Nguyen drove it through the throat of its former owner.

Shock showed in the eyes of their assailants as the king leapt back, flourishing the bloody blade. A dozen pairs of eyes turned to their fallen comrade, even now still grasping at his throat, desperate to stem the blood pulsing between his fingers. Then the eyes returned to the king, and Lukys glimpsed their rage.

"You'll pay for that, bastard," Cleo growled.

He advanced a step, freeing space for the last of their comrades to enter. Lukys clenched his fists, eyeing their weapons. Unarmed, he would be of little use, but perhaps he could disarm another of the guards as the king had—

A soft growl, barely audible, was the only warning Cleo and his companions had before Sophia fell upon them. The breath lodged in Lukys's chest as a man staggered back from her blur of movement, the side of his helmet caved in by an unseen blow. The steel had done little to protect him from the Tangata's strength, and with a gurgling cry, he crumpled to the ground alongside his dead companion.

The other men cried out and thrust their weapons at Sophia in panic, but these soldiers did not possess the same skill as royal guards, and Sophia easily evaded their attacks. Before Lukys knew what was happening, she tore a weapon from one of their grasps and sent it hurtling towards him. At the last second, he snatched it from the air, then moved to aid Sophia.

Not that she needed it.

The freshly unarmed man turned and fled, while Cleo and the rest tried to rush her all at once. It looked like Sophia would be overwhelmed, but she only bounded forward, dodging inside the range of the spear tips, and kicked out at the nearest of the men. An awful *crack* followed as her boot connected with his chest and hurled him backwards.

Snarling, Cleo tried to bring his spear to bear, but Sophia was faster, grasping another of the men by his chainmail vest. Unable to use his weapon, he dropped it and swung a punch. The blow connected with Sophia's forehead, but she barely seemed to feel it. A growl rumbled from her throat as she spun, flinging the man over her hip and into the path of Cleo. The two crashed together with an audible *thump* and went down in a heap.

As the two struggled to recover, the others came at her, spears held in trembling hands. A hiss escaped from Sophia as she swung on them, and Lukys glimpsed madness in her grey eyes, a reflection of the insanity he'd seen in the eyes of the Old Ones. The remaining men saw it too, and with a final glance at their fallen leader, they turned and fled.

For a moment, Lukys thought Sophia would chase after them. A growl rumbled from her chest as she watched them vanish into the corridor, but then she let out a long breath. The madness seemed to leave her with the exhaled air, and blinking, the tension fled her body. She glanced at him, and now he saw concern in her eyes, sensed it in the yellow fear of her aura.

Lukys said nothing, only crossed the room and drew her into a one-handed hug, the spear she'd thrown him clutched unused at his side.

"Impressive," Nguyen said softly.

A groan from across the room drew their attention to Cleo and the man he'd tripped over. Sophia must have thrown him harder than Lukys had thought, for neither had yet regained their feet. Releasing the Tangata, he levelled the spear at the royal guard.

"How did you get in here?" he snapped.

Cleo drew his lips back in a sneer. "I'll never tell you anything, Tangata fu—"

His words were cut off as Nguyen stepped up and drove a spear through his back. The guard's eyes widened and his mouth fell open, as though to say more, but blood burst from his lips instead, and he pitched face-first to the ground.

"I believe you," the king said softly. He turned to the second man. "And what about you?"

The plain-clothed man tried to retreat from the king, but his collision with Cleo must have left him with injuries, for he struggled even on his hands and knees.

"Please," he gasped. "I don't know anything!"

"I see." The king's voice was cold as the spear flashed out. A moment later, the man lay still in a pool of his own blood.

Lukys stared at the dead men in shock. Beside him, horror radiated from Sophia, and absently he recalled her dismay when he'd told her of the wars that had raged between humanity, how obscene the concept had seemed to her. The Tangata did not murder one another —or at least they hadn't, until the reappearance of the Old Ones.

Silence fell over the chamber as the last of their assailants breathed their last breaths. The king stood regarding them, his green eyes unreadable.

"Why did you kill them?" Lukys finally managed.

"Were you planning to take them prisoner?" the king asked. "I'd rather not have them come against us again while we're trying to escape."

"Escape?" Lukys frowned.

"You weren't planning on sticking around waiting for others, were you?"

Lukys shook his head, still staring at Cleo. The hatred had left the guard's face with death. Shivering, he looked to the door again, the empty corridor. Where had Tasha and her escort gone?

"None of this makes sense," Lukys whispered. Cleo he could imagine giving in to his hatred and going against the wishes of the Sovereigns, but Tasha? She might hate the Tangata, but the woman was a professional.

"When politics is involved, I rarely find things do," the king commented.

"The Sovereigns…" Lukys started.

"Forget the Sovereigns," Nguyen said shortly. "The guards will never let us near them after this, even if they don't have some hand in it. Come, we'd best move quickly if we're to escape with our lives."

Lukys's mind was still reeling from the sudden betrayal and he struggled to keep pace with the king's thinking. "Where are we going?"

"My ships," Nguyen replied.

Lukys and Sophia followed the man into the corridor. Outside, the hallway was empty, all sign of the men that had attacked them vanished. But if the royal guards were plotting against them as Nguyen believed, it wouldn't be long before more came to finish the job. As though to confirm the thought, horns began to sound in the distance.

"We'll never make it that far," Lukys said, turning to the king.

Nguyen grunted. Reaching into his shirt, he drew out a glass orb. Lukys frowned. The object had a strange sheen to it, as though there were some inner light within the crystal…

He jumped as light burst from the globe, raising his spear. But when the brilliance faded, he found the space where the king had been standing vacant. Blood pounded in Lukys's ears as he took a step back, touched by fear. What new magic was this?

"Step closer, and it will hide you as well," Nguyen's voice emerged from empty air, causing Lukys to jump for a second time in as many minutes. "Amina is not the only one with a few tricks up her sleeve."

Lukys swallowed and stole a glance at Sophia. Jaw clenched, her grey eyes were fixed on a point near where the king had disappeared. Without waiting for him to speak, she took a step forward—and vanished as well.

A shiver ran down Lukys's spine, but a moment later her voice whispered in his mind

It's okay, she murmured. *This king has an old magic.*

Lukys let out a sharp breath, his skin crawling at the strangeness of this new power. But circumstances left him no choice, and clenching his fists, he strode towards what seemed to be the source of the king's voice. There was another burst of light across his vision, then his companions reappeared before him. The hackles on the back of his neck stood on end as he looked around, finding the rest of the world stained a pallid grey.

"What is this?" he whispered.

"How do you think I was able to sneak into the court of the Sovereigns?" the king replied. "My Archivists and engineers managed to create this prototype from an artefact we discovered. A shame they were lost in the ruins of my fortress—they would have been excited to see how effective it has proven. Now come, we'd best reach my fleet before our new friends decide to up the stakes."

Lukys watched as the man turned in the direction of the harbour, but something held him back. There was a wrongness to all this, to the sudden betrayal of the royal guards, a question he needed answering. More than that, there was the threat of the Old Ones, the need for humanity to unite against them.

"Stop," he said abruptly. The king swung back, eyebrows lifted with irritation, clearly unimpressed by the delay. Lukys spoke over his objection. "We can't run," he hissed.

"Lukys, if we stay here, we die," the king said, his eyes hard.

Lukys shook his head, surprising himself with the defiance. But Nguyen was not his king. Not even the Sovereigns were now. He was his own man, the Tangata and Dale and Travis and all the others his people.

"If we flee, we die anyway," he replied. "When the Old One and her Tangata come, there'll be nowhere left to run, no safe place to hide. Millions will perish."

His words seemed to give Nguyen pause, and his gaze flickered to Sophia before returning to Lukys.

"The Sovereigns won't listen," Nguyen replied. "Not with the blood of their guards on our hands, not without my soldiers to protect us. It was a mistake coming here, I can see that now."

"No," Lukys said softly. "You were right to ask Perfugia to stand with you. You were right to seek unity. But we cannot turn from the path now, whatever the risk."

"Those who escaped will have already told their tales to the Sovereigns. They will call you monsters, name me a traitor."

"Then we will name them liars. We will make the Sovereigns see through their hatred," Lukys said, though recalling the look they'd given them in the amphitheatre, he struggled to believe the words himself.

The king regarded him for a long while, until Lukys thought the man must think him a fool. Yet he knew in his heart they could not run now. A fleet might wait for them in the harbour, but what use was that with no safe port to dock? If they fled now, all the world would stand against them.

I am with you, Lukys, Sophia whispered.

He smiled at her, seeing the support in her eyes. Whatever he chose, he knew Sophia would join him on the road, however long and arduous the journey might prove. Even should Nguyen turn back, he would not be alone in his confrontation with the Sovereigns.

"Very well," Nguyen said abruptly. He waved a hand. "You are right, of course. Though you'd best pray to those Gods of yours that the Sovereigns don't have us slaughtered on the spot. Alone, I fear there's little we could do to defend ourselves."

"They won't," Lukys said firmly, "and we won't be alone."

The others? Sophia said.

Lukys nodded, and silently he reached out with his mind as he had before in their chambers. This time, though, he persisted, sending out feelers for Sophia's brethren, for his family. The citadel was filled with minds, with the presence of other Melders, some barely a glimmer in his inner eyes, others a brilliant vortex of colours. But only a handful were familiar.

The Tangata.

Brothers, sisters, he called out, touching each of their consciousnesses. *They're coming for you.*

He sensed fear and concern as a dozen voices called back to

him, but he thrust their words aside. There was more to say, and he could not afford to delay.

Escape your quarters and evade the guards. Meet us in the amphitheatre of the Sovereigns. We will make our stand there.

As he finished, the fear radiating from the others subsided, giving way to quiet resolve. In his mind's eyes he glimpsed images of the Tangata and their human partners climbing from windows, bursting through doors, exchanging blows with blue-garbed soldiers. For a moment he was with each of them, felt the rush of their adrenaline, their desperate plights...

Lukys!

Sophia's call drew him back to his own reality. Shaking himself, he glanced at the others. They still stood in the bubble of strangeness, cast by the orb in Nguyen's hand. He swallowed, touched by sudden guilt. The others did not have the advantage of the king's magic. Would any of them survive to reach the Sovereigns?

"Our friends will join us in the amphitheatre." Too late to second guess himself now. He looked at the king. "Do you remember the way?"

❧ 31 ❧

THE EMISSARY

"**S**tay back!"

Fear gave Erika fresh strength and she scrambled back from the Old One. She found Cara, still standing unmoved, and managed to come to her feet. Grasping at the Goddess, she looked at the Old One, saw the shine in her grey eyes, the amusement.

"Should I tell you the truth, human?" the Old One said, stepping closer. Erika shrank against Cara, feeling the tremors in her friend, but there was no escaping the creature's words. "About what really happened all that time ago, when the world Fell?"

Erika shook her head, trying to deny the creature's lies, her darkness, but no words left her mouth.

"It was so long ago, centuries of darkness. No wonder humanity has forgotten," the creature continued, its voice soft, almost seductive. "Perhaps it has even passed from the memories of the Tangata." She swung back towards where Farhan knelt. "But *they* have not forgotten. Not with their long lives, their isolation. Their Founders made sure of it."

"No," the Old One continued, shaking her head. "My children may have forgotten the sacrifice of their forefathers, but I have not. For it was my own mother and father who helped light the match of humanity's destruction."

"They were the first of you," Erika murmured, more to herself than the creature. "The ones who stole the magic from the Gods?"

Then she frowned, glancing at the kneeling Anahera. That had been the legend, the tale passed down by human legends for generations. The Tangata had stolen their power from the Gods, the Anahera. But…that no longer rang true, not with everything she'd learned. Then how…

"My parents were no thieves," the Old One snapped. "Their power, the strength that runs in my veins still, even that which remains to the Tangata, it was a gift." Her smile grew. "From humanity."

Erika started. "What?"

The Old One stared back, unrelenting. "Yes, just as the Anahera later received their gifts, we were blessed by the magic of humanity." Her face hardened, the smile turning to a snarl. "Only your gifts came with a cost, one we became increasingly unwilling to pay: our servitude." She glanced back at Farhan, still knelt in the mud, unmoving. "Isn't that right, Anahera?"

Erika's heart throbbed painfully in her chest and she staggered, the pieces of the puzzle finally falling into place. The reason the Anahera had fled into the mountains, why their city was so pitiful compared to the pictures of the past, why the sight of her magic had triggered such a reaction from them. Even the notes from the journal, the regrets, the doubts of the long dead Founder.

Because *none* of it had been created by the Anahera.

The magic, the majestic city, the very existence of these beings, all of it had been created by humanity.

"Do you understand now, human?" The crunch of the Old One's footsteps whispered in Erika's ears as she came closer. "Yes, I can see it in your eyes, the truth."

Shaking her head, Erika broke away from Cara, retreated from the Old One's advance. Her mind was still racing, the whole of the puzzle taking shape. The legends claimed that the Gods—the Anahera—had thrown down the world to destroy the Tangata, that they had brought about the Fall to stop the stolen magic from spreading.

Lies.

Erika squeezed her fist, summoning the power of the gauntlet. Magic that could cause a Tangata to scream in agony, that could bring an Anahera to his knees. Just a fraction of the magics had once existed. All of it, created by humanity.

Until the Fall.

"My father told me the story," the Old One rasped, her grey eyes boring into Erika's, "about my mother's sacrifice—and the great alliance between our peoples, the union of Anahera and Tangata against a common enemy." Her lips drew back, revealing shining teeth. "Against humanity."

"No," Erika whispered, her whole being trembling.

No, no, no!

She stumbled back from the creature, struggling to deny, to reject the tale. Desperate, she looked at Cara. Two of the Tangata had approached on either side of the Goddess, ready for signs of treachery, but the Goddess did not seem to notice them. Her amber eyes were wide, fixed doggedly to the ground, avoiding Erika's gaze. Pain swelled in her chest, a gathering pressure, building, growing, screaming for release.

She saw again that glorious, wondrous city from the painting, rising from the waters of the harbour. The City of the Gods , created by her own people, sculpted by her ancestors hundreds of years passed, by humanity.

All of it destroyed, torn down in the violence of the Fall, by the cataclysm that had reduced humanity to beasts, clawing and warring in the dirt.

Not to destroy the Tangata, as human legends had told for generations.

But to destroy humanity itself.

Erika's entire being shook as she stared at the Old One. Every evil her people had borne, all the death, the destruction, the suffering, it had all been because of the creatures before her, a vile way to keep humanity in check.

And all these while the Anahera had hidden away in these mountains, holding themselves aloof, proclaiming their Divinity because they did not kill, did not lie.

They had committed the greatest genocide in all of history.

A soft crackling lit the yard as she ignited her magic.

"I will destroy you all," Erika whispered.

"Such anger," the Old One murmured, "and yet you call my

children mad, have treated them as monsters. No wonder my mother took retribution upon your kind." A smile touched her lips and she glanced at Farhan. "With your own Founders' help, of course."

Erika screamed.

It was a scream unlike any she had ever given, carrying with it all the torment of her life, the betrayal of her people, of a limitless rage. Without thinking, she leapt at the Old One, arm thrust for her face, the magic thrumming in her ears. Light flashed and the Old One stumbled in the snow, hands going to her ears…

…then she was surging forward, teeth bared, fist flashing out to strike Erika's chest. The agony of her broken rib flared back to life and suddenly she was on the ground, mouth stretched wide, straining to breathe.

The Old One gave her no time to recover. Growling, she caught Erika by the shirt and lifted her into the air. Erika tried to raise her fist, to bring the gauntlet to bear, but the creature caught her by the wrist and grinned.

"A curious thing," the Old One said matter-of-factly as she inspected the metal links covering Erika's arm. "Of all the power your ancestors once possessed, this was but a trinket, created at the end. Yet it is still enough to bring us to our knees."

"I will see your children burn for what you did to us," Erika spat.

Laughter rasped from the throat of the Old One. "Oh, I don't doubt you would try." Her face hardened, and a fresh darkness came into her eyes. "I do not intend to grant you the chance."

Suddenly the Old One's grip tightened on Erika's wrist. She cried out, twisting, trying to break free, but there was no escaping this beast. Iron fingers dug into the gauntlet, squeezing, crushing metal against flesh, until Erika could feel the bones grinding, crack-ing, *shattering.*

A scream tore from her throat as red-hot agony swallowed her arm. Through the pain, she saw the Old One smiling, the triumph in her eyes…

…then felt a *thud* as a blur of auburn struck the Old One, flinging her back, sending Erika tumbling to the snow.

Light flashed as she struck and stars danced across her vision. She lay in the snow, gasping for breath, screams still ringing in her ears as she fought the pain, sought to stave off unconsciousness. Agony rose in her throat to swallow her, threatening to drown her.

Somehow, Erika clung on.

Across the yard, the thud of fists on flesh sounded from the walls. Teeth clenched, Erika struggled to rise once more, to see what had become of Cara. Two bodies lay on the snow nearby—those of the Tangata that had tried to restrain her. Blood seeped from their shattered skulls, staining the snow.

Auburn and gold flashed amidst the falling snow as Goddess and Old One battled fist and boot and wing. She could barely follow the two as they warred against one another—not even the other Tangata seemed able to keep pace, and Erika's heart soared. Cara had already defeated two of the Old Ones in the caverns beneath the earth; surely she would emerge victorious now.

Snarls rose from the two, each punctuated by the heavy *thud* of flesh on flesh. In moments, the dirt and snow had been trampled to mud by the fury of their assault. Around the square, the Anahera watched on. Not one moved to aid their fellow Anahera—not even Farhan.

The Tangata had no such hesitation. Lying in the dirt, Erika watched as the creatures edged closer to their embattled leader, though they did not yet attempt to interfere. Gritting her teeth, she struggled to push herself up. Pain lanced through her chest but she made it to her knees. Erika could go no further though, could not help her friend this time, not in this battle. Just the slightest shift of her fingers ignited fresh agony in her gauntleted hand.

Horror stole Erika's breath as a sudden cry came from Cara. She watched as the Goddess stumbled, mud slipping beneath her bare feet. Her wings flared out as she sought to regain her balance, but the Old One would not grant her the opportunity. She pounced, boot crashing against Cara's stomach.

The blow drove the breath from the Goddess's lungs and she doubled up, only to meet the Old One's knee as she drove it upwards. A terrible *crunch* sounded across the yard as the blow connected, lifting Cara from her feet, hurling her back. Mud splashed as she tumbled across the ground, staining her wings, drenching her thin clothing.

Still Cara would not surrender. Groaning, the Goddess struggled to her knees as the Old One approached. The familiar laughter sounded in Erika's ears, but she could do nothing but watch as the creature caught a handful of Cara's hair and hauled the Goddess to her feet.

"At least one of the Anahera still has the heart to fight," she said, and it seemed to Erika there was regret in her voice. "A shame; you might have served me well."

Tears filled Erika's eyes as she watched the Old One send her friend crashing back to the ground. This time Cara struggled to rise, her wings flailing, hands slipping in the mud. Heart pounding, Erika searched for someone, anyone that could help. Maisie still lay unconscious, her leg twisted at a terrible angle, and not one of the Anahera even looked at Cara now. Their eyes were fixed to the mud, as though by turning their backs, they might ignore what was about to happen.

Then Erika saw Farhan. He still knelt like the others, but he alone of the Anahera did not look away. His amber gaze was fixed on his daughter, reflecting her pain, her grief…

"Farhan," Erika rasped, struggling to lift her voice above the wind in the mountain peaks. "Farhan, you have to help her!"

The Anahera's eyes flickered ever so briefly towards her, but he made no move to act, to intervene. Watching him sit there, Erika felt her rage stirring, the terrible anger that burned within her, the desire to rend and tear, to punish those that had so devastated her people, humanity.

"*Bastard!*" she screamed, her vision blurring. Agony engulfed her as she pushed herself to her feet, but the rage would not be denied. "You said you only wanted to protect her, to shield your daughter from the dangers without. Now you sit and watch her die, and do nothing? *Coward!* You deserve your slavery."

At that she turned away from the fallen God, from the Anahera and the Tangata. Her entire being in agony, Erika faced the Old One.

"You thought they would aid you?" The creature reached down to where Cara knelt at her feet and patted the Goddess's cheek. "This one has more courage than all the Anahera combined."

Cara still struggled against the creature's grip, but her strength could no longer match her foe. Diminished by captivity, by grief and exhaustion, Cara was all but defeated, the Old One resurgent.

Erika stumbled towards them, lurching from one foot to the other. Each step sent jolts of agony through her chest, her arm, but she did not stop. She knew she couldn't win, couldn't stop this creature. All she could do was stand with her friend. If they were to die, at least then it would be together.

The Old One watched her come, amusement showing in her eyes, in the cruel twist to her lips. She knew the end was near, that soon the city, maybe even the whole world, would belong to her. But it didn't matter to Erika, not now.

Suddenly she was standing before the creature, eye to eye, with Cara at her feet. The Old One made no move to intervene as she reached down with her good hand, said nothing as she helped the Goddess to her feet. She only stood and watched, smiling, always smiling.

Erika swallowed as she glanced at her friend, saw the pain in her amber eyes, but also the love, the warmth of the knowledge she did not face this monster alone. Just as Erika had said, they faced the Old One together.

"Are you ready then?" the creature growled.

A lump lodged in Erika's throat and she tensed, preparing for one last stand, one final attempt at resistance…

"*Old One.*" Erika's head whipped around as a shout came from across the yard. Farhan rose slowly to his feet. "*You will leave my daughter be!*"

Eyes burning, white wings spread, he advanced on them. For just a moment, the Old One seemed surprised. She watched him come, then abruptly turned from them. Her movements quickened as she stepped to meet her challenger.

"So another has the courage to fight," she laughed. "Come then, Farhan of the Anahera, come and meet your death."

Erika winced as the two came together, but she knew there could be only one outcome from this battle. The Anahera remained on their knees, unmoved by Farhan's defiance, just as they had been for Cara. The Tangata still held the child, the fledgling slumped in its hands. They would not act so long as she was in danger.

Erika looked around for Maisie, hoping against hope she might have recovered, but her hopes were crushed as she saw the Tangata had found the injured woman. Half a dozen of the creatures stood guard over her unconscious figure, grey eyes alert. There would be no saving the Gemaho spy.

Despair welled in Erika's heart as she looked to her friend. "Cara," she whispered, reaching out to take the Goddess's hand. "Cara, we have to go. We can't stay here, we can't help them."

The Goddess's eyes were still fixed on her father, on the ferocious battle between the two titans. Erika felt a tremor shake her friend.

"He cares," she whispered. She blinked, and a tear spilt down her cheek. "He…he…"

Her heart twisting, Erika stepped between the Goddess and the battle, cutting off her view of Farhan. "He saved you," she whispered, cupping Cara's cheek. "He saved us both. We can't let it be for nothing. Cara, we have to go."

Cara's face spasmed and she shook her head, a sob tearing from her throat. "No, no, I can't…"

"*You can,*" Erika insisted. "*You must!*"

"No!" Cara whipped her head from side to side, her eyes scrunched closed. "Please, don't make me."

Standing with her back to the two fighters, Erika couldn't see the blows, but she could hear each strike, the thud of pounding flesh and breaking bones. It grew more urgent, more violent with each second. But even if Farhan gained the upper hand, there was still the Tangata. There were enough in the yard to tear the leader of the Anahera to pieces.

"It's time," Erika whispered, hugging her friend tight. "Come on, before it's too late—"

Erika broke off as with a final scream, Cara hugged her back. Agony engulfed her chest, but before she could cry out, the great wings of auburn beat down, striking the air, pounding so hard that stones and sleet and mud were sent whirling away from them. Roars of anger came from all around as the Tangata realised what was happening, but it was already too late.

They were airborne.

Lukys raced through the twisting corridors of the citadel, surprised at the speed with which Nguyen moved. Sophia had no problem keeping pace, but still weakened by his time at sea, Lukys struggled each time they came to a fresh set of stairs. His heart pounded hard in his chest as they made their slow way up through the endless complex.

For a time, it seemed the king's magic would allow them to pass easily into the amphitheatre of the Sovereigns—until they finally turned a corner and found themselves facing a hallway filled with soldiers. They stumbled to a stop as one, their path blocked. The soldiers stood some thirty yards away, spears and shields held in preparation for battle, their formation tight.

And at their front stood Tasha.

Lukys swallowed, holding his breath as he felt the eyes of Tasha and her soldiers upon them, though he knew they could not be seen. It was eerie, the sun shining down upon those dozens of faces, their brows creased, eyes wide, as though in reaction to their sudden appearance.

"Oh by the Fall," Nguyen swore.

Jumping at the outburst, Lukys swung on the king. He started to raise a finger to his lips, then paused, his heart growing suddenly still. His gaze was drawn to the orb in the king's fingers. Its light was dull—had vanished completely, as a matter of fact…

Suddenly Lukys's heart was racing and he swung back to see the soldiers lowering their spears. Shock showed in the eyes of Tasha, though it was quickly replaced with rage.

"So it's true," she snarled, pointing at them with her weapon. Gone was all semblance of reason. Hatred seethed instead in her eyes. "See, comrades, how the traitors show their true colours? Quickly, we must stop them before they reach the Sovereigns!"

Ice spread through Lukys's veins as Tasha started towards them, the soldiers at her back. A cold wind swept through the corridor as overhead a cloud passed before the sun. Holding his spear close, Lukys swore at the king.

"What the Fall happened?"

"Ran out of steam," the king panted as he tucked the sphere back into his tunic and gripped his spear in two hands. "Don't suppose you had a plan B."

Lukys cursed, but before he could respond, Sophia spoke into his mind.

I do.

For a second, he thought his partner meant she would face the soldiers alone. But her eyes were not on Tasha and their foes at all, but rather on the sky, on the walls of the corridor stretching above.

"What are you thinking..." he started.

He broke off as Sophia caught him by the front of his tunic. Before he could so much as cry out, Lukys found himself airborne, hurled upwards by the astonishing strength of the Tangata, up towards where the ceiling should have been.

Only there were no ceilings here, no stone roofs to trap them, and Lukys's cry cut off abruptly as he landed with a thump atop the corridor wall. Gasping, he rolled onto his side, struggling to regain his breath. Shouts and the clash of weapons came from below, then another body followed him.

The king of Gemaho landed with a little more poise than Lukys had managed, though to be fair Sophia had probably given him more warning. He lost his grip on his spear though, and the pair of them watched as the weapon rolled over the stone ledge on which they crouched and disappeared over the side.

Lukys's heart clenched as a scream drew his attention back to the corridor. Below, Tasha and her soldiers were swarming Sophia, pressing her back against the wall. Fear rose in Lukys's throat, and gathering up his own spear, he rose to go to Sophia's aid.

Again though, it proved unnecessary. In a blur of rage, she caught a soldier that stepped too close and hurled him backwards into his companions. Several went down, and in the ensuing chaos, she turned and leapt.

Watching her hurtle upwards, Lukys couldn't help but marvel at her ability. Sophia could have been one of the Gods themselves, the way she moved, the grace with which she landed atop the narrow strip of stone on which they perched. Her eyes flickered from Lukys to Nguyen, a wry smile twitching on her lips.

Shouts came from below and a moment later a spear flashed up from the corridor. But the narrow space and sheer angle of the walls made the throw difficult and the weapon came nowhere near any of them. Even so, Lukys moved away from the edge and turned to survey the landscape.

He swallowed as he found himself looking upon the citadel from an entirely new perspective. The open corridors looped away from the complex of the Sovereigns like the rings of a labyrinth. The covered roofs of sleeping chambers dotted the citadel, creating a unique design when looked at from above—a pattern that only the Sovereigns would ever see, seated on the thrones atop their high balcony.

Voices came from below, drawing Lukys's attention back to Tasha and her soldiers. They were already organising themselves, some attempting to lift others onto their shoulders to reach the top of the high walls, but the majority were retreating down the corridor with Tasha, no doubt to reinforce the guards at the amphitheatre.

Lukys's gaze swept across the loops of the labyrinth to where the palace of the Sovereigns rose above them. They were close, might even be able to reach the amphitheatre before Tasha's soldiers. The way ahead was clear, and after a quick glance at the others, he set off at a jog along the tops of the marble walls.

With the soldiers trapped by the labyrinthine passageways, they soon left their shouts behind. The palace of the Sovereigns rose above them as they neared the amphitheatre. Even from a distance, Lukys could see that the great balcony was empty. The Sovereigns must wait within the dark alcove of their palace. He prayed they would listen, that he could convince them, but…

He pushed his doubts aside and came to a stop atop the stands overlooking the amphitheatre. The ground below was silent, unnervingly so, and he flicked another glance at the balcony of the Sovereigns. Nothing moved there, not even a breath of wind to shift the curtains of their chambers.

A shiver ran down his spine as he looked at the others. "What is this?" There should have been dozens of guards here already, hundreds even…

Whispers rose from below and he swung around, spear clenched tight in case of an ambush. A moment later, Dale and Isabella appeared, followed by Travis and Keria and half a dozen of the others. He was pleased to see they had armed themselves and his heart soared. Throwing caution to the wind, he started down the stands into the amphitheatre. It might still be a trap, but at least they would be together.

Concern showed in the faces of the others as Lukys and Sophia joined them, followed belatedly by the king.

"Lukys," Dale said, his voice low. "What's going on? The corridors are empty."

Lukys shook his head. A few minutes later, the last of the Perfugian recruits joined them with their Tangatan partners. Lukys's heart pounded in his chest as he turned on the spot, scanning the rim of the amphitheatre, the empty corridors leading into the bowels of the citadel. Something wasn't right. The royal guard could not have simply disappeared. And where were the Sovereigns?

His thoughts trailed off as a distant pounding carried to his ears. For a moment it seemed to match his heartbeat, the racing of his anxious pulse. But it soon grew louder, more insistent, until Lukys knew it for what it was.

The beating of boots on stone.

Standing with his Perfugian comrades and the Tangata and the Gemaho king, Lukys watched as the soldiers raced into the amphitheatre. Tasha led them still, and at a gesture from her, the soldiers spread out, surrounding the Tangata and their human companions in a ring of steel.

Lukys clenched his fists about his spear as he looked from Tasha to the empty balcony. Something was happening here, something he did not understand.

The soft tread of footsteps came from above. Lukys swung on the balcony and watched as the Sovereigns emerged one after another from the darkness of their complex. Others of the royal guard filed out behind them, moving quickly to place themselves on the steps leading up to the balcony. Garbed in their purple gowns with silver crowns upon their young heads, the Sovereigns looked down into the amphitheatre.

"What is the meaning of this?" The voices of the Sovereigns rang with anger.

"Your Majesties!" Lukys cried, taking a step towards the balcony. *"We came to beg—"*

"My lieges, blood has been spilt in our halls," Tasha called as she joined her fellow guards on the steps to the balcony. She paused, and then went on: "I left Cleo to guard your…guests, but moments ago word reached me that they had attacked his escort, killing many before they escaped. I led reinforcements to your defence as fast as I could."

"So the Tangata reveal themselves." The words of the Sovereigns carried down to those gathered below. *"Do you think to take us unawares, traitors, to slay us while our backs were turned?"*

"It was your own people who attacked us, Sovereigns," Nguyen called back calmly, stepping up beside Lukys.

"More lies, traitor king?" the Sovereigns shook their heads in unison. *"It should not surprise us to find your involvement in this betrayal."*

"Please, Your Majesties," Lukys tried again. "The Tangata are not responsible for this bloodshed."

"No?" the pair growled. *"Do not seek to deceive us, Melder. Against the knowledge of our forebearers, we granted you our trust, invited the creatures into our citadel. But the Tangata have proven their true nature. They are hateful creatures, just as we have always known."*

"Sophia and her people want only peace," Lukys responded, shouting to be heard by the two above. "It was humanity who attacked them, who stormed their villages and killed their children." He gritted his teeth. "Now they come to warn us of a new threat, to seek asylum, and what do they find?" He shook his head. "Deceit, treachery, an oligarchy as obsessed with purity as…" He trailed off as a thought came to him, unable to finish the sentence.

Mouth still open, he stared up at the Sovereigns. Something had just occurred to him, an answer to the question that had plagued him since their arrival in New Nihelm. In his mind, he recalled Sophia's words, the story she had told him all those weeks ago in the dungeons of New Nihelm. And later, her claims that he must have Tangatan blood in his veins, to possess their ability to Speak.

"Your people will be enslaved by Flumeer unless you heed to my warning," Nguyen spoke into the silence. "Queen Amina will not stop until all the kingdoms of humanity fall under her control."

Blood pounded in Lukys's ears as he shook his head, trying to blot out the words, to focus on what the Sovereigns had said. Surely it could not be true. There must be some other explanation. And yet…the hairs stood up on the back of his neck as he recalled their words.

So the Old Ones have returned…

How had the Sovereigns known that name? Nguyen had not known it, not even Cara had ever mentioned that name to him. Only the Tangata knew, only Sophia and her people.

"Lies," he murmured, then louder: *"It's all lies!"*

33

THE HERO

"*How dare you—*"

"*Liars!*" Lukys bellowed over the Sovereigns' objections. He stood staring up at them, hardly able to believe the scale of the deception that had been played upon his people. "You've lied to us all from the start, down through the centuries, you and all your predecessors." He drew in a breath, hardly able to believe what he was about to say. "We're not human at all," he whispered. "We never were."

His words were met with silence, as all eyes in the amphitheatre stared at him in disbelief. Even his comrades cast him sharp looks, as though afraid he had lost his mind.

"What nonsense are you talking, lad?" Nguyen hissed.

"*Madness,*" the Sovereigns snarled.

"Truth," Lukys said.

He turned to Sophia. Standing beside him, her eyes were wide, their grey depths a mystery, though…he could sense a familiar fear from her, that the world was spiralling beyond her control, that if things went wrong, she could not protect him. Smiling, he kissed her gently, just in case…then turned again to the thrones above.

"The Tangata sent us away," he said softly, matching the stares of the Sovereigns now, refusing to back down, "our ancestors. It was never the human wars the first Perfugian settlers fled from. It was the Tangata, in the early days after the Fall. Sophia told me, there was a time they sent away those who were born without the grey eyes, some they sent on ship into the endless ocean, never to be seen again."

"*More madness,*" the Sovereigns hissed. "Why would Tangata be born without grey eyes?"

Lukys hesitated, glancing at Sophia. *Can I tell them?*

She paused only half a moment before meeting his eyes. *I trust you, Lukys.*

He nodded, swinging to address Tasha and her circle of soldiers. "The Tangata are a dying race," he said, his voice touched with sadness. "Their strength dwindles with each passing generation, as fewer and fewer are able to breed amongst themselves."

Frowns creased the faces of his fellow Perfugians as he spoke, though he could not decipher whether their reaction was one of anger or confusion. Their auras, the emotion swirling from each man and woman, had become a bubbling kaleidoscope of colours.

"To survive, the Tangata have been mixing their lines with humans. That is how my friends and I came to know our Tangatan partners, to know their humanity." He drew a breath as he prepared to reveal the truth of their own ancestry. "But it was not always so. Once, those who became too human, who lost the grey eyes of the Tangata, they were sent away. Our ancestors, the first of the Perfugians, were amongst those banished, sent away in a ship to keep the bloodlines of the Tangata pure."

This time, silence answered his proclamation. Atop their balcony, the Sovereigns stood unmoving.

"Sent away, but not forgotten," Lukys murmured. "Sophia and her people, they never knew what became of us, but they never forgot their lost cousins."

Still the Sovereigns said nothing. A stillness had fallen over the amphitheatre, as every soul present stared at Lukys.

"But not all of those the Tangata sent into exile were without power, were they?" he continued. "Some of our ancestors who arrived on these shores, they retained the abilities of the Tangata, their ability to Speak, to communicate mind to mind. Powers that would become valuable through the years, cherished, protected, preserved. The abilities of your Melders."

He could feel the anger behind the Sovereigns' eyes now, the rage, and he wondered why they had not ordered him killed. Clenching his fists, he spoke on.

"Sophia, Isabella, Keria and their brethren, they *are* our people. You *know* they have not come to harm us, that they would be our allies. Why do you hate them so?"

Footsteps came from above as the Sovereigns slowly descended from their balcony. Lukys held his breath, watching as they came. The expression on their faces was unreadable, their aura carefully kept blank. Tasha and the royal guards formed up to either side of them as they reached the floor of the amphitheatre, spears held at the ready.

"Because they rejected us," the Sovereigns finally replied, their voices low, tinged by sadness. *"Because they sent us away for being weak, impure."* Their eyes met Lukys's across the floor of the amphitheatre. *"Because they deserve our hatred."*

Inhaled breaths whispered through the yard as those gathered swung to stare now at the Sovereigns. Lukys felt a rush of exhilaration, that he'd guessed right, that he'd discovered the truth the Sovereigns had kept from his people down through the centuries— that the Perfugians had descended from Tangatan exiles. Though, one question still remained unanswered…

You were not forgotten, Sophia's voice carried through Lukys's mind. He glanced around as she joined him, entwining her fingers with his, sharing a secret look before she turned again to the Sovereigns. *The lost ones,* she continued, bowing her head. *We always wondered, always regretted…what became of you.*

"We were the Banished," the Sovereigns rasped. *"The hated ones, judged inferior and forced from our homes, our families."*

"Yet now you do the same to our own people," Lukys said, gesturing to his friends. "While the Tangata have grown, come to embrace all, no matter their differences."

"Lies!"

Truth! Sophia responded.

Lukys shivered as images flashed into his mind, of New Nihelm as he had known it—humans living alongside Tangata, children of both races playing in the streets, eyes of grey and blue and brown shining in shared joy. He found his own eyes burning and a tear streaked his cheek as he recalled his days there, what he had lost.

"No…" the Sovereigns tried to refute the images, but they spoke in a whisper now, more a plea that what Sophia showed them was false.

An Old One has returned, Sophia continued inexorably.

The images changed, and Lukys saw the Matriarch falling to the hands of Maya, witnessed Tangata racing through the streets of New Nihelm, becoming more animal than human as they hunted down the humans living alongside them. He saw again Adonis in their courtyard, using his powers against them, speaking of his desire to rule them…

The images cut off and Lukys swallowed, finding himself looking again at the Sovereigns.

Your people need you, Sophia said again. *We will fall to the darkness without your aid.*

The Sovereigns said nothing, only stared at Sophia, brows wrinkled. Then their eyes flickered to Lukys.

"Is what she says true, soldier?" they asked softly. *"Have the Tangata truly changed?"*

Lukys glanced at Sophia, hesitating, then straightened his shoulders and faced his Sovereigns. "All my life, I have struggled to find my place, as a student, as a recruit, to find a way to serve my people." He swallowed, giving Sophia's hand a squeeze. "In New Nihelm, I finally found it. With this woman."

There was a long pause as the Sovereigns regarded them, until Lukys thought for sure that he'd failed, that whatever ancient hatred the pair carried would triumph and he and his friends would be slain. But finally the Sovereigns bowed their heads, and when they spoke, there was acceptance in their words.

"We have clung to this anger for long enough," they said softly, *"but that is for past generations. Today, let the peoples of Perfugia and Tangata be reunited."*

Silence hung over the square at their proclamation. Slowly the soldiers began to lower their weapons, to look from the Sovereigns to one another, confusion in their eyes.

"About time," Nguyen grunted, "And let the Gemaho stand alongside you. We will face our common enemies together."

The Sovereigns frowned at the king's interjection, but before they could respond, movement came from beside them as Tasha stepped forward.

"*No,*" she said softly, and Lukys staggered as her words rebounded inside his skull, amplified by her own power.

The Sovereigns too flinched from her, swinging to face the guard. "*Soldier, it is not your place—*"

"This is *wrong!*" Tasha roared the word this time. She took a step towards the Sovereigns. "How can you call them allies, these monsters that have plagued our peoples for generations?"

The Sovereigns stood staring at her, their strange eyes unwavering. "*We are sorry for your confusion, Tasha,*" they said gently, "*but—*"

"*No!*"

Suddenly Tasha was leaping forward, silver spear raised. The Sovereigns staggered back in shock, but the woman was too slow to escape the blow. A sickening *thud* whispered through the amphitheatre as Tasha drove her spear through the Sovereign's stomach.

Lukys gaped, unable to believe what he was witnessing, that one of the royal guard should so betray their vows. Face twisted with rage, Tasha tore her blade free and the woman Sovereign slumped to the ground, hand clutched at the terrible wound. Blood bubbled between her fingers, as alongside her, the male of Sovereigns screamed and fell to his knees, as though her agony were his own.

"I thought you would realise your mistake," Tasha hissed as she advanced on him. "That you would see the truth when they slew Cleo. I thought it would be worth the sacrifice, driving him to attack, to force the beasts to reveal their nature. But now all here have seen the treachery of the Sovereigns."

"It was you," Lukys gasped, staring at the woman.

Tasha had been the unseen influence he'd sensed, the one that had driven Cleo to attack them. By doing so, she'd thought to turn the Sovereigns against them, to convince the rulers that they'd broken the peace.

Ignoring him, Tasha looked to the others of the royal guard. "Ever we have guarded the power of the Sovereigns, protected their secrets—but not to treason! Not to the destruction of everything we hold dear. They would sell our freedom to the beasts, would see us become slaves to the creatures of our nightmares." She shook her head. "I will not allow it."

Abruptly she reversed her spear, and drove it down through the back of the male Sovereign. Still crouched beside his partner, he tried to straighten, to fight her off, but the youth was no match for a warrior's strength. Dragging back her blade, she looked again to the royal guard.

"Join me, brothers, sisters, and we will drive these beasts forever from our land."

Lukys's heart thundered in his ears as one by one, the royal guard raised their spears. Hatred shone from their eyes, swirled from their minds, a seething, festering green, so overwhelming that Lukys sensed it could not be natural, that Tasha was using her own powers as a Melder to augment their emotions. And it was spreading, passing from the guards to the soldiers. Metal rattled as the ring of steel surrounding Lukys and his companions began to advance.

Cursing, Lukys gathered his own emotions within, drawing them close, allowing them to build, to swell within him. Then praying their enemies remained open to more than hatred, he released them, broadcasting to Tasha and the soldiers and all those gathered in the amphitheatre, just as he had that day on the beach in Calafe.

But this time, he filled his mind with joy, with the shining hope he had found with Sophia, the love they had forged, with the warmth of companionship, with the sheer elation of existence.

It swept from him to strike the minds of the soldiers, to crash upon the hatred Tasha had fed them. For a moment, the two forces warred, love and hate burning against one another, a swirling vortex of colour.

The roar of voices died as the soldiers broke off their charge. Staggering to a stop, they looked at one another, bewilderment and confusion showing in their eyes. These were common men and women, not Melders. They could not understand the forces warring for their souls, but for the moment at least, Lukys's action had broken Tasha's hold upon them.

Not so the royal guards, and Lukys realised with a chill that all those garbed in blue-armour possessed the abilities of a Melder. With Tasha in their lead, they came on, their hatred more powerful than his hope, nourished by the lies the Sovereigns had fed them for generations. The Sovereigns might have risen above their resentment in the end, but their legacy could not be so easily severed.

Realising a battle could not be avoided, Lukys looked to his friends. "Recruits," he said, meeting the eyes of Travis and Dale. "On me."

His friends snapped to obey, raising spears and moving into place alongside him. Sophia and the Tangata made to follow, but Lukys waved them back.

No, he said softly. *This is our kingdom, our fight.*

Sophia hesitated, but after a moment she nodded and he saw understanding in her eyes. In that moment, he wanted to hug her close, to breathe in deep her scent and forget everything around them. Instead, he turned to face the advancing guards.

"It is not the Tangata who committed treachery!" he called, adding his Voice to the words, so that all would hear him. "Sophia and her people kept the peace—it was *you* who sent armed men to attack us, *you* have raised your hand against our own Sovereigns. You dare to call the Tangata traitors?"

Around the great room, the soldiers he had stopped looked to one another, and he could see the depth of their confusion, as they were torn between loyalty to their Sovereigns—and hatred for the cursed Tangata. The royal guards had slowed at his words, hesitating, though he knew Tasha would not turn back. The hatred she had kept so carefully hidden would not allow it.

"I fight for Perfugia," he said softly. "For the lives of all our people."

"Ha!" Tasha spat, a sneer on her face. Spear in hand, she marched towards him, the royal guards formed up behind her. "Don't believe a word from this traitor's lips," she snared. "See the Tangata with him, it is his mate. He has formed a Gods-cursed bond with the enemy."

A sad smile touched Lukys's lips as Tasha came to a stop a few feet from him. "I have only one enemy—and she stands before me. There is no need for any more to die this day—let this end between us two."

Tasha seemed to consider the proposition. Then she shook her head and laughed, gesturing to the other Perfugian recruits. "You think these sorry excuses for soldiers can stand against us? The rejects of our society, sent to die so they did not taint us with their weakness?"

"Obviously some mistakes were made," Lukys shot back with a smile.

Tasha's smirk turned into a scowl and she hefted her spear. "Enough talking," she snapped.

"I couldn't agree more," Lukys hissed.

Their blades met with a flash of sparks and snarls.

34

THE FOLLOWER

The child hung limp in Adonis's arms. She no longer struggled, no longer even cried. She was so still she might have been dead already, if not for the occasional sniff of her nose, the quiet hiccup of her sorrow.

Guilt hung heavy on his soul as he watched the child's despair. They had used her, this innocent of the Anahera, had taken advantage of her helplessness to crush their enemy. Now the spirits of the Anahera hung as low as the child in his arms. All around the yard, his brethren were in celebration. Their inner voices thrummed in his mind, rich with the ecstasy of their great victory.

But standing amidst it all, Adonis remained untouched. He could not lift himself above the shame of what he'd done, the stain upon his soul. Was it worth it, this victory? The Anahera had remained neutral for generations, had removed themselves from the conflict between man and Tangata. Everything they had learned here only served to confirm that truth.

So what purpose then for this conflict, to enslave such glorious creatures beneath the rule of the Tangata? Beneath the Old One?

His heart twisted, and he found his gaze drawn to where Maya stood above the corpse of Farhan. The Anaheran leader had fought valiantly, had bloodied Adonis's mate with his strength. With wing and fist he had driven her back, until even Adonis had begun to fear for her.

But there was nothing valiant about the way Maya had defeated her foe. Falling to one knee, she had claimed defeat, had begged the Anahera to spare her. But when Farhan had approached…

Adonis shuddered as he looked at the blood mingling with the ice and mud. There was no river here to carry it away, no swirling current to hide the atrocity that had taken place this day. There was only the Anahera lying dead before his fellows, white wings twisted and broken, eyes staring unseeing at the stormy sky.

Movement came from nearby and Adonis frowned. Two Tangata stood guarding a figure on the ground. They withdrew as he crossed to them, revealing a human crouched in the mud. Adonis's frown deepened, but this was not Erika, the human that had escaped. Idly he handed the child to one of his brothers—let *his* hands be stained now—and stepped forward to stand over the human.

She stared up at him, eyes hard, jaw clenched, but she did not flinch away. Unusual amongst her kind—usually even the bravest of human warriors tried to flee when they found themselves face to face with a Tangata. Something was clutched in her hands, but as Adonis knelt, he saw it was only a shattered globe of glass.

Footsteps approached and Adonis rose as Maya drew alongside him, dipping his head in deference.

Shall I kill her? he asked softly.

Maya's laughter whispered in his mind. *So eager, my mate,* she replied, then paused, contemplating the creature at her feet. For her part, the human glared back at them, eyes revealing nothing of her fear. *No, our war against humanity will depend on more than simple violence. They are unpredictable creatures, cunning, dangerous. They will not succumb like the Anahera. Their conquest will require…subtlety.*

Adonis frowned. *You wish to interrogate her?*

Perhaps.

Maya stared at the creature for a while longer, then flicked a hand. One of her guards moved forward and took charge of the human. She stirred at his touch, but her struggles were rendered useless by the leg lying twisted beneath her. Adonis watched as she was carried away, the Tangata he had handed the child prisoner following. They would join the other Anaheran fledglings—taking the rest captive had been the first priority of the Tangata, after Farhan's surrender.

This one you may kill, my mate.

Maya's words drew Adonis's attention to the youth that knelt beside the body of the Anaheran leader. His son, Adonis presumed. His wings lay in the mud as he sobbed into his father's chest. The sight sent another jolt of guilt through Adonis and he looked again at Maya, wondering at her cruelty.

His sister was the one who fled with the human, he said absently.

Is that so?

Stones crunched as Maya approached the youth and crouched alongside him. He did not look up at her presence, but as Adonis stepped closer, he realised there were words to the boy's sobs.

"I'm sorry…Father…should have been…better."

Shaking his head, Adonis looked again at Maya. Surely the youth had suffered enough. Let him be returned to the other Anahera, to grieve alongside them for their fallen leader. Greater suffering would come soon enough, he did not doubt. The creatures were weak, lessened by their years of peace. They belonged to the Tangata now, and his brethren would take what they wished.

"Dear, dear, cry not for the departed."

Adonis shuddered as Maya spoke the coarse language of the humans, though he sensed her Voice beneath, prodding at the youth's consciousness, seeking weakness. They were untrained, these Anahera, vulnerable to her power. Little wonder they had surrendered so easily, with an Old One playing upon their minds, influencing their emotions.

The youth could not resist her manipulations. His head lifted at Maya's words. Anger glinted in his eyes as he saw who it was, but Maya spoke before it could catch light.

"There was no need for blood to be shed this day," Maya continued, her Voice whispering, winding its way into the young Anahera's mind. *"Your father surrendered in peace, with nobility. It was not he who broke our accord."*

Some of the anger went from the youth at Maya's words and he frowned. "What…are you saying?"

Maya leaned close, her fingers reaching out to stroke the young Anahera's cheek, to brush the hair from his face.

"It was the humans who brought this upon your people," she whispered. *"Upon your father. It was they who tainted your sweet sister, who lured her to the darkness."*

"I…" the Anahera swallowed. "Cara…" He looked around, eyes lost, trapped. "She's…gone."

"Yes…*gone beyond my reach,"* Maya said, *"but not from yours. Humanity has claimed her soul, but you can free her, my child."*

He looked up at that, and for just a moment, Adonis thought he would refuse, that the youth would find the true cause for his hatred. Then the last of the fury faded from his eyes, leaving only a dull blankness, a final acceptance of his new master.

"Please," he whispered. *"Tell me how to free my sister."*

❧ 35 ❧

THE HERO

Lukys ducked as a blade flashed for his face, then thrust out with his spear, forcing Tasha to leap back. Immediately he retreated and sensed movement from behind. He grinned as Dale and Travis stepped up alongside him. Tasha had refused his challenge and sought to kill them all. No point in it being a one on one competition.

A frown appeared on Tasha's face as she found herself confronted by a line of spears. Though they wore no armour and only a few had scavenged shields, Lukys had to admit the Perfugian recruits appeared a ferocious sight standing together. Just as Romaine had trained them. His heart swelled and he thought the old Calafe warrior would have been proud to see them now.

Smiling, he faced Tasha once more. She had expected the royal guard to sweep them away with ease. They might have the advantage of armour, but he could see the hesitation in her eyes now, the sudden doubt. Time to press the advantage.

"Perfugians, forward!" Lukys cried, and gripping his spear with two hands, he stepped forward, trusting his comrades to join him.

Spear tips shone as the line advanced and Tasha leapt back, rejoining her fellow guards. Around the courtyard, the common soldiers stood fixed in place, eyes wide as they struggled to overcome the warring emotions the Melders had cast upon them.

That suited Lukys. The Perfugian recruits were already

outnumbered without the soldiers aligning against them. It would take all their skill and determination just to turn the guards back, though…

…perhaps if he could strike Tasha down, the rest might be reasoned with.

He jerked as a sudden roar crashed over the amphitheatre. Then the guards were charging.

Lukys had faced a Tangatan charge before, had felt their voices thrumming in his mind as they sung their chants of death in the face of battle. But this was something different. These men and women, they had no reservations about using their power, and now Lukys felt his legs tremble as fear swept like a gale through his soul. Around him, the recruits wavered, threatening to succumb to the emotion cast by their enemies.

Gritting his teeth, Lukys did his best to lift them, to nurture their courage, but he could feel the cracks spreading through his own strength. He was but a drop in a lake before the collective strength of the guards. Twenty Melders stood with Tasha—too many. In that moment he knew they would break, that the guards would sweep them away, crush them all beneath their boots…

Warmth struck him like a wave, sweeping through his body, his soul. It carried on through those around him, filling them with hope and love, casting off the fear. Suddenly the men and women of his regiment were straightening, their courage restored. Blinking, Lukys glanced back through the ranks of his companions and found the Tangata guarding their rear.

In this, at least, we can help, Sophia said, though he could not see her through the press of his fellows.

A smile came to him as he realised that she and her people were protecting them from the guards' mental assault.

Thank you, he whispered, and faced the enemy once more.

Tasha and her guards faltered as their powers failed, but that hesitation lasted only a moment. Then the battle was upon them, and Lukys found himself fighting again for his life. Despite their heavy armour, the guards moved with deceptive speed. As a spear almost took him in the throat, Lukys found himself wondering if the guards had retained more than just the powers of a Melder, for it seemed they moved almost as fast at the Tangata themselves.

"Friends, on me!" he called, fighting to keep his recruits in a line.

Dale and Travis formed up to either side of him, and together they pressed forward into the teeth of the assault. The other recruits would not give an inch so long as they three stood. The guards seemed to realise it too, for those nearest turned towards them.

Lukys thrust out a spear as a man came at him, then cursed as the guard evaded the blow. Travis intercepted a riposte that would have caught Lukys in the groin, then attacked himself. This time, his spear found flesh and the guard fell. Two more came at them. Teeth bared, Lukys joined with Travis and lurched to the attack. He felt a satisfying *crunch* as his spear slipped past his foe's shield and found a weak point in his armour.

They weren't so fortunate with the second. Rushing forward, he evaded their spears and slammed his shield against them. The weight of his blow sent Lukys onto the back foot, and for a moment Travis was left exposed.

Dale was there though, and together they drove the guard back, until finally he fell, dropping without a sound. Lukys glimpsed a flash of white surprise in the aura of the guard standing beyond. The man hadn't even lowered the visor of his helmet. Obviously these guards had not expected such resistance from the rejects of the Perfugian academy.

Lukys offered a grim smile as he re-joined the line and leapt to the attack. He was happy to be underestimated. The royal guard would pay dearly for their complacency. More of his recruits had recovered shields now and one tossed his to Lukys. As the next guard advanced, he found himself presented with three united shields and hesitated.

All along the line, the royal guards faced a similar struggle against Lukys's recruits. The enemy might have been better armed and trained, but they fought as individuals. They weren't used to facing soldiers trained for battle, working together as a unit, protecting one another's backs. Just as the Tangata had once struggled to break the formations Romaine had drilled into the recruits, now the royal guard found themselves under pressure.

They were losing.

Another guard went down before Lukys, and suddenly he found

himself facing Tasha across the line of their spears. Anger touched him. This bloodshed, all the death, it was all because of her.

Gritting his teeth, Lukys gathered himself as she came for him. Tasha moved faster than the others, her silver spear flashing at his face so fast he barely had time to raise his shield. The *thud* as it struck wood left his arm numb and instinctively he thrust out with his own blade, seeking to slow a second attack.

A *shriek* followed as the point caught steel, forcing Tasha to retreat. Lowering his shield, he studied her, seeking an opening. Her feet moved like water beneath her, reminding him of the Tangata, of their poise and balance. His fists tightened around the shaft of his spear as he cursed the hatred that had so blinded her. He knew it well, recognised its glow—it was the same hatred that had driven him to attack the Tangata on the shore, that had made him so distrustful of Sophia, despite everything she had done for him.

He wished he could make Tasha see the truth, the similarities she and her guards shared with the Tangata, rather than the differences.

Instead, there would be only death.

Tasha came for him again and he met her with shield and spear. All else fell away as they moved through the dance of death. Lukys sensed his companions retreating to grant them space. The sounds of battle receded, until it seemed they fought alone in the amphitheatre, as though the fate of the kingdom fell upon their shoulders.

She was a better fighter than anyone Lukys had faced before. Lacking the speed and power of the Tangata, she still moved with a subtly that hinted at the blood the Perfugians carried in their veins. Adding to it were the skills of years spent training, of an entire life dedicated to but one task—protecting the Sovereigns.

Against her skill, Lukys brought raw ferocity, a blunt talent learnt in desperation, skills drilled into him by the last warrior of the Calafe. Romaine might not have prepared him to fight someone so skilled, but he had trained Lukys to face the Tangata, to stand against enemies he had no right to resist.

And so he stood against Tasha and defied her with every inch of his soul.

He could sense the hatred radiating from her, the madness that had driven her to such extremes, to break her vows. Lukys reeled from it, shrunk from its fury, struggling to fortify himself against it. Yet still it pressed against him, her power as a Melder crashing against his thoughts, drawing his own anger to the fore, his own hatred.

Teeth clenched, he struggled to fight back with his mind, reaching out for the thrumming of her power. The emerald of her hatred washed over him, its awful power, seeking a home in his own heart, to drive him to corruption, to deal death. Something inside him responded to that power, the piece of him that had loathed the Tangata since childhood, that had been nurtured by the teachings of the Sovereigns.

But he could feel Sophia's presence on the edges of his mind. With her love, Tasha's hatred could find no purchase within him, no soil in which to take root.

Instead, he gathered it up, the twisting threads of her hatred, working by instinct and desperation, rolling it into a ball of darkest emerald, into a focal of hatred.

Then he cast it back at Tasha, hurled it back at its owner.

A scream tore from Tasha's lips as it struck and she lurched back from him, eyes bulging. An awful snarl hissed from her throat, a cry of such loathing that it sent tremors down to the souls of all who heard it.

Still shrieking, the woman hurled herself forward, driven mad by her own hatred, all caution cast aside.

Lukys's spear crunched through steel as it struck her throat.

Then Tasha was staggering back, eyes wide, blood gushing from her wound, staining the blue of her armour.

Lukys froze, his eyes drawn to Tasha's face. Shock showed in her eyes as the spear tumbled from her fingers, as her hands clutched weakly at the wound, as the strength went from her legs and she slumped to the ground, armour clattering against the stone.

Standing over her, Lukys shivered as she met his eyes, as the glow of her hatred gave way to fear, to the terror of failure. Whatever her deeds, Tasha had thought she stood on the side of right. Indoctrinated by a society that had preached of the Tangata's evil for generations, she had seen no other choice but to stand against the monsters, though it meant betraying the very leaders she had sworn to protect.

Then the light was gone and Tasha was tumbling backwards, lying still upon the stones, blood spreading out beneath her.

Lukys's vision blurred as he shook his head, tears burning in his eyes. He wanted to scream at her, to tell her she was a fool for choosing hatred, for going against her own Sovereigns, her own people. But it was too late now. If only…

The thought trailed away as he realised that silence had fallen over the amphitheatre. He blinked, looking from Tasha's body to the royal guards. At her death, they had staggered back from the Perfugian recruits, weapons slipping from their hands. Shock and horror showed on their faces as they looked to him, and he saw the regret there, the pain.

They too had been caught up in Tasha's hatred, in their own loathing for the creatures of their nightmares. Now that their leader had fallen, her influence had vanished, leaving them to stare in horror at what she'd done.

At the bodies of the Sovereigns, lying still on the amphitheatre floor.

❧ 36 ❧

THE EMISSARY

E rika was flying. Soaring. The mountains flashed by below, little more than a blur to her narrowing vision, the darkness pressing in. But still…she flew.

No…Cara flew. Somehow, the young Anahera held her, clutched Erika tight as her wings struck the air, beating frantically, straining to keep them aloft. Erika frowned as she looked at the Goddess's face. She was crying…no, screaming, the sounds ripped away by the mountain winds. Veins bulged in her neck and Erika realised her friend was at the limits of her strength, barely keeping them aloft.

Then her vision spun, another wave of pain radiating from her chest, from her shattered wrist. For a while she knew only a tide of red, drifting, floating on an ocean, in warm waters, swept away, carrying her to someplace else, to peace…

Thud.

A scream tore from Erika's lips as she found herself suddenly back in the mountains. Before she could recall how she had come to be there, she was falling, tumbling towards distant rocks. Arms clutched tight around her waist, straining against the buffeting winds. Something struck her arm and agony laced her mind—

Thump.

They slammed into the mountainside in an eruption of gravel, so hard Erika's teeth rattled in her jaw. A cry tore from her lips as stones ripped at her clothing, her flesh, as she tumbled down the jagged slope. Torn from Cara's arms, she rolled over and over, the world a flashing of white and red and black and blue…

…the warm ocean swallowed her again, and for a second Erika felt blessed peace, sinking into the depths of unconsciousness, away from the pain…

…a scream dragged her back. She fought against the call, but there was something in that scream, a need, a desperation, and suddenly the agony returned, forcing her eyes to open again upon the world.

Erika found herself lying on an outcropping of rock in the bottom of a valley. How far they had flown from the City of the Gods, she couldn't say, only that she no longer recognised the peaks rising high above. A stream raced past below, crashing over jumbled boulders lining the valley floor.

A flicker of movement drew Erika's gaze back to the gravel slope down which she had tumbled. A few yards above, Cara crouched, one wing twisted behind her at a horrible angle, face lifted to the sky as she screamed her agony. And above…

…above stood Hugo, shoulders heaving, wings stretched wide as he stared at his sister. His lips parted as he raised a fist. Below, Cara remained on her hands and knees, her screams echoing from the cliffs, only to turn to soft sobbing. Erika shuddered at the pain in her friend's voice. She tried not to look at the broken wing, at the terrible bend to the bone beneath her auburn feathers, at the blood staining the gravel.

Then suddenly the Goddess fell silent. Lifting her head, she looked at Hugo.

"Brother," she rasped, her voice breaking, "why?"

A spasm passed across Hugo's face as he looked down at her, but Erika could see his eyes now, glinting in the flickering light, the grey sheen. There was a madness to him as he stood over Cara, a rage.

"I must avenge my father," he growled. "I must free you from their evil."

"Wha—"

Cara broke off as Hugo surged forward, his boot rising to catch her in the chest. A cry tore from Erika as her friend tumbled down the slope to crash into the rocks alongside her. Desperately she tried to rise, to go to Cara's aid, but another wave of pain broke upon her and suddenly her vision was spinning and the cold rocks were pressing against her face.

"Brother...please, stop."

Sobs came from Cara as she tried to push herself back up, but the fall had only done more damage to her injured wing. The pain seemed to rob her of strength and she slumped, gasping, against the rocky outcrop, watching as Hugo moved towards her.

"I will give you peace, sweet sister," he was whispering as he reached for Cara. He lifted her easily, drawing her up by the shirt, softly, almost tenderly. "I will free you."

The sharp *crack* as he slammed her back to the ground was anything but tender. Erika screamed as Cara struck the rocks, her broken wing flailing useless, the arm she raised to break her fall crumpling beneath her weight. This time there was no scream, only a low groaning as she lay upon the stone, the soft sobbing of her pleas.

"Brother." Erika could barely hear the words from where she lay. Somehow, impossibly, Cara pushed herself to her knees. Agony twisted her face and her body was a mess of torn flesh and broken limbs, but still she faced her brother, amber eyes aglow. "Please, you don't have to do this," she whispered.

A flicker passed through Hugo's face, but he only shook his head. "I do."

Before him, Cara bowed her head, and Erika heard the soft cry of inhaled breath, the depth of her friend's sorrow.

Then abruptly the Goddess surged forward, her bent legs propelling her from the rock. She slammed into her larger brother, and on the uneven slope, Hugo lost his balance and fell. Cara was on him in a second, hammering her fist into his face, her incredible strength slamming him backwards into the mountain.

But Hugo did not have a broken wing. He recovered quickly from the shock of her attack and surged back, his greater bulk threatening to hurl her from him. Instead, Cara clung on, teeth bared, eyes burning, and the two tumbled across the rocky ledge— then disappeared over the side.

Erika cried out and crawled across to where the two had vanished. The drop was only a dozen feet. Below they had landed beside the stream, their battle carrying them into the waters themselves.

Still, neither would surrender, and Cara screamed again, her broken wing trapped beneath the currents. Her face went so pale Erika feared she would collapse, but somehow the Goddess dug beyond her limits and attacked her brother again. The slick stones shifted beneath them and suddenly Cara was straddling the younger Anahera, grasping him by the throat, driving him beneath the waters.

A fist slammed into Cara's face with desperate force, almost dislodging her. Blood ran from her mouth but she clung on, a shriek sounding from the depths of her soul as she drove her brother back beneath the surface. Her eyes were wild, swirling from orange to grey, tears streaming down her face.

"Erika!"

It was a moment before Erika recognised her name amidst Cara's cries. Shaking off her shock and pain, she stumbled to her feet. The movement sent her vision swirling again, but gritting her teeth, she swung from the outcrop and staggered down the shore towards her friend.

"Help. Me!"

Cara's screams took on a fresh desperation as Hugo surged back, mouth wide as he sucked in fresh air. His wings churned the waters, but weighed down by the currents, he could not bring them to bear, could not quite free himself before his sister drove him back into the icy cold.

Help her? What could Erika possibly do to help against one of the Anahera? Her gaze was drawn to the gauntlet, but she could not even make a fist, did not have the energy to fuel it, even if she could. Her legs felt weak and her vision was blurring.

Another cry came from Cara. Tears streamed down the Goddess's face and blood ran freely from her nose, her mouth. Still she held on, screaming, sobbing, though Hugo might be stronger, though she was injured, though she fought against her own brother. She did what she had to, not because of duty or family or for the greater good.

But to survive.

The blood was pounding Erika's ears as she fell to her knees beside the stream. Rocks lined the shoreline and she clutched at one she could lift. It was only the size of a small melon, jagged and broken, as though it had only recently cracked off the cliff face above.

Fighting back her own agony, Erika stumbled into the water, the rock held awkwardly in both hands. It hardly seemed enough, but she clutched it all the same. It was all she had.

Cara's face was a bloodied, purpled mess now, her wing twisted so badly Erika feared it might never heal, that after all they had been through, her friend might still lose her ability to fly. It hardly mattered now, not with Hugo here, trying to kill them.

Erika stumbled into the swirling waters, her boots slipping on unseen rocks. Then she was there, standing above her friend, above Hugo. Images flashed in her mind, of the young Anahera showing her to Cara's room, of him standing up to his father, speaking on Cara's behalf. Suddenly she found herself hesitating. Surely this could not be happening, surely they could convince him…

A roar sounded as Hugo's head broke above the surface again, his eyes shining the dark grey of madness, teeth bared. Cara slipped, almost lost her grip as his wings thrashed. She cried out, her eyes meeting Erika's. In that moment, she saw her friend's desperation, her grief, her pain. And she knew there was no other way. They were the only ones who knew what came, the darkness that now lurked in the Mountains of the Gods, the death that marched on mankind.

Hands trembling, Erika lifted the rock and brought it down on Hugo's skull with all her strength. There was a soft *crunch*, a gasp and a groan, before his head slipped back beneath the waters. His fingers clutched at Cara still, but the strength had suddenly gone from his struggles.

The end wasn't long in coming, after that. Sobs rasped from Cara's lips as she held him down, as she watched her brother die, until finally she released him. Swaying in the icy waters, she slumped against Cara. Together, the two stumbled from the stream and collapsed against the jagged stones of the shore. Neither looked back, could not bear to watch as the water claimed its prize.

Instead, Erika found herself staring up at the open sky, at the endless blue above. She'd done it. The Anahera was dead.

They were free.

This time when the darkness rose to claim her, Erika embraced it with open arms.

Silence had descended on the courtyard. Lukys could sense the eyes upon him, of his friends, of the Tangata, of the gathered soldiers and those Royal Guard who still lived. Even King Nguyen was watching him. They seemed to all be waiting for something.

He swallowed, still looking down at Tasha, hardly able to believe what he'd done. This was beyond anything he'd thought himself capable of, an act that seemed almost blasphemous. He'd used Tasha's own hatred against her, used his mind to practically drive her onto the spearpoint. He could see now why the Matriarch of the Tangata had forbidden her people from such abuse of their power.

A shiver ran down his spine and shaking his head, Lukys looked to the soldiers that still ringed the amphitheatre.

"Throw down your weapons," he said.

It was softly spoken, without hint of threat, but the rattle of steel blades striking stone was deafening. When silence returned, he met the gaze of every man and woman present, and nodded. Exhaustion hung heavy on his shoulders and he wanted nothing more than to lie down and rest, but there was still work to be done.

Lukys. He turned and found Sophia standing nearby.

He reached for her, then hesitated, aware that what he'd just done was forbidden by her people, considered a great crime. But she came to him anyway, and he let out a sigh of relief, that at least the two of them were okay, that he had not thrown everything away in a moment of rage. He closed his eyes as they embraced, savouring her warmth, her support.

She's still alive, Sophia said into his mind when they broke apart, so that only Lukys could hear.

He nodded. He had sensed the flicker of the Sovereign's aura, though she had tried to hide it from Tasha. Drawing in a breath, he took Sophia's hand in his and moved to where the Sovereigns had fallen.

They found the female Sovereign lying beside her brother, one arm outstretched to rest on his shoulder, as though she could not bear to be separated from him, even in death. For a second, Lukys sensed nothing from her, and he wondered if they were too late. But she shifted at the sound of their footsteps, her eyes flickering open.

And so ends our reign, her voice whispered into their minds. It sounded wrong, without the echo of her brother's.

Lukys glanced at her wound and saw it was true. There was nothing to be done for such an injury. Only the fact Tasha had driven her spear through the Sovereign's stomach, rather than her heart, had saved her from an immediate death. Though perhaps that would have been kinder…

How? Sophia whispered, crouching beside the Sovereign. *How… can you remember our people, our crime against you?*

The hint of a smile tugged at the Sovereign's cheek. *Without the…strength of the Tangata, we learnt to cherish the abilities of our Melders, in those early days on this wondrous island.* Even in Lukys's mind, he could hear her pain. *Eventually, two of us were chosen to lead…for eternity.*

Sophia shook her head, not understanding.

It is good…that we could better…those who rejected us…in at least one talent.

You would have been welcomed by my Matriarch with open arms, Sophia whispered, and Lukys saw that tears beaded her grey eyes.

I think…we would have liked to meet her, the Sovereign breathed. *Alas…our hatred was the end of us. We should have…forgiven long ago. Should have…led our people forward…rather than looking back.*

Silence fell and the Sovereign grew still. For a moment, Lukys thought she had passed, but then her eyes flickered and her Voice came again.

This Old One… she whispered. *You will need…aid.*

Lukys nodded. *The Gods—*

No, the Sovereign cut him off. *We allowed their legends, but…the Anahera have already failed humanity once. They cannot defeat the Old Ones alone.*

Then how? Sophia pressed. *I have felt her, Sovereign. She is too powerful. I would have slain my…love, had she commanded me to.* Lukys could hear her voice breaking at the admission.

He swallowed, wanting to say something, but the Sovereign was speaking again. *I do not know, children.* It was strange, being addressed as such by someone in the body of a child, but then those ancient eyes…

But…perhaps we have been wrong. Perhaps we have followed the wrong path, these past centuries. I do not know. Maybe you can do more with the Sovereign gift than we ever could.

Sophia had been watching her with curious eyes, silent, but now she spoke again. *Who are you?*

The smile returned to the dying Sovereign's lips. *Someone who witnessed rule of the Old One's…first-hand.*

What—

Lukys didn't get to finish the question. Even as he touched the mind of the Sovereign, something surged from her, a burst of Voice, as though she'd screamed into his very consciousness. He gasped, trying to withdraw, while beside him Sophia stiffened. But it was too late.

In a flash of white, images burst through Lukys's mind. Voices cried out within him as he saw an inferno fill the horizon, as he saw darkness and light and cities turned to dust. Gods fell from the skies and creatures that looked like the Tangata howled, as hours and days and decades swept past, as the world changed, castles rising where cities had once stood, as the Tangata crept from their holes and civilisations were reborn.

The Sovereign cried out as the images finally faded, blinking against the brilliance of the light above. His vision swirled, then crystallised, and he found himself staring down at a pair of bodies on the marble floor. The Sovereign frowned. One was *his* body, was it not? Images, memories, collided in his mind, and something else stirred. He sensed something…had gone wrong.

Another consciousness slivered through his mind and another

memory imposed itself on him, of the Sovereign looking up at…
himself? Agony tore at his head like a dagger and Lukys cried out.
A hundred other voices cried with him in the silence of his own
mind, the voices of the Sovereigns, every one of them from today
stretching back to the first settlers of Perfugia—and further even
than that. Their minds passed down from one pair of Sovereigns to
another, until today, until Lukys.

"Lukys?" a voice came from nearby.

He looked around, finding an unfamiliar…no, a *familiar* face
standing over him.

"Travis?" he croaked, looking up at the man. A barrage of
images assaulted his senses, flashes of the man who stood
before him.

"You okay, Lukys?" Travis asked, reaching out to grip his
shoulder.

Lukys shook his head, trying to sift through the memories. So
many memories. A hundred lifetimes of knowledge. He felt himself
getting lost in them again, felt those other consciousnesses pushing…struggling for supremacy.

No…

He pushed back, and reluctantly they sank. Lukys sucked in a
relieved breath, struggling to retain his sanity—and his breakfast.
Stars were still dancing across his eyes but he nodded to his friend.

"I'm…okay, I think," he croaked. "What about Sophia?"

Travis glanced to his side, and Lukys followed his gaze, finding
Sophia hunched in two. But as he watched, she straightened,
turning to meet his gaze. For a second, he saw the ancient gaze of
the Sovereigns and felt a pang of fear, that somehow they had taken
her. Then the gleam faded and when she blinked again, it was
Sophia who looked back at him.

"Are you okay?" he asked, too exhausted to use his mind.

Sophia managed a smile. "I'm okay, Lukys."

EPILOGUE
THE EMISSARY

With Cara's broken wing and Erika's injuries, it took them almost two weeks to reach the River Illmoor, to finally gain the safety of the Gemaho plains. In all that time, Erika expected wings to darken the sky at any moment, for one of the Anahera to come diving down upon them, for the Tangata to emerge from the shadows.

But none had followed after Hugo.

A tremor shook Erika every time she thought of the dead Anahera, of his battered corpse in the river, Cara's soft sobs as she mourned him. His blood still stained their clothing—no matter how many times they tried to wash in the freezing mountain streams, the red refused to fade.

Cara herself said little during the long journey, though there was no missing the pain, the agony in her eyes. They had used strips of their clothing to bind her broken wing flat to her back, but even after two weeks, the Goddess had not attempted to use them. Erika hadn't asked how long it would take to heal, or whether it would heal at all.

And so they had travelled in silence, haunted by the darkness they had escaped, by the failure of their desperate mission. Banished by her people, her father and brother lost, Cara had no one left, was as alone as Erika now.

Erika could hardly bear the thought of standing before King

Nguyen and revealing her failure, that the Anahera now stood allied with the Tangata, that Maisie had been left behind, had surely been slaughtered by the Old One in vengeance for their escape.

The thoughts made her cold. No longer could she imagine hope for the future. Once, Erika had thought she would return to civilisation and find her lost people, gather the refugees of Calafe and lead an uprising against the queen that had betrayed them. But what hope could she offer them now? Their Gods were a deception, cowardly creatures that would rather submit to terror than fight for their freedom.

No, only Nguyen could help them now. He was a true king, would know what to do, how to deliver humanity the victory it so desperately needed. The man was their only hope, their only chance for sanctuary now.

But when they finally stood on the shore of the Illmoor, they found the plains of the Gemaho aflame. As far as the eye could see, the fields were burning. Crops and pasture and livestock, all of it had been consumed by flames. Where before the horizon had seemed to stretch to infinity, now a sickly smoke stained the sky grey, and ash turned the land black.

"What happened here?" Erika whispered as they came to a stop before swirling currents.

She glanced at her friend, but the young Anahera said nothing, only stood with her shoulders hung low, eyes staring into the distance, as though they did not see the destruction. Erika suppressed a sigh. She needed her friend, needed her strength, her determination, but she could not find the words to lift the Goddess from despair. Maybe when they were safe, when she could finally rest, they could finally process all that had befallen them in the mountains.

But for now, rest would have to wait.

Together, they turned and started downriver. It would be a long march north to Solaris, the capital of Gemaho, but there were no other options. Whatever the source of the fires, they would find answers in Solaris. To the south was only fresh wilderness, only Badlands and the Dead Sea. But in Solaris was the king's court, the last bastion of freedom in a terrible world. There they could plan how they would defend their world, how they might stand against the Anahera and Tangata and the Old One that now led them.

Cara must have taken them north in their flight from the City of the Gods, for it was only another three days before they finally came into sight of Solaris. Built on a fork in the great river, it was said to be one of the great cities of the age, more wondrous even than Mildeth.

Looking across waters turned dark by ash, Erika found destruction in place of wonder. After so long on the road, on the run, she could no longer summon the will to be surprised. There had been signs on their march north, burnt villages and the river empty of ships. In her heart, Erika had known what they must find here, though she had clung to the hope she would be proven wrong, that the great Solaris might still stand.

It had not.

The Kingdom of Gemaho had fallen.

The lands of humanity belonged to Queen Amina.

Slumping to the soot-stained grass, Erika sat beside Cara and watched in silence as the great ship floating on the river swung towards them. Men and women scurried backwards and forwards across the deck, rushing to obey the orders of their captain, and soon oars beat the waters, sending them racing towards where Erika knelt.

There was no point trying to run. Erika was tired of running, of fighting, of *trying*. All that remained to her now was despair.

Swinging alongside the shore, a gangplank rose from the galley and fell to the shore with a *thud*. Soldiers garbed in steel and wearing the red of Flumeer rushed to surround them, swords in hand. Erika made no move to rise as the weapons were pointed at her throat, but as a fresh set of footsteps came from the gangplank, she managed to push herself to her feet. Reaching out, she took Cara's hand.

They watched together as the Queen of Flumeer walked down the gangplank, royal armour shining in the noonday sun. A sword was strapped to her side, but she did not draw it. What need did *she* have for a sword, with the might of her soldiers on hand, with an entire kingdom brought to its knees before her?

With the glow of the gauntlet she wore on her fist.

The soldiers parted as she approached, but her eyes never left

Erika. Despite her exhaustion, despite the despair that had robbed her of even the will to flee, Erika shuddered at what she saw in those eyes. There was a hatred there, a raw anger kept carefully in check. She drew to a stop before Erika.

"So, my dear Archivist returns to her maker." Amina smiled.

Then the queen raised her gauntlet.

Light flashed, then a sharp, shrieking noise sounded in Erika's ears, so high pitched as to be almost inaudible. And yet…a scream tore from her lips as pain split her skull, as though someone had taken a nail and driven it through each eardrum. Her mouth fell open and she tried to scream, but no sound came out, even as her legs went from under her. Mind aflame, she arced against the ground. Even as she sucked in the slightest breath, Erika knew she did not suffer alone, that Cara lay alongside her, engulfed in the same agony, the same doom.

Then the pain intensified, the nails turning to her eyes, her brain, her very being. White flashed and the world fell away.

Until all that was left to Erika was pain.

AARON HODGES

DREAMS OF FURY

DESCENDANTS OF THE FALL

PROLOGUE
THE SOVEREIGN

Standing atop the marble balcony, Lukys looked down into the amphitheatre of the Sovereigns, down at the thousands that had gathered below. The citizens of the capital were dressed in every colour of the rainbow, though Perfugian blue was most prominent. In one corner, a group of yellow cloaks marked where King Nguyen and his Gemaho waited.

A lump lodged in Lukys's throat as he felt the weight of all those eyes upon him, the hush of expectation. He had not expected so many to accept the invitation, not with the events that had led to this day, and the woman who stood beside him. And yet…come they had, from all across Perfugia, come to witness the inauguration of their new Sovereigns.

Lukys struggled to swallow the lump in his throat, and his stomach tied itself into a knot instead. A buzzing filled his inner mind, the whisper of a thousand voices, generations of lives lived, the knowledge of every Sovereign that had come before him, all screaming to make themselves heard. He clenched a fist and fought to press them down, to ignore his own inadequacy compared to those that had come before him…

All Sovereigns before this day had been chosen at birth for their strength as Melders—humans who had inherited the mental abilities of their inhuman ancestors. The chosen were trained to rule, prepared for their elevation to Sovereign, when the minds of all who had come before would be passed to them.

But for Lukys and the woman beside him, the process had been almost accidental, a desperate act committed by their dying predecessors. Now he felt exposed, a fraud before the gaze of his people. Surely they would see the truth beneath the purple robes, that he was nothing and nobody, a failed recruit who had been destined to die on the frontlines fighting the Tangata.

At that thought, he reached out an unconscious hand for the woman at his side. Sophia. Warmth touched him as she entwined her fingers through his and he felt the reassurance of her consciousness against his own. Smiling, he exchanged a glance with his lover, the woman with whom he had chosen to share his life.

The grey eyes of the inhuman Tangata looked back at him, though…he no longer saw the Tangata as inhuman. More…distant relatives, long lost to human history.

A glint appeared in Sophia's eyes as she smiled, and in that look Lukys saw a flicker of the knowledge she possessed—that they both now possessed. Memories, stretching back to before the founding of Perfugia, before even the creation of the kingdoms of the mainland. So many lives, they could each spend a lifetime sifting through the memories, and still not know them all.

So far, those memories had revealed much, and nothing. They were so convoluted, flickering of images without rhythm or reason. Some things they had managed to piece together—confirmation that Lukys's theory had been correct, that the first founders of Perfugia had been Tangata, not human.

In a way, those memories meant Sophia deserved to stand as she did, more so than Lukys himself. After all, the abilities of the Melders came from her people. But there was no convincing her of that. Even now, he could sense her fear, a doubt that matched his own reservations. The title of Sovereign was sacred amongst his people, a line of secretive, powerful rulers that had protected Perfugia since its founding.

But of course, that secrecy had only been a means to an end, a way to conceal Perfugia's true ancestry from its people. It had also protected those few amongst Perfugian society fortunate enough to possess the abilities of the Tangata—Melders like Lukys, though his ability had not been discovered until his first encounter with the Tangata on the frontline.

But that was all in the past, and forcing the memories aside, he leaned in close to Sophia. "Are you okay?" he said out loud.

A grimace crossed Sophia's face but she nodded. *Yes,* she whispered into his mind. Then turning to face the crowd, she opened her lips. "I will…be okay."

The words came out with the hesitation of someone unused to speaking. Indeed, even now the hairs on the back of Lukys's neck tingled to hear his partner's voice. No Tangata in living memory had possessed the ability to speak aloud, something that had no doubt contributed to their conflict with humanity. Now though, with the knowledge passed onto her by their predecessors, Sophia had rediscovered the ability to speak.

Lukys smiled back at her, savouring the musical accent to her voice, strangely similar to his friend Cara's. Something stirred in his mind at the thought of the Goddess, some long-forgotten memory of the Sovereigns, but now was not the time to delve into that labyrinth. Giving Sophia's hand another squeeze, he turned towards the stairs leading down into the amphitheatre.

Their guard responded immediately, men and women dressed in blue-stained armour falling into step around them, surrounding the two Sovereigns in a ring of steel. The guard in the lead glanced back before they started down, and Lukys glimpsed a cheeky grin on Travis's face. Lukys's fellow recruits and their Tangatan partners had seemed the logical choice for their guard. They were family now, the only ones either of them could trust.

When they didn't immediately start down the steps, another face looked back. "If you two are quite done dawdling, I believe you have a pair of crowns to accept," Dale grunted.

Lukys drew in a breath and nodded. "Let's get it over with then."

"About time," Dale muttered.

Their guards went first. Silver spears and kite shields in hand, they advanced down the stairs to the floor of the amphitheatre, clearing a path for the new Sovereigns. Silence gave way to whispers as the crowd parted before the blue-garbed warriors, their heads lifting in search of a glimpse of their new rulers.

Lukys shivered as they descended the great steps. The unpredictable Perfugian spring had chosen to gift them with a rare day of sun. Despite the warmth, Lukys couldn't help but feel exposed as they approached the floor of the amphitheatre. After months of war and battle, he was used to a spear and shield in hand. To stand before so many in nothing but a simple robe, defenceless...he felt naked, though with Sophia at his side, he knew no human assailant would dare attack.

And the gift of the Sovereigns had added something to Lukys as well. Not the raw strength or speed of the Tangata, but another sense almost, an awareness of their surroundings that neither he nor Sophia quite yet understood, but which he hoped might aid them in times of need.

Certainly Lukys's own talents as a Melder seemed amplified by the Sovereign gift. And so as they approached the crowd, he reached out with his mind to examine the aura of his people. They flickered before his inner vision, multicoloured hues augmented by their colourful clothing. Purples for fear and courage shone, pinks for love and greys for doubt, even some blues of sadness shimmered in the minds of his new subjects. Thankfully, the reds of anger and greens of hatred were blessedly rare.

It was surprising, the power of truth.

There had been resistance, of course. For centuries, the Sovereigns had spread tales of the barbaric Tangata, of a monstrous species that sought only to destroy humanity. But the reality Lukys had discovered in the south could not have been further from that lie. Sophia and her companions who stood with them now wanted nothing more than a life of their own, a chance to raise their children in peace, to create rather than destroy.

And those they'd left behind in New Nihelm...well, that was a worry for another day.

Lukys did not doubt there were still those who disbelieved the revelations, who refused to accept their Tangatan ancestry. But from what he glimpsed of those below, the people who had come here did so out of curiosity, rather than anger. After all, the public had never been invited to an inauguration for their Sovereigns. Perhaps that alone had been enough to quench their trepidation at Sophia's presence.

Or maybe they just wanted to see the monster.

Lukys's head whipped around at Sophia's whisper.

No, he said immediately, catching her gaze. *To see the Lady and her partner.*

A smile touched her lips at his words and they continued down the stairs, doing their best to move in what they thought was a regal fashion. The long robes were more than just uncomfortable—Lukys feared they would actively hinder them should it come to a fight. Only with his friends and their Tangatan partners around them had he agreed to the ceremony—and even then, only because Nguyen had pressured them. The King of Gemaho had insisted that an official coronation would help the people to accept their strange new rulers. Much to Lukys's irritation, the reaction of the crowd suggested that the old king had been right.

He caught a glimpse of the man himself now, standing amidst his Gemaho guard. Nguyen had shaved the unkept beard he'd grown over the past weeks, though he still looked more the part of a scholar than a king. The man kept his face carefully blank as they approached, though Lukys could see the sheen in his eyes, the amusement behind the mask. Even as he watched, the king gave a subtle wink. The man was enjoying their discomfort.

At Lukys's side, a snort of laughter came from Sophia. He shook his head, a smile of his own tugging at his lips. The pair had formed an inexplicable bond, even before Sophia had learned to talk. Since their ascension to the Perfugian throne, the king couldn't hear enough about her people and their past, their wants and dreams. It seemed Nguyen was as fascinated with the past as the Archivist Erika had been, though no one had heard news of the woman in weeks. Neither had they heard of Cara, and Lukys was left wondering what had become of their quest to find the City of the Gods.

Again a memory tugged at him, but they were approaching the floor of the amphitheatre now, and quickly he pushed it aside. Hand in hand, Lukys and Sophia stepped onto the stage and started towards the stone slab that had been placed in its centre.

A shiver touched him as they walked amongst the crowd, the

line of their blue-garbed guards keeping them back. He couldn't help but remember another day just a few weeks ago, when their fate had seemed far grimmer. Standing alone in a ring of swords and Melders, Lukys, Sophia and his friends had faced off against the old Sovereigns—and convinced them to cast aside their hatred.

The bloodshed might have ended there but for one of the royal guards. Consumed by her hatred of the Tangata, Tasha had refused to accept the decision of her Sovereigns. In her desperation to save Perfugia from what she saw as monsters, she had struck down the last Sovereigns, then used her powers as a Melder to turn the rest of the guards against Lukys and the Tangata.

But he had defeated her, struck her down with mind and spear, and in doing so had claimed the memories of the dying Sovereigns.

Now he and Sophia stood where those ancient rulers had, preparing to receive their crowns as thousands watched on. He could feel their minds now, pressing in from all around, adding to the strain of those secret memories locked within his head. What must these people think, watching the Tangata walk amongst them, seeing a monster from their childhood about to be crowned Sovereign over all of them?

Even now, he half expected the calm to break, for their rage to be unleashed, to see them surging forward against the thin line of blue steel. Yet there was only silence, only that hidden curiosity, only the waiting. He supposed this was the first time most had ever set eyes upon the Sovereigns. When the rulers were so remote, so mysterious, they might have been Tangata all along for all these people knew.

Besides, through the academy every child entered at eight years of age, Perfugians were accustomed to obedience, to accepting the decree of their superiors. If the last Sovereigns had chosen a Tangata and a failed recruit as their next rulers, would they even question it?

Lukys couldn't help but feel there was a wrongness to that. After all, was that not how the Old One had conquered New Nihelm? The Tangata there had been ruled by a Matriarch, an ancient creature of strength and wisdom. But the Old One had turned the Matriarch's guards against her, slaughtering her in order to take her place. That should have mattered to the Tangata, that betrayal. Instead, they had bowed to the Old One's power without question.

Coming to a stop before the granite slab in the middle of the amphitheatre, Lukys looked upon the silver crowns that rested atop the stone, awaiting their new bearers. Adorned with a fortune in sapphires, they were only ceremonial, a show for those gathered to watch, an object to give legitimacy to their rule, as Nguyen put it. The true Sovereign gift had been passed to them as their predecessors lay dying, just as it had for every pair of Sovereigns before them.

Lukys shivered as he sensed cold eyes looking down from the pillars that lined the amphitheatre. Atop each pillar stood two statues, Sovereigns of ages past, stretching back centuries. He knew each of their faces now, had *been* every one of them. A strange sensation, that.

Turning from the statues, he and Sophia paused before the crowns. Their minds were closer than ever now, almost as one since the transformation, their thoughts aligned by the hundreds of lifetimes they had shared. It scared a part of him, to sense her presence so close, always on the edges of his consciousness. Yet it was a comfort too, the knowledge she would always be with him, that he would not be left alone.

As one, they reached down for the silver circlets. Despite the sun, the metal was cold to the touch as Lukys lifted the first above Sophia's head, and she did the same for him. There they paused, and their eyes met, grey of the Tangata to his own plain brown. Time seemed to stand still, and Lukys felt he stood on the edge of an abyss, that this moment would forever change their lives, tie them to a path they might grow to regret.

Yet what choice did they have? The Old One was coming with her Tangatan army. No kingdom could stand against her, not alone. If they did not act, did not lead Perfugia to unite humanity, the Old One would prevail. The kingdoms would fall, one by one, and his people would be exterminated, enslaved. One day, there would be nowhere left for them to run, nowhere left to hide.

He saw the same thoughts reflected in Sophia's eyes and momentarily, he wondered if they were truly his own, or hers, or one of the hundreds they had collected in their fragile minds. A shudder shook him, but they could not look back now, could not pass on this burden.

As one, they lowered the silver crowns onto each other's heads.

And turned to greet their subjects as the new Sovereigns of Perfugia.

❧ I ❧

THE TANGATA

A light snow was falling as the Tangata moved from the mountains into the Calafe foothills. The cold did not touch Adonis as he paused to watch the passage of his people, but he couldn't help but be reminded of their last journey through these hills, the desperate march of the Tangata as they followed Maya into the unknown heavens, driven on by her Voice, by the power of the Old One.

A tremor raised his hackles as he recalled the swirling snow, the faces of those who had succumbed, of men and women, of the children who had fallen in the snowdrifts, never to rise again. The journey had taken a terrible toll on the Tangata, on his people, and more than once he had found himself doubting his partner—though he had helped raise her to Matriarch.

Now though, after their glorious victory in the mountains, Adonis joyed in her power, in the fall of the Anahera, of the creatures that humanity had named Gods. The cost had been terrible, but in the end, to watch the Anahera kneel at their feet, cowed by mere Tangata…it had been a glorious sight.

Smiling, Adonis looked up at the creatures, soaring on their cursed wings. They served the Tangata now, keeping watch for the enemy. Faced with Maya's power, the creatures had made their choice, had bowed to the Old One, surrendered their liberty to preserve their future.

Adonis turned as the sound of rattling chains carried above the soft patter of falling snow. The elation of their victory left him as he saw the group of prisoners approaching, watched closely by their Tangatan guard.

The children of the Anahera—fledgelings, as the creatures called them—marched with heads down, each chained to the next in line by collars of steel fastened about their necks. They walked in blessed silence, heads bowed and stumbling in the deep snow, cowed by the power of their captors, by the thrum of Maya's Voice, always present now, as she walked at the head of their column.

Adonis clenched his fists as he watched the fledgelings trudge past. They might have left them imprisoned and under guard in the Anaheran city, but Maya wanted to keep them close, needed them to ensure the obedience of her new slaves. Not even her Voice could keep so many of the adult Anahera in check without the threat against their youth.

His heart twitched as one of the fledgelings tripped and fell into a snowdrift. The icy stuff had ceased to fall, but the ground was thick with the last of winter's storms, making passage difficult for the young. And their wings, still too young for flight, only seemed to hinder them further on the ground.

Adonis couldn't help but wonder at a species whose youth were so defenceless. The moment he had caught one within his super-human grip, the fledgeling's life had hung in his hands. No wonder the rest had surrendered so easily.

Most of the fledgelings barely stood taller than Adonis's waist, and with the chains binding them together, the journey through the mountains had been difficult. It would only get worse. Now that they had reached the lowlands, the pace would increase. And if their parents resisted Maya's orders...

At least the Tangata were strong. From a young age, they were able to fend for themselves. And the Old Ones...legend whispered of their offspring, of new-borns able to walk within days, fight by their first year. Adonis felt a thrill of excitement at that thought and looked around for Maya. Her pregnant belly had grown large in the weeks they'd spent in the mountains, and he wondered whether it was right that they continue with this mad rush, that they hurl their strength upon the defences of humanity now, rather than wait. But Maya had been insistent.

A shout from the fledgelings drew his attention back to the captives. Another at the rear had fallen, his chain pulling short so that the others stumbled. Shouts came from their Tangatan guards, then one of his brethren strode forward. He held a rope in one hand and with a flick of his wrist, he sent it hissing at the fledgeling's back. A scream punctuated its impact as the youth's wings thrashed against the snow, becoming entangled in the chains. The Tangata raised the rope again, but a shout from the back of the line gave him pause.

"Hey!"

Adonis flinched at the coarseness of the human language—not so much the words themselves, but the manner in which they communicated. The creatures spoke aloud, so that all the world could hear their thoughts. Indeed, he had come to suspect they enjoyed the fact that their speech made it all but impossible to be ignored. Certainly this individual did not want for silence.

"Bastard, why don't you pick on someone your own size?"

Stifling a growl, Adonis marched to the rear of the line where the human was sitting up in her stretcher, waving a fist at the Tangata with the rope-whip. The human had been injured in the battle for the Anaheran city, twisting her leg in a terrible fall. For now, Maya had permitted her to live, though if she did not cooperate when they reached the human lands, her protection would not last.

Swathed in furs, only the human's golden complexion and long black hair was visible, but that was more than enough to show her displeasure. The two Anahera that had been assigned to carry her stretcher struggled to keep from tipping their burden into the snow at her erratic movements.

Adonis shook his head as he approached. They were such vulgar things, these humans. This one called herself Maisie, but Adonis rarely bothered to recall their names. He couldn't understand how so many of his brethren had taken them as assignments. Despite the old Matriarch's urgings, he could have never stomached the thought of bonding with one, let alone procreating—though until recently that had been the only way of preserving the Tangatan lineage.

For Adonis, even the Anahera would be preferable, cowardly as they had proven. At least they were powerful, elegant, maybe worthy of the Tangata. That had been his hope once, a union between their species, one that might save the Tangata from extinction.

Then he had discovered Maya, and the future of his people had changed forever.

Approaching the stretcher, Adonis looked to the Anaheran woman who was helping to carry the human.

Translate for me, slave, he said, then turned to glare at the human.

"You," the human spoke before Adonis could relay his admonishments through the Anaheran woman. "I know you…you're the first one, the one the Old One used to take the fledgeling."

Adonis scowled. "*I am Adonis, partner to the Matriarch of the Tangata,*" he hissed, and the Anaheran woman relayed his words. "*And you will speak only when commanded, human.*"

To his surprise, the human only rolled her eyes, a gesture he'd come to learn was one of disrespect. A growl rumbled from his chest and he took a step towards the creature.

"I hope you're happy," the human said, ignoring his warning and lying back in her stretcher. She gestured to her bearers. "I can't say I was the biggest fan of the Anahera, but to enslave an entire species…" She shook her head. "That's almost *human.*"

"*Quiet, prisoner,*" Adonis snapped, irritated despite himself. How dare this creature compare his people to their kind? "*Or you will soon outlive your usefulness.*"

"Ha!" Maisie snorted. "You and I both know I'd already be as dead as poor Farhan and his son if that was the case. Your master clearly needs me for something."

Maya is not my master, Adonis snapped back.

The human only stared at him, as though she had not caught the meaning of his words. It was a moment before Adonis realized the Anaheran woman had not relayed his words. Snarling, he swung on the creature.

Slave, why have you not translated?

The Anahera blinked, shaking her head as though coming out of some trance. "I…I…" she stuttered, seemingly unable to put together the words. Her face had paled, and he noticed now that her eyes were red, as though she had not slept in a long while. "I am sorry, Tangata, the human…she mentioned my partner…and my son."

Her face twitched at the words—then to Adonis's horror, tears spilt down the woman's face. Images flickered in his mind, of Farhan's death by Maya's hand, crushed by her power. Then the youth in his grief, bowed over the fallen Anahera's body. The son. Maya had sent him to kill his sister, the young Anahera that had escaped, but he had never returned. Adonis had no doubt that meant the son was as dead as the father. Such was the power of Maya's Voice that the boy would not have stopped until the sister was slain, or he himself was dead.

"I am sorry," the Anaheran woman said softly, struggling to straighten, to contain herself. "I…it is just…I do not know what became of Hugo. He so wanted to please his father…"

Your son is dead, Adonis said harshly. False hope would not help the woman now, as he knew was the human way. The woman's son was dead—no amount of lying would change that truth. *Likely his sister killed him. I suppose you can be pleased by that at least: your daughter lives.*

The tears had returned to the Anaheran woman's face, but she froze at his last words. Then she was shaking her head, fists clenched, her whole body trembling. "Cara…was not my daughter," she mumbled. "She was…the daughter of Farhan's first partner. She would not have…could not have…no, she was headstrong, but she would not have killed one of us, not Hugo, not her own brother—"

The Anahera broke off as Adonis struck her hard across the face, sending her crashing to the snow. Anger raged within him as he looked down at the creature's shock. She would be far stronger than him, faster, more powerful, but the steel collar about her throat revealed the truth of her nature. She had bowed with the rest of her kind and now her strength meant nothing. They were his, all their kind. Their lives belonged to the Tangata. How dare she waste his time with her tears.

Yet, as he looked into her eyes and saw the grief there, Adonis felt the harsh words wither within him. Instead, he only shook his head and glanced at the human.

Pick up your burden, slave, he said, adding venom to his words despite his sudden regret. *Perhaps hard labour will help you to forget the loss of your foolish child.*

The human watched him as the Anaheran woman rose from the snow, her simple tunic now damp from melting ice. She had not heard his words, could not have understood half the conversation, but knowledge still shone from Maisie's eyes as she watched him. A shiver passed through Adonis at that look, and he couldn't help but wonder at Maya's wisdom in keeping one of Maisie's kind alive. They were intelligent, scheming creatures. So long as this human lived, she was a danger to them all.

But he could not go against the wishes of his Matriarch. So instead he turned back to the Anaheran woman as she picked up her end of the stretcher. The second Anahera had remained silent throughout the exchange, and he couldn't help but think he'd picked the wrong translator. Even so…

You had best get used to the pain, Anahera, he said as she lifted the stretcher. This time his voice lacked anger, and his tone was soft, without antagonism. He spoke only truth. *I fear the suffering of your people has only just begun.*

2

THE PRISONER

Erika's world was pain. Agony, drilling into her skull, searing her flesh, twisting her very bones. Darkness engulfed her, the pitch-black offering no escape, no fleeting distraction from her suffering. Even when the convulsions subsided, and her mind began to return, she would hear the footsteps on the stairs, the soft creaking of boards beneath booted feet, the rasping of the queen's laughter.

And the sound would begin again. That terrible, soul-rending shriek that set her whole being aflame. No matter that Erika pressed her hands to her ears, that she screamed to drown it out—the sound found her anyway. Through cloth and flesh and bone, even in the depths of unconsciousness, it sought her out. There was no escaping the fiery lashes of the queen's power, no relief. Time fled in that dark place and reality with it, until there was nothing for Erika but the ebb and flow of her pain.

The pain—and the whispers of the queen.

"Give up, Erika, surrender, and be free."

Lost amidst the agony, Erika began to wonder why she still resisted. The insidious words crept their way into her soul, murmuring their promises of freedom. She wept at the thought of relief, of a world without the shrieking, without the agony.

But something within Erika would not allow it, a tiny fraction of her consciousness, one that remembered the queen's lies, that recalled the woman's treachery. And she knew the promises were ash, that the only relief the queen offered was the cold embrace of death.

So instead, all Erika offered her enemy were her screams.

Queen Amina didn't seem to mind. Between flashes of red and white, in moments of brief clarity, Erika glimpsed the woman's face, the cruel grin twisting her lips. The queen didn't care that Erika resisted, only that she had her revenge. Then the madness would rise once more, an ocean of agony sweeping Erika away on dreams of suffering.

She could not have picked the moment when the end finally came, when the tide of her pain receded—and did not return. Consciousness came to Erika slowly, her soul creeping back to the broken husk of her body, as though fearing some trap, a trick by the queen to catch her unawares.

But when Erika finally cracked open her eyes, she found herself alone in the hull of the ship. Pain still rippled through her body when she tried to sit up, aftershocks of the queen's magic, but for the first time since being taken captive, the raw agony had vanished.

Drawing in a breath of stale air, she sought to pull the scattered fragments of her thoughts together. Memories collided in her mind as she recalled her struggle to convince the Anahera to fight, to resist the Tangatan attack. Never could she have imagined that the noble creatures, proclaimed as Gods over humanity, could have submitted so readily.

In the end, only Farhan had resisted. Cold, uncaring Farhan. But he had proven his love for his daughter, twisted and controlling as it was. He may have saved Cara from the Old One, but only after coming so close to condemning her, to robbing the Goddess of the wings that gave her life, freedom.

Yet, what did it matter now? Farhan was dead…as was his son Hugo, who had perished at the hands of his own sister, Cara. A shudder shook Erika as she recalled that desperate struggle. Through the agony of Erika's broken arm and Cara's shattered wing, they had fought poor Hugo, Cara's half-brother, to the death. Driven mad by the Old One, he had fought as though possessed, screaming that he was helping Cara—even as he slammed her skull against the stones.

Now he was dead, drowned in the mountain stream, his body carried away by the currents. And Erika and Cara had found themselves a fresh prison, a new tormentor in the form of the Flumeeren Queen. How Amina had come to take the lands of the Gemaho, Erika could not comprehend, but it hardly seemed to matter now. They had fallen into her clutches, been conquered by her magic. There would be no escape now.

Erika still wasn't sure why she was even alive. The queen wanted the magic gauntlet Erika wore, but why not prise it from her corpse? Why go through the hassle of torture, of the demands for Erika to remove it? Unless…the magic could not be taken against her will. Erika hadn't considered that possibility, but now she wondered…

The squeal of hinges drew Erika's attention to the boards above her head and she flinched as a ray of light swept the gloom beneath the deck, illuminating stairs leading up to a trap door. Feet descended, followed by the queen herself.

Erika's heart raced as she watched the woman's approach, but there was nowhere to hide in the hold. She shrank into a corner, as though if only she could make herself small enough, she might avoid the queen's wrath. But there was little hope of that, and balling her fist, she tried desperately to reach for the power of her gauntlet.

Pain seared through her wrist as the broken bones grated together, still mending from the injury she had taken in the mountains. Despite the pain, a brief flickering of light appeared in the links of her gauntlet, but it quickly died, as Erika's energies flagged. She couldn't remember the last meal she'd eaten—even before their capture, she and Cara had barely scavenged enough from the land to stave off starvation. She had discovered in the mountains how the gauntlet fed off her own strength. Without sustenance, its power was useless to her.

A smile crossed the queen's thin lips as she watched Erika's pathetic attempt at resistance. Then she raised her own gauntleted hand and squeezed it into a fist. Light burst from the metallic links, so bright it was nearly blinding. Erika flinched from the display of power, her own mind withering at the pain it promised, the agony that would follow. A moan drew from the depths of her throat as half-mad, she turned and clawed at the boards of the ship.

Erika herself had once used that same power to dominate friends and enemies alike—to strike down Cara and the Tangata, even Farhan, the leader of the Anahera. Now that she found herself on the receiving end…she could barely hold onto her own sanity.

"So my Archivist awakes," the queen murmured, raising her burning fist.

The woman was dressed for war, with heavy chainmail draped across her lithe frame, a helm with a golden circlet set in the brow carried in her free hand. A sword hung from her side, though with the power of the ancient gauntlet, this woman had no need for such a primitive weapon.

Erika shrank further into her corner at the woman's voice, tears springing to her eyes. She could already feel the onset of the pain, the return of the madness. Those Erika had tortured with her own gauntlet had perished quickly, their insides torn apart by her magic. But Queen Amina had obviously spent time refining her power, had learned such control that she could torture Erika for hours without her victim succumbing to the silent embrace of death.

A sob tore from Erika's throat as she shook her head, scrunching her eyes closed. Now that she had regained her sanity, had escaped the pain for even a few hours, the thought of its return…

Laughter rasped in her ears and a brilliant light seared at Erika's eyelids, as though the queen were gathering even more power. But then the light faded and footsteps approached. Another tremor shook Erika as she clenched her fists, struggling to keep from screaming.

"Such bravery," the queen's voice whispered from close by.

Cracking open her eyes, Erika found the queen crouched alongside her. The woman's emerald eyes seemed to pierce Erika to the soul. There was a sharpness about the queen's face that spoke of power, of her unyielding will. This was a woman who had defied the Tangata, who had traded and manipulated and battled her way across the kingdoms of humanity, until all lay conquered at her feet.

Where had she come from, this warrior queen of Flumeer? Her father had been king before her, but he had not shown any inclination towards war—had overseen years of peace for Flumeer, in fact. Little was known of her mother, only that she had succumbed to a wasting fever when Amina was yet a child at the breast.

Somehow, the pair had created a conqueror.

Light bathed Erika's face as the queen reached out with the gauntlet and pressed a finger to Erika's chest.

"Why do you still fight, little Archivist?" Amina whispered. "You know you cannot resist. Eventually you will give me what I want, you must know this. So why suffer? Why put yourself through this agony? In the end, the result will be the same."

Fire lit in Erika's belly at the queen's words, at her arrogance, to think that Erika could not stand against her, that she would surrender so meekly. Staring into the queen's eyes, she found a spark of courage and bared her teeth.

"Because I am a princess of Calafe," she snarled, "because I will never surrender to the murderer of my people."

"Calafe?" The queen seemed surprised by that as she rose. "Since when? Did your people not chase you from your lands, steal the rightful crown from your head? Did you not come to me yourself and kneel as a citizen of Flumeer, swear yourself to my cause as Archivist?"

"That was before I knew the truth," Erika snarled. "Before your assassin revealed himself, before he told me about my father."

"Ah…" the queen sighed. "So Yasin found you in the end. I take it he is dead? A shame; men of his quality are difficult to find. Though he always did have a loose tongue."

"He killed my father on your orders!" Erika screamed, her rage coming alight at the queen's casual tone.

"A means to an end, my dear," the queen said, dismissing Erika's anger with a flick of her hand. Turning away, she clasped her arms behind her back. "While other leaders have fought and squabbled amongst themselves, I alone knew of the danger that was to come." She spun suddenly, golden eyes seemingly aglow in the dim light beneath the ship. "Tell me, Archivist, what did you discover in those mountains? What did you learn of *their* kind, of the Anahera?"

Erika's retort caught in her throat at the queen's words. "How… how do you know that name?" she whispered.

That was a name known only to the Anahera themselves. Surely Cara had not told her? No…looking into the queen's eyes, at the anger simmering those golden irises, Erika sensed there was more to this woman than she had realised.

"*They* were the ones who betrayed us, Archivist," the queen murmured, crouching before Erika. "The Gods we have worshiped, whom my father so loved—it was they who cast down humanity, who schemed to destroy our ancient ancestors." She paused, eying Erika a long moment, before nodding. "Yes, I can see it in your eyes; you found them, discovered the truth."

"How can you know?" Erika whispered, barely able to manage the words. The queen's words…they spoke a truth Erika had only learned from the Old One when she had invaded the city of the Anahera. How could Amina possibly…

"I have always known," the queen murmured, looking away. "My father discovered the truth. He knew they would come one day, that humanity's growing power would threaten them, and they would seek to destroy us again. He raised me to prepare for that threat, for the coming of the false Gods." She smiled bitterly. "When I heard your Goddess had revealed herself above the waters of the Illmoor, I knew that day was upon us. Alas, if you live, it means Yasin and his assassins failed. Time is short, Archivist. I will need every power at my disposal to defeat them. Come."

The last word was an order and Erika flinched, her beleaguered mind unable to process the command. How did the queen know all this? Cara would not have told her such secrets, no matter the pain Amina gifted with the gauntlet. Only the Anahera and the Old One had known the truth.

"*Come,*" the queen said again, and this time Erika managed to stagger to her feet.

The queen went first up the stairs. When she disappeared into the light above, Erika might have slunk back to her shelter, might have tried to hide again in her corner, but then the queen would only send her soldiers to drag Erika out. And besides, she had a yearning to see the world again, to discover what had become of Gemaho and its people now that Amina had conquered them.

Emerging onto the deck, Erika squinted against the brilliance of the day. The sun shone high overhead, announcing the noon meal —not that Erika would be offered anything. Her head swam as she looked around, finding massive cliffs stretching above the river on which they sailed.

Erika recognised their surroundings immediately—there was

only one place like it in all the kingdoms of humanity. They were sailing down the Illmoor through the pass that connected Gemaho and Flumeer.

"Come and look upon the fate of those who defy me, Archivist," the queen called to her from the bow.

Erika swallowed at the power in the woman's voice. Her back was turned and the crew on the ship did not seem to be paying Erika much attention. She might have fled to the railings and hurled herself into the racing waters. But Erika was weak in mind and body, and instead she found herself staggering across the ship to where the queen waited, her spirit crushed, defeated.

Amina gestured to the shore as Erika joined her. A dozen ships sailed around them, each flying the scarlet sails of Flumeer, while a hundred yards away, an army shadowed the fleet on the banks of the Illmoor. They too bore flags of Flumeeren red, the conquering army returning to its homeland. Their numbers hardly seemed diminished from the force that had stood outside the Illmoor Fortress and demanded King Nguyen to surrender. She wondered what had become of the man, how he had been defeated so quickly.

Then the ship sailed around a curve in the gorge, and Erika looked upon the truth.

Ahead lay the Illmoor Fortress itself, whose walls had defended the lands of the Gemaho. For generations, those walls had defended the kingdom against Tangatan and human foes alike. No foe had ever breached their granite expanse.

Now the fortress lay in pieces, great holes torn through the stone of its walls, as though a giant had swung his club to break them. Blocks the size of small houses lay scattered around each breach, and part of the citadel had been broken too, crumbling before some vast power. Black ash scorched the stone blocks, suggesting some fiery explosion had been behind the fortress's fall.

"Your Archivists Guild finally proved itself useful," the queen announced. "After your departure, I had my guard tear their school apart in search of any secrets you might have hidden from me. Turns out they had secrets of their own. Black powder. Seems you used it for minor excavations, but my engineers saw other possibilities. The Gemaho never knew what struck them."

A shiver ran down Erika's spine at the destruction the queen had wrought. If the Illmoor Fortress could have fallen so easily…

"You see now, Archivist?" The queen's words echoed Erika's thoughts. "You see the truth? There is no one left to save you, no one left to stand against me. Nguyen, your father, they stood in my way. Now they are dead. Whatever it takes, I will unite the kingdoms beneath me against the Anahera. There is no reason left now for you to resist, nothing left for you at all, but surrender."

Looking upon the ruin, Erika knew it to be true. She closed her eyes, her body trembling. She imagined returning to the stale air of the hull, to the torture and pain, to the unending agony without even a hint of hope. No one would come for her. Nguyen was gone, his kingdom fallen, the Gods made slaves to the enemies of humanity. Her future held only agony, and death.

But the queen was wrong. There was still one person left that Erika cared about, one good deed she might yet fulfil.

"Okay," she croaked, eyes still closed, unable to meet the queen's gaze. "I'll give it to you. But first, I must see Cara."

‍‌ ❧ 3 ❧

THE SOVEREIGN

"Well, I can't say the past few weeks went quite as I imagined when I set out from Gemaho," Nguyen said to those gathered in the room.

Holding a glass of whiskey in one hand, the other tucked behind his back, there was regal manner to the way the king paced the room while Lukys and Sophia sat together on a velvet sofa. Lukys tried to hold himself a little straighter to mimic the king's posture, but it was only a moment before he slumped back into the soft cushions. It was no use—Nguyen had trained all his life in the ways of royalty. Lukys couldn't hope to achieve the same poise in the span of a few days.

"You mean when you *fled* from Gemaho, right?" Travis interjected. Standing at attention by the door, he seemed to take his Sovereigns' silence as an opportunity to speak himself.

A scowl crossed Nguyen's face as he glanced at the newly made royal guard. "It's customary for guards to keep their silence in a gathering of monarchs," he said with a scowl.

"It's also customary for a king to have a kingdom," Travis shot back, face blank.

For a second, Lukys thought the king might explode at his friend's impudence. The moment stretched out as Nguyen stared at the guard, teeth bared. Then suddenly the man let out an explosive laugh. Waving a hand, he turned his back on the gathering and continued his pacing.

"Might be your man is right, Lukys," he said, glancing at their sofa. "Regardless of how we came to our current circumstances, we have what we wanted: Gemaho and Perfugia united."

"It won't be enough," Sophia spoke up.

Lukys looked at her sharply, his consciousness already extended, sensing the familiar fear she had carried since that day in New Nihelm when Maya had slain her Matriarch. There was more to Sophia's fear now though, augmented by the knowledge they had acquired, though they had still only glimpsed a fraction. The rest lay buried, like the iceberg concealed beneath the waters. But what they had uncovered so far of the Old Ones filled Lukys with terror.

Sophia did not reply to his silent enquiry. Instead, she reached for the table beside their sofa. Taking up her glass of rum, she raised it in silent salute, then downed it in one go. Lukys raised an eyebrow as he sensed ripples of the alcohol's burning from his partner. She seemed to have developed an appreciation for Nguyen's various liquors over the last week, though Lukys understood from the Sovereign memories that a Tangata's sense of taste and smell were far more sensitive than humans.

Letting out a sigh, he took a measured sip from his own glass. Unlike Sophia, he did not have the metabolism of a Tangata, though…it might have been his imagination, but his senses *did* seem augmented now, as though the imbuement of all those lifetimes had passed something else onto him. He held the rum in his mouth, savouring the caramel tones overlaid by wood smoke. Memories stirred at the taste, an image appearing in his mind, of shacks built of wood clinging to cliffs, a hundred at most, a broad harbour stretching out beyond.

Ashura, as it had been long ago.

Lukys shivered. Nguyen claimed to have uncovered the cask in the Sovereigns' private cellar, a vintage over a century old. The image in his mind suggested it was even older than that, stretching back to a time not long after their ancestors had first arrived on the island.

The king did not return Sophia's salute, only stared at the Tangatan Sovereign, as though he were still trying to communicate in the telepathic manner of a Melder. Finally he shook his head and crossed to his own chair. A servant stepped forward to fill his glass from the decanter as he sank into the soft leather.

"What would you propose, My Lady?" he murmured.

"I do…not know," Sophia replied, her eyes drifting to the open window that overlooked the harbour. Outside, in place of the shacks Lukys had seen, buildings of stone stretched across the cliffs. "Only that we must stop Maya before…" She trailed off, and Lukys shuddered as fresh images flickered through their minds, of a land overrun, of fields, forests, an ocean aflame.

The king sighed. "How many Tangata will this Old One bring against us?"

"Maya will have thousands from New Nihelm," Sophia replied, "but…others have been moving north to occupy Calafe. My people once had a bond with that place, with its people, in centuries long forgotten…" She shook her head at the distraction, at the memories rising from the depths of their minds, struggling to restore her train of thought. "If she gathers more on her way north, they could number ten thousand by the time she reaches the Illmoor."

Her words sent a chill down Lukys's spine. "Even amongst the younger generations, it would take thirty thousand human soldiers to match that force." The younger the generation of Tangata, the more their lines were mixed with humanity. Sophia was of the fifth generation, the others they had brought with them mostly sixth. "Perfugia has only three thousand regular soldiers," he finished finally.

"And my fleet six thousand," Nguyen added grimly. "What of your citizens, though? If we could recruit—"

"*No,*" Lukys cut him off, turning hard eyes on the king. "I will send no more untrained innocents to be slaughtered in a foreign kingdom."

The king scowled. "You would prefer them to be slaughtered in their houses when the Tangata come?" he snapped.

"I would prefer them not to be slaughtered at all," Lukys replied.

He thought the king might dig in his heels, but instead Nguyen waved a hand. "Fine," he said curtly. "Then what do you propose? A guerrilla campaign? We know the Tangata cannot easily replenish their number. If we retreat into the mountains and forests, avoid a pitched battle, we could whittle them down over a few years. It will cost Flumeer everything, of course. Turn the entire kingdom into a battleground, but I am prepared to play that game."

Lukys's skin crawled at the king's words, at the thought of condemning an entire kingdom to years of open warfare, to armies rampaging across their lands, resisted only by small freedom forces, striking the enemy where they could. He could never countenance such an option, even for the warlike Flumeerens. But there was another reason the king's strategy would not work; it was the reason the war needed to end, and end quickly.

"No," he replied softly, his tone so low that all eyes in the room turned to him. "We cannot afford to delay."

The king raised an eyebrow, but when he said nothing, Lukys swallowed and went on.

"It's different with this creature, with the Old Ones," he said, digging into those ancient memories.

The Sovereigns had only been created on their arrival in Perfugia, but even before then, the ancestors of the Tangata had passed knowledge between their generations.

"Maya, the Old Ones, they're fertile, virulent. In ancient days, they would gestate for a matter of months before giving birth to litters of half a dozen or more. Those children would grow to adolescence within two years, but even before that they could be dangerous. If you think *one* Old One is terrifying, wait a few years, and there will be dozens."

Lukys trailed off. A silence had fallen, heavy with the weight of his words, with the spectre of the danger that haunted them.

"Not even the strongest of the Tangata could stand against Maya's power. Give her time, and she will give birth to an army of her own kind, superior in every way to our soldiers, *and* the Tangata." He paused, those other memories stirring in the back of his mind. "Maybe superior even to the Gods."

There was more there, a flickering in the back of his mind, a memory of Cara soaring above, and others, winged figures in the sky, soaring through mountain peaks…

…then it was gone, slipping beneath the surface of a hundred others. He looked around, meeting the eyes of his friends, of the king, and let himself fall silent. Slumping into the sofa beside Sophia, he waited for someone to speak, to offer a plan, some semblance of hope. That had been his task for so long now, first as they marched south of the Illmoor on the Archivist's mad quest, then again on their desperate flight from New Nihelm, on the ship amidst the storm, even here in Ashura, when they had faced the condemnation of the old Sovereigns.

But now…this time Lukys couldn't see where to begin. If she chose it, Maya could remain at the seat of her power, safe in New Nihelm, far from any danger humanity might pose to her. Their only chance was the rage of the Old Ones, that her hatred for humanity would drive her to attack, to place herself at risk.

"You're right," Nguyen said finally, his voice reassuringly calm, though Lukys didn't know how anyone could keep their cool when faced with such an existential threat. "We cannot let this Maya go to ground. She must be destroyed…even if it means going through ten thousand Tangata to get to her."

Lukys nodded, but before he could ask what the king planned, a fresh wave of emotion struck him, a surging, bubbling, rippling red, of anger, of rage. He looked sharply to Sophia at the abrupt change in her state, though…it came not just from her, but others in the room, from the blue-garbed guards, from her brethren Tangata.

Sophia had grown so pale Lukys feared she might lose herself, might surrender to the uncontrollable rage of the Tangata. Silently he reached for her, but she jerked away and swung on him, eyes wide, shining.

"You're talking about my *people*," she said, and hearing her voice break, Lukys knew suddenly the grief that lurked beneath her rage. "About slaughtering thousands of innocents. How can you be so casual, so calm, as though they were no more than numbers on a piece of your paper?"

"They are the enemy now, My Lady," Nguyen replied softly, leaning forward in his chair. "They have chosen their side."

"They have chosen *nothing*," Sophia grated. "Maya controls them, just as she would have controlled me, or any of my sisters and brothers in this room, had she turned her mind against us." She shook her head, and Lukys's heart twisted as a tear streaked her cheek. "You don't understand, *can't* understand…"

She trailed off and Lukys reached for Sophia with his mind, seeking to comfort her, to reassure her that he was there, that he understood. But for the first time since they had been granted the gift of the Sovereigns, he was met by a wall of grey, so thick he sensed not a hint of what hid beneath.

The sudden absence of her mind made his heart begin to race and he sat frozen for a second, unable to focus, to pull his thoughts together. Sophia's grey eyes swept the room, and in them he saw the emotion she hid, anger and fear, and confusion too. She knew the threat Maya presented, the danger the Old One posed to all their kinds. Her people were not the only ones that would suffer should the Old Ones return.

But they would be the first, if humanity moved against Maya.

Abruptly, Sophia rose. Without another word, she strode from the room. Movement came from around them as the other Tangatan guards followed her out, until only the humans remained.

Letting out a long sigh, Nguyen sat back in his chair and entwined his fingers. "There is a time in every ruler's reign when he comes to realise a terrible truth."

"Oh, and what's that?" Lukys snapped. In Sophia's absence, he found himself suddenly agitated, anxious about their separation. He could feel the memories pressing on him, an enormous ocean on which his consciousness floated, waiting to swallow him up. He feared there were more perils to the Sovereign gift than either of them knew.

The king raised his eyebrows at Lukys's tone, but when the Sovereign did not offer an apology, he went on with his explanation.

"There are many who call me a coward, who hate me for my actions following the southern campaign."

Lukys frowned at that. The king was not wrong. Just over a decade ago, the four kingdoms had led an invasion into the Tangatan homeland—only to have it go disastrously wrong. Barely half of those who had marched south had returned. Afterwards, Nguyen had withdrawn from the alliance, leaving the other kingdoms to face the wrath of the Tangata without Gemaho's aid.

"Most would have had me remain faithful to the alliance," Nguyen continued, his voice soft. "To send more Gemaho soldiers south to the frontlines, to be used as fodder in the battle against the Tangata."

Lukys frowned, surprised by the admission. "It *was* a cowardly act, abandoning the alliance."

"Perhaps," the king replied evenly, "but also a kingly one. Others do not understand, but before all else, a king's duty is to his people. Our own wants and desires, our pride and vanity, our past loves and friendships, all of it must be put aside before the weight of duty." He looked away, gaze sweeping out to the ships at anchor in the harbour. "I faced the Tangatan charge once, on the plains south of Calafe. After the events of that day, I knew they could not be defeated, not in open battle. Resistance would mean deaths by the thousands. That was a price I was unwilling to let my people pay."

He looked back at Lukys, and in that moment he saw the pain in the man's eyes, the guilt at what he had done.

"And so I ordered the Gemaho to withdraw. I abandoned the lands of Calafe, the kingdom of a man that had been my friend. Had it only been me, I would have fought to the end to protect those lands. But as king…" He trailed off, spreading his hands as though he had said everything that needed saying.

Lukys swallowed as Nguyen's emerald eyes watched him, until finally his gaze fell to the floor. A lump lodged in his throat and he shivered, thinking of all that stood before them. The challenge they faced was daunting, the thought of protecting all of Perfugia, of defending the shores of this peaceful archipelago all but impossible. And yet…

Swallowing, Lukys rose to his feet and nodded to the king. "I'll talk to her."

❈ 4 ❈

THE TANGATA

Standing in the centre of the village, Adonis felt the very air thrumming with the Voices of the Tangata, with the growing excitement that always came before Maya's arrival. This was the third Tangatan village they had visited since reaching the lowlands. And it would be the third they left empty, abandoned as its occupants marched north, just as its former owners—the Calafe —once had.

Only the Calafe had fled before the Tangatan invasion, while Adonis's brethren would march north for conquest.

The murmur of Tangatan voices swelled to a roar in Adonis's mind, though beneath he could still sense the beating of Maya's own Voice as she worked her power on the crowd, feeding their anger, their lust for revenge against the humans that had tormented them. Old memories of the human invasion swelled in his mind, of brethren who had died to human blades, of youth put to the sword.

Despite knowing the source of those images and his strength as a third generation Tangata, Adonis's blood began to pound in his ears. He clenched his fists, letting the rage sweep through him, his own bloodlust surging along with that of his brethren. And yet…he was growing accustomed to his partner's presence, the pressure upon his mind, and finally he exhaled, relaxing as the anger flowed from him.

A shiver touched him instead as he scanned the faces of those gathered, and he glimpsed the prisoners in the rear, the human and her Anaheran bearers. How much longer must the human be carried, he wondered. A Tangata would have healed long ago. How such flawed creatures could have resisted his people for so long, he could not understand.

But it was not the human Adonis sought. His eyes settled on the Anaheran woman and he frowned. He had been harsh with her, forced her to confront the loss of her son. Adonis did not regret that, but…there was another guilt in his soul, a remorse for what Maya had done to the Anahera's son. Young and untrained in the powers of the mind, the young Anahera had never stood a chance against the powers of the Old One.

Silence fell in Adonis's mind, the Voices of the Tangata abruptly cut off. Only the dim pounding of Maya's Voice remained. Now it swelled to a crescendo as she walked amongst the low built stone buildings. The Tangata parted like water before a human ship as she strode to where Adonis stood.

Adonis's heart raced at her approach, at the sight of her swollen stomach. Smiling, she reached out a hand to cup his cheek, then pressed her lips against his. In a rush of heat, Adonis's concerns were swept away, consumed by the touch of her mind against his own, by the *roar* of her Voice.

Then the warmth faded, and he found himself standing fixed in place, watching as she turned to face the crowd. She raised her arms to them, her grey eyes, so like those of his own people, aglow with the power of the Old Ones.

"My children!" she spoke aloud, but beneath the human tone, her Voice carried to every mind in the village, caressing them, calling them, inviting them to join her. *"Come, hear me. The age of the Tangata is upon us!"*

At those words, the crack of wings came from overhead and half a dozen Anahera fell from the sky. Those of the Tangata who had not noticed Maya's prisoners gasped and leapt back as the creatures landed amongst them. They might not have worshiped the Anahera as humanity did, but even the simplest of his brethren knew of the creatures, that their power was not to be trifled with.

Now the Tangata of the village watched in awe as the Anahera fell to their knees before Maya, sinking into the soft mud at the centre of the Tangatan village. Standing over the kneeling creatures, the Old One raised her hands again to Adonis's brethren.

"See how even the mighty Anahera bow before us?" she cried. *"They have accepted the power of the Tangata, the power of your new Matriarch!"* Her eyes seemed to glow as she looked out over the crowd, and Adonis shivered at the thrumming in the air, the hiss of her voice upon his mind. He didn't feel the same elation he once had, watching her display, but he was still touched by her aura, by the glory of her promise. *"Soon, all the world will bow to our will,"* she went on. *"The humans that have plagued our people for so long will be vanquished, enslaved by their betters, as they were always meant to be. My children, join me in their conquest, in the heralding of our new world."*

A roar sounded in Adonis's mind as the Tangata that had followed Maya from New Nihelm responded. It was only a moment before those of the village joined in, merging their minds with the crowd, with the collective of the Tangata that marched beneath the banner of the Old One.

Hearing the glory in their Voices, the ecstasy, a tremor shook Adonis. Witnessing their rapture, he found himself wondering if these newcomers would meet the same end as their predecessors. Would they too be left behind when she judged them weak, cast aside as though they held no more worth than the human they dragged with them?

Shivering, he looked again at Maya. Her Voice rung above the din of the crowd, silencing any doubters, those who might deny her. His blood stirred as he stared at her swollen belly, the life that grew within her, and he felt his own doubt subsiding. The weeks were passing rapidly now, and it would not be long before his children took their first steps into the world. What possibilities then, with a new generation of Tangata, invigorated by the power of the Old Ones?

Adonis found himself dreaming of the days that would follow, when his children would stand alongside him in battle. Together, they would lead their people against the enemy. Whatever remained of humanity would crumble before their power.

Are you well, my mate?

Shaking himself, Adonis looked around, surprised to find that Maya had returned to his side. Concern was etched into her brow and he saw now that the crowd had dissipated, gone to prepare themselves for the journey, to gather their children and elderly and leave behind this place they had made their home…

…to be led to their deaths.

Shuddering, he shook his head, frowning at his mate. He felt her mind pressing against his own, the vastness of her strength, but for once he resisted, did not capitulate to the power of her Voice.

I…confess I am concerned, he said softly, taking a step towards her and placing his hand on her engorged stomach. *Our path forward, this campaign against the humans…are you sure it would not be best if you returned to New Nihelm? You could wait in safety, while I lead our forces against our foes.*

A smile touched his mate's lips and reaching down, she entwined her fingers with his. As she held his palm to her stomach, he felt the soft movement of the life within. Tears stung his eyes as images of a future yet to be flickered before his mind.

They are but a few weeks away, my mate, she said softly. *These children will be everything you have ever wanted.* She hesitated, her eyes growing uncharacteristically distant. *But I cannot do as you suggest.*

Why? he asked, reaching up to cup her cheek. *The fate of our entire world rests upon your survival. Should the humans strike a lucky blow, should you fall…*

I will not fall, Maya replied, a soft smile upon her lips. She turned away then, eyes drifting to the mountains above. *Still you do not understand what is at stake, Tangata,* she said. *Once, my parents delayed their assault upon the humans, sought safety that my siblings and I could be welcomed into this world. It cost them everything.* She turned abruptly, her deep grey eyes catching Adonis's. *They are a plague upon this earth, the humans, a flame that grows brighter with every day we delay. Did you not see the magic the one in the mountains wielded? Grant them time, and soon a hundred such will come against us.* She shook her head. *Or worse, rediscover the magics of their ancestors. No, we must crush them now, grind them back into the mud from whence they came.*

Adonis shivered at Maya's words, for they were accompanied not only by her Voice, but images of her past, of a man and woman standing in a cave, of skies stained red, of horizons turned black with ash, an abyss that would never be filled. He swallowed, wondering at such a time, at a world twisted by the old magics of humanity.

A warm hand touched his cheek, drawing him back, and he found himself staring into the dark eyes of the Old One. For a second he glimpsed something there, a flicker in her mind, a hint of yellow fear, of doubt. But what did Maya, a being capable of defeating even the Anahera themselves, have to fear? Surely she did not truly consider humans such a threat?

Maya stroked his cheek again, then smiling, she moved away, calling for the Tangata to join her, to make ready for the journey, for the next desperate race across the wilderness. They couldn't be far from the great river that marked the border of human territory, just a few more days. Would they meet the humans there, or would their human captive's words prove true, and they would find the creatures busy warring amongst one another?

Adonis shook his head at the thought. Maya might fear them, but it seemed to him that if anything, humans had become like the Anahera—a shade of their former greatness. How could a species that spent half its time murdering one another possibly pose a threat to the Tangata?

But there was no arguing with the Old One, no dissuading her with his own Voice. So they would march north and fall upon the enemy, slaughter them where they stood.

And then he would welcome his children into a new world…

"She's using you, you know."

Adonis started as a voice carried from the shadows. The soft tapping of wood against rock came from a nearby building as the human, Maisie, appeared. While she still required bearers to carry her across the endless wilderness, her twisted leg had healed enough that she could hobble around the village with the aid of a wooden crutch. Only one guard was with the human, but Adonis was irritated to see it was the woman, Nyriah. At least she kept her face stoic today, her grief concealed.

Scowling, Adonis swung on the human woman. *What would you know, human?* he snarled, before realizing belatedly that she could not hear him. Cursing, he gestured for the Anahera to translate.

Maisie laughed before Nyriah could finish. "Your words might be hidden from me, Adonis." He started at the use of his name, but the human went on before he could interrupt. "But the body language between you and your master does not lie. You get to know these things, when your survival depends on reading those around you." She leaned casually against a building, appearing relaxed, though she faced a creature capable of tearing her in two at a whim. "Yep, no doubt about it, she's using you."

A pounding started in Adonis's ears at her words and he felt the Tangatan rage coming upon him, felt its burning, the longing to grasp the pitiful creature before him and throttle the life from her.

In an instant, he snapped, launching himself forward. The human's eyes widened—then he was upon her, catching the woman by the throat, hauling her into the air. A squawk escaped Maisie as she struggled, but it was little use. Her face contorted in pain as Adonis shook her, her injured leg bumping against his shoulder. Gasping, she slumped in Adonis's grasp, helpless before his rage.

Still trembling, Adonis dumped the woman to the ground, not caring about the scream as she struck. Lips drawn back in a snarl, he faced the Anaheran guard.

Translate, he snapped, then turned to the human without waiting for a response. *"You know nothing, human. Maya is the only reason you still live. You had best show more respect to the Matriarch of the Tangata if you wish to see another day."*

The human lay panting on the ground for a long moment after the Anahera translated his words, gasping, moaning as she struggled against the pain of her leg. Adonis felt no remorse—she was only a human, a plague upon this world, as Maya had said. What need had he to pity such a creature?

"It was obvious…even back in…the Anaheran city."

For a moment, Adonis did not recognise the words amongst her gasps. When understanding finally dawned, he blinked, shocked at her continued defiance. Did this creature have a death wish? He frowned. Was that what this was about, a way out for her, to make a quick end of her imprisonment?

"She makes you do her dirty work," the human rasped, "had you capture the fledgeling, has you stand with her at each village. One of their own, mated with a creature of legend. All so they will not question, so you will not realise the truth—she cares nothing for any of your people."

"She is our Matriarch," Adonis snarled. *"She will lead us to glory."*

"She isn't even one of you," Maisie replied.

A growl tore from Adonis's throat and he fought the desire to haul her from the ground and shake her again. But lying on the snowy ground, unable to stand or even lift herself to a sitting position, Maisie was too pathetic to be worth his effort. Adonis could only shake his head at her wretched figure.

"She will be the mother of my children, of a new generation of Tangata."

To his surprise, Maisie began to laugh, though lying there in the muddy snow, it sounded like sobs, might have even been both, given the undoubted agony from her leg.

A growl rumbling from his throat, Adonis advanced on her. *"Why do you laugh, human?"*

Her eyes snapped up, brown against the pale white of her face. "It's only, I didn't realise the Tangata were so gullible," she replied softly, shaking her head. "After all, what makes you believe the children are your own, Adonis?"

$\text{❧}\quad 5 \quad\text{❧}$

THE PRISONER

The queen's cabin was everything Erika's confinement in the hull of the ship was not. The interior was small, but had been filled with an opulence the queen rarely displayed in public. A golden chandelier dangled from the low ceiling, candles swinging slowly in rhythm to the ships rocking, and several silver-framed paintings had been hung from the walls. Papers decorated a mahogany desk in the corner, the etchings almost unreadable to Erika, and she wondered again at the queen, the secret knowledge she had hidden from the rest of the world.

Erika shivered as her eyes passed over a standing mirror and she saw herself for the first time in weeks. The long blonde hair she had once so prided herself in now hung in a tangled mess, ends split where she had hacked it shorter with a knife. Shadows hung beneath her sapphire eyes, and looking into their depths, she searched for the woman who had set off into the mountains all those weeks ago, determined to save the world.

But the truth was, that woman had perished in those mountains, crushed by the weight of her discoveries, the knowledge of the Gods' betrayal. Her spirit had faltered, and now she could not bring herself to stand again, to face the evils that threatened.

Shivering, Erika swallowed that despair, and forced her attention to what had brought her to this place.

In the other corner of the queen's chambers, Cara crouched in a steel cage so small the Goddess could not even lie down properly. At least it was tall enough for the Anahera to stand, but her auburn wings hung limp, unable to stretch within the bars of her confinement. Erika was relieved to see the wing Cara had injured in the mountains had at least straightened. Did that mean the Goddess could fly again?

Cara didn't look up at the entrance of Erika and the queen, and Erika swallowed, wondering what torments her friend had suffered at the hands of the queen. Though…after what Cara had faced in the mountains—the condemnation of her father, the subjugation of her people, the brainwashing of her brother…who then died at her own hand…

"Cara." The whisper slipped from Erika before she could contain it.

The Goddess flinched at Erika's voice, but it was a moment before she finally lifted her head. Her movements were slow, lethargic, as though she hardly retained the will to move. Amber eyes, once so full of life, met Erika's gaze, now vacant, empty.

A tremor shook Erika, and ignoring the queen, she slipped across the room and fell to her knees beside the cage. "Cara," she said again, trying to reach the Goddess through the bars. "Cara, what has she done to you?"

But Cara only looked away. Defeat hung about her like a cloak, and Erika couldn't help but recall her own despair on the deck above, the realisation that she was doomed, that she could not hope to stand against all the power of the queen.

And yet…seeing her friend's pain, Erika recalled their desperate battles in the mountains, how they had stood against the wills of Farhan and Maya both. Erika had defied the Gods themselves—and lived to tell the tale. She had saved her friend from a fate worse than death. That had to count for something.

"Cara," she whispered, gathering her courage. Managing to reach through the bars, she wrapped a hand around the Goddess's fingers and squeezed. "Be strong. I'm going to get you out of this."

Cara didn't so much as lift her head this time. Erika's stomach twisted, but giving her friend's hand one last squeeze, she straightened.

Queen Amina shook her head as she approached the cage,

emerald eyes on the Anahera. "I thought the Gods would be regal, when they finally came for us. Still, I cannot ignore the danger they pose. It is fortunate you uncovered our people's lost magic, Archivist."

Erika swallowed as she faced the queen. How did Amina know such things, secrets that had been kept from humanity for centuries? It had been Cara who had first revealed to Erika the origins of the gauntlet she wielded, that it was born of human magic, centuries past.

Created in a time before the Anahera and Tangata had worked together to manufacture the fall of the world—and the destruction of human civilisation.

Tightening her fist, Erika faced the woman down, though the flicker of light that came from her gauntlet only set her swaying on her feet. Her vision swirled, as though she'd just run several miles on an empty stomach. Watching the queen, she wondered how the woman had come to master her own device so quickly, what poor souls she had tortured to perfect its use.

"How do you know about our ancestors, about the Anahera?" Erika demanded.

The queen waved a hand. "The source of my knowledge matters not—you cannot deny its truth. The Anahera will come for us with their Tangatan allies, just as they did in ages past. Humanity lies divided, unprepared and ill-equipped to face them. Our people will perish unless they unite beneath my rule."

"You're a traitor," Erika spat.

Amina snorted. "In more ways than you could possibly know," she replied, "but it matters not. The people believe the Anahera to be our saviours, that they will come at the hour of our greatest need, but you and I know the truth. They will turn on us when the moment comes. I must prepare the kingdoms for what they truly are."

At that the queen spun, a flash of light bursting from her gauntlet. Erika flinched away, a scream on her lips, but for once the magic was not directed at her.

Instead, it caught Cara in its terrible light.

Shrieking, the Goddess thrashed on the floor of her cage, back arched, wings beating against the bars, veins popping on her neck.

Her entire body taut, fingers bent like claws, Cara gasped, helpless within the steel cage, defenceless to the human magic. A moan rasped from the back of her throat—then abruptly, the Goddess stilled.

Swallowing, Erika took a step towards the cage—and then the Goddess looked up. Ice slid down Erika's spine as she saw the grey eyes watching her from behind the bars, the familiar madness swirling in their depths, the rage, the need to rend and tear and destroy...

The light from the queen's gauntlet vanished as the woman lowered her arm. In the cage, the fight instantly went from Cara and she slumped back to the floor, soft sobs whispering from her throat. Erika's eyes burned as she watched her friend, unable to comprehend the queen's casual cruelty.

"You see, Archivist? The beast lurks within your noble Goddess, waiting to emerge, to betray humanity as the founders of her people once did." The queen spoke in a quiet voice, untouched by emotion. Her eyes did not leave Cara, though Erika thought she glimpsed... something in their emerald depths. "Your treachery denied me for a time, but now I will show my people the truth. In Mildeth, humanity will learn what their Gods truly are."

"You can't do this to her," Erika whispered. "Cara is the best of them, the only one of the Anahera who believed in us, who refused to side with the Tangata." She was pleading now, desperate to dissuade the queen from her plan. "You're right, the others, they have allied themselves with the enemy, submitted to their new ruler, but Cara...she fought *for* us!"

"My dear Archivist, are you truly still so naïve?" the queen said. "I thought you would have learned something of the world by now, after all you have been through."

"I've learned," Erika hissed, clenching her fist, gathering what fragile energy she could muster. "Learned to trust in my friends." She drew in a breath. "To trust in Cara."

At that, she leapt at the cage, light dancing from her fist. Thrusting out her arm, she slammed it against the locking mechanism, and prayed she was strong enough to do what was needed. Red light flashed across her vision, followed by swirling darkness as the last of her strength drained away. Half-blind, she slumped to the floor, ears ringing, the metallic taste of blood on her tongue. Barely able to move, her stomach convulsed and she found herself retching acidic bile to the floor of the cabin.

A moan rasped from Erika's throat as she lay there, unable to see, to hear, to know whether she had succeeded. In the mountains, the magic of the gauntlet had broken locks easily. Here though, half-starved, she feared the effort might have killed her.

Finally her vision cleared and Erika found herself looking up at the brightly lit cabin.

Her heart sank as she saw that the queen was unmoved, her arms crossed, a smile playing on her lips as she watched Erika. Except...no, she wasn't looking at Erika, but at something behind her. Stomach still convulsing, Erika struggled to push herself to her knees, to look around...

...and saw that the door to Cara's cage had swung open.

Erika felt the darkness rising once more, the call of unconsciousness threatening to swallow her up. She fought it, clinging to her mind, to her sanity. If she lost consciousness, who knew whether she would ever wake again?

Inside the cage, Cara had come to her feet and now stood staring at the queen. Wings spread, face set, she looked ready to spring, and yet...something kept her in place. Erika swallowed the acidic taste in her mouth, struggling to speak.

"Cara," she croaked. "Run, leave me!"

But the Goddess did not flee and as Erika watched, she saw a tremor cross Cara's face. Erika recognised the fear in her friend's eyes, the knowledge that to go against the queen was to risk an agony that could threaten her very sanity.

Laughter came from Amina as she uncrossed her arms and took a step towards them. "It seems my dear Archivist has yet to learn her lesson."

Shaking her head, the queen raised the gauntlet. Cara flinched, but to Erika's surprise, the queen only gripped the artefact with her spare hand. A hiss followed, then the strange metal fibres released their grip on the queen's flesh. Erika inhaled sharply as the gauntlet slipped from the woman's wrist. Tucking it into her belt, she gestured Cara forward.

"Come then, Anahera, let us see your strength."

Standing in the cage, Cara's eyes had widened. Her feathers quivered as she watched the queen for some sign of a trap, but…the woman was only human. She could not face an Anahera, not without her magic. No human came close to matching the Goddess's speed, her strength.

Hesitantly, Cara stepped from her prison. When the queen did not reach for the gauntlet, it seemed to grant her confidence, and spreading her wings, she snarled. Then suddenly she was surging across the cabin, wings beating hard, fingers outstretched. Erika flinched at the violence of the action—in the mountains, she had seen Cara tear a man limb from limb in the grips of one of her rages. Only Romaine's dying pleas had brought the Goddess back from that madness. If she lost control here…

The harsh *thud* of a fist striking flesh reverberated through the cabin, followed by a *crash* as Cara struck the floor. Erika watched, shocked, as the Goddess thrashed, wings entangled, fingers clutching at the boards, unable to stand, to regain her feet. When she finally managed to get her limbs right beneath her, she struggled to rise, to regain her footing…

…only to meet a second blow from the queen. There was a sharp *crack* as Amina's fist connected with the Goddess's brow, then the Anahera went down in a heap. Her wings twitched, and this time she did not rise, did not even move. Instead, Cara's amber eyes slid closed as she slipped into unconsciousness.

❈ *6* ❈

THE SOVEREIGN

Lukys paused in the doorway of their apartments as he caught a glimpse of Sophia within. She stood at the edge of their balcony, looking down into the now empty amphitheatre, the wind tugging at her curly brown hair. From where he stood Lukys could not see her face, but he could sense her mind once more, the grief roiling within.

He swallowed at the depths of his partner's sadness. It came not just from Sophia's own personal loss, but that of all her people, the pain passed on by those who had perished a decade before, when the Calafe had led the invasion of Tangatan territory. Lukys shuddered to think how many lives had been lost on both sides because of that disastrous campaign. The war between their peoples had been born in those dark days.

But the past was fixed, unchangeable. There was nothing he could do for what had already come to pass—he could only hope to change what was yet to come. Drawing in a breath, he moved through the apartment, out onto the balcony where his partner waited.

"Are you okay?" Lukys asked as he came alongside her and leaned against the railing.

Sophia did not look at him, but he could see the tears shining on her cheeks. Drawing in a breath, he looked out over Ashura. The spiral pattern of the citadel spread out before them, its swirling

797

labyrinthine a testament to the arrogance of Sovereigns past—a masterpiece of architecture created only for their eyes. The passages of the outer citadel had no roofing, leaving them exposed to the elements and the eyes of the Sovereigns above. Lukys could see even now the men and women who were their subjects moving about the corridors. Various chambers housed nobles and dignitaries such as King Nguyen, and these formed domed circles amidst the spirals, like the compartments of some giant beehive.

Beyond the citadel, Ashura spread out across the slopes of the hillside, its multitude of marble buildings a stark contrast to the shacks their people had first settled in. At his back, Lukys could feel the icy chill of the mountains above the city, the endless depths of the fir forests. The Perfugians had built their city as a collision between civilisation and wilderness.

They were so like the Calafe, in that way. But there were differences here as well. Where the Calafe left no barrier between themselves and the wilds, living in small villages amidst the trees, the Perfugians built great stone walls around themselves, leaving the wilderness untouched, but separate from their lives.

But what did any of that matter? The Calafe had fallen, their lands taken by the Tangata, ruled over now by the Old One. Lukys wondered whether the creature would remain there, safe on the island of New Nihelm, or if she would march soon against the kingdoms of humanity.

The smarter tactic would be to remain, to consolidate her power, but Lukys's new knowledge whispered to him. The Old Ones were not patient. She would seek to use her newfound army, to lead the Tangata against her enemies, to strike first, before they had time to organise. Even now, the Old One might be leading a force through Calafe, intent on striking at the Flumeeren border. Unless forewarned, they could not stand against so many.

But if Lukys were to send a message, it would warn Amina of the new leadership in Perfugia, that the Sovereigns had allied themselves with her enemy, King Nguyen.

"I thought we'd left this all behind," Sophia said suddenly. Lukys started, glancing at her from the corner of his eye as she turned towards him. "I wanted to escape the wars, the killing, Lukys," she continued. "Not wage one against my own people."

A pounding began in the back of Lukys's skull as he sensed his partner's uncertainty, and for just a moment he imagined himself standing in her place, facing the choice between the lives of her people, and that of her adopted home. How would he react, had he been asked to fight against Perfugia? Not just Tasha and her guards, but the ordinary men and women of the city? Maya would bring all the Tangata who lived in New Nihelm. Young and old, they would be unable to resist her call, the power of her Voice. Even those such as they had encountered in the seaside village, innocents who had refused to participate in the war against humanity, would be coerced into joining her campaign.

His stomach twisted and he drew her into a gentle hug. Shuddering, Sophia buried her head in his shoulder and began to sob, but Lukys found he could offer his partner no words, no reassurance for the choice they faced. What could he possibly say? That it would be okay, that they would save her people, find a way to kill the Old One while protecting the Tangata she controlled?

It was impossible. Maya was too powerful, too dangerous. Even if they *could* reach her, somehow sneak past her armies and Tangatan guards and confront the creature, not one of them had the strength to face her. Cara was the only being he had seen match blows with the Old Ones, and she had vanished with Erika in the Mountains of the Gods. They may never see her kind again.

Their only hope was to use overwhelming force, to defeat the Old One with sheer weight of numbers. That meant an army, one that must first face the Tangata she controlled.

There was no other choice but war.

So Lukys held Sophia tight and waited for her grief to pass. And as they stood together, his eyes drifted to the fleet of ships upon the harbour, the hundreds flying the colours of Perfugia and Gemaho, more even than they had soldiers to field. Some would remain in Perfugia, they had already decided, to protect the kingdom should their campaign fail. As for the rest…

…the rest would bring fire and sword to the mainland.

And death to Sophia's people.

"I want to live, Lukys," Sophia rasped, lifting her head from his shoulder. Her eyes met his. "I want to laugh and love and grow new life."

Lukys swallowed. There was such longing in her voice, in her eyes. Leaning down, he kissed her, his lips hard against hers, pulling her tight against him, holding her desperately, as though at any moment she might be lost to him. When they finally broke apart, he was panting. A fiery desire burned in his chest, to lift his partner into his arms and carry her to their chambers, to grant her everything she desired.

Instead, he gently brushed a lock of hair from her eyes. "You will have it all," he whispered. "I promise."

A tear spilt from her eye as she watched him, streaking her cheek. Her lip quivered and when she spoke again, her voice was so soft he barely heard her words. "At what cost, Lukys?"

Lukys shivered, but reaching down, he entwined his fingers through hers, then leaning in, he kissed the hot tears from her cheeks. "Don't cry," he whispered. Drawing their hands up between them, he held her tight. "We will find a way, Sophia."

"How can you be so sure?"

Has he ever lied to us?

Lukys looked around as two figures stepped from the shadows. It was still strange to see Keria and Isabella, Sophia's sister Tangata, garbed in armour and equipped with the silver spears of their new position, but their support was welcome. He nodded his thanks as they approached, laying their hands on Sophia's shoulders as she stepped away from him.

A wry smile crossed Sophia's lips as she looked to them. *Are you ganging up on me, sisters?*

Laughter whispered in Lukys's mind before Keria, who had chosen Dale as her partner, turned to him.

No, sister, we stand with our family. We expect our strange brother here to do the same.

Lukys inclined his head at the respect they'd shown him, naming him as family. He and the other Perfugians who had returned from the south felt the same. After all, it had been their fellow Perfugians who had condemned them to a cruel death on the frontlines. Whereas Sophia and the Tangata… they had welcome the Perfugian recruits into their homes, into their lives. It was a kindness none of them would forget.

Yet, Lukys found himself haunted by Nguyen's words, by the

king's insistence they would have to choose, that the lives of his people must come first.

But were the Tangata not his people too? After all, the Perfugians shared common ancestors with Sophia and Keria and the others. There must be a way he ccould protect both, however impossible it might seem.

Clenching his jaw, Lukys nodded in answer to Keria's words. "We will find a way to free your people," he said softly. "We must, or we do not stand a chance."

He could already hear Nguyen's objections, but the king was wrong. Whether he liked it or not, the fact remained that even united, the forces of humanity could not stand against all the Tangata.

It will not be easy, Isabella said. *You have felt the power of Adonis's Voice —he is only of the third generation. Maya is infinitely more powerful, strong enough to hold captive the will of our people, even over some distance.*

Lukys turned to Sophia. "Ay, but we are no longer just Tangata or human," he said quietly.

As he spoke, he reached with his mind for hers, felt their consciousnesses reunited, the surging, burning force of their collective of minds, the power of a hundred Sovereigns long passed, all the way back to the ancient rule of the Old Ones. Those voices cried out in unison against the rise of Maya, at the threat to their people and Tangata both.

Lukys's mind thrummed with the power of their Voices, the harmony he felt with Sophia. Could they use this strength, these past minds and memories against Maya? Surely there must be a secret, some power, some weakness of the Old Ones they could exploit.

Finally they looked back at their friends and smiled.

We are Sovereigns now, Lukys and Sophia said in unison. *We will find a way.*

❧ 7 ❧

THE TANGATA

Adonis paced among the silent trees, ice crunching beneath his boots, ears still pounding with rage—even a day after the human's insults. Even now, he longed to find her and tear out the creature's throat for her impudence…

Instead, he shuddered, recalling against his will the Tangata who had guarded the old Matriarch, who had turned on her to join Maya's side. They had perished assaulting the city of the Anahera, but they had been of the third generation too. The Old One had spent long hours with them during the journey into the mountains, when Adonis had lingered with his people, helping them through the storm…

He ground his teeth, and clenching his fists, Adonis turned his mind back to the human, the revenge he would have against her. His heart raced at the thought of watching the life flee from her eyes, to see her fear as she realised death came creeping upon her…

…how it pained Adonis that he could not touch her, not yet. For now, all he could do was stalk the forest in search of another target for his rage. It would be a day yet before they reached human territory, and even then, they may need to search for their foes if Maisie's information proved true.

But when they did finally encounter the humans, when they destroyed the enemy armies and took more captives, Maisie would no longer have value.

Then she would learn the true extent of his displeasure.

In truth, only Nyriah had kept Adonis from unleashing his rage against the human. Despite her subservience, the Anahera had stepped between them, protecting the creature's welfare, just as she had been ordered by Maya.

But that had not protected her from Adonis.

Now he paused in his stride, turning to where the Anaheran woman shadowed him. He'd removed her from assignment with the human. She was too close to the cunning creature, it seemed to Adonis, and so he'd made her his own personal guard. To keep an eye on her…

…though looking upon her now, a shiver ran down Adonis's spine. She had defied him to protect the human, and so he had unleashed his rage against her instead. Now bruises covered Nyriah's face and arms, just reward for her obedience. The pale skin typical of the mountainous Anahera seemed to bruise easily, though surely his blows could not have caused great damage to one of their kind. Certainly, Adonis suffered far more with Maya, when the lust took his mate and she threw him down beneath her…

What makes you believe her children are your own?

Adonis's rage returned and he advanced on Nyriah. They were alone in the forest, and he saw the fear in her eyes now, saw her flinch at his approach. Instantly, he regretted his actions. It was the human that deserved his castigation. Not this sorry excuse for a god.

You should not have stopped me, slave, he said harshly, looking up at the woman. He had quickly come to ignore the wings. Far from being a symbol of the Anahera's strength and majesty, he saw them now as a reminder of their cowardice, of the unfulfilled promise of her people.

"I was ordered to watch over her," Nyriah replied meekly.

To keep her from escaping, Adonis spat. He turned away, the anger slipping from him. *She will pay for what she said, one way or another.*

"Yes, master."

He glanced at her. *That's not…necessary.*

The Anahera bowed her head but said nothing. Adonis shook his head. It didn't matter what this creature said, what the human thought. He knew the truth. His future, the future of the Tangata, was bound to Maya. The children she birthed would be his, would give way to a new era for the Tangata. Within a generation the greatness of his people would be restored, while humanity would fail, crushed beneath the boots of the Tangata, reduced to mere servitude…

A shiver ran down his spine as another image flickered into his mind, of bodies in the snow, of the dead children Maya had left in her wake. They too had been weak, too fragile to be worthy of her love, however much they wished to serve the Old One.

She isn't even one of you.

Adonis clenched his fists, hurling the words from him. Maya was harsh, it was true, but everything she did was for the betterment of his people. After all, look what had come of their sacrifice, of the sacrifice of those they'd left behind. His people had conquered the Anahera, a feat unimaginable before her coming. And now…

…now they marched children through the snow. He swallowed, a lump lodging in his throat. The young Anahera were the picture of innocence, with their pale wings and wide eyes. They couldn't understand this cruel world they'd suddenly been plunged into, the hardship and death and pain they faced.

She reminds me of Farhan.

Adonis looked around as Nyriah's words whispered into his mind. The Anahera's eyes widened at his attention, as though she hadn't meant for the silent words to escape. His frown deepened and he advanced on her, watching the fear grow in her eyes, even as she clenched her fists, as her wings lifted in preparation for a fight.

But he knew she would not resist him, not with the threat hanging over the Anaheran fledgelings. She might have lost her own child, but she would not risk the lives of the others.

What did you say? he murmured.

A tremor passed across her face and she dropped her eyes to the ground, wings slumping into the snow.

"Please, forgive me, master. I spoke out of turn."

I asked you what you said, slave.

"I…only that the Old One…she reminds me of my former partner, of Farhan."

The one Maya slew? Adonis frowned. *Explain.*

Nyriah shook her head. He could see that she regretted speaking, could read the terror in the white of her aura. "Only that she is powerful, that she dominates those within her control, just as…just as Farhan did for our own people." She hesitated, still looking away. "But…I would not think to speak for your master."

She is not my master, Adonis hissed.

This time Nyriah did not flinch away. Instead, she faced him, eyes wide with defiance, though her body was tense, awaiting his blows.

She is my mate, Adonis said instead, *my Matriarch. Soon to be the mother of my young. She is more powerful than any other being alive. It is her right to dominate, to control those too weak to decide their own fate.*

"So very like Farhan indeed," the Anaheran woman replied softly.

No, Adonis rumbled. *Your Farhan was weak, trapped in a past long since vanished.*

And it is so different with the Old One?

Enough, Adonis snarled at her words, angered again despite himself. He turned away, struggling to contain himself. Drawing in a breath, he sought to slow the racing of his heart, then faced her once more. *Your words deserve punishment, but you have already suffered enough. I will spare you this once, Anahera. But be warned: you must learn to still your tongue.*

The Anahera bowed her head in submission. *That is kind of you, master.*

You may call me Adonis, he said dismissively.

In another lifetime, you might have called me Nyriah. But now I am naught but a slave, and you my master. She finished there, but he sensed there was more beneath her words, a hint that she thought the same as Maisie, that he was as much a slave as the rest of them.

Be gone, he snapped before he lashed out again. *Return to your duties with the human. I have no more need for you, slave,* he snarled.

As you wish, master, Nyriah replied with a short bow. Turning, she vanished into the trees.

And Adonis was left alone with the ghosts of his doubts.

※ 8 ※

THE PRISONER

Anger shone in the queen's eyes as she watched the unconscious Cara. The moment stretched out, until it seemed certain she would strike again, would snuff out the life of the Goddess with a final blow. A cold smile spread across her lips as she looked to Erika.

"I should kill her for that." Lifting her boot, she placed it on the Anahera's throat.

Her eyes never left Erika and a shudder shook the Archivist. Still too exhausted to even pull herself up off the floor, she shook her head, eyes watering.

"Please, don't," she gasped.

The queen's emerald gaze did not flicker, but she removed her boot.

"I should have expected nothing less from my former prodigy," she said finally.

Leaning down, she gripped Cara by one of her wings and dragged the Goddess across the cabin. With a flick of her wrist that revealed again her impossible strength, she tossed the Anahera back into her cage. A clang sounded as the unconscious Goddess struck the bars and slumped to the metallic floor. Erika reached for her friend, but a boot came down on her hand, pinning her to the floor.

"The game is at an end, Archivist," Amina said softly. "All that remains is for you to concede."

Tears blurred Erika's vision as she stared up at her former

mentor, the woman she had aspired to become, whose approval she had sought to win for so long.

The same woman that had seen her father murdered, her kingdom cast down, her friend killed.

Who had just defeated one of the Anahera in hand-to-hand combat.

"How?" she rasped, still unable to comprehend the queen's power.

Laughter rumbled from Amina's throat as she removed her boot. Pain shot up Erika's arm as the blood rushed back to her fingers, and the barely mended bones began to ache. She made to sit up, but faster than she thought the queen lashed out, her boot catching Erika in the side. Breath hissed between her teeth as the blow threw her onto her back.

Gasping, unable to inhale through her winded lungs, Erika lay looking up at the queen's rage.

"Stupid bitch," Amina spat. "When will you learn to admit your failures? You're weak, Erika. Unworthy." Shaking her head, she turned away. "You will never understand the burden I carry, the responsibility placed upon my shoulders."

Finally catching her breath, Erika managed a groan as she rolled onto her side. She did not speak or try to rise, fearing the queen's wrath. Amina had not replaced the gauntlet on her hand, but it was obvious that the woman had never needed it, not for one so weak as Erika. What secret had the woman hidden all these years, to possess such power? Her vision swirling, Erika watched the queen cross to the mirror in the corner.

Then lifting her arms, she pulled off her heavy chainmail vest. The rings chimed as they slipped over her shoulders, then struck the ground with a jingling *thud*. The woollen tunic she wore beneath followed, until all she wore were her fine undergarments.

A hiss rasped from Erika's throat when she saw the queen's back. Suddenly blood was hammering in her ears and she found she could not look away, could not tear her gaze from Amina. Crouched on the floor, Erika stared at the scars the queen bore, at the twin circles of twisted tissue marking the skin on either side of her spine.

"Imagine my father's joy when my mother first revealed herself to him," Amina murmured, turning so she could study her back in the mirror. "And imagine his shame when years later she finally revealed the truth about her people." Erika could see the queen's rage in the mirror, furrowing the edges of her eyes, turning down her narrow lips. Abruptly, she spun and advanced on Erika. "He loved her. I know it, though I have no memory of the bitch."

Erika opened her mouth, then closed it again, unable to form a coherent thought—let alone words. How was this possible? How could one of the Anahera have sired a human queen? A murmur came from behind her, as Cara stirred in the cage, and an icy suspicion filled Erika's chest. Could it be?

"Your mother?" she croaked.

The queen looked away. "The creature seduced my father, convinced him he had been blessed by the Divine. Only during my birth did he learn the truth. With his own eyes, father saw my mother change, saw the beast that lurked within, the madness they share with the filthy Tangata. It broke his heart, but he knew he had to act, before that beast was unleashed upon our world."

"He killed her," Erika whispered.

"Eventually," Amina replied with a sneer. "My father was prudent. He knew there were truths to be uncovered, secrets the false gods had hidden from us. With fifty of his most trusted men, he tricked my mother, imprisoned her deep beneath the citadel in a cell not even her kind could escape." Amina shook her head. "The... creature admitted it all, by the end: the treachery of the Anahera, how they destroyed the cities of our ancestors, ground us into the dust."

Erika shuddered at the cold way Amina talked about her own mother, but already the queen was speaking again.

"They say she begged my father to spare me. Perhaps that is why I still live...why he laid this charge upon me, why he spent his final years preparing me to face the demons that hide in the mountains,"

Erika swallowed, horror still clawing at her throat. "He...he took your wings."

"The mark of demons," Amina spat, swinging on her. "My father hoped removing them would spare me their darkness, though he was prepared..." She trailed off, glaring down at Erika. "He took a terrible gamble, but he hoped I would have the strength to stand against them, to do what was necessary. Every moment of my life has been spent in preparation for these days."

"He created a monster," Erika whispered, slumping to the floor. Shaking her head, she looked up at the woman. "But why would you kill my father, when he fought against the Tangata?"

A cold smile crossed Amina's lips. "Your father served his purpose well," she replied. "Peace had made humanity weak, unprepared for the coming threat. The Calafe king was a fiery man, quick to anger, easily manipulated. He began the war that would forge humanity anew, but I could not allow one so flawed to lead us. When he fell, humanity was to unite beneath my leadership. Together, the four kingdoms would have crushed the Tangatan threat." She hesitated, eyes narrowing. "But King Nguyen ruined everything when he abandoned the alliance. I had to find other ways to bring about unity." She gestured back in the direction of Gemaho, as though in explanation.

Listening to Amina's words, Erika felt something die within her, the last remnants of her defiance. Her eyes slid closed, despair withering her soul. All along, this woman had been a step ahead of the other monarchs. Amina was right. Erika could not defeat this woman. She was too weak, her strength sapped, her last hope lying crumpled in the cage, defeated.

Abruptly, Erika's world spun as the queen grasped her by the shirt and hauled her up. Crying out, she struggled against the queen's impossible strength—until she glimpsed the fiery light of the gauntlet. Amina wore its silver threads on her hand again. Now its glow bathed the cabin, red and threatening, promising pain.

Watching that light, Erika found herself unable to look away, to fight back, to do anything but slump in her captor's grip and wait for the pain to find her, for the agony to sweep her mind away on a sea of madness…

…but that pain did not come, as instead the queen suddenly turned from Erika, her eyes drawn to the wooden walls of the cabin. A frown creased the woman's forehead.

"What?" she murmured. Before Erika could understand what was happening, her eyes widened. "So they have come. It is earlier than I'd hoped, but I am not unprepared."

Erika cried out as the queen hurled her backwards. The back of the open cage brought her to an abrupt halt and she crumpled atop her friend, drawing a moan from Cara. Before Erika could even roll off the Goddess's wings, the door to the cage slammed shut with a harsh *click*, the locking mechanism reengaging. Smouldering emerald eyes glared down at them.

"I will leave you to contemplate your fate, Archivist. If you still have the strength to use your gauntlet, I dare you try and escape. You will not make it far." She held up her fist, a flash of light sending tremors down Erika's spine. "And I promise, the attempt will make your end all the longer."

With that she turned away, disappearing up the stairs to the upper deck of her ship.

❧ 9 ❧

THE SOVEREIGN

Wind whipped at Lukys's cheeks as the ocean surged around the ship, sending water hissing over the bow to strike at his flesh like knives. He ignored the stinging, eyes fixed on the distant walls that rose from the swirling blue.

Mildeth.

He could still recall his last journey to the city, a brief stop at the end of a short voyage across the narrow sea. The crossing had taken only hours and the Perfugian recruits had not lingered within the city before beginning their march south.

This time, Lukys intended to make an extended visit.

The defensive walls facing the harbour were taller than those in Ashura, raised in centuries past to defend against pirates that had once plagued the coast. The rise of Perfugia had put end to those outlaws, as their fleet hunted them down one by one. But the Flumeeren walls remained, and now they barred the soldiers of Perfugia from an easy victory.

But Lukys had hopes it would not come to battle. Their intelligence was that Queen Amina remained in the south with the majority of the Flumeeren army. That suited Lukys's purposes. Their own fleet followed a half-day behind with Nguyen, but if things went to plan, they would not need the king's forces to take the city.

It was a risk, sailing ahead with but one ship. If those in control of Mildeth suspected a trick, they might bar the gates. Forewarned, the city would mass defenders atop those giant walls, making it difficult for the invaders to gain a foothold. They might extend the siege for weeks—long enough for the queen to bring reinforcements.

That was why Nguyen had wanted to attack immediately, using overwhelming force so the city would fall quickly. But Lukys couldn't bring himself to throw away the chance for a peaceful resolution.

After all, the Flumeerens had no reason to believe Perfugia came for conquest. The Sovereigns rarely left the shores of the island, but it would not be the first time they had ventured to the mainland in times of strife. He remembered when they'd come to the assembly called by King Micah of Calafe…

…Lukys shook his head, trying to separate himself from the consciousness of the Sovereigns who had come before, who had stood with the other kingdoms and set out to make war against the Tangata. Such a strange sensation, to know he had played no part in those events, and yet…

…he could picture the noble Micah perfectly as he called on their aid, could recall his righteous fury as he demanded support of Queen Amina, as he swayed the young King Nguyen to his side.

Lukys found himself turning in search of Sophia. Finding her alone at the railings, he wondered if she too had found that memory. How must it feel, to recall making a decision that had condemned so many of her people to death?

Even for himself, that memory was a knife twisting in his gut. The Sovereigns before them had been so cold, so calculating in their decisions, the product of a hundred lifetimes placed into the minds of children. Their predecessors had never had a chance to live their own lives, to develop a consciousness beyond that which they inherited.

Struggling with those memories, Lukys wondered whether he too would succumb to the tide, if one day he and Sophia would become as those Sovereigns before them, removed from the lives of mere mortals, incapable of measuring the value of a single life.

Would Lukys one day come to understand the logic of sending untrained recruits to die for the simple crime of failing an examination?

The thought made him shiver, but he shook off such dark

contemplations and crossed to where Travis stood at the tiller. His friend wore a broad grin as he directed the ship towards the safety of the harbour, though he offered a quick salute at Lukys's approach.

"My Sovereign," the man said in an overly dramatic fashion. "A million thanks for this ship you have provided. Much better than the last one."

Lukys snorted. "You mean the holey fishing boat you sailed across half an ocean?"

"I remember her fondly," Travis remarked. "A shame this journey is so short. I would have liked to see how this beauty did against a storm."

Lukys shuddered at the memory his words conjured. This one he had lived himself. "Let's just give thanks for the sunny skies," he replied with feeling.

Silence fell as they turned their eyes to the city. Two smaller vessels had detached themselves from the docks to escort them in, and Lukys couldn't help but feel his tension growing.

"I'll leave you and Isabella onboard with a skeleton crew," Lukys said. "If we don't return…"

"Don't be so grim, Lukys," Travis said with a laugh. "It's a few bureaucrats and those in their army who were too old or green to march south. After facing Tasha and her rebellion, the pair of you should have no problem with this lot."

Lukys sighed. He wished he could feel Travis's confidence, that everything would work out as they intended. But whatever his jovial friend said, things had a habit of spiralling out of control when it came to Lukys's plans. Ever since he'd first picked up a spear and lead them in defence of Fogmore's walls all those months ago, nothing had gone as he'd intended.

But he would press on regardless. There was no other choice.

As the Flumeeren vessels pulled up on either side of their flag ship, Lukys was relieved to see only a few soldiers aboard. He hoped that meant the Flumeerens remained unaware of their alliance with Nguyen. Even so, he watched the gates of the city as they approached, seeking signs of some trap.

But as they drifted into the port, no soldiers came rushing from the gates to attack them, nor arrows from the sky to strike them down, and Lukys finally let out a breath and moved to join Sophia at the bow. She wore a cloak with the hood pulled up, a veil drawn across her face. He quickly lowered his own to complete their illusion. The mystique of the Sovereigns was well-known across the human kingdoms, and he prayed the Flumeerens would not question the concealment of their faces. One glimpse of Sophia's grey eyes, and all his careful planning would fall apart.

"Peace, My Lady," Lukys said softly, reaching out to take Sophia's hand. "I promise you. Now, let's go trick some Flumeerens."

They were met on the docks by two dignitaries and their guards. Lukys had rarely seen such an odd assortment of nobles, although his experience with their kind was rather limited. An overweight man in a bright orange robe led the way, his face damp with sweat, as though their arrival had forced him to run through half the city to reach the docks in time. Behind him followed an elderly man with more wrinkles than even the most ancient of Lukys's history professors back in his academy. Supported by a cane, the man arrived a few steps behind the big man.

The two fell into a steep bow as Lukys and Sophia descended the ramp from their ship, and Lukys was struck by the difference a few weeks made. It seemed like only yesterday that their arrival on the shores of Perfugia had been met with armed soldiers and threats of violence.

Then again, if the Flumeerens realised that a party of Tangata stood amongst them, it might yet come to violence. After all, this kingdom had been at the forefront of the war with Sophia's people for ten long years.

"Exalted Sovereigns!" the large man wheezed, clearly still trying to catch his breath. "Please, I am Wallace, steward of the royal citadel. I must apologise for my queen's absence, but she is occupied by grave matters in the south. I welcome you to Mildeth in her absence."

"It is an honour to witness your arrival on our humble shores, your dignities," the elderly man added, his voice soft. "I am called Zayaan, chief advisor to the queen. As the good steward says, your visit is welcome—if unexpected. I fear you have come to Flumeer at a time of ill fortune."

"So we understand," Lukys replied, doing his best to adopt the haughty tones of the nobility. "Some trouble with Gemaho?"

"Yes," Wallace replied, his eyes flickering to the open sea. "We are on high alert for the Gemaho king. His fleet has not been seen since the coward fled down the Illmoor, escaping our majesty's righteous wrath. Your ships have not caught a glimpse of his presence, perhaps?"

"I'm sure the noble Sovereigns of Perfugia would have alerted us immediately had they encountered the coward king," Zayaan interrupted, hands clasped at his back as he shot the steward an irritated look. "As I am sure they would prefer to discuss such delicate matters within the protection of the city walls."

Lukys blinked, taken by surprise at the speed at which they had been invited into Mildeth. Despite their outward confidence, it was clear both men were nervous about the prospect of an attack on the city by Nguyen. If only they knew how close they were to the truth. Thankfully though, Lukys's veil concealed any emotion that might have given him away, and he only inclined his head in agreement.

"We thank you for your hospitality, Zayaan," he replied. "Shall we proceed to the citadel then?"

The men nodded quickly, but as they made to turn away, something behind Lukys and Sophia caught the steward's attention and he hesitated. Glancing over his shoulder, Lukys saw that Dale and the other royal guards were marching down the ramp onto the docks.

"Oh!" Lukys turned back as Wallace let out an exclamation. "You brought soldiers, I see. Excellent, excellent, every sword is welcome in the war against the traitor. Only…" He hesitated, glancing at the elderly Zayaan, then back to Lukys. "We have orders from our queen prohibiting the entry of foreign soldiers into the city, regardless of their allegiance."

Lukys's heart began to race as he saw all his carefully laid plans unrolling before him. They had hoped to gather the leaders of the city in an assembly and take them hostage with their own guard, preventing them from commanding their forces to defend the city. But without Dale and the others, Lukys and Sophia would be alone in the citadel. They risked becoming hostages themselves when Nguyen arrived with the bulk of their forces.

"My dear steward," Sophia spoke before Lukys could announce his displeasure. "It would be a difficult task for our soldiers to defend the city if they are forced to remain outside its walls."

Lukys glanced sharply at his partner, surprised not only by her words, but how they had been spoken. Gone was the singsong accent she'd adopted since receiving the gift of the Sovereigns—in its place was a perfect imitation of a Perfugian noble. For a moment, he was left questioning whether it was truly Sophia who spoke, or if another of those minds within her had taken control of her voice.

"I…" The steward wrung his hands, clenching and unclenching his fists as sweat dripped from his brow. "I am sorry, good Sovereign, but I…perhaps a message…the queen."

"Surely your queen could not have thought to apply such restrictions to the Sovereigns of Perfugia, her last remaining ally in this terrible war? To think we would enter a foreign city alone…" Sophia shook her head, glancing to Lukys. "It seems we were wrong to think our aid would be welcomed, my dear. Perhaps we should return—"

"No!" Wallace interrupted. "Please," he continued, lowering his voice, "our forces are badly depleted here. Should Nguyen appear, we could not hold the walls against him for even a day."

Sophia said nothing, only stared at the man from beneath her veil, waiting…

"I am sure we can come to some arrangement," Zayaan said finally, shifting alongside the steward. He had named himself the queen's advisor—perhaps that meant he had some authority to supersede her orders. "Perhaps we could permit…two of your guards to enter alongside your noble personage," he offered finally.

Lukys grimaced beneath his veil. His plan didn't require defeating the Flumeeren army, only that they took enough of their leaders hostage to prevent the organisation of the city's defences. Would four of them be enough?

It would have to be.

"Very well," he said abruptly. "Dale, Keria, you will accompany us into the city." Their helmets would conceal Keria's Tangatan eyes, and her Tangatan strength would be an added advantage. He inclined his head to the pair of nobles. "If you would permit our remaining soldiers to disembark, perhaps they could take refreshments outside the walls. That way they might be of some aid outside the gates, should the Gemaho fleet happen to make an appearance."

Zayaan nodded his agreement, and Wallace sighed his relief. "Excellent, excellent," he exclaimed, offering another short bow before spreading his hands in the direction of the city gates. "Then may I again bid you welcome to the glorious city of Mildeth."

Lukys sucked in a breath as he looked to the gates of the city, wondering whether they were making a terrible mistake. A glance back at their ship showed their soldiers beginning to disembark. He clenched his jaw, considering one last time the wisdom of this decision, before turning again to the two men. If things went wrong and this was all some elaborate trap, at least he would be able to communicate with the Tangata outside. That was an advantage the Flumeerens would not suspect.

And so he exhaled, and nodded for Wallace to lead them into the stronghold of their enemy.

10

THE TANGATA

The dark waters swirled as Adonis struck out through the racing currents. The river fought him, sought to drag him down into its murky depths, to steal away his warmth. But on the quiet spring night, it would not succeed.

His heart pounded with the thrill of what was to come, his mind thrumming to the beat of war, the Voice of his mate. The time had finally come for them to strike against the true enemy, to destroy the humans who had dared venture so close to his people's territory.

The ships had anchored themselves only a few hundred yards from the shore. Truly, the humans had grown bold while the Tangata had been occupied in the south. Now they would suffer for their arrogance.

The sight of the ships had driven Maya into a rage. Her hatred had swept over the ranks of her Tangata, their numbers swollen by the journey north, until all who stood upon the banks of the great river had yearned for the blood of their foes. With night already fallen, the distant lanterns burning upon the waters had become beacons, drawing the Tangata like moths to the flame.

Adonis led the attack, an assault that would finally break the impasse upon the great river. United, the Tangata would sweep the humans back from their barricades, shatter their defences. Without the natural advantages of the river to bolster their defences, it would only be a matter of time before the armies of humanity crumbled, before their cities fell, before their so-called civilisation was reduced to ashes.

His stomach churned strangely at that thought, and he found himself thinking back to New Nihelm, the human city the Tangata had conquered, that they had made their home. Though he loathed the creatures who had built the city, Adonis couldn't deny that there had been a beauty about the place. Those who had first raised the wooden buildings had long since passed, but their descendants continued their work, caring for the city, adding to it, until succeeding generations had built something grand.

Swimming through the racing waters, Adonis found himself wondering if one day his children might build such a city, if they might raise wonders from the stones of this earth…

…or if they too would bring destruction.

He shook off the thought as the shadow of a ship rose above him, the curve of its hull illuminated by a lantern hung from its rigging. Pausing, Adonis sought the Voices of his brethren, their rage, the thrill of their excitement for the battle to come. His own heart responded, his anger stirring, though he could not muster the same emotion he had felt at Maya's side.

A rope ran from the ship into the waters, taut with the weight of the anchor. Quiet now in the swirling currents, Adonis directed himself towards the rope, catching the coarse fibres in strong hands. As the others in the water grew close, he began to climb.

The night greeted him with a cold breeze that cut through his thin clothing. Water poured from him to splash upon the river, loud enough that he feared the humans might hear. But the creatures' senses were blessedly poor, and no shouts carried through the night to alert the sleeping soldiers.

A smile touched Adonis's lips as he continued his climb. He had missed the battle with the Anahera, being one of the few Maya had trusted to hunt the fledgelings instead. Now he once again had the honour of leading his people in battle. This was what he lived for, what he had been born to do. The third generation had been great warriors, the last of the true Tangata, possessed of the strength to run all day and battle all night.

The stench of humanity struck Adonis as he pulled himself over the railings, the reek of dozens of bodies crushed together in filthy conditions. He couldn't imagine how the creatures stood to live in such cramped confines. Even now he could hear them below, the whisper of voices, the snoring and the grunts. The ship must have held a hundred of the creatures, yet it could not have been larger than the villa he had occupied in New Nihelm.

Dropping to the deck of the ship, Adonis examined his surroundings, waiting for his brethren to join him. Most of the soldiers slept below and at first he saw no one. A small cabin was lit by a lantern at the stern, a pile of barrels stacked nearby. This was the largest of the dozen ships anchored on the river. Maisie had claimed it was the flagship of the Flumeeren kingdom, that it might belong to the queen herself.

That thought made Adonis's heart clench with anticipation. If the Flumeeren queen fell this night, the kingdom would not be long in following. That was the way of these creatures. Led by the right man or woman, they fought like demons, refusing to lie down and die when they had no right to fight on. But when that leader fell, her followers fell with her.

Adonis tensed as he sensed movement, and a human armed with a spear emerged from behind the cabin. He must have been making his rounds, for he continued along the railings, eyes on the water below. Adonis watched the man, wondering if the humans were truly so arrogant to post only a single guard. Surely this close to Tangatan territory, there must be another…

The squeak of a board was the only warning Adonis had. Spinning, he flung up an arm as the soldier creeping up behind him thrust out with a spear. Adonis wore no armour and the blow would have driven the blade straight through his back—if not for his inhuman speed. Instead, he twisted, wrist slamming against the haft of the weapon and deflecting it into the wooden boards at his feet.

The soldier's eyes widened as his attack failed, and snarling, Adonis leapt at him, seeking to silence the threat before it could alert others. But the soldier recovered his wits quickly, and a scream escaped his lips a second before Adonis tore out his throat.

Adonis stilled as the body struck the deck, fists clenched, praying that none had heard the cry, that the foolish humans would put it down to a trick of the wind, of the river...

Whoooorl!

Adonis cursed as a bugle horn came from the other side of the ship, the second soldier sounding the alarm. The note rose above the silence of the night, carrying to the soldiers below—and the other ships as well—alerting them to the danger that stalked them this night.

But it alerted the Tangata too, and the battlecry of Adonis's brethren rang out across the river.

Adonis's body reacted before his mind. Surging across the deck, he caught the human before it could blow another warning note. The horn struck the deck with a heavy *thump* as Adonis sucked in a breath, fighting off the call of the Tangatan rage. He could not afford the madness now, not if he was to lead his people.

Movement came from nearby, followed by shouts and a sharp *twang* as something fired in the darkness. Adonis spun and something *hissed* through the space he had occupied. A clacking sound followed that Adonis recognised as the reloading of a human crossbow.

Roaring, he charged towards the noise. From behind, he sensed his brethren as the first reached the top of the rope. Adonis needed to keep the enemy occupied for only a few moments longer.

The human with the crossbow saw him coming and tossed their weapon aside, its wire still only half loaded. He fumbled for his spear, but Adonis caught the wooden haft before the man could bring it to bear. Fear showed in the human's eyes as Adonis tore the weapon from his hands, but to his credit, the man did not flee. He was reaching for the dagger on his belt when Adonis's fist struck his skull. Despite the metal helmet worn by the human, he dropped without a sound, and Adonis turned in search of his next victim.

The first of his brethren had reached the deck now, but as Adonis watched, a door at the rear of ship burst open and humans half-dressed in armour poured from the darkness below. In moments, a dozen of the creatures stood against him, weapons held high, dull eyes scanning the darkness for hint of the creatures that had come upon them. The few lanterns burning were not enough for the pitiful humans to spy the Tangata in the shadows. Adonis might have laughed.

Instead, he roared and charged the group of humans.

The soldiers reacted instantly, swinging towards the sound. A dozen was too many for Adonis, even in the dark, but his charge drew their attention away from where his brethren still emerged from the dark waters.

Then Adonis was amongst them, slicing through their ranks like a dagger, fists flashing, leaping and dancing between their blows, striking soft flesh and hard steel wherever his foes lowered their guards. Cries of pain filled the night and in those first seconds several of the humans crumpled, clutching at broken ribs or shattered kneecaps.

Still roaring, Adonis ducked and weaved, narrowly avoiding the desperate thrusts of steel weapons. The humans found their spears almost useless in such close proximity, and several of the more intelligent tossed the weapons aside and drew short swords.

It was one of these that spilt the first of Adonis's blood that night. He cursed as the blade sliced his cheek and leapt back, twisting away from an awkward spear thrust in the process. Heart racing, he felt some of the rage leave him, reason returning. The human's blow had been just inches from his throat. It had almost ended him, snuffed out his life and left his children alone, with only Maya to raise them.

For some reason, that thought chilled Adonis and he took another step back from the humans, allowing them a moment to regroup—and for his brethren to finally join the battle. Their silent cries echoed through the night, unheard by the humans, so that they did not turn as the Tangata charged.

Adonis smiled, satisfied as his brethren fell upon the humans from behind. Of the fourth and fifth generations, human bones still shattered beneath their blows. Despite their resilience thus far, the humans crumpled before the surprise attack. Screams rent the night as they scattered—and one by one were hunted down by their Tangatan foes.

His victory achieved, Adonis was about to join in the hunt, when a figure stepped from the nearby cabin. Garbed all in steel and wearing a helmet engraved with a golden crown, the figure raised a sword high and charged a group of Tangata. Distracted by the human soldier they had been tormenting, Adonis's brethren scattered at the sudden assault, though not before one had fallen to the newcomer's blade. Spinning to face the others Tangata, the human raised its blade to the sky.

"Soldiers of Flumeer!" The woman's voice lifted above the chaos, calm, determined. "To me!"

❧ II ☙

THE PRISONER

Erika sat up in the cage as a scream carried down from above. Her vision swam at the sudden movement and she would have thrown up if there had been anything left in her stomach. The long days without food had more than taken their toll and now she barely had the strength to keep her eyes open. How she wished that they'd never left the mountains. Maybe she and Cara might have found peace somewhere amidst the endless peaks, far from the queen's darkness, from the rage of the Old One and her Tangata.

But no, instead Erika had brought them to a land torn by war, following the futile hope that she might help her people, might find a way to save the very kingdom that had turned its back on her as a child.

She had doomed not only herself, but Cara too.

Erika shook herself as another scream came from the ceiling, followed by the ring of weapons. Erika struggled to concentrate through her exhaustion. The ship was under attack, but who in the kingdoms of humanity still had the power to threaten the Flumeerens? Had King Nguyen escaped after all?

A chill touched Erika as she recalled the queen's words.

So they have come. It is earlier than I'd hoped, but I am not unprepared.

No, not the Gemaho at all. The Old One and her Tangata. Erika must have been locked in the hold longer than she'd imagined, if the creatures were already here, though it was a shorter route to cut through the fallen lands of the Calafe than the round-about way she and Cara had taken through Gemaho.

Her stomach twisted at the memory of the Old One, at how the Anahera had bowed to her will, the way she had looked at Erika. The creature loathed humanity above all else. No matter what preparations Amina had made, whatever strength she had inherited from her mother, the queen could not possibly be prepared for that.

Another scream sounded, high pitched and unending, as of some soldier horribly disfigured. Heart pounding in her chest, Erika turned to Cara. Somehow, they had to escape this cage. She didn't want to be trapped here when the Old One finally came.

"Cara, she's here, isn't she? The Old One?"

The young Goddess did not stir, only sat with her knees drawn up to her chest, eyes on the steel floor of the cage. Erika swallowed, then gently reached out and clutched Cara's shoulder.

"Cara, come on, I need you. We have to find a way out of here."

Still Cara did not stir and Erika feared she'd lost her friend to madness. But then the Anahera's head lifted, her amber eyes meeting Erika's. A tear streaked her cheek as she blinked and began to shake.

"I never gave up," she croaked. "Never stopped hoping she was out there somewhere. That one day I'd be flying over the plains, and she would find me."

Another tremor shook the Goddess. The tears were flowing freely now. Grief contorted her face and Erika felt her friend was about to shatter, to crumble beneath the weight of her pain. But Erika said nothing, only crouched beside her, waiting.

"After all these years of searching..." Cara's voice broke as words gave way to sobs.

Despite their danger, despite the screams of dying men from above, Erika hugged her friend tight. What else could she do? At the end of her strength, Erika could no more will the cage away than she could defeat the queen in single combat.

Amina, the queen of Flumeer.

And Cara's unknown half-sister.

Only one Anahera had left the city in the past decades—Cara's mother. The creatures had said little of the woman, only that she had vanished. Not even Cara had known her fate. Until now.

"She abandoned me." It was a moment before Erika heard the words in Cara's sobs. Suddenly the Goddess stilled. "Left me all alone with *Farhan*. All so she could be with one of *you*." She looked up then, and Erika could see the rage in her eyes now, fed by the depth of her grief. "And what did it get her in the end? Only more pain, only death. Maybe my father was right to hate your kind."

Erika swallowed, but she could find no words to reply, no argument for the grieving young woman beside her. It was difficult sometimes, to recall that Cara was in fact fifty years of age. Due to the slow development of the Anahera, she appeared no older than a teenager. Human blood from Amina's father must have aged the queen faster than her sister, yet looking at the Goddess now, Erika finally saw the similarities—the sharp cheekbones and scarlet shades of their hair, the large eyes that seemed to pierce you to the soul.

"I don't know what to say, Cara," Erika said at last, her own vision blurring, though she kept the tears from falling. "It's a cruel place, this world our ancestors left for us. Humanity is what the fires of the Fall made us—harsh and merciless. I know it cannot bring your mother back, but I am sorry for what we did to her."

The Goddess looked away at that, though every so often a tremor would shake her wings, the feathers standing on end. The sounds of battle were growing louder now, fiercer. Erika glanced at Cara, but there was no signs of life in the Goddess. The anger had died from her eyes, leaving only despair, only the darkness of the defeated.

She clenched her fist, wishing for the strength to summon the magic. She only achieved another bout of dizziness. A gasp slipped from her lips as she slid sideways, slumping against the bars. Cara frowned as she watched her, seeming confused.

"Why are you still fighting?" she said, her voice almost angry, as though Erika's lack of despair were an insult to her. "It's over, Erika. The Old One and her Tangata are here, some of my people too. I can hear their Voices—they're all around us. Not even my bitch sister can fight them. It's over. Maya has won."

"No," Erika hissed, forcing herself to sit up. "No, I won't let them." She gripped Cara by the shoulder and forced the Goddess to look at her. "I'm sorry about your mother, Cara. I know what it feels like to lose a parent to evil. But you're not alone."

"Of course I'm alone," Cara snapped, tearing herself from Erika. "My brother, my mother, my father, they're all dead now. My own people bow to the darkness of the Old One. I'm the only one left."

"No," Erika hissed. Gently she cupped Cara by the cheek. "No," she repeated, softly this time, looking into Cara's amber eyes. "You still have me, Cara, always. We're family now, you and I." Gently she pressed her forehead to the Goddess's. "I won't let her hurt you anymore. I won't let them take you."

She thought Cara would pull away, but after a moment the Goddess's eyes slid closed and she began to tremble. Silently she shook her head, fingers pulling at her torn leggings.

"I don't know what I'm doing, Erika," she croaked. "It's all wrong, all of this, what Father did for me, what happened to Hugo...there was so much blood." She was sobbing now, hugging Erika tight, clutching at her back. "I should have done something else, should have been able to save him. He was so young...never had a life...and now Mother...I can't..." Her words became unintelligible as she tumbled from one loss to another.

Erika squeezed her tight then drew back, carefully wiping the tears from the Goddess's cheeks. Cara fell silent, blinking at Erika in the gloom of the cabin, amber eyes reflecting the fading candlelight.

"You did your best, Cara," she said softly, "but no one could have saved Hugo. You said so yourself—he was under Maya's control. She's too strong for any one of your people. And your father chose to save you, to do right by his daughter. You cannot blame yourself for the choices of others. All you can do is honour their sacrifices."

The tears still slid down Cara's face as she hiccupped softly, shivering in the confines of their cage, feathers trembling. But finally she closed her eyes and nodded. Angrily she wiped away the last of her tears, then rose abruptly, eyes on the ceiling.

"Maya's close," she said sharply. "There isn't much—"

Boom!

12
THE SOVEREIGN

Standing at a window looking out over the harbour, Lukys struggled to contain the pounding in his chest. At any moment, he expected the alarm to sound, for soldiers to come rushing into the room and take them hostage, or worse. Wallace and Zayaan sat at a table behind him with a growing number of nobles, but the most important of their number had yet to join them—the officer in charge of their defences.

"This has been the strangest of times," Wallace was saying to Sophia who sat with them at the table. "Hidden Gods and traitorous kings and all."

He doesn't know the half of it. Lukys sent the silent words to his partner, and sensed a ripple of her mirth in response.

Earlier, Wallace and Zayaan had led them through the streets of Mildeth. The queen might have left with most of their army, but Lukys couldn't help but notice the frosty manner of the populace, the suspicious glances they cast at the strange group moving through their midst. Most relaxed when they noticed Zayaan, but Lukys still sensed their distrust in the sickly green of their aura.

Thinking of their reception, Lukys couldn't help but question his plan, whether the four of them would be enough. Even if they took hostage the members of this room, would the people on the streets submit willingly? Or would they rise up against the invaders?

"A strange time indeed," he said finally, moving from the

window to join those gathered at the table. "Though I am glad to find that Flumeeren hospitality has not changed."

Taking the seat alongside his partner, he allowed his eyes to roam over the gathering. Wallace and Zayaan had been joined by half a dozen others, minor officers and nobles from the south that had fled the Tangatan threat. Most of those with higher ranks would have marched with the queen, but Amina must have trusted at least a few of these men and women, to have left them in command of her capital.

"Indeed," Zayaan replied. "Though I admit, I had not thought them strange enough to merit your noble presence in our city, Sovereigns."

Lukys narrowed his eyes as the queen's advisor spoke, sensing the man's suspicion. Zayaan was seated at Lukys's side, while Wallace took the spare seat alongside Sophia. It was clear these two carried some measure of authority over the others, though neither were military men. He glanced at the door, but there was still no sign of the officer in command of the city guard.

"It has been some time, has it not, since your last visit?" Zayaan continued.

Sensing the question in the man's words, Lukys allowed himself a smile beneath the veil. It took a moment to find the memory he needed—those more recent seemed easier to uncover.

"Ten years," he confirmed. "Not since the gathering of kings have we stepped foot on the mainland."

Zayaan smiled at that. "I must say, I find your attire…puzzling. The veils must be quite the advantage during negotiations. I can hardly tell which of you is the man and which the woman, let alone the thoughts behind your words."

Sophia and Lukys turned their eyes upon the man. Though neither spoke, Lukys could sense his partner's unease. They both recalled the near disaster of their arrival in Perfugia, when Tasha had torn the blindfold from Sophia's eyes, revealing her true lineage.

Thankfully, Wallace came to their rescue, as his face grew red and he spluttered something unintelligible at the elderly Zayaan.

"My apologies!" he said finally, turning to them, "I am sure Zayaan meant no offence with his words."

Lukys proffered an exaggerated sigh beneath his veil. "It is a tradition of our people, you understand," he replied. "Only our own—and royalty, of course—may look upon the likeness of the Sovereigns."

That was only partly true. The memories he held recalled many occasions when the Sovereigns had revealed themselves, but there was no need to make exceptions here. At least, not yet. Not until all had gathered in place.

"Fear not, good Sovereigns, we in Flumeer respect the traditions of the ancients," Wallace proclaimed, flashing Zayaan a glare as he spoke. "Why, the good queen has often remarked to me the loyalty of your kingdom. Perfugia has never missed a tribute to the alliance."

Lukys's heart twisted at the man's words. He knew all too well what Wallace was referring to—the recruits like Lukys that Perfugia had sent each year to fight on the frontline. Only…

"It is a welcome arrangement for us all." Lukys forced out the words, though they made his intestines squirm. "Your generals receive more fodder to slow the Tangatan advance, and we…rid ourselves of wasted mouths."

Lukys, you know that is not true, Sophia's concern sounded in his mind, a wave a warmth accompanying her reassurance.

He smiled beneath his veil and sent back his silent agreement. Outwardly, he said nothing, though he saw shock in the expressions of some around the table.

"You are surprised at our candour," Sophia offered, picking up the conversation. "We believe one should always talk openly amongst allies—lest distrust be allowed to enter relations." She lifted her drink to offer a toast.

Lukys raised an eyebrow at her words, but the others were already following Sophia's lead and toasting her back. With a sigh he did the same, though it was difficult to pass the cup of liquor beneath his veil.

But as he sipped the burning whiskey, an idea came to him. Looking at those seated around the table, he realised they didn't seem so different from the Flumeerens he'd once fought with in Fogmore. Richer, certainly, but not the greedy nobles he had expected of those who followed Amina. Rather, their loyalty seemed…misdirected, abused by a woman who had abandoned them here, helpless to defend themselves against their enemies. No wonder they had welcomed their arrival so readily.

Lukys rose to his feet before he could doubt himself, drawing the attention of the others at the table.

"On that sentiment, my good lords and ladies—" he started, but as he spoke the door to the chamber banged open, and a man garbed in the red uniform of the Flumeeren army entered, a sword hanging from his belt.

Lukys tensed, but he spied the golden lieutenant's badge a second before Wallace leapt to his feet. "Finally! Lieutenant Ewan, what kept you?"

The lieutenant frowned as he crossed the room. "The safety of the city?" he said shortly, irritation in his voice. "You do realise we're at war, steward? I cannot attend every dalliance you decide to host on a whim. There was another protest amongst the Calafe camps that needed dealing with…" He trailed off, eyes noting the presence of Sophia and Lukys at the table.

"Yes, well, as you can see, Lieutenant, we have important guests," Wallace replied shortly. "My dear Sovereigns, may I introduce Lieutenant Ewan, the man in charge of our defences in the queen's absence." He paused, belatedly remembering that Lukys was on his feet and clearing his throat. "Er, Sovereign, you were saying something?"

Lukys hesitated, needles prickling at his brow as the attention of the room returned to him. This was their chance. With the members of this room captured, the city would be left without leaders. He cast his gaze to the back of the room, where Dale and Keria lurked. The Flumeerens had guards of their own of course, but none possessed the strength of the Tangata. With Sophia and Keria on their side, it wouldn't be difficult to take control…

…but what if violence was not the answer here?

"Thank you, Wallace, for your kindness," he said softly. "It is welcome after the difficulties we have suffered these last months." He drew in a breath as a frown crossed the steward's lips, then continued before the questions could begin. "In truth, we are new to our roles as Sovereigns. Word would not yet have reached you here on the mainland, but there has been a change in leadership in Perfugia. The old Sovereigns were killed…unexpectedly."

"Killed?" Wallace exclaimed. Seated nearby, the elderly Zayaan only frowned, lips pressed in a line, eyes fixed on Lukys.

"Slain by their own guards," Lukys confirmed grimly, gesturing for Sophia to rise. He sensed the tension in his partner as she came to her feet, felt it too from Dale and Keria as they edged towards the other guards. "We do not intend to make the same mistakes."

"I should hope not," Zayaan responded calmly. "Treachery must be quashed wherever it is found."

"That was not their mistake," Lukys said. "Their mistake was filling the hearts of their people with hatred, in clinging to the past."

Even as he spoke, images flickered in Lukys's mind, of a people exiled, of the former Tangata as they landed on a barren shore, of men and women coming together to create a new kingdom. But always those memories were clouded, distorted by the hatred of his predecessors, by their anger towards those who had seen them banished.

Lukys closed his eyes, exhaling. He knew what he had to do.

"We must find a new way," Lukys continued. "One of peace, of respect amongst equals. We can no longer blindly follow your queen."

✹ 13 ✺

THE TANGATA

Adonis shivered as he looked upon the human queen. Seeing
her standing calm amongst the chaos, Adonis realised he
knew this creature. He had glimpsed her from afar, at the height of
the human invasion so many years before, when the Tangata had
trapped the human army between their forces. The enemy might
have been crushed that day, had it not been for a calvary charge that
had forced the Tangata back, giving the humans time to retreat.

This woman had led that charge against his people, had saved
the humans from disaster so long ago. If not for her, the war might
have ended that day, with the strength of humanity destroyed in one
terrible battle.

Adonis would not allow her to save them again. Now, on this
night, she would finally fall. And the last resistance of humanity
with her.

Brothers, sisters, on me.

Standing in the shadows, he gathered his Tangata. Already the
humans were responding to their queen, retreating from the
Tangata-inspired chaos and raising their weapons in a defensive
formation. His people would need to change their tactics too, if they
were to destroy this creature.

Thankfully, the Tangata had already taken a heavy toll upon the
human forces. There couldn't be more than twenty left to stand

against an equal number of Adonis's brethren. Impossible odds, even for this queen.

Kill them all, Adonis said softly when the last of his Tangata joined him.

As one, they surged forward, charging across the blood-slicked deck, silhouettes in the night. The humans roared in answer and hefted weapons. But most had lost their spears earlier, the one advantage they might have had against the Tangatan charge. Instead, the humans met their foes with swords in hand.

And died screaming.

Ducking beneath a wild swing, Adonis shattered the ribs of the human before him, then leapt over the falling body, eyes on the woman who stood at their centre. Dressed in chainmail armour with a greatsword in hand, she alone amongst the humans stood her ground. Indeed, as Adonis watched, one of his sisters leapt at her and the queen spun, her blade slashing out to catch the Tangata in the neck. The blow almost decapitated the Tangata, and she fell amongst the other bodies littering the deck.

A growl rumbled from the back of his throat and fists clenched, he pushed aside one of his brethren.

Focus on the followers, he hissed. *The queen is mine.*

Encased in her armour, it would be difficult for one of his lesser brethren to pierce her defences, but one blow from Adonis would crush the metal like a hammer. This was the moment he had waited for, the foe he had been created to face.

The other Tangata stepped aside, splitting the ranks of human soldiers and allowing Adonis to pass. They were falling quickly, the queen's human guards, overwhelmed by the sheer power of the Tangata. The queen realised it too, for her helmet flickered left and right, and he heard her voice carrying over the clash of weapons. Her followers, though, could not hear her over the cacophony of battle.

Then the woman's eyes fell upon Adonis. The queen seemed to realise his intent as he started towards her, but to her credit, she did not try to flee. Rather, she squared her shoulders and took her greatsword in a two-handed grip. Adonis smiled at her courage, but it mattered not. This night would see her end. No human could stand against a Tangata of the third generation.

Crying his rage, Adonis charged, closing the gap with his foe in an instant. Her sword came up, reacting with the speed she had demonstrated with the others, but Adonis was confident in his strength, and his arm swept out to slam against the flat of her blade to turn it aside…

…except the blow felt as though Adonis had struck something hard and unyielding, as though the greatsword were fixed in some vice rather than held by a mere human. For a second, he felt bewilderment, confusion—then the point of the sword slammed into his shoulder, tearing through flesh and bringing his charge to a sudden halt.

A cry burst from his lips at the impact, and stunned, Adonis twisted, tearing the sword from his flesh. His cry turned to a growl as he regained his balance, swinging again at the human woman. She raised her blade, face hidden by her helmet, but Adonis saw the mirth in the ripples of the woman's aura.

A frown touched his lips. How had she held the sword against his blow? How could she move so quickly, keeping pace with even his own supernatural speed?

Baring his teeth, Adonis reached a hand to his shoulder, feeling the hot blood gushing from the wound. His right arm had lost some of its strength, but it should still be enough to defeat a human, even one dressed in steel.

Snarling, he clenched his fists and attacked again. This time the queen dropped into one of the strange stances practiced by the humans, sword extended, iron fist held across her chest. Adonis ignored the blade this time, trusting his speed to evade her next blow. All he needed was to land a strike, one with the force to crush her bones, to tear her flesh, and it would all be over.

But as he came at her again, far from awaiting his attack, the queen leapt forward to meet him. For half a moment, Adonis was left frozen. This human dared to attack *him?* Only the hiss of approaching steel snapped him from his stupor, and gasping, Adonis hurled himself aside…

…and again found himself too slow. Pain erupted from his side as the greatsword slammed against his ribs. Fortunately his retreat took most of the impetus from the blow, but even so, he felt something go *crack* as he staggered back.

Gasping, he stared at the woman, hot blood running from his side as well as his shoulder now. For the first time that night, fear touched him. This should not be possible. A human could not stand against him, not unless…

…his eyes widened as a suspicion touched him, and without thinking, he reached out with his mind.

What are you?

Laughter rattled from behind the iron visor, lifting above the screams of the dying. Reaching up, the queen tore the helmet from her head, revealing great eyes of emerald and flaming red hair.

"I am the saviour of humanity," she shouted into the night.

A roar came from nearby as one of Adonis's brethren, caught in the grips of the Tangatan rage, crushed his foe's skull—then caught sight of the queen standing nearby. Before anyone could react, he charged at her.

The queen didn't bother with the sword this time. Instead, she lifted her empty hand, and only now did Adonis notice how it rippled, how it was different from the rest of her armour. A burning light lit the night, and his brother fell to the ground, writhing against the wooden boards.

"I am the death of gods," the queen continued, even as Adonis's brother died in agony.

Adonis shook his head, staring at the human in disbelief. She *was* human, that he sensed, smelt, but…somehow she had Heard him, had matched him blow for blow, had injured him.

Abruptly, the queen raised her sword and shouted into the night. Too late, Adonis realised his danger as she charged. His brethren were engaged with the last of the humans, leaving him to stand alone against the queen, against whatever creature she was, and the human magic she wielded.

Watching her charge, Adonis realised his death was upon him. Even so, he clenched his fists and readied himself for battle, though its end seemed already written in the night sky.

A sharp *crack* came from overhead, then a shadow fell over them, black-feathered wings flashing out to slam against the queen's blade, finally tearing it from her impossibly strong grasp. Adonis barely had time to recognise Nyriah before the Anahera launched herself at the queen, fist and boot and wings lashing out, driving the woman back, leaving her no opening to use the magic of the gauntlet.

The queen roared as she matched the Anahera's blows, revealing a strength beyond anything Adonis knew to be possible for a human, for even a Tangata. His heart hammered hard in his chest as he watched the two battle amidst the flickering lanternlight. This queen could not be human nor even a descendant of his people. She was too powerful, her strength too pure for that.

No, this creature had come from the Anahera themselves.

But the false gods had their limits, and as the last human soldier fell, Adonis's brethren formed up around him. This was their chance. With Nyriah's aid, they could still win a victory. He could still salvage his injured pride. The creature could not fight them all.

With me, Tangata, he called. *The human queen falls this night.*

Across the deck, he saw the pale face of the queen swing in his direction and he cursed silently. She had heard him, knew they were coming for her. But what did it matter? The Anahera had the woman pinned against the bow where Adonis had first climbed aboard. She had placed a pile of barrels to her back to keep from being surrounded, but even that would not help against so many. There would be no escape for the human queen.

Grinning, he started across the deck with his Tangata.

An all-too-human curse slipped from the creature's lips and she leapt back from Nyriah, finally managing to bring up her gauntlet. Light flashed as its magic lit the night and Adonis rushed forward, his Tangata with him. He knew this weapon, its magic. The queen could not strike them all with its power.

Nyriah's wings swept down, hurtling her into the sky as the queen unleashed the magic. Adonis and the other Tangata charged into the gap the Anahera had left and one of his brethren went down, caught in the gauntlet's awful power. But not Adonis, and teeth bared, he leapt at the queen…

…but she was already turning from him, her magic vanished, reaching instead for a…lantern. The sight gave Adonis pause and he hesitated, watching as the queen wrenched the flaming light from a hook and raised it high. The whisper of wings from above announced Nyriah's return, but the queen paid no mind to her. With a shout, the queen hurled her lantern at the pile of barrels.

The *crash* of breaking glass followed as it smashed upon the wood, spilling burning oil across the barrels in a *whoosh* of heat. Even as Adonis stared, she swung on one of his brothers, bringing the Tangata down with a terrible blow to the face.

Then the queen was charging through the gap the fallen Tangata left. Reaching the railings of the ship, she hurled herself over the side before any could catch her.

Adonis had just a second to stare at the point where the queen had disappeared, pondering her plan, before—

Boom.

The night erupted in an inferno.

⚜   14   ⚜

THE PRISONER

Erika cried out as a wave of light and sound burst through the cabin, followed by such heat that she feared they had been engulfed by flames. Smoke seared her lungs as she drew in a breath to scream, and instead found herself choking. Her ears rang and stars danced across her vision, but the heat vanished as quickly as it had appeared, and she found herself lying again in the iron cage.

Except the cage was no longer standing upright, but rather lying twisted on its side. Groaning, Erika struggled to push herself up, even as her vision cleared and the first sound returned to her ears. Somewhere nearby she heard the roaring of flames and screams of men in agony, before a whisper from nearby drew her attention, desperate, urgent. A hand grasped her by the shoulder and shook her.

"Erika, are you okay? Please, I can't—" Cara's voice broke, as though she were already imagining the possibility of Erika's death.

Erika let out a moan, hoping it would reassure the Goddess, though truthfully she wasn't sure what condition she was in. She was already so weak…and now she could hear a roaring from above, of…flames, growing closer.

What had happened? That explosion…it had to have been the black powder Amina had mentioned earlier, when speaking of the fall of Fort Illmoor. She couldn't help but feel some small measure of satisfaction at that. It seemed only fair that the woman's stolen weapon had been turned against her. The Archivists knew the perils of the black powder well, and never stored great quantities in one place.

Deciding she was still in one piece, Erika managed to push herself upright. "I'm okay," she said softly, placing a hand on Cara's arm as she looked around. The walls of the cabin had been torn apart by the force of the explosion, but they hadn't been so lucky with the cage. Some of the bars had twisted, but otherwise it remained in one piece.

Fear touched her as she saw the fire flickering beyond the broken ceiling. Orange lit the night, illuminating the silhouettes of men and women still struggling on the decks of the galley. Erika didn't know whether to scream for their help or hope they didn't notice them. The queen did not appear and Erika could only pray she had been consumed by the explosion.

Swallowing her fear, she turned to Cara. They would get no better chance than this—if only they could free themselves of the cage. The Goddess seemed to have realised the same thing, for some of the life had returned to her. Seeing that Erika was unharmed, the Anahera turned her attention to the bars of their prison. Pale fingers closed around the steel and veins appeared on Cara's neck as she exerted her incredible strength. Erika held her breath; Cara obviously hadn't been able to escape this way before, but if the explosion had weakened one of the bars...

...but even as the Goddess strained, the steel bars resisted. They would not give an inch, not even to a Goddess made flesh.

Warmth touched Erika's cheeks, a dry, searing heat that swept through the broken cabin. The silhouettes beyond the shattered walls had vanished, the ship apparently abandoned, but the light of the flames only grew, creeping closer. She could feel the ship rocking sharply beneath them too, the floor pitching as the vessel sunk lower on the river.

Idly, Erika found herself wondering which would reach them first—the flames or the water. Whichever took them, at least they would be free of the queen and her torturous magic. Perhaps she had even perished in the explosion. The thought was cold comfort to Erika. She didn't want to die, not yet, not when there was still so much for her to do. Even after the agony she had suffered these past days, it was the hope for a new life that had given her strength to resist. Watching Cara strain to save them, seeing her own fear reflected in her friend's eyes, Erika found herself clenching her fist, wishing for a final whisper of power, enough to crack the lock again…

The power did not come, but looking at the silver chains she wore, an idea came to Erika. Starved and beaten, she had no strength left to summon her gauntlet's power.

But there was another option, a choice someone like Amina would never consider.

Reaching down, Erika squeezed the gauntlet around her wrist the way the queen had earlier. A soft *hiss* followed, then a tingling in her skin as the wires separated from her flesh, like a thousand tiny needles withdrawing from her arm. Finally, the gauntlet slid free and fell into her lap, its intricate threads shimmering in the fiery light.

"Cara," she whispered.

Her concentration still on the bars of their cage, it was a moment before the Goddess looked back. When she did, Erika saw again the terror in her eyes, the fear they would both be consumed by the flames.

"Take it," Erika said, holding out the gauntlet to the Goddess. "I…don't have the strength to use it, but you do. Break the lock, save us."

Cara's eyes widened at the sight of the gauntlet. Erika had fought so hard to keep this artefact, had feared and yearned for it in equal parts these past months. Now she offered it freely to the Goddess.

"It's forbidden for us to use human magic," Cara whispered, still staring at Erika's offering.

"Add it to the list of our crimes," Erika retorted. "At least we'll be alive."

The Goddess swallowed visibly, hesitation written across her face, but finally she reached out and took the gauntlet from Erika. Holding it in her hands, Cara paused, looking from the artefact to the broken walls. Fear turned Erika's innards to ice as she saw that the fire had reached the cabin. The air was hot to breathe now, and tainted with smoke, it seared her lungs. As she watched, another wall went up in flames with a *whoosh*.

"Quickly," she wheezed, swinging back to the Goddess.

Clenching her jaw, Cara slipped the gauntlet over her hand.

A burst of light flashed from the artefact, forcing Erika to turn away, but Cara did not hesitate now. A low buzzing filled the cage as she thrust out her palm, slamming it against the lock. The shriek of twisting metal followed as the Goddess drew on her strength, far greater than Erika's dwindling energies. But another scream echoed the breaking steel, torn from Cara herself, as though something within her were breaking, reacting to the artefact's power…

The light cut off again as a sharp *crack* came from the lock—then the door to the cage was falling open, crashing sideways to the wooden floor.

A moan came from Cara as she swayed on her knees, and Erika was shocked to see a trail of blood running from her friend's nose. The magic had cost the Goddess something, but there was no time to consider the price of their freedom. Grasping her friend beneath the arm, she pushed Cara through the opening, then scrambled out after her.

The heat swelled as they stood, Erika still supporting the Goddess. Smoke swirled about them, blinding, burning as they struggled to breathe. Dizzy from the darkness and her own weakness, Erika swung in one direction, then another, unable to find the direction of the door, of freedom.

"Erika!" Cara's voice rose above the inferno as the Goddess straightened. It seemed all the world was aflame now, the pair of them standing in a tiny oasis amidst the firestorm. *"Do you trust me?"*

There was no time to consider the answer. "Yes!" Erika screamed.

The breath hissed from Erika's lungs as Cara tackled her, picking her up, hugging her tight. Then they were hurtling towards the flames, towards the burning walls, towards the searing heat—

Dark wings enclosed them both, cutting off the brilliant light, the burning. A *crash* followed as they struck something solid, but whatever it was did not halt the Goddess's momentum and they tumbled on, swirling, falling, tumbling…*burning.*

Erika opened her mouth to scream her agony—and the icy waters of the Illmoor rose to claim them.

✣   15   ✣

THE SOVEREIGN

"We can no longer blindly follow your queen."

A collective intake of breath came from around the room at Lukys's words. Men and women rose to their feet, some banging fists against the table, others demanding an explanation for the insult. A spluttering came from Wallace and he rocked back in his chair as though Lukys had struck him.

"No!" the steward gasped. "You cannot betray her! You're Amina's closest ally."

"Amina has had other allies—all of them are dead now, their kingdoms broken," Lukys said harshly. Reaching up, he pulled off his veil and swept his eyes over the room. "I will not allow the same to happen to Perfugia."

To his surprise, the room fell silent at his words, those gathered momentarily shocked by the removal of his veil. Even so, not everyone was frozen. The guards in the corner had hands on their weapons, and Ewan was on his feet. His stomach tied in a knot, Lukys sent a silent message to Sophia and Keria.

Be ready.

Abruptly, Zayaan pushed himself to his feet. Around the table, eyes flickered, turning to the old man. A frown wrinkled his face as he studied the pair of Sovereigns, as though he already knew what lay beneath Sophia's veil. His frown deepened as Wallace continued to splutter, clutching at his chest as though in pain.

"Oh, calm yourself, Wallace," Zayaan snapped. Wallace's gasps cut off as he stared up at the queen's advisor, while Zayaan returned his focus to Lukys. "The good Sovereigns obviously did not come to conquer, or we would already be dead."

Lukys frowned at the elderly man. He'd expected Zayaan to lead the resistance against them, being the queen's personal advisor. Indeed, it seemed others in the room had thought the same, for with his words came an uncertain calm as the other nobles looked from Lukys to the elderly advisor.

Lukys drew in a breath. "We have received…word of a new threat to the south, of a creature beyond even the powers of the Gods. The ancient enemy of legend has returned—and your queen plays politics while the world burns." He shook his head. "Her tyranny has gone too far. You speak of the renegade King Nguyen, but the man did not start this war with your kingdom."

"Nguyen broke the alliance," Zayaan said matter-of-factly, as though he held no opinion about the events of which he spoke. Alongside him, Wallace whimpered. "Amina's invasion was retribution for that betrayal."

"You can't do this!" Wallace interrupted, pushing himself to his feet. Puffing, he swung on Zayaan. "You don't understand, it's impossible to resist her! We must remain loyal, she'll—"

"*Nothing* is impossible," Lukys cut the man off, leaning forward and pressing his hands to the table, eyes still on Zayaan. He sensed this was the man he needed to convince if they were to take this room without bloodshed. "If my presence here proves anything, it is the truth of those words. In just a few short months, I have witnessed Gods come to life, seen lost magics and the rise of creatures long thought to be extinct. I have…" He hesitated, glancing at Sophia before drawing fresh breath.

"If all that can be possible, if the Gods themselves still live, then we humans can find a better way. If we can stand together, as one, we have a chance for peace, for unity amongst the kingdoms. Can you imagine a world without war, without needless death? A world of peace." He drew in a breath. "Even with the Tangata themselves."

Finally the old man's face showed a change in emotion, as he frowned at Lukys's last words. Lukys could sense the tension building in the room, the doubt in the eyes of the men and women at the table. Peace with Gemaho and Perfugia was one thing, but these people still saw the Tangata as monsters, the enemy they had fought for ten long years to subdue.

But Perfugia *was* the Tangata now.

Lukys, are you sure? Sophia's words whispered into his mind, drenched with doubt, with fear.

Fists clenched, eyes still locked on Zayaan, Lukys nodded. He sensed movement alongside him as Sophia reached for her veil, but he did not take his eyes from the queen's advisor, did not so much as blink. If the man signalled for the guards to intervene, Lukys would be ready.

Slowly, Sophia lifted the veil, her grey eyes blinking in the lanternlight. Gasps came from around the room, and Lukys watched the colour drain from Wallace's face. Only the queen's advisor remained steadfast, though his eyes did flicker in Sophia's direction, widening a fraction as he registered the grey eyes of the Tangata.

"I thought it odd," Zayaan said at last, a quiver in his elderly voice despite his mask of calm. "The creature's accent…changed from sentence…to sentence." He hesitated, eyes flicking momentarily to Sophia before returning to Lukys. "Might I ask how you tamed it?"

"I needed no taming, *sir*," Sophia snapped, reverting fully to her singsong accent. "I grow weary of saying it, but my people are not the monsters you think us."

"One can be uncivilised without being a monster," the queen's advisor said softly.

This time a growl came from Sophia's throat, and Lukys sensed the anger building in his partner at the old man's words. Quickly he reached for her hand, seeking to calm her. There would be time enough for repudiation later. For now, they needed the people in this room on their side.

Probably shouldn't have brought us along if you wanted that, Keria's Voice carried from where she stood across the room.

They would have realised the truth sooner or later, Lukys replied, before focusing his attention back on the queen's advisor.

"Sir, I would advise you to remember with whom you speak," he admonished. "Tangata or no, Sophia and I *are* the new Sovereigns of Perfugia. We will not hear you insult our people."

To Lukys's surprise, Zayaan chuckled. "In that case, might I assume you slew your predecessors yourselves? Is Perfugia burning even now, Ashura lying in ruins?"

"No," Lukys shot back, looking from the man to the others at the table. He noticed several of those on their feet edging towards the door, but Dale had thankfully already moved to bar their exit. "The rest of our people are on their way here, in fact, with King Nguyen."

"I see." Clasping his hands behind his back, Zayaan stepped out from behind the table.

Lukys tensed and the man paused, one grey eyebrow lifting towards the fringe of his failing hair, as if to ask, *May I?* After a brief delay, Lukys nodded, allowing the advisor to move around the table. As he did so, Lukys sensed a distant call, as though one of the Tangata were reaching out to warn him of something. The horns began to sound from the city a few seconds later.

"I suppose that would be your fleet then?" Zayaan asked as he crossed to the window and looked out over the harbour.

Heart hammering in his chest, Lukys joined the old man and saw the blue and yellow sails marking the horizon. On the streets below the citadel, men and women scurried like ants, a steady flow making for the walls. Fists clenched, he looked to Wallace and Ewan and the others at the table, but none of them made any move to act. They all looked to Zayaan.

"It's not too late," Lukys said softly, his heart pounding. This was their chance, the moment they had been waiting for. If they could convince this man to turn against his master... "There doesn't have to be bloodshed, Zayaan. Call off the guards, surrender the city, and we will face Amina and the Old Ones together."

Unclasping his hands, Zayaan turned from the window, and for a second Lukys thought they would scream for the guards to attack, for the Flumeerens to resist at all costs. Then the queen's advisor met his eyes.

"No harm will come to our people?" he murmured. "Our city will remain undisturbed?"

"*None*," Lukys said, his Voice ringing silently in emphasis of his words.

A grim smile appeared on the old man's face. "Very well, Sovereign," he said softly. "It seems Amina's reign over Mildeth has come to an end."

"*No!*"

A scream from the table was followed by a *crash* as Wallace attempted to leap across the wooden boards. He tripped and fell, but moving with a speed that belied his size, he scrambled up again. Steel flashed as he charged at Lukys, but Sophia was faster still. Though the steward was four times her size, a blow to his sternum sent him crashing to the floor.

Lukys's gut churned as he approached the man. "Wallace, there is no need for this," he said, even as the steward struggled against Sophia's impossible strength. She was forced to push him face-first against the ground and pin an arm behind his back, but he still continued to scream and whimper, sobbing into the wooden floors.

A frown touched Lukys's forehead as he knelt beside the man, trying to make sense of his words.

"Please!" Wallace cried. "You don't understand, you don't know what she *is!* Amina, she does not forget. She'll kill us all if you cross her!"

THE TANGATA

The water was the only thing that saved Adonis.

Even as the fire licked at his flesh, he felt the force of the explosion lift him up and hurl him backwards, sending him tumbling through the air, over and over until he struck the river with a harsh *thump*.

The icy waters extinguished the flames instantly, though the pain remained, the lingering agony of burns to his face and chest, a shrieking from his flesh that he knew would only grow.

For the moment though, he had more pressing concerns than his pain. Submerged beneath the water, his lungs screamed and he kicked out, struggling in the depths, unable to tell up from down, to find the surface. Caught in the currents, he slammed into something hard—and moving. Another of his brethren, or the queen?

Regardless, he caught hold of the unknown figure, fingers latching onto rough fabric—not the queen in her iron suit, then— before he kicked out again, finally glimpsing the light of the flames. They would mark the surface.

He broke free of the depths with a gasp, sucking in great lung-fuls of air. Strength rushed back to his failing limbs as he looked around at a world turned to chaos. The screams of the dying and the roar of the burning ship thundered across the river. Gritting his teeth, he struggled to drag his burden up from the depths. Some-thing weighed the figure down, and it took all his strength to pull them above the surface. Only then did he see why they had been so heavy.

Nyriah coughed and spluttered as her head broke the surface, her water-logged wings churning the river as she struggled to keep above the water. It was clear she had no idea how to swim—and that with her heavy wings, she was in danger of dragging them both back into the depths.

Cursing, Adonis struck the Anahera across the face.

Calm yourself! he growled, his rage pressing upon her mind.

It did nothing to calm her panic though, and gritting his teeth, Adonis reached out again. This time he sought peace, to rid himself of the rage that had driven him for so long. Slowly the Anahera calmed as he sought to share some measure of tranquillity with her, until finally she stilled in his grip.

Lie on your back, he ordered. *Tuck away your wings, if you can.*

Adonis offered nothing more, but after a moment Nyriah obeyed. Cursing his own weakness and the growing pain of his burns, Adonis gripped her beneath the arm and kicked out towards the distant shore.

Behind them, flames lit the night as the human flagship burned. Adonis watched as it sank beneath the waters, and cursed the queen with all his being. How had she caused such an explosion? It had not been the magic of her gauntlet, but some other power, born of fire. Something the Tangata had never seen before.

For the first time in his life, Adonis felt a tremor of fear for the humans. This night, he had witnessed the threat Maya had predicted. Finally, he understood the danger these creatures posed. Worse, he knew now they were not led by a fragile mortal, but one of Anaheran descent, a creature that could stand against any of the Tangata, perhaps even Maya.

Lying in his arms, Nyriah said nothing as they swam, though she was shivering by the time Adonis's found ground beneath them.

We are safe, Nyriah, he said softly. *You can stand.*

Her overly large eyes blinked in her pale face. Unlike himself, it seemed she had escaped the worst of the flames, though the force of the explosion must have been enough to knock her from the sky. Her water-soaked wings would have dragged her straight to the bottom if he had not encountered her in those swirling currents.

"You saved me," she murmured, standing in the muddy shallows. Her wings spread wide and a tremor shook them, spraying water into the air. A frown touched her forehead when she looked at him, clothes clinging to her body in an…unseemly manner. "Why…master?"

Adonis gritted his teeth and quickly looked away. *Your aid proved vital to our cause,* he said vaguely. *And I needed information.* He looked at her sharply, recalling his earlier suspicions. *The creature we fought, the woman who led the enemy, she is not entirely human.*

"No…" Nyriah murmured, quickly glancing away.

He was on her in a second, catching her by the wrist, squeezing. Despite his burns, he was still strong, still needed to know.

What is she? he hissed. *Who is she?*

The Anahera lowered her eyes. "Only one of our kind has left the mountains in generations," she said softly. "Cara's mother, Farhan's partner before me. She disappeared one day. Though no one knew what had become of her, Farhan always suspected…she had a great interest in the humans."

Adonis narrowed his eyes. "But that was not her?"

Nyriah shook her head. "That creature was not full-blooded Anahera. But perhaps…a daughter."

Adonis nodded, his thoughts turning to the human Maisie. Had she known this? Was that why she'd sent him against the flagship, knowing the queen would be there?

Anger touched him and suddenly Adonis was striding from the water, leaving the Anaheran woman behind him. Could Maisie have been manipulating them all this time, using their anger and hatred, their excitement to destroy the humans against them? It seemed unlikely—Maisie had been isolated from her people for weeks. But the humans were manipulative, cunning creatures. After this night, who knew what else they might be capable of?

The sound of footsteps on mud came from behind Adonis as Nyriah followed, but even with his injuries, she struggled to keep up, her wings still heavy with water. Adonis clenched his fists, casting a glance over his shoulder at the river. At least two other ships were burning—had they taken inspiration from the queen, or had this all been a trap from the start?

He bared his teeth, wondering at the weapon the queen had

unleashed. Was this the extent of the new power, or was there more? How long did the Tangata have before the humans created other such weapons? In just the last few months they had uncovered magic gauntlets and explosives. But even before that, their war manoeuvres had advanced, as they learned to use their shields and spears as a unit against their stronger foes.

Maya was right. The humans had to be eliminated before they grew to threaten the entire world.

Movement came from the waters of the river and Adonis was thankful to see that others had escaped the inferno. He could sense the fear of his brethren for what the enemy had revealed. The queen had been within their grasp, but in an instant she had turned the battle, decimating the Tangata and escaping into the night. It was a humiliating defeat for Adonis.

A soft pounding came to his mind as he climbed the bank, a tremor of rage, a warning of what awaited him. Reaching the borders of their camp, he moved towards the source, towards Maya's fury. Her rage swept out across his people, stirring them from their shock, calling upon their emotions…

Calling them to war.

Adonis found his mate standing atop a small hill. Her golden hair shone in the light of the distant flames, her stomach straining against the simple Tangatan clothing she wore. Her grey eyes fixed upon the burning waters, she did not seem to notice his approach at first.

You have failed me, my mate.

Adonis flinched as Maya's Voice roared into his mind, so loud he staggered back from her, his entire being trembling. Looking up at her, he tried to meet the grey eyes of his partner—and failed. Bowing his head, he tried to retreat—only for her to surge forward. Before he could resist, her hand caught him by the throat.

Maya bared her teeth as she hauled him into the air, and in that moment Adonis finally realised his peril—for in Maya's eyes he saw not her usual calm, but the insanity he had glimpsed the first time he had woken her, the madness that had been passed down to her descendants, the rage of the Tangata.

Maya! he shrieked, reaching out with his mind in a desperate attempt to calm her. But he sensed only chaos from his partner now, only the terrible rage. *Please! They are led by one of the Anahera!*

Somehow, his words must have pierced the haze of her madness, for suddenly Maya blinked. The glow in her eyes softened, giving way to confusion. They narrowed then, and she lifted him higher, as though suspecting him not just of failure now, but treachery.

What is this? she hissed. *The Anahera are* mine! *There are none left to oppose me.*

One left their city long before our arrival! Adonis gasped desperately. *The ex-mate of their leader. Nyriah believes the queen who leads the humans could be her daughter.*

Impossible, Maya growled, and Adonis's gasp was choked off as her fingers tightened. *You lie to protect your own humiliation—*

"No," a voice interrupted.

Adonis's heart twisted as he glimpsed movement from the corner of his eye, then Nyriah stepped into view. Before Maya could react, the Anahera surged forward, slamming into the Old One's arm and tearing Adonis from her grip. He cried out as he crashed to the mud, while above Maya snarled, turning her fury against the Anaheran woman.

Adonis's vision swam as he lay in the dirt, as he struggled to catch glimpses of the battle between his partner and Nyriah. The Anahera's black wings hung limp against her back, still heavy with water, and she clearly was still suffering from the earlier explosion. Adonis tried to raise a hand, to call for them to stop, but he found Maya's mind was closed to him now, her power focused on the Anahera that dared oppose her.

And with all the strength of an Old One, she struck the Anaheran woman down.

Crying out, Nyriah slammed into the ground with a *thud,* her wings fluttering weakly, trying uselessly to carry her to safety. Bones crunched as Maya stomped her boot down on one, followed by a ghastly scream as Nyriah thrashed in the mud. The colour drained from the Anahera's face as she struggled to rise, to flee, but there was no escaping the Old One's wrath.

I warned you what would happen if one of your kind betrayed me, Maya hissed, boot grinding down, shattering the bones of Nyriah's wing. Her Voice pounded against Adonis's skull, rending at his mind, threatening to summon the madness within. *Tell me, Anahera, which of the fledgelings is yours, that I might exact a just punishment?*

"*None!*" Nyriah screamed. Tears appeared in her eyes as she slumped against the ground, suddenly limp. "None," she whispered, scrunching her eyes closed. "If there is punishment to be had, let it fall on me."

No, Adonis grated, struggling to rise, to force Maya to hear his words.

Her mind remained closed to him, but he saw her eyes flicker in his direction. A frown creased her forehead as she looked from him to the Anaheran woman.

So this is the source of your treachery, she whispered, tilting her head as she examined Nyriah. *I am disappointed, my mate.*

No! Adonis tried again. *No, I told it true. There is a half-blood who leads the humans, one of Anaheran and human descent.*

This time, finally, his words penetrated the barrier Maya had erected around her mind. Her frown deepened as she paused, seeming to consider his words.

If this is true, she said finally, *then the humans pose a greater danger than even I had thought. My plans must be advanced immediately.*

Still crouched in the mud, Adonis bowed his head. *As you will, my Matriarch,* he murmured. *My people will follow where you lead us.*

Silence answered his words—followed by a mad laughter. His head jerked up at the sound, only to find Maya leering down at him.

Your people? she murmured. *Oh my dear, Adonis, after this failure, what makes you think yourself worthy to stand at my side, let alone lead this army?* She shook her head. *No, after this, all will know of your humiliation at the hands of the human. They will spurn your authority.* The smile faded from her lips as she turned to regard Nyriah, still lying motionless beneath her boot. *You are as worthless to me as an Anahera who refuses to bow.*

With those words, Maya surged forward. Adonis lifted a hand to cry out a warning—but he was far too slow. With all the strength of her kind, Maya brought her boot down on Nyriah's neck.

A terrible *crack* echoed through the night.

Followed by a haunting silence.

And Nyriah lay still upon the mud.

No! A scream tore from Adonis as the rage finally split within him, shoving aside sanity, lifting him from the dirt to stand against his partner.

But she was still an Old One, and her power was greater than any he could imagine. With a backhanded blow, she sent Adonis crumbling back to the dirt. A groan hissed from his lips as his anger slipped away, despair replacing it, leaving him alone with the pain, with the guilt of another life lost.

I SHOULD KILL YOU, Maya's voice whispered in his mind, taunting, terrible. *But your blood flows in the runts I carry. For that, I shall spare your life, though from this day forth your people will curse the name of the cowardly Adonis.*

With that, the Old One turned and walked away.

❧ 17 ❧

THE PRISONER

Crouching in the long grass, Erika eyed the horse standing several yards away. It hadn't noticed her yet, though its soft snorts in the night revealed its nerves. Flames had scorched its saddle, probably the same ones still burning along the banks of the Illmoor behind her, but there was no sign of its rider.

She held her breath, watching the darkness, waiting to see if this was some trick, a trap set by Amina to ensnare her missing Archivist. It had to be. Surely it could not be that Erika's luck had finally changed. Fate had long ago decided it would not favour her. She couldn't believe she would be so fortunate now, to find a horse here on this burning night.

As the minutes passed and no movement came from the long grass, Erika finally allowed herself to hope. But still she waited, watching, shivering as the cold wind cut through her damp clothes. Though…at least she had not been burned in their flight.

Slumped beside her in the grass, the Goddess had not been so fortunate. Erika could not tell the extent of Cara's burns without daylight, but half the Anahera's hair had been devoured before they'd struck the water. Flames had kissed her auburn feathers too and Erika felt a pang of guilt—it had been Cara's wings that had protected her from the fires, and her friend suffered the brunt of the inferno.

The gauntlet still glinted on the Goddess's arm, and Erika felt a stirring of jealousy, that another wielded her power. She shoved it down—they were both too exhausted to even consider its magic now. They needed to get clear of the river, where even now the distant screams of men told of the battle being waged between the Tangata and Amina's land-based forces.

Whatever the outcome of that battle, the victor would soon turn north towards Mildeth. They needed to be long gone by then, and the horse was their only hope.

Swallowing the last of her doubts, Erika rose from the grass, taking care not to startle the gelding. Cara remained on the ground, the last of her strength consumed by their escape. She'd barely managed to pull them from the river before collapsing on the muddy shore.

The horse swung in Erika's direction at her appearance, nickering nervously in the dark.

"Hey there, greatness," she murmured, extending an empty hand, praying to the Gods she'd long ago discovered to be false that it would not flee. "Are you alone? Do you need a rider?"

The horse nickered again and for one horrible moment Erika thought it would bolt. Heart in her throat, she stood frozen in place as the gelding hooved the ground, but finally it seemed to settle. Abruptly it stepped forward and pressed its nose into her outstretched palm.

Erika stood, stunned, as the wet of its tongue licked her palm, blinking in the moonlight. Soft laughter came from behind her and she turned to see Cara sitting up, her amber eyes aglow in the moonlight.

"I didn't know you were a horse whisperer," she rasped, her voice sounding raw.

Erika found herself smiling back as she stroked the horse's brow, then gently reached up and took its reins in hand. Stroking its neck, she leaned closer to inspect the animal. The metallic tang of blood touched her nostrils and her hand found a wet patch on the hard leather saddle. At least that explained what had become of the horse's rider. She wondered if there would be anything left of Amina's army come morning. Recalling the terrible eyes of the Old One, Erika wasn't sure which side she preferred to win.

At least Amina fights for humanity, an inner voice reminded her.

"Erika," Cara's voice interrupted her thoughts. She turned to find the Goddess standing alongside her. "Are you okay?"

Erika nodded quickly, though as a distant scream carried to her ears, she knew it was a lie. Amina was the last hope humanity had of defeating the Old One and her Tangata. By fleeing this fight, was Erika placing her own life above her people yet again, against humanity itself? But no…surely Amina could not be the future for her people.

"Come on," Erika said softly, pushing aside her doubts.

Even if she'd wanted to, Erika could do nothing for the queen now. Not unless…her eyes drifted to the gauntlet Cara wore. Wielding her Anaheran strength and the twin magics of their human ancestors…could Amina have won this night?

It was too late for second thoughts now. Turning to the horse, Erika swung herself into the saddle then reached down and offered Cara a hand. The Goddess hesitated, eyeing the horse, but after a moment Cara accepted her aid. Warm hands wrapped around Erika's waist as the Goddess clutched her tight, before she felt her friend's head upon her shoulders.

"So tired," a whisper came in her ears. "So *hungry*."

Erika's stomach rumbled in agreement but there was no time to check the saddlebags for food. That would have to wait. Starved as she was, first they needed to put distance between themselves and the battle.

"Hold on tight," Erika said.

Then, praying she still had the strength to guide them, she kicked the gelding into a canter.

———

Morning found the pair still on horseback, but as the sun's glow turned the mountains a deep red, Erika knew they had best find shelter. She was swaying in the saddle by then, kept in place by sheer desperation and Cara's arms around her waist. Responsibility for the young Goddess sat heavy on her shoulders. The knowledge that Cara was also at the end of her strength forced her on.

They had ridden north through a passageway that cut through the rolling hills of Flumeer, but now as the daylight lit the open ground, Erika began to search for shelter. There were few trees left in Flumeer these days, with most cut down to create the ships and forts that had guarded the Illmoor, while the rest had been burned for farmland.

There were no farmers now though. Word of the armies amassing to the south must have driven them out, sending them north to shelter behind city walls. Directing their gelding along a goat track leading up into the hills, Erika wondered which would come for them. Would it be Amina, with her gauntlet? Or would it be the Old One with those terrible grey eyes?

A shiver passed down Erika's spine at the thought of the Tangata stalking their trail, following their scent from the waters of the Illmoor.

No, better that Amina emerged victorious. At least they might have a chance to escape human pursuers.

Erika drew her horse to a stop before a remnant of forest nestled in a small vale. Its steep slopes must have made it unsuitable for livestock, for these were the only trees she could see for miles. Their shelter would conceal them from sight of their pursuers, whether they came by land or air…

…but the trees would also be an obvious hiding place. Her eyes slid closed, exhaustion weighing heavy on her shoulders, but Erika's instincts whispered that they could not stop here. It would be the first place their hunters looked.

Skirting the treeline, she led the horse up towards the crest of the hill. There Erika took stock of their surroundings. Pasture and young crops of corn stretched out for miles around them, while flocks of sheep and cattle moved in the distance. She wondered what would become of all this should the farmers not return in time for the harvest. Did the Tangata know how to harvest crops or care for livestock?

Her eyes caught on a distant shadow—a farmhouse, she thought by the size of it. The hour was still early and a chill breeze blew off the snowcapped peaks to the east, but there was no sign of smoke around the chimney. Praying that meant it had been abandoned, she kicked the gelding into a trot.

A half hour later, Erika could hardly bring herself to believe they were safe within stone walls. She'd taken the time to lead the gelding into a small stall attached to the house, then had half-carried, half-dragged Cara inside. Still in a daze and murmuring softly with her eyes closed, the Goddess had hardly stirred. She was far heavier than she looked, and it had taken the last of Erika's strength to lower the young Anahera onto the down bed in the corner of the great chamber that was the interior of the farmhouse.

Darkness swirled at the edges of her vision and she could feel unconsciousness calling, but even then, Erika knew she could not rest. Their enemies might come for them while they were unawares, and besides, her hunger had only grown more urgent through the night, until it felt as though her insides were consuming themselves in their quest for sustenance.

Returning to the horse, she found some salted beef and dried fish, even some cheese wrapped in a wax cloth in the saddlebags. A quick scout about the farmhouse revealed an abandoned hen coop, its door left open by the departed farmers. The birds squawked and fled at her appearance, already feral from the absence of their owners, but inside she found several eggs. There was also an overgrown vegetable patch out back.

Returning to the house, Erika laid her prizes on the kitchen bench, her stomach rumbling with renewed desperation. There was enough to cook a stew or broth, but the smoke from a fire would be seen for miles during the day. If only a storm would sweep down from the mountains, she might risk a flame. The owners had even left a stack of wood in the hearth for when they returned.

Perhaps when night fell, if they were not discovered before then. In the meantime, she grabbed a piece of the salted beef and took a bite—and groaned as flavour filled her mouth. Her stomach rumbled in anticipation, but she chewed slowly, aware that after so long without eating she didn't want to overdo it. Finally she approached the feathered bed where she had laid her friend.

Cara still slept, though it was a fitful rest, her breath coming in ragged gasps, as though even in her dreams the demons pursued her still. Her feathers stood on end and Erika shivered as the light coming through the shuttered windows revealed the damage the flames had done. Her wings, so recently healed from their crash in the mountains, had been blackened along their edges, the auburn feathers scorched by the flames. There was a smell about her too, the stench of burnt hair, though at least her skin had been spared the worst of the flames.

Another moan came from the Goddess and she twisted violently atop the covers. Erika swallowed the last of her scant meal, clenching and unclenching her fists. It pained her to see Cara this way, and without thinking she climbed onto the bed. Taking the cover Cara had kicked off, she drew it over them both, then curled up beside the young Anahera, pulling her head to her chest, holding her tight. For a while, the Goddess lay tense in her arms, breath still coming in ragged gasps, hissing between clenched teeth.

After a time though, the tension leached from Cara's muscles and her breathing eased, her groans and twitching easing. Erika closed her eyes, still holding Cara safe in her arms. The fiery warmth of the Goddess soon drove back the chill of the day, the woollen covers weighing down on them both. She listened with relief as her friend's breathing grew regular. After all Cara had done for her, saving her, protecting her, this was the least Erika could do.

She just wished she could do more, that she could bring back Cara's mother, that she could have made Farhan see the truth about his daughter. Far from deserving punishment, Cara was an incredible, caring, loving young woman, deserving of pride, of love. If only she could have convinced the Anahera to see that truth, to abandon the folly of their own ancient ways, maybe then the world would have hope.

But instead, Erika had failed yet again, had returned from the Mountains of the Gods empty-handed. She knew now she would never change things, could do nothing to save her people.

All she could do was lie in an abandoned farmhouse and hold her friend tight, banishing the cold and the nightmares for a time.

Erika prayed it would be enough.

$\maltese$ 18 $\maltese$

THE FALLEN

Adonis lay in the dirt, rain falling softly about him, cradling the head of Nyriah in his lap. Hours had passed, slipping away like autumn leaves caught in the winter storm.

Adonis didn't care. He knelt there holding the fallen Anahera in his arms. She had saved him. Adonis struggled to comprehend what had happened, why she would have done such a thing. What had he been to her? Why would she try to stop Maya, put herself in harm's way for him? After everything he'd done to her, how he had treated her people, how was it that Nyriah had found the strength to defy the Old One on his behalf?

More hours passed and night turned slowly to day. The light found Adonis alone in the mud, lost, forgotten. Silence hung over the riverbanks, over his mind, the muddy field abandoned. His fellow Tangata had left, abandoning him to exile, gone with the creature he had delivered them to, the Old One that carried their future.

His future.

A shudder swept through Adonis and finally the dam broke, and he felt at last the rejection of his entire people, of the woman he had sworn himself to—and the loss of the Anahera in his arms too, the slave he had so hated, who had stood proud against Maya's Voice, even as all around her bowed in subservience.

A hiss escaped Adonis's throat and he doubled up, holding the cold body tight, wishing he could give her his warmth. He didn't deserve to live, to continue after his failures, when this noble creature lay dead. Nyriah had possessed more courage than he ever had. She could have left this darkness and forged another path had she wanted, despite Maya's powers, despite the fledgelings—but she didn't.

The human found him like that, knelt in the dirt holding Nyriah, his body broken by Maya's beating, barely conscious, barely sane from his grief. He sensed her before she crouched nearby, *smelt* her, even through the stench of smoke that drifted from the river. Immersed in his pain, at first Adonis ignored the creature, lying still, hoping her cursed presence would move on. But this human never could leave well enough alone.

"Are you alive?" Maisie's voice came finally, then when he did not move, "Adonis, is *she* alive?"

His head jerked up at that, and he fixed his eyes on the human. The grey eyes of the Tangata, enough to send one of her kind scurrying in their weakness. But this human did not so much as flinch as she crouched beside him, brown eyes meeting grey.

Instead, it was Adonis that looked away first.

"I see." Sadness crept into the human's tone, and when he looked at her again, a tear streaked her cheek.

Maisie sat back on her haunches, still eyeing him, watching closely. "I should kill you, you know," she said softly, and for the first time Adonis noticed the knife she held. Where had she gotten that? How was she free, in fact? "For everything you've done, you deserve it."

Swallowing his pain, Adonis gently laid Nyriah down, her black wings falling limp in the mud, then turned to face the human. She rose quickly at the movement, knife raised before her, and he felt a brief satisfaction. At least his injured presence was still enough to generate fear in the human.

But as he pushed himself slowly to his feet, it became obvious that Adonis could not defend himself. Pain ate at his leg where it had twisted in the fall, strong enough to cripple him. It would be days before the torn muscles repaired themselves. Based on the look in Maisie's eyes, he didn't have days, or even hours.

So instead he slumped back in the mud and stared up at her, lips pursed. For the first time in his life, he wished he could speak the language of humans, if only to demand she do it quickly, that she end his shame, his suffering, his…grief. He watched her with wide eyes, arms limp at his side, as though to say he was ready.

But the human did not act, only stared back at him, knife gripped at her side. "I won't though," she said abruptly. Shaking her head, she turned away, her gaze falling on the fallen Anahera. "I don't know why she saved you, but…I won't undo what she did." She flashed him a glare. "So you don't need to worry about me."

Adonis hesitated at her words, heart twisting in his chest. For a second, he felt the urge to throw himself at the human, to *force* her to kill him, to end his suffering. The Anahera's wings, so glorious, so beautiful, lay in the mud, dirt treaded into her soft feathers. Dead. Dead because of his foolishness. Because of what he'd done to her people.

He wiped away a tear of his own, then looked around. The grounds before the great river had been churned to mud by the passage of his people, but the Tangata were long gone now. They had crossed the river in darkness, following the eager drumbeats of their master's Voice, driven into a frenzy, into the madness his people had long sought to suppress.

Commanded by Maya.

"You're wondering where your beloved Old One has gone?" Adonis looked at the human sharply as she spoke, eyes narrowing, but Maisie's gaze was also on the river. "Afraid I have some bad news for you," she continued. "She's ditched you, bud. Gone off with that army you helped her win." She looked at him then, and he saw the accusation in her eyes. "You know, the thousands of Tangatan villagers and Anaheran slaves you recruited. Pretty sure they'll make short work of anyone standing in their way on the other side." She shrugged. "On the bright side, they were all in such a frenzy when they left, they seemed to forget all about little old me."

The queen, Adonis thought, reaching out to Speak without thinking, *the half-blood. Maya fears her.*

He trailed off when the human did not react, then belatedly remembered that Maisie could not hear his Voice. Adonis cursed softly in his mind. How could so many of his brethren stand to bond with these coarse creatures, when they could not even communicate with one another? His eyes fell again on the knife, wondering…

"I know, I know," the human mused, seeming to notice the direction of his stare. "I really should kill you. Only, I'm pretty sure you're my only hope of reaching civilisation." She gestured at her leg, and while the human stood now without aid, when she took a step, it was clear she couldn't put much weight on the injured limb. "I'm not in any condition to walk unaided. Looks like you're pretty beaten up yourself. Must have really pissed off that Old One of yours. Still, I'm hoping you're a faster healer than this old body of mine."

She hesitated, looking at Adonis as though waiting for something. He nodded hesitantly, and she cracked a smile.

"So you *can* understand me. I was beginning to think I was raving to myself."

Adonis offered a scowl, then ignoring her, he pressed his hands to the ground and forced himself up. Agony sliced through his left leg, the torn muscles screaming their outrage. Gritting his teeth, Adonis fought the pain, until finally he found himself standing. He looked at Maisie, teeth bared to show his strength, though in truth he wasn't in any better shape than the human.

At least the rain had ceased during the night and the morning fog was lifting, revealing the broad expanse of water—and in the distance, the flames of Maya's conquest.

The burning ships had long since sunk beneath the brown surface, but on the far distant banks, something else was aflame. A building, or perhaps an entire town, had already fallen to the fury of Maya's rage.

Even after her rejection, Adonis's heart lurched at the thought of his mate out there alone, carrying his children without him…

"I know." He flinched as Maisie spoke into the silence. "Sucks to be rejected, doesn't it? Let's face it though, she was out of your league, bud. Made the same mistake myself once, if it makes you feel any better. What is it about monarchs and all that bloodline business?"

Adonis clenched his jaw and flicked the human a look. Already her coarse voice was grating on him, but there was little he could do about it. If only she could Hear, he might make her understand her crudeness. Once he recovered his strength, he would be able to influence her emotions to a point, but for now he did not even have the energy for that.

Beside him, Maisie sighed. "I know, I'm talking too much." Adonis looked at her sharply, as her words reflected his own thoughts. "I don't…normally. Haven't in a long time. Part of being a spy, all that going unnoticed and whatnot." She chuckled. "I guess I'm…reverting. It's the fear, you know? Haven't been this helpless since…well that's another story." She glanced at the fallen Anahera. "She was going to be my ticket out of here, once we figured out how to rescue the fledgelings. But that Old One of yours…" She shuddered visibly. "She's insane, you know. Surely you know that?"

The human fell silent then, though her eyes remained unnervingly fixed upon Adonis, as though waiting for a response. As if he could. He bared his teeth at her words. Despite his fall, he remained loyal to Maya's cause, to the destruction of humanity, the elevation of his people above all others…didn't he?

Maisie's eyes drifted past Adonis, to the distant burning. "She'll destroy them all, you know," she whispered finally. "Humanity, the Anahera…even your Tangata. That thing, she doesn't care about any of us. You know that, right? Surely you have to see it."

Something deep in Adonis's soul responded to the human's words. Instinctively he reached for the warmth of Maya's mind, seeking reassurance from her presence, that the path she had set them on was righteous…

…and found only silence. Only emptiness. Since her departure across the river, Maya's mind no longer touched him, no longer spoke to his consciousness.

No longer influenced him.

In that moment, Adonis finally saw the last months for what they had been. Saw the grief of his fellow Tangata as they slaughtered their human partners in New Nihelm, helpless to resist Maya's commands. Saw again his brothers and sisters lying in the snow, the dead face of a child staring at him in accusation. He witnessed the conquest of the Anaheran city, heard the pain of the fledgeling as she fought against him, saw the anguish in the eyes of Farhan as he bowed before the Old One, and Nyriah's pain at her son's death.

And through it all, he recalled the pressure of Maya's Voice on

his mind, her silent whisperings, her influence upon his people—
and upon himself.

Finally he turned to Maisie, and nodded.

A smile touched the human's face. "Then what are we going to
do about it?"

🕸 19 🕸

THE FUGITIVE

Erika awoke with a start, aware that darkness had claimed the world. For a moment she thought she was back in the hold of the ship, that the flames, their escape, even the queen's true identity, had all been but a dream.

Then the darkness resolved into shadows and she felt the weight of the covers atop her, the softness of the mattress beneath. Except…the bed was cold, empty.

She sat up abruptly, looking around in search of the Goddess. She had been right about the darkness—sunlight no longer streamed through the shutters. How long had she slept? So much for keeping watch for the enemy. Anyone could have come upon them while they'd been unawares. A chill spread down her spine—they could be creeping up on the house even now, surrounding them with soldiers, or worse, with Tangata.

Throwing off the covers, Erika swung herself out of the bed and scrambled for her boots. At least she'd left her clothes on, but in the dark the holes of her shoes evaded her, until with a curse she let them fall and raced to the nearest window. Placing an eye to the blinds, she searched the ground outside, but clouds must have come across the sky as she slept, for there was no moon to light the world outside.

The sound of a foot scuffing the dirt floor came from behind

Erika and she turned, raising her fist as a matter of habit, though she had not recovered the gauntlet from Cara.

A soft glow lit the room, but instead of coming from Erika's hand, it came from Cara's as she ignited the gauntlet. A smile crossed the Goddess's lips as she raised an eyebrow.

"Don't worry, there's no one out there. I already checked," she said with laughter in her voice.

"Oh," Erika replied, then glanced over the Goddess's shoulders at her wings. "Are they okay…"

Erika trailed off as the smile fell from her friend's face.

"No," Cara said softly. Her wings twitched at the pronouncement, as though they too longed for the freedom of flight. "Another week now, I think…"

Erika's stomach twisted at the sadness in her friend's voice, and she drew the Anahera into a hug.

"A week then," she said, and gently she stroked her hand over the Anahera's feathers. She knew how sensitive they could be, and the soft murmur from Cara showed her appreciation. "We're free, Cara, a week is nothing."

The Goddess remained silent at first, but finally Erika felt her nod and draw back. "You're right," Cara said, looking away. "It's just…everything. The Old One, my mother, this queen of yours. How do you humans handle so much chaos?"

"To be fair, this all only started when you appeared, Cara."

Cara snorted at that. "All this started when you went digging in things that were best left buried," she replied, raising the gauntlet. She reached up and squeezed her wrist. The artefact gave a hiss as it separated from her hand. Cara held it out with a hesitant smile. "Here, you had better take this. I'd rather not be caught breaking any more of my people's prohibitions."

"Thank you," Erika said, swallowing back a wave of desire.

Whatever the Goddess had said in the mountains about the gauntlet's magic being harmless to its user, the power had a hold on her. The rush, the exhilaration she felt when she activated its power, it was addictive. The gauntlet may not have been responsible for the terrible things she'd done with it, but there remained a selfish part of her that did not want to see another use it. She slipped it onto her wrist and shivered as its silver threads melded with her flesh.

Light leapt from the mesh as Erika squeezed her fist, her strength at least partially restored by the earlier meal and sleep. Her stomach gave another rumble though, and she looked beyond Cara to where she'd left the food.

"Have you eaten?" she asked.

Cara's stomach gave an audible growl as a sheepish look crossed her face. "A few of the eggs," she said, wrinkling her nose. "I wasn't sure whether it was safe to light a fire," she added, glancing at the hearth.

Erika nodded. "It should be now, so long as we keep the windows shuttered. Come, let's see what we can cook up."

An hour later the pair sat back on the earthen floor with a warm bowl of stew in their laps. Inhaling the rich aroma of the broth, Erika began to salivate. But if Erika was hungry, Cara must have been moments from starvation, for the Goddess was practically inhaling her bowl.

Chuckling to herself, Erika ate more slowly, taking care not to burn her mouth. It was a shame they had no bread to give the broth substance, but the tubers she'd dug from the vegetable patch with her bare hands helped. The remnants of the salted beef added flavour too, and by the time she was finished Erika felt better than she had in…who knew how long. She hadn't had a proper meal since leaving the City of the Gods.

They helped themselves to seconds, then Erika let Cara finish the remnants from the beaten pot. The Anahera needed more sustenance to thrive than the average human, and it was obvious the past weeks had taken their toll on her friend. The flesh had sunken on Cara's face, revealing sharp cheekbones. Even the slim muscle of her shoulders and arms had withered. No wonder the queen had beaten her so easily, despite only being half-Anahera.

Turning her eyes to the gauntlet, Erika studied its shimmering links, feeling its innate warmth. They would both need to rebuild their strength if they were to stand a chance against Amina. This house would not be safe for long, regardless who won the battle for the Illmoor. But where *would* be safe for them? Gemaho had fallen and all of Flumeer was aligned against them. Perfugia was far and away, impossible to reach without a ship— and besides, they too were allies of Amina. The Sovereigns would turn the pair over the moment they appeared on those distant shores.

"You look worried."

Erika's head jerked up at the interruption. She frowned at the Goddess. Light from the gauntlet bathed Cara's face, adding a glow to her amber eyes as she leaned closer, as though to inspect Erika. Blinking, Erika considered her words, and struggled to contain a mad bout of laughter.

"Me, worried? Why would I be worried?" she asked wryly. "I mean, there's an insane creature and her legion of Tangata hunting us. And the only ally I had left is dead, his entire kingdom burned to the ground." Her voice grew in pitch as she spoke, tears welling in her eyes as the weight of what they faced fell upon her shoulders. "Then there's the Flumeeren queen, your half-sister, the woman I served for years, the same woman who killed my father. A woman with the powers of the Anahera and an army at her back, who would love nothing more than to torture me until the end of my days."

A tear streaked Erika's cheek and she turned away from the Goddess, fixing her eyes on the fire. She felt just like a vase that had been heated by the glass blower for too long, filled to bursting, ready to shatter into a thousand pieces at the slightest touch.

Then strong hands were wrapping around her, holding her close. A sob burst from Erika's lips as she turned to Cara, the pressure within bursting, and all her pain and despair and anger came gushing out. Gasping, she buried her head in the Goddess's shoulder.

"Whatdamigonnado?" The words rushed from her between sobs. Fists clenched, she clutched Cara as though she were a true Goddess, as though she possessed the power to lift her burden, to free her from their danger.

"You'll find a way, Erika," Cara's whisper came through the darkness. "I believe in you."

A hiccup burst from Erika's lips as she finally pulled away, eyes still hot with tears, cheeks wet. The Goddess offered a hesitant smile as they drew apart.

"What if I can't?" Erika whispered. "What if it's beyond me?"

"You will," Cara replied firmly. "It's what makes you special, what made me—" She cut off abruptly, and it seemed her face brightened in the flickering firelight.

Erika frowned. "What?"

The Anahera shook her head, her feathers rustling as she turned towards the fire. Silence fell, before Cara breached it with a new topic. "Maybe it was because of how different you all are from us," she murmured.

"Huh?" Erika asked, her confusion deepening at the Goddess's cryptic speech.

"That made my mother fall in love with your people, with the queen's father."

"Oh…" Erika exhaled. She couldn't help but shudder at the memory of Amina's naked back, the terrible scars left from her amputated wings. "What are you saying?" she added at last.

"There is so much *life* in humanity," Cara said, eyes still on the flames. "The clothing, the art, the music, in everything you do. It's like you fit a dozen of our lifespans into every year of your own existence, every moment. Each of you are so different, so unique, even the Tangata must wonder at it." She looked up, eyes locking with Erika's. "When I first saw you, I thought you must have been a different species than the others—Romaine and Lukys and the Perfugians. They were warriors, rugged and unkept, their hair and beards so tangled and…*filthy*. The other villagers in that place too."

She drew in a breath. "Then you appeared. Dressed in silk, with your hair kept long, tied back for riding, clean and tidy and elegant…I was entranced."

Erika felt her cheeks grew warm and she shook her head. "I was an arrogant fool," she said, recalling the day she'd arrived in Fogmore. "I thought I was better than everyone in that place, even Romaine, a man with ten times my courage."

"A man who believed in you," Cara insisted. "You might not be a warrior, but you have just as much courage as Romaine. You've proven it every day since we stepped into my mountains, in the way you faced my father and the Anahera, the way you stood against the Old One and her Tangata. Even on the ship with Amina. You are elegant and glorious and strong, Erika, everything your people need."

"My people are dead," Erika whispered. "I failed them long ago."

"Your people are every human who does not wish to be enslaved by Maya or my sister, every man and woman who resists their tyranny. Forget your petty kingdoms—they don't matter, they have never mattered. Even the differences between human and Tangata and Anahera are nothing. In this world, there are only the free and the enslaved now, Erika."

Swallowing, Erika looked at the Goddess, wondering at the change in her friend. Just a short time ago, Cara had been in despair, defeated by her sister, crushed by the death of her brother and father, the enslavement of her people. Something had given her hope…but surely it could not have been Erika?

She shivered, unable to meet the Anahera's eyes. Looking at her hands again, she clenched her fists, watched the shimmer that lit the gauntlet. It was the artefact's magic that had gotten her this far, that allowed her to do the impossible things Cara spoke of. She was no leader, no princess as she had once claimed to Romaine. That wasn't why he'd followed her. It was not her own reputation, but her dead father the king that Romaine had believed in. Her father had led Calafe to glory, before betrayal had cast him down.

She could not be that leader, could she?

A shiver shook Erika as she recalled the vow she had sworn the day Romaine had fallen. She had promised to return to Flumeer and help her people, the Calafe refugees that had been condemned by the queen's cruelty. An impossible task, surely, and yet…

…on her last visit to Mildeth, there had been thousands camped outside the city walls. Her people all, the last remnants of the fallen Calafe. Impoverished and homeless they might have been, but they were Calafe still, proud and unbroken, trained as youth to survive, to fend for themselves, even to wield a blade. Could they form the beginnings of a resistance against the mad queen?

A shiver ran down Erika's spine as she stood suddenly, looking at Cara. A grin spread across the Anahera's lips as she rose beside her.

"You have a plan?"

Erika swallowed. "The beginnings of one."

❧ 20 ❧

THE SOVEREIGN

Lukys paced the floor of the royal chamber, his footsteps echoing up through the overlooking rows of empty chairs. The nobles of Mildeth had mostly marched south with the queen, and those few who remained had been imprisoned once the Perfugian forces had entered the citadel. Zayaan had been helpful in identifying those likely to keep their loyalty to Amina and those who might be persuaded to the Perfugian cause.

For now though, Lukys had other concerns on his mind.

How many days will it take for your people to reach the city? he asked, glancing at Sophia.

She stood fixed in place while he paced, but Lukys could sense the same fear within her, the same doubts. Everything had changed with the news from the south, and now it seemed the weight of the world fell upon their shoulders. Neither had been prepared for such a burden, not yet. Abruptly he crossed to where Sophia waited and drew her into a hug.

A shudder wracked them as they stood alone on the floor of the giant chamber. Less than a week had passed since their bloodless conquest of the city, and they'd hardly had a moment of peace since. Their time had been consumed organising the city's defences, with their first act inviting the Calafe refugees into the city.

Zayaan had argued against it, claiming that the presence of the so-called barbarians would disturb the fragile peace in Mildeth and turn the people against them, but Lukys had not forgotten his old mentor Romaine. The last warrior of the Calafe had been the only who had believed in him back in Fogmore. No one had heard a word of Romaine in weeks, but Lukys would not abandon the man's people when the Tangata came.

And come they would.

Word had reached the city in the night, carried on the lips of the first refugees—the Tangata had crossed the Illmoor. Amina's forces had waged a great battle for the river, but in the end her fleet had been destroyed and they had been forced to retreat. General Curtis, the man who had commanded the southern defensive for nigh on a decade, was said to have fallen defending the walls of Fogmore, and a sizeable chunk of the Flumeeren army with him.

For the first time in living memory, the Tangata had gained a foothold north of the Illmoor. And it did not look like they would stop there.

Somehow, Queen Amina had survived the conflict. Riding a white stallion, she had led a charge against the enemy in a replica of her efforts so many years before. This time though, the charge had failed, faltering as the winged Anahera came against her forces. Witnessing the Gods themselves turn against humanity had sown chaos amongst the Flumeeren ranks, and the last resistance had finally crumbled, turning the battle into a full-blown rout.

The news of the Gods' betrayal had turned Lukys's blood cold, and he could feel a memory stirring within, a whisper of a truth long forgotten. The last Sovereign had warned them not to trust the Anahera, that they had failed humanity once before, but the memory of that failure still escaped him.

Days. No longer.

He shivered as Sophia finally responded to his question. Meeting her gaze, he saw the pain shining in her grey eyes and hugged her tighter, wishing he could make this all easier, that he had the answers. But they possessed the same memories, the same knowledge and power. They both knew what marched towards them, the death that followed in the footsteps of the Old Ones.

We will find a way, was all he said, though he knew Sophia saw through his words. Their minds grew closer each day, and he could feel her thoughts fluttering against his own. *What if…we tried to speak with them, with your people?*

Sophia let out a sigh as they drew apart. *If even the Anahera have bowed to Maya…* She shook her head. *What chance do my brothers and sisters have against the power of her Voice?* She hesitated, and he saw her doubt. *We are not a people used to questioning, Lukys. It is a part of our fabric, obedience, subservience to our Matriarch, to the most powerful amongst us.*

Lukys shivered, reaching out to lift her chin so that they stood eye to eye.

"I don't believe that," he whispered, gently kissing her lips. "If that were true, you and Keria and the others would have killed us back in New Nihelm, when Adonis commanded it of you. If that were true, you would not be with me now, doing everything in your power to stop her."

"Maybe," Sophia replied. She looked across the debating chamber towards the south, as though her Tangatan eyes might pierce the stone and distance, might allow her to look upon the darkness that came for them. "Maybe that is what we had been striving for, what our Matriarch wanted for us—the freedom to choose our own fate. But…" She sighed. "Lukys, I fear she died too soon. This Old One, she cares not for the weak, whether Tangata or human. She wants only to dominate."

Lukys sighed, reaching out to squeeze her fingers. "We will find a way to free them."

"We'd better," a new voice spoke from the side of the chamber. They looked around as Nguyen entered. Isabella and Travis followed, looking apologetic for the interruption. They'd been posted outside as guards, but the Gemaho king was a difficult man to deny. "If you can't find a way to bring at least some of your brothers and sisters to our side, this war will be over before it even begins."

"Thanks, Nguyen," Sophia said, adapting a wry tone. Lukys was impressed by how quickly she had learned to adjust to the inflections of spoken voice. "As though the fate of my own people wasn't enough pressure, let's just add the existence of humanity to the burden as well."

The king chuckled and his gaze lifted to the rows of seats that ringed the chamber floor, a hundred in the first tier, another two hundred in the second for minor nobles. The only piece of furniture on the floor of the chamber was a golden throne. Zayaan had explained how the queen held her court here, seated beneath the gaze of her nobles, allowing them to participate in debates over the kingdom's future, as well as witness her judgement against those brought before the throne.

The size of the chamber was but a fraction of the Sovereign amphitheatre back in Ashura, but that theatre had been kept empty, all semblance of the public excluded from the presence of their rulers. They intended to do away with that tradition upon their return. Perhaps they would draw on the queen's custom, though with true citizens of Perfugia, rather than a few privileged nobles.

A part of him cried out against that idea, a dozen minds deep within that resisted such an indulgence of the public, but he pushed them aside. They were the voices of the past—it was time Perfugia had new ideas.

First, though, they had to survive. He looked again at Nguyen, who had seated himself in the golden throne and now lounged with his legs draped over one of the arms.

Lukys raised an eyebrow. "How do you think Amina would react, knowing you sat in her chair?"

"It's our chair now," the king replied with a wave of his hand. "Amina will behave, once she realises we have her city. She knows she cannot face the Old One alone. If she wants to have any chance of survival, she will have to accede to our conditions."

Lukys frowned at that. "You would let her through the gates?"

The king shrugged. "I don't see any alternatives."

Lukys sensed a stirring of anger as Sophia stepped forward, eyes burning. "That woman is responsible for the genocide of my people," she hissed. "For starting a war that has slain thousands on either side. You would greet her as a friend?"

"I would greet her as the enemy of my enemy," Nguyen said softly, unflinching from the rage in Sophia's eyes. He grimaced, glancing around the room. "This is her city, Sophia. She will know best how to defend it. And she still has an army. Better them on our side, rather than fighting against us." He sighed. "I don't like it any more than you do, believe me. But it is as I said back in Perfugia—a ruler must set aside his own principles and do what is best for his people. Justice will come for Amina one day. For now, we must stand together, or risk annihilation."

Sophia said nothing at that, only stared the king down, her aura a burning red. But it was clear that Nguyen had won the argument. Lukys shivered. The man was right. Whatever her crimes, they needed Amina now, needed her army. Though he feared she would sooner see them all dead than stand alongside them.

Is there not another way? a new voice said, and Lukys looked around at Isabella. The Tangata rarely spoke in these meetings, and he nodded for her to continue.

She hesitated, placing a hand on Travis's arm, as though it granted her courage.

It seems to me, she said, and Sophia translated for Nguyen and Travis, *that ever since we encountered your people, you have been able to do the impossible.* She hesitated. *Or rather…find a way to make the impossible possible. When faced with an immovable barrier, instead of giving up, you simply find another way.*

"What are you saying, Isabella?" Travis asked, entwining his fingers with hers.

A smile touched her face as she looked at him, then back at the room. *We have been trying to find a way to defeat Maya's army, to match her power, but however we look at it, the task seems impossible. She is too powerful, our brothers and sisters too numerous.*

"And what would you suggest?" Nguyen asked.

That we look at our problem another way, Isabella replied. *There is much we do not know about the Old One, but it seems to me there is a question we have not yet asked.*

And what is that? Sophia said hesitantly.

What does she want? Isabella responded.

Something stirred within Lukys at the Tangata's words, a memory buried deep. He shuddered as he sensed Sophia alongside him, realising she felt the same stirring. They stood together in silence, concentrating on that lost past, on secrets hidden inside their own minds. Images emerged slowly from the depths, and Lukys held his breath, waiting, watching with Sophia as faces took shape from the shadows…

Ten pairs of grey eyes stared around the circle of

those gathered, but Lukys sensed that these beings were not Tangata, that this memory was older even than the arrival of his ancestors in Perfugia, before the kingdoms of man had risen, from a time when the old world had Fallen.

These were the first of their kind, the Old Ones in flesh.

A shiver ran down his spine as he recognised Maya's face amongst those who had gathered.

"How many years have passed now, brothers, sisters?" The speaker stood with Maya, and Lukys realised from their closeness that they were partners. "How long since we unleashed the doom upon this land? Since we last birthed a new generation?"

"It has not been so long," another replied. He shifted nervously on his feet, reaching for the female who stood with him, clutching her hand. "Only a few years. The children will come."

"No." It was Maya who spoke now, her voice touched by anger. "The winged ones have betrayed us, betrayed the sacrifice of my sires." She bared her teeth. "There are those who speak of sightings in the mountains. We should go to them, take our vengeance, before the end comes."

"It was your own father who brokered the peace," the first speaker argued. "I will not break it now, not when our strength wanes."

"You would rather a slow death?" Maya's partner replied. "To see the noble Chead fade away, lost to the annals of history?"

"It has not come to that, not yet," came the reply. The Old One hesitated, and Lukys could see the doubt on his face. "And...there are still the humans. We know from the past—"

"A false hope!" Maya snarled. "You would see us debased, our powers corrupted by those creatures? No, I say it must be war. If not against the cursed winged ones, then with humanity itself. You know the danger they pose.

Pockets of their civilisation remain, hidden beneath the earth, protected from the darkness we unleashed. We should seek them out, destroy them once and for all, before they rise again. And…perhaps they might hold the key to our survival, some secret in our creation that could save us."

Many of those who stood with Maya stirred at that, and Lukys sensed their agreement. Even then, hundreds of years before the Sovereigns and the war started by the queen, it seemed there had been hatred between their peoples. But he noticed that others dissented, and now the male who argued against Maya and her partner stepped forward.

"We are tired of war," he said softly, shaking his head, "of death. For years we have dwindled. I will see no more of my people's blood spilt in senseless violence."

"You would rather waste away, the glory of our people lost to time?" Maya's mate questioned.

"I would rather live to face whatever glory, whatever doom fate has dictated for the Chead," came the reply.

"So be it," Maya spat. Shaking her head, she turned her gaze on the rest of the circle. "Follow Tangata and Chiara if you must, but I will not go quietly into the night. Raxion and I will live as did my sires when they saved us from humanity's wrath. Any who wish to see the Chead rise again, follow me, and I will lead you to glory."

There was a pause around the circle, but as Maya and her partner turned to leave, several broke ranks and followed. Lukys watched them go, realising belatedly that he recognised some of those who left. Their faces were etched into his memory, terrible and twisted, maddened as they sought to slaughter him. These were the creatures they had unearthed in the hidden chambers so many months before, the ones the Archivist had uncovered, and Cara had slain.

Slowly the memory faded and Lukys found himself standing again in the debating chamber. Beside him, Sophia slumped against him, her eyes wide, entire being trembling. He held her close, feeling the same shock at what they had seen, though it was impossible now to know whether it was his own, or hers. The sight of Maya in that ring of Old Ones, of her disdain as she regarded those who would not follow…

"She will kill them all," Sophia whispered to the room.

The hairs on Lukys's neck stood on end at her words. Sophia was right. Maya loathed humanity. She cared nothing for the creatures that had become the Tangata, who had mixed their blood with her enemy. They were beneath her, unworthy. All that mattered to this creature was the survival of her own people.

The survival of the Old Ones, the *Chead.*

And Lukys knew now what she wanted.

A true mate, another of her kind that had lain sleeping through the centuries, one that might restore her race to its former glory.

He opened his mouth to speak, but before the words could leave his lips, a *boom* came from the entrance to the chamber. Lukys stumbled, still struggling to return his mind to the present, to the grand chamber in which they stood, as the queen's former advisor burst inside. Eyes wide, Zayaan's gaze swept the room until it settled finally on Lukys and Sophia.

"Your Majesties!" the elderly man cried. "Please, you must come quickly. The Calafe refugees, there's been an uprising. They're marching on the citadel!"

THE FUGITIVE

E rika struggled to make headway as the crowd pressed against her, the dense bodies threatening to swallow her up. Refugees from all across southern Flumeer had converged on Mildeth, fleeing before the retreating army and the Tangata surging across the kingdom. The chaos had made it easy to enter the city unnoticed by Amina's guards, but it complicated her plans. The unwanted Calafe, after more than a year spent camped outside of the walls, had finally been allowed into the city. If she could not find them, she would fail.

Alongside her, Cara struggled with the crowd even more than Erika. While she had healed enough to fly on their journey, she now wore a jacket they had taken from the farmhouse to cover her wings. Rumours of the winged creatures that harried the queen's army had raced ahead of the battle, and now instead of looking upon the Anahera in awe, the Flumeerens spoke of them in the same breath as the monstrous Tangata.

But it was the crowd itself that was causing Cara problems. She had coped fine in Fogmore, but that had been a backwater village compared to the population of Mildeth. Thousands surged around them, more people than the young Anahera had ever seen before, and Erika could see the anxiety in her friend's eyes, could feel it in the strength of Cara's grip around her hand. She was pretty sure that grip was the only thing keeping the Goddess from fleeing into the sky.

Thankfully, Cara kept her feet on the ground, at least for now. They were chasing a rumour that the Calafe refugees had taken up residence in a plaza not far from the citadel itself. She wondered what Amina would think of that, should the woman survive long enough to return. Erika still prayed the Tangata would strike the queen down, but given her Anaheran strength and the human magic she wielded, the odds seemed stacked in Amina's favour.

A princess could dream, though.

Finally the crowd began to shift. The girls went with the flow rather than trying to force themselves in a particular direction. All roads in Mildeth led towards the citadel—it was only once you reached the mountain on which the citadel perched that the way would be barred.

Still, the crowd thinned as they approached the citadel, as the refugees were taken in by those households and taverns willing to help, or more often found a spot on the sidewalks, plazas or parks— wherever they could find space not already occupied by another lost soul. Compared to the tranquil city she had last left just months before, Erika could hardly believe the difference now.

But then, the Tangata were coming.

They found the plaza crowded like all the others, but it was difficult to tell immediately whether the rumours had been true, that the Calafe were the ones who occupied this space. Certainly, the plaza seemed better organised than others, with makeshift tents set up in long lines, creating avenues through which foot traffic could pass.

Still clutching Cara's hand, Erika led them into the square. It wasn't long before she heard the rough southern accent of the Calafe amongst those camped there. Her heart quickened at the sound, and she found herself studying the faces of the men and women they passed, noting their differences from the average Flumeeren. While the locals generally preferred spears and swords, these refugees carried axes, clubs and maces. The weapons were older too, their handles worn with use, though Erika saw not a speck of rust upon the blades.

The final confirmation came when she noticed that the women

carried weapons too. The warrior queen of Flumeer was an exception to the norm in Flumeer, where most women went unarmed.

Which meant Erika had found the Calafe, her people.

As though summoned by the thought, a rough hand grabbed Erika by the wrist, jarring her to a halt and spinning her in the direction of her assailant. Heart lurching, Erika raised her fist, but the man spoke before she could summon her power.

"Who are you?" he growled, spittle from his swollen lips flying between them, such that Erika took a quick step back. The man released her, but advanced after her retreat. "This is Calafe territory," he continued. "Outsiders are not welcome."

Erika struggled to contain her surprise—she hadn't expected her presence to be noted so quickly, let alone confronted. Now she found herself staring up at the gruff stranger, dwarfed by his size, by the bulk of his massive barrel chest. The hilt of a greatsword rose from between his shoulders and he wore an old chainmail vest, its links polished so they shone. Such was his size, it was a long moment before Erika noticed his missing arm, the empty sleeve where his left hand should have been.

Her heart lurched at the sight and she remembered Romaine, how he had lost his arm protecting her in the caverns. But the man had not been alone in his loss—amongst the Calafe, many had suffered similar injuries in the decade long war against the Tangata. Though…most had not continued the fight as Romaine had.

Remembering his courage that day in the mountains, so long ago now, when Romaine had fallen, Erika drew herself up. "I am no outsider," she snarled at her accoster. "Who are you to question me?"

The man raised a bushy eyebrow. "I am Darien of the Calafe," he rumbled. "And I know all of my people in Mildeth, those who survived the death of our kingdom. And I don't know you."

"And yet I am Calafe."

"Did you come from the south then?" Darien asked, his voice taking on a mocking tone. "Perhaps you've lived amongst the Tangata all this time, sharing their beds, breaking your fast with them." He snorted and waved a hand. "Begone, women, look for shelter elsewhere."

Movement came from behind Darien as two others stepped

from the crowd with clubs in hand. One sported a missing eye, the other a nasty scar that started at his exposed shoulder and disappeared beneath his shirt. Erika shivered again at the evidence of their lost war. Most of the Calafe had refused to flee from the Tangata. Only those too injured to fight, or with families to protect, had fled willingly. Even Romaine had only survived because of a head knock that had incapacitated him during the final battle.

Alongside her, Cara shifted at the sight of the men and Erika sensed her friend's tension. Quickly she stepped between them. She didn't want to see what would happen if the people of this city witnessed the Goddess in all her glory. After the rumours that had spread ahead of the fleeing army, they were unlikely to be friendly…

"Ay, I came from the frontier," she said softly, allowing the accent she had worked so hard to squash the past decade to slip back into her words. She kept her eyes locked with Darien. It was obvious he enjoyed some degree of status amongst the refugees. "I stood with Romaine of Calafe when he marched south against the Tangata." She hesitated then, knowing she carried news the world had not yet heard. "And I was at his side when he died."

"Romaine is dead?" the man asked, shock showing in his eyes. He lowered his hand, the tension going from his body. "It cannot be true."

Cara stirred at his words. "It is," she said softly. "He died saving me, protecting me from a terrible man."

For the first time, Darien took note of Cara. His eyes narrowed as he looked her up and down and Erika's heart clenched, fearing Cara would be recognised as the Goddess that had revealed herself on the Illmoor. This man could not have been there, but rumours would have spread…

"It is said that Romaine journeyed into the mountains to protect a…woman with fiery hair and eyes of amber," he said softly, and Erika realised this man knew the truth. But he only inclined his head to Cara. "I am glad to hear his passing was not in vain. Long did our champion seek the release of death."

The Goddess swallowed at his words, her eyes shining in the afternoon sun. Erika felt a sting in her own eyes, but she clenched her teeth and forced the grief aside. How much easier this would have been, if Romaine had lived to stand at her side. They could have worked together to reunite their fallen kingdom…

…but there was no use wishing to change the past. There was only the present now, only her. Drawing herself up, Erika nodded to the Calafe.

"He died fighting for his kingdom," she added.

A frown touched the man's face, and he looked at her, perturbed. "Who *are* you, girl?"

"I am no girl," Erika said, inserting every inch of authority she possessed into her voice. These men must not view her as a child, and so she drew about her the practiced air of the Flumeeren court, the skills she had acquired in her years training beneath the queen. "My name is Erika, daughter to King Micah, and the rightful Queen of the Calafe."

The man stared at her, eyes wide, brows lifted into his ragged mop of black hair. Then abruptly, he threw back his head and let out a booming laugh. Erika jumped at the sound, flinching back from him, before a scowl crossed her face. Instinctively, she clenched her fist.

The sound of Darien's laughter drew the attention of the nearby crowd, and as his laughter faded, Erika and Cara found themselves surrounded now by onlookers. Embarrassment rose within Erika as she felt the weight of their gazes and her cheeks grew warm.

But they fell silent as the heat grew in her hand, their eyes drawn to the light seeping from her fingers. Swallowing her doubt, Erika raised her fist, the gauntlet aglow, its magic bursting out to bathe the faces of the onlookers. Even Darien's eyes widened at the sight and unconsciously he took a step back.

"What sorcery is this?" he whispered.

Erika ignored him. Instead, she scanned her surroundings, settling finally on an appropriate place to stand. Crossing to a nearby fountain, she climbed up onto the rim. The water within had long since dried up, probably one of the first luxuries to be halted with the approaching war. There was a statue within of a man upon a horse, probably queen Amina's father, Erika guessed, though she could not have said for certain.

Ignoring the now silent crowd, Erika crossed the barren fountain and pulled herself up onto the statue, climbing higher, leaving behind those below, until she stood upon the back of the horse and looked out across the plaza.

A thousand faces stared back at her, mouths wide, eyes fixed upon the glowing gauntlet. Erika grimaced as she looked at them, at their pain, their poverty, the cruelty the world had dealt them. Once, she had condemned these people for their misfortune, but now she saw more. A mother who wore a sword upon her belt as she supervised a group of children. Warriors like Darien and his friends amidst the crowd, eyes alert for troublemakers. The orderly placement of the tents, though they had only been in the plaza a few days.

The Calafe might have lost their home, but they had not lost their pride.

"Hear me, people of Calafe," Erika called, speaking in a soft voice, though such was the silence now, that her words did not fail to reach the ears of a single watcher. "My name is Erika. You do not know me, but my father was Micah, our fallen king. My mother and I were driven from New Nihelm upon his death. Perhaps you know the story." She hesitated at that, memories flickering into her mind, of a life lost, of suffering and hardship, of her heartbroken mother doing her best to raise an ungrateful child. Then she exhaled, and let go of that pain. "In truth, I have lived much of my life hating the Calafe for what was done to me." She drew in a breath. "But that time has passed. I have learned much these last weeks, the truth about my father, about our kingdom."

Erika paused, eyeing the crowd, knowing that what she said next would change everything. Revealing the truth would set the Calafe against Queen Amina, and all who stood with her. But there was no choice. However she justified her treachery, the woman must pay for the crimes she had committed against the Calafe.

"It is time I shared that truth. It was not the Tangata who killed my father, our king, but an assassin. Sent by Queen Amina, he slew Micah at the height of the southern campaign, when our forces were committed to battle, so that the Calafe would collapse, leaving our lands unprotected. All so Queen Amina could play the hero, so the other kingdoms would turn to her in fear."

A rumble rose from the crowd and she sensed their disbelief, their anger. She had felt that same doubt herself. How could anyone be so selfish, so cold-hearted, to commit such an atrocity against her fellow man? And yet her words were truth. She caught sight of the man that had accosted her as he pushed his way to the edge of the fountain.

"Is it true?" Darien called up to her, his face twisted, anger shining from his eyes. Cara hovered at his side, looking from Erika to the Calafe man.

Erika clenched her fist and light burst from the gauntlet. "Every word I have spoken is truth," she proclaimed. "I served beneath the woman for years, trusted her, loved her. But I cannot allow her treachery to stand. No longer."

Darien stared at her for a long moment. "And what would you do about it, Erika of the Calafe?" came the question.

Erika clenched her jaw. "I would lead my people against the one who betrayed us."

Darien nodded, then dropped to one knee. "Then I will follow you, My Queen."

Erika eyes widened at the man's abrupt change of heart. But his gesture was already spreading around the plaza, whispers passing through the crowd as they looked upon Darien. In that moment, Erika realised she'd been correct in her assessment, that Darien was someone important amongst the Calafe.

Standing atop the statue, Erika watched in disbelief as one by one, the Calafe gathered below fell to their knees and pledged their loyalty. In that moment, looking out over her people, Erika's worries evaporated, and she felt a warmth within, a quiet confidence. If she could do this, then nothing was beyond her. Not with her people united behind her.

Her eyes flickered towards the mountain that rose from the centre of the city, the walls of the citadel twisting up to enclose it. Amina was still marching north, the bulk of her forces with her. Most of the Mildeth's remaining defences would be committed to the city walls, leaving the citadel relatively unprotected. But if the queen was allowed to retake the city, that would change.

There was no time to hesitate.

"People of Calafe," she called, lifting her arm to point the way. "Let us take our vengeance upon the home of our enemy!"

❧ 22 ❧

THE SOVEREIGN

Lukys stumbled to a halt as he turned a corner and was greeted by the roar of raised voices. Sophia stopped beside him, even as Nguyen and their guards fanned out around them. For a second, all Lukys could do was stare at the Calafe as they advanced up the street. Weapons glistened in their hands and a burning red aura rolled out ahead of the crowd, thrumming with their rage.

Instinctively, he reached out with his mind and felt Sophia moving with him, seeking to cool the heat of their emotion, to restore calm to the approaching mob. For once, though, they resisted, and Lukys sensed a flickering of images from their minds, of a man with wild black hair cut down, of burning villages and the fall of New Nihelm, and…

…he started as a woman's face emerged from the images, one he knew, that of the queen's Archivist he had known once, though it seemed a lifetime since he'd ridden south with Erika…

"*Lukys!*"

His head jerked up as someone shouted his name over the roaring of the crowd. His heart lurched and his mouth fell open as a figure leapt into the air, wings snapping open, beating down, sending their owner hurtling upwards. Screams sounded from the crowd as the Anahera soared higher, and curses came from his guards as they raised spears and shields to protect the Sovereigns and the king.

Lukys hardly noticed their actions. His eyes were fixed on the winged woman, on the figure spiralling down towards him, taking in the brilliant auburn wings and copper hair, the ringing voice calling his name, the joy upon the face of the Anahera.

Only when he heard the clacking of crossbows did he take note of his guards.

"*Stop!*" he shouted desperately, using his inner Voice too. The crossbow winches fell silent as Travis and the others looked at Lukys, eyes wide, and in the air, even the Anahera seemed to falter at the power of his Command.

With a soft *thump*, the Anahera landed on the cobbled streets a few yards from where their party stood. As one, Dale, Travis and the other guards spun towards her. Only then did recognition bloom in the eyes of Lukys's fellow Perfugians.

The Anahera standing before them was Cara, their long-lost friend from Fogmore.

"Lukys?" Cara said his name again, but this time he sensed her hesitation, the doubt in her mind.

Lukys couldn't blame her. As far as she and most of the world had known, he and his friends had died south of the Illmoor. For Lukys to be standing there alive, let alone in the garb of a Sovereign…well, even he had trouble believing it at times.

"Cara?"

Another voice spoke before Lukys could greet the Anahera, as Travis stepped from the line of guards, tearing off his helmet.

"By the…well, you, I guess, it is you!" he exclaimed, a sudden grin stretching across his lips.

Then he was racing forward to drag Cara into an embrace, lifting her from the ground and spinning her around, wings and all. A chuckle whispered in Lukys's mind at the sight and he glanced at Sophia, seeing the grin on his partner's lips.

So this is the Anahera you're all so fond of.

So it would seem, Lukys said quietly, then hesitated, wondering if he should reveal more. But…Sophia would sense the truth from him anyway—there were no secrets between them now. *Travis in particular…*

He trailed off as Isabella stepped hesitantly after her partner, lifting the helmet from her own head. Still embracing Cara, Travis noticed her approach and turned from the Anahera, still wearing his grin.

"Cara, there's someone I want you to meet!" he said with his usual enthusiasm. Releasing the Anahera, he stepped up to Isabella and kissed her quickly, before looking back at Cara. "This is Isabella, my partner!"

Lukys's heart twisted as he watched the smile fall from Cara's lips and she took an abrupt step backwards, eyes wide, suddenly shining. There was no missing the shock on her face, even if he had not seen her aura change from pink to white. Her mouth opened and closed, but the surprise of seeing her former…crush with another had obviously robbed her of words.

"You must be the Anahera who protected my favourite human from the Old Ones," Sophia interjected quickly, stepping forward to offer Cara a hug. The Anahera had regained a little of her composure by the time Sophia stepped back, and Lukys smiled at his partner's quick thinking. "It's a welcome sight to see one of your kind on our side," she continued, though Cara was still staring at her in surprise, no doubt wondering at her Tangatan nature. "We have heard terrible rumours of the Anahera fighting alongside the Old One."

"I'm afraid that much is true," a new voice interjected, and Lukys's heart clenched as the face he'd glimpsed in the minds of the crowd approached. So Erika *was* here. Behind her, the Calafe lingered, apparently shocked to a standstill by Cara's appearance. "I thought you were dead, recruit."

An audible groan came from somewhere behind Lukys at the Archivist's appearance. He cast a sharp glance over his shoulder, catching Dale's eye, but the guard only shrugged. Erika wasn't exactly their favourite person, after she'd forced them all to join her on her mad quest south. Regardless, Lukys shook off his hesitation and stepped forward to greet the woman.

"Archivist," he said, keeping his tone pleasant regardless of his true feelings about her. "It is good to see that you have endured these past months." He did not offer any explanations for his own survival.

"I have a new title now," she replied somewhat hesitantly, glancing over her shoulder. Several men of the Calafe moved to join her and Lukys thought he glimpsed what might have been a nod from one missing an arm. Apparently reassured by their presence, Erika faced Lukys and Sophia again, though only for a moment, as her eyes registered another presence.

"King Nguyen," she greeted, arching an eyebrow. "I am surprised to find you here. Don't tell me you've allied yourself with Amina after all?"

Nguyen chuckled at that. "The Sovereigns and I decided we liked the look of Mildeth, so we took the city for ourselves."

A frown creased Erika's brow at his words. "Sovereigns?" Her eyes flicked back to the pair of them and widened. "I see…" She hesitated, then made to offer her hand. "It seems we have all moved up—"

Before she could come any closer, the one-armed Calafe man leapt forward, grabbing her by the shoulder and dragging her back. "Beware!" he cried, a blade appearing in his hand as he placed himself between the former Archivist and the Sovereigns.

"Darien!" Erika gasped, struggling to retain her balance as she staggered. "What in the—?"

"A Tangata stands with these kings," the Calafe man hissed. "See the eyes of the two women?" he added, gesturing to Sophia and Isabella, neither of whom were concealing their faces now.

Blood began to pound in Lukys's ears as he watched the colour drain from Erika's face. Light burst from the familiar gauntlet she wore, even as the Calafe warriors raised their weapons. Her head whipped around, focusing on Sophia as the glow of her gauntlet grew brighter.

"*Stop!*" Lukys bellowed, unleashing his Voice for the second time in as many minutes.

Erika stopped dead, hand half raised, that strange glow dancing around the metallic links. But she did not—could not—bring herself to open her fist and unleash her power. Drawing in a breath for calm, Lukys placed himself between the new queen and his Sovereign mate.

"Peace, Erika," he said softly, hands raised. "Wait a minute, before you make a mistake you will regret. Sophia and her brethren are on our side."

Rage shone in Erika's eyes and her face twitched. Abruptly,

Lukys's spell broke and letting out a sharp exhalation, she retreated from him, gauntlet still raised in readiness for an attack.

"What was *that?*" she hissed, looking from Lukys to Sophia, then back at Cara. "It…it was like he was in my mind."

"The Voice of the Tangata," Cara replied, still frowning. "Lukys has it, though it has become far more powerful since I knew him in Fogmore." She looked to Sophia. "And it should not be able to have such an effect on a human."

Erika watched the Anahera a moment, then shaking herself, she swung on Lukys once more. "How can you say they're on our side?" she hissed. Flinging out a hand, she pointed to the south, in the direction of the approaching armies. "Don't you know what's happening out there, the danger that marches upon this city? Their kind are slaughtering people all across Flumeer."

"I know," Lukys replied, refusing to retreat from the rage in her eyes, nor the fear behind it. "And the Anahera too, if the rumours are true." He looked pointedly at Cara. "But it is not the Anahera, nor the Tangata, who are our true enemy." He swallowed, staring at Erika, recalling the darkness of the tunnels they had uncovered, the stench of rot and death thick on the air. The creatures that had stalked them in that darkness. "Do you remember what we found… that day beneath the earth?"

Erika started at his words, her eyes widening, revealing her shock. For a moment, he thought she would deny his words. She had been knocked unconscious during that conflict, had only caught a glimpse of the Old Ones before Cara had slain them.

Then the former Archivist lowered her fist, the light dying from her gauntlet, and she nodded.

"So you have seen her too," Erika whispered.

23

THE FALLEN

For days, Adonis and Maisie followed behind the Tangatan army, trailing in the shadow of their conquest, surviving off the scraps they left behind, watching, waiting. There was nothing else for them to do, no alternative path either could take. After all, where else could they go? The lands behind them belonged to the Tangata, but they were mostly empty now, their inhabitants swept up in Maya's power.

And so Adonis followed in the wake of his former mate, tracking her passage through the human lands. Maisie's people had retreated before the might of Maya's army, avoiding a pitched battle and forcing the Old One to give chase if she wished to bring the half-blood queen to heel.

Even so, they still found bodies scattered across the hilly land-scape, the remains of skirmishes between the Tangata and the enemy, only…it was strange how Adonis had never noticed before how difficult it was to distinguish between the two in death, how similar his people looked to the humans, lying side by side with them.

A week after his fallout with Maya, Adonis's wounds had at least partially mended. The same could not be said for Maisie with her human frailty, and after a few hours walking each day, she often resorted to her makeshift crutch for support. Or failing that, his shoulder.

Despite his own improvement, it would be obvious to any they crossed that neither was up for a fight. Thankfully, the attention of Adonis's brethren remained focused on the human army. Whenever they drew near the fringes of the Tangatan camp, he could sense their rage, like the distant pounding of drums, sounding to the beat of their conductor, to the Voice of Maya.

Even at the edges of her influence, Adonis found his own emotions stirring, his fists clenching tighter, his anger rising at the human's incessant chatting. Fortunately, Maisie tended to grow quiet at those times too. She might not hear the Voice of Maya, but that did not entirely spare her from the Old One's influence. Adonis couldn't help but wonder if it was that power which had broken the human army. If Maya could stoke the rage of so many Tangata, might she also be capable of influencing the humans, of fuelling their fears until they fled?

Such a use of the Voice had long been forbidden amongst his people, even on the smaller scales capable of by the Tangata. Adonis had argued against such restrictions, but their former Matriarch had denied him, enforcing the principles of ancestors long since perished.

Now, watching the madness that had consumed his people, Adonis at last saw her wisdom. His people might have won the battle for the river, might have driven the humans back, might even soon claim a final victory…but what had they lost in doing so, in bowing to the greater power of Maya? What remained of his people now but a mindless mob, thirsty for the blood of their enemies?

No, this victory had cost his people their souls.

Standing atop a hill at the top of the valley, Adonis looked upon the Tangatan horde—and the walls of the city that towered beyond. Mildeth, Maisie called it, the capital of the Flumeeren kingdom. The humans and their half-blood queen had finally run out of places to hide.

Instead, they had readied fortifications beneath the great walls and turned to face the Tangata. Perhaps suspecting another of the queen's traps, Maya had not yet attacked, but Adonis was sure the Old One would not wait long. Above, he caught glimpses of shadows in the sky, the winged Anahera scouting out the enemy formations, no doubt.

Shivering, Adonis tore his eyes from the mass of Tangata and looked to the human, Maisie. Even after three days, he was still not sure what to make of her. Half the time they'd spent together, he found himself regretting sparing her life. She spoke constantly now, her voice grating on his nerves day and night, and her presence only slowed him now that his wounds were healing. Perhaps he should put the creature out of her misery. After all, there would be nothing left for her kind after Maya's inevitable victory. Death would be a mercy, rather than the enslavement that waited when the new dawn rose.

But with a sigh, Adonis dismissed the thought. The human could have slain him as he lay injured from Maya's beating, but she hadn't. He would not harm her now. He had at least that much honour. Though…

…they were close enough to the Tangatan camp that he could feel *her*, could sense the darkness of her Voice upon his mind, upon the minds of all who resided in the valley. Despite that dark touch— or perhaps because of it—Adonis found himself confused when his thoughts turned to Maya.

Even far from her presence, he found himself longing for her touch. The pain of her rejection had not healed with his other wounds, remaining instead a gaping hole in his soul, a nightmare from which he could not wake. His vision blurred as he recalled the promises she had made him, the children she carried, the future he had envisioned at her side.

Adonis clenched his fists, his entire being trembling. If only…

An image flashed into his mind, the memory of Nyriah, of her body lying cold in the mud, her feathers twisted and broken, empty eyes staring…

Gasping, Adonis tore his gaze from the distant army and staggered back from the crest of the hill. The human made some sounds of concern, but he ignored her. How had it come to this? The great Adonis, third generation Tangata, strongest of his people, now trailed after the woman that had spurned him, yearning like a lost puppy for a second chance. Why did he want her still, when all she had ever done was cause him pain?

A shudder racked him and Adonis squeezed his eyes closed. He'd been wrong to come here, to follow. The human thought

Adonis planned to help her, but…he did not have the strength for that, did he? No, he had come to hand Maisie over to his mate, to earn the Old One's praise, to restore himself in her eyes, to…to…

"You still want her back, don't you?" Maisie's voice came from behind him, soft, yet firm. She snorted. "Why not, I suppose? Maybe you can present me to her on a platter, a human that has completely outlived her usefulness. I'm sure it will *entirely* make up for the queen you failed to kill back on the Illmoor."

She laughed, the sound harsh, bitter. Her eyes remained on the army and the city beyond, but as he looked in her direction, they narrowed. "Well, isn't that something?"

Adonis followed her gaze, expecting to see some disturbance amongst the opposing armies, but there was nothing. He turned back to Maisie and raised an eyebrow in question.

"That wily bastard," she muttered by way of reply. When Adonis only raised his other eyebrow, she sighed. "Seems you're not the only one with an ex-lover on this battlefield. See those flags above the city gates? That one means King Nguyen is in residence." She pointed to another flag, and then another. "The Sovereigns of Perfugia too, and…what's this, the Calafe?" She blinked, glancing at Adonis in disbelief. "Haven't seen that one in a long time. I wonder…"

She trailed off, still looking at Adonis, as though waiting for him to say something. He shrugged and glanced at the flags she'd indicated, but they were only flapping pieces of fabric to Adonis. Humans were so strange, the way they divided themselves, pretending that differences of geography meant something. No wonder they had warred so readily against the Tangata, when they could not even keep the peace amongst themselves.

"You know, Adonis, you're terrible at small talk."

Adonis glanced sharply at Maisie but the human did not elaborate. After a long moment, he snorted at her, a stubborn smile touching her lips. Again, he found himself wishing he could respond in her coarse language.

"It's true, you know," she said, smiling herself.

Retreating from the edge of the hill, Maisie seated herself on a boulder. Her face was pale and she was puffing by the time she sat. Concerned, Adonis followed her, gesturing silently to her leg.

She shrugged. "It's fine," she said, though her expression betrayed the lie. Reaching out with his mind, Adonis glimpsed the swirling grey-black of her agony. "It just needs to rest."

Adonis hesitated before nodding. Dark lines of pain still radiated from the woman, mingling with her usual rainbow of fear, anger and sadness. After a long moment, he knelt beside the boulder and reached for her leg.

Maisie flinched away from him, her hand dropping to the knife she wore at her belt. He paused, looking up at her brown eyes, but did not move away. Eyes narrowed, Maisie stared back. Despite their days together and her incessant chatting, she clearly still did not trust him. That was smart, considering his earlier thoughts. But finally she seemed to relax, removing her hand from the dagger.

Adonis took that as a sign he could continue. Carefully, he lifted her calf and gently rolled up the cuff of her pant leg. Her skin beneath was pale and the uneven line of her shin revealed where the bones had knitted poorly from her injury. Adonis could do nothing for that, but the muscles of her calf had locked tight, swelling as they cramped from the long journey.

Slowly, gently, he trailed his fingers along her calf, his touch turning to gentle prods, senses extending in search of knots. Maisie flinched again at his touch, her entire body taut, but this time it seemed less due to mistrust, more the pain of her injury itself. Adonis continued, taking care not to press too hard, though he did slowly increase the pressure, seeking the deeper knots, the twisted fibres that had built through the long weeks of disuse.

Seated on her boulder, Maisie gritted her teeth against the pain but did not try to stop him, nor reach again for her knife. Instead, she turned her gaze again to the city.

"It's terrible, isn't it?" she whispered.

Adonis paused, but when he looked at her, he realised she wasn't talking about him. He frowned, then decided she was just trying to distract herself from the pain. He continued the massage in silence, and Maisie went on.

"When I first realised Nguyen was manipulating me…well, I knew he was a king. What else should I have expected? We're all just pawns to their kind." She sighed. "Still felt terrible though, to be used by someone I loved. At least with me…well, I think it was for a good cause. But you…" She gestured in the direction of the Tangatan army. "You think she cares about them? Your Tangata? She certainly doesn't care about the Anahera. Those kids you helped her capture, they'll be dead before this ends, mark my words. They'll live as long as the adults prove useful, but the moment the Anahera fail…"

She trailed off as Adonis stood abruptly, his task with her injured muscles forgotten. His heart beat faster as he returned to the crest of the hill and looked down on the Tangatan camp. Even as he scanned the distant campfires, his mind filled with images, of the Tangatan children lying in the snow, of Nyriah's pain as she collapsed to the mud, defending him. Adonis owed the Anahera a debt he could never hope to repay. Not unless…

"Oh, that *is* a bold thought," Maisie said softly, as though she had read his mind. Rising, she moved to stand alongside him, following his gaze to the distant camp. "But do you have the guts to pull it off, Adonis?"

❧ 24 ❧

THE QUEEN

Sitting in the parlour of her former chambers, Erika struggled to piece together the warring revelations of the past few days—and the insane political situation she had found in Mildeth. She had arrived in the city expecting a battle, to lead her people in an uprising against the tyrannical Queen Amina, to take back what had been stolen from them.

Instead, she had found that someone had beaten her to the punch, that the city had already been conquered—and by no less than the once-incompetent Perfugian recruit she had thought long dead.

No, not just him, she reminded herself.

There was the Tangata as well, the creature that had partnered with the man, who shared with him the title of Sovereign. Erika clenched her fists, heart racing just at the memory of her unveiling. She should have noticed it sooner, likely would have, if not for the sheer shock of seeing the Perfugian recruits alive. Or…perhaps not. Even after learning of the creatures' intelligence, who would have expected to see one garbed in the fine silks of a Sovereign?

When Darien had shouted his warning, Erika had thought for sure they'd stumbled into a trap, that somehow Maya and her Tangata had infiltrated the city and her followers were about to come swarming from the shadows. The truth, if anything, had been stranger still…

It seemed not all of the Tangata followed the Old One. Lukys's…friends might be few enough, but their presence threw fresh complications into the war between their species. Sophia claimed many amongst the Tangata had only ever wanted peace with humanity. Only her own father's invasion of their land had changed things, forcing them to defend themselves, to fight back.

A shiver ran down Erika's spine. Could it be true? Could her father have led a genocide? He had called for war in response to raids along the Tangatan frontier, to the slaughter of Calafe innocents. But if Sophia was to be believed, the Tangata had not been responsible for those attacks.

It wasn't difficult for Erika to guess who that might have been.

Recalling Amina's words on the ship, her resolve to prepare humanity for war against the false gods, Erika felt the truth in her very bones.

Amina was behind it all.

But the Sovereigns were not the only ones who carried grave news. It had saddened Erika to tell Lukys and the other Perfugians of Romaine's death, to see their pain as they heard how their mentor had fallen, protecting Cara from the queen's assassin.

But Romaine's death still paled in comparison to what else Erika had discovered, the truth about the Anahera, how they had worked together with the Tangata long ago to bring about the Fall of humanity. She had told only Nguyen and the Sovereigns, though she still struggled to think of Lukys as anything but an inexperienced recruit—and the Tangata as anything but the monsters that had stolen her kingdom.

Erika had left them to contemplate her news—and to ponder their revelations herself. Now she could only shake her head as she considered the past, the secrets upon secrets their ancestors had kept from the world.

With a sigh, Erika forced her mind back to the present. The past would have to wait—she was an Archivist no longer, and had responsibilities of her own now, people that looked to her for answers. Glancing across the room, she noticed Cara slumped on the velvet sofa, her wings drawn around herself in a feathery shroud.

Erika's frown deepened, sensing the change in the young

Goddess. The Anahera had been delighted at the sight of Lukys and his little band of Perfugians, but her mood had darkened since. Rising from her armchair, Erika crossed the room and sank onto the couch beside the Goddess. Another shiver raised the feathers on Cara's wings and she gave a muffled sob.

"Cara?" Erika murmured. "What's wrong?"

The Goddess slowly lowered her wings to reveal her face, flicking Erika a glance. "Nothing…" she muttered, her eyes drifting sideways, taking on a distant look. "I just…I never thought…" The words faded, leaving Erika no closer to deciphering their meaning.

Hesitantly, she reached out and ran her hand down Cara's wing. "What's the matter?" she tried again. "Clearly something has you upset."

Tears shone in Cara's eyes when she looked at Erika again, and abruptly she rose. Stalking to the window, her wings snapped open, and it seemed she would hurl herself into the sky. But the Goddess paused at the windowsill, and finally her auburn feathers drooped.

Stumbling back to the sofa, she slumped to the floor alongside it and drew her knees up to her chest. "It's stupid," she muttered.

Erika smiled. "We humans are always dealing with stupid things," she replied. "You might say it's our specialty."

A sigh slipped from the Anahera and she looked up from the floor. "One of the Perfugians," she said quietly. "Travis. I…liked him, once." She snorted. "Like I said, it's stupid, I…there was too much happening…I thought he was dead, and with Romaine and Maya and all your luggage…with my long-lost sister…"

Cara's voice cracked. Sliding onto the floor alongside her friend, Erika hugged the Goddess to her chest. She stroked the young Anahera's hair as another shudder shook Cara, cooing softly beneath her breath the way her mother had once, when Erika had still been innocent. Those days seemed a hundred years ago now.

"I thought…" Cara said, then began to truly sob, the tears coming hot and fast. "I thought…for just a second…when I saw him still alive, even after all this time, after everything we've been through, I thought maybe…"

She gave a violent shake of her head, and Erika sensed the girl's anger—not at this Travis or Lukys or anyone else, but at herself.

"I'm so stupid," she croaked, looking up from Erika's shoulder, eyes shot with red. "Of course he found someone else." She hiccupped, then swallowed them down and went on. "I don't know why I was surprised. The Tangatan lady…seems nice. I'm happy for him…really, happy he's alive, but…" She trailed off.

Erika nodded as fresh tears welled in the Goddess's eyes. There were no words for this kind of thing, nothing either of them could say to make it better. So she hugged the young Anahera tighter, letting her sob and cry and curse, safe in the knowledge someone was there, that Erika would not let her go, that she would be there until Cara found the strength to face the world again.

Or until the world came looking for them.

As one, the pair flinched as a distant horn sounded from outside the window. It was followed by another, then another, as others picked up the call. The hairs on the back of Erika's neck stood on end as she recognised the pattern, the message the watchers on the wall were conveying.

One was the signal for an enemy sighted, for the arrival of the Tangata in the valley of Mildeth.

The second was a greeting.

Queen Amina was at the gates.

25

THE SOVEREIGN

Standing atop the walls of Mildeth, Lukys looked out across the valley and wondered what madness had brought him to this place. Sophia and their guard stood with him, and Erika and Cara were nearby, Nguyen and Zayaan too. But in that moment, looking down upon the vast army gathered beneath the walls of Mildeth, Lukys had never felt so alone.

I am here, Lukys.

He smiled as Sophia joined her mind with his, but not even her presence could relieve his terror, the sense of inadequacy he felt. Below, a woman sat alone on her horse, garbed all in steel armour, a helm marked by a crown upon her brow.

The rightful Queen of Flumeer had come to claim her city.

Amina sat in silence, without advisors or generals or guards to protect her. She knew her enemies were too noble to strike her down unprovoked. She did not even seem overly concerned to find her city held by enemies.

Beyond the queen, the sprawling mass of her army filled half the valley. Lukys's heart was divided at the sight. Her forces appeared mostly intact. After the rumours that had spread ahead of her arrival, they had feared little would be left of the Flumeeren army. It meant they might stand a chance against Maya's forces, that humanity might yet survive.

But only if they could avoid a battle between the forces of humanity.

Most of those Amina led were mounted, and Lukys wondered what had become of the others, the soldiers that had manned the forts along the Illmoor River, who for years had guarded the kingdom from Tangatan invasion. Judging from the coldness of Amina's face, Lukys suspected this woman would not have hesitated to leave them behind if it meant her own survival.

"Well, well, well," her voice carried up to them, surprisingly powerful despite the distance, *"it seems the mice came out to play while the cat was away."*

Lukys shivered as he felt an echo in his mind, the reflection of Amina's inner Voice. So it was true. Erika had told them about the queen's heritage, but it was one thing to hear of it, another altogether to witness it for himself.

And it meant Erika's other revelations must be true as well. Lukys swallowed a lump in his throat, memories of Romaine rising to swamp his thoughts. Somehow, a piece of him had known the great warrior had fallen. Otherwise, there would have been word of him somewhere, rumours of his presence. The Calafe warrior wasn't one to run from a fight.

Even so, to learn the truth, to think of his mentor lying alone in the cold Mountains of the Gods…

Amina's heritage might have greater import for the fate of humanity, but somehow, it was Romaine who lingered on Lukys's mind.

Shaking himself, he focused on the queen. Despite her ability, she didn't seem to be using her Voice in a deliberate manner. He prayed that meant she was unschooled in her powers. The last thing they needed was another Melder influencing the battle. And it might prove an advantage they could exploit.

"Amina!" he called finally, shaking himself from his silence. "We have co—"

"My, my, is that Nguyen I see up there?" the queen interrupted. "And unless my eyes betray me, my Archivist has come to greet me as well. I might have guessed you would have survived the inferno, though…you should have left your pet to burn."

A growl came from nearby and Lukys glanced at Cara, but

Erika had already raised an arm to bid the Anahera wait. The two seemed to have grown close in their absence.

"Oh dear, and Zayaan, they turned you as well? I had thought you at least would remain loyal to my father's cause." She *tsked* softly, and Lukys leapt at the opportunity.

"*Amina!*" he bellowed, adding his Voice to his words. "*Your treachery has been laid bare. Will you submit yourself to the judgement of the Sovereigns?*"

Below, the queen's eyebrows lifted in surprise. "So it's true then?" she said softly, though the words still carried to those above. "The Sovereigns have finally left the safety of their island. I did not think you had the courage." Then her eyes narrowed, her lips thinning into a cruel smile. "But no, I see the truth, even from here. The eyes betray you, Tangata. It seems I find monsters everywhere I turn, these days." She looked again at Nguyen. "I am disappointed, brother king. I did not think you so cowardly as to ally with the enemy."

"The only enemy I see here waits outside these walls, Amina," Nguyen's reply came from beside Lukys.

"Oh?" Amina asked wryly. "And where was the bold king of Gemaho when the Calafe begged—"

"Don't you *dare* speak about my people as though you care," Erika snarled, stepping up on the crenelations. Light appeared in her hand as she ignited the gauntlet, though Amina must have been far behind its range. "It was *you* who betrayed my father, who provoked him to attack the Tangata. You have been behind every death, every pain and loss my people have suffered this past decade."

"Oh, they're *your* people now, are they, my good Archivist? And where were *you* while the Calafe suffered? While they fought desperately for their survival? When everyone else fled, whose soldiers fought alongside them? Who gave them shelter when their kingdom fell? Where were you, *Archivist?*"

Erika lowered her head, but she did not back down. "I failed the Calafe once," she said softly, then looked up to meet the queen's gaze again. "I will not do so again. I am an Archivist no longer—the Calafe have elected me their queen, at least until this war is done."

"Queen, is it?" Amina's eyes narrowed as she appraised the

group atop the walls again. "Bold claims you all make, but I see the truth. You are all little better than common thieves, sneaking into my kingdom, stealing my city. Your treason will not save you from my armies."

"Your people stand with us now, Amina," Lukys said, and Sophia stepped up beside him, granting him her strength.

"And *her* people are behind me," the queen snapped. Lips drawing back in a sneer, she gestured to Erika and Nguyen. "Truly you must be desperate, to ally yourselves with such creatures. Is your hatred for me so great that you would see us all destroyed?

Nguyen stirred at that. "Everything I have done was for the survival of Gemaho."

"And everything *I* have done is for the survival of our species!" Amina snarled. "But your treachery threatens to destroy everything I have worked towards, the union I have built."

"*Your union was built on lies*," Lukys said, and now Sophia spoke with him in unison, as the Sovereigns of old had done. There they hesitated, and Lukys glanced at his partner, knowing what they said next could tear their fragile alliance asunder. But there was no other choice, and looking again at the Flumeeren queen, they continued: "*Yet it is not too late to negotiate a true union.*"

"*What?*"

Lukys did not look around as the cry came from Erika, instead keeping his gaze fixed on the queen. Amina's eyes narrowed at his words, but for the moment she said nothing. Erika, on the other hand, roiled with a burning rage.

Lukys could hardly blame her after everything the woman had done to the Calafe. But the crimes of the past could not change one, immutable fact.

Queen Amina commanded half the forces of humanity. Without her on their side, Maya and the Tangata would crush their piddling army without breaking a sweat.

"And who are you to speak of these matters, Sovereign?" Amina called from below, her gaze flickering to Nguyen. "Nguyen I can imagine perhaps seeing reason, but the Archivist..." She trailed off as her eyes settled on Erika, and Lukys knew without turning what she saw. He could sense the rage bubbling from the former Archivist, a burning, scorching thing.

"No, the self-styled Queen of Calafe clearly does not consent to your idea," Amina continued, eyes returning to the Sovereigns. "Who are any of you to think you could lead such an alliance? Not my dear Erika, who until yesterday fled all hint of responsibility. Surely not Nguyen, who abandoned the last alliance between our peoples, surrendering an entire kingdom to the enemy." Her eyes settled on Lukys and Sophia. "And surely not the Sovereigns of Perfugia, who have hidden on their island for generations, who shirked their duties to the last alliance, just as bad as the coward king."

She shook her head, as though to dismiss them all. "None of you are worthy. There is only one who has fought for all our peoples, only one who saw the threat that lurked in our mountains, who did what was necessary to unite humanity against the coming threat."

Lukys gritted his teeth at the woman's words. "Do not seek to present yourself as the saviour of humanity, Flumeeren Queen," he growled. "You have never cared for the lives of those beneath you." He shook his head. "And my predecessors might have shirked their responsibilities, but I have not. It wasn't long ago that I served beneath your own general, fought in a war that *you* started, against a people that wanted only peace."

"Monsters," Amina replied coldly, her gaze flickering to Sophia before returning to Lukys. "Creatures from the dark, ruled by base emotion. They possess no civilisation, no civility. Just like our so-called gods, they would have betrayed us in the end. There can be no peace with such creatures."

A growl came from alongside Lukys as Sophia stirred. "Yet in the end, it was not my people who broke the peace," she called back. "It was not the Tangata who sought bloodshed, who oversaw the slaughter of innocents on both sides, was it, Queen of Blood?"

Amina raised her eyebrows at Sophia's speech. "So you taught the beast a trick." She snorted, then glanced behind her, in the direction of the distant hills. "But it matters not if one can speak. Make no mistake, her kind *are* the enemy, along with our cursed false gods. When the battle is joined, only one species will emerge as victors."

"The Tangata and Anahera are controlled by another," Lukys

struggled to explain, to fight back against her attacks. "An Old One by the name of Maya. She seeks only destruction—of humanity, of the Anahera, of the Tangata even. All so she might one day restore her own kind to life."

Amina chuckled at that, before abruptly turning her horse, presenting them her back. "Very well." Her voice carried on the breeze. "Then I will make my last stand here. At least my death might give courage to the faithful of Mildeth, that they might cast off your tyranny."

"Amina!" Lukys cried, suddenly panicked, that she might truly lead her army in a suicidal charge against the Tangata.

Below, the queen glanced back, one eyebrow raised.

Lukys swallowed, glancing sidelong at Sophia. He could sense her anger, a reflection of the others, of his own, but there was no choice.

"As I said," he continued, clearing his throat. "We came to negotiate. Humanity cannot stand divided against this threat. Whatever the cost, we must work together, or face annihilation alone."

A stirring came from along the wall but Lukys did not take his eyes from Amina. Instead, he ploughed on, not daring to give the others a chance to object.

"Your people will be permitted into the city, on your agreement there will be peace between them and those inside. What crimes you have committed..." He paused, then finally finished, "will be forgiven, at least until the war has ended." He drew in a breath, guilt weighing heavy on his soul. "I warn you though, do not seek to betray us."

Amina watched him for a long time, and reaching out with his mind, he struggled to pierce the fog of her thoughts, to sense her mind amidst the swirling colours. Grey doubt flickered, the purple of hope too, but a hundred other hues too, mixing and changing as she considered his words...

...until finally Amina shrugged, as though his offer was of no more consequence than a pebble beneath her horse's hoof.

"So kind of you, Sovereign, to offer me safe passage into my own city," came her reply. Then a smile touched her lips and he saw a flicker of triumph in her eyes. "But very well," she said, gesturing with a hand. "My soldiers are disciplined. They will not break the peace." Her grin spread and her gaze turned on Erika, who seemed barely able to restrain herself. "Just be sure to keep your monsters and the barbarians under control. My soldiers will not hesitate to defend themselves."

Abruptly she raised her hand. Horns trumpeted from the gathered lines of her army, sounding the call to advance, as though she'd known they would allow her entrance all along. As one, the Flumeeren army surged forward, marching in ranks towards the waiting gates.

For a moment, Lukys stood frozen atop the city walls. Terror rose in his chest as he watched the army approach. Had Amina outmanoeuvred him? If they did not open the gates now, chaos would ensue, and anything might happen in the confusion. Sensing Erika's rage, the pain of Sophia and her Tangata, already he found himself regretting his decision. And yet...

...there was no other choice. The weight of humanity's survival —of all their survival—settled on his shoulders.

Turning, Lukys nodded for Dale to signal the attendants below to open the gates for the Flumeeren queen.

⚜   26   ⚜

THE FALLEN

Adonis and Maisie slipped into the Tangatan camp beneath the cover of night. Once the Flumeeren army had retreated into the city, they'd waited all day to see whether Maya would attack. But as the sun dipped beneath the horizon, it became obvious the Tangatan army was making no move towards the granite walls. Watching Maya's hesitation after her previous aggression, Adonis couldn't help but wonder whether something had happened, if perhaps the children...

His heart quickened at the thought, but he pushed it aside. He couldn't think of that now, could not allow himself to be distracted. It was difficult enough to concentrate with the thrumming of Maya's Voice in his mind again...

All was quiet as they slipped through the long grass of the hillside, down towards the waiting camp, towards the shimmering bonfires in the Flumeeren night. It wasn't long before movement appeared in the darkness. A Tangatan guard stepped before them, her face creased with confusion.

A...Adonis? her voice whispered into his thoughts, hesitant.

True to Maya's word, knowledge of his exile had obviously reached even the lowliest ranks of his people. Still, Adonis was not without his own strength, his own cunning.

Yes, he replied, reaching out with his Voice. He might not have been a match for Maya, but Adonis still had a power over the lesser generations. *I have been gone on a secret task for Maya, but now I have returned.*

You were...banished, spurned, the guard whispered, struggling against the waves of Adonis's mind.

But she could not have been more than fifth generation, her resistance futile.

You will let us pass. The human has vital information for our Matriarch.

With these words, Adonis felt the last remnants of the guard's resistance crumble. She bowed her head and stepped aside, allowing Adonis to pass. Gripping Maisie tightly with one hand, as though she were his prisoner, he strode into the disorganised camp—though he kept his grip on the guard's mind still, infusing her with confidence, with a joy that she had served her masters well. It would suppress her doubt, for a time at least.

Shadows shifted in the night as they made their way through the camp. With their enhanced vision, the Tangata were bothered little by the dark, though he noticed how Maisie tripped and stumbled. Adonis found himself wondering how it would be to find oneself blind, unable to discern the shadow of an enemy from that of a tree or shrub. Such a terrifying, helpless existence, pitiful, when compared to the greatness of the Tangata...

Adonis gave his mind a mental shake. Maya's voice was growing louder now, seeming to vibrate his entire being, though he steeled himself against it. Her influence would only grow greater the longer they remained in the camp, and carefully he gripped the human's hand tighter. Maisie had not seemed overly affected by the Old One's presence, but neither could she defend herself against its affects. If something caught her anger, Maya's influence might drive her to ruin everything.

For now, all he could do was take them in a broad circle around the centre of the camp, where Maya's Voice was strongest. Even so, he could feel its effects within him, the growing desire to turn towards that centre, to go to his mate, to deliver the human to her judgement...

Teeth bared, Adonis resisted and kept on, though his hold on the human tightened even further. He could sense her glances, the concern swirling in her mind, and wondered how she could bring herself to trust him. She couldn't even begin to understand his kind. He certainly did not trust her…did he?

Adonis paused, glancing at the human, and Maisie raised an eyebrow.

"Hey, stay with me, bud," she whispered, clicking her fingers. "The plan, remember? Where are those kids?"

Adonis hesitated, watching her, wondering, then abruptly he nodded. He turned towards the dense clot of fear, the terror radiating from a group that could only be the Anaheran fledgelings. The poor creatures only wanted to see their parents again, the noble beings he had made into slaves. He wondered how many of the Anahera would fall, never to see their children again, before this was all over.

No more, if we can help it, he told himself.

Yet there was another voice within him, a deeper voice, one that whispered that this was madness, that they would never escape with these innocents. Even should they pass the boundaries of the camp, the city was a mile off and morning was fast approaching.

One step at a time. He tried to suppress the doubts, but it was a struggle now—one Adonis feared he would soon lose.

Maisie took a sharp intake of breath as a pair of shadows moved to bar their path. Adonis drew to a stop, fearing for a second they'd been discovered, but he soon realised the reason for the presence of his brethren here. The knot of terror lay just beyond them—these two were guarding the fledgelings.

Who goes there? the first of the guards hissed.

There's a human— the second started, but he broke off as Adonis quickly invaded their minds.

This was a greater challenge, even for one such as Adonis. No amount of trickery would convince these Tangata to part with their charges, not without approval from Maya herself. And they were stronger too, of the fourth generation. To prevent them from raising the alarm, Adonis pressed his Voice upon them.

Do not move, do not Speak, he ordered, before turning to the first of them. *How many of you are there?*

A tremor shook his brother's face as the Tangata struggled, but there was no resisting Adonis's Voice, and finally the guard broke.

Five! came the gasped cry, even as the Tangata slumped to his knees.

Adonis held up a hand, stilling the human at his side, then reached out with his mind for the other guards. He found them stationed amongst the children, alert for signs of treachery. The fledgelings might have been young and apparently helpless, but they were Anahera still. Thankfully, Adonis's brethren were not alert for treachery from their own.

One by one, he took their minds, swamping their thoughts with his Voice. When he had them all, Adonis ordered them to where he and Maisie waited, until finally all five stood rigid before him. Spasms racked their faces as they strained against his Voice, struggling to break free and sound the alarm, but Adonis held them—at least for now.

Trembling with the strain, he turned to Maisie, and nodded.

The human stood wide-eyed, staring at the guards, as though waiting for them to leap forward and tear her limb from limb. At Adonis's gesture, she looked at him, her features knitting into a frown.

"You're doing this?" she whispered, shaking her head. "Incredible."

Teeth still clenched, Adonis gestured again in the direction of the children. Their time was short—he could not hold these creatures long. They couldn't waste a second if they were to somehow escape with the fledgelings.

The human finally seemed to understand and a look of resolve crossed her face. She disappeared into the darkness, leaving him standing alone with the Tangatan guards. Adonis could sense their eyes on him, their hatred as they fought his mental bindings. Silently he prayed for the human to hurry. Against these five, his strength would eventually fail and they would fall upon him, tearing him to pieces before turning on her…

…Adonis's stomach twisted at the thought and he straightened, determined to see this through, to…to…

Maisie reappeared from the gloom. Adonis had no idea how she'd managed it so quickly and without struggle, but a group of tiny figures followed just a step behind. Their wings tucked close to their sides, the Anaheran fledgelings looked from Adonis to the Tangatan guards with open terror in their eyes.

Adonis's heart swelled at the sight all the same. For the first time that night, he felt that they might actually accomplish their mission. But even as the thought came, he sensed a surge of emotion from the Tangatan guards, a terrible rage as they realised his plan and truly began to fight. A gasp escaped him as they stretched against his restraints. Quickly he refocused his attention on the five figures, commanding them to be still, to silence.

A sound like nails on a chalkboard sounded in his mind as the five consciousnesses fought back, determined to defend the charges the Old One had given them. Sweat dripped from Adonis's forehead as he panted, his entire being focused on his prisoners, struggling to hold them.

"Adonis?"

He flinched as Maisie's voice intruded on his concentration. One of the Tangata leapt at the distraction, throwing his strength against Adonis and almost breaking free...

Kneel! Adonis hissed, putting all his remaining strength behind his Voice, seeking to regain control before it splintered into a thousand pieces.

A tremor shook the Tangata and he thought they would repel him. Then the moment passed, and one by one they fell to their knees.

Releasing his breath, Adonis finally risked a glance at the human. Maisie stood alongside him, her eyes as wide as those of the Anaheran children, though in her case it might have been something her kind did to see better in the darkness. But the way she looked at him, the lines that creased her forehead, he could sense her concern.

"Adonis, I have them," Maisie said quickly, flashing a glance at the kneeling Tangata. "Come on, we have to reach the city before they sound the alarm."

Adonis said nothing. He couldn't. All he could do was stand and stare at her, hands at his sides, hoping she would understand. She had to, surely? The perimeter guard had been easy enough to influence—they had no reason to suspect. But these five? They had witnessed his treachery firsthand. And they were stronger too. No compulsion would last once the force of his presence left. Neither would Adonis kill his own kind, whatever it might cost himself. They were his people still, his brethren. It was his own fault that Maya controlled them.

Maisie stared back at him, lips pursed, fists clenched. He watched as realisation finally came to her, the truth dawn in those dark eyes. In the night, drained of their colour by the silver moon, they could have been as grey as his own. Indeed, her courage, her strength in the face of their enemies…she was as bold as any of his sisters.

"I see," she said at last, looking from Adonis to the guards. "You knew…this was to be a one-way journey." She swallowed. "This better…better not be some convoluted plot to see your lover again, you know…" A shiver shook the human as she turned to him. "She'll kill you, you know. After this, when she learns what you've done…"

Adonis inclined his head in a nod. He knew. Maya's rage had been terrible to behold when he'd failed on the river. Now he plotted openly against her, had freed the Anahera. He could only pray to his ancestors that his death was quick.

Exhaling, Adonis looked towards the distant city, where the dark walls were shadows even to his eyes. It would take Maisie more than an hour to cross the terrain with the fledgelings. Could he hold the guards until the dawn arrived? Even as he considered the prospect, he felt them fighting again, their collective wills pressing against his own.

Quickly he made a gesture, a dismissal in the direction of that distant city. Still the human hesitated, until a whimper from the children caught her attention. She glanced quickly over her shoulder, and in that second, he glimpsed her own fear, the terror she struggled to conceal. A lump lodged in Adonis's throat as he felt his regret. Everything that had happened to this woman, to these children, to his people—it was all his fault. If he had not woken Maya, had not led her back to New Nihelm, had not supported her against the old Matriarch…

…but it was too late for regrets now. With a final nod to the human, he turned to his prisoners, taking a firmer hold of their minds. Stones crunched behind him as Maisie finally led the fledgelings away. Thankfully they were positioned near the edge of the camp and he hoped they could slip away unnoticed.

If not…well, Adonis could do nothing more for the human now. All he could do was hold the Tangatan guards for as long as possible. So gritting his teeth, he stared down at his captives kneeling in the dirt.

Five pairs of eyes stared back at him, hatred burning in their grey depths.

An hour passed and the sun had touched the distant horizon when their collective strength finally broke him. By then Adonis was on his knees as well, gasping for each breath as he threw every ounce of his strength into the battle. But as the sun lit the walls of the distant city, the last of his strength slipped away and he collapsed to the dirt. Abruptly, the flow of power reversed, and the crushing strength of five Voices crashed against his mind.

The cries of those five Voices echoed through the Tangatan camp, sounding the alarm, alerting his brethren to their peril.

Chaos ensued as the Tangata responded, leaping to their feet in preparation for battle. At first their response was one of confusion, their minds fixed on the humans, expecting an army to descend upon them at any moment.

It was long minutes before the Voices of the five guards cut through the chaos. Their panic turned to anger then as realisation spread through the Tangatan ranks.

That one of their own had betrayed them.

Adonis shrunk as the collective will of his people turned in his direction.

But before it could strike, another stirred, a mind beyond all others, a rage that made the thousands around him seem like candles before an inferno.

The Old One came for him.

❦ 27 ❧

THE QUEEN

Erika had never known such rage. It burned in her veins, filling her with the need to destroy, to unleash the gauntlet against her enemies, to see them writhe and scream and beg for her mercy. How satisfying it would be, to watch the queen fall, to see her die slowly by Erika's hand, in recompense for everything the woman had done?

A tremor shook Erika and the image faded, replaced by one of Queen Amina standing over her, matching gauntlet aglow, whispering for Erika to give up, to surrender. A moan tore from her lips, a sharp, rasping cry in the peaceful darkness of the dawn.

Erika struggled against the urge to flee.

Because the truth was, beneath her anger, a terrible fear held her tight, a terror for what the queen would do now that she had regained her city.

Rising from the pile of straw she had used as a bed, Erika knelt in the gloom of her tent. She had spent the night with the Calafe, in the square still called their own, rather than in the citadel. Just the thought of sleeping under the same roof as the Flumeeren queen made Erika sick with terror.

And if Erika had been enraged by Amina's admission into the city, the Calafe had been livid. It was all Erika could do just to keep them from storming the citadel. She still wasn't sure whether it had been the right decision to stop them, to accept the peace Lukys had brokered. She knew Amina. There was always something more to the woman's actions, some ulterior motive that would see her enemies crushed.

Steeling herself, Erika finally gathered herself and rose from the straw mattress. Leaving Cara to sleep in the corner she had claimed for herself, Erika stepped from the tent. A shiver ran down her spine as the brisk morning air greeted her. A flicker of movement nearby announced Darien's presence. The man had appointed himself her guard and was never far from her side now.

She nodded a greeting that the man returned. "Couldn't sleep, Your Majesty?"

Erika suppressed a frown at the title. She might have asked for this, but it still sounded strange to her ears. Shaking off her own doubts, she shrugged, and her gaze was inevitably drawn to the citadel towering on the hill above. There was to be a meeting of monarchs this morning. She would have to be present, to stand in the same room as the woman who had killed her father and listen to her speak. Just the thought of seeing Amina's smiling face was enough to spark a flicker of light from her gauntlet.

Shivering, Erika forced herself to exhale, then turned to stroll down the lines of the Calafe camp. The refugees were only just beginning to rise, and she watched with interest as they prepared kettles over freshly-lit firepits, as they hugged and waved greetings to one another. Her people. It was still difficult to believe it, that they would welcome her so freely after all these years in exile.

"Why, Damien?" she asked suddenly, turning to the stoic warrior who shadowed her.

"Why what?" he replied, a frown wrinkling his brow.

"Why did you kneel?" Erika elaborated. "Why did you decide to follow me?"

"You mean besides the magic gauntlet?"

Erika didn't respond, only stared him down, knowing there was more. It had been bugging her, how easy it had been, to convince this warrior to kneel, for the Calafe to follow her.

After a moment, Damien offered a shrug, nodding to the surrounding camp. "You know how long we have been here," he said softly. "For more than a year we have been camped outside the city walls, refugees without a home, without a leader. Without hope." He shook his head. "Maybe that's why I chose to accept your claim. Your stories could have been fabrications for all I knew. But... at least you offered us change, a chance for vengeance, maybe even fresh hope. Figured that was worth taking a risk."

"Thank you," Erika whispered, struck to the core by his words.

They finished the rest of their loop around the plaza in silence before returning to her tent. Cara's snores still came from within and Erika hesitated to wake the Goddess. She feared going to the citadel alone—very little could stop Amina now that she was within the city. In fact, Cara might be the only one capable of going toe to toe with the queen. But the Goddess needed rest after their time on the road, after everything the two of them had been through, and Erika was about to turn away when a harsh cry came from within the tent.

Cara appeared a second later, still only half-dressed, wings spread, amber eyes aglow with…something. The Goddess swung wildly from side to side, before finally seeming to notice Erika.

"*Erika!*" she gasped. "Something's happening, beyond the wall, with my people. They're *terrified!*" The words tumbled from her mouth faster than Erika could follow, then ceased abruptly. "Their voices…" Cara murmured, before her eyes widened. "*The fledgelings!*"

"Cara, what—" Erika tried to make sense of the Anahera, but Cara cut her off.

"*The fledgelings!*" she cried again. Abruptly, the Goddess hurled herself into the air, leaving Erika and the other Calafe staring dumbly after her.

Erika's heart pounded hard in her chest as she watched her friend spiral upwards, auburn wings flashing in the light of the rising sun. Panic spread through her soul as Cara disappeared beyond the rooftops, leaving her behind.

Whispers spread around Erika, growing quickly as the Calafe emerged from their tents in search of the source of the commotion, only to find their bedraggled queen standing in the middle of the street, eyes on the heavens. They followed her gaze, confusion in their eyes.

It was long seconds before the importance of Cara's words

finally struck Erika. The fledgelings, the children of the Anahera…it couldn't be, could it?

Something swelled in her chest, a sudden hope, the glimmer of a possibility. Then she was spinning on Darien, drawing an aura of authority about herself, igniting the power of her gauntlet.

"Darien, gather as many of our warriors as you can, *now!*"

The one-armed warrior didn't hesitate to ask questions. In an instant he was turning from her, bellowing out orders. Despite the ramshackle camp and the ragged appearance of her people, they obeyed with the discipline of trained soldiers. Those still fit for battle cast aside loaves of bread and mugs of coffee in exchange for great-axes and broadswords. Within minutes, a force of a hundred men and women had gathered around Darien in answer to their queen's call.

Erika swallowed as their eyes fell upon her, taking in the glittering weapons and hard faces. Only once had she led soldiers into battle, when she'd forced Lukys and his Perfugian regiment to follow her south of the Illmoor River. It had ended…badly. But she could not hesitate now.

"Calafe, my friend needs our aid," she said shortly. There was no time for long speeches. "Follow me!"

At that she spun on her heel and raced from the plaza, praying that her new authority and Darien's respect amongst their people would be enough to convince these warriors to follow. It might have been her imagination, but there seemed to be a pause, before the pounding of boots finally chased after her. Her eyes on the sky, Erika exhaled in relief, but she couldn't count her blessings yet.

Above, she glimpsed Cara as the Goddess soared back over the city. Spying Erika below, she gestured violently in the direction of the gates. Then she was gone again.

Baring her teeth, Erika charged through the city after her friend. The Calafe ran with her, Darien drawing alongside her, others moving ahead. With the early hour, the streets were mercifully quiet, and those already outside stepped quickly aside at the sight of the charging Calafe.

Then they were bursting into the courtyard before the city gates. The gates themselves stood barred to the enemy without, though in truth they would make little difference as the Tangata could scale the walls in seconds. The guards on watch snapped to alert at the sight of Erika and her Calafe. She waved urgently to them as she raced across the courtyard, gesturing at the gates.

"Lift the bar!" she bellowed. "By order of the queen!"

Knowing she had no power over these men, Erika neglected to say *which* queen. Panic showed in the eyes of the Flumeeren men at the sight of a hundred grizzled Calafe charging towards them. Whatever objections to her command they might have had were forgotten as Erika and her followers reached the gate, and the guards belatedly leapt to obey her.

The doors swung open with a soft squeal of old hinges. Erika caught a glance from Darien, the flicker of doubt in his eyes, but there was no time for explanations now—even if she had fully understood what was happening. So instead, she darted through the opening, and summoned the power of her gauntlet.

To their credit, the Calafe followed Erika despite her apparent madness, though it was definitely not her imagination this time that several hesitated. She could hardly blame them. Whatever her claim to the throne and the magic she wielded, Erika was still an outsider, yet to fully earn their loyalty.

Open ground stretched beyond the gates. The land around the city had been cleared just days ago in preparation for the siege, to ensure there would be no shelter for the Tangata to come creeping upon the defenders. The sun was just beginning to peek above the distant mountains, its heat washing across the land, lighting up the long grass…

…and the distant ranks of the enemy.

Erika paused to catch her breath as she looked across the mile that separated the city from the Tangatan camp. And in that pause, she caught a distant rumbling, as of a thousand feet pounding the earth, of a hundred voices raised in anger.

Icy fear lodged in Erika's throat, and she struggled to inhale as she glimpsed the cloud of dust rising from the horizon. Her stomach tied itself in knots and she scanned the sky, seeking, searching…

"*There!*" Erika shouted, pointing.

Cara plummeted from the air a half mile out, swooping towards the ground, wings snapping wide to slow her moments before she alighted amongst the long grass. Fist aglow with power, Erika set off at a sprint, though her lungs were already burning from their headlong race through the city. As Darien and the other Calafe glimpsed Cara, they chased after her, impressing Erika with their bravery.

Blood pounded in Erika's ears as she ran and she scanned the long grass ahead, searching, praying, hoping. It grew higher as they drew farther from the capital, untamed but for the few lines that were Flumeer's roads. Surely they must be somewhere…

Erika's heart lurched as a figure burst from the grass ahead, brown eyes wide, face panicked as she glanced back, urging others behind her to hurry.

Maisie, the Gemaho spy.

Such was Erika's shock, she almost staggered to a stop right there. She thought Maisie was dead, fallen in the Mountains of the Gods. How many more of her former companions were destined to rise from the grave this week?

Shaking herself, she leapt forward. Maisie's eyes widened as she glanced towards the city and finally noticed Erika and her Calafe, shock showing in her face, though it turned quickly to relief.

"Erika!" her cry sounded above the distant pounding. Only… that pounding was no longer so distant. *"They're coming!"*

Erika hardly heard the spy's words, as suddenly more figures were bursting from the long grass in front of her. Gasps came from around Erika, then the Calafe were stumbling over themselves to stop, staring open-mouthed as the tiny Anahera darted amongst them, adolescent wings flapping uselessly as they struggled to keep pace with the human they followed.

Several of the Calafe reached belatedly for their weapons—the Anahera had sided with the enemy, after all—but these were quickly lowered again when they saw the terror in the eyes of the youths.

Only then did Erika and her people return their attention to the distant rumbling, to the pounding on the air, the vibrations of a rage so terrible Erika swore she could sense what Cara had never quite been able to describe in words.

The Tangata were coming.

"Calafe, on me!" Erika screamed, lifting her fist to ignite the light of the gauntlet.

The sight of her magic steadied their line as Darien fell in at her side. Maisie had vanished after the fledgelings. She was no warrior, and would be needed to shepherd the young to safety. That left Erika and her Calafe to deal with the enemy.

One hundred Calafe warriors and their mad queen.

Against a Tangatan horde ten times their number.

"Form up around me, weapons to the fore!" Erika bellowed, doing her best impression of Romaine when she had seen him commanding the Perfugian recruits.

The last of the fledgelings passed between the Calafe ranks as her followers pressed together, and Erika risked a glance over her shoulder. The gates were barely in sight, half a mile off at least. She gritted her teeth.

"Controlled retreat, weapons to the enemy!" she called.

Darien nodded alongside her, and though the Calafe were not trained soldiers, they began to withdraw, eyes never leaving the direction of the enemy. It seemed to Erika that they held a collective breath, waiting for the first of the enemy to emerge from the grass, to leap upon their line.

A shadow on the horizon drew her eyes to the sky, and her heart twisted as she spied distant wings, too far and too many to be Cara. The Anahera. She and her people might hold a few Tangata, but her hundred would be decimated by even one of those creatures attacking from above.

Then with a roar, the Tangata were upon them. The first exploded from the long grass and leapt at Darien, but Erika reacted without thought, directing a burst of power at the creature. The shriek of her gauntlet struck, bringing the Tangata to its knees, where a swipe of Darien's sword took its head from its shoulders.

Others soon took its place.

Step by step, the Calafe continued their retreat, struggling as the dark creatures launched themselves from the grass, as the strength of the Tangata sought to break their lines, to recover the fledgelings their master had worked so hard to capture. There were only a few at first, the fastest of their kind. They attacked in madness, driven to such a frenzy that they barely seemed to notice the warriors that stood between them and their prey.

But even mad, the creatures were more than a match for a tiny band of Calafe. Erika did her best to use the gauntlet to slow them, allowing Darien and his fellow guards to strike the finishing blows, but she could only protect the centre of their formation. On either side, the line was quickly buckling beneath the Tangatan assault.

"Hold!" she cried as they stumbled back, but Erika's voice was drowned out by the screams of her followers, by the deaths of those who had trusted her to lead them.

Chaos engulfed the Calafe as the tide of Tangata swelled. There was no time to glance back, to check how far they were from the gates, from safety. No doubt the guards would have barred their entrance by now anyway. Erika could only pray Maisie had managed to lead her charges to safety, that their sacrifice would not be in vain.

A scream tore from Erika's throat as she unleashed another burst of power at a creature that evaded Darien's sword. It crumpled before her magic and she screamed again, frustration building within, that after everything she had been through, this was how it would end.

She might have fallen then, might have lain down and died, but instead Erika lifted her gauntlet and fought on. She could feel the strength draining from her with each flash of light, but she would not surrender now. She would go to the void screaming, before she failed her people again.

Darkness fell across the battlefield as another Tangata came at Erika and she flinched back, raising her gauntlet to strike it down. Light flashed from her fist, but already more of the creatures were stepping up to take its place, snarls upon their faces.

She staggered back, sucking in a breath, struggling to stay upright, to gather energy for her next attack.

Before her strength returned, a sharp *crack* came from overhead, then a shadowy figured plunged from the sky. Another followed, then another, until dark wings all but blocked out the sky. Despair swallowed Erika as she looked upon their doom.

The Anahera had come.

28

THE SOVEREIGN

Standing in the great throne room of Mildeth, Lukys looked around at the gathered rulers and couldn't help but feel himself an imposter. It was a familiar sensation by now, but one made all the worse by the presence of Amina. The woman stood pointedly opposite her throne, and even now he could sense her eyes on him, could feel her disdain. That emerald gaze seemed to pierce him to the core, to know the doubt in his soul, regardless of the outward illusion he presented to the world.

It is not an illusion, Lukys, Sophia whispered. *You and I, we deserve to stand here. It is only your own doubt that does not allow you to see it.*

He offered her a smile at that, though they did not say more. They knew now what Amina was, the danger she presented to them. She might have been unfamiliar with the mental powers of the Anahera and Tangata, but that did not mean she was ignorant to them.

I just pray we made the right choice, Sophia, he replied finally.

She pursed her lips, eyeing the Flumeeren queen. *She will never be a friend to my kind,* Sophia said at last. *Her hatred is too great. But…we had little choice, given the circumstances.*

Lukys nodded, though he could feel the whispers of other minds within, the memories of Sovereigns that screamed to strike Amina down before she could betray them. But…he wasn't sure they could have harmed Amina anyway. She wore the gauntlet of the Gods—

or rather, of humanity, as Erika had explained to them. And with the strength of the Anahera coursing in her veins…

…well, he would feel better when Erika and Cara arrived. The pair might hate him for the decision they had made, but they were likely the only ones capable of controlling Amina now that she was within the walls. They had spent the night in the Calafe camp, but with sunlight streaming through the broad windows above, the pair should have arrived by now. The hour of their meeting had long since passed, and he could sense the patience in the room growing thin.

Not that impatience was the greatest of their problems just now.

In his mind, Lukys could feel the distant pounding, the weight pressing upon his emotions. The influence of the Old One. He could hardly believe the strength of her Voice, to reach them even here. He had tried to counter her, to fortify the courage of his people as she toyed with their fears, but even with the strength of the Sovereign gift, he felt as a pebble before the endless currents of the mountain river. He knew too little about those minds within, feared losing himself in their terrible depths.

Even without her influence, Lukys hardly knew where to begin with this meeting of monarchs, how he could possibly unite the warring factions within the city—let alone set aside the personal grievances between those present. Amina had not even allowed Zayaan into the meeting, claiming she would not recognise the authority of traitors, though the old advisor had run the city in her absence. It was a miracle she'd consented to the presence of Erika and Cara. And now they were late…

Lukys sighed, sharing another glance with Sophia. How far he had come since his arrival so long ago in Fogmore, when he'd first faced the Tangata. Romaine had saved his life that day, a whirlwind of power that had shielded him from death. How he missed the man, his strength, his conviction that what he did was right. Even now, he wondered what the man would think, how he would judge Lukys's decision to parley with the Flumeeren queen, despite everything the woman had done, the atrocities she had committed.…

He would understand, Lukys, Sophia said, interrupting his thoughts.

Would he? Lukys murmured, staring at Amina now. *She betrayed his people, destroyed his nation. She was probably behind the death of his family.*

No, I think Romaine would have killed her the second she set foot in this city. Who is to say we're right, to keep others from their vengeance?

It is as Nguyen warned us, she replied. *Rulers must set aside personal convictions, their own grievances, for the greater good of their people.*

The words whispered into Lukys's mind, granting him strength, quieting the voice deep down, and finally he nodded. *We will find a way to save your people, Sophia,* he replied, recalling their conversation in Perfugia. *I promise.*

I know, Lukys, Sophia said in response. *I believe in you, in us.*

"Well!" Amina's voice broke suddenly over their conversation. "Had I known this alliance would involve so much standing around, I might have chosen war after all, and spared myself the boredom."

Lukys ground his teeth. "We are waiting—"

"I'm done waiting," Amina snapped. She strode the length of the chamber, passing Nguyen and Lukys and Sophia, crossing directly to her throne. There she paused, glancing pointedly at the others, before lowering herself onto the velvet cushion. Crossing one leg over the other, she entwined her fingers and arced an eyebrow in Lukys's direction.

"It seems the good Archivist will not be joining us after all," she continued. Lukys narrowed his eyes, suddenly suspicious that the woman had done something to Erika, but she continued before he could question. "I suggest we begin, unless you'd prefer we wait until your Tangatan friends break down the gates." The queen looked pointedly at Sophia as she spoke, and they could both sense the emerald of her hatred.

A soft growl, barely audible, whispered from Sophia's throat, but to her credit, she did not rise to Amina's bait. Instead, she took a moment to gather herself, then nodded her consent.

"I agree," she said firmly, looking to Nguyen and Lukys. "We can apprise the Calafe queen later of what we discussed—for now, there are urgent matters that must be addressed, before *Maya* seeks a final confrontation."

After a moment's pause, Nguyen inclined his head in concession, though Lukys read his concern in the yellowish tinge of his aura. Letting out a breath, he clasped his hands behind his back and positioned himself in the centre of their circle, attempting to draw the attention away from Amina.

"Very well," Lukys said, his words echoing from the high ceiling.

Beyond the throne, a great map of the valley around Mildeth had been laid out by the citadel staff, complete with tiny statuettes representing the warring factions. He moved to the edge of the map. Nguyen and Sophia joined him, and with an accentuated sigh, Amina abandoned the throne to stand with them.

The map had been updated in the night to show Amina's troops in the citadel, along with the arrival of the Tangatan army. Maya's forces seemed small beside their own, representing numbers rather than raw strength, but with the strength of the Tangata on her side, numbers were deceiving. The Old One had already surrounded the city by land, ensuring there would be no escape into the foothills. Lukys might have thanked the gods she had no naval ability, but...

...the gods themselves, the Anahera, would harry any attempt to flee by sea. Such was the power of Cara's people, it wasn't beyond reason to believe a single Anahera might sink a dozen ships....

Lukys shook himself. It would not come to that. They would make their stand here.

"With your soldiers, Amina, we should have the numbers to hold the walls for a time," he said softly. "Only..." He trailed off, glancing at the queen.

"Holding our own is not enough with this creature," Amina finished for him.

She crossed her arms, tapping one finger against her elbow as she stared at the red figurine placed in the centre of the valley, where their scouts suggested the Old One had stationed herself. Lukys frowned at the queen's words, wondering what she knew.

"My mother...revealed certain truths to my father, before he put the demon down," Amina elaborated with a smile. Lukys's stomach twisted, and he decided he was pleased that Cara had not come. The "demon" Amina spoke of had been Cara's mother too. Amina's father was the reason she had never returned to her people, to her first daughter...

Gritting his teeth, Lukys did his best to ignore the comment and nodded. "We are aware," he said, still staring at the red statuette.

Surrounded by the dense ranks of Tangata, Maya's position was unassailable. But he still carried Isabella's words in his mind, that perhaps there was a way to manipulate the creature, to separate Maya from her followers—before the worst came to pass.

"According to Erika, the Old One may already have been with child a month ago, when she invaded the Anaheran city. The gestation of her kind was often as short as three months before the Fall."

Amina lifted an eyebrow at that. "That is more than my mother knew," she remarked. "My father made sure of it. How could you know such details, *Sovereigns?*"

Lukys pursed his lips at the scorn she placed in the word, but he ignored the taunt. "We have our methods. Needless to say, there is no time to waste if these reports are true."

"Indeed," the Flumeeren queen replied, looking from Lukys to Sophia. "Though…if you can uncover such secrets, perhaps you might also unlock the secrets of the ancients, how they first cursed these Old Ones, removed their ability to procreate."

Lukys bit his lip, sharing a glance with Sophia.

"That…" Sophia started, then sighed. "They destroyed the world," she continued. "It had…consequences. The males of Maya's race, our ancestors, were made sterile."

"Then how did *your* kind survive, my dear Sovereign?" Amina pressed.

You don't have to answer her, Lukys said silently to his partner, sensing her tension, but Sophia only shook her head.

"Our ancestors splintered," she replied after a pause, recounting what she and Lukys had witnessed in that ancient memory. "Some, like Maya, searched for a cure amongst the ruins of ancient humanity, from their magic. Others…they chose peace, unity. They went to the remnants of humanity that had survived the Fall. They bonded, created new lives for themselves, peace. Only…" She looked up, catching the queen's eyes, holding her gaze. "It was not to last. Divisions appeared, tensions rose, and eventually those with Tangatan blood were ostracised, pushed out for their differences."

"A tale as old as time, it seems," Nguyen commented. "Even in the texts my own Archivists recovered, they speak of such divisions within humanity from before the Fall. Hatred without reason."

"Or maybe there was every reason," Amina interrupted, her eyes still on Sophia. "Perhaps your people betrayed the peace."

"Maybe," Sophia murmured. "Or perhaps it was humanity. Such details are lost even to our memory."

Lukys shivered as an uncomfortable silence fell, watching the swirling colours of Amina's aura. It was strange, how openly they displayed despite her Anaheran ancestry, as though this were a part of her she had no control over. It revealed the truth of her mind to Lukys, the hatred that contaminated her, the distrust she held for Sophia, for even the Anahera.

"Gladly, we no longer possess the power to destroy worlds," Nguyen stepped in, playing the peacemaker despite his own grudge against the queen. "So we cannot repeat the errors of the past. But that still leaves us with the question: how do we defeat this Old One?"

Silence fell at Nguyen's words as they exchanged glances. Lukys looked at Sophia, then drew in a breath.

"We might have a way."

"Oh?" Amina asked, one eyebrow raised.

He nodded hesitantly. "There is…something she wants. Or rather, *someone*. Her former partner. He was with her at the end, with those who sought a cure."

"I thought she was the last."

"She might be," Nguyen interjected. Clasping his fingers behind his back, he nodded to Lukys. "By the false gods, I hope she is. But does *Maya* think that? If she has slept all this time, perhaps this partner of hers did as well.

"Okay," Amina replied, eyes narrowed. "How does any of this help us?"

Lukys smiled, glad to be a step ahead of Amina in this at least. He opened his mouth to say as much, but before he could speak, the doors to the chamber burst open with a bang. As one, the four of them swung towards them, hands raised, weapons at the ready.

But it was only Erika. She paused a moment in the doorway, shoulders heaving, face slick with sweat, as though she had run the entire way there. Lukys frowned, taking a step towards her, before he noticed the tears in her clothing, the blood…

"Erika?" he asked, his concern growing with each pulse of his heart. "What—"

"Your Majesties," Erika spoke over him, advancing into the chamber, before stepping to the side.

Behind her, a second figure loomed in the doorway. Wings spread wide, Lukys thought at first the figure was Cara, but a second followed behind it, then a third. Steel rattled behind him as Dale and the other guards raised spears towards the creatures, but Lukys could only stare as the Anahera crowded in the chamber.

"May I present to you, the Anahera," Erika continued as though this were an entirely expected event. "It seems they have decided to join us in the fight against Maya."

❧ 29 ❧

THE FALLEN

Adonis no longer struggled as his captors dragged him through the Tangatan camp. His body was an aching mess and he lacked the strength to even stand now. And his mind…

…his mind was a shrieking torment, a vortex of self-hatred and regret and…ecstasy, joy that he had won, that in the end he had achieved the impossible, freed the Anaheran fledgelings, freed the Anahera themselves.

The Tangata had beaten him for that, had unleashed their pent-up fury against the traitor in their midst. But in the end, their blows could not harm him, could not change what he had done, could not bring back the escaped children.

It was only when the silence fell, when his assailants suddenly retreated from him, that the darkness had invaded Adonis's mind. He knew what it was, recognised her touch. He'd clung to the memory of his freedom, the light of what he had done, and yet…

Adonis could not stand against her.

Now with each step his captors carried him closer to her presence, to the darkness that bombarded his mind, crashing against his consciousness. With each passing second, his hope shrivelled, the light of his defiance dwindling, the despair in his soul swelling.

Until finally he was thrown to the ground in the centre of the camp. The sun rose slowly into the distant hills, but where Adonis lay was shadow, the sky blotted out, darkened by the figure before him.

Adonis's mind withered as he looked into the eyes of Maya. Rage shone from her face, and the force of her hatred battered him, tearing and rending at his consciousness until he felt the very fabric of his being coming apart, the substance of his mind unravelling…

Abruptly her mind released him and Adonis gasped, sinking to the ground before her, sobbing, shuddering.

You should have stayed dead, Maya's voice whispered into his mind, dark, deadly. *You have no understanding of what you have done, the danger you have unleashed. The Anahera are no different from humanity. They would see us exterminated if they held that power in their hands. They have already tried once before.*

No! Adonis struggled against her power, against the weakness of his own body.

But as he tried to stand, two Tangata leapt forward, capturing his arms, forcing him back down, to bow before their Matriarch. Even so, Adonis would not allow himself to be silenced, not so long as he still possessed his sanity.

These Anahera are not the ones you fought in ages past, Maya. Nyriah, her people they want only—

He broke off as her anger slammed into him again, the strength of the Old One's rage silencing his own Voice. He gasped as images invaded his mind, of the Anahera swooping down, fighting, battling against Tangata…no, not his people—Old Ones. Maya's people, from a time unknown.

The Anahera will fall, she hissed. *They will feel my retribution for the crimes of their ancestors. That is my sole purpose, Adonis, to see my enemies extinguished, to see those who betrayed my people cursed to extinction.*

Adonis struggled against those words, against the depth of her hatred finally revealed. But however he resisted, still he felt his own emotions responding, his own hatred swelling in answer to her call.

You too shall pay for what you have done, Maya's voice hissed in his thoughts, sending tremors through his very being.

This time when Maya invaded his mind, it was not words or emotions she pressed on him, but a pure agony, as though she had poured molten iron over his skull, as though she were running ragged blades through his veins, crushing his chest upon an anvil, tearing each nail from each of his fingers, peeling the skin from his flesh…

A scream burst from Adonis, harsh and unending, tearing at his throat, and he began to thrash. His captors released him and he fell to the earth, digging burning fingers into soft dirt, as though its dampness might extinguish the flames within.

But there was no escape from Maya. Eyes locked open, Adonis looked into the depths of her grey gaze and saw no mercy there, not a hint of the love she had claimed for him. Nothing but hatred, the rage of centuries.

Adonis cried and begged, pleaded for his fellow Tangata to save him, to strike him down and end his suffering. But his brothers and sisters stood in silence now, watching without emotion the fall of one they had respected, had followed. There was no Nyriah to save him this time, no Maisie to drag him from the muddy ditch. Adonis was alone, abandoned, discarded by all he had trusted.

No, rose the thought through the pain, *not abandoned. I chose to be here, to stand against the darkness, to help my people. To put right my wrongs.*

Abruptly the pain vanished.

For a moment, Adonis thought he had succumbed, that the agony had driven the spirit from his body, freeing him from the punishment of the real world. But then sensation returned, the touch of the earth beneath him, the reek of the camp, the whisper of Voices nearby. Slowly he gathered the will to sit, and discovered Maya still standing over him. He flinched away, but she knelt beside him and reached out to stroke his cheek.

I feel your defiance, my mate, she said softly, *the hope you cling to.* Adonis shuddered as laughter whispered into his mind. *Fool. You think you have saved the Anahera? Their freedom will be short-lived. The human city will fall, then nothing will be able to protect those fledgelings from my vengeance.*

She looked into the distance then, where the stark walls of the city shone with the morning sun. *No, my dear Adonis, your resistance will fail.*

Adonis's eyes widened at her words and he struggled to retreat from her, but instead he found himself fixed in place, body trembling, unwilling to obey his own will. A sob tore from him as he found his eyes locked with Maya's, and felt the doors of her trap swing shut.

Consider this your reward, she continued, a hand falling to her swollen stomach. *For the service you provided me.* She smiled, and taking Adonis's hand, she drew him to his feet. The darkness surged, robbing him of will. *You will be the executioner, will stand at my side as we slaughter the humans.* Laughter rasped in his mind. *And when we capture your precious fledgelings again, it will be your hand that snuffs the life from their pathetic bodies.*

No…

He tried to resist her, to fight back, but his mind rang with the vibrations of her Voice, twisting his emotions, changing him, until…

…Adonis felt a terrible shame within, a swelling horror as he realised what he had done, the trick the human had played upon him. She had manipulated him, turned Adonis against his own people, caused him to commit the greatest treachery the Tangata had ever known.

A moan tore from his lips as he prostrated himself before Maya, before all those who stood in witness. Crying out, he begged for her retribution, for her to send him against the humans, so that he might die in honour, might escape the knowledge of the terrible thing he had done.

And Maya stood before him, before all of the Tangata, and smiled.

Now you see, children. Her Voice carried over the crowd, to the ears and minds of the multitude. *Now you see the power of the humans, their corruption. Not even the greatest of us could resist. Their whispers must be silenced, their power crushed, until every one of their kind has been erased from this world.*

An ache swelled in Adonis's heart, a pain that threatened to tear him in two. Such was his shame, he could not look upon the eyes of his people, could not face their condemnation for what he had done. He found himself sobbing, begging.

Please, my Matriarch, he whispered. *Please, kill me. I do not deserve to live, after what I have done.*

Maya smiled down at him, and there was something in her eyes, a mocking laughter that he should have sparked something in him, something other than the awful, terrible shame. Yet there was nothing else within him, only an emptiness, a void where the rest of his mind had once been…

He begs for death, children, but am I not a merciful Matriarch? Maya spoke again. *No, sweet child, I will not give you death, but life! I will grant you—*

Maya…

The Old One broke off abruptly, her eyes swinging to the west, the colour draining from her face. For a second, Adonis felt a spark of something within, a flicker of life, of will…

Maya, where are you…please…so weak…

Raxion! Maya's voice boomed across the open field, echoing through the minds of all present, searching, seeking. *Where?*

Images flickered through Adonis's mind, of twisting corridors, of endless darkness, of waves crashing upon cliffs. He shuddered, seeking the source, the mind from which they had come, but the images were already fading, the presence withdrawing.

Please… a last whisper reached them. *Others…hunting me.*

Abruptly, the presence vanished, and Adonis's mind returned to the field outside the human city. He gasped, the flickers of life returning to him as Maya's distracted mind released him. She stood looking into the distance for a moment longer, eyes wide, as though contemplating what they had just heard.

Then she turned her gaze back to Adonis, and the vice closed around his mind once more.

Well, well, well, she said at last, her Voice thundering in his mind. *What have we here? Perhaps I will not need your mongrel offspring after all, Adonis.*

———

A MILE AWAY, STANDING ATOP THE WALLS OF MILDETH, LUKYS AND Sophia gasped as they came back to themselves, as they surfaced from the depths of the Sovereign gift. Lukys shuddered as he shared a glance with his partner, unable to believe they'd managed it, that their mad idea might have worked.

That ancient presence within was so utterly foreign, so unlike their own minds, a part of him screamed to hurl it from him. That mind had been an Old One like Maya, a *Chead* as it thought itself, but unlike Maya, it had chosen humanity over hatred. They had hoped the power of its Voice might have been similar enough to

Maya's mate, Raxion, that she would not recognise the difference, not if they limited their words.

It seemed their gamble had paid off.

The trap had been set.

Now all that remained was to spring it upon the Old One.

❦ 30 ❧

THE QUEEN

Erika watched as the cliffs rose from the crashing waves. They stretched high overhead, towering above the swirling ocean waters, making even the masts of the ship seem small by comparison. Ripples ran through the stone, lines of gradient colours that seemed more a reflection of the ocean below than true rock.

It seemed too strange to be natural, and yet…the truly unnatural feature of the cliffs lay not in the layers of stone, but at their base. There, the strata abruptly gave way to plain grey stone, untouched by the invisible forces of erosion. This was the stone that defied nature, refusing to bend before the will of Mother Earth.

The stone left here by her ancestors, waiting for its creator's return.

A rowboat carried their unlikely party ashore. Cara might have ferried them across one by one, but she needed to preserve her strength for what was to come. Even so, Erika would have rather been anywhere but a damp rowboat seated alongside the Flumeeren queen. For her part, Amina had said nothing on the voyage, even as she suffered the glares of Erika and her Calafe guard. One-handed or no, Darien looked ready to drive a blade through the queen's cold heart at a moment's command.

Seated across from them, Maisie was similarly quiet. The Gemaho spy had said little since her victorious return, and Erika wondered what the woman had been through during her weeks of captivity. She doubted the Old One would have treated her prisoners any better than Amina. And yet…Maisie's morose silence seemed to go deeper than that.

Perhaps it was the Anahera. Freeing the fledgelings had released the adults from their bonds with Maya. They would fight for the enemy no longer. But while the creatures had professed their gratitude at the release of their children, the truth was, most were not warriors. A few had elected to fight with humanity on the walls of Mildeth, but many others had been needed to ferry their fledgelings to safety. And on this journey…

…well, of all the Anahera, only Cara was willing to face the presence of the Old One again. Erika just prayed their collective strength would be enough.

Clenching her fists, Erika shivered as she watched the light play across the threads of her gauntlet, and wondered if she should have done more. Perhaps she could have taken one of the fledgelings herself, as the Old One had. The Anahera would have fought for them then…

…but no, that would only have created a lifelong enmity between their peoples. If humanity was to survive, it could not be through darkness. They needed to be better than their ancestors, to rise above their terrible past and forge a new future, one where all could prosper.

The rowboat thumped down on the crest of a wave, shaking Erika back to the present, reminding her there was a battle to be won before any could plan a future free of war.

The sailors deposited them on the shore not far from the unnatural streak of rock. The four of them moved quickly, scrambling from the rocking boat onto the exposed reef at the base of the cliffs. Maisie stepped onto the slippery surface with her usual confidence, while Amina still somehow managed to move with the air of a queen. For Erika's part, she tripped stepping from the vessel, and would have plunged headfirst into the icy waters had Darien not caught her.

When she finally gained a purchase on the damp rocks, Erika did her best to ignore the smug smile on Amina's face. The meaning of that look was clear—that *she* was the true queen, and Erika nothing more than an imposter, the lowborn offspring of a courtesan rather than the daughter of a king.

The whisper of feathers on air announced Cara's arrival. She landed between Erika and Darien, keeping a wary eye on Amina. The young Goddess's distrust for her half-sister was obvious, a sentiment Erika could well understand. And for her part, Amina made no secret of her hatred for the Tangata and Anahera both.

With them all gathered, Erika finally turned her attention to what had brought them to this place. This had been the first ancient site Erika had explored in her quest to uncover the secrets of their Gods. Little had she known then the truth that waited.

The shadow of a cave marred the strange rock. In her explorations, she had discovered this was not one of the original entrances to the site, but had been exposed when a section of rock had finally given in to the unending pounding of the ocean waves. The original entrance was somewhere above. That was the entrance the Sovereigns had shown Maya. Cara had already checked its iron casing—it remained barred to the world.

The Old One had yet to arrive.

Shivering, Erika glanced at her companions to see whether they were ready. Lukys, Sophia, and Nguyen had remained behind in Mildeth—someone had to oversee the defence of the city, and they weren't about to trust Amina with the task. Given that neither had Erika's magic or the strength of an Anahera, the three had seemed the natural choice.

Even so, Erika found herself questioning that decision. They might have been as new to their roles as Erika, but Lukys and Sophia carried an air about themselves, a quiet confidence that lent strength to those around them. How she wished for such an ability, to squash her inner doubts and stand as a natural leader, confident in her command.

But Lukys and his Tangatan partner were far from them now, and instead it fell on Erika to see the Old One defeated. So after a moment's hesitation, she led their group up the shore to the cave. Stepping into the darkness, Erika found herself recalling her first visit to this place, the excitement of entering its forbidden darkness, the secrets that might lie within. She had been disappointed that first time, though she had known so little then. Perhaps she had missed something…

Erika shook herself, forcing her thoughts back to her more pressing danger. This was no expedition into the secrets of the past, however she might wish it to be. Maya might not yet have arrived, but she would not be far behind them. They needed to be ready before then, to find a chamber to make their stand. Clenching her fist, she allowed the gauntlet to light the way.

Cold walls swallowed them up, beckoning them further into the darkness. Erika's chest constricted as they stumbled ever deeper, her nerves betraying her. She would have preferred to face the Old One in the open, where they could see the creature coming, but their lie had to be believable. And this was the closest ancient site to Mildeth.

Well, the only one that could be reached by sea at least. There was another, the site where she had discovered the gauntlet and the map that had revealed the locations of other such sites. A shudder ran down her spine as she recalled the tale Lukys had told her, of how Maya had come to rule the Tangata. They had taken that map from Lukys's mind. Just as it had led Erika to the city of the Anahera, the map had led them to where Maya had lain sleeping.

And so the world had changed forever.

How she wished now she'd destroyed it, burned it where it lay and left sleeping demons buried. But it was too late for that now.

"So what do we do once we're inside?" Maisie murmured as they crept deeper into the tunnels.

"We get ready for Maya's arrival," Erika replied. "I explored this place for weeks, the first time I visited. It's empty, but there are some areas that could make for good ambush sites."

Alongside her, Cara nodded. Erika could read the tension in the young Anahera's wings, the way her feathers stood on end. Her eyes kept flicking to Amina, and Erika prayed her friend's distraction would not cost them against the Old One.

"I'm not sure what good we mere mortals are going to be," Maisie offered, nodding to Darien.

The one-armed Calafe grunted and reached down to pat his sword hilt. "I'll fight," he replied shortly. "There's no other choice."

Cara's eyes flickered to the man, while Maise offered soft laughter. "I suppose that's true." She drew her own blade, a short sword, and hefted it.

Erika nodded. "Maya may not come alone."

Word from the Sovereigns was that the Tangatan army had remained outside Mildeth and was even now preparing to attack, but some of the creatures might have joined Maya on her journey. Though the Old One would outpace the weaker of the Tangata, there were some that could match her speed, at least for a time.

"If she has company, we'll need you to keep her followers distracted while we fight her," Erika added after a pause.

Maisie grunted. "Definitely feeling some second thoughts about joining this quest. Who knew a city under siege by thousands of Tangata would prove the *safer* option."

"There'll be no chance to run this time, Gemaho," Darien said, his voice hard. Erika grated her teeth. Though the blame for the southern war now fell squarely on Amina's shoulders, the Calafe would not be quick to forget how Gemaho had abandoned them in their hour of need.

"Enough," was all she said, and was grateful when Darien obeyed.

They were in the true tunnels now, where multitudes of passages branched off from the main corridor. This would be a poor place for an ambush—the side chambers they passed were too small, and the narrow hallways would only aid the Old One, making it difficult for more than one of their party to attack at a time.

"So this is one of your precious ancient sites, Archivist," Amina said as they moved through the corridors. She paused, eyeing another chamber as they moved past it, then wrinkled her nose. "Delightful. Truly, if your interest in dust and dirt is exquisite."

"These were the places where our ancestors created beings like the Tangata and the Anahera," she replied. "The things we could learn—"

"Yes, yes," Amina smirked, waving a dismissive hand. "I'm sure you could discover another trinket or two, given time. But there are more efficient ways of extracting secrets than digging in the dirt, my dear Archivist."

Erika ground her teeth, but forced herself to ignore the woman's gibes. "Come on," she said instead. "I wish I had my maps. I think there was a larger chamber this way—"

She broke off as her light caught on something in the tunnel ahead. Freezing in place, Erika squinted into the gloom, struggling to pierce the darkness at the end of the corridor. Surely it had only been her imagination, her mind playing tricks in this haunted place.

As the others drew to a stop behind her, Erika raised her fist, and ignited the full power of her gauntlet.

31

THE SOVEREIGN

Lukys stood with Sophia on the ramparts of the Mildeth and watched as the Tangata gathered in the distance. Their rage radiated across the open fields, their hatred pressing against his mind. Maya had vanished, but her dark presence remained on the battlefield, her influence still touching those below, driving them to a frenzy.

Against the raging emotion rising from the enemy, he leaned against Sophia, drawing on her strength, on her love to keep the darkness at bay. Yet amidst her own consciousness, he could feel her pain, the terror she felt for what was to come.

A shudder ran through Lukys and he drew her closer, though the blue-stained armour they both wore was cold beneath his hands. In that moment, Lukys wished they could be anywhere else, that they had gone with Cara and Erika to face the Old One. But…he knew his place was here. They both did. He had not yet given up hope for the Tangata. If anyone could reach them through the haze Maya had cast over their minds, it was them. The future would be decided not just in that dark place beneath the earth, but here on this battlefield.

And humanity needed to win both to survive.

A roar rolled across the battlefield as abruptly the Tangata surged forward, their powerful legs sending them bounding across the open ground. Lukys tensed as their cries crashed upon the battlements, and releasing Sophia, he took up his spear. Travis and Dale and their other guards shifted around them, determined to shield their Sovereigns from the worst of the assault.

All along the wall, calls went out from sergeants and regiment leaders as the human forces prepared to face the deadly Tangata. Nguyen had organised their defences, placing the three surviving kingdoms on separate sections of the wall, with the Calafe waiting in reserve as reinforcements. The proud Calafe had not been pleased by the assignment, but Nguyen had pointed out their numbers were too few to stand alone.

Lukys couldn't help but agree. In fact, if it had been up to him alone, he would have seen Romaine's people far from the battlefield. Enough Calafe blood had been spilt in the last ten years. It was time the other kingdoms stood against the darkness.

Watching the Tangata charge, Lukys felt the emptiness of his failure, the pain of knowing those who came against them did so not because they desired war, but because a dark creature had fed them lies. The Tangata attacked now because they feared there was no other choice, because they believed humanity would destroy them if they did not strike first.

Maybe they were right. Maybe one day those like Amina would come to rule all the kingdoms of humanity, would seek the extinction of the non-human species. Perhaps the Tangata were right to fear humanity, to loath them and seek their destruction.

Yet recalling the days he had spent in New Nihelm, living side by side with the Tangata, Lukys knew things did not have to be this way. There had been peace between their peoples, if only for a brief time.

Maya had stolen that peace, but if it had existed once, they could have it again.

Are you ready? he whispered to his partner, eyes on the approaching hoard.

No, came her reply. Yet he saw her gathering herself. *But I will fight regardless.*

Lukys drew in a breath, then called out for the archers to nock arrows. A sharpness touched his mind at the order as Sophia tensed alongside him, and he shuddered at the weight of what he was about to do.

But there was no other choice.

"Fire!" he bellowed.

The sharp *twang* of bows followed as arrows rose high into the air, only for gravity to take hold, plunging them down into the ranks of the Tangata. The first screams rose as a new colour blossomed amongst the chaotic aura of the charging enemy—the grey of pain.

Lukys… Sophia's voice came to him.

He pulsed a wave of reassurance to her, though he knew worse was yet to come.

Below, the Tangata line barely faltered, as many dodged the flashing arrows or continued regardless of their injuries. They charged into the teeth of a second volley, Voices raised in defiance. As they drew nearer, Lukys saw that many carried pieces of rock the size of his fist. Understanding struck him a second before the first drew back their arms in preparation for their own attack.

"Down!" Lukys bellowed, adding his Voice to the command.

The Sovereigns and their guard dropped even as Lukys spoke, his mental warning reaching them heartbeats before his spoken words. A second later, rocks flashed overhead and the sharp *crack* of stones striking the crenelations sounded over the cries of the enemy.

Heart beating hard in his chest, Lukys clenched his spear tight and lifted his shield from where it rested. Sophia and her brethren did not carry any weapons, and he gestured for her to take shelter behind his shield. Keria, Isabella, and the other Tangata did the same with their human partners.

Only then did Lukys have the chance to assess the damage to the rest of their forces. Those soldiers nearest them had been able to heed his warning, but he saw many others slumped on the stone battlements, great dents in their steel armour revealing how they had fallen.

Fists clenched, Lukys stepped back to the edge of the ramparts, shield raised cautiously in preparation for another volley.

Instead, a flicker of movement was the only warning he had before a Tangata launched itself over the crenelations. It would have had him then, if not for Sophia. The creature seemed almost surprised as she leapt forward, moving with unnatural speed to place herself between them. Cast all in steel, it would not recognise her Tangatan eyes, and her appearance gave it pause.

But only for a moment, as with a snarl, it charged the Sovereign. Sophia met the Tangata with an iron fist that stopped the male with an audible *crunch.* Then it was tumbling backwards, disappearing through the gap between the crenelations.

And as it fell, Lukys sensed a scream, a shriek from his mate's mind, even as a sharp sob rent the air. He stepped forward quickly as she stumbled, a groan rumbling from the depths of her soul.

Sophia! He forced the words into her mind, and within he found a terrible pain, a shock at what she had done. *Sophia, are you okay?*

I…I killed him, she gasped, and Lukys gritted his teeth.

You did what you had to, he replied, pushing her behind his shield and aiming his spear at the gap in the crenelations. He would not be taken unawares again, would not force Sophia to… *This is not you, not us,* he said to her, embracing her mind, shielding her from the horror. *We wanted only peace.*

But even as he spoke the words, he saw the aura rising from the tops of the ramparts, the emotions of his fellow humans. They matched the dark hues of the Tangata below, a roiling squall of anger and hatred.

Lukys recoiled from the sight, though he felt the same emotions within, the war between his desire to reconcile—and the part that had feared and loathed the Tangata for so long. He had almost forgotten those emotions these past weeks, but now they came rushing back. And with them came a terrible realisation.

There could never be peace between their peoples.

Humanity would never tolerate Sophia and her kind, would not break bread with the creatures that had haunted their nightmares for a generation. Even if they could end this battle, it would only postpone the inevitable, would only delay the darkness…

Lukys…something is happening.

He shivered as Sophia's warning whispered into his mind, struggling to free himself from the dark thoughts. They clung to him, seeking to draw him back into their depths, but he resisted, clinging to the light of Sophia's consciousness.

As he rose, withdrawing his senses from the greater battle, Lukys turned his consciousness to those nearest him, on Isabella and Travis and his friends. Their aura shone with red and yellow, with fear and anger, but there was no hatred amongst them, no darkness.

This was the hope he clung to, that if these men and women could surrender their hatred, so too could the rest of humanity. That was the truth, not the whispers of his despair…

…or perhaps it was not his despair at all.

Looking out across the walls of the city, Lukys finally saw the pattern to the auras, the swirling of darker forces, and knew they were not the only Melders influencing this battle.

Maya's mind was at work here.

Panic touched Lukys and he scanned the surging bodies below, seeking the Old One, fearful suddenly she had not taken their bait at all, that she had remained with the Tangatan army. Without their strongest warriors, they would be helpless if she came against them, unable to match her strength, her speed…

…but no, her touch was present on the battlefield, but it remained faint, where before it had been a radiant glow at the centre of the Tangata, corrupting all it touched.

Where then? he whispered.

Sophia stirred alongside him, and he sensed her joining in the search for the Old One. The creature had disappeared from their view the day before, after their message, but surely if she were working her influence here, they could find her.

Perhaps if they worked together…

Reaching for Sophia's aid, Lukys shivered as their consciousnesses overlapped, the lifetimes of knowledge they possessed uniting within their twin minds.

And looking to the sky, they saw finally the darkness of the Old One, the tendrils of aura criss-crossing the battlefield, feeding the base emotions of the warring men and women. They rose from the gathered ranks, trailing towards the distant horizon.

Their hearts beat quicker, and as one, the Sovereigns set out after those threads. They could see the truth now, that Maya was far from this place, still somehow able to influence the battle, but…that influence was waning. With their united power, they just might…

There!

The Sovereigns touched the Old One's consciousness, but recoiled from what they sensed there. Not anger or fear, not even desire. Within Maya's mind they found only darkness, only a hatred that consumed all it touched. This creature's sanity had fled long ago, leaving only the husk of a person, a remnant with but one goal, one desire.

To destroy.

What is this?

The Sovereigns shuddered as a Voice grated upon their consciousness. They drew back, seeking to escape, but it was already too late. The Old One had sensed their presence. Their hearts twisted as her attention fell upon them.

Is that a human I sense? There was curiosity in her voice, confusion too. *No…something else? Not one of the Tangata…nor even the Anahera… something…older?* There was a pause, as though the Old One were contemplating something. *What are you?*

The Sovereigns shuddered as the pressure upon their minds grew, the Old One seeking to pierce the veil of their thoughts, to infect their minds with her madness. But they were not what they had once been, not a naïve boy who dreamed of war, nor the innocent Tangata in search of love. Those parts still existed, but they were something else now. Something *more.*

We are the Sovereigns of Perfugia, they replied in unison, hurling the words at the Old One. *And we stand united against you.*

The Sovereigns felt a moment of satisfaction as this time it was the Old One who recoiled, the barriers of her mind rising to guard against their power. For a fleeting moment, they glimpsed something more amidst the madness, a flicker of gold. Fear?

Sovereigns? No…no, that is a lie. You are something else, yes, but… She trailed off, then a brilliant light flared, and Lukys sensed shock from the ancient creature. *Yes…I sense you now, Tangata, Chiara. What magic did you discover, that you persevere still?*

Something responded within the Sovereigns at those names, a roiling deep within their souls, as consciousnesses long dormant struggled to wake. They were the names of those who had stood in the circle all those centuries ago and opposed Maya, the first to have passed their memories on to their descendants, to form the tradition of the Sovereigns.

Shivering, Lukys tore himself from those memories, from the drowning ocean. As he did so, he felt his consciousness separate from Sophia's, emerging from the depths of the Sovereigns.

Suddenly alone, he found himself drifting before the Old One, before their enemy.

And for the first time, Lukys sensed the images flicking through their enemy's thoughts, of a cavern cast in darkness, of chambers deep beneath the earth.

To his horror, Lukys recognised that darkness.

She was already in the tunnels beneath the earth, the ancient site in which they sought to trap her.

But it was his friends who were walking into a trap.

Cara! he screamed desperately, reaching for the young Anahera. *Beware!*

❧ 32 ☙

THE QUEEN

Erika cried out as a face appeared in the darkness. A voice behind echoed her—then Cara was there, hurling her back, spreading her wings to fill the narrow corridor.

For just a moment, Erika longed to retreat, to turn and flee back the way they'd come, to escape the tunnels, the darkness, the *history* of this terrible place.

But then she saw Darien standing alongside her, face hard, eyes on the creature that lurked in the darkness. His blade was already in hand, ready to face the enemy, and Erika knew she could not flee. Her duty was here in this darkness, to her people, to humanity.

Drawing in a breath, Erika turned and stepped up alongside Cara. Movement came from their other side as Amina joined them, barely able to fit in the narrow space. Erika cursed inwardly. This was the last place they wanted to face a creature such as Maya.

Laughter whispered in the darkness, low and haunting, empty of mirth or joy or…anything. Hairs rose on the back of Erika's neck as she watched Maya emerge from the gloom. Her long hair hung around her shoulders, bleached of all colour in the light of the gauntlet, and her eyes…her eyes were like two empty voids, watching them from the face of the Old One.

"Magic wielder," the creature whispered, and the darkness fixed on Erika. "I know you, do I not?" She nodded, taking a step closer.

"Yes, the human who escaped with the young Anahera, the same one I see here, I suppose."

A growl came from Cara and Erika quickly grasped her friend's arm, steadying her. This creature was far more deadly than those Cara had once fought, the pair she had defeated alone. Those had been weakened by their long sleep, while Maya…Maya had been awake for months now.

No, if they were to attack, it must be together.

Though…Erika's stomach twisted in horror as her suspicions were confirmed. The Old One was with child. And while only a month had passed since the City of the Gods, Maya looked to be ready to give birth any day now.

"It was a clever ruse," the Old One continued, leaning her head to the side. "Luring me away from my followers, bringing me here." She cackled suddenly, advancing a step. "Or was it I who lured you here? My greatest enemies all gathered in one place, ripe for the slaughter?"

A chill spread through Erika at the creature's words. That couldn't be true, could it?

The laughter continued. "Your scheming matters not, human. The Tangata are mine now. They will destroy your precious city, whether I am with them or not." Her voice hardened and she took another step. "As for you…well, I will ensure your deaths are long, for taunting me so with the promise of my mate."

Erika shuddered as she felt something dark touch her mind. Her fear responded to that touch, swelling to terror. Even as she recognised the touch of the Old One, had known to expect it from Lukys and Cara's warnings, still she found herself trembling, her knees shaking, the strength fleeing her limbs…

… abruptly, the sensation lessened, dwindling, as though someone or something had turned off the tap of her terror.

The Old One didn't seem to notice, though, as turning to the walls of the tunnel, she ran her hand across the stone.

"What memories these places hold," she said softly. "You have no idea the atrocities humanity committed here, the ghastly experiments they committed against our kind, against *her* kind." She paused, leaning her head to the side.

Cara screamed. Erika spun to the Goddess, expecting an

attack, some surprise assault from the darkness. Instead, she found Cara staggering backwards, wings thrashing, fingers clawing at her face, mouth stretched wide as her amber eyes lit the darkness. A moan rattled from the back of her throat, building into another scream.

The Old One was doing something to the Anahera, showing her something. Before Erika could react though, Cara's screams died away, leaving only the echoes calling back to them through the endless tunnels. The Goddess stilled, her wings still stretched wide, poised as though about to flee. The rasping of her desperate breaths filled the silence.

"Cara." Erika took a step towards her friend, hand outstretched.

A shriek came from the Anahera as she leapt back, eyes wild, their colour swirling from yellow to grey. Erika froze, as behind her, the Old One's voice whispered in the darkness.

"Now she knows," Maya murmured. "Now your pet has seen the truth, human. Do you think she will forgive the terrors your kind committed upon her ancestors, the torture and abuse and death?" She turned her attention to Cara. "Her people tormented ours by the thousands, child, tore us limb from limb and put us back together, again and again, all for the pursuit of greater power. Will you serve her still, even knowing their crimes? Or will you finally throw off your chains?"

A tremor shook Cara as some of the light returned to her eyes, the yellow glow, though as she looked at Erika, a new emotion appeared in her friend's eyes.

Fear.

"Cara," Erika said urgently, seeking to drown out the Old One, though the creature might even now be whispering into the Goddess's mind. "Cara, it's me. You know me. I am not my ancestors. I will not allow my people to repeat the mistakes of our forefathers."

"Won't you?" Cara whispered, the words seemingly torn from the depths of her throat. Her eyes fell to the gauntlet on Cara's hand. "Truly? You wield their magic, have dug into their hidden places, sought their secrets."

"Yes, child, see the truth," Maya's voice came again. "See them for what they are—wild, reckless. This creature would do anything for the power of her forefathers, would commit any crime for their secrets."

Erika opened her mouth to deny the charge, but found the words would not come. She swallowed, wondering…how much truth there was in Maya's claim. She looked again to Cara, knowing a part of her could not deny the Old One's words, only…

…that was the old Erika, was it not? The Archivist who had dug so recklessly into the past, who would have done anything to fill the void left by her father's death, by her exile.

Erika was no longer that woman, but she had responsibilities of her own now, to her kingdom, to her people. If the powers of the ancients could save them…

"I…" Erika trailed off, struggling to find the words. "I…we are not them, Cara," she said finally, the words lame, even to her.

"Aren't you?" her friend replied, and Erika saw her eyes flicker, shifting to where Amina stood nearby. The Flumeeren queen stared back, face betraying none of the emotion hidden within. "Aren't you *exactly* like them? Didn't your people torture my mother, twist her, break her, *murder her*? And all for what? For her knowledge, for the secrets she possessed."

Erika let her hand fall to her side. Cara stood staring at her with those soft yellow eyes, and she could see the pain there, the hurt the Goddess had carried since the day they'd realised the truth, had discovered the fate of her missing mother.

"You're right," Erika said at last. Her eyes caught the queen's, and she saw the slightest of smirks there, the satisfaction. This woman held no regret for Cara's pain. "Some of us are terrible," Erika continued in a whisper. "All of us have that capacity, whether we be human, Tangata, or Anahera. But I swear to you, Cara, there are others amongst us who want to do better, who would create a world for all of us." She drew in a breath. "But I can't do it without you, Cara, without your light to guide the way. Please, I need your help."

She trailed off, watching the silent Goddess, staring into those golden eyes. Hesitantly, Erika offered her hand again. The moment stretched out, a silence hanging in the air as the others watched on, waiting.

Until finally, Cara reached out and clasped her hand around Erika's.

"Okay," she whispered.

Laughter answered the pronouncement. "So disappointing," Maya rumbled. "I thought for sure the child would throw off your shackles, human." She grimaced. "Alas, it was not to be so. Her kind were always weak, their will easily corrupted." She paused, then turned, the dark pits of her eyes fixing on another. "And what of you, half-blood queen? Are you ready to embrace your true power?"

Footsteps sounded in the gloom as Amina advanced into the light of Erika's gauntlet. Her smile did not falter as she looked from Erika and Cara to the Old One. She shook her head as she appraised the creature.

"All my life," she snarled, "I have been waiting for your arrival, *Chead*. You think I would join you now?"

❦ 33 ❦

THE FALLEN

Hidden in the darkness, Adonis listened to the thrum of Maya's Voice. She had brought him with her, her repentant servant, the only one she had trusted to bring to this place. Watching from the shadows, he listened to her converse with the humans and wished she would unleash him, set him upon the vile creatures. He could feel her strength within him, the swirling of her hatred...

...then abruptly, he felt it weaken.

An inner gasp escaped Adonis as he emerged from the pain, from the crushing agony of his own regret, as Maya's influence over his mind retreated.

A shudder shook him as he returned to himself, looking across the tunnel to where the humans stood. What did the creatures think they were doing, coming here, thinking they could face the Old One alone? The Anahera might fight for a while, resisting the power of Maya's Voice, but even he could sense the divisions amongst the others. The Old One would turn them against one another before any managed to strike a blow.

She played the calm Matriarch now, but when they had arrived in this place earlier, her rage had been terrible to behold. To discover her mate's absence, that the humans had tricked her, manipulated her...

...no, none would leave this place alive. Maya could have crushed them already, could have broken their minds as she had his.

Why she had not already, Adonis could not comprehend. Neither could he understand why her influence on him had lessoned. Her Voice still touched him, fixing him in place where he stood hidden in the shadows. But the unrelenting agony she had used to torture him had at least vanished.

He was not surprised to see the human and young Anahera from the mountains, the ones that had escaped. Even less so the half-blood queen. After witnessing her fight on the river, Adonis had known she would come.

But why had Maisie followed them here?

Beyond the three with power, she stood with another human, armed only with a simple blade. No magic or strength to protect her, just a regular sword, barely enough to fend off a feeble human, let alone the strength of the Old One.

When he'd first seen her, he'd wanted to scream for her to run, to flee. But even with his mind restored, his Voice remained mute, unable to reach out in warning to the Anahera, let alone the Voiceless Maisie. He couldn't save her this time. He couldn't even save himself.

Instead Adonis remained hidden, locked in his master's mental grip, waiting for what was to come, to witness the doom of humanity and his own kind both.

"Give up, Maya." To his surprise, it was Maisie who finally spoke. "You're all alone, outnumbered. Your time has come."

Laughter answered the human's words. Adonis might have laughed with the Old One. Little did the poor human know the darkness she faced.

"Human, it seems I underestimated you. I should have realised one of your kind, even injured and alone, would find a way to survive. Had I known Adonis could be so easily influenced by your words, I would have killed you both that day." Maya's words turned to a cackle. "But you are wrong, my dear child. I am not alone."

At her words, Adonis felt a compulsion, the pressure returning to his mind as the Old One refocused her attention on him. Though her Voice was weaker than it had been earlier, it was still enough to propel him forward. Head lowered, Adonis stepped into the light of the human's magic. A hiss of inhaled breath followed his appearance.

"Adonis."

Despite Maya's compulsion, Adonis's head jerked up at that, surprised at the emotion in Maisie's voice. But his ears did not deceive him, as looking upon the swirls of her aura, he read the impossible rainbow of the human's soul.

He wanted to speak to her, to ask what had become of the Anaheran children—but instead the full force of Maya's Voice returned, crashing upon him like a landslide. And instead of reaching out with his Voice, a soft rumble came from his throat and he drew back his lips, the hatred in his heart responding to Maya's own. In that moment, Adonis saw again the truth, that this human was the creature who had tricked him, that had caused him to betray his own people.

Fists clenched, teeth bared, he took a step towards the human.

"Adonis," the human gasped, retreating from him. "No…"

Anger raged within Adonis, at his naivety, his foolishness, that he had allowed this pathetic creature to manipulate him, to trick him. He wanted to reach out and tear her apart, to finally earn redemption.

Only Maya's Voice held him back.

"I suppose it was for the best," the Old One mused, her words mocking as she addressed the human. "Tell me, how are your new allies, the Anahera? I do not see them here, apart from their rebellious daughter." Her smile grew as the humans said nothing. "Oh my poor dears, did they abandon you?" Laughter echoed through the tunnel. "It is good to know they shall never change. The Tangata might be weak and foolish, but at least they are not craven."

Her words pierced the fog of Adonis's thoughts, and for a moment he was as a man drowning, struggling to keep his consciousness above the miasma of Maya's power. He clenched his fists, yearning to turn and strike at his captor, but…

…instead all he managed was a growl. Maya laughed again, though this time it seemed her mirth was directed at him.

"For what it's worth, human, know that the Anahera will not escape me," Maya whispered. "When your civilisation burns and the world belongs to me, I will have my servants hunt them down, bring them my retribution. Just as extinction beckons for humanity, so it will come for them."

A growl answered Maya's words as the winged one straightened, eyes flashing in the darkness. "The only extinction that beckons is yours, Maya."

Silence fell as the Old One regarded her foes, a smile touching her lips. "An unusual alliance," she mused. "I have read your hearts, know your minds. If this is the best your kind can send against me, I am not impressed. Three women, rejected, spurned by their own blood, by their people. How far the world has fallen." She spread her hands and grinned. "But very well, children. Come to me, and I will gladly grant the death you seek."

Snarling, Amina leapt at the creature, Erika and Cara just a step behind.

❧ 34 ☙

THE SOVEREIGN

A snarl tore from Lukys's lips as a Tangata leapt at him, evading his guards and reaching for his throat. Reacting faster than he'd thought himself capable, Lukys spun his spear and drove the point up through the creature's heart, sending it screaming into the void. But he barely heard the creature's Voice as it cried out—his attention was only half on the events in Mildeth, the assault upon the walls.

The other half was far away, tangled in the minds of his friends, supporting them as they fought in the darkness. The queen had led the charge against the inhuman Old One, Erika and Cara joining in the battle while Maisie and the Calafe Darien held back. Yet with Maya's Voice filling the underground tunnels, they would have been incapable of throwing a single punch without his own Voice to reinforce them.

Yet despite his efforts, they were losing.

He could sense their furious battle, the exchange of blows and screams. But even as those in the caverns struggled, Maya worked her mind upon them, peeling at the layers of their consciousness, feeding on their base emotions, seeking to turn them against one another.

Only Lukys's desperate efforts kept her from succeeding, as he used all the strength of his Voice to bolster his friends' courage, to keep the Old One from their minds.

His efforts were slowly failing, as Maya crept through the gaps in his defences, or tore them apart when a distraction on the walls drew his mind back to Mildeth. Her raw power, her mastery, was far beyond Lukys's amateur efforts, even with the memories of the Sovereigns crowding him. This was a fight he was destined to lose, and yet he struggled on, did his best to keep his friends safe, if only for a moment more.

Alongside him, Sophia struggled as well. On the battlefield of Mildeth, she fought for the hearts and minds of the human defenders, of her people. But despite the distance, despite her own innate knowledge as a Tangata, she too was losing. The passion of battle was too great, the fear and rage and hatred too deep between their peoples. Maya had only to nudge the minds of the warring factions to drive each to ever greater madness.

But like Lukys, Sophia would not give up, would not surrender so long as hope remained. If only they'd had time to practice this ability, or had greater allies to support them. The Anahera who had remained in the city had raw ability, but the creatures were unpractised, easily distracted by the chaos around them. Perhaps together—

Lukys gasped as the overwhelming strength of Maya pressed against him again, her hatred washing through him, and for a moment he felt as though he stood alone, that he would be consumed...

...screaming, he tore himself from the battle in the caverns, surfacing for a moment on the walls of Mildeth. His vision flickered, clearing in time to see a Tangata leap over the crenelations. Quickly Lukys moved to shield Sophia from the bloodshed. He felt her pain with each death, but he could at least spare her the agony of fighting her own brethren. For now, at least.

But despite the memories crammed into his skull, Lukys was still human, and his strength was waning. Their guard were struggling too. He saw Travis fighting desperately at Isabella's side, glimpsed Dale down on one knee as Keria stood protectively over him with another of the Perfugian guard, fighting off a maddened Tangata.

Slamming the butt of his spear into the face of another Tangata, Lukys reversed the weapon and drove the razor tip through its throat. It fell back, crumpling to the ground, and he forced his will back to the cavern, even as he felt his friends wilting.

His protection was failing. Eroded by distance, he could not match Maya's strength, not for long. Sooner or later, she would find her way into the hearts of one of the allies. When that happened, their fate would rest on the strength of that soul, on what lay in their heart, whether they had the will to resist...

Thinking of the mistrust held between the three women, Lukys shuddered. He gathered himself for one last effort, then hurled himself at the darkness surrounding his friends. He would not surrender, would not abandon them to the Voice of the Old One. He held the knowledge of generations in his mind, the will of all the Sovereigns who had come before him. It would be enough.

It had to be.

Withdrawing from the battle atop the wall, Lukys found himself back-to-back with Sophia, with his love. Without seeing her face, he could sense the tears in her eyes, her pain as she tried again and again to find the love in her people's hearts, to remind them of the peace of New Nihelm.

They're dying, Lukys, her voice came to him.

He scrunched his eyes closed, turning to hold her tight, even as chaos reigned around them. They fought and fought and would keep on fighting, but he no longer knew why. They were losing, crumbling. Maya could not be defeated, would destroy them all. It was inevitable.

Why suffer, why continue?

Why not finally give up, and have peace?

"I can't lose you," Sophia whispered to him, lips warm on his cheek as they held one another.

Lukys tightened his grip on her and said nothing. What more was there to say?

You do not have to perish with the rest.

A shudder slid down Lukys's spine as the Voice of the Old One spoke into his mind. He tried to force it away, to close himself to her, but there was an exhaustion upon him now, a weariness he could not simply shrug off. It left cracks in his consciousness, gaps through which the Old One continued to whisper.

I sense my brethren, the true strength of the Chead, entwined in your souls.

Surrender to it, give yourself to the power. Return to me, brother, sister, and we will rule this world as we were always destined.

Lukys's skin crawled as she spoke, and something within him stirred in response to her command. Opening his eyes, he found Sophia staring back at him, saw the terror upon her and knew she felt that same stirring, like a giant that had long lain dormant, now waking…

An icy cold seeped through Lukys as he found himself frozen, his body torn between the memory of a creature long dead, and his own self. Looking around, he saw the bloodshed upon the battlefield and felt that creature grow stronger, sensed it gathering, its anger, its rage…

No!

With an effort of will, Lukys fought back, clinging to Sophia, sensing her own battle, her own fear. Instinctively, he reached out for her, their minds mingling, uniting in their battle against those other consciousnesses, filling them with strength…

…and with relief, they sensed those other minds subsiding, returning to the depths, to dreams of a world long since passed.

Letting out a long breath, the Sovereigns found themselves standing once more atop the walls of Mildeth, arms clasped around one another. They shivered, thankful for their sanity, and wondered…they were a hundred miles from the battle beneath the earth. Why then had Maya turned her attention towards them, tried to bring them to her side? Their minds raced, their thoughts as one as they came to a singular conclusion.

She fears us.

It was a spark of hope in the darkness of night. Together, the Sovereigns realised they no longer felt the oppressive weight of Maya's Voice, the darkness that had weighed on their thoughts these past days. Something had changed, a discovery of fresh power, of strength that kept the Old One's influence at bay.

We work as one.

Realisation struck, the truth that had been staring them in the face, ignored, avoided for fear of what it might mean. Separated, they could not stand against the Old One. What they had been doing, dividing their attention between their friends and the battle for Mildeth, it was not enough. Maya's mind was greater than either of them alone.

They needed to act as one. And yet...

We must decide, the Sovereigns thought together. *We must choose.*

The thought struck fear into their souls, and for a moment Lukys found himself separated from Sophia, though her emotions still roiled alongside his own, raw, exposed. He felt her pain, her fear, but beneath that, a steely resolution.

We cannot abandon our friends, she whispered, and Lukys saw her attention was not on their battlefield now, but had turned to that dark place, where Erika and Cara and the others were now fighting for their lives.

For a moment, Lukys watched the three fighting, their magic and power flashing in the darkness.

Then his mind returned to look out over Mildeth, at the thousands of lives joined in battle, at the terrible hatred shared by Tangata and mankind alike. Hatred that had been born from the mouths of men, crafted by callous rulers to bring war from peace. Maya was only the latest of those to exploit these peoples, to use them for their own purposes.

But what if that hatred could be healed, if the minds of humanity and Tangata alike could be opened, so that they saw one another not as the monsters of childhood tales, but the men and women they truly were?

What if they could bring peace from war?

If the Sovereigns could heal the wounds of centuries, not all the power of the Old One could tear them asunder again. Humanity, the Tangata, they would live on, would survive and prosper in a new world.

In that moment, Lukys realised it was not the battle beneath the earth that their fates rested upon, but the one before him. Turning to Sophia, he reached out to embrace her.

No, he whispered, and felt her frown, her confusion. *No, it is our people,* all *of our people, that we cannot abandon.*

What about our friends? she whispered back, though he sensed the swelling of her hope.

He kissed her then, and as he did so allowed their minds to

unite, to become the Sovereigns, to feel that joyous sense of Oneness.

We must trust them to do their part, the Sovereigns said, even as they released their protection from the caverns, turning their attention instead to the battlefield. *Our attention is needed here.*

And together, the Sovereigns reached out to undo the destruction wrought by Maya, by Amina, by kings and queens and Sovereigns past, by all those dark rulers that had come before them.

❧ *35* ❧

THE QUEEN

Light burned in the darkness as Erika and Amina ignited their gauntlets. The brilliance of their power reflected off those unnaturally smooth walls, catching on Cara's scarlet feathers. Erika's heart raced as her strength rushed into the strange links of the gauntlet, its power gathering, preparing to strike. In the City of the Gods, she had seen Maya resist its magic—but back then Erika had been weak, exhausted. Let the Old One stand against her true strength.

She exchanged a glance with Amina, who nodded. There was no love lost between them still, but the queens would stand together, at least against this enemy. As one, they raised their magic, preparing themselves.

"Ahhh!" A cry of joy, of victory, burst through the chamber as Maya suddenly straightened...

...and Erika staggered, a weight suddenly falling upon her, a crushing darkness, terror and despair that burnt away all hope, all thoughts of resistance. Tears welled in her eyes and she watched as the power bled from her fist, slipping away until the light all but died. Only the softest glow remained, casting their world in shadow.

A whimper slipped from Erika's lips as she sank to her knees. Sobs came from nearby and she saw that Cara had already crumpled, arms wrapped about herself, wings spreading to hide her face. The sight sent terror rushing through Erika, and she felt desperation, a need to act, to protect the young Anahera she had come to see…come to see as…

"And so we come to the end."

Maya's voice sounded in the darkness, banishing everything else from Erika's mind, leaving only the despair. On her knees, she looked up as footsteps approached, as the terrible eyes of the Old One fell upon her.

"I admit, your Sovereigns resisted far longer than I thought possible." She smiled as she stood over them. "But I knew their true nature would reveal itself eventually, that they would choose themselves over their friends."

A cry tore from Erika as she felt the world shrinking about her, as childhood terrors rose to drown her, as she came to realise her every hope, every dream had been a lie, the foolish whims of a child. She had never been a queen, did not deserve the love of her people. She was no one, a pretender, a fool for denying the majesty of this creature before her.

"Still," Maya mused. "I will have to deal with them eventually. Who knew my old rivals would be so cunning, as to find a way to thwart me even now, long after they were gone? I will have to prise that secret from their hosts before I rip them apart."

The Old One leaned her head to the side as a whimper came from nearby, and the dark eyes fell on Cara. "So considerate of you to lure yourselves out here, so far from your friends and followers."

Erika shuddered, shrinking farther and farther towards the floor. Her entire being unravelled as she relived her every mistake, her every terrible decision, the lives she had cost, the evils she had committed. Again and again she had led those who'd trusted her to their deaths, and now…now she had done it again, had brought Darien and Maisie and Cara to this place, had failed them, failed herself, failed her people.

The Old One stepped past her, advancing on Cara. The Anahera was sobbing, trying to crawl away, but Maya caught her by the wing and dragged her back, laughing, cackling as she threw the girl down in front of Erika.

Pain burst within Erika's heart, threatening to tear her apart. Desperately she sought something, anything to sustain her, some spark amidst the suffocating despair. But she couldn't breathe, couldn't think, couldn't see anything beyond the darkness, the doom. Not a hint of love or hope or joy. It was all gone, washed away, sponged from her soul.

She watched as Cara sobbed on the floor, unable to summon the will to defend herself, and knew that her friend would die, that here, now, Erika had truly failed her.

No...

Somewhere in the depths of her soul, a piece of Erika fought against that thought, resisted. She had made a promise, had sworn...sworn to protect her friend, to do better, to *be* better. Somehow, her hands found the cold stone beneath her and she froze, no longer sinking, no longer slumped in defeat. Teeth clenched, she struggled, fought to push herself back, to rise again.

The weight upon her redoubled, the despair swelling within, trying to crush that spark, to drown her. Erika clung to its light, to its determination, even as she felt it slipping from her, knew that no matter her strength, this was an enemy she could not fight, not alone...

...but she was not alone. Her eyes found Cara, lying on the ground beside her, saw the Old one pinning her wing beneath a boot, saw the death shining in the creature's eyes.

Desperately, Erika sent up a plea to the sky, to the Gods she knew did not exist, had never existed...and yet still she begged, pleaded...

Please, give me the strength to help her.

But of course there was no answer

Erika cried out as the Old One slammed her boot into Cara's chest, punctuated by the sharp *crack* of breaking bones. The Anahera doubled up from the blow, gasping, sobbing her pain, but still she did not fight back, could not. Another blow landed, then another, the harsh *thud* of each impact whispering through the tunnels, until Erika was forced to squeeze her eyes closed, unable to watch, to witness...

Very well, human, a voice—no, voices—whispered into Erika's mind. *You have...proven your word once. Perhaps you are proof that humanity truly can change.*

And suddenly, the spark to which Erika clung exploded, sweeping outwards, washing back the darkness. Where before there had been despair, Erika found an unlikely hope, an unyielding joy for the voices in her mind, the possibility of a future. The weight of responsibility no longer felt so heavy, the doom she had foreseen not so inevitable.

And she found herself rising.

We will not see another world Fall, the voices of the Anahera whispered to her. *This Old One, she is too strong, too powerful. We cannot risk leaving the fledgelings, not again, but this, at least, we can do. Stop her, Erika of the Calafe.*

"Impossible," Maya whispered as she swung to see Erika on her feet.

Erika reacted without thought. Light burst from her gauntlet and she threw out her hand. Screaming, Maya staggered back, retreating from the power. Erika had not gathered enough to strike the creature down, but the attack still served as Erika wished, driving the Old One away from her friend. Quickly she advanced, placing herself between Cara and the Old One.

A groan came from Cara as, trembling, the Goddess rose. She clutched at her chest and one wing hung limp and broken, but despite her obvious pain, the Anahera stood, teeth bared at the creature who opposed them.

We will watch over you and Cara, came the voices again, followed by a pause. *The other…she clings to the darkness. She will not let us in.*

"So the Anahera have found their courage after all," Maya murmured as she straightened. "No matter. Their Voices will not be enough to save you, human."

Erika had a moment to process those words before a figure joined Maya in the darkness. A dark smile crossed Amina's lips as she looked at them. Erika sensed the vibrations in her mind, could almost read the words of Maya as she gestured to the queen.

"Kill them."

And smiling, Amina advanced.

———

Hatred blew through Adonis like a storm unleashed, tearing every other emotion from his soul. Setting his sights on Maisie, he advanced with a snarl, hands outstretched. He made no move to rush—the human could not escape him, could not fight him. Trapped by the Voice of the Old One, she could only stand there and die, just as her friends were dying even now.

Indeed, she watched his advance, eyes wide with fear. Then abruptly she spun—and vanished.

Adonis staggered to a stop, confusion penetrating the haze of his mind, struggling to comprehend what had happened. The human had no power—how could she have resisted Maya's Voice, let alone disappeared into thin air?

Movement came from nearby, and he spun as a one armed man charged him. Adonis's eyes widened at the creature's nerve, but it stood no chance against his power, and brushing aside a blow from the man's broadsword, he struck the human's chest.

The man crumpled, collapsing to the floor with hardly a sound, and Adonis turned back to the darkness.

Back to the hunt.

His ears caught the soft thump of retreating footsteps and he grinned, striding up the tunnel after his quarry. The human might resist Maya's mental powers, might have been capable of vanishing from sight, but she could not hide from his other senses. He trailed after the whisper of her soft movements, after the sharp scent of her humanity. No, she would not escape.

The chase carried him away from where Maya and her new servant battled against the Anahera and the human. Adonis's master did not need him to defeat two such as them, though as the distance to Maya grew, her presence upon his mind lessened again, retreating as it had before, until only her Command remained, the order to hunt, to kill. A growl rumbled from Adonis's throat as he stalked the tunnels, seeking his prey, desperate to finally watch her feeble life fading into the dark. She would pay for corrupting him, for luring him from the path of his Matriarch.

"You're a fool, Adonis." The human's voice chased him through the shadows, taunting him, ever just out of reach.

He growled, bounding forward, before he realised her scent no longer hung in the air of the tunnel. Retreating, he found the side passage down which she had fled, and continued after her.

"A lovestruck idiot, lost, alone, *weak*," Maisie mocked. "Better you had died than this."

They continued the chase, Adonis ever just behind, though he sensed at times the shift of movements, the human's presence. She had no stamina, this creature, especially not with the aftereffects of her injury. This could not last—eventually she would fall, would stumble or trip, and reveal her position. Laughter rasped from his throat as he imagined his fingers closing upon her soft flesh, her screams as he wrought his revenge.

"Nyriah, she would weep to see she died for nothing." Her voice came again, and this time the words struck Adonis like a hammer, bringing him to a halt. "You are a stain upon her memory."

A tremor wracked Adonis and he swung this way and that, his snarls echoing in the narrow corridor. Where was she? How he longed to destroy her, to cease her tormenting—

There!

He leapt, bounding forward at a flicker of movement. The human had cried out, but there was no escaping Adonis now, as his fist met with flesh. He heard a soft *crunch* as of breaking bone, followed by a *crash* as glass struck stone. Abruptly, whatever magic had protected Maisie vanished and she appeared before him, broken wrist clutched in one hand, eyes wide.

She retreated from him, cursing beneath her breath, but the rock was damp beneath her feet and she slipped, collapsing to the stone. Adonis loomed above her, breath hissing in and out as he drank in her fear, her terror. The time had finally come, his vengeance, his redemption.

"They're alive," she said suddenly, eyes wide as they met his glare. "The fledgelings, they're safe. She'll never find them. Thanks to you."

Adonis stumbled to a stop. Her words pierced the darkness upon his soul, the fog of his mind. Those words, they should have enraged him, driven him to a fury, for they proved the magnitude of his treachery.

Instead, he felt a thrill, a sharp joy that swelled within, growing, swirling as it burned up his hatred, his anger. A gasp tore from his throat and he staggered back from her, shuddering, struggling.

"I know you're in there, Adonis," Maisie's words chased him.

Placing her good hand on the stone, she pushed herself up, her legs struggling to support her. One was slightly crooked, its bones healed poorly. She was so weak, he should never have let her live. And yet…

"I know you can hear me," she spoke again, taking a step towards him, reaching out a hand. "I know you don't want to do this."

Another shudder shook Adonis and he twisted away from her, then back. A moan built in his throat, a pressure, a battle within that threatened to tear him apart. The pain in his soul grew to a crescendo as the twin forces of Maya's Voice and his own did battle.

I…can't… he whispered to himself.

And still the eyes of the human watched him.

❧ 36 ❧

THE SOVEREIGNS

The Sovereigns shuddered as they looked across the battlefield, taking in the chaos of war. Fear and rage and hatred swirled, mixing and swelling as human and Tangata clashed, the screams of the dying and the victors rising until it seemed they were one and the same. Watching the flicker of their auras, they couldn't help but think it was true, that a part of both of their souls was lost with the death they dealt.

The darkness of Maya, and those who had come before, had consumed these pour souls. Even now as the Sovereigns worked to sever the Old One's influence, the darkness fed upon itself, upon the battle, upon the pain and loss and death. These men and women, they no longer wished to see the light, to believe in a better world.

A piece of the Sovereigns broke with each death, with the loss of every brother, every sister. In their minds' eye, the terrible waste of war was laid bare, revealed for the tragedy it was, brothers and sisters murdering one another. Looking upon that horror, they knew they had made the right decision.

And together, they reached out to grasp the scarlet threads of rage, the emerald lines of hatred. Speaking as one, they sought to crush those dark emotions, to press them back, to contain them in the bounds of compassion and empathy that had once held them in check. Across the battlefield their Voice rang out, muting those terrible passions, trying to heal the wounds their foe had dealt.

Only as they came to an end and looked back did the Sovereigns realise the futility of their actions. As they moved from one part of the battle to another, the fighting paused, but only momentarily. For as the people looked and saw the dead and dying around them, their hatred crept back, and the battle was re-joined.

No, they thought to themselves, watching the chaos resume, the darkness sweeping through the ranks of human and Tangata alike, all across the walls, except…

…except where they themselves stood, surrounded by the glow of their guard. Of all the souls on the battlefield, the Perfugian recruits and their Tangatan partners alone stood untouched by the darkness. Instead, they shone with the rosy hue of hope, of joy and love. And looking upon their friends, the Sovereigns realised their mistake.

We cannot hold back the darkness, but we can spread the light.

Gathering their power, they swept back into the chaos, immersing themselves in the surging emotions, feeling the hatred that had torn them asunder, that had led humanity to first attack the Tangata, that had unleashed the Tangatan rage upon humanity. But it was not those emotions, those memories, they sought this time. They were entrenched, experiences that could not be ignored, would never be forgotten.

Yet there were other emotions amongst them, buried deep by Maya, smothered by her hatred. Buried, but not destroyed. One by one, the Sovereigns dragged them from the depths. Images flickered through their minds as they passed above the battlefield: a Tangatan man and human woman in one another's arms; a human spear raised above a helpless Tangatan child, withdrawn; even images of themselves as they walked the streets of Mildeth and Ashura. Memories still fresh, suppressed but not forgotten. Now they returned at the bidding of the Sovereigns, to remind the people of what *could* be.

More and more, the images of hope rose from the past, of families left behind, of children and loved ones waiting, praying for their return, of joys forgotten in the depths of their darkness. The reasons they had first taken steps down this path, but which had been forgotten in the pursuit of Maya's conquest.

Amidst it all, the Sovereigns felt their own joy swelling, their memories sweeping outwards to join with the others: the warmth as Lukys danced with Sophia in the courtyard of New Nihelm, the joy of the children in the streets, the hope they'd felt, watching their peoples protect one another, and a future they had once envisioned.

Of peace between their kinds.

Atop the walls of Mildeth, Lukys opened his eyes, sensing a change had come over the battle. Beside him, Sophia stirred too. Blinking, he struggled to adjust to his return, to separate the links of his mind from his union with Sophia. Relief touched him as he found Dale back on his feet, Keria at his side. And Travis too, standing nearby, an enormous smile on his face.

Lukys frowned at the sight, and straightening, he stepped cautiously to the edge of the wall. And only as he stood there, looking out across the battlefield, did he realise the change that had drawn them back, the impossibility that had come to pass on the walls of Mildeth.

Silence.

Erika screamed as the energy gathered in her fist, burning, boiling, blinding. With another cry, she threw out her arm, directing it at the blur in the dark that was the Old One. The figure staggered, but the Old One's momentum still carried her clear of Erika's magic.

Laughter whispered from the shadows as the figure straightened and Erika panted, struggling to gather her strength. The harsh *thunk* of blows on flesh carried from elsewhere in the dark, as Cara and her half-sister did battle.

She caught a glint and rustle of feathers as the two darted past. In the narrow corridors, Cara's wings were only a hinderance against the maddened Amina. Light flashed as the queen snarled and unleashed a burst of her own magic. Twisting, Cara somehow managed to avoid the debilitating effects of the gauntlet, her smaller size and agility aiding her against the larger woman.

A *crack* followed as Amina's fist collided with the Anahera's cheek, sending her crashing back. Erika winced and in her mind the voices that aided her rose to a cacophony, the Anahera's terror swelling.

Clenching her teeth, Erika forced herself to ignore them, to turn her back on Cara's plight. She had to believe in her friend, trust she would survive, would distract Amina long enough for Erika to do what needed to be done. There was only one way to win this fight—by killing the Old One.

With Darien down and Maisie vanished, somehow, impossibly, that task had fallen on Erika's shoulders.

She balled her gauntleted hand into a fist, allowing the power to grow, to light the dark. Its brilliance revealed Maya standing a few feet away, smile still stretched across her lips, eyes glimmering in her magic's glow.

"You know you cannot win, human," she rasped, "and yet you fight on." She shook her head. "Such is the arrogance of humanity."

Abruptly she darted forward. Erika screamed, hurling herself to the side and bringing up her fist, unleashing the power. Light flashed from her, silhouetting the Old One, tearing a scream from Maya.

Then Erika collided with the wall of the tunnel and tears of pain sprung to her eyes. Stumbling, she struggled to see, to spot the Old One before she attacked again. Laughter sounded in the narrow confines, but Erika's magic must have had some effect, for the Old One retreated again, merging with the dark. Words echoed through the tunnel and Erika swung this way and that, chasing shadows.

Nearby, Cara screamed and hurled herself at Amina, catching the queen about the waist. Amina stumbled but did not fall. Instead, she bared her teeth and clenched her fists together, then brought them down on Cara's back, driving the Anahera to her knees.

A snarl tore from Cara as she released the queen and tried to leap away, but the half-blood was faster still, catching one of the Goddess's wings as they fluttered outwards. Cara screamed as the queen dragged her back, before several feather tore loose, freeing her.

She staggered away from the queen, spinning, eyes wild as blood dripped from the ends of one wing. Glimpsing the beginnings of madness in her friend's eyes, Erika cursed, but there was nothing she could do for Cara, nothing she could say to draw the Goddess back from the edge.

Instead she turned and sought the Old One.

"It is not arrogance that makes us fight," she whispered, more to herself than in answer to Maya's whispers. "It's hope." She swung her gauntlet in an arc, seeking out her foe. "Maybe I cannot win. Maybe you'll kill me. But it won't end here, Maya. Even in death, my people will remember my sacrifice. They will fight on against you. Maybe one of them will have the strength to defeat you."

Laughter answered her words and Erika suddenly felt foolish, sensed the ridicule of her enemy. Even with the support of the Anahera, she sensed her doom. She could not win this battle, would find only death down here in this darkness. The Calafe would forget her brief reign—if they survived to remember anything at all.

And Maya would persist, would give birth to more of her terrible kind, nearly as strong as herself. Then it would only be a matter of time before they took the world.

A scream built in Erika's throat as she foresaw that dark future. Another flicker of movement came from a nearby corner and she threw out her hand, unleashing the gathering power. Light burst from the gauntlet, catching Maya midstride.

The Old One staggered as the power struck, bending her in two, freezing her to the spot. Shocked, Erika kept on, pouring her energy into the gauntlet, feeding the magic. Gripping her wrist with the other hand to steady herself, she staggered forward, knowing this was her chance. A dark sound whispered from the Old One as her frame bowed, as her body shook, trembled…

… then straightened.

Erika stumbled to a stop as the Old One's laughter echoed around her. Abruptly the creature darted forward, catching Erika by the wrist and yanking her hands towards the ceiling, directing the gauntlet's power away from her.

"Ahhh, but I had forgotten that sting," the Old One hissed, leaning in close so that they were face to face.

Erika flinched away from that face. Her power had not been without effect. Scarlet tears ran from Maya's grey eyes and her cheek twitched with the aftereffects of the pain. Yet she still stood, teeth bared, that terrible insanity watching Erika from the grey depths.

A scream came from nearby, and Erika's heart twisted as she saw Cara go down. Before she could recover, Amina leapt forward and landed upon the Anahera's back. Grasping the youth by the hair, she drove her face into the stone floor. Screaming, Erika struggled to free herself from Maya's grip, but the Old One only smiled, amusement playing across her lips as she too watched the end of the battle between sisters.

Snarling, Amina drew Cara's bloodied face back, then slammed her into the stones again. And again and again, until finally the Anahera lay limp beneath her.

Only then did the Flumeeren queen rise. Magic lit her fist as she gathered power there, readying herself to finish the Anahera.

"No!" Erika screamed, fighting hopelessly against the Old One's sheer strength. "Amina, don't you see? She has made you the very thing your father raised you to stop!"

To her surprise, Amina glanced up at that. A frown played across the queen's face, but her hesitation only lasted a moment. Her eyes met Maya's, and something seemed to pass between the pair, before Amina turned back to Cara and raised her fist once more.

"Witness, my dear human, what becomes of those who stand against me," Maya whispered.

"No."

Erika jerked as a voice spoke from behind them...

...then a blur charged from the darkness, and slammed into the Old One.

✤ 37 ✤

THE TANGATA

The breath burst from Adonis's lungs as he collided with the Old One, hurling her back, freeing the human from her grasp. He attacked again, driving a fist into his master's face, straining to do the impossible, to stand against Maya's Voice, against her power. Yet even as he struggled, Adonis felt her mind turning towards him, felt the full force of her consciousness as it focused on him…

Movement came from the floor as Maisie helped the other human to her feet, yet Adonis could not stop to consider them. He launched himself at Maya again, snarling, screaming, determined to stop her, to prevent her from leading his people to disaster—

Light exploded across his vision as the Old One finally recovered, her shock turning to rage. She moved faster than thought, faster even than his Tangatan senses could follow, and abruptly Adonis found himself on the cold stone, the metallic taste of blood filling his mouth.

"Adonis!" Maisie screamed.

His heart lurched at the thought of Maya turning her gaze upon the human, and snarling, Adonis pushed himself back to his feet, placing himself before his foe. Maya's eyes widened, as though unable to believe his defiance. Even Adonis struggled to comprehend it, the animalistic desperation that fuelled him. The buzzing of her Voice increased in pitch, scratching at the layers of his mind, but fists clenched he fought back, clinging to his freedom like a drowning man to a log.

Gathering himself, Adonis charged again, determined to stop her. But this time the Old One was ready. She caught his fist in one hand, a look of disgust on her lips, as though she considered it beneath her to spar with one so low as him. Her fist came up, and not all Adonis's speed or skill was enough to avoid the blow. It collided with the side of his head, sending him careening into the wall. Red flashed across his sight, and this time when his vision cleared, Adonis found he no longer had the strength to stand.

A scream pierced his sluggish mind, and teeth clenched, he raised his head, struggling to remain conscious. Light burst from the fist of Maisie's friend as she unleashed the power of her ancestors, though this time she used it not against Maya, but the other, the half-blood that had fallen to the Old One's power. The queen's face contorted as the magic caught her, and she staggered, clutching her ears, crumpling to the ground.

The light faded as quickly as it had been unleashed as the human lowered her arm. Adonis frowned, his addled brain confused, struggling to track the players in the room. Nearby, Maya appeared equally as surprised, but the human ignored her, focusing on the fallen half-blood.

"Amina, get up!" Her voice echoed loudly in the narrow space. "We need you!

On the ground, the half-blood queen stirred, and Adonis realised that her eyes had cleared, that the human's attack had disrupted Maya's hold on the woman. The Old One realised it at the same moment, unleashing a scream, she leapt towards them.

Recovering with the speed of the Anahera, the half-blood surged to her feet to meet the Old One, turning aside a blow meant for the human. Maya stumbled, and light lit the darkness as the human raised her gauntlet. This time there was no mistaking her target, and Maya snarled as the power of the ancient humans struck.

Adonis had already seen Maya resist that terrible power, but roaring, the half-blood ignited her own weapon, the matching gauntlet she wore. Too late, the Old One realised her peril, as the half-blood queen unleashed the magic of the second gauntlet.

A terrible scream shook the tunnels beneath the earth as Maya fell to her knees, hands clasped to her ears before the assault of the twin magics. A snarl hissed from her lips, and even as blood spilt from her eyes, she tried to rise, to leap at one of the two, to bring them down.

But even the strength of the Old Ones had its limits, and Maya reached hers now, her feet slipping on the smooth ground, sending her crashing back to the cold stone.

Only then did she turn, her bloodied face twisting, her desperate eyes searching the dark, finding Adonis. They shone as their gaze met, as she looked upon his fallen figure. Even through layers of his mind, the defences Adonis had raised against her, he heard Maya's call as she placed a hand to the mound of her stomach.

Adonis, please! she begged. *Please, save me! Save our children!*

His heart wrenched at the words, and despite everything she had done to him, to his people, Adonis almost went to her, almost stood and struck down the human and her awful magic.

But he resisted. He knew it could not be, that the Old One's words were but ash upon the wind, her lies greater than any humanity had ever told. She would see him dead, would murder his people, slaughter thousands to feed her hatred. Even the children she carried would be consumed by her cause, discarded in her pursuit of her revenge.

No, Maya could not be allowed live, or she would doom them all.

And so, though a part of him was breaking, Adonis bowed his head and sat back. Closing his eyes, he waited for the end.

Until finally, the vibrations of the Old One ceased, and silence fell over the ancient tunnels. Her presence, her touch, vanished from his mind.

It was done.

The threat to his people, his world, was dead.

And all it had cost was his own future.

Voices whispered in the darkness as the humans conversed. He wondered if they would kill him, but finally they seemed to decide to leave him, that they would return to the surface. Still he did not move, barely breathed as their footsteps retreated, finally disappearing into a distance too great for even his enhanced senses.

Only then did Adonis finally lift his head and look upon the creature he had loved, that had lifted the hopes of his people to the heavens, that would have born his children. Sobbing, he dragged himself across the floor to where Maya lay and cradled her body against him, held her tight.

And wept for the future that might have been.

EPILOGUE
TWO WEEKS LATER

Standing on the shores of the Illmoor, Erika looked to the north, where a fleet of ships was slowly disappearing into the morning fog. Raising a hand, she bid farewell to Nguyen and the Gemaho as they returned to their lands. What they would find there, no one could say—Amina had disappeared after the fall of the Old One, fleeing into the tunnels. She must have learnt something of her own mental powers during that desperate battle, for not even the Sovereigns had been able to locate her since.

Erika could only shake her head at the thought. Perhaps it was better that the woman had vanished. Though she longed to bring Amina to justice, there were still many in Flumeer who supported her. Had the queen chosen to resist, she could have started a civil war amongst the Flumeeren people.

As it was, a fragile peace had finally come to the four kingdoms, to human, Tangata and Anahera alike. Erika couldn't help but wonder whether it would last, if the darkness that had so stained their history would rise its ugly head once more, but for now, she was willing to give it a chance.

And so she led her people south, back to the vast forests and wilderness of Calafe. Despite their fears of what they would find there, her people had followed, had placed their faith in their young queen and set out on a journey to reclaim their homeland.

Though perhaps *reclaim* was too strong a word.

For nearby, journeying separately, yet never far from the Calafe column, came the Tangata. Their numbers were greatly reduced from the host that had marched north to assault the Flumeeren capital, numbering similar now to the Calafe. Despite the efforts of the Sovereigns, distrust still lingered between the two groups, remnants of a hatred fostered over a decade of war, and yet...

...here and there, Erika saw where the groups had combined, where children of each race played as one, drawn to one another by a shared curiosity, by a desire to discover, to explore the unknown. And where the children went, the parents soon followed, nodding greetings to their former enemy.

Watching such scenes, Erika felt hope for what they would discover once they reached New Nihelm. With both groups decimated by the Old One's campaign, there would be no shortage of housing, and Erika's heart quickened at the thought of seeing her childhood home again, the future she might discover there.

A shame Maisie and Cara had decided not to join her. Cara had set off in search of her people, promising she would come find Erika in New Nihelm. Erika worried for the young Anahera, but she had faith the Goddess would return.

As for Maisie...she too had not been seen since the death of the Old One. She had ventured alone back into the tunnels, to seek out the Tangata that had saved them, but...the pair had never re-emerged. By the time the party had gone looking for them, both had vanished—along with the body of the Old One.

Erika feared for her friend, but Maisie had trusted the Tangata...had perhaps felt more than that. Erika could only hope Maisie had discovered a safe place, had found joy in the peace of the wilderness, in companionship with Adonis.

As for herself...Erika shivered, looking out across the broad expanse of the Illmoor, at the swirling mists. To the north, she had built a life for herself, had had status and authority as the queen's Archivist. But she was no longer that woman consumed with advancement, obsessed with power. Erika might still wear the gauntlet of her ancestors, but in the darkness beneath the earth, faced with the madness of the Old One, she had finally set aside the follies of her past, and become a queen in truth.

So looking out across the Illmoor, Erika smiled, bidding one last farewell to the woman she had been, to the queen's Archivist…

…and turned to lead her people forward into the wilds of Calafe.

———

ADONIS MOVED CAREFULLY THROUGH THE TREES, TREADING SOFTLY, creeping closer as the deer lowered its head to tear a clump of clover from the ground. Its head came back up as it chewed and he froze in place, watching, waiting. He was almost close enough now, just one more second…

…the deer lowered its head again, and silently Adonis darted forward, crossing the dozen yards in a heartbeat. Leaping forward, he slammed into the creature's back with all the power of the Tangata, and felt a satisfying *crack* as the beast's spine snapped at the impact.

The deer struck the ground with a *thump* as Adonis stood over it, panting softly, his breath fogging in the dawn air. After a moment, he looked around, checking for wolves or other predators that might be interested in his meal, before returning his attention to the fawn. Slinging the dead beast over his shoulder as though it weighed no more than a sack of feathers, he set off through the forest.

Maisie had a fire burning in the cave when he returned, and a smile touched her face at the sight of him. Rising, she crossed the stone floor and greeted him with a kiss, before wrinkling her nose and gesturing to the carcass he carried.

"Did you have to kill Bambi?"

Adonis creased his brow to show his confusion, and Maisie laughed, gesturing with a hand to the depths of the cave, where they were preparing a larder for the winter.

"Don't worry," she explained as he wandered back to lay out the carcass for butchering. "It's just a story from our children's tales. I'm glad we won't be running out of meat when the snows arrive."

Grunting his agreement, Adonis returned to the fire and embraced the woman. She drew him into her arms in response, her brown eyes lifting to meet his, lips parting to draw him in. They kissed, and he felt the rush of blood pounding in his ears, the burning in his veins…

"Waaaah!"

Flinching, the pair broke apart as a shrill cry echoed from the stone walls. It wasn't long before a second voice joined the chorus of screams, followed by a third. Cursing, they crossed to where they'd stacked a pile of furs high near the fire. Leaning down, Maisie lifted a baby in each hand, while Adonis took the third. They stood together like that for a while, rocking the children gently in their arms.

"You know, Adonis," Maisie said as the cries of the children slowly faded. A smile touched her lips as she looked up from her burden. "They have your eyes."

———

WELL THAT'S THE END (FOR NOW!) BUT TO FIND OUT HOW THE Tangata were born and this world ended, check out the prequel with ***The Evolution Gene***. And don't forget to ***leave a review***!

NOTE FROM THE AUTHOR

Ooof. That hurt to write. Goddamn bad guys, they never give up do they? But there was no way the scheming Amina was going down without taking **someone** with her, and given how much she hated the Tangata…

…well, you saw what happened.

Obviously I'm not quite done with this world yet. In fact I'm hoping to begin work very soon on my next series in the Four Kingdoms. There'll be a time skip again, although nowhere near as long as after the secret sequel (***The Evolution Gene***). So you'll get to see your favorite characters again soon.

Well, most of them…

In the meantime, if you'd like to discuss my dastardly plot twists with other readers, be sure to join me on Facebook or my newsletter…

FOLLOW AARON HODGES

Join Aaron Hodges on his newsletter to **receive TWO FREE novels and a short story!**

https://aaronhodgesauthor.com/newsletter

ALSO BY AARON HODGES

The Sword of Light

Book 1: Stormwielder

Book 2: Firestorm

Book 3: Soul Blade

The Legend of the Gods

Book 1: Oathbreaker

Book 2: Shield of Winter

Book 3: Dawn of War

The Knights of Alana

Book 1: Daughter of Fate

Book 2: Queen of Vengeance

Book 3: Crown of Chaos

The Evolution Gene

Book 1: Reborn

Book 2: Havoc

Book 3: Carnage

Descendants of the Fall

Book 1: Warbringer

Book 2: Wrath of the Forgotten

Book 3: Age of Gods

Book 4: Dreams of Fury

The Alfurian Chronicles

Book 1: Defiant

Book 2: Guardian

Book 3: Conquest

The Swords of Heaven and Hell

Book 1: <u>Darkstrider</u>

The Four Circles

Book 1: Help! My Wizard Mentor Had A Heart Attack And Now I'm Being Chased By A Horde Of Giant Spiders!

The Untamed Isles

The Path Awakens

9 781991 018106